| 10-11 | | | |
|---|---|---|---|
| ILL SVDL | | | |
| | | | |

# The End of Sparta

By the Same Author

*The Father of Us All*
*Warfare and Agriculture in Classical Greece*
*The Western Way of War*
*Hoplites* (editor)
*The Other Greeks*
*Fields Without Dreams*
*Who Killed Homer?* (with John Heath)
*The Wars of the Ancient Greeks*
*The Soul of Battle*
*The Land Was Everything*
*Bonfire of the Humanities* (with John Heath and Bruce Thornton)
*An Autumn of War*
*Carnage and Culture*
*Between War and Peace*
*Mexifornia*
*Ripples of Battle*
*A War Like No Other*
*The Immigration Solution* (with Heather MacDonald and Steven Malanga)
*Makers of Ancient Strategy* (editor)

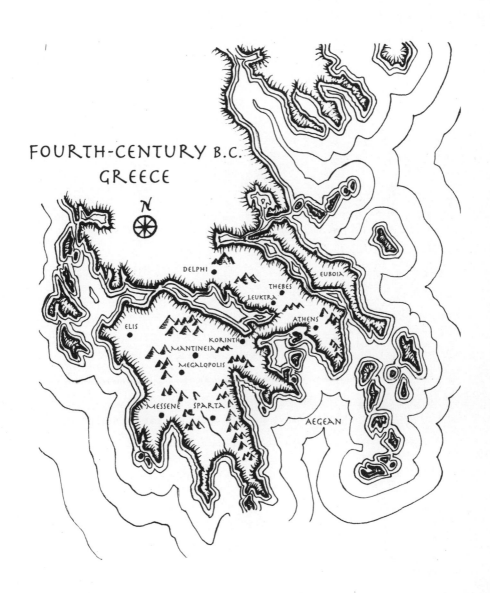

FOURTH-CENTURY B.C.
GREECE

N

DELPHI

EUBOIA

THEBES

LEUKTRA

ATHENS

ELIS

KORINTH

MANTINEIA

MEGALOPOLIS

MESSENE    SPARTA

AEGEAN

# The End of Sparta

*A Novel*

VICTOR DAVIS HANSON

BLOOMSBURY PRESS
New York   Berlin   London   Sydney

Published by Bloomsbury Press, New York

All papers used by Bloomsbury Press are natural, recyclable products made from wood grown in well-managed forests. The manufacturing processes conform to the environmental regulations of the country of origin.

LIBRARY OF CONGRESS CATALOGING-IN-PUBLICATION DATA

Hanson, Victor Davis.
The end of Sparta : a novel / Victor Davis Hanson. — 1st U.S. ed.
p.   cm.
ISBN-13: 978-1-60819-164-2
ISBN-10: 1-60819-164-8
1. Epaminondas, b. ca. 420 B.C.—Fiction.   2. Generals—Greece—Thebes—
Fiction.   3. Thebes (Greece)—History—Fiction.   4. Sparta (Greece)—
History—Fiction.   I. Title.
PS3608.A7233E63 2011
813'.6—dc22       2011013805

First U.S. Edition 2011

1 3 5 7 9 10 8 6 4 2

Typeset by Westchester Book Group
Printed in the U.S.A. by Quad/Graphics, Fairfield, Pennsylvania

# Contents

# *Preface*

This is the story of the great march against Sparta, the dream of the general Epaminondas of classical Thebes, whom the ancient Greeks and Romans acclaimed as the greatest man the classical world produced. Today we hear little of him. We know even less about all that his armies accomplished in a dramatic two-year period between 371 and 369 B.C.

Most contemporary accounts of that war were long ago lost. Our few extant historians apparently did not like the Thebans and so often misrepresented them or left them out of their narratives entirely. Most often Greek writers focused instead on Sparta and Athens. All that helps to explain why Epaminondas has faded from our memories—and why I offer a novel about what he accomplished.

Sometime in July 371 B.C., the Theban Epaminondas and his Boiotian Greeks shattered the phalanx of the supposedly invincible Spartans at the battle of Leuktra. They killed the Spartan king Kleombrotos, and crushed his warrior elite. The next year, not content with that stunning victory, Epaminondas—a follower of the philosopher Pythagoras who believed that our souls lived beyond our bodies and were judged by our deeds during our incarnate existence—led a grand coalition of Greeks southward to overrun Sparta.

The plan was to liberate the people of the Peloponnesos and apparently to reorder Greece itself. They were to found great citadels to hem in a weakened Sparta, and to free forever the serfs of its colony across the mountains in Messenia. That way, Epaminondas might cripple Sparta by robbing it of agricultural labor and thus ensure that no Greek people should be serfs to other Greeks—and that the Spartans, like other Greek militiamen, would finally have to grow their own food rather than train constantly for war.

Still, we cannot quite fathom all the reasons why tens of thousands followed this mystic general—plunder of course, strategic necessity probably, idealism perhaps. We only know that his preemptive invasion of the Peloponnesos began the end of Sparta—at least as the preeminent power as the Greeks had known it for centuries.

Nor do classical scholars understand the degree to which Pythagorean idealism energized these Theban liberators. Pythagoras was always a shadowy figure even to the Greeks. He had long been dead by the time of Epaminondas. Contemporaries derided Pythagoreans and their practices as a subversive cult. They certainly seemed strange. The embrace of vegetarianism, equality between the classes and sexes, reincarnation, reverence for nature's harmony and order, avoidance of extremes, and fascination with numerical symmetries all frightened traditional Greeks. Apparently the soul could achieve its lasting perfection and rest only by denying the earthly appetites. It was almost considered trapped within matter of some sort—in cyclical fashion reentering a plant, an animal, or a human until it was cleansed of temptation, and at last set free to become incorporeal and immortal.

The divine was visible around us for those willing to train hard to appreciate it. Prime numbers cannot be divided. Man, not nature, creates artificial and unnatural notions of diet. Social intercourse and rank should be dissolved. Plants and animals have souls and are one with men and thus sacrosanct. Suppression of the ego and material acquisition alone help us to glimpse the godly.

For the Pythagorean farmer, the divine was found by cultivating symmetry out of savage chaos. For the statesmen, the ideal was to return men to their naturally free state without arbitrary rank. For the citizen, he should avoid eating meat and not be embarrassed of using the left—and traditionally unlucky—hand. Somehow for Epaminondas and his circle all that translated into an idealism of freeing the serfs of Sparta—or at least the philosophical veneer of a shrewd strategy to weaken rival Spartan military power.

The catalysts of this story of Epaminondas are the farmers of the clan of the Malgidai—Mêlon, his slaves Chiôn and Nêto, and their fellow rustics from the highland orchards and vineyards of Mt. Helikon. These characters—unlike most others in the novel—are not found in the historical record, but they are the sort of people who so often appear as farmers in the *Works and Days* of Hesiod, various comedies of Aristophanes, and the letters about rural life that have come down to us under the name of Alciphron.

A word is needed on the use of dialogue. How can Greek-speaking literary characters, belonging to a foreign world some 2,500 years past, sound authentically ancient and yet be understandable to a modern English reader?

Classical Greek authors themselves wrote in what we today might call a formal style. Their own elevated vocabulary and complex syntax certainly were not realistic, and would have been recognized as such by the proverbial man in the street. Indeed, both public orations and recorded private dialogue—whether found in Thucydides's history, Plato's repartee, or the verses of Sophocles—were not intended to reflect actual speech.

Much less did Greek prose mimic the spoken word heard daily in a Thebes or Athens. Even at their most colloquial expression, Greek literary prose and poetry were a world away from the accessibility of American popular slang.

So I have tried to strike a balance—avoiding both the extremes of the formal prose of nineteenth-century English historical fiction (written in large part by novelists who knew Greek and Latin and emulated the complex syntax of ancient authors), and the now common practice of making ancient people sound as if they were American suburbanites.*

My editor at Bloomsbury Press, Peter Ginna, offered countless editorial suggestions that have improved the narrative. Glen Hartley and Lynn Chu of Writers' Representative once again proved invaluable friends, advisors, and agents. I profited a great deal from close readings of the manuscript by Curtis Easton, Susannah Hanson, Jennifer Heyne, Raymond Ibrahim, Yishai Kabaker, and Bruce Thornton. I would also like to thank the editorial staff at Bloomsbury Press for editing, advice, and patience in bringing the book to fruition.

---

*All quoted Greek by convention is rendered into the Attic dialect.

# PART ONE

# *Holy Leuktra*

# CHAPTER I

## Mêlon Comes to Leuktra

A cart approached raising a high dust trail. A few more hoplite soldiers for the outmanned army?

Atop the hill, in the center of the plain of Leuktra, a lookout
man of Epaminondas was already yelling out the news. Proxenos, the
Plataian, had spotted the wagon in the distance—but only one, a single-
ox cart maybe, making its way up the switchbacks from the town of Thespiai. That surely meant Mêlon from Mt. Helikon had come to battle at
Leuktra as he had promised. He was late, but here nonetheless for the final reckoning with the Spartans. And it looked as if he came with two
other men as well.

"He's here. Mêlon of Thespiai is here with Epaminondas, or least almost here." Proxenos did not wait for the wagon to near. He ran down to
the camp of Epaminondas to tell his generals that the apple, the *mêlon* of
the Spartans' dreaded prophecy had at last come to battle—as if the
awaited man were now worth a thousand, if not five thousand at least.
The presence of Mêlon, the apple, would win over the hesitant horsemen
and the scared farmers and the ignorant tanners and potters as well.
Could not the council start this very night and muster the army for
battle? Oh yes, Proxenos thought, all the silly superstitious Boiotians
would at last fight now. They would battle not for right or even their land,
but buoyed by the idea they would destroy the Spartan army with this
aging cripple of prophecy, Mêlon, son of Malgis, at their side and General
Epaminondas at their front.

Mêlon saw ahead the lookout running down the hill, but made no point of it. He was in the back of the cart and stretched his legs out. The Thespian also ignored the singing of one of his slaves, Gorgos, beside him. Instead, he pointed to the other with the reins, Chiôn, to find the good ground and let old loud Gorgos be. Mêlon's feet without sandals were now dangling from the open backside. His old, twisted leg was wrapped. He had bound it with leather straps for battle. Mêlon had wedged himself among the food and arms, propped up in the back of the deep cart—and had just woken up again, when a wheel jolted out of the stone ruts and slammed back in.

The groans of the ox Aias, as the wagon kept uphill a bit longer, had helped to rouse Mêlon from his dark returning dreams of a high mountain hut. The shack was not the one on his own farm on the uplands of Mt. Helikon. Not at all.

Instead, it was alien and had something to do with this impending war, and seemed to be shared somehow with Gorgos. But it was far away, cold—and, he sensed, to the dreaded south. How he wished the dream interpreter Hypnarchos were here, with his red-lettered scrolls that made sense of the nonsense of the night visions, and taught which dreams were false and which could prove true. In these apparitions, this shed was also shrouded in rain and winter fog, high in spruce trees somewhere amid the clouds. The hazy peaks around it were foreign, and not those of his Helikon. His Gorgos was there too, just as he was here now, still singing his Tyrtaios, but different looking and sounding as well. His other two slaves, Nêto and Chiôn, they were also in this far-away vision. He remembered that much and accepted that the dreams became more frequent as the war loomed closer.

But Mêlon was now fully awake and he sensed Gorgos was, too—likewise rousted from the same dream. Mêlon looked about Boiotia again as the wagon slowly creaked past the hill's summit to a flat meadow. He saw no shed of his dreams anywhere, but he heard his name shouted by some guards off to the right. Otherwise, the cut grain fields were quiet and empty. Not a Spartan yet to be seen. A brief lull had taken hold of the countryside. The early summer threshing was long over. The grapes had their first color on the greener hillsides.

So all was quiet for tomorrow's battle. For all the summer heat, his Boiotia was not nearly as dry, not so barren as he feared it might be. Towering Mt. Parnassos was at his rear. A peak higher than Helikon, with a touch of the undying snow even in summer. To his left rose rocky Ptôon by the sea. Up there was the temple of Apollo. He had hiked the pathway with Malgis—even after his father had stopped seeing the older Olympian gods, and had turned instead toward worship of the Pythagoreans, whose god was Lord Logos, and whose priests were philosophers, claiming that the divine was not just more powerful than men, but more moral as well. On behalf of this god, long ago his father Malgis had died at the battle at Koroneia. For all this land, long ago Mêlon had ruined his leg against the Spartans. And for all the Boiotians, his only son, the best of the three of the Malgidai, was tomorrow willing to ride into the spears of the Spartan horse.

As he scanned the plains and hills around Leuktra, Mêlon saw now how the farmer creates his own better world of trees and vines. He gets lost in it, and needs someone to bring him out of his refuge. His son had now done that for him and so brought him to the grand vision of Epaminondas, but then, again, Lophis had never fought the Spartans. Any who did, as Mêlon had, might wish to never again, and so would remember why the world of the orchard and vineyard was far safer than the chaos of what men produce in town. Yet then again, no man can be the good citizen alone on his ground, although Mêlon had tried that for thirty years and more, in between his service for the Boiotians. A farm may hide failure, be a salve to hurt and sorrow, even disguise fear and timidity, but it cannot be a barricade of peace when there is mayhem outside its walls. And there was now plenty of that at Leuktra.

As he neared the creek of Leuktra, Mêlon saw again from the jostling wagon that his Boiotia was a holy place. It was no pigsty of marshes and dullards the way the Spartans slandered it. If it were, why would they be here this day to take it? It was time anyway for this settling up tomorrow, Mêlon thought, even if it meant that the Malgidai would have to mortgage their all—himself, Chiôn, Gorgos, and Lophis, maybe even the farm itself. The fight was not yet about Epaminondas freeing the slaves of the south, he assured himself. Not entirely tomorrow. Nor about the Pythagorean dream of "we're all equal" that would take the gods to enforce. Nor about the promises of oracles and seers that Mêlon was the apple who had to fight at Leuktra for Epaminondas to win—and for a Spartan king to die.

Apart from all that, Mêlon and his son Lophis would battle just this once more to push the invaders off his soil. Or at least he thought he would, since he had not yet met this Epaminondas—this huge jar into which everyone seems to throw their dreams, fears, and hopes. The seers said the men of his age were not like the grandfathers of their grandfathers, who had saved the Hellenes from the Persians at Marathon. Mêlon's debased generation was said not even to have been the equal of their grandfathers, who had helped the Spartans stop Athens from gobbling down Hellas. But now the Boiotians—right here, tomorrow—they could at least end Sparta? That would prove that the polis was not through yet, that the blood of the old heroes of Hellas, of Miltiades, of Lysander and of Pagondas, still ran in the veins of the Boiotian farmers at Leuktra.

So a sense of contentment, of *eudaimonia* had come over Mêlon, son of Malgis, as they had left his farm this past morning. For its vines and trees, and tall grass—and for fear of being found wanting in the eyes of the dead—he would pick up his spear. For his son Lophis, and his son's young wife Damô and their boys and their neighbor Staphis who had braved the hoots of the Thespians in the assembly—and for the simple folk of his Thespiai who never had harmed Sparta—he would fight Sparta and seek to end Sparta. Staphis with the smelly single cloak and a bleary eye and his stick arms was the least likely hoplite in Thespiai—and the only one who had joined the Malgidai for battle. Even now Mêlon recalled the rabble in the assembly back home, who had hooted the vine man Staphis down when he alone had called for the town to muster with Epaminondas.

"We know," Staphis had screamed back at them, "that the Pythagoreans will join Epaminondas, whoever this general is." Vine growers rarely had the ear of the assembly and he was not about to lose his moment as he bellowed out more. "And we know his fellow Thebans will as well. And those who could use plunder from the dead on the battlefield may wish to go to Leuktra. Others who hate Sparta will line up in the front rank. But why should we farmers on the high ground of Helikon care whether these Spartan invaders torched the wheat land of the lowlanders below or trample our vines? Why would I, with two daughters and a gout-footed wife, risk a spear in my gut, when my grapes are overripe and rot on the vine for want of pickers? Why? Well, I will tell you: for the name of Helikon, of course. And for the pride of our Thespiai, and for holy Boiotia that bore and raised us. Yes, for the idea that no Spartan will ever again barge into the ground of their betters, and that on the morrow, we shall end Sparta for good as we knew it. For all that, I, Staphis, will walk alone to find a slot in the front line of my general Epaminondas."

Now remembering all the lofty words of the defiant Staphis, as he neared the enemy encamped at Leuktra, Mêlon sensed, like Staphis, that decay was not fated. Decline was a choice, a wish even, to idle and to lounge and willingly to become lesser folk, rust that appeared to feed on the hard iron of what their parents had wrought. If Boiotia were to fall, it would not be because of Lichas and his Spartans, or Persians from across the sea, or the wild tribes who swept from Makedon, but because lesser Boiotians simply let them in, preferring wine and flute-girls to blood and iron.

The farmers of Helikon had the good on their side. They had never yet marched down into Lakonia to bother the Spartans. Mêlon had never sung war songs like the war-loving Spartans did. But now, today, they were burning his homeland of Boiotia, and nearing his polis Thespiai. Until now, for much of his life, he certainly had not had much feeling one way or another about their helot slaves—at least not until this summer. But the Spartans had provoked Epaminondas, and now the general in fury would risk thousands of Boiotian farmers killed for the freedom of the Messenian serfs and to end Sparta for good. Is that the nemesis that the hubris of Sparta has earned—and their ruin that was to come at last? But was there another way to stop them? Surely not, at least not for good. A wall of stone, a mountain perhaps could block a line of advancing Spartan hoplites, but not other mere men, at least as he had known them until now. A man, Mêlon now smiled at his wild thoughts, could think of a lot as he rested in the back of a cart on the way to war.

Each spring, the tall men of Sparta from the south came to torch when the grain of Boiotia grew heavy and dry. This summer, almost on a town crier's schedule, King Agesilaos had ordered the other king, his royal partner, Kleombrotos, to bring in another army. The two promised that Boiotia would be theirs before the rumors of war and promises of revolution spread to the south and took flesh—before the rest of Hellas got drunk, they also said, on the mad idea that the poor man with nothing could vote in the assembly right alongside the noble with everything and put the worse in charge of the better. All that would ruin what was once good in Hellas. Or so they also said.

Boiotia knew that Kleombrotos, if his army won at Leuktra tomorrow, would then unleash his henchman Lichas to kill the Pythagoreans of Thebes. Lichas would round them all up, since their talk about equality was at the root of this democracy—and their notion that their one god judged men on their merit rather than, like the Olympians, by their power and nobility. The Spartans warred not just against the Boiotians, but against the notion of democracy itself.

Mêlon knew Epaminondas was right to face the Spartans down, even though he did not believe he was fated to kill a Spartan king or that any such silly prophecy was needed in the ranks to win. He was here instead to do some big thing. He would accomplish something different from the last years, to end his quiet and plunge into the roaring storm's surf rather than hear it crash from a safe distance. Perhaps the muscles of his Chiôn and his own skill with the spear would put an end to it all. Who better than these two veterans could stop the Spartans? Tomorrow was as good a day as any to start, here at this fight beside Leuktra creek.

Then a strong breeze blew across his face from the south, and Melôn was back out of his dreams of the day and fully awake again, once again the lame farmer from Helikon and no longer the would-be savior of Hellas. The wagon had pulled up well beyond the outer edge of the Theban camps, almost alone on the upland plateau. A thousand tents spread down the slopes to the gully at Leuktra. The "white" creek of Leuktra was mostly a trickle by summer, more fouled and black with moss than white with running foam. Finally the three neared the flat top of the hillock most distant from the center of the Theban camp. Some oaks and a laurel tree there shaded a small spring that fed a clean stony pool. Only a few Theban tents were this far up, across the way on the neighboring rise above their army below.

Gorgos was still singing his most peculiar Spartan tune—"It is a noble thing for a good man to die, falling among the front-fighters, fighting on behalf of his fatherland." The harsh beat sounded like some nonsense from an ancient Spartan war song of the poet Tyrtaios—even though the three in the wagon were supposed to be Boiotians, pledged to fight for General Epaminondas, the final arrivals from Mt. Helikon to the Boiotian camp.

Gorgos had kept on with his song even as the wagon passed by the Boiotian campfires—all the louder, the more numerous the enemy tents appeared on the hills across the gully. In his defense, he often claimed that before the Malgidai had captured him he too had been a helot, a noble of Messenia born far to the south, but one Spartan freed and Spartan trained. Now with seventy summers and maybe more behind him, his gravelly voice kept croaking out Doric song lines like, "fighting on behalf of his fatherland." But whose fatherland did he mean?

The closer the wagon had come to the army of the Boiotians, the wilder the mind of Gorgos became. He decided now that he did not like at all this idea of fighting against his old benefactors, the Spartans. Not even if they were here up north tramping on his master's ground and he had not been with them for more than twenty years. Only with the threat of the lash had Mêlon dragged him with armor to the stream here at Leuktra. And Gorgos suspected that these Boiotian pigs were not fighting tomorrow just as defenders against the Spartans' invasion, at least not entirely, or even that this bloodletting would be the end of it. Instead if they won tomorrow, if they beat their betters, they would promise endless battles to come in the south for Epaminondas. He was their ragged dreamer who got them drunk on notions that they were going to be liberators and freers of chattel slaves and so become better even than the slave-owning gods on Olympos themselves—notions far more dangerous than fighting for mere plunder, pride, or revenge. Could not a brave man kill that faker, slit his throat, cleave off his head—and so save untold men from dying tomorrow?

Yet Gorgos still kept arguing with himself as he chanted, not quite a Spartan lover, for he was also loyal to Mêlon in his way, and had also known as a young helot the hard stroke of a Spartan lash, one that cut far deeper than did the Thespian. His grudge was more with the madman Epaminondas who wanted endless war, not mere battle of an hour or two—a total war and not just to defeat Sparta but to end the Spartans. And not to free a helot or two, but to free all of them.

Even his recluse master Mêlon would no doubt listen to the firebrand Epaminondas. His entire clan on Helikon already talked of setting up democracy, such a fantasy where dogs and birds could vote alongside landowning citizens—of marching into his Sparta, of building vast free citadels in the Peloponnesos of towering stone, of liberating the helot serfs so that the Spartan lords would finally have to farm and could not fight, of turning Hellas upside down and putting the worse over their betters.

And all this craziness for what, old Gorgos now asked himself on the eve of battle. If his master in the back of the wagon was mumbling in his dreams, why could not he as well? The Boiotians claimed a Pythagorean lie that all creatures who bleed are equal and all our souls become happy in the hereafter for lives well lived. If victory tomorrow led to that lotus-land, well, then, better defeat and death for his master and himself in the noble Hellas rather than to live on in the new bastard one.

As Gorgos kept dreaming and chanting out his poet Tyrtaios on the ride to the battlefield, he forgot again they were already passing amid the army of Epaminondas. Soon he was back in his trance as his singing returned to his childhood in Lakonia. The slave closed his eyes. He could still dream, more so now than ever. Chiôn had the reins, not he. Here on this eve of the end, all the more he could feel thousands of Spartans were nearby in the hills across the plain. He thought he could see, even feel the front line of the enemy Spartans ahead, thousands of tall men in red capes and long black braids. They would be grim still—just like he remembered them as a boy the first time he saw hoplites under Brasidas. The Spartan *Homoioi* had all been marching to pipe music, just like they did when he was later captured at the Nemea battle. Their shields would be out chest-high, the spears all lowered. Breastplates, helmets, greaves all would be dazzling in shiny bronze—horsehair crests bobbing, scarlet cloaks flapping in the wind. All in perfect order. A porcupine, as deadly as it was beautiful—with quills out and ready for stabbing.

Gorgos thought he could almost see that death walk of his noble red-caped killers. Oh how he wished he were with them and not here with the soon to be losers at his side. Sparta was always short of men, and here he was untapped, unused, a Boiotian slave no less. The helot even began tapping his foot, even in the back of Mêlon's wagon, alongside the dozing master. Who cared, since they would all die anyway in a few hours. Boiotians always fall when they meet the better men of Sparta. So it did not matter that an old helot in Boiotia sang the songs of the enemy or woke up his sleeping master.

Then a hard slap. Gorgos almost fell off to the road. The song ended. The other slave, the driver Chiôn—"Snowy" most thought *chiôn* meant—had let loose of the reins, turned, and given Gorgos his backhand. He slapped Gorgos for no more than his bad verses, or so it at least seemed. Chiôn stayed silent, even as he stood tall again, always a head higher than any around him, now driving amid the rising dust. He was the young one, Gorgos the far older slave. In his years of his pout and isolation, their master Mêlon had let both of his two farm slaves run almost wild. They managed the vineyards on Mt. Helikon more than did their master. Now with this new notion of Epaminondas and talk of freeing of the helot serfs to the south, not much longer could a liberator own other Hellenes anyway.

Mêlon himself woke yet again to the sound of the slapping of Gorgos. In the back of the wagon, he had fought with his own visions. Maybe he should have long ago killed these two slaves, inasmuch as both were smarter and stronger—and far angrier—than their master, just as he thought he was to all others on Helikon. If Chiôn and Gorgos survived the battle, if they were freed, even in his dotage Gorgos would kill too many of the good, as if he were some whip of the Spartans; and Chiôn would kill too many of the bad, as if he thought he had the rights of some fury god. It was a dangerous thing to free slaves with good minds and longer memories. Who could guarantee that they would kill each other and so cancel themselves out, before the corpses of the guilty and innocent alike piled up?

War, Mêlon at least knew, is the great torch that brings such heat and light to everything and everyone. Nothing can hide from the god Polemos, not even the clever mind of Gorgos who now sang like a traitor. But then he saw Chiôn smiling; did the Spartans have any idea of how many of the red capes that one would kill? Mêlon went on and imagined that, like some high mountain bear, his Chiôn might take down all these southerners, drag them to the nearest oak, hang them up by their heels with their red tunics, and let the dogs and birds do the rest. Or so he remembered Chiôn mumbling, that and more still: that spearing was too good for them. Chiôn talked more like that because he was now close to the moment of battle, to being freed at last to make all things right, as he promised, for his master, for his slave Nêto, for the good son of Mêlon, Lophis, for freeing slaves of the artificial laws of the polis that said some are free, others not.

The cart stopped. Gorgos unhitched a sweaty Aias. He roped and hobbled the ox to the tongue. The helot gave enough slack so that the beast could drink from the creek water. Cagey Gorgos had guided Chiôn well here. He laughed out loud, as he thought how clever he was to have known the spot in advance—maybe as a back escape path down the hill should the slave Chiôn turn feral and try to kill him right here? Or was it a way to get out the backside, should the Boiotians lose—or even win? About four stadia away on an opposite gentle rise, the three could make out through the haze where King Kleombrotos and his horde of Spartans had settled down for the night. The ditch and brush ramparts of the invading Spartans were already finished—and all done in just the two days since the king's arrival in Boiotia. The outline of shadowy Mt. Kithairon loomed to the enemy's rear.

Mêlon knew how to compute numbers. He had long ago measured borders when the farm squabbles broke out on the upper plots on Helikon. Now he saw there was a far larger army of invaders than there was in the new Boiotian tent town of Epaminondas below them. What had his son Lophis talked him into—and into what had Epaminondas talked the Boiotians? The old man turned to Chiôn. "I gauge at least ten thousand of them, maybe twelve or even fifteen thousand more Spartans over there, who need killing. Three to two, against Epaminondas, maybe closer to two to one. For all his fine talk of freeing the unfree, that is all that is left. Either they keep ravaging Boiotia or we stop them. You stop them only by knocking down the royal Spartan bunch on the right wing where they need killing the most. Only the spear arm stops them. Nothing else. They won't parley, won't surrender, won't stop—until killed. No need to count them. They aren't going anywhere. Why should they when they outnumber us?"

Chiôn paid him no heed. Mêlon could smell the campfires of the Spartans as they roasted their sacrificial goats for their early meal. He kept talking to himself. For stadia well beyond their ditch and camp wall, early evening fires were flickering everywhere on the hills opposite, on the other side of the gully in the growing twilight. The whole world tonight seemed Spartan. How were they to beat men like that, said to be better and known to be more numerous? King Kleombrotos, Mêlon said to himself, if he wins, he will be supping inside the seven gates of Thebes. By tomorrow at dusk we will all speak Doric on our way down into Hades as well.

The two slaves still ignored their babbling master and kept unpiling their gear.

# CHAPTER 2

# Lichas the Spartan

Across the way, the Spartans were working, not thinking—stacking brush as a wall on their backside. They had the dry streambed and now a ditch as rampart at their front. Unlike the Boiotian camps, there was order here in their huge circle—a *taxis*, a plan of marching hoplites in drill and to pipe music. On this night before the battle, the stewards on cue brought kettles of black barley soup and spits of roasted goat. Over there, Gorgos knew, stalked bald Lichas, son of Lichas, the best of the old Spartan breed. Lichas had fought the Athenians forty summers earlier. He knew enough of Epaminondas that if the fool had his way in making everyone equal who were not, then there would be no place for the better ones like Lichas himself in the new softer Hellas. Only Lichas and a few of his Spartan henchmen stood in the way between the old and better ways of the Hellenes and this polis-wrecker Epaminondas.

Now in confidence Lichas went from campfire to campfire rousing his men on. "Comb your hair who have it, men. Shave your upper lips clean. Look like the better men you are when we face these pigs. We are no different from the tall men who once broke the Persians at Plataia. Why, we could still sail into Athens, as our grandfathers did, and tear down its walls. So chant your Tyrtaios. Tomorrow, right at mealtime we eat on their acropolis, atop their Kadmeia. The Boiotian pigs? Why, they will soon sup in Hades. Listen to your king. Our Kleombrotos, king of Sparta, speaks at torchlight."

His hulking son Antikrates followed. He was a giant of a man outfitted like a battling Ajax or Achilles depicted on the red clay pots from Athens. The panoply was all Spartan style, but heavier and thicker and better than most armor of the peers, his scarlet cloak a deeper hue and with a silver trim. Few others could carry the weight of such bronze. His willow shield was ten palms wide, as round as the best turned cartwheel, hewn from the copses on the low slopes of Taygetos. Bull leather padded the inside, and on the outside was hammered a tin lambda for Lakedaimon, the home of Sparta. His thick left forearm alone could hold it chest high. Two dented bronze greaves covered his shins with an olive oil sheen—and each with two intertwined serpent bosses, no less, hissing and biting as they wound around each other down to his feet. More oily leather sheets were stitched to the greaves's insides. Antikrates wore the old-style chest plate, all cast and hammered bronze, with silver clasps joining the back sheet to the front. Small finger-length silver running stags with six-pointed horns were hammered about, all with eyes of gold, of intricate design, patches that covered the holes and cracks from twenty spear thrusts from Arkadians, Athenians, and Boiotians, fool hoplites all who died thinking they could reach the flesh of Antikrates through the bronze scales of his armor.

His *pteruges*—wide leather straps weighted with iron square rivets— hung down from his breastplate, flapping about to protect his lower parts, should the long leather apron on the bottom of his shield fail. The helmet crest of Antikrates—black stallion hair, mixed in with a white mare's tail—bobbed a foot higher than his head, making him seem taller, more savage still. A bit of beard and two narrow eyes were all that peeked out from his bronze helmet, as if there were some beaded lizard behind the horrific metal mask. Or perhaps there was, since few had seen Antikrates without his helmet. *Haima*—"blood"—he called his spear of cornel wood with a black iron head that went nine feet from its bronze butt spike up to the sharpened point. The shaft was a thumb or more thick, too heavy for any but his father Lichas to stab with. All this was worth more than five oxen, or a field slave of thirty years. The panoply had once been worn by Lichas in his flower until he passed it on to Antikrates, lest one day the old man fall in battle and have *Haima* carried off by an Athenian or Theban lord.

The Spartan even with the weight of his armor was as straight as his father Lichas was stooped. Antikrates scowled and slapped any helot servant who was slow to get out of his way: "Shield against shield—crest against crest we fight. Ares is our god. Artemis and Pan are our henchmen." While the Boiotian generals across the gully parleyed and bickered and voted, these invaders were united, all eager to raise their spears. They were worried only that the Boiotians might run rather than fight them. The enemy camp told this story of Spartan order well enough. Shields, thousands of them, were arranged in neat concentric circles. Most rested on wooden tripods. A lean-to of twenty spears—not one out of kilter—stood next to every fire. Helots ran from campfire to campfire with pots of oil and jugs of wine. Order governed the camp, so too order on the battlefield—Spartan *eunomia*.

As the hoplites prepared their mess, dutiful Messenian slaves had taken out their sheepskin rags. They dipped them in olive oil, polishing their masters' breastplates and greaves. Others brushed their horsehair crests. Still more braided the long tails of their masters' hair. Amid them all, Antikrates now left the side of his father. He marched through the camp after an older and toothless red-cape Sphodrias, who liked to sneak into the enemy camp and slit the throats of the snoring. The two kept bellowing out as they stalked past the fires, "Get out your whetstones. Sharpen your cleavers. Our blades will go through these pigs as spits do fat pork. Sharper still. Always file your iron, men. Ready your iron for your king."

Finally King Kleombrotos himself appeared and yelled out to his Spartan subjects. He was standing on the back of a wagon surrounded by a throng of his royal hoplites. The lord was a young sort, maybe no more than forty years. As the king of the Agiad line, he had already held his office for the past nine. Kleombrotos had not wanted to fight this day. He had headed north for Thebes only because he feared the wrath of Lichas and the ephors—overseers who audited the king's campaign—should he slink and file out of the plain without battle. Although he knew his Spartans would win, Kleombrotos did not expect to survive the battle. Even back in the south he had heard of the helot Nêto's prophecies of his own doom at White Creek where he would meet her master Mêlon. Kleombrotos feared Epaminondas as much as he did Zeus. Now the eye blinks he had suffered since childhood, and his bad head tilt of the past year, made him talk more in the fashion of a slave or half-helot than a king of Sparta.

"Men of Sparta. Another spring in Boiotia, so another victory over the pigs. Nothing ever changes for us, the better men of Sparta—unchanged since the days of the founder Lykourgos. Right after our breakfast and wine, we go out. You know the Spartan way: We fight each other for targets and enemy hoplites. Pray there will be enough of them for our spears. We go always to the right across the field—rightward all the way to their rear without a break in our stride. Tomorrow we mass twelve deep—not our eight shields of the past. All the better to crush the Theban pigs at the first spear thrust. No worry about our flanks. Men of Sparta, *Homoioi tôn Lakaidaimoniôn*, we have more good men there than we need. Our army has wide horns, more men than we need on the flanks."

But the voice sounded too high, too shrill for a Spartan king. The king spoke as if battle with Epaminondas were to be avoided rather than sought. He finished weakly, "If every Spartan peer, if every ephor, if even a Spartan king should fall tomorrow, so be it. It would be worth that great price to kill Epaminondas and stop his democratic madness. Follow me to victory. Follow me up their Kadmeia."

His army murmured. Only a few raised their fists at their king's notion that any Spartan would need die at all against these pigs. Most of the companions in disgust turned to finish off their wine. Then the pipes took up and the king's guard took the frightened royal into his tent. Before the men laid out their reed bedrolls, and smothered their cook fires, Lichas the ancient ephor climbed back up on the wagon bed. He bounded up as if he were no more than twenty. The brute Kleonymos, captain of the king's guard, stood on one side, Lichas's son Antikrates on the other, his shield still on his forearm. Both were a quarter royal and, better yet, claimed bloodlines from Brasidas himself. The two always had fought side-by-side and argued only over the number of their kills. Yet the sly night-killer Sphodrias came too and towered behind them all, even if he usually sought to hide rather than strut his size as he crawled about the campfires of the enemy. He planned this very night to go behind the lines and bring back a Theban shield—or, better, a hand or foot.

Lichas was becoming tired of his reluctant king. He could care not a whit whether the odds, or the omens, or the weather, or the battleground favored either Spartans or Boiotians. He was of the old ones, a Spartan like Leônidas. An ephor. In defeat or victory, Lichas, son of Lichas, of the greatest polis of Hellas, in its greatest age. He would fight like his grand-

fathers at Thermopylai. He would kill Boiotians and he would bring untold misery to them and endless glory to his own. If their own king was
fated to die, better to rid them of a royal not fit for the Spartan office. The
women of Sparta claimed Lichas was even uglier than Kleombrotos, and
they boasted it was due to the scars of battle, not the bad draw at birth.

"My peers, my equals. We muster before dawn. This time the pigs
claim they will go over us tomorrow and on into Sparta. The fools claim
they will not slink back into their sties as in the past but will fight for all
sorts of silliness under the silliest of all, Epaminondas. They want us to be
all the same, to ruin Hellas and to call it democracy—to end our beloved
Sparta as we know it. We say the best men are best to keep the weaker
ones secure. That's why we come into pig land to collect our rent for keeping the swine penned up and safe."

He liked the sound of his roaring voice. Lichas could not stop.
"Whether we have to fight the Titans or Olympians, the verdict is the
same, always the same. You Spartans are born, raised for the fight against
anyone, at any moment we please. We all will die without it. I ask our
seers here—will it be young Kleonymos, the tower of the phalanx, or my
boy Antikrates, who breaks the guard of Epaminondas and sends him
and his fools to Hades? Which one? Tell us now. Place your bets before
sunrise when we throw the knucklebones. As for me, your Lichas here—
Lichas, ephor son of the ephor Lichas? I vote for none of them. Only for
me. I'm the one, the best killer of them all."

He let out an eerie high-pitched laugh, even as more Spartans drifted
back from their campfires to hear him. The growing throng was calling
out Lichas as loudly as they had been quiet listening to their stuttering
king. The more he swaggered and talked, the more the men in their long
capes cheered Lichas. Behind such a Spartan, they felt safe. They could
boast they were no worse men than those Spartans of old who had followed King Leônidas against the Persians. If there were *dikê* still in the
vale of Lakonia, any justice at all, this man Lichas, without birthright of
a king, long ago rightly would have been their king. Or so they mumbled
in admiration at the four tall men on the wagon.

Let the Boiotians talk of the faker god Pythagoras, who preached
that all men were equal to the worm or sparrow. Let them shout for
Epaminondas and the new fantasy cities to rise in the Peloponnesos. Let
them do all that and more. The Spartans had Lichas, Lichas of the old gods

and the ways of the south, and that would be proved more than enough tomorrow.

But even now Lichas was not quite done. He then roused them with a final taunt, as he seemed to know all the Theban generals and why they had begged Mêlon to come down from Helikon. "So who of us kills the counterfeit Epaminondas? Who then kills the other general Pelopidas and with them their Theban plague of *dêmokratia*? Who sends this Thespian would-be savior, the broken-down farmer Mêlon who, the hag priestesses say, will kill us all, if he dares to show up—the so-called apple of women's fables that kills our king. Who sends him to the houses of the dead?"

"Who? Who?"

"*Egô Lichas. Egô.* Not your Kleonymos. No, not my Antikrates. Not even sneaky Sphodrias here. No, I say it will be your Lichas. I am your Leônidas at Thermopylai reborn. The gods say no free man born of a free woman can kill me. Not tomorrow, not ever. You bet on others. I wager on Lichas—on myself. Sparta is as it was always before. We take the power we need and let others worry whether it's fair. For all we care, these pigs are no better than Persians, and they will die as badly as well." Then Lichas lumbered down. The other three followed him with a shout. The leaders of the *lochoi* rushed up to the wagon, pushing and shoving the crowd ahead to touch the old man. They wanted their Lichas as king—Lichas their man of hard oak, by his speech and zeal capturing the hearts of thousands that the green-stick king Kleombrotos had lost despite his birth.

As Lichas finished, back across the plain in the Thespian camp high across the creek bed, Mêlon and his slave Chiôn were almost finished digging their armor from the wagon, cursing at the frayed straps and patched clasps since they had not put the full bronze of Malgis on in more than seven summers—since the last spear crossing near Tegyra beneath Mt. Ptôon. Finally at late dusk the two began to make their way slowly toward Epaminondas. His tent was in the gully below.

Gorgos was left back alone with the ox. The helot slave was sitting on the ground against a wagon wheel, happy enough to be alive with Chiôn gone. In vain, he once more strained for even more Doric sounds from his godly poet Tyrtaios, as those sweet melodies wafted in from the Spartan campfires across the gully. The music of old brought dreams of his son

Nabis, the beardless boy he had left as an orphan long ago in smoky Lakonia, when Malgis had captured him up here in pig land.

Gorgos had been more than a helot in the south. He had risen to leader of the helots in Messenia, renamed by his masters Kuniskos, or so he claimed to the slaves on Mêlon's farm. In his youth he was freed by the house of Lichas for his battle courage and had once become known even as Lord Kuniskos—Lichas's fixer, the eyes and ears of the Spartan ephor and hero. Gorgos now dreamed that after the victory of Lichas at Leuktra perhaps he would return to Lakonia and be known this time as Kuniskos the Terrible—no longer Gorgos the snake man. Once the two, side-by-side, had spear-charged the Thebans at the great battle at the Nemea River—only to have Gorgos fall stunned, brought down and dragged out by Malgis the Thespian, bound with a rope on his way to servitude on Helikon, land of the pigs. Gone forever from his beloved master Lichas. Now he was old and had ended up as no more than Gorgos the dung spreader, who for twenty and three winters had emptied the slop jars in the vineyard of Malgis.

With Chiôn gone, Gorgos was soon napping at the wagon amid the flies of Aias. As he dozed, he chuckled out loud, as he went deeply back into the old dreams of his highland hideout, on his beloved mountain of Spartan Taygetos, far to the south in the Peloponnesos, where he was once more Kuniskos meting out justice for his lost son Nabis. Now he was cooking in his own hut, and laughing in his slumber that Nêto, and Chiôn, and Mêlon had just walked into his house, his own house, where his dinner, quite a meal, was ready for them all. There on Taygetos, the slaves were masters, and masters were slaves—though not in the way that his fellow dreamer Mêlon had thought.

# CHAPTER 3

# *General Epaminondas*

**M**êlon was trying to pick up the soft sounds from the playing of Kopaic reeds as he and Chiôn neared the main tents of the Theban generals of Leuktra. The two were let inside by a few leather-clad sentries with felt caps, stoking the evening fires of Epaminondas.

At last here was the great Epaminondas. Their general, who would lead all the Boiotians tomorrow, did not look like much. Was this short fellow really the god who claimed he could chase a myriad of Spartans back home and turn Hellas into a single polis?

Epaminondas seemed to Mêlon dark and wiry, with shoulders almost too broad for his small frame. His beard was flecked with gray. Most of the head was without hair. But it was hard to tell since his scalp was leathery and dark from the wind and sun. Eyes, nose, mouth—they were all dark too, and blended in with beard and crusty face. He was neither old nor young, neither fair nor entirely foul—just burned and wrinkled. He was covered in something that looked more like hide or bark than real skin. No wonder, Mêlon thought, folk like this talk of freedom, and deathless souls and all the other code of the wild Pythagoras. Most ugly sorts on the wrong side of four decades usually do babble of god and the good they will do as their end nears—like the great rationalist Perikles himself, who wore an amulet around his neck and invited in the witches to chant in hopes that they might abate the boils and fevers from the great plague that ate his body away each hour.

The gear of this Iron Gut—*sidêroun splangchon*, his hoplites called

Epaminondas—was cheap bronze, as dull as the panoply of Antikrates shone in the campfires across the way. The breastplate was cracked and dented. Cheap bronze patches were badly hammered on everywhere. Epaminondas wore no greaves. But he should have. His lower legs were scarred from ugly wounds. A tattered green cloak blew up over his shoulders. Mêlon's eye fixed on his bare right spear arm. It was nearly as wide as Chiôn's. A long scar went from his shoulder to his elbow. A worse *oulê* had reached his neck, right above the edge of his breastplate.

Mêlon looked for a general's horsehair crest, a leader's scarlet cloak, surely a gold sash of the usual Theban *stratêgos*. There was none—just an old round-topped Boiotian helmet and a cracked wooden shield without worn blazon. All those cuts and scars and he had still ended up a bald man with no money about to die fighting the Spartans. He was no peacock general. Or maybe one so marked by Ares that he more often suffered than gave blows in the mix-up. Whatever he believed in, he had believed in for a long time—and had fought for it, too. The nondescript, the poor and needy looking, these are far more dangerous revolutionaries than those with gold clasps and purple cloaks. Mêlon knew that, but he also sighed to Chiôn at his side, "Poor ugly Theban. He's a walking wound. They must call him *ho traumatias*. And he is to lead us tomorrow?"

Five or six other *stratêgoi* of the Boiotian Confederation—the elected Boiotarchs of substance and repute—in new armor, were there to urge Epaminondas to start talking with King Kleombrotos. The generals chimed in that it was time to back out of the valley and beg Kleombrotos for peace. The army was outnumbered and out-positioned, the Boiotarchs protested. They offered talk and money as well to pay the Spartans to leave. The best of the Boiotarchs, Ladôn of seventy summers, who owned five hundred pomegranate trees near Anthedon on the coast and was too old to earn a fist for his slurs, threw his wadded-up cloak in the face of Epaminondas and spat out, "Blood will be on your hands, Pythagorean. I figure Lichas would gladly take in payment some cows and grain to leave. Then he might let us be until next year. Unlike you, he prefers to do business than kill us."

Epaminondas ignored them. They all had white beards or big bellies, or wore purple cloaks or had hammered silver blazons to their shields, and so seemed to Epaminondas to think that their property mattered more than their honor. The generals were terrified that they would die en masse soon, given that they believed neither themselves nor any in the tent could stand up to the wall of Spartan shields and spears. And most liked the sun on their faces in the morning and were not about to give it up for the price of having Sparta ravage their grain each spring or some olive limbs in the fall, and install a few of their bothersome fixers on their *acropoleis*. Meanwhile the officers of the army looked only at their Epaminondas for a nod to fight or a sigh to go home. One look of hesitation, and seven thousand Boiotian hoplites would pack up their armor and head back to their fields. A fight broke out in back and knocked over two torches. Mêlon drew his curved knife—and wondered whether to unleash Chiôn, who cared little how many trees or years Ladôn claimed.

It now was almost dark, and the meeting was still little more than shouts and shoves. The Thebans of the Sacred Band, the three hundred elite hoplites who followed their general Pelopidas, were again playing their flutes in disdain, mocking the wavering generals and throwing the brawlers out into the latrine. Now they quietly put them away on the smile of Epaminondas. Mêlon saw again the blazon on the general's shield propped up on a wooden stand, and could now make out that it was a crude picture of Orpheus—as if this Pythagorean would descend, like the flute player of myth, into the Hades of the Peloponnesos to bring the helots down south out of their serfdom, and thereby ensure their liberators that their souls, suddenly eternal, would be even happier in the hereafter once freed from their brief-lived bodies. Pelopidas and the rest of the Sacred Band, one hundred fifty pairs of warriors in green capes, had now ringed the camp. The uneasy crowd was mostly made up of the lesser officers of the *merê* from the outlying villages, the boroughs far from Thebes. Mêlon looked in vain for his son Lophis in the tent. But at least he heard horses outside, perhaps on the far hill, where the cavalry and his boy were camping. He noticed the snake eyes of Epaminondas watching to spot a shaking knee or a stained cloak of the trembling among his officers. Find that, Mêlon knew, and then get that man out, before his look swept over the entire group.

Ainias the Stymphalian had enough of the noise and shoves and he shouted above the crowd with a mere point to Mêlon, "He's here, here from Helikon." Ainias was an Arkadian mercenary, born by the gloomy lake at Stymphalos, with rumors of slaughter and gore to his name from the south below the Isthmos. He had earlier left word for the command to watch for "the hoplite Mêlon of Thespiai, of prophecy fame." It was he who had sent his newfound friend Proxenos out to the high ground to look for wagons from Helikon. At least some were relieved at Mêlon's sudden appearance. Ainias paid heed to the seers who had promised victory should an "apple," a *mêlon*, join the army, and he knew that was the only way to win back the ranks for war. Even the generals now quieted when they noted the arrival of two such killers from Thespiai for the front line, old as one seemed to be, and even though the other brute was a branded slave.

Mêlon was pushed into the center of the crowd. Retainers stepped aside in deference to the son of Malgis. They knew he had fought at the Nemea, and the same year at Koroneia, and then later at Tegyra—and, in fact, in all the battles of the last thirty summers, after he went out with Malgis at his first battle at Haliartos and beat the Spartans back. In the three-sided open tent were another twenty officers of the provinces, crowded together in a closed circle around the general. As Chiôn strode in with Mêlon, no Boiotian wished to ask of his business. Most knew of this slave from Chios. They remembered that a few years earlier Chiôn had bashed Spartan skulls at Tegyra as he left the baggage train and joined in the pursuit. His branded face and bull's neck won him offers of seats, even from men of Anthedon under the rich Boiotarch Ladôn. He said that he was here at Leuktra for his master. But who knew—maybe also for their own farms as well, or even to restore the name of disgraced Thespiai, since he planned to kill a Spartan king and walk over the corpses of the royal guard to get to him—Lichas's most of all.

This was at last his moment. Chiôn, the "Chian" who never knew the island of Chios of his birth; Chiôn the "snowy white one" who had no affinity with the whiter Thrakians; Chiôn the slave who hated the slaves he knew far more than he did any free man. Chiôn was of nothing to anyone, nor anyone to him—except in battle, where his killing of the Spartans, or so he thought, would do far more for Hellas than any philosopher Alkidamas or Platôn.

Epaminondas moved over to a small bench, sipping some light barley and pork soup out of a black clay bowl with a long handle. He looked back over at the *misanthrôpos* Mêlon. He had never met the hoplite, but he sensed a kindred outsider who likewise had earned the distrust of the mob. Both perhaps would know each other by creed and need no formal greeting. Epaminondas rose in silence and laid an arm on Mêlon's shoulder. He sat him down gently. Then the general began to laugh as if all these bad things had in fact turned out as he wished—as if he enjoyed the ruckus and the brawling over his plans.

"Kleombrotos has come in from Kreusis by the sea—not where I thought by Chaironeia beneath Helikon. Now I reckon only seven thousand of our Boiotians bar his way from the agora of Thebes itself. They will have us as well for their relish." Epaminondas paced in tiny circles, and pointed to a few stools at the front of the crowd. "Sit down in front of us over here, Mêlon of Helikon. The seers cry out that you, the lame one from Helikon, will not lose this battle. Yes, he—you—will cut down a Spartan king. Or so the mouths of the gods quietly sing in prophecy. Your name alone is worth a thousand hoplites. Most came here to join my army for you—not me—convinced a king would fall if you fight in the ranks beside them. But I knew you would come even without the prophecy, you alone of the Thespians, because you are the son of Malgis, the greatest hoplite that we Boiotians have yet put on the field of battle. You had no choice, you are of the Malgidai, and I wager you will prove tomorrow as good as or better than your father whom we knew well."

"Well, Chiôn and I come as we are," Mêlon softly replied. "The two of us fight in the ranks. Somewhere, my son Lophis, my only one, is with the horse. Take care of him. I wish only that we break their ranks tomorrow and kill their king or Lichas or both—then go home to Helikon without fear of Spartans in our vineyards." Mêlon was suddenly restless. He got up and continued as he paced, pointing his black iron sword at Epaminondas. "Die or not, yes, we three will battle for the name of Malgidai. As for the rest of you—you, Lord Epaminondas—may say it is justice, for the equality of Pythagoras and for the freedom of helots to the south, and for democracy where men end up equal when they were not born that way, and for the promise that your souls will live on forever after your bodies rot—or for anything that you wish."

Epaminondas smiled at that. But then he rose and raised his voice as he strode into the center of the throng with his arms extended at last to address the crowd of officers. He knew the men were scared, but at least they were not as terrified as they had been before the arrival of the Malgidai. "The men of Sparta will go nowhere until it is over. The king is here to stay and to fight. He cannot leave—even if he wished to—until he knocks us out of his way. Lichas the Ephor, they say, is with him—to force their poor king to spear us. No, this time they will not run back to their Lakonia. Tomorrow we will become Spartans or they Boiotians. There is no third way. Leuktra is not the end of things, but the beginning of the end of the Spartans. Our road from Leuktra leads on to their hearths beneath Mt. Taygetos a thousand stadia to the south."

Epaminondas in a blink had silenced the crowd, as the Boiotarch drifted to the back of the tent in the shadows. The Boiotians whistled for their leader to go on, and had forgotten the old Ladôn and his five hundred pomegranate trees on the high ground above the Euripos. The general walked back over closer to Mêlon and changed his topic and voice. "The deserters from Sparta tonight claim as well that we will have quite a royal parade tomorrow. Their Deinon the *polemarch*, and Sphodrias, our friend who used to rule Thebes as Sparta's harmost, their overlord, are here. The son of Sphodrias marched out as well, the big one, Kleonymos, the favorite of the royal blooded Archidamos. Kleonymos, I remind you, sent ten Thebans to Hades at Tegyra. The spies also say the Theban killer Antikrates, the son of Lichas, comes as well. They swear that he will kill most of us in this assembly. The worst of the Spartans are here at last. I know them all from my trip to the south last summer. If they die in Boiotia, there are none like them to bar the passes of the Sparta to the south. Pelopidas will show us how."

Three of the Sacred Band stepped forward on cue to pour two baskets of sand over the ground and rearrange the torches in a circle. Then they sprinkled water over the surface to make it hard. They smoothed it all out with straw brooms and a long board, and let Pelopidas with a spear butt mark out the armies. But for some reason, the foreigner Ainias, the Arkadian from the lake at Stymphalos, south of the Isthmos, now stepped up with his own shaft. To murmurs he stood right at the side of Pelopidas. Was this outsider to have his own hand in the battle planning of the Boiotians—a bought Peloponnesian advising them how to kill Peloponnesians? Mêlon muttered to himself, "We have come to fight. Not to draw lines and boxes with Spartan-lovers." But the more he watched this mercenary, noticed his wide shoulders and big hands, heard his measured speech, the more he liked what he saw—especially his shredded right ear. He looked as dangerous as Chiôn and had the same stare as the slave as well. Before Ainias began talking, Pelopidas had been able to put the scouting reports of his own Sacred Band into some sort of larger sense. Now he quickly marked out two rectangles, faced off against each other. The Spartan phalanx in his drawing was nearly twice as broad. Both its flanks went well beyond those of the Thebans.

Pelopidas and Ainias huddled and were whispering a bit. Those around Ainias had welcomed this killer and knew that he would cut down untold Spartans—and yet might cause themselves even greater grief. Now Pelopidas began poking the sand in places as his voice went up and he pointed with the spear end. "There is a king there, Kleombrotos, along with his royal guards; we at least know that much. They will all be on their right wing as usual—the Spartan Right that scares so many of us. Maybe two thousand or three thousand of Sparta's finest, I reckon. All on the right wing. At least three, maybe four *lochoi*. The gods alone know how deep they will stack. Most likely at least eight. But I also reckon this time maybe even twelve shields in mass." Pelopidas went on. "You know the Spartans. The middle of their long line will be riffraff. Those are always the half-helots or the freedmen from Lakonia. Some of these northern scavengers from Herakleia and Phlios will drift in. But on the left, these are the good allies from the Peloponnesos. They are the tough farming lot. Mêlon over there knows these southerners well from the fight at the Nemea." He repeated himself for a moment, "I said these are allies, not enemies. The hoplites of the left wing of the Peloponnesians that the king counts on to hit our best on our right."

"That is not the worst of it, Pelopidas. We must fight in the morning." Epaminondas calmed him and strolled to the middle of the map because he knew the reaction to what would follow next. He began to add in the sand some lines of retreat very slowly and carefully with his own spear. "We cannot hold this army together for over a day or two ourselves—not outnumbered as we are and with even more cracks in our alliance than the king's army. Too many Boiotians and northern tribes are wagering that the Spartans will march over us when the flutes begin to play. Or that we will crack as we did at Nemea. They always wait to praise us should we win, and join the Spartans if we lose. Their only creed is to be the winners—whether with us or not."

The Stymphalian Ainias still stayed silent, but edgy, at his side. Next Epaminondas turned around quickly and addressed the assembled officers directly. "We must fight these invaders by tomorrow or there will be no *dêmokratia* anywhere north of Athens. Otherwise we won't even have seven thousand of this army left. The traitors promise that our farms will be spared. They boast at least everyone would be better off with the *dynasteia* of Spartans back in control." Epaminondas glared at Ladôn, and then backed up a bit. "But Pelopidas—step out of the way for a moment. Ainias of Stymphalos over here and I have been talking. We've worked something up a little different from what our enemies—or you generals here—expect. Let our southern guest speak."

Ainias took off his cape and stepped forward again. His helmet was on the floor at his feet. His gloves and arm bands were off. His pockmarks were shadowed in the torchlight. Long matted oily hair covered his shoulders, his half-ear now and then hidden. His black beard stubble highlighted rather than covered the furrows and creases on his face. From what cave in Arkadia had Epaminondas dragged this wolf-beast out? He made Epaminondas look soft. The captains whispered he'd worked for that rogue archon down south, Lykomedes of Mantineia. Still, few in Boiotia apparently had ever seen him, much less knew of any Ainias of Stymphalos—that wild Arkadian place where the birds of Ares once flung their iron feathers at Herakles by the vast and gloomy lake.

Ainias eyed Pelopidas's sand map. He pushed away others who stood in his light. For all his gaze at the sand below, Ainias looked as if he'd been out in the byways the night before, robbing and throat-slitting for his pleasure along the taverns on marshy Kopais. The Thebans listened in fear that he might draw his long sword and take off a nose or ear, Persian-style—the way his own ear had been lost.

Instead he startled them by talking, much louder than the voice of either Epaminondas or Pelopidas. "Your wars of trumpets and boasts are over. Over. We live in the age of *logos,* of science. I kill by an art, a skill, a *technê.* Not by the livers of goats. Not your prayers to Artemis. Not even numbers and muscles win battles. Battle is as much of the mind as the heart." Few wanted to argue with this man's blasphemy—but what a voice, what long words came out of the mouth of an uncouth killer. "Listen up to the new war. We all know what Kleombrotos and his royal guard will do tomorrow: what they always do whenever they fight. A suckling child without teeth could tell us in advance."

Ainias then waved his hands as he went through the Spartan way of war bit by bit. The entire crowd was hypnotized; those who had just before been punching each other were now pushing to get nearer this curious sand map. "The flutes will start up. The army will walk out on their heavy feet. They stare. They do their slow two-step. The king and his wing slant. They swerve to the right. We will be blinded by the sun at their backs. Or scared by the glare of their polished shields—a thousand and more of the Spartan Similars, all shuffling in the king's charge. Flute music all the while. These shaved lips come on. On always—like the crab we see on the seashore that can only walk sideways and at an angle. They hope, they *expect* to break you rustics from the provinces. Their strong right wing faces off against our weak left. Then they get to your rear. Then stab you in the back. Then turn. And they come up behind your best Thebans on your right. Then you all die. And we are burned and float away as ash. I know this. I did just this as an ally alongside them for twenty seasons. I killed many of your fathers at the Nemea and Koroneia."

He calmed and with almost a murmur finished, "But this they will not do. Not tomorrow. Not ever. I swear to you all that Leuktra will be no Nemea." Ainias, bathed in sweat under the summer torchlight, tore off his leather tunic and was focused on the captains. Epaminondas then stepped up and yelled to his men, "Watch and learn."

"Says who, Arkadian?" a loudmouth interrupted the trance of the crowd, and yelled in a high pitch. They nicknamed the barker Backwash. He was some sort of low official of the Confederation, who had borrowed his father's breastplate and agreed to a safe slot in the back of the phalanx for the price of haranguing the officers before battle and upping the hoplite pay to a full silver drachma. But if he could not talk the army out of battle, then he had some lamb's blood in his pouch that he would smear on his helmet as he peeled out at the back of the column before the first collisions with the Spartans. His real name was Menekleidas. He was from Aulis, on the narrow strait between Boiotia and Euboia, and thought he could steal the crowd back from the Arkadian. "Tell us something we do not already know, foreigner. My lads from the Euripos can stay put and hide well enough from the Spartans over on the big island of Euboia. Tell us why we need to fight and how we can win. Does this foul bird of Stymphalos think he can wing in here and squawk to us, scratching up a fantasy victory from his fancy drawings in the dirt?"

Laughs and growls arose from behind. "You tell them, Backwash." Menekleidas turned around to bask in them. Mêlon had had enough. He pushed away two or three rustics to grab Backwash by the neck, then bent him down and kicked his rear so hard with his good right leg that the would-be orator flew out like an arrow into the goat carcasses outside the tent—and to greater laughs than he had just earned with his smart talk. Backwash was lucky Mêlon had struck first; Chiôn had been about to use iron, not a fist or kick. The council was again almost reduced to a brawl. The Stymphalian hadn't even begun his attack plans. Across the ravine the Spartans were ready to follow Lichas. Here the Boiotians were fighting each other.

Mêlon raised his voice, "Shut up, all of you. Especially this slimy eel from the Euripos. I know my Homer and this here man is an ugly Thersites. Remember the poet's words: 'I swear there is no worse man than you are.' Yes, this Thersites, this Backwash, knows well enough to charge us jacked-up tolls for those who pass over to Euboia. Like the double current, his men know how to collect coming and going. But so far he won't fight for his fellow Boiotians." Then Mêlon, son of Malgis, gave his own brief speech in the way he did to his pruners on Helikon. "I've heard all this before. It leads nowhere—except to a few fistfights and a Spartan army over there at Leuktra already chopping down our olives. They're trampling our vines while we bicker and moan. You decide, all of you, whether you wish to be the dragon-sown men of Old Thebes, the bronze giants of our grandfathers' age—or the connivers and trimmers of this new low era of Backwash." Mêlon then put his arm around Ainias and raised his voice even louder. "Let this stranger from Stymphalos speak and finish his work in the sand—unless you know the Spartan better than he. But I recognize none of you from the battle at Haliartos. Is there any more than a handful here from the fights at Koroneia? See whether the Stymphalian bird has talons or not. I have fought him and his kind from Pellene before at the river Nemea. I would not wish to again. If you know spear work like he does, go on; if not keep still."

The crowd grew quiet along with Backwash. Murmurs went around that this fellow was the son of Malgis of myth. Here was Mêlon of prophecy of the falling apple—and here no less with his brand-faced slave.

Ainias resumed drawing in the sand. "As I said, this they will not do. No, no—tomorrow the best of our army on the right will *not* kill their worst on their left. Our lesser folk won't be harvested by the king across the field on his right. Instead Epaminondas and Pelopidas with his Sacred

Band will take the harder path. They will veer toward the royal Spartan spears. They and the veterans of Thebes *muster on our left*, facing Kleombrotos and his royal right. Chiôn and I, with Mêlon here, go helmet to helmet with Lichas from Pythagoras's noble left."

A louder rustling began at mention of the strange trick. Ainias once again raised both hands to warn them all he would finish. "I said *on our left*. I promise to you this: The Thebans and their generals will fight on the unlucky side of our battle line, head-to-head against King Kleombrotos to the death. We few will end everything once and for all tomorrow spear-to-spear. Let their royal right hit our choice left—best against best. Let your gods on Olympos at that very spot decide who wins Boiotia. We live or die with one blow."

A wave of silence struck the crowd, as if the apoplexy of the sight of the lame Mêlon had not been enough. How could a man with a scarred face and stubble talk like he was a sage of hand-to-hand spearing, the eloquent master of *hoplomachia*? Officers far better than Backwash pushed and squirmed for a better view of his crazed battle plan in the sand at their feet. The Theban elite was now to be on the bad-omened left side? The dirty side. Spear-to-spear, shield-to-shield set against King Kleombrotos. Mêlon scanned the tent. The provincials in the past always used to face directly the enemy king and his guard, while their own city grandees of Thebes stationed far to their right were untouched—slaughtering the allies of the Peloponnesos and calling it their victory.

Since the time of Kreon, the nobodies of Hellas in the battles between the city-states had been the fodder to die on the ill-fated left wing. Mêlon was always told by the Boiotarchs not to lose the battle before their good men could win it over on the easy right. Malgis his father used to joke, "A funny sort of war it is, when the weak fall to the strong—on both sides of the battlefield." Then Ainias called out some more. He would either convince the Thebans or enjoy bashing the heads of the shouters. "Yes, on the left. It's been done before in the south and maybe elsewhere as well. Do you hear me, the left—the good-omened Left Hand, the divine Left of Pythagoras, where our strong hits their strong. There it will be for most of us in this council tomorrow. I and this Mêlon and Epaminondas and Pelopidas over there."

Ainias went on. "But that is not all the Spartans will see at noon." The raspy voice of the torn ear had three cups of wine behind it, so he was louder even than before. "We will not stack sixteen men deep. Not like your fathers did at Nemea. We will not crowd even up to twenty-five shields—as your grandfathers fought at Delion. No, no, no. Epaminondas will lead a column of fifty deep. To push over the king from our left. Fifty shields deep, I say."

Fifty? Fifty shields on the left. How? Why? Now at more of these crazy *taktika*, the throng began pushing to see this map of Ainias in the sand, to find out whether he was mad or drunk or both. In the midst of the crowd's chattering, a tough Boiotarch of wide shoulders from Tanagra came forward, with cratered face, a burn scar down his chin, and a smashed nose. He was no trembler like the whiny wide-butt Backwash or lord of pomegranates, Ladôn. No, this veteran scowled and he forced his way to the fore in a well-earned swagger. Hoplites parted since they had seen him cut a similar wide swath in the mess of battle. Ainias himself was not sure whether to hit this man—or, better yet, pull his sword out. For now the Stymphalian kept his blade in his scabbard on his shoulder.

"Enough of this sophistry. Philliadas, I claim to be. Son of Philostratos. You all know me," he yelled as he turned back to the crowd. The coarse farmer had cleared his barley ground near the battlefield of Tanagra. He was covered with ugly welts and healed-over rips, from both spears and goat horns. Grime and splinters were under his nails. Worse was on his hob-nailed sandals. This Philliadas also knew his numbers. In the past he had earned an Athenian drachma a day settling fights as a surveyor on the borders at Panakton near Attika. Philliadas could measure boundaries in his head—and box any who questioned his number reckoning. He would have done the judging free, just for the chance to kill a man without the charge of blood guilt.

He stared down Ainias. "I wouldn't try to slap me, sophist. Keep that shield still, or we'll settle it here." He stuck his finger almost into the chest of Ainias. "But listen, Arkadian, all you big fellows over there on the left will be only sixty men wide in your square—if even three thousand of you show up tomorrow and I can square my numbers. I figure Kleombrotos and his Spartans on the right wing will add up to twenty-five hundred, if not three thousand—at least as much as the men of Thebes. They may be eight shields to the rear. Or they may be twelve deep at most. Either way, with your sixty shields wide in the front row, you men on the left will be facing two or three hundred of them. I say you will be swallowed up in an eye blink one against four or maybe five. You Pythagoreans talk big about numbers and the good left hand. But these you don't have a clue about."

This Philliadas had the crowd's attention, even though most could not add or subtract, much less multiply his numbers. But they grasped well enough his point: The king's wing of the far bigger army would be broader and quickly outflank the narrow deep column of the outnumbered Epaminondas on the left. It was madness to put your small head into a wide Spartan noose. Philliadas was chewing on the stem of a dried fig as he growled. "With that wider bunch, the king's Spartans will go around you in no time. They'll be at your rear and in the baggage in eye blinks. Even if my boys of Tanagra are out of the storm, soon they will be left naked in the center. We'll be cut and spliced from our backsides. You Thebans will spear nothing but shadows way over on the naked left."

Voices of agreement followed. This torn-nose Philliadas had seen his share of crashing shields. "Maybe this will happen," Ainias nodded, "*if* our mass charges straight ahead or to our right, dear Philliadas, as you seem to think. But why in your Apollo's name should we when fifty deep?" Ainias then threw out the rest of his wine on the dirt. "Instead Epaminondas and Pelopidas with the mass will veer left from the left. They lead their Thebans leftward to the king himself—at an angle, or *loksên* as you say. The rest of the line must follow them. The whole army will go out double-time at an angle leftward. Boiotians too can be crabs in their walk—although left-clawed crabs at that."

As he talked, Ainias clapped his hands to signal the collision of the armies, and then hit the dirt with his spear. Most in the crowd could not see his lines in the sand. But the hoplites felt that he seemed to know what he talked about to be able to draw and talk numbers at the same time— and not get a stab from Philliadas for his efforts. "No, our left mass will angle left for the king. It will kill him. Kill his flank guard, too. Our strong against their strong. We'll hit them fifty shield deep from their open sides before they encircle us. The red-capes have not a clue of our ship's ram that will smash them tomorrow with full oars." Ainias finished, "If the Thebans do as we say, the Spartans will carry off their dead king in defeat packed in honey, back to the River Eurotas before Sparta itself— and the rest will flee."

Philliadas was left mumbling something about himself and his men filling in gaps when the left wing went on its slanted march. Then he headed back to the rear of the crowd, which hooted in approbation that one of their own had at least stood up to the Arkadian high talker.

Epaminondas had quietly translated Ainias's talk into even more crude lines and arrows in the sand. Then he paused to add a few twists of his own. To the hipparchs, about ten or so of the cavalry commanders of Thebes, he pointed. "You ride better than the Spartans. They scoff at horse battle. Why not move away from the flanks and ride out at our front? Why not begin the killing at the fore, as the better men you are—shielding with your dust our new moves from the king?" When he saw the light in the cavalry commanders' eyes, Epaminondas went on. "Kleombrotos will not expect our horsemen in his face. Even he will not think that fifty shields are coming his way behind our cavalry. Their king will see something different at Leuktra—something that no Hellenic general has ever witnessed. I plan to hit him right after his midmorning meal. Then his men are full of food and wine—slow on their feet, and dizzy in their ranks."

Epaminondas paused again. Too much battle talk, and now he could see the eyes of his hoplites wander. But he pressed a bit more. "Allies on the right—give us a little time tomorrow to hold fast. Do not move against the spears of the Peloponnesos. Don't cross the battle line. Watch us first kill their idle Spartan overlords. Stay put. Hold. These allied farmers of Sparta need not die. Our business is only with the braid-hairs and smooth-lips. We have no killing lust for the allied yeomen of the Peloponnesos. They plow their own ground. Do not kill today who will be a friend to-morrow."

He finished with a warning. "Today we talk about killing Spartans on our ground, but that I fear will not be the end of it. Better to ask how we let Kleombrotos in here in the first place. Or why he comes with praise from the Athenians and most others who do not so much hate us as fear and worship him. But there will come a day soon that Hellas, as we know it, ends—and ends, I hope, for the better. There shall be no more unfree in Messenia—and beyond that no slaveholders anywhere even among us, the liberators who free serfs. This is a war not just to free us from Sparta, or even to free the helots from Sparta, but to free us all in Hellas from what makes some masters and others slaves. We fight to free ourselves from ourselves."

## AINIAS DRAWS THE BATTLE PLAN OF LEUKTRA

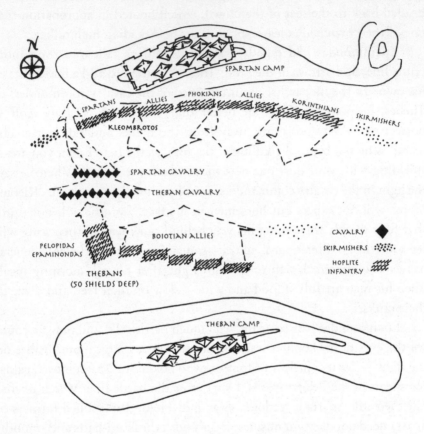

Mêlon murmured to Chiôn, "This man is either crazy or himself a god, and I suppose we will find out by daybreak. He seems as worried about keeping us alive as he is about killing Spartans. Does he know that most Boiotians here are scared, so scared that they would bolt at the sight of a Lichas or Sphodrias, even with all the war lore of Ainias and Epaminondas?"

The slave answered only, "That is why we are here, master—to make sure none runs." But the assembly was not quite over. On some sort of cue, Proxenos, the Plataian aristocrat, strutted to the center like the oligarch that he was. It was fine and good to have new ideas like a deepened phalanx, a slanted march, and the left wing stacked to fifty shields deep. But most of the ignorant and superstitious could not follow the logic of the tactics. That is why Nêto and Proxenos, long ago on his estate above the Asopos, had figured a far better way to rally the Boiotians: to remind them that the gods, the Olympian gods of the ignorant and superstitious, had promised victory to them should the Thespian Mêlon join the ranks.

Now Proxenos began to walk and point. He wore a white cloak and heavy gold around his neck and on his fingers. He trampled over the sand without a care, as he did his polished marble halls at home over the Asopos—and the chart of Ainias disappeared beneath his boots. His newfound protector and friend Ainias did nothing. If the ragged Epaminondas was willing to crash into the red-capes for ideas and helots and freedom, well, then, it was likely because he was poor, and old and without wife or child. But why so, the hoplites wondered, was this rich man, with a deep-breasted wife and sons, and plow land above the Asopos? Why would a Plataian with a big gold ring fight for Thebes or, worse still, for things beyond Thebes? He knew well enough the answer if others did not. He had come to leave the idle rich estate owners of his Plataia, to build entire new cities rather than hang a city-gate in a backwater polis of Boiotia.

Nêto, the slave girl of Mêlon, had drifted into the council this evening, and said she had joined the circle of Epaminondas to free her kindred helots. But she told herself that she was here to free her master Mêlon as well, and bring him down the mountain to fulfill the prophecy of the apple—and turn his mind from the mountain back to the world of the polis below, where men marry women if they proved to be their equals. Nêto trusted that her master cared not for any women except for herself, a lowly slave from Messenia. When off Helikon, she rarely saw any need to talk of him to others, to stand near him, to worry even that slaves are more often beaten than yoked by their masters. So she would do her part for him: She would be freed by the Thespians for joining the Boiotians at Leuktra when most of the craven of the small towns would not, and the two could then be one on Helikon. Because of all that, Nêto also reasoned that there was not much need even to talk to Mêlon, given they were as fated to be one as the Pleiades to rise or the magnet stone to find iron. After all, he was Mêlon, she Nêto, and that was all that the two or any others needed to know. It was just that simple.

Proxenos was an architect, a wall builder, known in Thebes for his good sense and for his devotion to the logic of walls and gates. There was none more believable to deliver the oracles and signs of the gods. His father had taught him about Pythagoras, but then his father had also died seeking gold with Xenophon and the Ten Thousand in Asia. The Pythagoras of the son Proxenos taught the Hellenes that their souls were not one with their bodies, but can live on after death, in the next world where they suffer or prosper on the records that they compile here. Fail, Proxenos lectured his new friend Ainias, mar the soul with the lust for gold, women, or power, and the need to find yet another body—of an eel or snail, perhaps—to house an errant soul becomes endless.

The meeting was about over, when even this man of Pythagoras reported the wild things he had just seen that morning. If the sober Proxenos saw omens, surely most had as well. "Boiotarchs and you other leaders of the files: Listen. Today the doors of the temple of Herakles in Thebes flew open. The statue of Herakles himself stands without his armor. It has vanished. The god himself is in the field. He is calling us to follow him against his impious kin from the Peloponnesos. The virgin daughters of Skedasos are to be avenged. Yes—those who were raped long ago on the rolling hills of Leuktra by men from the south. Listen to the wails of their ghostly spirits. They will fly out to help us kill Spartans."

Proxenos left the center and walked amid the crowd, to and fro, patting the heads and backs of the Boiotian commanders. "The spirits of these maids of Boiotia, once molested here at Leuktra by men from Sparta ten generations ago, have guided us here for revenge against their attackers from the Peloponnesos. Their ghosts hover over us tonight. Their shades shriek for our vengeance against the Spartans. Smoke of the offerings drifts in black patterns into the wind. The seers tell us the livers of their victims lack their full lobes as the gods demand vengeance. The insides of the animals are night-black with a foul stench. A few goats are without any organs at all. Some lungs stink and shrivel in the air when touched by flames."

Proxenos raised his hands to the top of the tent, and went on. "That is only the beginning; ribbons blow off our officers' spears and then land on the tombs of the dead to warn of more to come. The snake god at Trophonios warns the Spartans of their death. The stone statue of Athena bent over and picked up the shield sculpted at her feet." The crowd was rapt at the rich man's words that offered far better promises of victory than all the complex sand drawings of Ainias and big talk of Epaminondas put together.

This Proxenos was as handsome as the foreigner Ainias was ugly—

and one of their own Boiotian aristocrats for relish. Who cared for the *logos* of Epaminondas? Who needed Ainias's *technê*? Listen to the prophecy of their own Mêlon, a Boiotian. There were gods on Olympos. They listened not to the numbers of Pythagoras—but spoke through the omens that Proxenos, another man of Boiotia, related. "Hear me out. All the prophets sing of our Mêlon the Thespian. This man the oracle of Pasiphai from far-off Thalamai warned. He is the lame one—come here tonight from his high farm on Helikon. He is the one the king was warned about. This I can prove. I have talked to the priestess of Apollo on Ptôon. She too has heard the gods' voices: *"Should Mêlon live till tomorrow and see the face of a Spartan king, then the sons of Leônidas, they will be no more."*

Proxenos grew even quieter in speech. "Some of you have heard the rumors about the Thespian Nêto, near Askra. She's the virgin helot, the slave on Mêlon's farm. She has sworn that the priestess of Trophonios, the snake-goddess of Lebadeia, promised us victory—if only the son of Malgis would fight. Ah, she is here with us now."

Then on cue a blood-curdling shriek filled the tent. *"Alalalê. Alalalalalêêê . . ."* The war cry of Helikon. Tall and thin, Nêto stood on a chair above the hoplites. She had sneaked off from the farm, once Mêlon had left with Chiôn and Gorgos, and had spent yet another day at Thebes with Proxenos studying the omens. Now with her hair in waves and her eyes rolling, she posed like those wild gorgons in stone, carved high on the big temples, with mouth and teeth wide open. Back on Mêlon's farm, Nêto had learned to sound her war cry in Boiotian, when guiding the oak plow that Chiôn drew—always in fear that the snorting, sweating slave would break her plowshare on the half-hidden boulders ahead. She had been born a helot but had been bought here in the north by Mêlon. He claimed her seller had told him that the little girl was daughter of a disgraced priestess of Pasiphai to the south. Now she was the oracle of the Thespians in the woods of Helikon. She acted no more like Mêlon's slave than did Gorgos or Chiôn.

Then this wild Kalypso went on again, louder in man speech, winking at her master as she began. "Here is Mêlon. Among you Mêlon, son of Malgis. Don't you see? Mêlon. Listen to our one God. Mêlon of Thespiai is chosen. Yes, yes he is the one they fear to the south. Mêlon will kill a Spartan king. Why? Why? He is the *mêlon* of course, the "apple" the seers say will end the Spartans."

Now she was quite out of her steamy breath. Shaking, swaying, almost tipping off the chair, near collapse, she offered gibberish all mixed up in clumsy hexameters. One hand went up and flailed the air. The other was stabbing the breeze with her reed pipe. The hoplites had never seen anything quite like this. The sudden shouts, followed by her eerie calm voice, kept them still. All this ranting in cadence came from what looked like a slave and a woman. In Boiotian with some Messenian strains—delivered with a high pitch that cut the ears. She appeared as odd as her verse. Nêto was as tall as most men, cloaked in the rough wool of a man. Her nose was a bit long. Her lips were too wide. Her ears were big enough that her long hair could never quite cover them. Yet she was pretty, perhaps even goddess-like—or so she seemed to the eyes of her master Mêlon, who let her roam all over Boiotia.

They could see all that right now, so at least she was humankind. Nêto's face balanced out well enough, as if its parts could not do without each other. Her legs were long. She often ran up to the dam above the farm of Mêlon, with the fawns and does. "Deer Legs," Chiôn called her. Yes, Nêto of the fast legs that outpaced the stags on Helikon. Some of the Thebans murmured that she was a wood nymph or worse than a naiad. But who could get her off that high chair? She must have jumped up with those panther thighs to get there. Without much prompting, Nêto threw off her cloak and hood. As if possessed by the Pythia's vapors, she slowly sang out a few more phrases as she pointed to Mêlon. "Him. Him. The Spartans must kill or lose tomorrow morn. Keep him safe. Do that and the king will die. The Thebans are mightier in war."

Even the glum ones such as Philliadas were stunned silent once they heard that the violated virgin ghosts of Leuktra were to be in the skies floating above them in battle, tearing at the red-capes. They would keep away the winged demons of death from the Thebans. These were the Kêres, the blood-sucking goddesses who appeared, at one time or another, at all the battles of the Hellenes, drawn from afar by the shouts of battle and the smell of gore—with their craws full of man-flesh and sharp claws plucking up any who were tottering—assured that the life-threads of these victims were already spun by Klôthô, measured by deathless Lachêsis, and then cut by their partner Atropos, and that all three of the divine Moirai had nodded to their flying henchwomen that the doomed could now be stripped, their carcasses feasted upon, their souls whisked off to Hades.

In battle, the untouched hoplites saw none of the Kêres of this nether-world. Only the blood-spattered and dying were given the sudden vision of these feathered vultures, who grew fat from the carnage. When sated, the women of the night landed in weariness among the flies and dung to walk off their meal, and vomit and crap out tooth and bone, and then fly up for more. They flapped off cackling and farted out the fumes of human blood. Yes, on oaks around the battlefield the Kêres perched and fouled the ground with their red pus dung. They stank, as they always dove back, eye-level over the battlefield, with their pale breasts, bloody tunics, and long white fangs—eyeing any falling hoplites that could be grabbed and torn apart before the souls went down into Hades. The foolish among the dying saw their female full-white breasts and long red nipples, and paused—only to find fangs in their necks and talons under their arms as they were snatched up. All these would fly above the battle tomorrow—and yet the hoplites were encouraged that perhaps the good ghosts of the virgins of Leuktra might keep the black daughters of night away from them.

Nêto quickly covered up and looked around for Mêlon. Then she jumped down and took her place with the servant girls who scurried about the tent to clean up the mess of eating and loud men. Finally she went over to Proxenos, and amid the commanders, Nêto whispered despite the din of the tent. "I had a shudder. The Olympians speak through me, even if I damn them and instead worship Pythagoras. Yes, you and I claim we understood these signs, but not all of them. If there is truth to the prophecy of the *mêlon*—there is also truth to another warning that Proxenos, son of Proxenos, lord of Plataia, shall not cross south of the Isthmos."

He laughed. But she only grabbed harder on the arm of the Plataian. "The gods on Olympos hate our arrogant Pythagoras, who has stopped so many of their sacrifices and the burnt meats men offer up to their greedy tastes. I hear these old ones, petty, spiteful, and full of envy, at night. Yet they do not always lie to me, especially when I sleep. They hate him and his *logos*." She was weeping in this, the moment of her joy that the army was about to fight and would win, she knew—and then would go south and free her Messenian kin after all, even if thousands of helots down south as yet knew nothing of Thebes, of Pythagoras, or the idea of democracy.

But then Nêto frowned and grabbed the cloak of Proxenos. "Listen, again. Do not go south after our victory tomorrow. We will win. But you lose if you do not stay north of the Isthmos. You are no Mêlon, who even in his age is stronger than you, and is the god-loved. Nor are you an Ainias who can oversee your walls to the south. There are no black clouds above that man, either, and yet he cannot keep you safe. I see only corpses of enemies at his feet, never his own. He will die with a white beard and a walking stick at his own choosing."

Proxenos the architect laughed, this time even louder. He was young and tanned more than he needed to be from his days fixing the walls of Plataia. Birth and money, and his white teeth and black beard, gave him a certain arrogance that comes when a man feels bigger and stronger and richer than those around him. He had been born into wealth and bred to think less of slower wits. Women, he knew, he could always persuade. Nêto would be no different: No doubt she was entranced by his vigor, looks, and silver, and now worried that she might lose the chance to enjoy them all the more when the war ended.

Proxenos had met this Nêto the previous year at the shrine of Eurynomê on the Asopos River below his red grape vineyards. A chance occurrence, he had thought, to see a naiad alone in the wilds of Boiotia. But now he was not so sure of that long-ago accident, as Nêto had come often for most of the past spring. She had taught him of Pythagoras, and soon no longer was he the bored aristocrat lamenting that the capitals of his atrium were Doric rather than new Ionic. Instead the new Proxenos became a devotee of her Pythagoras when she told him that his genius could raise walls of new cities to the south taller than those of Troy—his work for thousands rather than for a few aristocrats who wanted a new portico on their mansions. He could draw the plans in the north, and let others follow them to the south.

Now, in reply to her warning, Proxenos's soft words flew out as pained concession, or more condescension from lord to master. "Nêto, Nêto, my Nêto. We go to all the trouble to consult these fat priests. If that is not enough, we give heavy silver to the virgins of the temple to tell us of their signs and visions. And now you tell me to go home to the Asopos? Some day, if the One God wills, we will march into shadowy Messenia and at last live up to our divine *logos* that says no one is born a slave—and just as we start, you tell me all that reason, that faith in numbers is but a lie?"

Nêto grabbed the arm of Proxenos. "But my Proxenos, reason or not, don't press too hard the dying gods who like to give short lives to those too certain of themselves. Run from Nemesis." She was almost ranting again. "Because we ignore some of the omens does not mean we are smarter than the old gods—or the duller mortals who believe in them, much less that they no longer exist and cannot hear us right now. They grew old, yes, but they were here before the wisdom of Pythagoras dethroned them. That is why the reason of our god Pythagoras may explain what exactly saves our souls and what not, maybe nine tenths of what we do each day, but not always the last tenth part of our lives. Only faith and belief do that. The other voices tell me. I warn you, if you cross the Isthmos this year or next, it will go badly for you, Proxenos—as badly here as it will be square and good for your soul with the One God later on. The others, they can or cannot come back. Their fates are their own. But not so Proxenos, son of Proxenos, of youth, and riches and bottomland on the Asopos, who has the most to lose of us all. Epaminondas can win here and in the south without you. You were to build the ramparts, and you have drawn up such plans, but you were not to cross spears—or so said Pasiphai to me."

Proxenos felt a sharp pain across his flank. It burned right below his navel on the lower left, as if cut by iron. She had the powers of a witch. But the aristocrat and the rationalist forced a second laugh. "Why ruin tonight with words of gloom and darkness? If you believe in our One God, if you really do, then you know nothing bad ever happens to the good man who lives his life according to reason. Did you not see, woman, that I was dead when I was idling on my farm, wondering whether I had the good number five thousand forty or the bad number five thousand forty-one of olive trees after all? I am not here to save Epaminondas. I am here to be saved by him, just like you persuaded me once."

Nêto turned and headed out of the tent before Chiôn and Mêlon could scold her for having snuck to the battlefield.

# CHAPTER 4

# *Helikon*

H old up, man." Chiôn and Mêlon yelled to the approaching riders. The two Thespian hoplites had beaten the throng out of the assembly. Now both were looking for a place to sleep near the tent of Epaminondas. They had decided to let Gorgos stay back by himself at the wagon up on the hill. As they spread out their gear, four horsemen galloped up—Thespians like themselves. "Lophis is here." Chiôn immediately yelled to his master.

Lophis pulled his reins and tossed his head up. "We rode out yesterday and camped on the water by White Creek across from the Spartans last night." He teased his father, "I figured you three had gone back in your old men's wagon to Helikon to hunker down in the farm tower and wait all this out." He had his helmet off. Lophis liked riding bareheaded around the camp. His hair was braided Spartan-like for show. He was taller than his father, thinner as well, with fairer skin.

The hoplite grabbed the saddle cinch of his horse, Xiphos, as his son slid off to greet Chiôn. "Hoa, you! Well, here we all are in the Thebans' cauldron, it seems." Chiôn nodded and looked to see if the hooves were cracked. Mêlon did not wait for the slave's answer but walked around Xiphos, his eye checking the leather flank guards that Nêto had stitched, worried that his son could afford no lapse if he were to survive the charge into the Spartans. "Your lance, son, does it go well with Xiphos?"

"Well enough," and the three young longhairs at his side assented. Mêlon knew none of them. But he grabbed his son's lance to test its balance. As Lophis watched his father jab with the huge shaft, he was reminded that none of us knows the whole past of even those we see each day. But arise a chance moment, a move, a word, perhaps just a gaze, and a keyhole opens to a hidden, larger life on the other side. It both frightens and excites us to see that one so dear to us has another, an unknown, perhaps a deadly side.

Lophis watched Mêlon take up his clumsy lance as if it were a light spear. As he stabbed about, even Lophis cowered a bit. His father's round shield was larger than most, closer to four than three feet in width, with stains of Spartan blood and brains soaked deep within its grain. The breastplate was one of Malgis's and had patches of tin and bronze and layers of paint that hid cracks and dents. Bora, his spear on the ground, had notches at its head, thirty and more, to mark all the Spartans who had fallen from it at the hands of Malgis and Mêlon. His father, Lophis could see now, handled a cornel spear as if it were not much more than a pruning hook.

Lophis then felt even smaller as he tried to stop his father's shadow jousting. "Epaminondas has told us that he has about three hundred of the horsemen of Boiotia. We will hit the Spartans first. We will give you hoplites some summer dust for your surprise. No doubt Sparta will send its horse first out as well. We'll have a real mix-up for all of you to see. The Spartans are not mounted folk. We will kill them for sport. All can watch. They will have no warning that you with fifty shields are on the left about to cut down their king."

"If only it were so plumb and square," his father replied, unsure what would happen when his son learned that battle was an awful thing, a *deinon*, nothing like the stabbing and romantic spearing of the stone Amazons and Lapiths far above on the friezes and pediments of the high temples. Still, it was good that young men like Lophis talked so—without fear and ready to go to blows for a bad look or less. Stout hoplites and daring horsemen were needed to face the Spartans. Who would otherwise if they knew such killers firsthand? Without the innocent Lophises of the world no one would fight for anything—but instead would count the risk, the gain and loss, worried more about the coins in the strongbox that might not be spent if he were gutted in the fields of Boiotia. Lophis had never seen the Spartans in battle, had only as a boy watched them cross Helikon to Koroneia from the mountain vineyard. He had never been in

a melee with thousands of longhairs bearing down on him. When he got
his down beard, he had stayed put during the killing at Tegyra to guard
the farm while Mêlon took along Gorgos and Chiôn to the battle. He had
been left behind to watch in case the Spartans sidestepped the patrols and
raided the mountain. Now he resented that he had been the one son, the
only son, to be saved at all costs—and thus had been deprived of just
those ordeals that make fathers proud of their boys. Men with brothers
have more freedom, since fathers know that a death in battle does not kill
the entire line.

Still, Mêlon was trying to show his pride in Lophis when all the other
mounted rich men of Thespiai either had hidden or had gone over to the
Spartans. "Perhaps, Lophis, it will be as easy as you say, since you and
Nêto first taught me of the thinking of Epaminondas. But we left orders
for your wife Damô all the same to prepare for the worst, should we fall.
Nêto came here to Leuktra as well. But after her oracle-mongering is
done, she is to go home to guard the farm with our Sturax. They are supposed to go up into the tower and bar the door. The only Spartans who
will reach Helikon are a bone or two of them that we bring back for the
dogs."

Mêlon was surprised at his own confidence. But he was feeling better
with this plan of fifty shields, left wing, and attack at the slant—except
for a final thought as he looked over his son. "One last thing, Lophis.
Trade breastplates. Trade now. Mine is the heavier. Its flared bottom stops
the downward jabs. You won't mind its heavier weight on Xiphos. It is
dull and patched, but it can turn any blade made by the Spartans and
covers the shoulders far better. Let me wear my father's gaudy inlaid plate.
On you I fear it will be the magnet stone for any who think they can kill
one of the Malgidai. It's bright with too much gold inlay. Remember
Malgis stole it at the battle near Haliartos. It is Spartan and foul. He
should never have brought it home, though the metal is worth five hundred olive trees if not more. Did I tell you that the plate was once worn by
the demon Lysander? Lichas and his folk miss it dearly. All that will only
make you a bigger target, when the sun soon breaks through and the
shine draws Spartan eyes to your chest."

Lophis laughed. "Wars are not won by worries, old man, you know
that better than I. The bigger the target, the better, Father! I will ride right
into their ranks. I will break them like Malgis did. Those around Kleom-

brotos will fear these men that wear without shame the armor of their dear Lysander." With that final exchange, Lophis climbed on Xiphos, tipped the end of his spear to his father, and galloped down the hill to battle. He was a man with everything to lose. Damô, his wife, was known on Helikon as Helen for her beauty. He had three boys and would inherit the finest farm in Boiotia. And he rode off to be among the first of the Boiotians to collide with the Spartans—galloping to ensure he was at the fore of the cavalry attack. Mêlon turned to Chiôn and sighed. "My dull plate would save him. His shine may well kill him. He is brave—but I fear that it is the bravery of the noble ignorant. My boy forgot that Malgis never broke the Spartans at all. I wish he were here beside me in the ranks, between my right arm and your left. No Spartan, not even Lichas there, could touch my son. And I wish I had never heard the name Leuktra."

Chiôn said nothing. He assumed that he would kill enough Spartans on their right wing himself to keep both his masters safe, even if Lophis were mounted and in front of the phalanx. As Lophis disappeared, the two lay down beneath a mountain oak and soon were asleep for the few hours left before the sunrise draw-up of the phalanx. Chiôn and Mêlon, as if by consent, were alike dreaming of the farm back on Helikon. Both were pruning and talking in these dreams before battle—as if they would soon have no more chance to meet again in this life.

Where was this high farm of Mêlon and Chiôn that drew them home in their last sleep before battle? Mêlon's ground was not far from Leuktra, high up the eastern side of the massif of Mt. Helikon, two stadia above the floor of the valley. The farm was right below the hard frost line, at an elevation at which olives can thrive. It was a good, safe place to grow things, to keep away from the Thespians and all the other Boiotian villagers below—mostly hidden as it was from the invaders from the north or south, and too hard a hike up for the raiders on the coast. The slopes of Helikon itself were a divine place, the center of Hellas—a place where the Muses could speak directly to a man. Helikon was south and to the east a little of snowy Mt. Parnassos. Along these mountains the clouds piled up to hide Apollo when he visited his oracle Pythia beneath at Delphi, navel of the world.

For his part this night at Leuktra, Chiôn could see the land almost as if he were floating above it, like Ikaros with waxen wings. From the farm it was an easy gaze at the mountain passes of Parnon to Attika and

Athens. To the south were the high woody crests of ill-omened Mt. Kithairon, on whose backside the Spartans this morning, if they lost, were going to sneak away along the cliffs above the sea. Farther in the distance rose peaks of Pentelikos and Akonthion, the ridges that kept out of Boiotia the bad Athenians, the false democrats whom the Boiotians hated more than any of the Hellenes. Chiôn for his part could see craggy Ptôon and the green island of Euboia lying far off into the west. The farm of Mêlon was right above the great plain of Boiotia—"cow-land," those arrogant Athenians called it. Few went up to Helikon. Even fewer on Helikon wished to go down.

Over fifty crops before this morning's battle, the founder Malgis, father of Mêlon, had staked out his plot on Helikon. He cleared virgin ground from the mountain. Hyacinth, amaryllis, and wild Attic orchids followed. Once the sun hit the land shorn of thousands of strawberry trees, dense beech, and poplar copses, tulips sprouted. "I did it," the hoplite Malgis used to yell to the skies. When he patched broken tiles on the farm's high tower roof, he could take in the view of his thirty years' worth of work. "All this—it came off of my back, with help from the prophets of the One God, all led by Pythagoras who set me right on my course." Farming, Malgis the founder said, was a lot like war. It needed the same order and discipline if you were to survive it. He came to worship Pythagoras, the god of order and reason, rather than the overgrown child-gods on Olympos. All they wanted were libations and burnt offerings, just like babies in diapers who cry when the teat slips out of their mouth.

Mêlon had been told all this by Malgis, his father, and how the old man had once planned their farm on the number principles of his god, who explained how the perfect world beyond is revealed to us through the eternal laws of the *arithmoi*. On a rocky expanse of about a hundred *plethra*, the farm's 720 olive trees and 5,040 vines spread across the terraced ground in a careful grid. He had dug in all the cuttings and rootings himself. The holes of the pattern he marked out with chalked rope. The farm spread all the way up the slope—terraced grain fields on the rich black soil, the wine vines higher up to catch the cooler breezes, olives on the poor rocky soils atop, each crop suited for each step higher up the mountain, no soil idle, no change in temperature or wind wasted. The harvests were serial, as the clan moved through the year from grain to vines to olives—the Malgidai busy always, slack in their labor never. No ice storm could kill their triad, as the harvests of the diverse crops and their leaf-break dates were never the same. A spring frost hurt the grapes, but not the barley—in the way a fall rain cracked open the grapes, but did nothing to the unripe olives. And the farm was the goddess Amalthea's horn of plenty, as Malgis called it: olive oil for the light in the clan's lamps and for cooking on the stoves, or even to lubricate the wagon's axle; grapes for raisins all winter, for fresh fruit in summer, for wine all year round; barley and wheat for their bread and gruel. Who needed anything more? Only war could stop the farm—by sending in Spartans to burn their wheat or trample their vines, or, worse yet, letting the foul Kêres harvest the farm's harvesters.

Walk into the orchards and vineyards anywhere on the slope, and the symmetry brought forth the voice of Pythagoras. On the farms of others, chaos reigned as three vines encircled a crooked row of four olives, or goat pens were plopped down amid apples. No order in the farms of others— and no reminders of the perfect world that we all must strive to glimpse and at some point enter. Malgis, the creator, told his son that in matters of great things, such as this carving out of an entire estate from the flank of Helikon, men tend to look only at the finish. The envious never remember the hard beginning or even the worse middle of doubt and remorse. Instead, without shame onlookers come to covet what they used to mock. "I can see them below from here, and that's close enough for me. Soon the Spartans will turn on them, and they will climb up here looking for our spear arms." Malgis taught the household to distrust the superstitious majority and to join it only when it acted in according to the precepts of Pythagoras—in other words, rarely at all. Even though the son Mêlon doubted that creed, he kept to his father's admonitions to shun the crowd and keep it away—and earned both the advantages from the ensuing tranquility of solitude and the dark moods that resulted from thoughts and suppositions untested and unquestioned that grow unchecked by others.

Freedom—Malgis added in his daily sermons to his son Mêlon— wars with equality. Always. The fathers of the polis had once marked out the grid of bottomland farms. Originally they were all equally sized and portioned out to the hoplite farmer citizens of equal wealth. Within a generation those belonging to the luckier, or better, farmers were larger, while some of the poorer or unfortunate farmers lost their portions altogether.

Mêlon still dreamed on this early morning before Leuktra that his father had warned him of those who demand equal slots in both the end and the beginning: Beware of the phalanx, the agrarian grid, and the assembly hall, where all are declared to be equal who in fact are not. So beware of those in the phalanx who look equal but do not protect their position as do others. They can kill you.

The farm craft of Malgis gave the vines' canes, high up and long in the air, the full sun for the entire day. That was why his grapes made the sweetest wine on Helikon. Malgis got the idea of the arbors from a farmer outside Syracuse he met who read and wrote block letters on long scrolls. "The sun makes the grapes, and the grapes the wine," this Sikilian Lysis told Malgis. He showed him charts and graphs, and when he returned home to Thespiai, Malgis translated all those lines and letters into *plethra* of arbors and pergolas, roofed with grape canes twenty feet long and more. But then Lysis also had lectured on the right dirt, the perfect eleva- tion, the type of water, and so Malgis thought it wasn't just the arbors that made his vintage. Good wine needed sparse soil. Grapes liked just a little water. Crisp mornings were good for color. A cold nip at night gave taste, as did the hot sun on the leaves of the vine. Vineyards would be planted above the wheat and below the olives.

The Malgidai themselves produced the bounty, not just prayers to Dionysos or cries of the Bakkhai that the ignorant shout who are without the reason of Pythagoras. When a man fails in body or soul or wisdom, he always prays to the Olympians. Or so as Mêlon kept dreaming before battle he remembered all that Malgis once had said. For fifty and more harvests before Leuktra, the Malgidai rarely came off Helikon except to fight for the Boiotians. They had enough coins and enough grapes, wheat, and oil to need none of those below—and no more desire to die in the phalanx of the Boiotians on the doomed left wing in the battles against the Spartans. So they were a confident bunch, and came to forget that the wages of *hubris* are *nemesis*.

Finally in the year before Leuktra, Mêlon had opened his ears a little to Pythagoras. For he tired of meat, and found his left arm as strong as his right, and no longer felt himself better by birth than his slaves, all in the manner of Pythagoras. He wanted to believe that he had an eternal soul that would be judged in the hereafter by its brief entrapment and struggle within an all too human body; or so he also told the believer

Chiôn, who was determined not to return as a sparrow or snake, but to free his soul forever with deeds he deemed good. And yet Mêlon had hesitated until now, worried by the rumors that Epaminondas might make the worse better and so replace the tyranny of Sparta with the chaos of freedmen.

For all their farming expertise, the Malgidai's strongboxes were heavy with coins that had not come entirely from the soil. No one ever quite makes a living on farming alone, although all always insist that they do. Instead the money had come from Malgis's campaigning when he once sailed for fifteen days to Sikily to join a Spartan attack on Athens. He came back a rich man with the loot of the dead at the Assinaros River. His new strongbox, with the lumps of gold beneath the coins, proved so heavy that he finally sent young Mêlon for a chain at the town forge to haul it up out of the well. No mere hemp rope would bear all the weight of his profits. War, it turned out, was a good way to make or lose money. But profit depended on what side of a war you ended up on. Always it was the wiser choice to fight on the side of the Spartans—even if that meant halfway across the ocean in Sikily or Asia. The Spartans would enrich Malgis for most of his life. At his end, they would kill him when he broke his own rule.

Mêlon remembered how Malgis, in the days after Athens had lost its great war with Sparta, liked to talk deep into the night with the big men from Thebes. Years before Mêlon came of age, the Theban friends used to walk on his farm's paths, talking of spurning earth's pleasures. Most of these city-folk were like Alkidamas, all self-acclaimed peripatetics who thought they were the true children and stewards of Pythagoras keeping the master's teaching alive in the backwaters of Boiotia, as they lectured amid trees and shrubs.

The dream of Helikon continued as the sleeping Mêlon tried to make sense of this night at Leuktra. Like all who renounce wealth and the tawdry pursuit of it, the philosophers who trudged up to the farm often came to enjoy its fruits all the more. Affluence adds a veneer of authority to knowledge—if it can be displayed without the ugly scars of its acquisition. Mêlon knew that as well, and how someone else's money had allowed him to think he could keep himself away from the mob below. He was at Leuktra this morning for yet one more reason as well: not just because of the prophecy of the apple, or to keep Spartans off his ground, or to replay the battle of Koroneia with a different ending, but also to prove, as he had at Nemea and Koroneia, that money gave him no exemption from the ordeal of the phalanx, and that he at last did believe men, even his Boiotians, could in a season or two set right the wrongs of ages.

The hoplite had thought that his senses, which had saved him so many times in the melee, had been dulled by age. They had not. Smell, hearing, even touch were all heightened this summer before Leuktra as never before. The light off Helikon had been much clearer, the hot wind of late afternoon through the shiny leaves of the olives stronger. Ever since word of Epaminondas and the failed peace at Sparta had spread and war had neared, everything had turned crisp. Nothing was as before. War was in the air. In this lull before the spearing, his touch, nose, ears, and eyes were burning and told him he alone was standing still as the world moved beneath his feet.

What was this mystery of Epaminondas, Mêlon asked in his dream? Whence came his zeal to face down the king of Sparta and then march south, down one thousand stadia into the heart of the Peloponnesos to build new cities of freedom for others finer than their own? These Pythagoreans, with no doubt, no second ideas, thought they had ushered in the new age of Hellas. All the city-states would become one state, one community of equals. All would worship the god Logos, and would teach that there are no masters, no slaves, no right hand better than left. No man would be better than woman—but all with free will to play the fool or the good man—and suffer the consequences at the blink of death. That was the power of Epaminondas to save the souls of the would-be saviors of others for the judgment to come. So these Pythagoreans had become the godfathers of Epaminondas, well before Leuktra. When Mêlon came down to fight in the year of Leuktra, he knew well enough where the fight of these men would finally lead.

This was also the arrogance of the Pythagoreans, Mêlon saw in these pre-battle visions. They thought they alone knew the good and alone could implement it among the Hellenes. They taught that everything we do—eat, sleep, crap, talk—must be in measure, according to *meson*, the golden mean. Once a man knew the rhythm of living—and he could not without the help of Pythagoras—then work was not work. Money was only for independence from the mob, never to be used for indulgence.

Women and slaves were to be as free men; and dumb animals, who had inside them the souls of the departed, were to be untouched. Maybe even the olives and grapes were the stopping stations of the souls seeking to reform this time around.

For most who improve their grandfather's house or ancestral vineyard, this temptation is never distant—to destroy and start over from the beginning rather than to correct the wrongs and burdens of the long dead. Malgis the killer was given a great gift not to farm the plot of his father Antander, but to start on the wild Helikon anew. This was the creed of creation of the Pythagoreans. The restlessness was also the danger residing in an impatient Epaminondas—to tear down all the ancient good along with the old bad and start over afresh. Sparta was a tired city of crooked streets and cobbled-together plots. But Messenê, the capital of free Messenia to come? This dream of Epaminondas's new city would be a grid. All new streets and blocks as perfect as the new vines and trees to be planted around it, their city to practice on with the newly freed helots—like the famous farm of the Malgidai, but for thousands.

After his father Malgis had terraced the hillsides, fashioned the big courtyard with a view of Boiotia below, planted the vines and trees, leveled and smoothed the wheat fields, built the pens and threshing floor, got the big press working, lined the farm's paths with flat stones, and worshiped his god of Pythagoras—after all that, three things that no seer imagined had followed. First, he ended up not with a man's refuge, but with the finest-looking farm in Boiotia. The orchard and vineyards proved better even than those on Sikily that he had copied so well. Malgis the founder became not just an *idiotês*—not just a recluse—but a wealthy one at that, whose wine and oil brought in gawkers and buyers alike. Then he buried his young wife, Kephesia. She died ten springs after the battle of Delion, from the stiff-jaw right after giving him a single son up in their new house on the mountain. Last of all, at sixty years still hale, Malgis himself fell.

Fell? Hardly. Malgis was gutted by the Spartans—knocked down by no less than Lord Lichas himself, at the spear clash at Koroneia, ten seasons after the great war with the Athenians—caught in the final mad Theban crash against the king Agesilaos. There the Boiotians in folly threw away the fight they had earlier almost won, losing thirty years after they and

Malgis's Thespians had won at Delion. But, of course, they were now fighting Spartans, not Athenians any longer. This last muster at his age was Malgis's death sentence. But still at Koroneia, Malgis did all that the Theban generals wanted, as a *lochagos* leading his son Mêlon and six hundred Thespians head-on against the Spartan king Agesilaos in the battle's bitter finale—on the Boiotians' weak left against the choice Spartan royals on the enemy right wing. At first he was blocked from nearing the king, but he soon found a way over them, as the men from Thespiai behind pushed their front files through. These images came more quickly now to the dreaming Mêlon as sunlight neared and with it the approach of battle.

Malgis had hit the royal guard under Lichas, who stabbed better with the spear than any on either side of the battlefield. Malgis had first wounded Sphodrias. Then he took on Deinon as well, and got close to King Agesilaos, almost through the last circle of the king's guard under Lichas. Finally, with the king's crest in sight, Malgis in desperation had thrown his thrusting spear—and it had hit the royal thigh itself. The wound would cripple Agesilaos, but not kill him. Malgis could not withstand the fury of a stunned Lichas. No man could. The Spartan caught Malgis without his spear and stabbed him right under the chin, above his breastplate. Then Lichas called in vain for his henchmen to strip the Thespian and take the gleaming armor that had once belonged to the Spartan general Lysander.

Mêlon saw his father collapse in the dust. Now he battled his way forward to keep the murderous Spartans from desecrating the body of Malgis; somehow he carried the body away from the fray. Lichas stabbed him above the knee and almost took him down, too, but the royal guard fell back and circled Agesilaos. They carried their king out rather than go after the Theban vanguard under Mêlon. The next day Gorgos, the captured helot, packed dead Malgis back to the farm, and he wrapped the leg of Mêlon as he drove the cart to Helikon with his dead and wounded masters. The Thebans set up a small black stone hidden away on a corner of the Kadmeia in the center of town, reading just as the Boiotarchs promised: *Tode mnêma Malgidi, Antandros huiô, tô Thespiaô, hon Spartiai eidon kalon en Koroneia. Eis Hadas elthe makairpistos tôn Helikonidôn hina Boiotia pasa ê eleuthera.* (This memorial is for Malgis, son of Antander, the Thespian, whom the Spartans knew well at Koroneia. He went down to Hades, most blessed of those Helikon way, so that all of Boiotia might be free.)

The Spartan iron had bored in a palm's width above the back of Mêlon's knee. To the bone and deeper Lichas had driven his spear tip to roll up his tendon. If he were to meet Lichas this coming day at Leuktra, then the reckoning had been yet another reason to follow Nêto's prophecy and come down at last from Helikon. But Lophis had filled him with talk of Epaminondas, and freedom from Sparta, and something greater still. The result was that he thought himself not so old and crippled as much as wise and experienced—and needing to settle with Lichas. But even before that for twenty years and more, he picked up his spear Bora, put on his panoply every other evening behind the shed—bronze breast- and backplate, concave round willow shield, banged-up greaves, slashing sword, and heavy helmet—and then did his ten or so jabs and set moves. Right foot forward with the spear thrust; right back to bring the enemy in off balance; the shield bash with the left foot leading; the underhand stab to the groin; the overhand thrust down into the enemy's neck; the wild right hand cross slash with the cleaver; the sword chop down on the helmet; the crouch to one knee behind the shield; the right-wing drift; the steady walk ahead; the double-time trot. These were all the moves, the *hoplomachia*, that his Theban drill masters had once taught him before the battles at the Nemea and at Koroneia, and that he had repeated three thousand times and more these years so that perhaps one day he would come down his mountain and kill Spartans without end.

At fifty Mêlon was on the downhill course without a rock or stump in his way, with a better farm for his boy Lophis than what Malgis had given him—and with a better son in Lophis than he himself had been. Lophis riled Mêlon with new talk of helots and Epaminondas and grand marches and Lichas and how he must come down to fight the Spartans if he were to claim he was a citizen and a man of the polis. But shortly after making his decision to fight, Mêlon had begun to see black visions sent from the gods—the dream changing on alternating sleeps. He always saw two cities to the south, far beyond the Isthmos, and now at Leuktra those old dreams came back and turned his mind from Helikon.

The first one was a rising city of tall stones, with ladders of men at work, and black cut rock stacked everywhere amid the growing ramparts. Two big levers with pulleys and hooks lifted squared blocks on a temple wall. A theater was half-finished. Workers swarmed on the embrasures, singing with the oxen-team drivers in a thick Doric. An agora was crowded. Farmers in peace flocked in to sell their wares. Squabbles were settled in a large *dikastêrion* by swift-mouthed *rhêtôrs* and voting jurors. Women brought their men apples in baskets. They sang to them as they hauled stones. On a *bêma*, a tall orator lectured to his listeners, who jeered and clapped—but then voted in peace and praised their freedom as their walls always rose higher. Calm and order reigned.

On the other gloomier nights when there was no moon, Mêlon saw these same towers and walls, but unfinished, with many more black blocks ready to be stacked. This other vision of the city was longer, darker and louder. There were rotting Hellenes hanging in nooses from the gates. Dogs and birds fought over even more corpses in ditches and refuse piles, pulling on their putrid ankles. There were more bodies half-eaten outside the towers, clubbed and knifed, with their purses and packs stolen. Men were killing and raping at will, and packs of cutthroats in the chaos of the city's license roamed over the unfinished city that was full of trash and worse, as slaves dumped their slop jars into open pits. Always upon waking Mêlon asked himself how could this same city be two different cities, and which dream was the real, which the false. Somehow he put himself in the answer: His presence in the south could ensure the good city of this Epaminondas, holy Messenê to come—while his absence would mean its failure and descent into chaos. But, he asked himself, would Gorgos, would Chiôn stay or go with him, and if they went, who would keep the farm and the family of his son Lophis safe?


A spear's length away, Chiôn on this hard-baked ground this night now saw these same images, but he had more of his own dreams and memories before Leuktra that would not easily give way. Malgis, he knew, had roped the slow-moving pursuing helot Gorgos in the free-for-all after the Theban phalanx had broken at the Nemea and the battle lines had been crossed. The prisoner Gorgos had squirmed on the ground and whimpered that he was the prized shield carrier of a Spartan noble. Maybe the manservant to the big ephor, to Lichas himself he was. Now the Messenian slave was somewhere around six tens, maybe more, or so he claimed, though his arms seemed too hard for a man that old. On feast nights for the two meat-eaters, Chiôn saw Gorgos crush a piglet's head like he did a squash. Gorgos said he was nearly blind—though the helot saw more than others the bad spots and crooks of the farm. Most days he shuffled about and was just worth the food to keep him going, although Gorgos talked as if he owned the estate itself. Chiôn's dreams now stayed on Helikon.

Nêto did more work than the Messenian. But she never stayed put as she wandered throughout the hamlets of Boiotia. Years earlier Mêlon had bought her as a twelve-year-old; he'd put down twenty good Boiotian silver coins, the new minted ones of the Confederation with the stamped shields. Down at the harbor at Kreusis some Spartan renegade had sneaked in at night in a leaky boat, eager to barter her away along with four other helots and a bronze breastplate. The trader had charged more for her than for the others, and had spun stories that she was the aborted daughter of a fallen virgin Messenian priestess. Artemis, he said, had struck her mother when she had found her pregnant. Then the goddess had cut out Nêtikon alive from the shaking womb and had bellowed, "You live and are cursed to be damned when you reveal today what will happen tomorrow." Mêlon told Chiôn he had bought her to help Gorgos; but he told also the tale of her birth, because, he reasoned, if she thought she was a priestess, well, then that was better than a slave after all, was it not?

The girl was more than twenty seasons now. Gorgos had tried to poke her twice. But Mêlon had beat him hard with his stick both times. A third time was even worse when Mêlon slapped him with the shaft of his spear, the heavy one of ash—even though the helot had fancied his Nêtikon would not fight back once she had had a taste of his horn. The last time his back bled from the hit so much that Gorgos dared to snap back at his master that he was beating the saddle rather than the willing mount. Yes, he'd try to settle up soon enough, Chiôn suspected, and with all of them if he could. Chiôn had heard Gorgos boast that Nêto needed a brand on her soft face to take her down two pegs—just like the one on Chiôn's own cheek.

Nêto had whispered to Chiôn, "For all his singing of lions, Gorgos has no thought of what floor he will end up on—or that he will die one day at the hand of another helot. But that is what the divine whispers say." She warned Chiôn to either kill or free him. The bit of freedom that the master Mêlon gave him, she knew, made the slave hate them all the more that it came late and in such small measure. At least that was how Nêto accounted for what she saw as the unaccountable, since the petulant Gorgos was treated as if he were free, and fared far better than any down in the Peloponnesos. Always Chiôn watched them from the high grain fields, as he pried up an oak stump with an iron bar and ax. Kill this broke-back now, Chiôn had thought. Or later, as Nêto foretold? For sport here—or soon in battle, no difference. Why just him? Why not even the score, since one killing makes the murderer as much as five or so. The neighbor below, Dirkê, and her slaves, the Spartan-lovers, would those traitors be good relish too? All this Chiôn went over in these dreams, just as if each choice were a different stone to be stacked and fitted into his grand terrace on the upper five *plethra*, or another notch on the windlass of the new olive press. When you live to kill the bad, you can do more good than the good, or thus Chiôn claimed his own ideas had the sanction of Pythagoras and called his plans to kill the god's wisdom to save his own soul.

Chiôn had been told that Malgis, the slave collector, had picked him up cheap—for almost nothing—at age three, when Malgis was on the way home from the wars in Asia. Malgis had once marched with the Ten Thousand and then stayed on to fight for better pay with the lords of the Spartans. Before Derkyllidas and the Spartan fleet sailed west, the Egyptian plague swept the islanders. Most island clans were selling off their scarred orphans—those few survivors who were free for life from the boils—for an owl coin or two from Athens to the ships as they passed to the Peloponnesos.

Chiôn also had been told that Malgis had paid only three obols—a half Athenian owl—for the pox boy with the ugly Spartan brand. It was a lambda burned into his cheek. Scars covered most of his face and arms from the *nosos*. "This sick worm, not much to be sure," the Spartan pilot had offered when he sold him to Malgis. "He's an ugly white toddler, too, maybe a snowy Thrakian. But then three obols is not much of a gamble either, is it, for a raggedy thing splashing about the currents of death?" Malgis had made the exchange. Only then the Spartan had grumbled, "No buyer's second anger for poxy boy—but the priestess of Artemis on Chios told me to kill this half-dead thing, since the pox and the hungry belly couldn't. She says he is a killer of Spartan royalty, Lichas's bane. Beware—or be happy—over that."

The words of the island trader had been forgotten, even if Chiôn had heard them enough. What was pock-marked and yellow soon grew on Malgis's farm into a near giant. Six-cubit Chiôn he was, with the stone shoulders of the Titans of old. Just like the vines on the high trellises that got stronger with the more sunlight, Chiôn had taken off on the mountain, and his remedy for a day behind the ox was "More work." He chanted no Tyrtaios as did Gorgos, but strains from Helikon's native Hesiod as he pulled Nêto's plow: *"Ergon epi ergô, ergon epi ergô*—work on top of work." As the great year of settling up with invading Spartans approached, Chiôn often went out alone to the sycamores on the crests of Helikon. He stalked the wilds, eating berries and killing game for the poor for days at a time—as if he were a hunter, perhaps a hunter of men with no need of the polis or even the meat for his own belly. "The Panther Chiôn," Nêto called him, the all-beast *panthêr*. With that, the dreams of Chîon ceased and black sleep held him a while longer.

But not so Mêlon, whose mind still saw visions as he snored. For all the tranquility of the farm, rumors of a new war had bored deeply into Mêlon. He knew that. They never really left him in peace again. It was not a mere battle anymore to showcase courage but something quite different—a struggle to overturn the ancient order itself that needed a hoplite like himself who could put his lore to good use for thousands of democrats. That bothered—but intrigued—him. Worried him that a man who promised to change the world would enlist a broken-down man like himself, and yet goaded him on that Epaminondas might see in Mêlon, sore back, and a deaf ear, and a locked knee, something he sensed untapped in himself as well. Now Mêlon joined Chiôn in a final slumber, blank and without memory, as if both were ordered by the One God to banish both dark and light dreams and rest for Leuktra and the sunup.

Up on the hill above, Nêto was not dreaming of Helikon, but still awake. Proxenos, the Plataian, was sleeping under the wagon nearby, sent there by Mêlon after the meeting to guard against Gorgos, who grew reckless as he neared his Spartans. The One God had this night sent to her the dreams of Chiôn and Mêlon, and now at last she too would sleep, relieved that they would fight and battle well, as the images of those on Helikon reminded them both of who they were on this eve of battle. What a strange clan, these men of the soil of Helikon, Nêto thought. Richer than the rich who despised them—and yet rich from Malgis's killing in Sikily rather than from the great bounty of his vineyards on Helikon. Gorgos and Chiôn were as free as their master—two forgotten slaves out on the uplands of mountain Helikon with no need of town who yet boasted to themselves that they were gods who would shake the very cities of Hellas. Damô, the wife of Lophis, and Nêto more like men of action than wives or servants. Mêlon, the center of it all, the savior of the Boiotians, said to be the apple of the prophecy about to fall on the Spartans who knew not how to farm, the master whose slaves acted as his master, the great farmer with but a single son, neither all Pythagorean nor Olympian—and with his bad leg and bald head somehow pledged to Epaminondas, although why or how he hardly knew. All this, Malgis had wrought from the word of Pythagoras and booty from Sikily, even as Nêto assured them all that they had been chosen to be carried along according to the order and plan of Pythagoras.

# CHAPTER 5

# *Spartans*

Mêlon and Chiôn roused themselves right before daylight. Chiôn woke up pondering all the grand talk of fifty men deep. True, fifty pushers should have more power than twenty-five. If they did, why not a hundred or a thousand? Better, Chiôn thought, to mass four or even eight deep, and then outflank the Spartans. That way each man could fight his way into the enemy rather than be pushed through. Better to forget all this *taktika* and instead remember that spirit, *arête*, alone would get him to Kleombrotos. "Kill him," he muttered, "and then nothing else much matters."

Mêlon heard the waking Chiôn at his side mumbling. He too had his own fears about this ragtag army of Boiotians. Some had cloaks, some did not. The men on his line were supposed to have the club of Herakles on their shields, but some had betas for the Boiotians, others their own family and tribal blazons—poorly painted crabs, and flies, and birds and the like. Sloppy men fought sloppily. They feared all the more those who looked like real hoplites, the Spartans most of all. There were dozens of different helmets in the army of Epaminondas—crest, no crest, cone shaped or flat on top, open, or close-faced. His peers should have the old-style bronze on their chests—but most had only linen with some metal woven inside. Those in the middle and some at the back had little at all. Only the officers of the *lochoi* wore greaves. Not all from the outlying towns had a sword on their shoulders, and their spears were of all lengths and types. Could such a rabble—little more than a people's army—stand up to the red mass of Spartans across the battlefield, where every man was outfitted identically to thousands of others?

This day of battle had begun oddly dark for the summer. Now it was humid as well. A few gray clouds even drifted over the battlefield. Now and then the gray cut off the early sun entirely. Beneath the clouds there were only brief flashes from the bronze of the Spartan phalanx, a twinkling from the shields and helmets of the Similars, all shined to a high gloss with oil. Suddenly, thunder rumbled in the hills.

A chestnut filly galloped across the Theban line out between the two armies—only to be roped by five hoplites of the Sacred Band. Pelopidas ran out. He cut the horse's neck. Then for the army he offered a prayer to the Olympians. He called out that Poseidon had sent the equine gift to the Thebans to show them the way of victory. At that, the Thebans began to regain their senses and yelled in approval to this other general bathed in horse blood.

The Spartans as expected marched out first. Lichas put on a show for thousands of rural folk who had flocked to the nearby hills to gaze on the spectacle. Each man filed into neat rows to the sounds of pipes and the signals of flags. The teeming crowd of their camp was slowly unfurling into a red line that grew ever deeper across the gentle rolling plain of Leuktra. One by one, files of twelve deep walked out—and halted on the crest of the low rise to the blare of trumpets. Slowly, side-by-side, these columns filled out the phalanx. Hoplites in long lines raised their bronze-coated shields, with even their red lambdas, the insignia of Lakedaimon, visible in the distance. The army was stretching fifteen stadia along the crest above the streambed.

Suddenly on a trumpet blast, helots of Sparta ran among the ranks and stripped off their masters' cloaks. The bronze fronts twinkled now and then in the darting sunlight—outlined at the shoulders, and arms and waists, by their red chitons beneath. Mêlon focused on the battle line where the enemies' tall black-and-white crests bobbed. Now they lowered their spears and jostled shields just a stade away. Spartans had no pause in their walk. They seem to have emptied their whole damn city.

Then, for a blink only—the first and final time at Leuktra—Mêlon lost his nerve, as he thought about their spear work to come. Dying was no dread, he thought, not even losing Chiôn or Nêto, or even his son Lophis with the horse. No, the rub was the sound, and especially the look, of the death-bringing Spartans across the way. The bristles of their phalanx and the pitch of the music made all afraid, if just for that moment, about how they were to die, the pain and cutting to take them into the final sleep. Are these killers even human as other hoplites? he wondered. His bowels rumbled and his bladder felt full. The men from the south across the way looked like hemi-gods on the high stone altars who did not tremble, drink, or tire as other men did. No living thing could get between their solid line of shields. There was no reprieve from their spears. These men did not lag or slow. It would take a god, he feared, to stop their onset. No, they came on at a steady pace—always to the tune of pipes, never too fast, but never slow, either. They stopped only when cut down.

Then the terror vanished as quickly as it had come. The madness of the war god Pan had no more hold over him, a god that left the glens at the sound of bronze and the chance to confuse thousands. In hopes the madness would not infect his men, Mêlon stared back at the ghost of the hoofed god in front of him in anger. "Be gone, foul god. Back to the herds and flocks!" Mêlon took in the Spartan line opposite him, ever nearing and now little more than two hundred paces away. He imagined that he could see these brutes smiling, even in their helmets, stomping their stiff legs on the ground in unison, in their eagerness. He looked at them with reason rather than fright. Spartan targets offered little open flesh. Maybe a spot beneath the shield in the upper groin, maybe some skin of the neck between the breastplate and the chinstrap. Always there was a peep of bare flesh or an open fold of their chitons when they turned, on their sides between the front and back plates.

For all his efforts, Mêlon could not calm all the men at his side. Too many other young Boiotians at his side shuddered at such killers. They had let the shade of clever Pan into their ranks as the ghost god galloped toward the front lines. They trembled at the shrieking of the horned spirit, of the wild goat god in their ears who struck men dumb before the crash with his screeches—oooha, oooohaa, ooooohaaa. And they for a moment ignored their officers who went among them answering the god. "No fear," bellowed Pelopidas. "No fear of these red-shirts. Forget the mad goat-horned ghost of Pan who gallops across the field and strikes your shield with his back kicks. Forget him and watch him vanish back into the woods where he belongs. There is no *panika*, no panic here. Forget the Spartans. It is show—all show, their pipes and shine. Herakles the strong is our god, always the stronger god. Herakles of Thebes. A better god by far. He fights in our ranks. Hold your shields high. Take up your spears. We file up and go out *now*."

Across the way Lichas, waiting for just this moment, trotted on a black stallion in and out of the wings. Kleombrotos was king, but all looked to Lichas to form up the phalanx. For a moment he reared his horse on its back legs and waved his helmet in his right hand, motioning for the Boiotians to come and take it from him. "They're already upon us. The pigs are here at last. Wait until the horsemen are through before marching out. Let me and my cavalry fight first, you later."

For all his bellowing, Lichas worried that the Boiotian army had formed up too quickly and had caught his red-capes unawares. The Spartans had wine in their mouths from the late breakfast, and a few were unsteady from too much. The ranks were not as tight as usual, and already enemy horsemen were charging from across the way. Too much drink, too much hubris this time. How could these pigs be more ready to charge than his own taskmasters of war? No, this was not the Spartan way, Lichas knew—and with a coward like Kleombrotos at the head of his army and drunken Dionysos, not Ares, their god this morning. Nonetheless, his hoplites raised their shields high and hit their spear shafts against the bronze shield blazons. The clash bellowed across the vale of Leuktra.

Mêlon across the field could smell the stench, as if in reply to the Spartan spectacle too many Thebans in the line had soiled their legs in terror. He noticed piss too in the dirt. Even some of the older ones emptied their bladders in the ranks. Their ground was becoming a sewer. Mêlon hit Chiôn on his broad shoulder as they found their slots on the left wing. "Our time, islander. You and I, we will stand firm—always the lead geese who break the wind for the weaker flyers behind." He was talking as if he were Epaminondas.

Chiôn paid his master no mind—even though he heard well with his helmet up on his forehead. He tapped his spear on Mêlon's shield. He was full of the good spirits, the *daimones* of courage and audacity. The slave was *entheos*, a god was inside him. As for Spartans over there preening to the mounted Lichas, he would kill plenty and rout the rest—happy to teach the Hellenes that there were men at Thespiai still. If he were killed? Well, nothing—he knew that well enough—nothing bad, no *kakon*. Nêto had promised him that: nothing bad would come to the souls of the good. He would return in his own fashion, fly back out of the whirl to his haunt on Helikon in a shape and with a voice he could hardly imagine—a free soul as an ant or leaf with no memories of who or what it had been as the slave Chiôn of Helikon.

Mêlon was not quite free yet from that vision of neighing Pan—and so once again he grasped Chiôn's arm and finally, in these last moments before the charge, he spoke to him as the equal Chiôn had always really been. "It matters nothing whether we are eight or fifty deep. We care little about how long Kleombrotos's line over there ends up. Men alone count on the battle line." Then he turned to his slave. "If it is the will of Zeus that every Boiotian die this morning, still you and I at least will not fall beneath the spears of Kleombrotos. Never. There is not a hoplite nor a god yet born that will break us, Chiôn. Not this day. Not on this plain of Leuktra."

But Chiôn was already eyeing the king across the way. He pulled his helmet down and heard not a word. Then a Thespian trotted up to the front out of breath. "Son of Malgis. I came late with the slaves." Staphis? It was the farmer the Thespians all knew as Dried Grape. Here was the lowly vine owner from Helikon who ran up from the back of the phalanx. Too old, with bad armor, thin arms, and knock knees and his empty head with no notion of the spears to come, only that he wanted to do some great thing on the front line before he fell to the earth beside his ox in aged weariness—the sort of idea that so often gets the best of us killed.

Staphis had marched from Helikon along with Nêto the evening before. Then Staphis had spent the early morning looking for the tent of Epaminondas to learn where were the files of Mêlon and Chiôn of Thespiai. Staphis had little skill with the spear. But he would prove the braver man if genuine courage is, as the philosophers said, not the raging of the desperate, but the risking of all when all in life is most dear and most to be hoarded. For this Staphis, his tiny vineyard on the rises below Helikon was his Elysion, paradise on earth for many seasons to come and a rather valuable thing not to be thrown rashly away in a morning in the muck at Leuktra, when the presence of a vine grower would not change the verdict of the battle either way.

Being ungainly and aged can suit a good man, when a spirit looms larger than what it is trapped in—and a certain rare beauty follows from the very contrast. On this morning facing the old guard of Sparta, the ugliest farmer from Helikon was not ugly at all. So Mêlon saw for the first time on the front line of the army of the Boiotians. Staphis was, in fact, the most beautiful of the Hellenes in Thespiai. He was at Mêlon's side ignoring a death sentence in hopes to fight head-on against the king of Sparta and his guard. The tiny teeth of the field mouse would have had a better chance against a green field viper. "Staphis," Mêlon called, "fight here. Head with us into death. Right through the swinging doors to the other side."

The line was set and about ready to charge out. The tanner Antitheos, on the other side of Staphis, kept his gaze fixed ahead. He held his shield too high, to show all the power of his strong left arm. Now he was raging out of the side of his mouth to Mêlon. "If you limp to the king first, Mêlon Chôlopous, all is forgotten. But I think we Thebans over here on your left, we will be the ones to cut off Kleombrotos's beard." Every man in the phalanx was boasting something like that. But not more than one or two in their immediate midst could hear a thing. Staphis muttered to himself, "Here we go into the storm. Pray Herakles and any gods who roam Helikon that I prove worthy of these better ones at my side." Staphis had cut the throat of a young goat the night before. He had offered it up to Zeus Eleutheros who frees those on the eve of battle shackled in fear. But the blood had not flowed. The victim had a half-liver. The spongy lungs had put the sacrificial flame out as well. Now the vine man wasn't sure that even if the god listened, and gave them victory, he would shield Staphis of Helikon. Then the grape grower stepped out even as he trembled. Mêlon felt his shaking and so he moved his shield a few more palms to cover more of the farmer's right flank. "Don't worry, my neighbor. We will laugh at all this, at harvest next, in the victory halls of Malgis on Helikon, my Staphis. These are the days that will bring us joy to recall back on Helikon."

On the other side, Antikrates frowned as he focused on the Boiotians across the field under the banner of Epaminondas—just out of bow shot, no more now than three hundred paces away. Like his father Lichas, he saw for the first time the Boiotian weight: too many spears there facing the royal right. The young Spartan thought, "Here is trouble right at the beginning, right in our path." His boys had drunk too much of their red wine as rumors swept the camp that the Boiotians would run and there would be only women across the way, and no need for a fight after all. His father, Lichas, had been circling on his pony, too far out in front of the phalanx, eager to charge the Boiotians and be the first to kill on either side, before he dismounted and joined the king's guard. "Still, our best may die, but if so, they are not our best. We follow no rules, no *nomima* of the Hellenes for us. We know no heralds. We pull back no spears from the wounded. No shaking of hands when we beat them. We ask for no quarter. Nothing but death now, death to them. We pray to no gods but Thanatos." With such pride, Antikrates lowered his gray spear Haima. He aimed its tip at a big hoplite opposite, with the tallest crest on the line. He had spotted a big one from Thespiai, not far, not far across the way.

The Boiotian hoplites across from Antikrates jostled to keep rank. Then Epaminondas stepped out without his own shield or helmet. Seven thousand spears were shaking. The general trotted down the front line of the Thebans beneath their raised spears. He was hitting the wooden shafts lightly with a large cleaver, an iron *klôpis* of the type the Spartans favored. "For Thebes, for Boiotia, and for Hellas!" he repeated as he made his way across the front rank to the clattering of struck wood. A few enemy arrows from the strong bows landed harmlessly ten paces from his feet.

Then he stopped in the middle of the Boiotian front line. Here Epaminondas yelled out a final time, "We are better men than the Spartans, better in peace and far better men in war. I swear a great oath to every man here: We will kill their king today. It is fated. I will not live after today if we lose. I will not breathe the air of Boiotia in shame and laughed at by all. We shall not lose this Holy Leuktra. Follow me into their spears. Follow Herakles who roams above us. Avenge the daughters of Skedasos. Follow me into song and story. Give me one more step forward still. The Thebans are mightier in war."

The army behind him shook their spears and clapped them against their shields. They let out a thunderous roar with their own paean to death, "Death, death, death—*thanatos, thanatos, thanatos*—the Thebans are mightier in war. The Boiotians are better than Spartans." They were immediately cut short by the ping of metal against wood and flesh as a thousand Spartan horsemen galloped out and hit the Theban cavalrymen head-on. Lichas led them, with a spear in his right hand and a cleaver in his left, reins in his mouth, his own men behind likewise chanting "*Thanatonde, thanatonde*—deathward, to death." To no avail. His horsemen were outnumbered, and they soon proved to be mere boys compared to the skilled riders of the plains around Kopais. The Boiotians had hit them in a massive rhomboid and then sliced through the thin line of Spartan horse, forcing them all back into their own ranks. Then the Boiotians threw javelins at the confused jumble of foot and horse, as they split off and rode back to the wings—even as the Boiotian phalanx now bore down on the men of Sparta. Dust engulfed the wine-soaked Spartans, and the oncoming hoplites of Boiotia could see only the raised spear of Lichas, as he shouted in vain, "Rally to me, my riders, rally to me!"

Pray God that Lophis my son was ready for that *hippomachia*, thought Mêlon. But then without warning almost everything in the ranks began to move, as the pushing from behind started up. Dust rose again. A cloud of it was already hanging in front. The phalanx of the Boiotians was on the move as the horsemen parted ways and yelled to them to finish their own against the jumble of Spartan riders and hoplites. More summer dirt blew into Mêlon's face. Staphis—or was it the pressure itself pushing Staphis?—crowded him and knocked him off balance into Chiôn. The men at his side were all moving at a double-step, with their spears held underhand. He could feel that much. The butt of Mêlon's Bora caught on something to the rear. The men behind were that close, their shields battering the back of his own shoulders. Even though the hoplites of the Peloponnesos were a few cubits distant across the rolling field, an enemy horseman broke through on his right. He was a Spartan *hippeus* and he had got turned around after the cavalry collision. The fool, with his flying braids, had galloped back into the wrong army. The Spartan rider was quickly stabbed on all sides—but not before taking a few hoplites down with him as his horse crashed over onto the men of Tanagra.

Next Mêlon heard an even worse sound than the neighing horses, worse even than the straps and shields bustling, and wood hitting iron as spears and shields bounced together: the sickly sweet music of Dorian flutes. Or was it women's shrieks in the air above them? No, it was enemy flutes, as the Spartan infantry were upon them and at last slanting into the leftward march of the Theban massed wing, each side now desperate to outflank the other. Mêlon could not even hear Epaminondas in the ranks a few feet away. His ears were instead full of Nêto's Thisbean flute, as if she were playing it inside his head to drown the death music of the enemy. He chanted to himself to blot out the enemy tune. His general was pleading with the men at his immediate side. "The sound of the Spartan dirge. Ignore it. The music is coming for them. Not for us. You hear the pipes of a dead city. A dead people. The enemy is lost. They are fleeing. Their flutes are sweet music to our ears."

Epaminondas might as well have been on Olympos. His men were charging ahead. They were already running in the *dromô*. Their heads were encased in bronze, tucked behind their shields, ready for the crash.

# CHAPTER 6

# The Breaking Point

Like some tawny hedgehog that is riled by the hunter's dog out of his deep field hole with spines erect, the Boiotian phalanx had shuddered and then, at last, had lumbered out to face the red Spartan line—this, the best army of men Boiotia had ever fielded in the memory of the elders, better even than the men at Delion who beat back the Athenians over fifty summers before. Never had Mêlon marched leftward. He squinted out the eye-holes of his Korinthian helmet. But he could see no helper god Herakles yet at his side. He thought he saw a glimpse of some deity in the sky, but it was a harsh one—in black with white incisors, and a pale female one at that. She flapped her long wings of ugly skin and feather, the length of two, maybe three hoplites. Ugly pale breasts with black braids bounced about on this thing, this monster, the Kêr, scavenger of the dead, the courier woman of Hades. Where were the virgins of Leuktra, who were promised to fly up and bat away the smelly daughters of night?

Then Mêlon's trance ended as the two armies kept on course for the crash. Spartans ahead. A long spear line of them. Now not more than twenty paces away. Their death music louder. He could hear that much. They would come on, shield touching shield—not like the farmers of Boiotia running with underhanded spears hoping to crash in and break through the slow-moving wall.

Lichas had already led the Spartan cavalry against the Theban horse and saw his mounted men beaten back and mostly killed. Now he leaped down and headed to the king's guard on foot, his side braids flapping out of his helmet, his retainer taking his mount behind the phalanx. Lichas was laughing in joy to be spearing as a hoplite, even as he yelled to the flutists, "Play them louder still, my pipers. It makes the pigs mad with the god Pan. We will eat them by noon. Look how they herd up. All good and ready to be slaughtered. All in a neat bunch. Follow me to the kill. Keep in step, not a gap in the ranks. Don't let them get to our sides! Shields chest high. Forward into the spears—*eis dorata*. Slow, steady in our walk of death. Spear, bleed these pigs. I rout their horsemen as play. Hear our Tyrtaios, hear him—'Let you never relax from war.' Where are you now, my Antikrates, where is my boy killer?" He screamed on without worry that not a one of his helmeted Spartans heard him and that the mass of Thebans was heading right for him.

Mêlon across the way knew that none could hear him either, given the clatter of gear and their bronze helmets, and the war cry of the Spartans. But the same advice came out nonetheless to Chiôn on his right and the quivering Staphis on the left. "Run. Keep moving. Shields out. High and out. Bunch together. No gaps. No gaps. No stops—all eyes ahead. Look at the men you kill. Steady, men, steady. Spears level. All at once. All at once, aim for their throats. Hit them as one, all together. Chiôn, my Chiôn, here they are, the eyes of these Spartan snakes. Endure it, men. Endure it, my Staphi. Staphi, Staphi stay left. Left. Left, left—drift to the good side. Always to the good side move. Hit them on their right, from the flank on their naked right. We go left. *Pros t'aristeron. Eis euônumon.*"

Still, few heard a word. There was too much iron and wood—and, for most of the terrified, the shrieks of the circling black Kêres above. Mêlon's helmet was down. Dust was in his mouth and ears. He was dizzy and wondered why he was running. No more trot now, he was running with the bad leg—faster even to the hated left, faster than he remembered from the old battles. The rear ranks are pushing me ahead, he thought. They're knocking me over, my own men, the fifty *aspides* from the rear. My elbows are free as we run. Good sign, good sign in these early moments. Yes, the big shove, the *ôthismos* that knocks us ahead. Do these doomed reds, these blurs up ahead, do they have any notion of these fifty shields at our backs? Poseidon's wave is about to knock them over. Yet they walk, walk into our charge?

What would the others, these young ones—Mêlon kept thinking— these who had never stood down the Spartan, what would they do with this wave, this push of their friends' shields breaking on their backs? They might panic. Or be knocked over before they hit the wall of the red-capes. He could hear the Boiotian paean, the war cry—*eleleleu, eleleleu, eleleleu.*

Chiôn alone was quiet and a step ahead, worried that his master's slow leg meant they could not be four or five paces closer to the oncoming Spartans. The Boiotian front lines hit the enemy at a run, shuddered, recoiled, bunched back up, and then began to push, stab, and pour into any gaps where Spartans had gone down. In a few moments, it was all Mêlon could do to keep his feet, even as he was struggling to move to the left with the others on the front line and get to the flank of the Spartan right wing. His left arm was battered and stung. The hard rims of the friendly shields from the rear kept pushing on his back shoulder to force him forward. He could not hear his Chiôn yell, "Forget your hobble. No Chôlopous now, master. Let them at our backs do the work. Jab our spears into their faces."

The Spartans were upon them all. Mêlon revived from a brief moment of darkness after the crash of the armies. Spartans everywhere—horsehair, braids, and plate bronze in a sea of red tunics and wooden shields, the lambdas on their shields eyeing him. His own to the rear kept blindly pushing him through these crimson lines. Shafts hitting at all angles, the battle now a maze of wood, round shields, and tall spears that not even the god of war could sort out. Mêlon's long Bora struck something and shuddered, first before most others. Why not—his tip was four palm's widths longer than most of the first line. He at least knew where they were—at the *symbolê*, at the first hit between the two armies. Then came the terrible counterblows from Spartan spears. At first only a few spent jabs glanced off Mêlon's breastplate. But soon his shield shuddered and cracked from hard spear thrusts. In these first moments none of the stabbers of the enemy line had hit his throat. His groin was untouched. Not so with the enemy. Thebans here on the left had struck the enemy royals at an angle, hit an entire line on their unshielded right sides as they had tried in vain to move to their right and behind the mass of Boiotians—who had won the race to the flank.

The noise reminded him of a hard spring hail on Helikon, when he worked on the olive press in the cold shed, under the din of Zeus's storm. It was like clattering ice on the roof tiles above. Amid the clanging, Mêlon was stabbing and bashing with his shield as the Spartan resistance stiffened. Soon he was nearly crushed between the pressure of spear points ahead and his own shields behind—before breaking deeper into the Spartan mass ahead. Then as the line plowed on, Spartans inside on his flanks grabbed at him amid their ranks. "Just keep on your feet, fool," he muttered to himself. Mêlon tried to steady himself, as the shields behind continued to send him forward, as he sought to keep his own shield high on his left to give Staphis cover, as he took safety in Chiôn's wooden shield on his right, as he stabbed over the shield rims of the enemy, as shafts from the rear grazed his helmet, as he went ahead in unison with his own, as he stepped over spears and shields—and men—on the ground. The best hoplite was not the strongest right arm, Mêlon knew, but he who could cover his neighbor, stab, advance, keep his balance amid the flotsam at his feet, and hide in the shield cover from his right—all at once.

At Mêlon's side, a husky Spartan broke through a small gap that just for an instant had opened between himself and Staphis. The long-haired killer—he was known in the south as Kobôn of the large hands—had plunged too deep into the Theban lines with not a Spartan shield in sight for his cover, and then fell to the stabs from the butt-ends of a half-dozen spears to his rear. "Lizard-killers"—*saurôtêres*—hoplites called these bronze squared spikes. Those with their spears still upright shredded anything that moved on the ground at their feet. This gnarly-hide Kobôn, even in the bronze of his grandfather Artemôn, was hammered apart by the feet and spikes of six men. "Keep rank, fools, keep rank, stay together," Mêlon yelled, more to himself than down the line. He knew that if just two or three more of these red-shirts like Kobôn had made it through, the Boiotian front line would have split asunder. A phalanx was like water: It flowed through the easiest hole. A current soon became a deluge if there were quick-witted officers (and in the Spartan army there always were) to cry out, "Push"—*ôtheite, ôtheite*—when they found a channel to widen.

In the brief death lock of the two armies, three or four Boiotians toppled to the ground from the enemy spear jabs, over to his left beyond Staphis. They were hard hill men from the slopes of Messapian, and below near Oinoi and Tanagra, a few of Philliadas's folk that seemed now to be always at the hottest spot in the fray. But they learned it was not so easy to hit these killers of the Spartan phalanx, who as one and with precision stabbed at their throats. Despite their small numbers in this pocket, many of the red-capes still penetrated three ranks in, before being swarmed by Thebans who filled these holes and put them all down. Yet for all the pre-battle bluster of Lichas, for all the royal pride of Kleombrotos, the masters of war so far had been outsmarted by the plans of Ainias the tactician. The Spartans, in their arrogance, had let the smaller Boiotian force mass deeper with no idea that the shorter front had marched at an angle to their own right flank. They were dumbfounded how to get around and outflank this narrow fist of Epaminondas that slammed into them at a run. Somehow the shorter front had reached to the flank of the longer.

Soon the force of fifty shields began to grind down the enemy's depth of twelve, as the Boiotians to the rear dug in their heels and pushed their own into the Spartan phalanx. Time, quick time was everything in this choreography of death: to break the lambda-shields before they got to the flank. Battle hinged on *kairos*, the moment, the *akmê* of position, of the first blow, of hitting hard men on their open sides. "With me, Chiôn. You, me, Staphi. Get to the king now—before they get to our rear. Plow on to the king." Who decided who lived or died this day at Leuktra? As in getting the harvest in, not always the greater nerve and muscle, since a coward might stab on the blind side and hit the hero's cheek. As often it was luck. The length of fate's long thread determined who stayed on his feet and who did not. The goddess Tuchê, or at least Klôthô and her two sisters of the Moirai had as much say as man's right arm in massed battle. If by chance he lined up across from lesser enemies—the allied Peloponnesians or freed helots—then a Boiotian farmer might live; but should he draw the lot to face the peers of Lichas, then even those of the Sacred Band could well die before such killers.

The line of killing peaked and ebbed. In this *klonos*, this frenzy of battle, those who were hit and went down at first were quickly replaced. In the world of the phalanx, the Thebans stepped forward to close and isolate these pockets of Spartan intruders and yet still keep the files and ranks tight—and the wall of shields unbroken. The Spartans were like their fathers of old in closing ranks and keeping even the most brutal of enemies from boring into their phalanx. A few Boiotians, Antikrates knew, would have their necks crushed this day by the edges of Spartan shields. Like the scaly serpent's jaws, the rims slammed shut on any fool who stuck his helmet forward into the Spartan wall.

Antikrates, still advancing on the Spartan right after the crash, almost alone cared little that his wing behind was buckling under the Theban weight. He thought that he could give room to Kleonymos and his guardsmen to range out to kill these pigs, even as enemy hoplites from three sides started to bang their shields against his collapsing wing. We can't kill enough of these men, Antikrates knew now, to stop the mass— even as he bashed down Eurynomos from the hills of Kithairon, and speared in the groin his brother Antalkidas who rushed in to take his fallen sibling's place. But it was not easy to kill brothers like these, not here on their soil. They did not run, these gnarled farmers who took three or more blows before stumbling. Nonetheless, Antikrates kept telling himself, we can kill the Malgidai and still save our king. We of the line of Lichas, alone the professional killers of Hellas, can kill Epaminondas, kill their best and teach others before we die the price of fighting men like us.

Or so he thought, but for every Eurynomos and Antalkidas of the enemy who were on the ground, four Spartiates had already been ground down. And they were the best of the Spartiates: Dorrusas, nephew of Agesilaos, himself screaming as a black iron spearhead broke the barrier of his teeth; the ephor Araios buried beneath five spear stabs—under the jaw, in the armpit, below the navel, above the knee, through the groin; and now even Anaxilas, the henchman of Antikrates. Anaxilas had married his cousin Kreusa, was hamstrung and flailing like a crushed scorpion on the red ground of Leuktra, as the rustics under Philliadas from Tanagra shredded his thighs, slamming down their butt-spikes. Worse still, few Spartans stepped up from the files to plug the holes. The Boiotians were now even into the middle ranks. And the terrified Spartans were backing up, some even turning about, and fighting their way through their own hoplites to flee the crazed men of Boiotia. It was not just Antikrates who noticed the novelty of Spartan failure; the catastrophe was spreading throughout the army as the royal guard screamed orders to stay fast, commands that were never heard and were as shrill as they were brief.

At this moment beside the stream of Leuktra, for the first time in three hundred summers, the dreaded thrust of the Spartan Right ended and went for good from the memory of the Hellenes. Instead, the unaccustomed stiffening of the enemy already sent a shiver throughout the entire Spartan column. The king's guard felt the unease in the ranks that an enemy line had not collapsed when hit hard, but had grown rather than receded with the blow. Of course, the old hands like Deinon and Kleonymos and Sphodrias, too, were spearing the Thebans as they always had. Yet why, Antikrates wondered, were even they not moving forward, not even holding their ground, but slowing being pushed backward? Antikrates through his eye-slits saw the bobbing crests about him. The horsehair plumes of his confused men began nodding in all directions. The circle of Spartans was collapsing around their king.

Far too late, Kleombrotos and Lichas ordered Sphodrias and his folk at the tip of the spears to get the men moving to the far right, to bypass this onrushing mob so much deeper than anything they had ever fought. Mêlon was now right in front of the king's line. Yes, he was to face Lichas once more, perhaps as Malgis had. But now Mêlon took heart that once more Lichas would bear out a Spartan king on his back, perhaps this time dead rather than wounded. He pressed on; yes, this time Lichas would carry out a dead king.

Mêlon could feel that gaping holes were opening, as yet more pockets of Theban rustics surged in. Too few Spartans stepped up to plug the gaps made by such spearmen. Mêlon and Chiôn, with Staphis and Antitheos and his men to the left, were already, at this very beginning of battle, three or four ranks beyond the Spartan front line. They were almost as far into the enemy phalanx as Pelopidas and the Sacred Band fifty or so feet farther to their left on the wing. Over there out of sight, the Sacred Band had avoided the crash. Instead they had already trotted around the Spartan line, and well past the king. From the side and now from the rear, the Sacred Band began to encircle the Spartan horn. Pelopidas's men were herding the enemy back into the spears of the advancing left under Epaminondas, Mêlon, and Chiôn. Already the Spartans were nearly surrounded, their entire right flank blocked at every side. Mêlon's Thebans were like Helikon goat dogs, nipping the ankles of the rams, herding them together as they were forced into the pen. The Spartans were in danger not of losing, but of being destroyed to a man.

Across the way, Lichas saw the disaster. Almost alone he felt this doom of his royal right. He pointed to the king's guard to keep to the right. "Break out of the pig jaws. Trot out. We break out of their ring, quick time, now. March on the double-step. Listen to our pipers."

As the Spartans tried to spear a way out of the closing circle, Staphis, Chiôn, and Mêlon held firm. The three were drifting more and more to the left as planned, batting down spear thrusts, jabbing Spartans as they worked their way onward toward the royal guard itself. More Spartan bodies lay at their feet as they stepped ahead—twitching like the fishermen's speared tunny, but trapped in their scales of armor. Staphis crushed

BATTLE OF LEUKTRA
(THE COLLISION)

SPARTAN CAVALRY IN FLIGHT

SHATTERED SPARTAN PHALANX

THEBANS
(50 SHIELDS DEEP)

THEBAN CAVALRY

a prone man's throat with his hobnailed sandal. Those coming up behind with their still-raised spears finished him off, slamming their butt-spikes straight down through his eye-slits, once the Spartan's shield was splintered and then hammered down flat. For these in the rear who would not meet the first storm of the Spartan, their grand tales back home at the pottery stalls would be of pushing their friends ahead and smashing their spear-butts, their *saurôtêres*, into hundreds of Spartans that they trampled and stepped on. Soon the Thebans, as song would have it in the years to follow, were walking over the dreaded schoolmasters of war—Spartans cast down like mere scraps of meat on the dirty floor of the raucous banquet hall.

Just then Mêlon felt a surge of warm power in his arms, a flow, a *rheuma* of heat. It came without warning over him. As he moved more freely, his muscles became fluid, no longer stiff, his leg limber, his knee no longer fused, his back loose. I am now an ephebe, he thought, younger even than at Koroneia some twenty-three seasons ago, more like at Haliartos when I was a down-beard. Just as if Mêlon had left the tall trees over the gloomy pass of Mt. Kithairon and reentered on the downward hike the sunlight of the rolling foothills, so he pressed on as fewer spears glanced off his wood and bronze. The battlefield had changed yet again. He now had far more space to swing wide his arms. Above Helios had long ago come out; the clouds of gloom were gone. He could hear and see far better now. For all the dust and noise, his senses sharpened with each step ahead as he saw fewer shapes and shadows. His shield felt as if the willow was instead oak, his breastplate more like iron than thin bronze, his helmet impenetrable to a jab from Zeus himself.

Everything was clear. This was the *aristeia*, the surge of victory and power that Homer sung of Achilles in battle. Now it was infused in him. He was light on his feet, his arms were supple and hot—and he would win this day. No more Chôlopous. No, he was Ôkupous. Lord of the fast feet. Like swift-footed Achilles of old. Then Mêlon felt that the grip on his shield was not quite right, that the straps and clasp, the *porpax* and *antilabê*, had been torn and bent and were out of balance. His shield string had long ago snapped. From the corner of his left eye he saw the problem: a Spartan spearhead and two fingers' worth of the wood of its broken socket still stuck into his boss. How forceful the collision a moment earlier had been with the front line of the enemy.

But even his shield mattered less now. The willow of all the Thebans of the front line rattled less frequently as fewer blows bounced off their *aspides,* following the grand *pararhexis* of the enemy front. Soon the lines would open up even more as the Thebans' push sent his own men on through the Spartans. Now the hoplites at his rear would have their own room to swing their shields and stab down over the enemy's shield rims. Mêlon was ready to go for his sword on his shoulder, since even his father's spear Bora was cracked. But for now it was enough to keep heading left. Always lean, Mêlon remembered, lean left. Cover little Staphis with the shield. Cover him. He lives yet.

Mêlon knew that from the feel of the man at his side. Staphis had matched his own step. This farmer of grapes could yet make it through the din, if there were no longer a solid line of Spartan spears ahead. With Chiôn always a pace ahead, and Staphis on the left one to the rear, their small bulge in the line went ahead at a sort of diagonal—just as Ainias had foreseen for the entire Theban left.

As in any great enterprise, the surge of passion comes not from the enjoyment of the success, but mostly in the immediate anticipation. There are only a few moments in this life when a man can gauge that all good things are just about to happen to him. Not even the gods can stop what surely is fated. The Spartans, Mêlon felt, were being obliterated. They were all stumbling, falling, turning. He let out another yell. How could he have stayed back on Helikon while the men of Boiotia bled on the ground of his Leuktra? For the next ten summers he would not have sat in the shadows of the wheelwright, with head down at the smithy, only to hear other, lesser men boast of their kills here at White Creek. Mêlon clobbered another bare neck of a falling Spartan with his shield rim and kicked at two squirming at his feet. How good he was at the work of war and how easily in a mood like this he would kill any men in his way.

No, he liked this leftward plunge, as the new Theban army pushed him ever on toward a collision with the Spartan king. "Stay with me, Staphi, stay close with your fast foot, my *taxupous.*" As the Spartans gave way, still more Thebans surged from the rear, left their files, crowding forward in the blood lust for killing. Just then Mêlon felt iron from the rear tear his forearm. The same fool Theban behind him—Aristaios he thought this olive-crusher was—a moment later hit the back of Mêlon's helmet with his shield. But Aristaios's hot breath on his neck ended when a long Spartan thrust went over his right shoulder and into the tall Theban's throat. That was about all Mêlon could tell. A taller Spartan, one of these guardsmen of the king perhaps—Mêlon would later learn his name was Klearchos, son of the famous drill-master who recruited the Ten Thousand—jabbed his spear right toward Mêlon's jaw. The Spartan aimed to hit somewhere between his nose guard and the upper rim of his shield. Mêlon ducked well in time from the clumsy effort. Then he rose to bash at the man's face with his shield rim.

Klearchos was knocked to the side into Staphis. The slight rustic held firm. With a jab of his spear shaft he hit the falling Spartan in the back of the neck as he strove to keep pace with Mêlon. Staphis knew more than just how to prune the choice canes of his winter vines. For the first time he had hit living flesh, and so robbed the strength from a Spartan peer no less. Is it ever an easy thing to kill the better man? Staphis in his greenness speared too deeply. Now, if just for a moment, his point stuck on the enemy's backplate near the rim by the neck, and threw him off balance. That pause gave the dying Klearchos a last opening. On his way down, the broad-shouldered Spartan grabbed at Staphis's thigh—just as Chiôn crossed over in front and in an instant finished off the falling Spartan with his spear.

Chiôn nearly tore Klearchos's helmet off with a single thrust to the back of his neck. He pulled out far more gore than did Staphis. For the arms of the slave were as thick as the lower legs of the vine grower. Yet the dying Spartan—he was young and stout, this Klearchos, and like his father also of large arms and thighs and just as cruel—still clung to Staphis. Both arms were frozen around the Thespian's shins in his final death grip. Klearchos would take Staphis down with him to the lower world. As the two intertwined, they rolled in the dirt and were smothered by the hobnails of dozens of oncoming Thebans. The killer Spartan opened his mouth, flashing his white teeth against his black beard as he gave up the ghost.

The last words of Staphis were a desperate shriek to his protectors at his side, "Mêlon, Mêlon, he kills me—*me apokteinei! apokteinei me!* Chiôn. Mêlon . . ." Then he disappeared. Even in this fluid final stage, Mêlon was pushed ahead by pockets of Thebans still in file. Might perhaps Staphis have risen back up and survived the stampede to come over him? No. When a hoplite went down, he rarely rose under the weight of his armor. Mêlon answered his own question. Once flat on the ground only the veterans survived if they could cover with shield and ride out the stomping above. Still, Mêlon for a blink had tried to withstand the pressure at his back, to ward off the thrusts in his face, to stop and grab an arm of the downed Staphis. But the farmer from Helikon was already buried amid legs, bodies, and shafts, as if he were a crushed rabbit in the coils of the long grass snake that had wrapped him from head to ankles.

Mêlon and Chiôn in the front ranks strode ahead, banging as much with their bosses as they stabbed with spears. Bora shattered for good. Mêlon was using the broken back end as a sword. In fury at the loss of his Staphis, Mêlon had switched weapons. He was swinging his shield sideways in offense, hitting Spartans with the rim, while he kept them back and protected himself by fending with the broken spear as if it were some long dagger, its butt spike and most of the shaft gone.

The lesser folk of Thebes, those who had chosen the safety of the middle ranks and back, saw even more of an opening. In their frustration at pushing rather than killing, some of these farmers tried to burst through their own ranks and beat the front line to the shrinking enemy circle, at last feeling a chance to boast about glorious war—and get a bit of Spartan blood splattered on their breastplates to show their womenfolk back home. The killing, all thought, was almost over and now easy. Thirty, maybe forty rows of the Thebans were deep inside or even beyond the enemy phalanx and spreading sideways among the files of the Spartans—if there were any files left to see. The greater danger for the advancing Thebans was mostly the dead at their feet, not the living in front. The soil was strewn with bodies and flotsam—cracked shields, broken spears, and the carnage of an army slowly being ground down as Spartan hoplites backtracked, tripped, fell, and were in turn stepped upon as their friends gave way.

For a moment Mêlon turned to his right, held his shield up high, and gave another hard bash to the neck of a falling Spartan. Leobotas, a royal cousin to King Agesilaos himself, had tumbled into the gap, grasping the waist of Chiôn. He hoped to take him down, as Klearchos had done to Staphis. But Chiôn was not like Staphis, and Leobotas was no Klearchos. Instead, the dying Leobotas was dragged along the ground. Chiôn paid Mêlon no attention nor did he pause for his help. He just quickened his pace. Without much bother, he slammed his shield rim on this nuisance, hard down on the neck of Leobotas between his backplate and helmet rim, cracking his upper spine in two. Freed from the mossy barnacle on his greave, a maddened Chiôn resumed his charge toward the king. No one heard him yell, "Off, dead man. Get below." In battle, a wide arm like Chiôn's was worth far more than fifty *plethra* of vines or two chests full of gold.

All these dying Spartan lords had names and past stories of brave kills in battle, and wives and children, and fathers as well, all in Holy Sparta under the shadows of Taygetos and Parnon to the south. But to the slave Chiôn, did any of their lineage and honor matter now? No more than the now dead Staphis, the vine man who had only wanted to do some big thing for his Thespiai. That Leobotas owned one hundred *plethra* on the Eurotas as it roared down from Taygetos, or that his grandfather's grandfather Hippokratidas had speared nine Argives at the battle of Sepeia and then died over the body of Leônidas at Thermopylai, swinging his *klôpis* as he fell to one knee as the Persians sought to cut off the head of his dead king—all that meant nothing at all in faceless battle, battle without memory, class, heritage. No, again, this was the new age of Chiôn, where rank was earned, not given. This was his own *aristeia* as the towering slave slaughtered six of the Spartan elite on his frenzied path right through the royal guard. What did it matter to Chiôn that Staphis's killer, the dead Klearchos, claimed his ancestor was an Agiad king—as if his exalted ghost would save him from a poxy slave from Chios?

Here next went down Mindauros and his son, Isidias. The boy had failed the brutal training of the *agôgê* and was later branded a *tresôn*—a "shaker" who trembled in battle. With them fell bald Glaukôn with his twin boys of twenty, Deinokrates and Adamantos. These two grandees proved to Chiôn to be neither "terribly powered" nor "unbreakable." The beardless bad-eyes Kleomenes too fell to a Boiotian brute, Polyneikes, who farmed near the Phokian border. The mother of Kleomenes had ordered her near-blind son to the front ranks, hoping he might kill a Theban lord and then die with wounds on his breast. Only that way might he match the fame of his unhinged grandfather, the Argive-killer who had burned his captives alive. Fool—he never saw the spear thrust from Polyneikes to his gullet until it came out the other side and three Kêres came shrieking his way.

# CHAPTER 7

# *The Circle Closes*

S hattered islands of Spartan hoplites—all that was left of the king's proud phalanx—were completely surrounded by the Boiotians. Most of these attackers held their shields high and unbroken, so sure that this pathway behind the farmers of Helikon led straight to the threshing of the king and, with his fall, to glory. A few more hotheads, Boiotian rustics from the backside of Ptôon, kept pushing past Mêlon. Even when defeated and trapped, the Spartans were still deadly. They drove their spears deeply into the Thebans who rushed too far in the front of their lines. These southerners welcomed the final moments to ensure their king matched the fame of Leônidas at Thermopylai, who had gone down and into legend with all his guard. The king's hoplites knew all retreat was forbidden—and by now futile anyway. Only within a final ring of spearmen was there any chance to kill more of these Theban pigs, to take as many with them into Hades as they could, to end the nonsense of freeing helots, and to bring renown to their wives and boys at home. The phalanx of the Spartans was broken. But a smaller force made a crescent moon, five or six men deep, around Kleombrotos to ward off any foolish enough to leap in after their king.

Mêlon began to hear a little—and, if only for a bit, to sort out the cries of the living and the groans of the wounded. Then he sensed a louder voice on his left cut the air, with the refrain, "One more step—O give me one more step, my men, and we can break these southerners!" Epaminondas. Or was this an apparition of a hero with his spear and shield in each hand, raised for a moment to the skies, as he rallied the ranks forward? Later Mêlon swore that this strutting hoplite was something more than Epaminondas—huge, twenty feet and more tall, and his shield the size of three normal men, a towering ghost striding ahead into the mist, his step worth six of others. Then this *Megas Epaminondas*, or whatever it was, vanished in a sort of smoke wafting toward the Spartan ring, pointing out the pathway to Kleombrotos.

In the open-rank fighting, the slave Chiôn was at least ten cubits ahead of his master, battering the wall of the Spartans. What was left of his spear had long since been thrown away. His shield was cracked and had finally been abandoned, its foil blazon shredded. Greaves were gone as well. Only his helmet and breastplate kept away the Spartan iron. With his lone sword and in the free-for-all attack on the shrinking Spartan circle, Chiôn, like an unshielded hillman from Akarnania, finally made his way up toward Sphodrias himself, the leader of the royal guard and tent-mate of the king. Sphodrias had once boasted to his peers that he had cut down a hundred Thebans and Athenians in his thirty years of work on the Spartan front line. The killer saw an easy target in this onrushing slave without either a spear or shield, but in glee he let down his guard, and so ensured his own destruction.

Sphodrias paused, thinking he knew the stride of his attacker. He did not, even though the Spartan had once been harmost at Thespiai under the rule of Agesilaos and should have recognized the slave coming his way. In his swagger as occupying lord of those Boiotian rustics, Sphodrias had once promised two Athenian silver owls to the young sandy-haired slave in the food stall with Nêto in exchange for fetching him grapes and apples from the farm of the Malgidai on Helikon. But when he got his fruit, Lord Sphodrias had given the unarmed young Chiôn a kick and had ordered that his henchmen run Chiôn out under the town arch. Ten summers earlier was that, but Chiôn—now the jury and executioner in his own capital court—remembered the slight far better than did Sphodrias. He had planned to kill this man for all those hundred months. To find Sphodrias out in front of his kin was just what Chiôn had hoped.

As Sphodrias hesitated, trying to place the Boiotian who faced him, another Theban had bolted in front of Mêlon from the left side. It was the tall loudmouth, Antitheos, eager to make good on his boast that he would be first to cut down Kleombrotos. And now the Theban raced at the Spartan off balance and with his neck and groin wide open—worried too much for his own glory, his *kudos* to come in the agora of the The-bans, and not for the advance of the men at his side. Antitheos got no-where near the enemy before being hit by two spears. Both points caught him on a downward arc in the lower stomach. Blood spurted out right beneath the breastplate.

Deinon, next in line to Sphodrias, was one of the pair who tore the guts from Antitheos with his spear. Now as he yanked out the shaft from the dying Theban, Chiôn was on him, too. He could do that much for dead Antitheos. So he hit the Spartan stabber on the neck with his sharp blade. It cut through halfway to the bone. Deinon yelled to warn Spho-drias at his side for help, but got no more out than "*erchete*" before falling. Without a pause, the slave swung his sword back and stabbed into the face of the frozen Sphodrias. He tried to cry out, but all that came out of his mouth was a gurgle of blood.

Now at his end, Sphodrias remembered that he knew this Thespian Chiôn. Then he knew no more. A sword plunge for an old kick, and the ledger for Chiôn was at last even. Nor did the slave care that he was bathed in the blood of the two Spartan lords, that with ease he had just ended Deinon and Sphodrias—heroes both, who claimed Lysander and Gylippos as their uncles. Hardly, Chiôn thought; I curse only that these dead men shower me with their own gore. I care that a third of my blade slid inside beside the nose guard of Sphodrias and was rammed between his eyes. Yes, I care only for that.

Chiôn thought to himself this war has no balance scales, nothing quite fair at all in it. The phalanx looked as if all were equal, but the man with the best right arm, and quickest feet, and stoutest heart, he was king of the faceless mass. Let these Spartan invaders fear a slave on Helikon, not talk in their drunken boast of long-dead Leônidas. The Thespian looked for more who barred his way to the king, in fear the Spartans would be called off and flee to camp, as the battle ended. He ignored the weak spear-jabs that either missed or now and then glanced off his cheek plates, as the Spartans targeted this lone raging slave without spear or shield. "For Helikon and Malgis, for Thespiai," Chiôn yelled. He ducked, lurched, and jumped ahead after Kleombrotos through the gap of the circle left by the dying, thinking always, "Freer than any man on this battlefield."

Mêlon tried to keep up with Chiôn. But what mortal could? His slave was unrecognizable, his face, arms, and breastplate all scarlet with gore, almost indistinguishable from the red-shirts under the armor of the Spartans. In this free-for-all, once the Thebans had broken inside these last Spartan ranks, it was a *pankration* of sorts, tooth against nail, finger in the eye, stomping the man who fell. Kleonymos, the king's best surviving man, tried to blurt out from the Spartan island, "We live for this, for this we live! Where is that damn *mêlon*? Pick the apple. Kill that Thespian and we win. Kill him and our king lives." Some Spartans kicked. Others slapped and clawed. Spears, swords were for most long lost. The enemy flute players were dead or silent. Chiôn saw two of them at his feet—one youth without a beard, but with a cracked reed stuck like a dart right through his cheek.

Still another crazed Spartan threw himself at Mêlon. He no longer held a shield or spear. This brave Eurypon was trying to tear off a Theban helmet or an arm maybe. Or maybe he wanted a bite out of Mêlon's wrist. He was a Spartan of the past age who thought his sacrifice might save his king or at least the name of Spartan prowess. But Mêlon had put both hands on his sword, pointed it upright, waited, and caught the Spartan in the lower belly as he had come on, lifting him a palm or so high, as his blade went through the groin and nearly hit the backplate. It took all his strength to yank it out and then kick the shrieking Spartan off with his good knee. Then he stepped on this Eurypon's shoulder and lumbered ahead. Eurypon had a high farm above the Lakonian gulf, near Aigeiai and the lakeside temple of Poseidon. His cross-eyed wife Kuniska, toothless father Eurysthenes, and tiny girl Chloê—they were all this summer safe in the tower and on watch for pirates while the men of Sparta were far to the north fighting Epaminondas. But all Eurypon did this day was ensure that no one would be there next year to protect his father's olives and vines when the mob of ravagers under Lykomedes of Mantineia swept down to the port at Gytheion—tearing down his tower and dragging his now orphaned Chloê in ropes to the slave-sellers. But what Spartan here at Leuktra ever might imagine that his family would soon be unsafe, far to the south in the stronghold of their tribe?

Mêlon and Chiôn then saw something not Antander nor Malgis nor Mêlon himself had ever before witnessed. Not more than a few feet behind the shredded king's guard, straight ahead of them were the crests of their own Boiotians, who had rushed out from their left wing, outflanked the king, and gotten to the Spartan rear. This final pocket around King Kleombrotos was sealed and surrounded. The Sacred Band of Pelopidas now headed toward Chiôn and Mêlon, slicing in two what was left of the final Spartan circle. Mêlon slowed at the sight of these last efforts of the king's hoplites and their Spartan empire. For a moment only, he lowered his sword and looked sideways and back for his Boiotians. Not since the Persians had cut off the head of Leônidas at Thermopylai had any man seen a Spartan king go down in battle.

To pause was a mistake even for a moment, since in that one stop Mêlon forgot that Spartans never do. Kleonymos, favorite of the Agiads, the son of the dead Sphodrias—who hated Lichas and his Antikrates for their claims of preeminence—came from his side and bashed Mêlon with his shield. It was a blow with the boss to the side of the head, hard enough to brain most men. Mêlon's horsehair crest flew off. The concussion sent Mêlon's helmet rattling against his temple and cheek and nearly knocked him off his feet. His skull's insides crackled deep from within.

He could no longer quite make out all the blurred shapes of battle. In this new netherworld of the wounded and dead, Mêlon strained to hear the garbled cries of Epaminondas, "One step more. Give me one more." But then Mêlon heard something else: the screeching of one of the stinking Kêres he had seen before battle, but no more than ten feet above the fray, circling and diving into the melee—and headed for him? Suddenly he was given proof by this blow that the vulture women did live and kill and were no myth after all. For the first time this day, Mêlon in his dizziness, swaying on the threshold of death, could easily make out these hazy women birds that must have been hovering all along above the battlefield. Two of them, Nyx and Melainê, flew with talons outstretched, just as the wounded veterans had warned—the winged and deep-breasted daughters of Night, who swooped down over the heroes to pull them skyward by their ankles.

For now the son of Malgis managed to stay on his feet. He beat these harpies off and sent his sword right through the mouth of Melainê fluttering above him. She without flesh let out a shrill laugh nonetheless at the effort, veering away in anger at her lost meal. Swinging his sword in frenzy, the Thespian kept both these carrion *daimones* and the hoplites around off him as he regained his senses. Not quite yet was his thread cut, even after taking the last and best blow of the fading Spartan elite. His head had stopped ringing. The greedy Nyx knew that when she alighted instead on the nearby groaning Eurypon, who was far closer to death, and picked him up by the heels. Chiôn later swore that his master for an eye blink or two had been stabbing at shadows, as had Aias in his madness. But Mêlon saw them as clear as crows nonetheless. After the winged Nyx flew off with Eurypon, Melainê lighted on Boiotian Mantô of Oinoi way, the tile-baker whom Eurypon had stabbed before he went down. Then Nyx returned and the two hags were flapping their stinky wings, shrieking at each other in the air to let go of their prize, each with a foot of the dead Boiotian, trying to fly off in different directions.

Drops of blood ran out Mêlon's mouth. He knew that what he had done to ten or so Spartans that day, Kleonymos had nearly done to him, with far greater strength and youth. After these brief moments of daze he discovered that five Boiotians or more had fallen while he had spun and thrashed at the Kêres. There was nothing of the enemy now but the towering Kleonymos, stabbing and swinging his shield wildly in the air, like the crazed she-bear that bellows and paws the very air between her cubs and the oncoming hunter. As Mêlon stumbled to regain his balance, he had enough sense to raise his shield to eye level. He saw that he had been pushed almost to the king himself. For now he heard no more cries of the Kêres, just the final pleas of the Spartan Kleonymos, calling out to keep his King Kleombrotos alive.

# CHAPTER 8

# The Battle Above

In the camp above the swale of Leuktra, not all were so scared or unhappy at the sight of their own shaking hoplites of Boiotia lining up for battle. "Loud and proud, my Spartans—big thing to see." Gorgos winked in a manner Nêto had not quite seen before. He stood up on the wagon bed. He had a better view than any below and thought he could predict what those lining up for the collision could not. Gorgos scoffed at the idea that anyone in Boiotia would dare go up against such men of Lakedaimon. "Look, look, Nêto. At the hills beyond—how our rabble of Boiotia awaits slaughter below. They're hoggies backing into the corners of their pens as their butcher enters. Ah, look. Even the blood-fanged Kêres will soon fly in the air. They will have their pork feast as they land on your Boiotians. You should have gone home as ordered last night, and been spared the sight of your bloodied Boiotians below."

Gorgos was freed of Mêlon, freed of Proxenos, freed of all memories of his twenty seasons and more as a slave on Helikon, so sure he was of a grand Spartan victory below. He too was a Messenian, and, like Nêto, born a helot. But the old man cared not a whit for any of those serfs, and he liked their masters better than their slaves. There was no law that said Spartans must prove strong, and helots weak. Sly Gorgos knew that the weaker usually hide behind their race, their color, their homeland—refuges all for failure. So now for the first time Nêto talks of her helot birth. More than that still, a liberator of her people—this slave who can't remember the look of Mt. Ithômê or even tell helot talk from the Spartan

Doric. She was not like him, not like Gorgos, he thought, who chose his race, his people, his land as he saw fit and so trumped a mere accident of helot birth. Spartans were his because they, like him, were better than the helots. In contrast, his master was worse and only by silly laws kept the true master Gorgos his slave. How odd that these Boiotian liberators brought their slaves like Gorgos to battle. But then again, Gorgos still liked his master and was, after all, born a helot as well, whose people were underfoot from the Spartans that he now boasted about. He figured that he could hate helots and their masters, both Spartans and Thebans, praise Lichas and at times his master, too—mixed up at least for a while more before battle.

Gorgos climbed down from the wagon. "So much, Nêto, for your gods yesterday. Your omens will get Boiotian men killed. Close your mouth, and we all live—paying money, fair tribute to Spartan occupiers and their ruling harmosts, and as you know, keeping our masters alive. These are our betters—yes they are—from Sparta, who rule with the iron hand. We helots, you and me both, know they earn what they enjoy—and how the two of us can prosper with them. But bet me—will our Boiotians run like Thespians or die fighting as they do in Sparta?"

Nêto paid this two-shoe no heed in his dotage; traitor long ago to the cause of the helots, traitor he seemed now to her master Mêlon. She packed her bedroll and then moved farther away from the wagon where she had slept the previous night. Nêto led the ox Aias over to taller grass. The master and Chiôn were far below. Apparently, Nêto thought, Gorgos cared little who heard him as he yelled out at what he saw below. For the first time in their lives the two farm slaves, Nêto and Gorgos, were alone without Chiôn or Mêlon somewhere nearby in the vineyard. They kept eyeing each other as the sun rose and the armies below marched out to crash. Nêto gasped when she suddenly realized that Gorgos no longer limped. She was struck mute when he pulled off his ragged cloak to reveal the broad chest of a man more forty summers than seventy. Maybe he been faking his age to avoid plowing on the farm, secretly scything and pruning after dark to build such muscles. Or perhaps this brute was a demon god—maybe some foul half-animal from Hades that had taken over the body of the old slow-wit Gorgos.

Had he taken some drink from the fountain at Hippokrenê on Helikon that had smoothed his wrinkles and put muscle where his fat used to hang, and made him talk as if were a lord? Surely he was no Odysseus whom Athena made young and strong in moments of crisis. The voice of Pythagoras had taught Nêto to scoff at these child stories of the Olympians. But she thought she would soon see hooves as well on this new Gorgos, who might have been a foul offshoot of Pan all along. Then this fresher, taller helot stood erect and blared out in a stronger voice and a better way of speaking. His Doric seemed purer now and with all trace of Helikon twang gone.

"By the gods, I wish this day we were on the other side of that battle line. You see, my Nêto, I was a slave up here only by name, not by heart— not like you and Chiôn, who found your proper station as the property of Mêlon. In Sparta I was free—only to see my freedom end when reduced to a slave on Helikon. All this is the logic from the would-be liberators of serfs. Slavery is good if you and those servile like you obey their betters, bad only to the degree that a natural lord like Gorgos sometimes trips on the battlefield and finds himself reduced to your lot. But in Sparta they know all that and so keep down the Messenians as the serfs they are, and make free those like me who soon prove that they were born to the wrong parents. Perhaps Sparta needs me as her men run out and her serfs increase. Watch below—the king steps forward. Now the music starts, Nêto. The most beautiful sounds to ears of men. Come here—*akouete*. Hear the Spartan pipes with me."

So this slave-turned-philosopher dropped all pretense and raised his voice in delight at the sight of thousands of Sparta's best below. A mania was in him at the sight of Spartans after twenty years and more. Nêto hoped those below might hear his loud treason, his high traitor talk, as if the dirty helot farmhand could have spoken like a Spartan lord all along. He went on without fear. "The killing begins as the sun warms. It peeps through the clouds, peeps through to show its face, Nêto. Look, sassy helot, at Spartans in their pride. Look at me. Look what Spartan men can do. Their fine steps, their shields chest-high, not a crest, not a spear tip out of order. That is the real *eunomia*, the real law. Tough and hard. It gives obedience and order. Not your freedom. They've had their late-morning wine. Hot they are for battle. Hot and ready, all up with the desire for warcraft—with their *erôs polemou*." Then this new Gorgos turned directly to face Nêto and at twenty feet distant beckoned with his right hand, as he hummed and danced to a Spartan war tune. "Come nearer, woman. Sit next to your Gorgos as we watch our men from our Peloponnesos, our shared birthplace. You too may come to see the power of Sparta and how we can help the winners take care of their children, we two who still speak with the Messenian accent. Your Gorgikos will tell you a long story of Spartan lore. Sit here. Learn of the Spartan way. Let me sing the Spartan poets, Alkman especially, to his Nêtikon, or some more Tyrtaios."

The maddened Gorgos had moved downhill and left Nêto back near the wagon, so intent was he on getting an even better view of the great slaughter below. He hiked down to yet another hillock of scrub cedars and tamarisks, wanting to get far closer to the battle than even the rise below the camp. From his early years with Brasidas, he had a sharp eye for terrain and the pulse of fighting. The son of Mêlon had ridden right out at the head of a column of cavalry, the first of the Boiotians to hit the Spartan horse. In a moment, the reckless Lophis at the point had been swallowed in dust and horseflesh. But before Lophis was lost to the mob, Gorgos determined that he had been knocked off and disappeared into the melee—unhorsed but perhaps alive.

"Don't wait. Save our master," a voice yelled at him from his rear. It was Nêto again, who had crept down with blade in hand. In her own wildness, she too had thoughts, but of killing Gorgos, cutting his throat from the rear. She believed in her visions at night that Gorgos could still, even at his age, even if the Spartans lost today, do great evil; and she thought some far better than he might live if he bled first. Nêto was worried too that he saw the false in her, that the more she had forgotten the distant helots of Messenia, the more she made up stories about them, the less she sounded like one, the more she tried to. But upon observing the cavalry charge below, she decided that she needed Gorgos to save her master's son, and put away her knife.

Gorgos barked back, "Leave woman. You deserted our farm. Go. It's man-killing here. In the raw. Look. Your Lophis fallen. Slaughtered. Or will be."

Nêto replied, "He is your master, too, or have you forgotten who saved you so often from the lash of Mêlon? If you won't go down, I'll go. Lophis is buried in men, not yet deep in dirt. No Spartan can beat him in the one-on-one, not our Lophis. The phalanx is on them now. If we can

get down there, if he survives the trample, we can save him from the locusts that will strip and kill him on the field. If your mania leaves you,
the two of us can drag him to the wagons."

As the two helots looked out, they saw that Lophis's charge had sent
the Spartans reeling. His horsemen had stunned their hoplite advance.
Before the reds had recovered, the Theban phalanx was upon them, killing all those who had not been trampled by their own horse. The Theban
left wing seemed as one iron hammer, its head battering and flattening a
sheet of bronze. Suddenly Gorgos cowered a bit. "Fire burns Spartans
and enflames the king." The two had no hint that they in fact were
watching the acme of Epaminondas himself and the Sacred Band under
Pelopidas—in concert with the furious onslaught of Chiôn. After their
cavalry charge, the Theban hoplites on the left had rammed obliquely
into the Spartans. They tore apart the slow Spartan march, as if order and
music meant nothing to the mass of farmers who split that red line in
two. Then the defeated Spartan horsemen galloped back into the ranks
and only fouled the king's reply.

Nêto could see that almost immediately a *lochos* or so of Thebans,
maybe six hundred, were well inside the Spartan ranks and were burning
their way through to within a few paces of the king himself. For a moment only she stopped begging Gorgos to rescue Lophis. Instead she
yelled to the sky, "Chiôn's swell"—*to oidma Chionos*—and it would be
named just that for the big slave who first cut the Boiotians' way in. From
here above, it looked as if the entire right wing of the Spartan line was like
some pitiful mole caught in the jaws of a huge fanged hound, being
shaken and torn apart, as the forest of spears was thinned out, ten or
twelve at a time.

The two helots above the battle had not forgotten Lophis. But for just
a blink the scene below stunned even Nêto. It would have scattered the
wits of any Hellene who saw the death throes of the Spartan army. When
the Theban mass went left and plowed through the Spartans, the allies of
Peloponnesos on the left wing fled to the hills of Kithairon. For all the
Boiotians' fear the night before, the grand battle of Leuktra ended up just
as Epaminondas and Ainias of Stymphalos had always foreseen—a Spartan king with his head in a Boiotian noose and his Peloponnesian friends
happy enough to see it. Then Nêto, who likewise had predicted this end
of the Spartans at Leuktra from the livers and lungs of the sacrificial ani-

mals, turned to Gorgos. "Lophis lives. My—our—Mêlon is near, near him somewhere. You foul gorgon, go down there; wherever the killing is hottest, his spear will be there. Our Chiôn, too. This is a great day for the Malgidai and the farmers of Helikon. Go down. Your new friends have lost. This is your final chance to prove yourself and get back to Helikon without your head in a noose. Lophis was good, or so you used to swear."

Gorgos nodded, for Lophis as a boy had ridden atop his shoulders in the high-trellised vineyard, spanking his back and calling the old slave his centaur. And when grown, he had cut off the flank of the goat and the tongue of the bull to take out to the shed of Gorgos and make sure the helot had his good share of meat from the sacrifices. But the head of Gorgos was now downcast, as the sound of the Spartan pipes faded and end of the king's army was growing clear. Gone for now were his wild visions of his old masters marching into Thebes, perhaps with Gorgos as new retainer, maybe even the new Lord Kuniskos, Spartan harmost of Thespiai. Instead he muttered to Nêto, now back in his simple helot voice of Helikon, "Our kin, our Dorians, all in Hades. Dead. Go back to the ox. Go home as you were ordered. Else I take lash to you. But for the sake of the good Lophis, I hike down to find our master. I will carry him to Helikon, just as I did the dead Malgis. Our Sturax comes with me. He will find the scent of his Lophis. Yes, give me the dog of Lophis. Wait for us at the camp of Epaminondas." For all his talk of Spartans, Gorgos would plunge into the din to find his master's son. He at least believed that he would do so also for Mêlon, for all his Spartan boasting, still the loyal slave of the Malgidai.

Nêto went for the wagon, confident that mania had passed and Gorgos was at least divided between his Spartans and Thebans, and so would get down to the battlefield to find Lophis. But first she turned to watch the path of the helot down the hill. She clenched her blade as she grimaced, determined to ensure he descended to the battlefield to Lophis. Then without a word, Gorgos quickly hiked down to the battle, out of sight beneath the crest of the hill.

The entire plain below was thick with the dusty haze of the Dog Star days. A light drizzle up on the mountains had long ago stopped. The late-summer ground coughed up its dust under thousands of heavy feet. For all the swirling dirt, Nêto grasped better the true picture of the battlefield below, as the hordes of the Peloponnesian allies were beginning to throw down their gear and flee to the hills beneath Kithairon. Their dust trail wafted hundreds of feet up into sky. Perhaps Lophis had risen to his feet after all. He might have made his way through the advancing hoplites to find a new mount.

From this lookout, Nêto saw the Boiotian allied right wing stop its pursuit of the panicked Peloponnesians—also just as Epaminondas had ordered. Then these allied Boiotians below turned to their left, to help the advancing Thebans under Epaminondas surround and annihilate the final Spartan stand. The few alive of the vaunted Spartan royal wing were surrounded and trapped. No farmer, she sensed, wished to miss out on the bloodletting of a Spartan king. She didn't either. "Oh, One God of us all, look." Nêto turned to the dumb ox at her side. "They are broken. So ends Sparta. Here, right here, is the end of Sparta." Now on the road downward Nêto climbed into the wagon, hitting Aias with a switch. She would drive the creaky wagon around the gentle slope of the hillside to find Lophis below and perhaps reach Mêlon and Chiôn as well. But as Nêto reached the trail that led to the camp of Epaminondas, a stream of rustics swarmed ahead of her, all unhinged in their bloodlust. Hundreds of Boiotians—wives, men, archers, horsemen, armed or not—were calling out in unison, "On to Sparta, on to Sparta." Then a new chorus rose of "O Epaminondas. Crush the head of the snake."

Another madness had taken hold as the mob of onlookers scrambled over the mess of the battlefield. Hundreds of the widows of Boiotia were on their knees, tearing off the jewelry of the dead Spartans, indeed fighting one another for their red tunics and clasps. Nêto thought from the bench of the wagon that the battle was over and won. All that had once been ridiculed was now accepted as dogma: "Like wheat stalks these Spartans—and mowed down by the scythes of our Pythagoras."

# CHAPTER 9

# The King of Sparta

Leuktra had ceased to be an *ôthismos aspidôn,* a push of shield against shield, since most of the enemy who were not trapped here were either dead or running. The Boiotians were battering with their shields the few stumbling Spartans who were left. Some fell and were stabbed by oncoming ranks, a few tried to join the shrinking circle around Kleombrotos. "Their king is trapped. Drag them away," rippled out through the Boiotian ranks. Always they were answered with a chorus from the mob rushing forward, "On to Sparta. On to the Peloponnesos."

For a moment only, both sides of the battlefield paused at the sight of the surrounded Spartan king and his huge Kleonymos barring the way forward. The king's man was swinging fiercely with spear and shield as he hit Thebans foolish enough to charge alone such a man. A skilled bowman from Phokis tried to bring him down from a distance. His missiles bounced off Kleonymos's shield and hit more of his own than of Sparta.

Four or five Spartan guardsmen rushed in behind Kleonymos. All raised shields to block the way to the king. In some places Spartans in the ring were nearly back-to-back. A tiny but solid mass was moving backward and for now was unbreakable. Maybe three hundred, maybe four were alive and had not fled, still killing all the Thebans who bounced off their spears. But this last circle was tightening, ever smaller, as it was pounded on all sides. Where was their Lichas? Where his son Antikrates?

It mattered little. Neither of those two talkers, Kleonymos swore to himself, had ever deserved their honor, their *timê*—not over himself, the best son of Sphodrias. Kleonymos turned and aimed his spear once more at Mêlon. He would spike this apple and finish off the faker for good if he dared to come on again. But a hoplite on his right blocked the Spartan's lunge. In the blur of bodies, Mêlon, as he would recall in the months to come, was pushed aside by one of his own, and so was not hit again by his attacker Kleonymos. Instead the Spartan pressed forward past him, eager to spear this new bigger target. Only later would Mêlon learn that Kleonymos would have stabbed his thigh, had he not been struck down almost at once by Chiôn—his Chiôn along with at least three retainers of Epaminondas. All their spears hit Kleonymos in the neck and groin. This legend of Sparta had gone down three times already at Leuktra—but always had regained his feet. This time the blows were mortal. The son joined the father Sphodrias in the dirt at the feet of their king.

As Kleonymos tottered, the melee cleared for a bit. Mêlon stared directly at the face of King Kleombrotos. The tall king was not more than five cubits distant. For a blink, he was alone. The royal had the look of a young man—far younger than Mêlon had imagined—even in these glimpses through the nose guard and bronze on his faceplate. This Kleombrotos had not wanted to be king, though the honors and the big house on the acropolis were good enough. His brother Agesilaos had fallen sick at Olynthos. So by accident the lot of the Agiad royal house had fallen to him, the lesser sibling. He was no leader in battle. The partner Eurypontid king, crippled Agesilaos of the lesser line, had shunned him as womanly. Now in his ninth year of kingship, Kleombrotos right here at Leuktra would crush the Boiotians and restore the honor to his Agiads. Or so the reluctant king had thought.

Again, where was his Lichas, the king now fretted, where was young Antikrates to save him? Traitors. Nothing in Kleombrotos had warranted royal rank other than birth and the unlooked-for fall of his elder brother. He was hardly the caliber of Agesilaos, the other king now sitting at home, who was glad when spears came his way, and—so the priestesses of Artemis had promised him—who would live on in his dotage to block Epaminondas from the acropolis of Sparta itself.

The *rheuma polemou*, the surge of war, gave Mêlon strength for a final burst, strength he had not known even in his youth. His spear was gone, his sword now in his right hand. He aimed his blade right over the edge of the king's shield with all the power of his good farming arm. His royal victim was frozen—in faith perhaps that his wood of Mt. Taygetos would save him for a bit longer, or that Kleonymos would rise up a fourth time to his defense. Or that Lichas was not dead, but would come down from the air to lift him away.

Fool. Nothing of the sort followed. Mêlon's thrust just cleared the top curved edge of the shield above the rivets. The sword's point found Kleombrotos's mouth. The tip entered between the cheek guards and beneath the bronze bridge over the nose. Mêlon's arm rammed the blade a good way into the Spartan king's head, snapping it back. Instinctively he raised his shield to prepare for the swarm of spears from the onrushing guard to follow. It came with no delay. Four or five blows knocked him back into shields of the Thebans to his rear. Too late. Mêlon had killed their king.

"King down. The king is down—*Basileus epesen, peptôken hameteros basileus,*" the guard called out. "Rally to us, men of Sparta, rally to us!" But there were few men of Sparta now to rally to anyone. Most of the guard were dead or wounded. A few even of the boldest had backed away looking to flee. Now others were trying to draw out of the circle to re-form the army or to prepare some rearguard to save the body of Kleombrotos. Losing their dead king would be worse even than losing this battle. Spartan hoplites such as these could not see their wives or boys again, even if they returned alive to Lakonia, if they did not save the body of Kleombrotos. They would be forever forced to live as spat-upon beggars, the *tresantes*—the tremblers who had lost their courage and their war and their king and their state.

The dark goddess Mania took hold of Epaminondas, the father of the Spartans' disaster, and goaded him on toward Kleombrotos. The Boiotian general was enthused with the divine as he now cut in on Mêlon's left. Boiotians from every direction reached at an arm or a leg of Kleombrotos, who had fallen to one knee and was about to keel over. "To the Kadmeia with him. Drag this dog to Thebes," they yelled. Chiôn was at the fore. He was dodging spear thrusts to his chest, trying to join his general and help drag Kleombrotos out. In the confusion, the patched armor of Ainias caught Mêlon's eye. Proxenos also was with Epaminondas, as the best men of Boiotia swarmed the body.

But just then from the retreating Spartans a spear thrust flew right under Mêlon's jaw. Swoosh. It slammed instead into Chiôn, squarely inside the left upper arm at the shoulder. The blow knocked him off his feet—Chiôn, who thought he had killed nine of the red-capes so far without receiving even a scrape. The slave shuddered and struggled to rise, for the hit had come from someone as strong as himself. For a moment those to his rear froze as the white flame that had blazed a path for them flickered and went out. Then their Chiôn got halfway up, tottered, and fell again, not far from the dead Kleombrotos.

Mêlon tried to make out the blurry figures in the jumbled mass of fighters. Here came a shadow out of the Spartan past, one of the breed left of the type that once had broken the Persian Mardonios at Plataia, and smashed the Argives at Mantineia. The Spartan was splashed with blood, his helmet long since torn off. He cared little whether he wore any armor or none. Bald on top with a forked beard, he looked like a besotted Satyr, but with blood, not wine, his drink. This was Lichas. And he now stalked from the shadows to the fore. He had ranged across the battlefield to find twenty Spartan hoplites in isolated pockets, rallying them to march over to the last stand of the Spartans and save their king. Two braids of his side hair were swinging wildly in the air. As his mouth opened there was not more than a tooth or two in his ugly head. Mêlon thought he was not grimacing—but smiling. Yes, this was Lichas of legend, who had killed his father at Koroneia and ruined his own leg.

Wrinkled almost beyond recognition of being a Spartan hoplite, scarred, and bald, this monster stormed into the final killing, scoffed at the spears tips bobbing in his face, and tried to save his dying lord whom he had ridiculed the last nine years. His huge son Antikrates followed him, eager to outdo the father, and himself prepared to carry out both their corpses, if need be—father and king one on each shoulder. Lichas and his son were frantic. "Save the king! To the camp! All alive back to the camp! *Eis to stratopedon.* To me, rally to me!" Neither cared anything for the collapse of the Spartan ranks, much less the truth that the day of his parochial state was over. No, it was enough this day that they were Spartans—now in the joy of battle, with their grip on shield and spear, whether that be here in the north or far to the east. Lichas's last son was with him. Good men lived—even if his other boy, Thôrax, was gasping now for breath, after Chiôn's spear had torn apart the sinews of his neck behind the ear.

Whether in the heyday of Spartan power or amid its twilight also counted for nothing. He was stalking proudly upright despite his age. If the Spartans were to lose, they would lose in the way of Leônidas and Lysander—and Lichas—killing as they protected their king with all blows to their front. The stabbing in this last battle grew fiercer still. But Lichas laughed as he heard the dying around him in vain begging the Kêres to pass them by, the vultures of death back above Mêlon and Chiôn. The black deities kept their wide distance from Lichas—lest such a man strike even these deathless ones a fatal blow. No, Lichas laughed, even Nyx, queen of her dark brood, fears my smell.

Then, without missing a step, Lichas stepped toward the downed Chiôn's chest and tried to spear his throat. The wounded slave rolled away as Theban spears covered him. Lichas moved on to finish off others less dangerous. But in that moment the slave stumbled somehow to his feet, bellowing, "Kill the king. Where is Kleombrotos?" Then he fell a third time to the ground, muttering as the battle raged past him.

Lichas whirled to meet a challenger: He slammed his freed spear shaft with an upward flat stroke against the helmet of the onrushing Epaminondas himself. Before Epaminondas could recover from the blow and with his men swarm this killer, Lichas stooped down. With one fluid motion, more a god than human, he picked up his limp king, slung him over his back, and used his body as a shield to batter himself a way out back through what was left of the guard. Antikrates backed away, face to the enemy, as his father headed to camp. He was trying to warn all those Spartans alive to follow his father's path. "We and our king are the way out. We are the way back. To camp. To the ditch. *Eis taphron, phugete pros taphron.*" They were aiming at an escape, perhaps back through the shattered circle and on right through the Sacred Band to the open country—slashing as they went. "Turn, Spartans. Turn back. Draw back from these stinking pigs. *Apostrepesthe tôn suôn.* They will not have our Kleombrotos. No Spartan king for their slop. Not today—not ever."

There were only two hundred Spartans alive in the circle who broke out with Lichas, as their bald hoplite god roared on, "Not today. Not ever. Not today, not ever—*ou sêmera, oupote, ou sêmera, oupote.*" They had been abandoned by their allies and were surrounded by the Boiotians. But the Spartan remnants were buoyed by the late appearance of their bloody Ares Lichas. He had always found a path out for them. Now his indomitable son Antikrates was his rearguard. The two would outdo each other for the laurels of battle. Both would clear a way for the rest to get out and home, or so the last of the Spartan hoplites thought.

With Lichas leading, the Spartans remembered their training of the *agôgê*, and as if awakened from a trance they backpedaled in column. With Lichas, almost magically they wheeled around and plunged ahead through Pelopidas's men to their rear—who had thought the battle long over. One man, a single god-like Lichas, was worth a *lochos*, or maybe more still than six hundred mere hoplites, and now he intended to save the best of those still alive for wars yet to come.

Many of the Theban Band in the rear had already begun stripping the bodies. Fools again. Ten or so of them, the best hoplites in Thebes, were impaled by Lichas's charge. Their ashes would soon send the big houses of the city into mourning for the year to come. Where this foul apparition came from, no one afterward knew. Perhaps some fissure in the earth had spat him back out from Hades below? Survivors claimed he had been on all sides of the battlefield, on and off his horse. That his neck and fore-arms were a bloody mess made him yell in delight, "The pigs bite us like children. Like children. They sting like wasps, no more."

Lichas stalked his way through the raining blows of the Thebans to the front of the retreating column. In disgust, with a quick overhand slam he sent his spear into the throat of Saugenes, the high officer of Pelopidas's Sacred Band who stepped forward to block his passage. Like his dead father at Delion, Saugenes only earned himself another black marble grave stele on the road to Thebes for his trouble. Lichas, even under the weight of his king, was making headway with level Spartan spears at his front and side. Mêlon had bolted back up after ducking his blow, followed the retreating band, and picked up the fallen spear of the king. He tried to cast it in anger for the stabbing of Chiôn, but it was a heavy thing not meant for throwing. Mêlon was aiming at the body of the king, since he thought the limp Kleombrotos might have survived his head wound.

Lichas turned and saw something out of the corner of his eye. He bobbed his head a little. The iron point of Mêlon's throw only cut through the ear of the Spartan's bare head before hitting the thigh of the king draped over the shoulders. Lichas's shredded ear on the side of his unhel-meted head spurted blood. He ignored the scratch. "To the hill, to the hill and form up. A thousand in camp await us there. A thousand others and more live. Across the ditch and on home," he roared. Kleombrotos was dead, having breathed his last even before Mêlon had thrown his spear. Now it fell from the king's limp thigh. The bodyguards pressed even closer to Lichas and their slain lord. In moments the Spartans were through the crowd of Thebans. Now they were marching across the bridge over the ditch under a hail of missiles. The Boiotian light-armed ran up to get in their blows, once they had a clear fleeing target.

Antikrates was last. With his massive shield, the son of Lichas brought up the rear. He was pushing the Spartans ahead. He waved his spear this way and that before throwing it at the Boiotians who had slowed in their pursuit. He took up a cleaver now. As his father rushed ahead into the camp, Antikrates turned about and paused, eager to kill one more Boiotian before he too was across the ditch—a sight to encourage his men who watched him cross.

Ismenias, son of Ismenias, the firebrand of the Theban *dêmos*, had ordered his men not to let them away. "At them. Follow me across." But Chiôn was now wounded and down. Mêlon, Epaminondas, and Pelopidas were wobbly and stunned. So Ismenias found himself far out in front of the pursuers, riffraff who waited for archers and javelin throwers to come up to pelt the retreating Spartans. Antikrates didn't wait for the fool Ismenias to reach the bridge over the gully. Now he charged back out to give his swing more power. With a clean cut, Antikrates sent the head of Ismenias flying off and up, his helmet strapped tight, a half yell already out of his mouth: "No escape! *Ou phugê*!" Antikrates turned once again in scorn and lumbered toward the camp. He crossed. Then the Spartan knocked away the two boards across the ditch and joined his father.

Lichas was already up on the rise of the Spartan camp where more than a thousand Spartan stragglers had found safety. They were forming up the phalanx to greet their rearguard. Lichas laid down his dead king carefully, strutting back and forth, smiling to the defeated Spartans. He was already making order among the mess and confusion of camp. It was better, he thought, that the king was dead, and now the better man, ephor Lichas, could take command and lead home what Kleombrotos had nearly ruined. Lichas commanded rank after rank of his survivors to kneel, shields down on the ground and spears resting on their knees. "Stay fast, my sons of Herakles. Stay fast. By our spear arms we get home. I bring you all home. There are no *tresantes* here. Not one. Not one of us is a trembler."

The battle of Leuktra was over. It became legend for the widows at the looms in Thebes and the blind bards in the halls to work over. The larger war to end Sparta itself now began. Hundreds of Boiotian onlookers swarmed the battlefield and began to tear at the bodies of Kleonymos and the corpses of the royal guard. Then back on the killing field Mêlon himself stumbled to the ground, in exhaustion, right where he had toppled Kleombrotos, amid a pile of corpses, bloody capes, sandals, helmets, and entrails. He drifted off, and his eyes closed. He was once again under a better blue sky on his vineyard beneath Helikon, where he saw the good Gorgos of old, and two-armed Chiôn in the vineyard driving in stakes in the rocky ground, calling to him to bring the iron bar to make more holes down the row. Lophis was the overseer of all, barking orders to get the planting done before the great ice storm came from off Helikon. He was happy to linger with Nêto at a pond by the vines, gazing at the dark images of storm clouds piling on Helikon in the growing ripples of the water as Nêto bent over for an icy drink. Wind rustled in the oaks and the scent of cedar came with the breeze from the storm. In the air always was that pipe music, the playing of that goat tune of Epaminondas, or was it Nêto with the reed at her lips and her strain from Thisbê that loosened his limbs, that strain that always came to drive worry and care away?

"Wake up, Thespian, you cannot cross over. Not yet."

It was the Stymphalian Ainias, the planner of Leuktra, who had sat down next to the son of Malgis. Throughout the entire battle the Arkadian had never been more than two files away in battle, always with Proxenos at his side batting away any thrusts aimed at Mêlon. Now from his wine sack Ainias poured some water into his bloody helmet. Then he beat away the flies that had covered Mêlon's head and cleaned the wound.

# CHAPTER 10

# The Wages of Battle

Mêlon's head cleared a bit and the Thisbean music in it abruptly stopped—no more cedar scent in the air, no pond, no Nêto, no Chiôn, no family at work on the slopes of Helikon. The sun of the long day was speeding westward on its home leg toward the mountains. He blurted out to anyone nearby, "Good men. That is all that matters. We had them. Hoplites like Lophis, Chiôn, and Ainias and Epaminondas can do anything—good men, far better than anyone in the king's army. Good men, that's all that counts."

Now Mêlon went on with his ramble, "I paid Lichas back in kind. I think you will find something of his ear, and maybe of the king's spear as well." Mêlon vaguely sensed that Ainias was treating his wounds. For an eye blink, he thought it was Lichas back to finish him off—since this Ainias spoke Doric and was a rough-looking sort, a frightful thing to see as well on the battlefield, nearly as ugly a hoplite as Lichas himself. "Thespian. Your spear fell from the dead Kleombrotos, but only after your sword went into his head bone. Few hit a Spartan king. None twice. That spear—it will hang in the temple of Herakles at Thebes. Or perhaps the *ekklêsia* will vote to send it to Proxenos's new Boiotian altar at Delphi."

Ainias was looking more carefully over Mêlon's head wound, wondering whether the larger tear across his brow should be seared or stitched. "You are the only Boiotian who has ever drawn blood from Lichas. The prophetesses from the south say he is the favorite of their gods. These seers boast that even in his seventh decade that bald head cannot be killed by any Theban—or even perhaps any free man of Hellas. It is not easy to stand up to Spartan men in battle when they believe that the gods favor only the strong, and live and talk inside their chests."

A growing circle of hoplites neared the dazed and bleeding Mêlon, wishing to walk over the very soil where he had just spilled the blood of the king Kleombrotos. The Thespian's arms and neck were laced with gashes and scrapes. Ainias, who knew well the nature of mending torn skin and stopping oozing blood, put a cream of honey and animal fat in the deeper gashes. He rubbed olive oil on the bleeding shallow cuts, and wrapped them in linen to keep away the flies and gnats. He counted out loud eleven spear slices. Mêlon's armor showed another batch of new dents. The blow from Kleonymos to Mêlon's head had closed an eye. Half his face was unrecognizable. Where, he wondered, was his son?

Mêlon squinted back and at last weakly muttered, "Where is Lophis?" "Where is my Bora? At least go find the spear head at the *trophê* where the Spartans turned. The king's guard of young Spartans nearly gored me. We fought from the left, Stymphalian. Just as you said. But their spears over that way were longer and sharper. Lichas was the better man. I know that now. He has a son as well—who is bigger yet. Antikrates is better still. And where is Lophis, where is our Chiôn to deal with these enemies."

"Wait until we know more. We are sure only that your sword first went into the mouth of Kleombrotos. The king is chewing on it in Hades. His henchman Lichas can thank you for another cut. It made him look even more the dogface than he was. Though he won't miss an ear since they say Lichas listens to none anyway. You and Chiôn have sent the royal house of Sparta across the Styx. Think of it—the king dead, and with a sword no less, a sword wielded by a farmer on Helikon. *Machairion* I should call you. But here is what is left of your Bora. We keep it and make a new shaft this spring."

Ainias held up the huge iron tip with a broken shaft about an arm's length left. A Tanagran had just found it near Chiôn. Mêlon was coming back for longer moments to his senses, "Where is my Lophis? Is he already at the gulf? Where Chiôn?" But there was no Chiôn to answer him. Mêlon finally began to fathom that his slave had toppled. "Chiôn? Did Lophis bring out his body?"

"Proxenos was near you all the time. That's his nature. The hard stone in a crisis. He was there right behind you. To steady you; so much for your Nêto's warnings to him that he too would go down." Ainias had spied a crowd around Chiôn with shouts that he lived. He also had forgotten that Nêto had warned Proxenos not of Leuktra, but of crossing the Isthmos in its aftermath. "It was Proxenos who saved your brute. Chiôn is warm, but whether he will live, I'm not sure. Your son was with the horse, and our riders routed them easily. No doubt he is far off, in the shadows of Kithairon riding down those who bolted." Mêlon nodded at news of his son and that Chiôn breathed, thinking that he must have been asleep as Ainias had searched the pile of the dead. He hadn't really thought that any Spartan could kill Chiôn.

Mêlon was confused as Ainias finished, "Lichas's spear cut into Chiôn well enough. But his bronze plate warded most of that hard blow away from his heart. The Plataian is sewing on him now, at least the smaller tear he cannot burn. They say he can patch flesh as well as build stones. Though I have healed more than he and I'll go back there to check on the wound to make sure he has put in enough honey and wool. I don't like thread. The hot poker is the only way to close a real tear. I brought my doctor box. I'll need to take the bronze prong and scissors and cut away the bad skin, and pull out the splinters before we melt the wound closed. I may want to bleed him—and purge him too while I'm at it. Or maybe a leech or worm to eat away the rot to come."

By now, as Mêlon alternately slept and awoke, it was almost dark and the torches were lit. Epaminondas had himself re-formed a tiny phalanx a few hundred yards ahead and his men right in the dark were squared off against Lichas and the Spartan survivors on a nearby hill. But Mêlon's head seemed caved in. The pounding of the waves roared in his ear. Bodies—he could see them in the twilight—were dragged and piled in heaps. The battlefield was becoming an agora as thousands of Boiotians crisscrossed the carnage. Who was that strange man in the long cloak over there? he thought. He stares here too long. An aged white-haired fellow crossed by, with a lanky, bleary-eyed attendant carrying off a corpse, a mess of a hoplite of forty or so from Thebes. There was a severed arm tied flat to his chest with twine, at least something like that under the flies. Are they afraid the dogs will get it? That must be the work of that Kleonymos, or maybe Antikrates, or so Mêlon thought.

Ainias's voice now kept Mêlon awake, as he muttered of this trio off in the distance, "There goes dead young Kalliphon, the orator and son of

Alkidamas, the greatest speaker of the Hellenes, and the godhead behind the freedom of Messenia, tutor to Epaminondas himself. They all had no business out here. The man was no fighter. You can see from the sad look of the father and their thin slave from the north. That son Kalliphon's first day in bronze was his last. His father and that sorry shield-carrier of his, they must burn him as they can. Though one is wrinkled and stiff and that other servant of his, a northerner with a half-Hellene tongue, thin and green."

Was this Alkidamas again? Why did he hear always of the mythical Alkidamas somewhere? Mêlon heard a familiar voice at his back, "You breathe still, my master. But you look dead to me."

Nêto.

The Messenian girl put a cloak over the cold Mêlon. Now she poured him more warm water from her own pouch and swatted away the blue-black flies. But hadn't he left her with Proxenos, just last dusk before the battle, with orders to start for home on the morning of the battle? He knew that he was not on the wrong side of the Styx. Or maybe this was Helikon, and he was working in the hot vineyard as his Nêto brought them his afternoon water from the spring above.

But none of this was so. Nêto cried out again, "Lophis is gone. Gone across—do you know?"

Let her babble. His son was safe and on Xiphos. The bright crackling torchlights were leaving Mêlon's head. The failed agents of death winged away for good now, still screeching as they quit their hovering above. Mêlon fully reentered the world of the living. Or at least he thought he had. But his hearing and sight for a time were no more than half of what they had been, and he was swarmed by these strange shapes and sounds.

More than a thousand enemy dead were piled in heaps on the ground. Four hundred, it would turn out later, were elite Spartan *Homoioi*. Thousands of Boiotians were walking the fields, more curious to see what Spartan hoplites looked like, when safe and dead, than just eager for booty. Mêlon remembered the Theban cries during battle, "A dead army. A dead poliso."—*Apethane to strateuma, hê polis apethanen*. Now he saw that it was no lie. In the torchlight, he made better sense of the mob about him. Some mounted longhairs scoured the battlefield for stragglers. Farmers tended the wounded. Their women were breaking out packs of rations and shooing off a new mob of looters and sightseers who were swarming over even the Boiotian corpses. Yet another heap of helmets, breastplates, shields, greaves, and spears was growing not far away beneath an old oak tree. Near it arose an even larger heap of capes, sandals, and cloaks. Silver coins were piled in the hollow shields.

Most of the dead Boiotians were being carried home by their folk. Pelopidas had posted guards over these piles of loot. Eurybiades the booty-seller and a small army of helpers were already buying plundered armor—paying for it with the very coins his slaves had scavenged from the battlefield. A dead Spartan stared at Mêlon not more than five cubits distant. He was naked, just stripped, and already stiffening. His legs were covered with flies and worse. A spear had gone up under the jaw. Or at least something like that had crushed in half the man's face. "Cover him," Mêlon yelled. He had no desire to see any more of the dead. The mangling of the face gave the corpse an eerie frozen look about him, almost a grotesque smile. One hand was extended in the dirt with all of its fingers cut off, except the index, which was pointing right at Mêlon. For a moment he thought the dead man was whispering that he had killed Lophis. But then Mêlon shook himself out of another trance, just as two slaves ran up, grabbed the nude body by the heels, and dragged it over to a long line of Spartan corpses.

Soon most of the plunder would be sold off by the states to pay for an annual festival to the victory goddess Nikê—and for a *trophê* of their victory at the spot where Kleombrotos had fallen and the enemy had at last turned. Mêlon was finally clear enough to understand that Nêto had, as ordered the previous night, hiked back up to the camp with Proxenos and joined Gorgos. But then somehow she had not gone home to the farm in the morning. Everything after that was a blur.

On her way down the hill, only with luck had she fought off the Boiotians who wanted her wagon for their own wounded. She finished her story to Mêlon with news that they had seen Lophis in the first charge fall—and then nothing more. She was uncomfortable with the crowd that had drawn around Mêlon. They pointed to him as a hemi-god and murmured, "He, that one, killed the king. There he is, the lame Thespian of the prophecy. Right there, the killer of Kleombrotos. The gods do not lie about the *mêlon*." Yet even amid the mob, Nêto thought it better that her master hear the end of his son.

She threw back her hood and stumbled on, "I saw Lophis from the hill yonder. He charged at the first trumpet blast, out too far from the rest. A Spartan knocked him off. I saw that much, and then dust rose and there was nothing more. Then Gorgos, our Gorgos ran off below into the field. He said he would fetch him. But no, it seems? He too vanished into the dust and never came back—dead or captured by our enemies or perhaps even turn traitor, I don't know. It was chaos by then."

She was weeping and then clear for moments, as she tried to tell her master that either his son was dead or his slave Gorgos was a traitor or martyr—or neither. "More of Lophis I heard than saw, since when I hit the flatland just now, I grabbed two bloody horsemen, wounded men from Orchomenos, one a with broken spear stuck in his mount. They told me that our Lophis had been knocked off with a huge spear, a lance larger than any on the battlefield. Lichas had targeted Lophis, the riders said. In the melee Lichas went after him. They heard Lichas yell: 'Fetch the armor, Spartans, drag the kill with us. Bring home the armor of Lysander.' So they told me before they too were beaten back. Right then I went farther with the wagon to pick up Lophis. Instead I found myself here with you and Chiôn. Master, I was swarmed by a mob. They tried to tear me off the wagon. I sliced a few arms and hands to keep Aias free. My new friend, this slave Myron, saved me from the mob. But no Lophis. He's dead, I fear. But I tried to find him. I tried."

Mêlon knew no slave named Myron. But the more he told Nêto that Lophis lived, that the Boiotian horse had broken the Spartan cavalry, that Gorgos would carry him out alive as he had once brought the wounded Malgis from Koroneia, the more he suspected that his son was dead—too far ahead of the horsemen, the strange role of Gorgos and his current absence, the glitter of the armor of Lysander, and Lichas, always Lichas. Too many of Nêto's details proved too true. He sat back down and kept mute. Lichas was alive. Lophis was dead. So the good die and the bad live on.

"I just saw Chiôn!" It was Proxenos who had walked up. As always the architect kept his head while others lost theirs. "First, listen. Chiôn talks. He lies back in the camp of Epaminondas. His left arm will never lift a shield—at least if that wound heals like others I have treated. Nêto, go to Aias. Drive your wagon a bit closer. We will put these two in and then you can get them back up to the farm."

The wagon was just over a gentle rise, just where Nêto had left it with Myron. The runaway slave had accompanied her from Thespiai in hopes of freedom, and was waiting on the battlefield. Proxenos stammered, but went on, "But I have other bad reports, Mêlon, now that you are back among the living. Your Gorgos is gone, at least if he is the old slave that hoplites saw head to the camp of the Spartans with a body over his shoulder. Worse still it is. Pelopidas reckons that this old man, if it is your Gorgos, probably went willingly to the Spartans. Many in the Sacred Band had seen him cross over to their camp. There is word among the horsemen that he carried off Lophis, and a pathway opened for him amid the rearguard of the Spartans."

Nêto had walked away and returned with Myron, who had stayed behind with the wagon. He had collected some helmets and breastplates off the dead Spartans, along with a sword or two that was probably Boiotian. What better way to find a new household than to offer himself along with presents? The slave was a rich man's runaway and worried that he would be flogged, though he had followed Nêto in hopes that any who walked at Holy Leuktra would be freed back home at Thespiai. Nêto bent over to the sitting Mêlon. In front of the small crowd, Nêto nodded to Proxenos. She likewise blurted out that there was more to her story than she first had admitted.

"So I feared what came to pass. I think now we know where Gorgos is. He is the servant of Lichas his true master. They will know him as Kuniskos—'Puppy' in the south. Nikôn, the leader of the helot firebrands, sends word to me from the Messenians who once knew of his trickery. And he talked such nonsense on the hill above the fight, as I said. A loyal man-footed helot—so he will serve Sparta once more, if he has not all these years."

Mêlon was tired of all these speeches. Nêto ignored Mêlon. She went on with more in a shrill voice that replaced her tears. "He didn't save Lophis. I see that now. And you see, too, that he joined Lichas. I speak true things, always *t'alêthê*. Over the fire before the battle, he was talking of the good days with Brasidas. The best helot killers were always helots. I can smell his stink, even from here."

Mêlon stopped her. "Leave it be. Tomorrow, tomorrow. This is all a dream. All a nightmare. I will hear all this when the sun rises. Not now, not any more."

Ainias grabbed Mêlon's arms. "Look, your head rings. But don't listen to your wounds. Gorgos is over there. Maybe it was his work that Lichas

has your dead son. Or at least he found his way or wanted to. Maybe Gorgos is dead or maybe breathing, we don't know. Lophis I fear is gone or will be after they dragged them to their camp. The Spartans, what is left of them, stand at their camp, and with spears ready. There's at least a thousand or two left ready to march home. The son of Agesilaos, the young Eurypontid Archidamos is almost here with another Spartan army on the coast road. The dregs of Lakonia are on the way here. We must decide tonight to let them all go home or kill them all."

Mêlon was glad to change the talk. "Then we can kill two royals this season. Finish off the rest who will never see their Eurotas. And then we will rescue Lophis."

Proxenos looked over at Ainias. "That's my wish as well. No doubt Epaminondas will soon tell us as much himself. But look at us, Thespian. The Boiotians have gone mad in their victory. The allies are plundering the field. Our army is going home. The battlefield is nothing but shit and flies now. We stopped Sparta today, but we did not end it."

As they argued, Epaminondas walked up. Before he reached them he threw down his shield. "Ainias and Proxenos. Where is my Thespian? Stand up. All of you. The war goes on." With that Epaminondas pointed at them in the torchlight. "Our friend Lichas is in command over there. He's sent us a herald for parley. He wants out of Boiotia. Pelopidas is over there, meeting with his henchmen. All their other big men are dead."

Proxenos, as always, thought more clearly than most. "Lichas will want free passage for his hoplites to the coast. So the rub is whether we want to lose five hundred hoplites to kill Lichas and maybe a thousand that are alive or not scattered. He has enough men to get across the Isthmos. Or maybe he hopes the young royal Archidamos can do the same coming up from the south to save him. Those Spartan allies who ran away—well, they are scattered in the hills and will rejoin him tomorrow. They have nowhere else to go. If they can all meet up with Agesilaos's son, the red-capes will easily make it out of here. So let them skulk home instead right now and in shame. Let them go."

"No, no," Mêlon pleaded as he got to his feet a third time, limped around, and then slowly sat down again, as the dizziness returned and his head throbbed. If he once had been reluctant to march out to fight, now he was adamant to finish what Epaminondas had started, even though he was in no shape to pick up a shield. Lophis was all that mattered now. But he would have to break through the Spartan camp this very night, and, as a half-dead hoplite, take back his son, dead or alive—or perhaps kill Lichas at parley or go back into battle this evening.

Mêlon had changed, into what he didn't quite know—just that he was no more the same recluse he once had been on Helikon. If his son were captured, he would take him back. If he were dead, then his life as he knew it on the farm was over, and his vineyards would be a mere respite between the unending campaigning for Epaminondas against the Spartans. Either way he wished to find out this very evening—and do something about it.

"Do not be fooled by such men. The Spartans are hungry now, without food. Trapped here in our country. Surround them. They came here to destroy our democracy. Lichas will be back to finish us off soon. Winning a battle is not the same as winning a war—unless we destroy the army who started it. Remember, the Thessalonians will be here soon as well as our newfound friends. We will have even more spears to deal with them when the word gets out about the victory here at Leuktra. The Hellenes like to pile on the loser."

"Mêlon is right. We beat them all day, Ainias. Didn't they lose, or am I possessed?" Epaminondas was talking to tough folk of his own rank who had just killed the king of Sparta. But they were tired. They wanted to enjoy, not second-guess, their victory. Still the Theban went on, "Nothing in war is as dangerous as to wound but not to kill the enemy. Sparta is defeated, but not humiliated."

"Enough of this idle talk." Mêlon struggled a bit before Proxenos offered both his hands to pull him up. "They wish to kill Lophis, so be it. I will kill them. Ten for my boy, twenty if I can. Re-form the ranks, such as they are. Tonight all together, one more time, all of us on this long day. We will kill this Lichas, hang his Antikrates up by his feet. If the light is already gone, we can at least muster the troops by our torches. I did not ask to fight this battle. But now that I am here, I finish what we started."

Proxenos cut in one last time. "With what? You were lame before the battle and are lamer still after. Count us. Most have gone home as we already said. We have no more than a thousand—if that still. Good men all. But not everyone is alive who was this morning. The best are dead or will be. I could build walls for us—but in one year, not one day. There are far more than Antitheos that lie over there. The flies are on them already.

My Plataian Lakôn, of our city's oldest family, has no throat and his nephew Archias with a bashed-in head won't make it until dawn. The work of Lichas again. Sour Philliadas has done his hard work and taken his bunch back to Tanagra. The men near Kalamos are all gone or dead. No, our Ainias even without his charts and maps is right. Have words with this Lichas and we will let him run in shame out of Boiotia to spread the word of our warcraft."

Mêlon then gave up as his head beat inside harder and in a quieter voice sighed, "But if the beast limps home, if it crawls away, well then like every wounded lion of your fables, it will lick its wounds to healing. It will come back right here and many of us will die in other battles—some far from Thebes. Lophis knows that, he would tell you the same." Epaminondas and the rest picked up their arms. With a hundred or so Theban hoplites, the small band of bloodied veterans headed with torches for the nearby hill to parley with the Spartans. There under light Pelopidas and the rest of the phalanx—maybe a thousand or so in armor, it turned out—were squared off against Lichas's formations.

Only the ditch and some rough thrown-up brush stockade separated the spears of what was left of the two bloodied armies. Mêlon looked around at his men in arms. Ainias and Proxenos were with him, dressed in their full armor. Dozens of guards followed around Epaminondas, all of them covered with the gore of battle. The Boiotarchs had already dismissed the ranks for the night. But Pelopidas's men had cobbled together enough of an army to guard the Spartan camp through the moonlit darkness. Mêlon had left Nêto with this new fellow Myron, the ungainly slave whose wide neck at least rested on broad shoulders and could help her shoo looters away from the wagon. Myron watched over Chiôn and put him under blankets on straw in the wagon—since he knew this hoplite was not quite dead but might prove a fair sort with a good memory if he lived.

The hound Sturax that followed Gorgos was nowhere to be found. But some of the Thespian slaves who had tagged after Nêto from the assembly to the battlefield had trickled back. They were fighting over the wagon, pilfering food and the good red wine of the farm in between knife jabs from Nêto.

Pelopidas ran up. He had made sure the Spartans stayed on their side of the barrier, and that none of his own men tried to storm their ground until Epaminondas arrived. "This killer Lichas is over there." Pelopidas pointed to two Spartan hoplites with torches and a raised spear. Both were now walking down from the camp and across the broad trench on a wobbly tree limb. "For a moment I saw his bald head."

Epaminondas then gave orders. "Ainias and Proxenos and you, Mêlon, you who killed Kleombrotos, will all come with Pelopidas and me. We speak for Thebes and the Boiotian towns around it. Keep your chin straps on, hands on your spears. Lichas should know that a man like Ainias from the Peloponnesos is with us as well. I would have liked to have Chiôn, if he could walk, with us as well. So that these Spartans can look upon the slave that took down their best and sent Kleonymos into Hades."

The five set out with torches about halfway between the two bands. Mêlon noticed in the glare that Ainias and Proxenos were even taller than Pelopidas. He in turn towered over Epaminondas. Yet the general was broader than any of the three and gave the look of one the Spartans would be most wise to avoid in battle. His arms were in constant motion, pointing, slapping Pelopidas on the back, waving others to follow—still dripping blood from a bandaged deep cut along the back of one arm.

A fierce-looking Spartan hoplite now came into view. His shield blazon was torn off, there was a crack in the concave willow planks. His right arm was also streaked with blood. Half his head was already shaven in mourning for the Spartan loss or in shame over defeat. "I am Teleklos. Royal blood. Regent now. I say Lichas talks for Sparta. You listen."

Another man with him stepped up. He was a red-haired pale sort, Lykos, a Eurypontid bastard youth, who was the "eye" of the surviving King Agesilaos and an ephor who reined in Lichas when he could. They planted a torch pole in front of them. For a moment the Boiotians let out a gasp. The Empousa, the bogeyman of their baby stories, was a few cubits away as this last Spartan hoplite finally came out of the shadows. His finger was already pointing in their faces. He blurted out before he even reached them—and sounded as if he had sand in his throat. "Cow-lovers and eel-catchers. Who claims to be good enough to speak to Lichas? Speak. Where are their hoplites? Not these beggars, these vendors in rags? Where is this faker, the general of this *ochlos*?" Lichas appeared as large as he had earlier when Mêlon had faced him in the melee. Yet the darkness, flame, and shadows made him more foul-looking still.

So he was older, after all, than Mêlon, as old maybe as Gorgos. Lichas was like the Satyrs or foul father Selinos he had seen on the pots from Athens: high pock-marked forehead, snub broad nose and jutting jaw, completely bald on top, with two white horse tails braided that grew from around his ears and hung halfway down his chest and lay on the breastplate—his son's bronze. The Spartan, then, had stripped the armor of Malgis from his son, and so was most likely his killer. Almost immediately Mêlon froze and looked down, careful not to betray his hatred. He then looked up carefully to see what sort of man he would have to kill and how.

In his shock, Mêlon noticed too that the Spartan's forearms, encased in leather and rivets, were larger than those of any on his own side, as stout as Chiôn's, or perhaps even more so. Lophis had had no chance against a spear jabbed by those. Lichas had done his own part to make what little nature had given him even worse, looking more like some ossified carcass that Mêlon had kicked up on the high cow pastures of bare Mt. Mesapion. One long scar ran from the bridge of his nose down his cheek across the jaw. Below his cratered forehead were plenty of holes and the marks of stitches and once-seared flesh.

If he had any teeth, they were invisible, or maybe black as his tongue itself. Then Mêlon caught another glimpse of the elaborate bronze under his dirty cloak—the aegis of Athena that Mêlon had kept in the tower of Malgis. This Lichas was by far the best man Sparta had on the battlefield that had escaped the death spears of both Chiôn and Mêlon. If Leuktra had been their best day—indeed, had gone beyond what either could ever again match—and this foul man had survived, surely no one in Boiotia could stop him.

Epaminondas glared at Mêlon, grabbed his shoulder, and took a step closer. Then the Stymphalian took hold of Mêlon's other arm. They all saw that the stub of what was left of Lichas's ear was oozing blood. A ball of wool had been stuck in the hole, and honey had been smeared on the side of his head. Lichas had another bad wound in his thigh, with a rope tied above it and a bloody cloth over it. He had walked up leaning on his spear—defiant, as if he were hale and forty, commanding at Koroneia perhaps, with ten thousand unbeaten Spartans or more at his back. Another four or five younger Spartans suddenly came out of the darkness to join Teleklos and Lykos. But on the sway of Lichas's back hand they stopped at the edge of the shadows with spears and torches, and let their master speak.

"I said hear your Lichas. You won a battle. A big one. But not this war. A bigger war—*megas kindunos*. That you will have in days. Then my men from the coast get here with our other king's son. Or now we march out home. Then go home. Or will we stay here? And kill you all?"

Whether he smiled or grimaced, few could tell. So far his talk was nonsense. "We go in the night. It is written by the gods that Sparta survives Leuktra. You do the second thinking; Lichas does the first killing of the enemies of Hellas. No, you won't kill me, the last true Hellene. You'd miss, need me too much. Kill me? Then you would kill Sparta. Then who would protect you weaker ones from the wild men from the north and east?"

Pelopidas came up and raised his spear, but he was checked by the hand of Epaminondas. Still, Pelopidas thought it better to kill this man now. Ainias nodded to him and grasped his hilt. Never again would such men as their own be together to get this close to the Spartan. If it was not done now, both sensed that this man would bring them and their own catastrophe upon catastrophe in the year ahead. But it was the softer Proxenos who already had his spear out. He was lowering it in the shadows for a groin stab, for a foul black mood had come over him as Lichas and his brood neared. He was a man of vast lands and black soil and halls with marble columns, while these lords of Sparta lived in hovels and knew not a plum from an apricot. Proxenos did not believe Nêto's prophecies about a bad end across the Isthmos, but he did sense that one day he would march safer in the Peloponnesos without the evil of Lichas and his tribe.

Epaminondas stepped even closer, to within five palms' width of the Spartan's face. "You claim to be Lichas? You carried the dead king out. I apologize—for not killing you myself. But we had others of the royal blood today to deal with first. You yourself have lived too long, old man."

Lichas blustered at that. "None of us ever explain what we do. We do all for Hellas—make her free. I keep the good on top to take care of the weak like you on the bottom. You only talk of making the bad equal to the good so that we all end up bad. Yes, what you cannot be, you would tear down. But we are the Hellenes, you its polis destroyers. Sparta is Hellas, Hellas Sparta, nothing more, nothing less." Lichas spat out some of the dried goat meat he was gumming on. Then he continued, looking at Mêlon. "Is it to be more war? Or do my Spartans march out under truce? No difference to me. I killed ten of you today, and got back Spartan armor from the babe in diapers who thought he could wear it." Then he laughed at all that and stepped a pace closer.

Mêlon hobbled up closer to the side of Ainias. In his own wounds, old and new, he looked as torn as Lichas himself; a knot on the side of his temple was as large as the egg of a hawk. Its blue sheen better reflected the torchlight. From the eyebrow to his jaw the side of his head was black with swabs of dirt and dried blood. Some cuts were wet and seeping, around the massive bruise to his face. His arms were bloody and his skin beneath his shoulders everywhere was torn like latticework. Every man, however small his stature and reasonable his nature, has his limits. Mêlon cared little whether he lived or slept for good, as he eyed the man who had killed his son. He had just woken from his trip to Hades, and did not find the change so much of a relief, this living without a son on his Helikon. Suddenly the fear of Lichas left him, and he quit scanning his enemy in worry about how to kill him. He knew he would kill the Spartan, and it mattered little whether it was here or next year in the south. Going to the house of the dead was a small coin to hand over—and would save the lives of others later on. This Lichas talked grandly of killing, but he had not killed either Mêlon or Chiôn. They had in turn sent most of his own to Hades.

Lichas first grunted as Mêlon came into his torchlight. "Hold up. I thought I killed you, yes, peasant boy of Helikon? So remind me. Did I hit you today? I am sure I killed you, cripple-leg. Is not this Mêlon, son of Malgis of the old women's tales? I remember you, Thespian. You're not the *mêlon* to fall, but the sheep to be slaughtered. I know our tongue and your *mêlon*—*mâlon* to me—means sheep, not apple. So bray for us."

Mêlon laughed. Any small fear of the Spartan had vanished. Only hatred for the killer of his son remained. "Not yet, Lichas. You are old, only good for carrying away dead kings, not for protecting live ones. We meet again, not for the last time yet. The voices of Nêto's seers ring in my head as well. This time you gave me an ear. Now give me back my helot Gorgos and my son he carried in."

"Your Gorgos? You mean my Kuniskos? Our long-lost puppy? That creaky helot would not fetch more than an Athenian drachma or two on the auction block in Delos." Unlike the other Spartans, Lichas had been a harmost and had traveled all over the Aegean. If he wished, he could talk more like an Athenian than any Boiotian. "But Gorgos was—is—mine again. I missed his service these long years. I needed my puppy's little teeth. He could have had better things to do for me than prune vines for you and drink in his stupor. He wagged his way back home to me. Of his own will. Like any good little dog that has lost his master and, when at last he picks up the scent, comes yelping back to his kennel, with a crushed hare in his mouth, a gift for good will."

Lichas went on. "The body that Gorgos lugged into our camp just now I keep safe in good faith—or what is left of him. Ah. I see now, he is your son. I thought until now it was you I had killed, you who had taken to riding horses with your bad leg that I gave you at Koroneia. I see that I have these years killed both the father and son of yours, Mêlon." Lichas smiled as he saw the Boiotians edging toward him. "Men like us sire plenty of boys to fight and die—at least if they are to be good men at all. I have another son you saw today, *megas* Antikrates. He killed Boiotians, better even than Kleonymos. Neither of you can escape, not from him. My big son, this one, is a sort even we fear at Sparta. You're already dead— so's your general and that branded slave we cut down this day." Lichas stayed fixed on Mêlon. "But, Mêlon, why was your young upstart on a black pony with armor not earned or worn well? One thing for your son to wear Lysander's plate, another to fight like a Spartan—a lesson your dead father learned at Koroneia."

Mêlon replied, "Lysander was a thief himself. Like all you Spartans who make nothing, but steal all from others. You neither farm nor build yourselves. You live in a city of wood, not stone. You have no money, no iron, nothing except what you steal. You are the true polis destroyers. Without your helots, you can't tell an oar from a winnowing fan. If we bind you, Lichas, perhaps your folk will hand over my Lophis in exchange. "

Epaminondas now stepped up. "Go, Lichas, before Mêlon puts a spear in your face. It is written that with you goes the last Spartan who will ever walk under arms in Boiotia," He saw the logic of letting the enemy regroup his army for the long march to come. "It is better this way, Lichas, to settle it down south in your courtyard anyway. Some day when there is new snow on Parnon and Taygetos, look for me when you least expect a winter horde from the north. On the banks of your Eurotas, we will meet you when its waters roar in winter."

With that the parley broke up and the two sides went back to their lines. Left unsaid was that the Spartans before light would be given passage to the mountains, and that the body of Lophis would be returned. As the two Spartans lumbered away to their awaiting guard, Mêlon kept silent, knowing now that his Lophis would not rot among dogs and birds, and that Lichas would not live long in the south.

The trailing Lykos turned around before the shadows swallowed him and faced the Boiotian. Lichas had already disappeared into the night. "Bother us no more, cripple of Helikon. Your time is past, Chôlopous. The dreams of Pasiphai warned us that you would kill our king. So our king you have killed—the worse one. But we have another. The gods tell us that by tonight you have no more power over us." Then Lykos, a peer of royal blood, gripped his sharp sword with his left and lowered his spear with his right, and backed off a few feet as he ended his lecture. For all his bristling, he was a Spartan man of his word, who did not break oaths or lie. "Gorgos leaves your son—or what is left of him—at the coast road tomorrow before night, with a hag at the seaside shrine. Lichas keeps his armor. It belonged to our big man Lysander. You keep the mess that was once your son. Lichas knocked him off his black horse. He was thinking it was you. Be proud, for he was a hard kill like your father, or so Lichas said. Four or five stabs and his eyes would not stay closed. And proud he was this day that he was the first of the Boiotians to die. He spat that in our faces when Gorgos laid him down. Lichas cut his throat to ease the pain of his spear wounds. Gorgos then turned to go home to Helikon, but we convinced him that he wanted to stay with us. And then he nodded he did."

With that Mêlon fell silent as the five walked back to the phalanx of Thebans. Pelopidas in his melancholy quickly sent all the Boiotians on home who were sated with plundered armor and the coin pouches of the dead. Mêlon turned darkly to Epaminondas. "Not quite over. You and I will see this Lichas again, and it will not be in Boiotia."

# Ripples of Leuktra

Epaminondas fell in with Pelopidas and the Sacred Band as they trotted off in silence under the moonlight on the road back to Thebes. It was full night and Mêlon was alone. Proxenos and Ainias went south in the darkness in the opposite direction toward Plataia, promising to visit Helikon within the year. Proxenos had sent word to his wife, Aretê, that both had survived the melee and would be home on the Asopos before the sun came up over Kithairon. Neither wanted any plunder and never liked the look of an army as it breaks apart. Both, as the new partners they had become, were plotting the rebuilding of Mantineia to the south and the greater citadel of the Arkadians at Megalopolis, the new democratic fetters that would hem Sparta for good inside the Peloponnesos.

The sound of Lakonian reed pipes filled the air. A clamor rose of moving wood and bronze. Mêlon did not look back. What was left of the Spartan army would before dawn march out with torches from Boiotia. A huge fire roared, consuming what dead they had managed to carry out and what Spartan corpses they had been given by the Thebans. Mêlon was stumbling about. The blow by Kleonymos had done more than close his eye, and after this long day he was nearly done for. He heard a high note and feared there was a daughter of night flapping in the air—or at least a shrill Kêr perched on a low limb of an oak, waiting for him to fall. But the sound was a better strain and from the living, not from Hades and not a Spartan reed, either. As it entered his ear, he recognized the familiar soft piping of a Thisbê song—the strain of safety and health that always brought him home. It was Nêto's old tune to him, the sign to come down to the house from the vineyard. He followed the sweet sound of pipe back to the wagon.

Nêto and Myron met him with the ox and the wounded Chiôn in the cart behind. She put her reed *aulos* down and recoiled in fright at her master's swollen head, now half blue and covered in blood and shiny in the torchlight. His eye was completely closed. Still, she soon had the two resting in straw. Sturdy Aias would pull all four back to Helikon. The ox was eager to reach once more the hay and quiet of the stalls even after the tall stand of green grass by the stream on the parched hills above Leuktra. There would be no shaking off this runaway Myron. He feared his master's wrath and begged only to sleep one night in the shed of Mêlon and a chance to care for Chiôn.

As the wagon rumbled home, Nêto sang softly and reflected that she, Chiôn, and even Myron now would be manumitted and claimed as heroes of Thespiai, who had helped break the Spartans—in Myron's case for merely following her around the wreckage of the battlefield. This night she concluded that the Myrons of the world always survive war and peace. They are not scroll-smart and can't recite a line of Homer. But they stay immune from the vanities of ambition, always knowing their own station in life and the narrow limits between which they must live. Earned pity is their currency. Even the hardest man would be hard put to lay a hand on Myron. His smile they said was from stupidity, but if so, it gave him more power than any shield, and came from a craftiness that even the wise could not match. Gorgos surely couldn't. Yes, in this war to free the serfs of the Peloponnesos, a Myron would survive a Proxenos or Alkidamas—as he all along had known he easily would.

She was stitching verses as was her wont, lines about the Spartan enemies in her midst—Lichas of the one ear and Sphodrias and Kleonymos who supped together in Hades with Klearchos and all the other Spartans that her heroes this day had killed. Her master Mêlon, always her master Mêlon at the van, side-by-side with Chiôn, sire of Lophis, all her men of the soil. She felt an anguish over the death of Lophis, and not only because she regretted that Mêlon had learned of it from other lips. If Nêto were to list all the ways Lophis had kept the Malgidai together, her tally, she feared, might be small. Likewise, she could not point to the tower roof or the oil press beam and say "Lophis made that." But she knew that without him there was no young heart left on the farm, no laughing, no energy from youth, just the void of his loss, and the wounded and old, and perhaps the end of the farm as they knew it, if she could not rouse the three boys to become men by first frost.

Mêlon lay numb next to the bleeding Chiôn, who took most of the cart's space. The slave murmured in his forced breath that his good right arm had already been pledged to avenge Lophis's ghost. He tried to lie on his side to give his master the greater straw, mumbling in the evening, "No worry, no worry. Lichas dies next time. It is written. Gorgos with him, even if he hides in the mountains to the south. I will hunt him down—and string him up."

Mêlon grumbled only, "If he fights next time like today, we'll both be dead. I liked the wagon ride over here far better than the return." Flat in the bloody straw, the heroes of Thespiai—the killers of Deinon, and Sphodrias and tall Kleonymos, and the king Kleombrotos as well—returned on their backs to Helikon from their day at Leuktra—and on into the myths of the Boiotians.

When Nêto finally drove the wagon up to the farm, it was still half a night before dawn, although the massif of Helikon blocked all light. She hailed Damô, wife of the dead Lophis. The farm woman had seen the torches of thousands plundering in the plain below but had not known whether they were Spartans coming her way or her own men soon to be rich from the loot of the Peloponnesos. Now Damô saw the wagon's torch moving along the winding road up the low spurs of Helikon. So she was waiting in the courtyard. The three boys helped Myron carry the two wounded hoplites onto oak benches in the stone hall. "Xiphos." Damô looked to Nêto. "The wretched horse of ours. He galloped in at dusk, and with blood on his flanks—without his bit or Lophis's reins. Dried blood. I smelled our own. Saw the light on pyres to the south. I thought Lophis must lie on one."

Her hair was torn, her face was gouged with grief—and her sorrow was made worse when she saw the proof in the limp arm of Chiôn and the swollen face of Mêlon—and no Lophis. No battle that had maimed the brute slave could have spared her husband. "These are the wages of your Pythagoras," she hissed at Nêto and then let out a loud *uluh-uluh-uluh* before returning to human speech. "Why us on Helikon, why us? Where were the blowhards of the assembly? Is there a son of Epaminondas among the dead? Is there a boy of Pelopidas without an arm? Did the big talkers like Backwash lead the charge?"

Damô finally sat down on a small bark chair, muttering to the hound Porpax on his dung heap. "Even your Sturax is gone. Everything's gone from this farm. Just as if the Earthshaker had knocked us to the ground."

Nêto spoke quietly. "We all knew what we were doing. We should have no second thought. Today is a great moment for the Boiotians. Though a sad one for the Malgidai."

Damô glared. "Try saying that when you've buried sons or a husband, but don't you dare in your virgin purity. You, barren womb, and your childless Epaminondas get too many killed. Too many rot for your visions and high words. Leave me be—*parthenos*, no-child, no-husband, no-mind, busy-body. No, the nice like you get too many killed who do their bidding."

Mêlon was half-awake. But when he tried to get up, he saw darkness and nearly fell over. Nêto—Nêto, he thought, would set things right, if Damô were to see her grief turn to madness. Then he saw no more of the torches of the courtyard. As he fell into the whirl, Mêlon also heard the voice of Malgis reminding him that in all great crises, but in matters of death especially, there are a few who come forward to do what no one should be asked to do: close the eyes of the dead, wash the corpses, and prepare the funeral for the departed. Then when their hard work is done in the worst moments of shock, they fade. They retreat into the shadows before the ensuing ritual and staged talk of weaker others that follow, when the public crying and group lamentation by a new, a lesser cast begins. Mêlon, as he went back into the dreams of sleep, knew it would be so with Nêto. She alone would keep the farm in the time after Lophis's death when he and Chiôn lay in the netherworld spread out in the hall of the big house. Nêto, freed from the anchor of Eros, or the goads of money and of pride, would do the right, the necessary thing as she always had. So Mêlon fell back asleep muttering to her that the Spartans had told him that Lophis would be found on the sea road to the south.

Nêto prepared to go fetch Lophis, certain that the word of Lichas, at least as her master related it, was good and that her young master's body was safe in some lean-to shrine. She unhitched the wagon and led Aias into the shed, where she soaked his back with a wet sponge and rubbed some olive oil into his wounds. She spent what little was left of the night taking off the armor of the two men, tending to the bandages and poultices of Chiôn, and putting oil and honey on the face of Mêlon. She even readied a stew of greens, beets, and wild cucumbers for the three boys to eat in the morning when they woke.

The three now had no father, only a crippled henchman in Chiôn. Gorgos was gone. There was not a hale man on the farm. Mêlon, the grandfather, was dazed and wounded—and already mumbling in vain about rising to harvest fifty baskets of red grapes before they rotted on the vine. The crops would not wait for Mêlon and Chiôn to heal. In a blink at Leuktra, the three sons of Lophis had gone from being boys to being farmers.

Care of the farm of the Malgidai now rested with Eudoros, Neander, and Historis, in the manner in which long ago a crippled Mêlon had inherited responsibility for the grape and olive crops from his dead father after Koroneia. If the three boys could scramble up the olive ladders, together hold the plow firmly behind the ox, and pack the grape baskets into the press, the family might keep the land; if not, even its coin box could not for long keep nature at bay, and soon Dirkê the neighbor would steal what she could at the first sign that there was not a man of the Malgidai with a long knife in his belt overseeing the orchard. The olives, the grapes, the wheat and barley, they all cared nothing for the health of the farm, but simply grew, ripened, and decayed in a natural cycle of oblivion without the human overseer to intervene to weed, fertilize, and harvest. Wound and illness matter nothing to a rotting olive or weedy field—or so the small orphaned boys of Lophis would learn this autumn after Leuktra.

The house slept the next day until the sun was high. Then finally Nêto took the boys out to pick strippings from the vineyards, the final red clusters of the dying year that they would put on the trays to dry into the sweetest raisins. When all else failed the household returned to what it knew best. But as dusk neared of this first day after Leuktra, Nêto took a rough wool blanket and some rope. She hid her jagged long knife in her tunic as well. No sleep, she shrugged, not a blink since the night before the battle, near the wagon on the hill with the long arms of Gorgos. At dusk then Nêto mounted the rested but lame Xiphos. His hoof was sore, but Nêto had filled its crack with lard and axle grease. They went slowly down the mountain and off to the east. Porpax, as best the dog could, followed her down the trail, in the direction of the stale scent of his Sturax, or maybe to find a hobbled deer on the lower folds of Kithairon. Damô would notice her absence not at all. For most of the next day the widow of Lophis would yell out to the shed below, "Nêto, come up here, my Nêtikon."

But Nêto was far away, headed for the coastal road to Kreusis by the sea and its junction with the main Theban way along the sycamores and ash trees, on the spurs of Kithairon and the rough pass up and over to Aigosthena by the sea. There Lichas and the Spartans would have earlier turned south for the trek home to Lakedaimon along the cliffs above the gulf. They were hugging the mountain, along the goat path above the surf. The survivors of Leuktra had been marching since before sunup and already had left Boiotia via the shore.

Mêlon had said only to find Lophis on the "sea road." Yet the trail along the gulf was long, and Nêto did not know exactly where it started and ended. The best way was just to head to the cliffs and surely she would intersect it. Almost as soon as Nêto found the pathway southward along the sea, she noticed even in this second night after the battle that the countryside was alive with Boiotians. Thousands of them in all directions were streaming back to their demes to the north. Most had packed up armor and spears, with carts full of wounded and dead, victims and heroes and gawkers to be sure, but brigands and throat-cutters as well. Some of those who appeared to Nêto to be the worst were fresh over the pass from Attika—Athenian rabble with the scent in their noses of booty and stories of unarmed Boiotian folk in the night countryside. Once the euphoria was gone, those waiting in the shadows came out to claim their due. Phokians, she could make out, too. These tribal kind, without cities and the ways of the polis, were riding and spearing stragglers still. They were after men with armor and coin—whether Boiotian or Spartan, it mattered little.

Nêto felt for her knife. She whistled for Porpax to come close. Then Nêto patted the neck of the tired Xiphos to prepare for a hard go should these foul riders turn to her. Some farmers had nooses around the necks of a few captive Peloponnesians, the allies that had run from the battle at the first crash and might be put to work or ransomed. She had some idea that it was the will of Epaminondas that these southern prisoners be spared. The ideal of the left wing, at least in the mind of Epaminondas, had been to leave the allies of both sides out of the fray—with good intent for the next act of the war. In the new Hellas of Epaminondas to come there would be no Hellene slave to any other, no ally to die for the hegemon.

But all that had been before the death of Lophis, and of Kalliphon, son of Alkidamas, and before the wounding of Chiôn. Nêto thought of these captives hardly as kindred souls. She thought to herself out here alone, "These Peloponnesians are like slaves after all. Now they are learning that every Hellene is always a day away from waking up a servant." She trotted past one miserable fellow on the road. He was a tall southerner without sandals. The captive was led by a fleshy farmer from way up on Skourta who had noosed him around the neck. Nêto showed no pity to the Dorian, though the Peloponnesian captive asked for water that she had plenty of to spare. As she passed him by, she put out of her mind the thoughts of Pythagoras and again thought that slavery was not so bad for those who enslave others. "These lost Spartans are helots now. In their pride these invaders gave no thought to helots, to those who were always as they will be now. Herakleitos says 'War, the father of us all, makes some free and others slaves.' So it is for this captive—slavery for him, freedom for me."

She soon arrived at the edge of the steep cliffs by the glistening water—the waves catching the early rising morning fingers of dawn. Far off in the distance Nêto could see the occasional fading glint from the spear tips of the army of Lichas. His Spartan army was marching on its second day without sleep, winding the way home over the high trail above the sea and back toward the Isthmos—beaten men, all of them. All eager to get back into the safe folds of the Peloponnesos, but fearing more the cursing of their Spartan women on their return.

Porpax had a few scrapes with some mangy dogs as he kept close to the heels of the slow-moving Xiphos. It was all Nêto could do to keep awake on the pony. Then she remembered that it was not just the previous night, but for the past three days and two nights that she had not slept, whether in fear of Gorgos above Leuktra, or in her long talk with Proxenos about their One God of Pythagoras. Then Nêto stopped. After some wild riding in circles, at about a stade beyond the road junction she smelled something foul. Nêto found the body of someone, not far from the sea, near a small mud-brick shrine to Kreusian Dionysos, about where Mêlon had told her to look. An old widow who tended the shanty temple said that she was standing guard over a corpse to keep the dogs and birds away.

"He yours, slave girl? A red-cape from the south—he told me, he said a Thespian would come here. You her? But I need another owl to give him up, though he stinks and is hard as a plank. Took you long enough. Name is Kallista—'the best of all.' Me Kallista—and I need an Athenian coin." She shrieked more, but had two teeth, so the howl came out as only whistling gibberish. This Kallista was covered in a black cloak, head to toe, and had only a scrawny hand out to catch her silver.

Nêto looked her up and down, to make sure it wasn't some demon. No, she was human, a hag with rump back. Kallista spoke Boiotian coast, that much was clear, and seemed a near twin to her neighbor on Helikon, Dirkê—if not the shrew herself in disguise. Nêto jumped down. She followed the woman's point to the shanty shrine. There was the body of Lophis. Kallista had already washed much of the gore from him, dead a day and a half now. The Spartans Teleklos and Lykos, for all their gruff, had given her a coin to keep the Thespian whole for his kin, a better gesture, Nêto thought, than what she herself would have done to the dead of Sparta. Lophis lay on the bench in front of the stone statue, the broken body that had been ridden over by the cavalry of the Spartans. Her master's throat was cut. It was caked with dry blood as the Spartans had said. But there were enough ugly wounds below the armor line that made Lichas's final slice no matter. These spear jabs to the lower stomach had finished Lophis anyway. Nêto finally looked away. How hideous Lophis had become—stiff, swollen, and blue-black and ghastly in expression like Medusa's face.

Was this the war she sang about—and urged others to risk their all for? All Lophis's grand dreams had been reduced to this contorted mess of flesh, to be thrown across the back of his tired horse by a slave girl? This— not Epaminondas's "one step more"—was the face of war. Perhaps she herself, if freed, would not vote for Epaminondas as Boiotarch, since he would only lead his people into more Leuktras south of the Isthmos. She flicked a maggot off his neck and poured some wine over his hair to flesh out more crawlers. The broad nose of the Malgidai was bent flat on his face, his strong jaw smashed and mangled apart from its joints. This certainly was not the battle that she'd seen from the camp above Leuktra, not the grand prelude to the march south to free her helots. How many Boiotians—she should ask the grand planners like Epaminondas or

Alkidamas—was a new Messenê on Ithômê worth? Surely her One God must give her a number. A thousand? Five thousand were worth it?

Meanwhile, the dog Sturax was nowhere to be found. Yet Porpax soon smelled the hound's death scent on the blood of Lophis. Then another odor hit the hound, and he was off toward Kithairon. Nêto thought he'd be back after the smell of a dappled fawn proved false. She gave the woman of the shrine a bag of raisins and figs—and another silver Athenian owl for good measure. Then Kallista helped her douse and scrub off Lophis with oil and sprinkle him with wine, and wrap his stiff corpse in Nêto's blanket. They tied it into a bundle and then slung him gently over the back of Xiphos. The horse jumped at that, raw as he was with cuts from the battle. Nêto shuddered; she had seen this picture in night visions before of her strapping a dead body on a horse in front of a shed, but was it this one now, or was there another corpse in yet another bad night in the future?

A bony hand grabbed her shoulder. "Stay here the night, pretty one? Don't go off in the dark with killers on the road. I hear the wild man-bear is out tonight, come down from Helikon out your way to harvest some Spartans. For another three silver pieces, I can lead you to my hut up the draw over there." But Nêto pushed Kallista away, flashed her knife, and decided to wait no longer for the marauding dog Porpax to return. She turned Xiphos around and slowly led the horse by the reins, careful that the body remained balanced on his back.

On the way back, an Athenian—or at least he sounded like one in his loud Attic—ran up to her in the darkness and grabbed the tail of Xiphos. The pony kicked hard. Nêto waved her blade in the air. She glanced back at the robber in the dirt, a boy, with two or maybe three more friends, out for easy steals in this blur between peace and war. During the trip back there were small parties of Spartans to watch for, trailing the army that by now was well past the Megarid. She remembered the warnings of her master, Mêlon, who had told her everyone has a choice in this life—a way to either live in fear or to give fear to others. So don't be a slave to your terrors, Nêto spoke to herself. Let those robbers worry what Megalê Nêto, the Amazon warrior, will do to them with this sharp knife, not what they might do to me. At that she pulled out her blade and pointed it ahead as she rode.

She went faster on her way north, and by midmorning Nêto could see the farm's tower in the distance on the slopes of Helikon. The Dog Star sun was warming up. She wanted to get Lophis inside the cool air of the bottom floor of the farmhouse where the water from Helikon was piped in, and she knew Mêlon would be waiting. Then she heard loud voices far in the distance, but thought at first it was only the Athenian robbers, accosting some fool without a horse and knife. It was nothing but sounds on the wind, as a hard breeze came up from south of the Isthmos.

She yelled out anyway in the direction of the noise: "I am Nêto of Helikon. Make way—or die."

# PART TWO

# *Between Peace and War*

# CHAPTER 12

# The Lizard's Tail

Off in the distance a world away, far to the south in Messenia, maybe a thousand stadia away from Nêto on Helikon, at this very moment hawk-eyed Nikôn of the helots, would-be leader of the revolt, stared out fixed on the late summer moon. His helot rangers had backed off from their leader and let him scream in his drink on his rocky perch, as he did on occasion when they walked on the high mountain trails of Ithômê far above Messenia below. This Nikôn was a tanner and smelled of hides and lye, and he was unlettered. Yet he knew knife work and had led the fiercest of the helot rebels. Let the Messenian leaders parley with Lichas for a quarter, a half of Messenia. But he would free it all, and kill every Spartan caught on the wrong side of Taygetos. Now he was perched on a cleft on Mt. Ithômê in the land of the Messenians, and he kept repeating to the stars under the moonlight, "I am Nikôn of Messenia. Make way for me—or die."

This same night Nikôn was on his second bag of sweet wine, and calling out to anyone under the same sky of Hellas. Did the men of Boiotia care that the *heilôtai* were whipped and killed and in the best of their moments pelted with rotten fruit, poked and lashed by the drunk Spartans at dinner in the *syssitia*? Did they know the Spartan overlords sang of "Messenê good to plow, good to plant" as if Ithômê were theirs, as if helots were but ants of their soil? Nikôn may have been the rabble-rouser of the helot rebels here on the upland. But the wine and the starry night on Mt. Ithômê had put him into a trance, as if his saviors in Boiotia, half the length of Hellas away in the north, might hear him—but only if he called out loud enough to their shared sky. He had heard voices of prophecy, of Epaminondas and Mêlon, of great armies to come, and of the Messenian woman to the north, Nêto of Helikon, who was promising a great reckoning this coming winter or next. Or so he told himself that there were real sounds and talk in his head, and not just gibberish brought on by two pouches of unmixed wine. He had no runners to send north for news, no money to visit the oracles at Delphi and Olympia for the gods' plans. So the illiterate Nikôn yelled to the stars in hopes that an oracle, a priestess maybe in Boiotia far to the north might hear him.

"Who said who was to be free and slave? What god did this thing? The Spartans? Is their Lichas an all-powerful Zeus Sôter? Why for three hundred and fifty harvests have the Messenians been the asses of the men of Sparta, while all the rest of Hellas has been free?" But Nikôn was talking only to himself. Only his henchman Hêlos, who knew how to write the block letters and put his master's thoughts onto scrolls, followed him on the high path on the cliffs of Ithômê. Loyal Hêlos had his own bladder bag, but one of icy spring water; and the good partner tried to get Nikôn to drink and dilute the raging heat in his head. It was also Hêlos, the finest scribe in the west of the Peloponnesos, who saw that the illiterate Nikôn alone of the rebel bands knew the mind of the Spartan, how to ambush him, how to goad the helots into killing their landlords.

The rest of the helots had taken the other path down after their nighttime patrolling. The rival Doreios yelled to them, "Join me—not this anvil-head Nikôn. His name spells defeat—not victory." All this meant nothing to the mumbling Nikôn, who this night kept up his helot shouts at the moon. "I watched my daughters with horse tails, clipped to their butts, forced to neigh, poked by Spartans at the symposia. Or made to bellow like cows, mounted from the backside, to the strains of their bastard poet Tyrtaios. Or my son Aristomenes, flogged and kicked as he howled like a dog to the laughter of the Spartans, hit with their black olives and mushy apples and then dragged like a side of beef from his pony."

Nikôn, in desperate appeal, thought he could plead to the female voice in his head from north in Boiotia. "Is there anything worse than for a man to pick his grapes, stomp them, filter the juice, store the amphora, and age the wine—only then to cart it over to the Spartan acropolis? To give them as *apophorai*—to be whipped for the service as the idle red-cape soldiers gulp down a year's work, most of it ending up as piss and vomit on the floor?" Now Nikôn went on to the black night above, "Don't forget the cleft of Kaiadas, the black abyss on Taygetos. Where we are thrown and then broken at the bottom, waiting at night for the wolves to eat our dying flesh as our tortured souls fly out from our ruined bodies." Soon his dwindling band split off on the paths between the wild figs. They laughed at the wages of wine, for now they saw that their captain Nikôn, silhouetted on a rocky outcropping across the vale, was taken with one of his periodic manias, as he talked with voices that wafted in the air.

He was drunk. Dionysus had sneaked into his head. Or worse, he had chewed some of the wild weed with the bitter white flowers that made the horses and cattle bellow and fall over. Alone of all the leaders of the helots, Nikôn could see that an army would come, and that some men in Greece were for justice and not just plunder and their own pride when they marched to battle. He looked more to the gods above, as the late-night fog lifted, and he saw the yellow moon of the coming Dog Days, smiling at the very thought of the liberation to come.

"I am Nikôn. A Messenian. No helot. A free man. Born here in Messenia. Citizen of its Messenê to be. Messeeeniiiaaa. On free It-hooomêee." Like the gray night wolf he yelled. He wanted his howl to reach the Spartans in their drink below and in dance behind their walls.

"Quiet, Nikôn." From a distance across the ravine the rival helots of Doreios on their way to the villages called back. "Shut up, drunken fool. No more wine boasting—unless you want to bring back Lichas from the north and his helot henchmen to string us up. Hush, mad dog. *Siga.* Go home. Hêlos! Hit him, Hêlos, won't you? Some leader—this fool who wobbles down a tiny path. Chew your bone alone, far off this holy mountain. Dry your gut out." The helots sang and laughed, far away, at the fading cries of their would-be leader.

Let the others talk of revolt while only Nikôn's men freed helots. Now Nikôn bayed at the moon all into the night. He clung to the ledge that pointed north to far-away Boiotia—as if in his sudden fit his godly Boiotians could hear him a thousand stadia away. "*Eimi Nikôn. Eleuthe-rios gignomai.*" I am Nikôn . . . I am born free.

Yet for all the prophecies of Nêto and the drunken calls of Nikôn on his ledge, Epaminondas did no more marching this summer after Leuktra. Nor the next spring did he call out the Boiotians to descend on

Sparta and free Nikôn's helots. Most Boiotians instead thought that the great, the seemingly final victory at Leuktra had proved war to be the parenthesis and peace the natural, more common order of things. So in the hamlets around Thebes the yeomen hoplites went right on after the victory into their cycles of the farming year. The timeless soil cared little what its temporary human tenants thought or did. The ground mute beneath the farmers just endured and went on whether Leuktra was won or lost. War or no war, for free men or slaves, the tasks of the season—sow, weed, reap, cut, and thresh—continued day in, day out. For most of the other vineyard men on Helikon, the battle was no more to be remembered than the severed tail of the stone lizard who proudly wags his growing stub without a thought of the old one, rotting in the dirt.

After finishing the later vintages of summer, the three boys got to work on the autumn harvest of the olive trees. For all the visual splendor of the estate, there was a well-thought-out economy to it as well, as in its irrigation ditches from the pond above that meant less carrying of the water with the donkeys. The three threshing floors spaced near the grain and barley fields made the harvests far easier. The eighty *plethra* could produce twice the food of the neighbor Dirkê's similarly sized place with about half her labor and expense. That gift—only vaguely appreciated in the past—was sensed by all in these days of loss. Mêlon had tried to let Myron go. But the awkward slave stayed on. Soon he followed Chiôn on the farm and even into the woods, like and not like him—both enormous, but Chiôn's maimed arm impairing his stride far less than did Myron's natural clumsiness. Myron had been freed by his presence at Leuktra according to the decree of the Thespians, and now earned his wages from the Malgidai.

Myron's skill in the collection and spreading of dung hardly meant he knew pruning and tilling. But he met rebuke for his poorly cut spurs and his crooked furrows with a shrug. Like the Korinthian mirror glass in town, he turned the harshness back on his master. Chiôn was freed, but as a one-arm he was more unfree than he had been as a slave of two hands. He saw that a man's body is his only master after all. Thoughts are nothing without the leg and arm, which alone turn word into deed. Yet he bore the hale newcomer Myron no grudge, praising his new henchman as he climbed high into the olives with his tree saw. "Myron is my left arm I lost at Leuktra," Chiôn laughed to Mêlon. "This freed slave is not so

bad, once his dung stink wore off and he picked up rocks in the field and quit collecting the mess of the public toilets. I wager no master ever will pry him off Helikon."

"Yes, he's our Sturax and Porpax come back alive," Mêlon offered, "the new watchdog of the farm. Our lost tail has grown back longer, and the farm is as good now as can be without our Lophis." Myron winked or twitched at that, since he knew them better than they knew themselves. So he let praise roll off his back, and looked down as they lauded him to the skies. Myron was working for different, better sorts now, and on a wage, no less—and so he no longer bore pots of dung from the city stalls to his master's vineyard, in fear of the lash of his owner Hippias, who each summer morning galloped on his pony down the rows of the vines, hitting the backs of his slaves with his mule-tail whip. This Hippias often came by Helikon on his black horse to take back or sell off his Myron. But Mêlon's spear and the dark look of Chiôn shooed him off, and reminded the mounted grandee that the assembly of the Thespians had freed all the slaves who had flocked to Leuktra to fight—a fact known to Hippias, who now wanted to keep the silver buyout from the polis and yet get his slave back for a double profit. No concern. Soon Hippias was no longer seen near Helikon—nor seen at all.

On a late summer morning, a year after Leuktra, it was Myron who found the rotting Medios, the Thrakian slave of Dirkê, the neighbor, hung up by his heels on a short pine tree far above the farm on Helikon— dead half a month or longer. Dirkê, Mêlon, and Chiôn soon followed Medios's trail—he had been cutting oak for plowshares above the farm of the Malgidai, so Dirkê said—but uncovered no others tracks of his killer. Now in fear of a demon-like man-bear on Helikon, Dirkê for a while came less to the farm of the Malgidai. She certainly said no more about Medios. Dirkê told no magistrate, and wanted no talk of where Medios had been—or how he'd been hung up and sliced, and how there was a man-beast killer loose on Helikon. Otherwise, despite the warnings of endless war against the Spartans by Epaminondas, the long months after Leuktra proved among the most peaceful in recent memory in Thespiai. Soon no one missed Medios.

Meanwhile, the Spartan booty—helmets, breastplates, mess kits, swords, and even a few coins—from the battle turned up from the Attic border all the way up to Phokis. Farmers hiked often over Kithairon to

Attika to buy stock and more slaves with their newfound money from the sale of plunder. The Thespian trader Eurybiades grew rich beyond his wildest boasting. His wagon full of pots and bronze creaked for days over the roads beneath Helikon to garner some of the captured Peloponnesian armor and coin in trade. At least ten thousand Spartans from the Peloponnesos, Eurybiades figured, had left most of what they had brought up. His practiced eye would find the final remnants of what they had cached in stone crevices and in cusps of trees.

"Not since my beardless days, all this money. Then I used to loot both sides of Kithairon. I'd strip the high border farms below Panakton of their roof tiles. Yes, and even the woodwork in the great war. But not like this. Never such a full cart like this. At this rate, I will buy another wagon. Maybe I'll hire this new Myron of yours, to follow me in my dust with another ox for my wares. Why, there are even Athenians who pay to ride back over the pass with me, just to look at the soil of Leuktra, to boast that they have walked on its holy ground. I've got my boy over there peddling clay toy Boiotian shields to the fool gawkers, with the sides notched out just like yours in the shed, and stamped on the front side with EPAMINONDAS."

"Oh, no, you won't take our Myron, king peddler. I've taken a liking to his empty head and wide shoulders. He stays here with Chiôn." Mêlon grabbed Eurybiades by the arm, "He's worth more than any three of them. Even his master, the whipper Hippias, won't get him back with a chain around his ankle."

There were to be more battle monuments for Leuktra, and victory decrees and temples from the booty. Thebes for most of the winter after Leuktra and following spring had sent its best monument builders and stone-cutters up to the sanctuary at Delphi. Of course, the architect Proxenos was hired to accompany the first party to survey the site. He would barter with the holy shrine keepers over the fees for buying a spot. The Boiotians were to build their own treasury on the Sacred Way, right in front of the Athenians' Parian marble eyesore.

Proxenos had become a court builder for the Boiotians. He traveled with scrolls stuffed with charts and lines drawn to make sense from the wild rantings of Epaminondas. Why he left his estates and horses on the Asopos, none were too sure, only that he came up to Thespiai more even than to Thebes, and to his home Plataia not at all. He was at work rede-

signing the walls, building clay models of vast new cities and for weeks taking trips south of the Isthmos with his packs of scrolls. Perhaps he wanted to build anew entire shrines and cities even, without the bother of old temples and the burden of poorly placed stones to hamper him—straight streets and right corners of fresh cities to rise, and not the hard work of straightening winding pathways of their fathers' cramped and dark poleis. Maybe too Proxenos wished to bring the mind of Epaminondas to stone, so that when his words were forgotten the ramparts of Megalopolis or Messenê would not be.

Soon Proxenos designed a white marble monolith right at Leuktra itself, on the spot where King Kleombrotos had fallen. The polished stone *trophê* was shaped like a cucumber of sorts. At its base the trademark notched Theban shields ran continuously around the circumference. Mêlon visited the builders at the big monument at Leuktra four times over the winter and spring. The tall column was as high as the new pyramids outside Argos on the Tripolis road, but of better stone than the plastered Herakleion at Thebes. For all the talk of Leuktra as the beginning of a new Hellas, it now appeared to have been the end of that idea, especially since nothing much had happened after the battle. If the tenure of Epaminondas were not renewed at the winter solstice, the new Boiotarchs would end all talk of a grand march into the Peloponnesos.

Widowed Damô was slowly regaining her looks. With her glow came back her power that had once reduced Lophis to teary entreaties to win her from the other nine suitors in Thebes, who had as much land and money, but also the coveted flat black earth around Kopais. Beauty is the great leveler among men, Damô remembered after Leuktra. She knew that folk didn't like some men because they were short, or dark, or had the barbarians' blue eyes and red hair, or could not speak the language of Hellas or owned only a cloak, rather than bottomland along Kopais. But the unspoken prejudice was really against their ugliness. In turn, the favor and advantage went not so much to the well-born, or the male, or even the moneyed, but to the beautiful. Children had suited Damô's look, and had widened her hips a bit only, but had added a sheen on her skin and a sway to her walk. This new Damô, hair black and skin without a blemish, with the high mountain *narkissos* of spring in her hair, went quickly through to the agora and the stalls, lest the women pelt her with roof-tiles and flower pots as she called them out.

Had she wanted, she could have robbed the mesmerized peddlers' stalls to their own applause. In this way each six days as she went into Thespiai, Damô shamed and confused and laughed and swore at those down the hill in the town of Thespiai below the farm on the spur of Helikon. She spat at them that they had sent no hoplites to help Lophis and their fellow Boiotians at Leuktra. "Gaze out at our monument to Leuktra, built by our Proxenos, a hero of Leuktra. See it from the acropolis of Thespiai, and feel shame," Damô barked at the Thespians as she shook her head and her black hair flew in the breeze. Without a husband, but with plenty of silver, she was bolder than ever now. All that only gave her sensible words even more credence, but it hardly stopped the rumors that Chiôn was up in her tower when the torches went out. Would that be so bad after all, the older one-toothed widows countered and hissed?


Despite the unexplained murder of Medios, the winter and spring after Leuktra on Helikon were ending in quiet—almost. After the summer solstice, Hippias, the former master of Myron, was found dragged by his horse on the mountain road to Aigosthena. His hand had strangely been caught and wound up in his reins, or so they also said, even as he boasted he was on his way with a decree from the city archon to get back his Myron from the Malgidai. No doubt, the horse bucked and bolted with Hippias trailing for a stade or two on the ground, his skull battered on the rocks. A freak accident, it was.

Or so they said.

# CHAPTER 13

# The Fall of Mêlon

The dizziness and head shakes Mêlon had suffered after Leuktra had finally stopped by the new year. His skull cleared from the blow of Kleonymos. He was alive; Kleonymos was not. So the pain had meant nothing. Mêlon's slaves were free. But still, he found that he missed the sharp tongue of Gorgos and the goat the two used to roast in the evening in the shed. Myron did his best at the shed talk, but he was a dense head. Even the dogs were gone. Sturax had gone into the belly of Lichas, as the Spartan had boasted, though dog-eating was usually the work of barbarians, both north and across the water. Nêto had lost Porpax along the coast. Perhaps the dog had gone wild with the wolves on Kithairon once he had tasted man-flesh, feeding among the corpses of the wounded Spartans. No doubt he too was gone for good.

The recovery of Damô, Mêlon saw, had mostly to do with Chiôn— just as the gossips said (and the slurs were spoon-fed by the neighbor hag Dirkê and her surviving Thrakian, Thrattos, who was finishing the oak cutting of the dead Medios). Damô hunted Chiôn down in the high fields and tamed him with soup and bread, and soon they talked of Pythagoras and how the spirit of Lophis was among them, awaiting both of them in the vortex, or perhaps even now in a new body—walking among the believers in Thebes with one or two more lives yet needed until perfection.

During the first winter after Leuktra, all during the month of *Prostatêrios*, it had been the neighbor gossip-monger Dirkê who reminded Mêlon of how much he had lost—hinting he might want to sell the worry of his farm to her. She went up too often as the new year approached. The shrew wanted to see whether stories were true that the harvest of Malgidai was slow and would be lost. Were the terraces of Mêlon's crumbling and overgrown with weeds? Surely the path up there was eroded and needed gravel? Was it true there was a great march to the south in the works—and perhaps the farm of Malgis might be sold for want of up-keep? Would not the hero of Thespiai know best the mind of Epaminondas? "*Eleutheria* is not so sweet, eh, hero of Thespiai and giver of freedom? Or at least for those who are foolish enough to be tricked into doing the dirty work of your helot-loving Epaminondas?"

"Sweet enough, and sweeter to come still," he answered.

"Boast like that when you're spear-gutted on black Ithômê—while some helot woman, with a Spartan rope around her ankle, slits your throat. Then you'll lie in the dirt on a hill of thistles, and with a toothless smile, no less. I know you'll die with a spear in you in the south. It will be far from home, far in the Peloponnesos. Or so it is written." Dirkê then trudged farther up to the vineyard and the shed, as far as her bad hips could take the climb. There was always money to be made in the after-math of battle. She wanted to rent out her slave Thrattos as a wage-hand to help her crippled neighbors with the olive pressing—and also through him hear the gossip of the Malgidai and get someone planted on the farm of Malgis. "Even your big oil stone press is not good when you don't have men to run it. The best oil is long past. Your fruit is black. Too long on the trees. Prance in armor all you want. It won't get your olives picked."

Dirkê seemed quite unconcerned about the past killing of Medios (she had even let his Thrakian corpse stay out there to rot where it was found). So she poked her head into the shed and kept on jawing. "With your Lophis gone, and Chiôn no good and free to boot, you might give us down the hill one of your second thoughts. That Myron slave, if he is even that, is a dung gatherer. He's no field hand. I've been told you will hear soon from the son of his dead master Hippias. Yes, you know him, new Lord Hipponichos, will go to the courts to get him back from you soon, as his father tried. They called me to come in as juror. So Mêlon—give me two obols a day. Add in some food. Yes, yes, for the belly of my big Thrattos and a bought vote or two to keep your Myron free up here. Thrattos will be yours for the winter. At least until your oil is pressed. Or are you short of coin? They tell me at the fountain that even your gold-inlaid breastplate is gone. Godlike Lichas the killer wears it down south, or so they tell." She kicked a few clods and then leaned on her stick. Then she spat out the seeds of a dried gourd, smiling with her one tooth over the lower lip. How had all that felt to the Malgidai? she wondered.

Mêlon liked the idea of an extra hand, but not a Thrakian. Dirkê had noticed that Chiôn was in the grove also striking the short limbs with a long reed stick from Kopais. Deftly he hit with his good right hand. She saw Zeus's black cloud over her Thrakian whenever he got near. "No worry, master," Chiôn yelled from the nearest olive, "I handle all of them as easily as before. Myron promises he will stay until the winter solstice to finish the picking. No need of her Thrakian; less of Dirkê. Send the no-goods away." With that he put down his pole and started his way over.

" 'Master' is it still? Small talk for such a big man—Chiôn the new lord of Hellas, hero of Thespiai." Dirkê sneered at him and went on, since she knew it was futile to get a pass from a man like that, and she might as well play out the hand to the end. "A conniver, your quiet cripple Chiôn is. He gets the farm without a silver owl or a Boiotian gold shield upfront? Dirkê works hard to buy it—but he stumbles into it? But I'd say instead maybe that tall tower of Mêlon's, and Damô's big melons along with it, is what he's got his eye on. So here we have a branded slave from Chios, with the scar on his poxy forehead. He ends up as lord and master of the estate of Malgis, swimming in the billows of a dead man's wife. You won't help your Dirkîkon a bit by hiring my Thrattos?" With that she hustled off down the trail in fear of a stone or kick for her venom. Being old and ugly and bent over is a better guard than a breastplate and shield.

"She is an Hekuba all right, Chiôn," Mêlon grumbled as his slave approached, "But the hag sorts out the chaos nonetheless." He stopped and put his lame leg on a stone and parted a few strands left back over his bald spot. They were outside the shed, around a smoky fire of green olive prunings. "Look, Chiôn, she believes in nothing, nothing at all—no love, no hate, no future, no past. Her memory is washed always by the waters of Lethe. She gets up each morning fresh without baggage or learning. She is guided only by that long nose for money and the bitterness that comes from feeling she is of lesser stock. Envy and spite, these are the twin oxen that pull men and women like her along. The *logos* of profit alone pilots her thoughts. I listen to her far more than I do to your Pythagoras."

How strange, Mêlon went on to lecture his Chiôn, that the odious among us can teach us the most—if we only can endure their cuts and jibes and then learn from their very mouths how not to view the world about us, and yet how with just a slight shove we might become as they are. Then he paused and thought to himself that had he not inherited the *paradeisos* from Malgis, had the gods not blessed him with Lophis, had he not been the *mêlon* of prophecy, perhaps he too might have become a Dirkê—or even a Lichas had he been raised in the *agôgê* of the Spartans.

Nevertheless, after Leuktra, Mêlon explored all these forbidden ideas further, and he now started up again to Chiôn. "Dirkê was as bad and yet right as much as our Lophis was so good and so wrong—about how the oligarchs at Sparta would come even to accept Pythagoras. But thank the gods for these Dirkai. She is the voice of all the dark thoughts in the world. Chiôn, Dirkê has been a great gift to me these years, sounding out and exposing the bad that is in me. She gives me a chance to hear my dark thoughts spoken, hear it all said by another, not me. Then I redeem myself by sneering at it, and claim the high ground from it, when she turns everything so foul and has no shame to voice the evil in us that we too feel."

Chiôn ignored his high talking and started to return to the olives—until Mêlon grabbed his rough wool cloak. "But Chiôn, she has reminded me that you were the better man at Leuktra, and one freed by the town fathers of Thespiai. So you marry Damô. Raise my son's boys to take this farm. More if you carve out another slice of the mountain with your one arm. Damô is still not three tens. She has three or four boys more in her yet. I can't pay you to stay on the farm. But stay you will. All that Malgis gave me will be your own to care for—at least until the boys of Lophis and your own to come are of age."

Chiôn and Eudoros, with Neander, Lophis's second born, were a small phalanx now. Chiôn was right. There was no need to hire slaves of others. Not when Chiôn and the boys had handled this olive crop, late but well enough in the absence of Lophis, and crippled as Chiôn was. Myron in his dung boots was strong and loyal, so he might work out as well. The wheel of luck would turn yet again for the farm. The upswing would be as good as before. The battle was over. Calm had arrived. Even the gossips of Thespiai would say little about the marriage. Chiôn was becoming the big talk of the forge loungers, jawed to the skies to the sound of hammer and anvil. They would all say the union of Damô and Chiôn was good farming—to keep the land safe and the free slave on the farm without paying wages, and the widow Damô from begging coins in the agora.

"Chiôn," Mêlon spoke slowly as the two made their way up to the high vineyard again. "You are my son now. The father of my son's sons. I claim my right as her legal guardian to pick who Damô marries. Those in Askra, and Koroneia and even Thespiai, too, will live with it—if for no other reason than all of Boiotia fears our two right arms." Chiôn said little. But his master was pushing him hard, to make him lord of the estate, father and husband and free man, citizen of the high property qualification, a rich *hippeus* should he wish to fight from a horse—all the honors Mêlon himself was tiring of as he waited for the call to go south. If Mêlon wanted a yoking on this farm, why not then he and the freedwoman Nêto? Were not they the better pair to stay home and guard the vineyards and pass the farm on to the boys of Lophis?

Yet Chiôn said to himself that he would try all this, at least for a while. Who would not wish the pleasures of Damô? Still, the wild, the high land of Helikon called, the better place—or maybe the strange piney, wilder mountain to the south, the slopes of gloomy Taygetos, where his mind went in his sleep to a highland hot on its slopes. He would try this plan of Mêlon, for they were all still in peace, and his master was the killer of Kleombrotos and so to be obeyed, even if Chiôn was no longer a slave. He would try. But he had his doubts. He and his master after Leuktra were each trying to make the other the custodian of the farm. Yet neither of them any more wanted to stay the man rooted to the soil, not with the scent of the south in their noses. "It is as you say master, as you say, at least for now."

Mêlon was coming off his mountain every other day, far more even than Damô. No longer was he the *misanthrôpos* and *erêmos* of old. The famous king-killer walked proudly on the narrow winding streets of Thespiai. He nodded to the admiring looks of the town folk from their balconies, those who had all voted to stay put, to keep themselves safe rebuilding their walls. He had been cured by Epaminondas and his fame of Leuktra from the disease of solitude, but the medicine had done far more than end the malady. His visits, he said, were meant to keep gossip about Damô and Chiôn within reason, and to learn what Dirkê was up to. Mêlon wanted to shame any he heard talking the dark stories about the heroes of Helikon. Or so he said of his time in town. But to Chiôn and Nêto, this new busybody was not their Mêlon, and they feared he was falling into something worse even than his years as the recluse before Leuktra.

As Mêlon strolled into town, sometimes he stopped at the potters' quarters to teach the idlers about Chiôn. They must know of the *prostatês* of the phalanx who had yelled "For Thespiai, for Helikon," as he slew Deinon, and Sphodrias, and cut down terrible Kleonymos in his proud youth. Chiôn, Mêlon lectured the craftsmen, gave his arm for these here, for the idea that they could idle in town. Mêlon went on and slapped the faces of the pot turners and kicked the kiln feeders. "It was your Chiôn, Chiôn of Thespiai. He killed the kings' best, when my Bora was shattered. He took on Kleonymos. He took that blow from Lichas so that I could spear Kleombrotos." Praise in town for his own clan—and for himself—was now as dear to him as the Thespian's disdain had once been to him out on the farm before he had heard the name Epaminondas.

A year and more after Leuktra, Damô and Chiôn were yoked. As a pair they had often driven Aias down from the farm, with Eudoros riding on Xiphos and the other two boys in the wagon, always just as the sun came up over the spurs of Kithairon to the east. They drove through the rubble walls into Thespiai to buy a litter of Lakonian hounds that the new henchman of Eurybiades had hauled over from Kithairon. Murmex was his name. He bought and sold dogs, blacks and spotted browns, with clipped tails and upright flat-topped ears—Lakonians not as large as the lost Molossians, Sturax and Porpax.

When the small caravan of the Malgidai made its way through the main gate and the roaring stone lions, and on by the theater, those at the forge yelled out to Chiôn, "For Thespiai." The hoplite stood up, turned, and roared back, "For Thespiai. Always for Thespiai." The widows at the looms shook their heads wondering how it had happened that Chiôn— the islander branded at birth by the Spartan hoplites of Lysander and sold to Malgis for two obols—had become his son and keeper of the name of the Malgidai. For all her three boys, the townsmen remarked that Damô was the real Aphrodite of Boiotia—and that Mêlon's rich soil grew goddesses as well as heroes.

# CHAPTER 14

# The House of the Goddess

In these autumn months, between *Pamboiôtios* and *Boukatios*, well after the first celebration of the Leuktra with its hekatombs and feasts,
and the union of Damô and Chiôn, Mêlon found he could still not
keep away from town, and he praised those on his farm as much as he
sought to avoid them. The Spartans were defeated—and yet not quite
defeated, given that thousands had escaped under Lichas. No doubt the
surviving king, lame Agesilaos, was raising an army to stop the democracy madness, which like the black spills from the ink bottle was staining
the entire Peloponnesos.

In the great uncertainty over quitting while ahead, or marching southward, some *daimôn* had turned Mêlon's thoughts back and forth, to solitude and then company, to being alone and to following the tug of the
mob, and all in a blink. From relief that he had survived Leuktra to restlessness that something else was promised, something far bigger in the
south that remained a rumor. So in his mix-up Mêlon began seeing Phrynê,
the newly arrived courtesan from Athens—though she claimed she had
been born at Thespiai and worked hard to sound Boiotian. For his part,
Mêlon claimed he only needed news in his calm after the battle, though, as
Chiôn worried, his master liked too much the back pats of town when
it would have been better to join his former slave on his treks across the
mountaintops of Helikon or Parnassos. Nonetheless, Phrynê knew the whispers of thousands—knew them and whipped them up or put them down
depending on whether or not they favored Epaminondas, whom she hated

more than any man north of the Isthmos. She did not quite know *why* she hated him, and she gave differing accounts to her friends about the wifeless, childless Epaminondas and his reluctance to visit her salon. To her clients, she cooed about the Theban at first, praised the general for his philosophy, and then only slowly showed her doubts about democracy, helots, new cities to the south, and all the dreams of Epaminondas.

Mêlon heard Phrynê's stories from both the peddlers of fruit and her own clients. Famous she was at Athens for having posed for the stone-artist Praxiteles himself. At ten and six years she had killed another prostitute, Lalagê, who claimed the tighter flesh. Phrynê had slashed her with nails and teeth, before finishing her off with a sharp mirror handle. Once when the young *rhêtôr* Hyperides, her lover, could not win an acquittal from the Athenian court for her profaning of the mysteries, she tore off her cloak in the *dikastêrion* and showed the Athenians her divine chest. She won the not-guilty verdict with her *mastoi* that the green orator could not. Then her *titthoi* pointed always upward. Her backside was hard as marble, curved, wide and full. Her tiny waist went in like the yellow-wasp's middle, and then out again. "Crescent moon," Hyperides had called her, for the bulge of her backside.

The Athenian sculptor Praxiteles was known to visit Thespiai to call on her girls to sit for all his stone goddesses—though he rarely asked Phrynê any more to model. In this great year of Epaminondas he saw the little pockets and rolls on her thighs, and the flesh that hung too much from the back of her upper arms. As she sagged—and she did so only a little, but still enough for the sculptor's falcon eye to notice—she bore him no ill will. Instead she turned her hate of aging to men in general, and men with power in particular. Phrynê fought the cruel law of her lord Erôs. The belly and bald head of an old man—just like the Satyrs' on the pots from Athens—did not mean he could not taste young flesh if his money and his vineyards grew with his years.

But for women? When the flesh spotted and its glow faded, when the hair thinned and the breasts drooped, then so did Erôs, the cruel god who saw only the wrinkled skin of the raisin, never the sweetness inside. To bear a child after lovemaking—and Phrynê had borne more than one—was a different sort of thing than a man's single poke. If she would no longer be seen in stone, and tired of men, Phrynê turned her head to counting coins, and what it cost and what it brought in to please the citizens of Thespiai. She grew rich from her shop of love in a house built into the corner wall, and added tall talk and Theban pipers to her business of pleasure, piling up more silver than she ever had as a poser and seller of love. For dessert she sold the Spartan agents secret plans, ideas, and agendas, and all the things the powerful blurted out as she mastered their passions.

Better than Naïs, the courtesan of legend, she wanted to be. With her money, she would find a man of action to whisper to, to taunt, to flatter, to play an Aspasia to a Perikles, and through him to defeat age and the laws of the Hellenes that say women alone must be trapped in their cages of aging flesh while stupider men were not. So Phrynê charged the estate owner ten silver Boiotian shields, but the philosopher or general sometimes nothing. Perhaps this bias came out of love of wisdom, but more likely she was careful to win high friends—all except Epaminondas—who could keep her exempt from both the fickle mob in the assembly and the angry wives of Thespiai.

She had come to Thespiai to stop the town from fighting the Spartans; it was said that she had a box of Agesilaos's gold. But, again, why did she hate Epaminondas more than did any Spartan? Perhaps she had lost business to the war, when the Boiotians invested in bandages and canes and not myrrh and frankincense. She worshiped at the altar of order and oligarchy; she knew clients by wealth, land, training, birth, accent, and parentage. Give this great leveler Epaminondas a cubit and soon he would take a stade and turn Hellas into a mixed-up rabble, where Phrynê would have to peddle her refined wares like the cheap harlots that lurked in the cemetery or the pottery kilns and took on all customers. Only *hoi aristoi* had the refinement to enjoy her houses of pleasure. In the world of Epaminondas to come, her slaves would be masters, her house frequented by smelly tanners and stained butchers who would choose always the younger flesh, never the smarter and more seasoned.

Phrynê claimed that she was not near thirty seasons (in truth, it was more). She had twenty strongboxes of coin to Mêlon's two. The farmer's visits to her house had all started when one of her girls had sent a message for "the hero of Leuktra" to visit the new symposia—a world away from Helikon's vineyards suffering under Seirios, the Dog Star's heat. Phrynê thought having the hero of Leuktra in her halls would be good business, as she reviewed the ways to praise the coming invasion of the south in a manner that might stop it.

Not happy just with the foreigners' money, Phrynê had refurbished the Thespians' temple to Erôs off the town square with a new fluted column and a hundred fresh roof-tiles. She even had paid for a new statue of Aphrodite near the south gate. Then she repainted the roaring marble lion at the city gate, added blue crystals for his eyes. "We get travelers from the islands, and from Thessaly way. They all hear of my house of Phrynê, and my statues. If I live another season, I will hire more potters from Athens. They'll paint what my girls do on clay, and we will last forever." With her silver, Phrynê stocked the back rooms with four looms and hired the widows in black to weave rugs and to sell to all her men what they could. That way the fools could go back home to their wives with gifts, and not just the scent of younger women on their cloaks. Always she sent them off with a word to stay home and forget the mad plans of Epaminondas. Phrynê still had beauty for most, and she knew it trumped all the philosophers' pretensions and the dour reserve of the generals. Phrynê had reduced both to no more than street-corner beggars, eager to touch her hair, even a toe or finger—at least for a year or two more before her beauty faded altogether.

The woman's given name was Mnesaretê. The Thespians had dubbed her Phrynê, "Toad," on rumors that at Athens she had hopped on the couches from one prone lover to another with her long thighs. Despite her beauty, the foul name stuck. In any case she was tall for a woman— maybe as tall as Nêto and half a head higher than some men. Mêlon at first liked her because alone of the ripe women in Thespiai she had no eyes on his farm—nor on him, or so he thought. "I am the scarlet grape at harvest," this Phrynê laughed to Mêlon, "plump and sweet. Yes, full of juice in the shade of my tendrils here in Thespiai. Why go up to thrashing the wheat stalks as Helios dries you out? I live for our god Love. Not for a man's ox or even always for a coin or two. Better for you to come down here. I can teach you the ways of the polis. Perhaps with my teaching, within the year you will be Boiotarch or *stratêgos*. Think of it—General Mêlon, lord of the federation. Yes, side-by-side with our noble Epaminondas. That's what wars are for—to winnow out the smart and brave and give them the fame to make them rich or powerful."

In these months after Leuktra, the town's *timê erotos*, its reputation for lovemaking, was as powerful as it had once been for war in the long-past age of its grandfathers. "No Spartans, no Thebans to worry about anymore, just love. We can turn our noses to what matters—and what we know too little about." Soon Phrynê was a philosopher of war as well, and lectured her customers that Herakleitos and that young Platôn from Athens were all wrong. There really was an end to war for all time. This was the age of the end of war, *to telos polemou*. The previous year had been the season of Epaminondas's war, and this year was to be the season of Phrynê's peace.

Better men of this new age ate well, and they read and wrote on papyrus, and they made machines to keep time, and track the heavens, and lift stone, the *polla ta deina* of Sophokles. They were no longer like the savage warmaking Thrakians or Makedonians—bushy-haired primitive folk in hides who believed in killing for killing's sake. Polis man, the new sophist Phrynê proclaimed, well, he was simply not as he had been in the past, and so no longer need a hoplite be. Lovemaking was stronger than the urge of pride, and honor, and fear and self-interest. Phrynê told anyone who listened, "It takes two phalanxes to fight. When we won't, there won't be war. I will rebuild the walls of Thespiai some day taller than those of Thebes, taller even than the new cities of Proxenos to the south, and then we will have no more need of spears. Why not have an *erôpolis* here in Thespiai? At my temple, here where our men can at last enjoy their own spear work? You stiff-legged Mêlon, don't you know that song of your love-poet Mimnermos—"The crippled man pokes best of all"?

He nodded at that. The tall statue of her nude—carved as Aphrodite—always stood in the courtyard, shiny with a fresh sheen of olive oil. She had paid Eurybiades to have it carted off from Athens and the studio of Praxiteles. That brought as many into her house as did her ripe girls. Mêlon found himself wondering who was more alive, the stone or Phrynê herself. Soon she had the statue brought into a special antechamber and charged an Athenian drachma a look. Many from Athens and beyond trudged over Kithairon to gaze at the godly marble work. Yet the statue and her courtyard of pots were only a foretaste of what Phrynê had prepared inside her tall halls. There were torches around a large common room. A shallow splash pool in the middle was usually full. When Mêlon entered, there were often naked fat men whose slaves tilled all their fields, with two heavy-set girls each, all entwined in the water. Though from the look of it, Mêlon scoffed to himself, the bald-heads looked more in pain than in the thrall of Erôs. Did any of these shield-bellies, men or women, ever plow or prune?

Stone couches with pillows lined the room. Carved arms and legs served as arm rests. A mural ran around all four walls above the heads of the dozen or so who were drinking wine. A flock of airborne *phalloi,* erect with feathered wings, were painted above, like harpies attacking naked girls in flight. One had eyes wide and was spitting out from its fanged mouth at a targeted woman below with legs wide open. About half of these figures had penetrated the fleeing in every way imaginable. In two scenes, six or seven of the winged shafts had cornered a smiling yellow-headed Amazon and were hovering over her erect nipples as she fought them back with a club. Instead of the gnarly bark of the olive and the rocks of the barley field, this was now the afternoon view of Mêlon, son of Malgis, whose hands became more polished than cut.

On one table was an array of leather dildos, *olisboi* of various sizes and shapes soaking in olive oil. If that weren't enough, the bottoms of all the wine cups of Phrynê were decorated with even worse, Satyrs and centaurs mounting men and women who themselves were mounting each other—the painted scenes all visible to the guests each time a man put wine to his lips. Yet Phrynê's actual guests seemed far older than those frolicking on the walls and pots. Still, all this was of no concern for Mêlon, or so he said to himself, since it was usually enough for him to lie down, drink some wine, and listen to the gossip of the Thespians—especially the mention of the growing war circle of Epaminondas. He often met the roustabout Murmex and his master trader Eurybiades in the house of Phrynê as well. They had three wagons, as he once boasted, and they made the trip over Kithairon every ten days. Each month the two also went northward to the hot gates and the great plains of Thessaly and the vale of Tempê. "Democracy in Thebes and Athens at the same time?" Eurybiades laughed. "So border peddling is good for us. It will stay that way—unless that philosopher Epaminondas objects. That faker with Orpheus on his shield may get one of his war ideas again. He thinks he's god and so starts up the war and heads into the morass down south." The profits of Eurybiades from love piled higher even than those from the loot after Leuktra, so he now praised Erôs and damned the war gods Artemis and Ares.

Phrynê had claimed friendship with the sophists in Thebes. When she first opened her salon, she had courted the famous Alkidamas—who few saw, but whose words many heard. In the days before Leuktra, he had told Phrynê (so she said), "I say you are as firm as Naïs, my Phrynê, and with a livelier tongue. I knew her at twenty-five, but not at your thirty."

Phrynê wanted even more from the man. "Did she sing her Simonides and Alkman? Did she dance on her toes, or swing from a limb, or have breasts as these? How many of the Spartan *bibases* can she do? Can she jump up and hit her buttocks with her heels, hit them five hundred times as I do? Did she speak with Platôn in Attic, and dally in the bow and arrow with an Iphikrates?"

"No, no to all that," conceded Alkidamas. "She bore me a son, the one Lichas or his foul son cut down at Leuktra. As handsome as I am ugly, Kalliphon was, though his shoulders were narrow and bottom too wide—like his mother's. Now the earth of Leuktra covers his ashes. His name is carved in black marble with the others on the road to Tanagra, since he died for the dream of Epaminondas."

"Our beloved general," Phrynê spoke softly of Epaminondas to Alkidamas, "is some idol that we worship as if he were gold and ivory. And why not, given his strong right arm and his honey tongue and simple dress? For your Mêlon of the prophecies, Epaminondas promises that the lame-leg's genius is at last appreciated, that he has an ordeal only worthy of a few select like himself, at least enough to pleasure us with his godhead as he now puffs himself up and struts down from his vineyard. For our dear Nêto, she thinks not just that she is a helot again, but has invented herself, of course, as a lord of the helots, our new Penesthelia, the Amazon general, at the head of some great serf horde that shall take down Sparta—quite something for a raisin seller just last year in the stalls weaving her webs to trap her rich master. And you, our brilliant Alkidamas, in your arrogance you believe your Epaminondas will make you first philosopher of Hellas, or maybe the new ruler of helot Messenia. Oh yes, then we have the gold-bags wall-builder Proxenos, who builds himself a castle and playhouse above the Asopos, and when that is not enough wants entire cities for his sport—as he frolics on his marble couches with that troublemaker Nêto. He too says he "is for Epaminondas," without a clue that he is building these huge citadels for those who will turn on Sparta— and perhaps eventually on us. I've even had the great hoplite Ainias of Stymphalos in my halls, the best killer of all the circle of Epaminondas. He wants walls for his beaten-down Arkadians, and pledges his spear craft to Epaminondas in the exchange, the most honest thug of the lot. Touch a hair on the head of Lord Proxenos of the golden coins, the builder of Ainias's fantasy walls, and you earn a spear in the gut from

Ainias, who prides himself a "Tactician" after Leuktra. Oh, I forgot Chiôn. Chiôn always loose at night, even as he dares prance in here in day as first citizen of Thespiai, as if we must praise his killing of the far better men at Leuktra. Quite a crowd, this circle the childless, wifeless Epaminondas has conjured up. My, my, I must talk with him again some day."

Mêlon had heard the same from Phrynê. He took solace in the knowledge that she, as the spurned lover, was now obsessed with the circle of Epaminondas, and that should the great man ever walk in, Phrynê herself, like some Kappadochian plaything out of the great king's harem, would kowtow before the Theban. Mêlon still told himself he was here, he insisted, only on business and so saw Proxenos the Plataian on the fourth day of each new moon as he came into the halls of Phrynê covered with the dust of bricks and stone and the smell of lead and iron. Phrynê gave him free rein of her house, since Proxenos had promised that her salon would stay untouched amid his rework of the fortifications of Thespiai. His new walls would go out around her crumbling corner tower, built into what was left after the Thebans had dismantled the circuit. After Leuktra the frightened Thespians, who had abandoned the cause of the Boiotians, had hired Proxenos to raise their walls, lest Epaminondas pay them a visit. As for Proxenos, he wished to try out some of his circular towers on the town before he built a new one thirty cubits high down in the Peloponnesos. Proxenos and Ainias had been down in the south each month, busy with what they called "the big things," *ta megala pragma* that were turning Hellas upside down in the land of the Spartans. So here in the house of Phrynê, Mêlon began putting together from the rumors of guests something more also about this Proxenos who appeared now to be committed to the plans of Epaminondas. And he assumed as well that anything he might tell Phrynê would up in about six days in the ears of Lichas himself—and on to the shadowy Lord Kuniskos of Messenia, the new master of the helots known even in the north.

As Mêlon pondered this Proxenos, more memories came to him. He knew of old talk of a a rich Proxenos, an oligarch who had lived on a farm with a high tower near the battlefield of Plataia, along the reedy banks of the Asopos River. The older Proxenos was a killer, with great chests of silver (and more still that Mêlon did not know of with gold), who foolishly went east to Babylon for pay under the Spartan Klearchos—the Spartan thug whose son had killed Staphis at Leuktra.

The shadow from his father's past, he learned from Phrynê, was the father of this present Proxenos, this dusty man on the couch beside him. The older Proxenos, Mêlon remembered as well, had been murdered by the Persians while he parleyed for the Ten Thousand. Unlike the father, this aristocrat Proxenos spoke softly to Mêlon, in a careful Boiotian more like Attic as some did from the border town of Plataia. Watch these tame ones like Proxenos, Phrynê warned Mêlon later, these men who plan vast new cities that will only cause more war for the price of their craft— and their vanity and their sense of entitlement and their desire to be pure and loved and all the other fat fruit that the carrion Nemesis gorges on. In their cases, she hoped the furies would be Lichas and his son Antikrates, who got their prompts from tall-ears Phrynê up north.

Yes, the dreamers smile and keep their bile inside, or so Phrynê preached to her clients who followed Epaminondas. Give me your ugly Lichas at Leuktra any afternoon, who is what he is by his own scars. So Phrynê spoke to any who would listen and flirted when Proxenos entered, often with Ainias to discover the when and where of a winter march to the south: the one to found the great cities of the Arkadians, the new fetters of the Peloponnesos, the other to ensure that the Plataian would live to remake his fatherland in stone, and so at last keep it free from the hated Spartans.

Mêlon listened to her bile, but wondered perhaps if he, the hide-clad farmer on Helikon, might still match the aristocrat Proxenos, might earn Phrynê's hatred as well with some great deed to trump even Leuktra. The delusions of the town now had him and squeezed him nightly. Yes, Mêlon, son of Malgis, might himself plan some big upheaval to the south, something of the sort his son Lophis had once boasted about. Yes, he might do even greater things to the south. He liked the rumor and big anger from Phrynê about Leuktra as he came in from Helikon and greeted the obsequious townspeople on his way to Toad's house. No longer deemed crazy, he was no longer even mysterious, but was seen and trusted when the Thespians went to the assembly to vote for the blocks on the wall and to pay fair prices for the emancipated slaves that had earned their freedom when they went to Leuktra.

The road from eccentricity to respectability is not as long as one might think. Both rely first on being known. Mêlon's name was certainly on the lips of most before, but especially after, Leuktra.

# CHAPTER 15

# *Nêto Unbound*

During these dog days on the farm in the calm year after Leuktra, when the midday sleeps were the longest, Nêto moved out of the estate and prepared to head south on the scent of an autumn war and upheaval. She was, of course, her own person after the emancipation decree of the Thespians for all those who had gone to Leuktra—even those slaves in the camp who had not put on armor and joined the ranks. Nêto had known no other home but Helikon, since her sale ten and more years earlier. Nêto was now renowned in Thespiai as the conduit to the voice of divine Pasiphai. She was acclaimed as the one seer of the north who rightly had seen in her sleep that her master Mêlon, the apple, would kill Kleombrotos. She had promised that the Thebans would prove mightier in war at Leuktra. That too had happened. That she knew even more about the fates of Proxenos, Chiôn, and Gorgos, perhaps even Mêlon and Epaminondas, she now kept quiet.

The new freedman Myron was about town as Nêto once had been, talking up the Malgidai and soon to reopen the family fruit stall that Nêto had begun. Myron talked with much more zeal, since for a collector of dung it was quite a rise in life to sell cucumbers and raisins as a free man, in the shade of a stone stoa no less. Of course, his master Hippias had been murdered and could not sue to reclaim his property, and he had no agenda about helots and Spartans and such things in the south. Few on Helikon cared that Nêto had found and hired Myron—only that he was the new Nêto without the babble. Soon she was now as irrelevant when freed as she had been valued when a slave despite her fame in town. Eudoros and Neander needed no guide, either. She even faulted herself for the dead Sturax, who had gone with Gorgos to the camp of the Spartans, but never returned. Worse still, she had lost the other Molossian hound Porpax as well. All these thoughts, both trivial and fundamental, piled high in her mind. Each was like the stones on Chiôn's terraces, and together they pressed her down to a sort of *mania*—that she was now the enemy of her own people, now the exile in her own land. Be careful, she remembered her Pythagoras, of getting too much of what you dream for.

Added to these constant second thoughts and regrets was the growing paradox of her long harangues about the freedom of the Messenians delivered from her safe perch on Helikon. Was it not more honest, as Damô had lectured her, to agitate when actually on Mt. Ithômê with Nikôn and his helots, where such talk meant often death? After Leuktra, with her freedom and the fame of her master, she thought at last Mêlon might wed her. He was a recluse, a *duskolos* anyway and would care little of what the Thespians might say about taking a freedwoman as wife. With Chiôn and Damô and the three boys of Lophis, and her boys to come, the farm would enter its greatest phase and would no doubt carve even more new fields from Helikon. Instead Mêlon had ignored her and talked more of the rumor-monger Phrynê's salon than the high pond where they used to gaze out at the hillsides below when she put him to sleep with her Thisbean strains. Nêto had tried to purge herself to cleanse out the black bile. A doctor in Thespiai had bled her as well. Still the cloud surrounded her. Night became more welcome than day.

With her pupil Proxenos gone often to the south, Nêto had also met a strange new teacher, this Alkidamas, who kept his hands out of her chiton and instead encouraged her visions. On the day before she decided to leave Helikon, she saw him coming out of the house of Phrynê, outside of which she had developed a habit of lingering and watching when she finished peddling the farm's harvests. His admonitions had helped to convince her to leave, although that was not necessarily his intent. "You are our bridge to the Olympians. As their superstitions fade with the bright sun of *logos*, they impart shadows of things to come to you as their final gifts. Use them for us, Nêto. Leuktra was not the end of things as they say. But as the Olympians whisper, the beginning of them all. Things are on the move to the south, though we cannot sense that yet in the quiet up here."

Be careful of surrendering completely to geometry and measures and numbers, Alkidamas had also taught her—lest she build her house on false reason, one weak foundation supporting ever more mud bricks of logic before collapsing altogether. *Logos* is a cold god. It could not explain all that he promised to explain. Reason might tell us why and how black and yellow bile differ, or how to measure the distance to the moon. But *logos* cannot say why one farmer suffered so from the bad air and fevers and another didn't. Or why one man was run over by a wild cart and another veteran of five battles lived to eighty. No, she needed faith in a moral god as well, not just pure reason and not just the deathless ones on Olympos who were worse than men. On the afternoon after listening to Alkidamas, Nêto passed Mêlon on her way down the trail and sealed the parting. "Whoa master, it is too hot to hike up in the sun. Look at you without your broad hat. Fetch it from the shed."

"Is that where it is?"

"Yes. Put it on."

"Nêto, Nêto, always the slave. Though you are freer than any *politês* in Boiotia and all that you saw came to pass. So well did the gods—or at least Pasiphai in the south—breathe into you the ways of the future. But remember, Hellas is wild. You are weak and a woman and going where such kind do not venture—even if you claim to be a priestess and a freed-woman at that, and under the protect of Chiôn and Mêlon of Leuktra. I gave you freedom, and you trumped it, but that does not mean others see that way. If I was foolish enough to come up bareheaded in the heat, why are you so silly coming down alone and without a hat as well?"

"Let me worry about the heat, man of the city."

"Well, you alone on Helikon have a fountain pipe to bring you cold water. Here are five silver shields I got for the bag of dried pears I carried down today to peddle in town, though I hear I did not do as well as you did yesterday."

"Pay me nothing, Mêlon. I eat more on your farm alone than I earn these days. I am going to see Theanô, the widow of Staphis, to help her with the vintage. It is not safe anymore with even tough Thrakians murdered in the wild—and Hippias, master of Myron, killed like a dog. Yes, this man-bear that killed Hippias and maybe Dirkê's two men, he is out there above the timber line. They say that Hipponichos, son of Hippias, bars himself in fear in his tower—although I figure he may already be rotting up there hung from the rafters, and can't answer the door. Theanô is a Messenian—again like me, a helot at birth. "

"Theanô is good and poor, you mean, Nêto," Mêlon went on, "But you have chores here. Neander wants to learn your block letters. Damô says you must nurse Chiôn's new one. It comes with the spring. Your shovel-head Myron needs help. He is a dull one, an empty skull to begin with. The vintage is good. But only because you clipped off the excess bunches. We—I most of all—have more need for you than ever. I miss your tune of Thisbê to call me down from the high orchard."

"Not at all."

"Always."

"Never. I am needed only to keep the farm so you may not, to stay in the orchard, so you can go into town."

Mêlon ignored this final chance to show her proof of his devotion and instead offered only lame small talk. "Who will hear my tales of spear play at Koroneia? Now I'm boasting only to the ox Aias and the pigs of Leuktra."

Nêto blushed and then laughed, "Even they forgot you. The only pigs you know are the fat men in the halls of Phrynê. Damô runs the agora. When she prances in, they either leave or keep quiet if they know what is good for them. The agora is your home now. Or so Dirkê whom you love so well tells me of this Phrynê. Oh yes, and her soft pipes and full table and more still. Beware of such a woman who will roast you even without fire, who wishes to be mistress on Helikon to the hero of Leuktra and lord over our widow Damô. Each word you utter is known to Lichas in the south. She might as well brand a lambda on her forehead. Peace used to bore you. Beware that victory ruins us as much as defeat."

Such a strange thing, Mêlon knew, that those who have no formal bond, and no history of physical love between them, nevertheless expect each other not to taste the flesh of others. Stranger yet that they both understand and honor such a pact though no words are ever spoken and they themselves are resigned to wait for each other—without worry that the wait may prove endless and outlast the flesh. He had half-expected that Nêto knew that he wanted her as his wife, without ever asking her—or even making her his wife. Wasn't the idle wish of his enough? Did she not know that he had risked his all to stop the Spartans, the oppressors of her dear helots? And had he not accepted Pythagoras on her prompt, and then let her roam over Boiotia, flirting with Alkidamas and Proxenos as they recruited for Epaminondas?

He grabbed her shoulder and made Nêto look him square in the eye, despite the glare from the stones. Mêlon felt a sort of pity for Nêto. Her ambition put her hopes into something greater than the greatest battle of the age that had just passed—as if to be alive during Leuktra was not enough for any mortal, much less a helot girl on Helikon. Did she know how small her world really was? Or how those far greater than her determined whether she and her kind lived or died?

Just over a year earlier, when the black clouds of Sparta hung over Helikon, all in town had listened to her prophecies and begged her to repeat her strange promise that the Thebans would be mightier in war. But now? Those were her great days lost. Then Lophis was riding about and Mêlon let her run the farm. Then Chiôn and the dogs were at her side. Gorgos was lusting after her blush, in the long afternoons of the spring and summer of the previous year, before everything had changed at Leuktra. The rich man Proxenos thought he would free and marry her, or so he boasted. She alone was the ear for Mêlon. He was the recluse eager for the news of the world below. She had once been his only conduit to the polis people beneath. Mêlon thought how foolish men lament that the long days are always the same. They are not, he knew. We change even as we speak. So in his folly he judged that the world had passed young Nêto by. In his new fame from Leuktra, and life in town, he felt sorry for her. Or was it that he feared that she might well not need the farm and tower anymore—and that she talked in confidence rather than hurt? Or that she might be as wary of wedding as he? Mêlon's last words of lament surprised him. "Nêto, come back with us. Theanô can hire Thrattos. She is better off for Leuktra and is no helot, but the widowed hero of a great man Staphis and with coins for his death no less. Come back and let us both avoid town and work the vineyard, side-by-side."

He took his hand off her and looked down, "You are the one that all the men of Thespiai talk of—some with many vines and six hundred *plethra* of the bottomland at their call. They would all yoke you this very summer. Come back to us. Stay."

Nêto flashed. "I earn my keep as all free women do: with work. I have no need of the men of Thespiai. Like women they stayed in the theater when we all marched to Leuktra. They watched you and Chiôn and

Lophis and Staphis carry the yoke of Thespians. Believe me, I have no love of the Thespians, men or women. Some are like Backwash, the others Phrynê. Their backsides from sitting are wider than the shoulders they never use. They would as soon kill as free a helot. Nêto as you knew her is gone and for good. And so is the old Mêlon of Helikon."

Mêlon was drawn to her even more by her defiance. But he saw finally that she was already gone from the farm. She would not come back. Not unless perhaps he would offer her what he would not yet give. He liked the idea that some day they might run the farm as two, but he saw too late that for too long he had liked even more the notion that she would wait for that moment without really thinking it would ever quite come. "Go then. Be the helot you are. Scrub the floor of Theanô. Forget the needs of the boys of Lophis. Go play the Thisbean strain to Lord Proxenos. Sit at the foot of Alkidamas."

"*Siga*, calm, master. You speak only in anger and hurt. What I see and hear of the army to come is not really of my doing," Nêto quietly countered, "but only what the goddess warned me long ago. I don't believe in these Olympians. I know only their anger at my treason, and my loyalty to the One God of Pythagoras. So they have put voices, wild ones, in my head. Because of them, I am not leaving you as much as beginning the trip south, where I think we two will see each other a last time and perhaps for good."

She continued more slowly. "There is a Nikôn to the south. He is a tanner, a poor man but one who fights. His better helots just talk. But Nikôn kills Spartans. I hear his voice in my head. He says he needs me soon, needs a prophet of things to come as guide for his gangs, needs a voice to counter the lies about us that Phrynê up here sends down there. And Alkidamas says there is a poetess as well that will go south with me before this summer ends. She's a great charmer who can help stir up the Messenians as well. Helots should help helots free themselves. And you, master? Some day you will stop thinking you, in your quiet arrogance, are not quite part of the world and join us who are in it up to our necks."

With that, Nêto passed him by as she made her way down. Mêlon noticed that she had a short double-edged blade, a Spartan *xiphos* that she had probably taken from one of the corpses the previous summer at Leuktra, to go along with her jagged single-edged chopper. Mêlon left her with, "It is hot today, girl. But your wits were long ago cooked. Be happy with a free Boiotia. Let the Spartans be—unless you must dress up your desire for Alkidamas with talk of trumpets and banners. Unless you have your eye on some helot lord, some tanner Nikôn to the south if it has not been Proxenos already."

Nêto kept her head down and moved down the path alone, chattering away, her words heard by no one as Mêlon was already up the trail. She was chanting, stitching together words of a song that came into her head, between Thisbean strains on her reed pipe. "Farewell—until the winter, until the winter when we will meet far away on Ithômê." But he was already long gone and well around the turn, with only a stade left to the tower and home.

She missed him at the first bend; and Mêlon for his part began to miss her the very moment she turned away.

# CHAPTER 16

# The Healing of Mêlon

By mid-autumn, Phrynê was shooing strange customers from her house and angry even as her coin boxes filled with the new business. Their accents were not Boiotian, even in out-of-the-way Thespiai. These bounders were not mere northern pilgrims on their way to consult the Pythia at Delphi. They had no religious business with Apollo of Ptôon. Most were fighting men of scars and dirty leather. Now they camped outside the walls of Thespiai and said little to the natives, as they drilled and sparred in bronze. Thebes would be mustering soon, and thousands of foreign hoplites were spreading over the countryside of the Boiotians. Phrynê sent messengers to Lichas, in silly fashion thinking that after Leuktra there were still enough Spartans left to come north—when, in fact, those who had survived the battle still woke with the night terrors of seeing again Epaminondas, Mêlon, and Chiôn in their armor.

Some at the campfires danced the Pyrrhic with their shields and spears and bought women. They sang the *enoplia* war songs in Doric. Their tents and shacks surrounded the walls. Even when sleet showers of winter came, men camped in the cold in the last months of the year, as if the foreigners and *xenoi* knew more than the Thebans themselves what would happen next. Mêlon had no luck hiring any of these itinerants for the final end of the olive harvest. Many were not like hoplites of the polis, but had the look of hired killers. They talked of money to be made from plunder in the south. What were they doing here—when it was the coming of the cold solstice, and the season of arms long past? What rogue, Phrynê screamed in her halls, had summoned them here?

Then arrived more winter roadmen, at first all northerners, later from almost every region of Hellas, marching on the trails leading over the northern passes into Boiotia. Lokrians came. Horsemen too rode in from Thessaly on taller ponies. Then trudged in later islanders from across the strait of Euboia and beyond. All of these by the first frost walked in the streets of the Boeotian cities as if they owned the polis. Chiôn saw that his Aegean folk were rowing in ahead of the winter storms. Some came from as far as Lesbos and Samos with accents like the Aeolic Hellenes—maybe his kin from Chios as well, or so a stocky Melian down at Kreusis told him in town when Chiôn hiked over to watch some of these island sorts sail in (and to turn upside down Nêto's prophecies that he should not view the waves and breakers).

Even Arkadians from Mantineia were marching northward to Boiotia in twos and threes. All heading now for Thebes, all going over the gulf road near Aigosthena along the water and up through Kreusis. Five hundred Messenians had come east along the coast from Naupaktos. These were the children of the helot refugees in the north freed at Pylos during the Athenian war. Thirty years later they swore to deliver their kin from the Spartan yoke. Most still had their Doric talk. Mêlon tried for a time to race against this great shaking up in Boiotia and finish the olive harvest in his own world on Helikon.

As the family team worked in the shortening days of late autumn during the month of Boukatios, Chiôn proved the natural father all along to Mêlon's grandsons. The dead Lophis for all his spirit had had no heart in either the land or its sons. He too often swore when the deep mud caked inside his long fingernails, and the boys tried to mount his sleek charger Xiphos and pile on behind their father. "We are not all men of the soil," Malgis once had warned his grandson Lophis. "You find keeping this farm for your sons hard, but keep it nonetheless you must. A farm is the stored work of a man's life. Lose it, and the rope snaps, with you, the weak weave. Then the boys will not have what you were given. You inherit, and see to it that you add to it—so others get more than you did. We Malgidai, we will buy the soil of others, or cut out more from the mountain, but we will not sell, not now, not ever."

Mêlon suddenly thought of all that now. How had the gods accomplished that the farm would be saved by a slave that his father had bought in Chios, land that otherwise might have been lost had his own son, who thought of town more than a hillside of olives, lived? Still, he missed his Lophis in the morning. No more did his son climb up bleary-eyed and full of talk from his nighttime rides at the marshes and beyond. When sons die before fathers, it is soon time for fathers to follow. Even if their hair is not all white and their joints are not yet frozen with the swelling and stiffness; and even if their son proved a worse sort than the father, himself a worse sort than his own father Malgis. Lophis had proved just the opposite; as good as Mêlon or better still. He had a year, or maybe two left, and that was perhaps all Mêlon deserved. No need to be greedy and take more than your son had—and so this thought too began to make the Thespian think Leuktra had not been enough and he might go down the mountain to talk to these growing hordes of hoplites who were camping in the orchards and vineyards of Boiotia and do yet one more big thing before the end. Slowly all thought of town soured him. And he felt shame that he had spent even a single afternoon in the Thespian agora rather than with a ladder in the orchard.

Only out on Helikon did his head clear and could he think again. Wars were not just won by hands like himself and Chiôn, the killers and gray-heads that hold firm in the spear crossing and don't flinch when iron tips rattle off their nose. There is need of young zealots such as Lophis who could ride head-on into the Spartan horse, with no foreknowledge of the gore of battle and no fear of Hades. Without young men who know it not, there could be no war brought to the land of others. So war is a sort of madness. It requires young men in their pride and recklessness who have no wisdom about how thin the threads of all of us hang—and so are willing to confront evil. Hoplites not yet much beyond their twentieth year believe their fate is a hardened iron chain that can't be cut by anyone or anything. So they fight even to get into the first bloody rank of the phalanx.

In the long nights in the shed behind the farmhouse Mêlon grasped how sorely he missed Nêto, whom he now regretted having driven off the mountain—though of course he really had not driven her off. Indeed, only by deluding himself that his words had banished her could he accept that he feared she had tired of him and the farm and the neglect which he had shown for both her and the crops after Leuktra. He was afraid this

Nikôn or Doreios—or worse still, the wealthy and landed Proxenos—had stolen his Nêto. Alkidamas had "taught" Nêto, but Mêlon scarcely knew what had been the nature of his lessons. That she had left for her helots, he knew; that she had left to raise her own station, and in that way at last to win her Mêlon, he had not even a small sign.

Almost as a revelation during the olive harvest, Mêlon now saw the broken terraces, cracked clay pipes, and trellises that had gone unrepaired in the vineyard in his absences down the mountain in the long months since Leuktra. How mad to have played the hero in Phrynê's house and left his own to decay. Just a year of neglect and nature gets the upper hand. Nature never rests as man sleeps or dawdles in town. Nature gives us mold, rust, and wrinkles as occasional evidence of her silent, ceaseless work—the poisonous mushrooms that sprout out of nowhere after the rain. The farm fights the wild daily, but without man to stem the tide, feral nature reclaims its own in one season of weeds, and insects, and floods. Mêlon rediscovered himself as the land slowly began to heal him and bring him back to what he had once been. Yes, he was a *geôrgos* of Helikon, a farmer of civilization. He was no wild bacchant on Kithairon. His were not the maenads who danced on Mt. Ida in worship with her cymbals to Kybele. Those fools liked nature in the raw and laughed at the hard work of bringing culture out of savagery. Instead, his gods were the sober makers of things, divine Athena and the bitter Hephaistos. They were not wild and untamed Dionysos of Asia. They were not the Spartans' huntress Artemis. Yet he was not a townsman either, who in softness had forgotten how to read the south breeze and the storm warning of birds and hoppers in the air. He was not to be a gawker or lay about in the halls of Phrynê, the seductress who had taught him so well that it was the land, not his own character, that kept him at work and away from the idle and slothful.

No, Mêlon son of Malgis was a *mesos*, a middle-man, neither feral nor tamed. From now on in these last days before the muster of the army, he would stay up on Helikon and tend to what he had neglected. He would go back to farming, and grow food from scrub and wait for a call from Epaminondas. The way to be ready for another battle was to ignore the talk of it in town, and instead ensure that his right arm was hard from pruning and he was once more used to sleeping on boards rather than reclining on the couches of Phrynê. Yes, that was the key, to be ready for the moment when it arrives even if that rendezvous be distant and unsure. If he wished to see beauty, it would have been far wiser to have gazed at Nêto for a blink between olive pickings than to have stared at Phrynê all day in her house of sloth.

So Mêlon was no longer hero of Leuktra, big man of Thespiai, but now cured once more and back to bald, lame Mêlon of Helikon, shorn of his slaves, and a mere tiller of the soil. As he stayed up on Helikon one evening about dusk the new dogs of Damô, Phylax and Hormê, began yapping at noises. But theirs was a different sort of bark. It was the rarer sort of yelp on lonely Helikon that most always foretold the scent of man, and strangers at that. Mêlon stopped the pressing to walk a bit out of the back room of the shed. What would the dog noise augur this time? Dirkê's new Thrakians, or those left-handed conspirators of Pythagoras? Was the man-bear lurking near? And were the old myths even true, that man-bears still roamed like the half-gods Agrios and Oreios, whose mothers had mated with wild beasts in the high mountains? Were they again sweeping down from the north—now human in appearance, now in their fits assuming the shapes of half-bears with the cunning of men but the claws, fangs, strength, and savagery of animals?

From the crossbeam of the shed Mêlon grabbed his new Bora, the replacement spear that he had turned out from a log of cornel, with its iron head resharpened. He made ready outside the pressing room to stand his ground. Then to his surprise he met both Proxenos the Plataian and Ainias of Stymphalos—the first he had seen recently in town, the second not so often since the long day at Leuktra. The dogs ceased their barks as they saw the master put away his weapon. The one was well-groomed with his ink-black beard, combed hair, and clean tunic. But Ainias not so. The mercenary's face was of stubble, and he had stitches and patches all over his leather jerkin.

Mêlon himself was covered with oil and pith. The king-killer was worn out at his twentieth straight day in the pressroom, having often worked the evenings alone to catch up to the picking of one-armed Chiôn and the boys. The two visitors came through the shed to the backside in the flickering torchlight. Both were shifting baskets of overripe olives to find room to sit on the slippery stone floor. Proxenos the builder stared in amazement at the elaborate machine that Mêlon had built. With the help of Chiôn and the tutelage of the peddler Eurybiades, Mêlon had spent years improving it—finally perfecting the original design of Malgis.

Murmex, the dog peddler and henchman of Eurybiades, had brought in parts for the press from Athens as well. The peddler knew more about such levers and stones than he let on, since he spent time boating along the islands off Argolis where his own folk proved clever with such machines. There was nothing quite like this press in all of Boiotia, the entire floor of the room finished in shiny hydraulic plaster. The surface was waterproofed like the fountain bottom in the square in Thespiai—as well done, Eurybiades claimed, as the famous public pools of Megara. Mêlon had cut channels that led to giant *pithoi*. Receptacles were set into the floor at the corners of the room. These cuttings seemed to run slightly downhill from the center, where rested a large round polished limestone drum. It was a smasher of sorts. It was set atop a stone casing, where crushed half-black olives were piled. A fifteen-foot oaken beam held the stone. On one end it was attached to the wall on a heavy axle, resting on bricks of the building.

The other end of the beam near the opposite wall was anchored by heavy ropes on a pulley to the ceiling and cranked further by a windlass. That machine forced the beam downward. With it, the attached stone smasher in its middle pressed the olives. It had taken Mêlon three seasons to build, and a lot of talk with the peddlers to learn of the strange design. Proxenos, the architect of walls and gates, gazed at the ingenuity of the press. He would have liked to stay here on the farm, and have built one like it, only better, since he already saw ways to improve it. "Mêlon, you should be in charge of the walls of Thespiai and those rising to the south. I have not seen anything like this. Well, once maybe at Haleis. There a fellow I know on the coast of the Argolis, a Diôn, son of Diophanes, has built such things—before in jealousy his neighbors broke it up with mallets. The envious were slave-dealers, of course, who wanted no such machines."

Before Mêlon could reply, an impatient Ainias got up and probed the press. He stroked his stubble beard, and wondered whether it were not salvaged from one of the belly-bows, or maybe parts of a catapult frame that killed men from two stadia. He hit the beam with his shoulder. He pulled at the lever a bit. "Show us how this thing of your gods works. I have no notion of it. It looks like the funny machines they play with at Athens that keep our time and chart the heavens. Is it a toy? A weapon perhaps? One of Homer's automatons? Clearly it works. How else would your jars be overflowing with oil?"

Mêlon kept quiet. He leaned back and cranked the windlass on the beam's end two more notches. Then he put a foot-long wooden peg in the holes of the gear. That held taut the ropes. The beam could not spring back up from the resistance of the pile of olives. A thud followed. The heavy ropes had pulled down the end of the beam. In turn, it forced the stone press weight at its middle farther down on the pile of olives in the receptacle. As Mêlon relaxed, the two observers clapped as a fresh stream of oil spurted out through a small cutting beneath the stone and into the channels on their way to the jars. "Before Malgis died," Mêlon spoke as he rose back up, "he had brighter ideas still. We were to put this entire business on a high foundation, with three steps up to the floor of our new room. That way we would not have to ladle out the oil from the storage jars. The ducts instead would lead to pipes that would go through the wall. All onto a cart with jars outside. Clever?"

Proxenos frowned. "Perhaps. But you are the smarter one. You work with what you have rather than dream and idle about something you haven't. Why, you can turn out more oil with this beam than four or five of the old-style rollers and hand-pressers in town. Still, your neighbors will gossip. They hiss that you'll have no need of slaves with this machine. Without work, what will slaves do—set up a democracy with Epaminondas and walk as free as us?"

Ainias likewise teased his host. "You are no longer our friend—but instead act like some god who lives here on your Olympos with his henchman Chiôn. First a recluse, then a town-monger, and now what are you, my Proteus?"

Mêlon laughed. "A little of both. At least I know you are not another muster officer here to take us down to battle. Every time some stranger from the flatlands hikes up, one of the Malgidai dies."

"Or goes into song."

"Or rather you mean into Hades."

Ainias turned from the fire, got up, and kicked the press, "We come to say good-bye. Our year after Leuktra here in Thespiai is over. The archons of the city are glad we are finished with their tiny walls—and the townsfolk won't carry the stones any longer. Phrynê bade us hike up here. She never sees you in town as before—and wondered whether you had taken sick with the fever of the highland swamps, or had grown tired of her yapping. Or was it that you thought this toad's big breasts had sagged to near her belly and were no longer worth the hike down?"

"Oh no, it's the olives. Even this short crop proved too much. Now that Chiôn has one arm only, I have to pull the lever as I used to. I must finish before the muster." He ignored the question of Phrynê below in Thespiai, whose breasts hardly sagged and which he, in fact, had never felt. Instead, she had turned foul in his eyes not because of her looks, which never dulled, but because of her slurs and her boasts and her hatred of helots and Epaminondas—and his suspicions that she was plotting against Epaminondas. Besides, she asked only about the missing Gorgos and talked only of Lichas, and seemed to praise Sparta more than Thebes.

"As I meant to say, we are heading south—to killing and to war, before Epaminondas," Ainias offered. "Or at least as far as my lake at Stymphalos and then maybe down to the plain of Mantineia. The archon of the city, Lykomedes, promises to deal with the Spartans there. They are just sorting out Leuktra down there, and eager to get something back of what they lost up here."

"Both of you?" Mêlon was puzzled, especially by the mention of Mantineia, the great killing-field of the Hellenes where the Spartans had once crushed Argos and her democratic friends. "What's a Plataian doing heading across the Isthmos to Mantineia? Are you tired of the low wages of the Boiotians? Has it come to that already—an invasion into the south and in midwinter no less?"

"The whole countryside is not afire just up here. So it is too down there," Proxenos said. "We know it. Hear it. See it. The end of Sparta is near. The men of Mantineia barred entry on the borders to King Agesilaos. He and Lichas are hobbling about the countryside trying to spear enough rural folk to settle them all down. The empire of the Spartans to the south is unraveling as we speak. It is for us to rip it finally apart."

Ainias broke in with his thick Doric, tapping the broad beam of the press. "Proxenos goes south to build cities of my Arkadia—to oversee their rising. To finish two citadels that he has designed. They are not small. Not circuits like Plataia or Thespiai. No—vast and new, at Mantineia, with all the villages of the plains and hills inside. The first is done, or almost. Hellas has seen nothing like it since the days of the Cyclopes that stacked up the stones of Mykenai. He weaves the stones, *emplekton* they are. The walls in turn weave over the ground." The Stymphalian pointed to Proxenos, who on that prompt pulled out of his leather bag a long papyrus roll. He spread it carefully out along the floor of the shed. But first Proxenos scattered straw beneath to keep the oil away. On the map there was a circle with carefully drawn small boxes and lines. A plan of sorts, of a round city of stone, but topped off with mud brick. Proxenos promised that this citadel was to have walls twenty-five stadia in circumference, with more than a hundred towers.

Below it, farther down the roll, Mêlon recognized sketches that looked like the new towers of Thespiai. But they were drawn to such a size that they were more like the ruins of Troy. Or maybe they were the old parts around the Kadmeia of Thebes that the Titans had built. As he looked at these charts of Proxenos, Mêlon scoffed, "These walls of your southern cities look Boiotian. Your corner drafts, and gates and towers, all are like ours. You're building a Thespiai all over again, bigger, and many of them, to my eye—all for the southerners to keep out the Spartans?"

Ainias pointed to the towers. "Why else would he stay here for months in your one-whore town, Mêlon?" Then he looked at Mêlon again. "No, we can finish this new city in Mantineia in months, not years—and then head on for even more."

"More? And finish what else?"

Proxenos ignored him. "For a man so smart you have become so dense. The Peloponnesos is on fire, in open revolt against Sparta now that its hoplites were crushed at Leuktra and Boiotia is filling up with hoplites. Just as Epaminondas knew it would be after the victory. Do you ever think why we are up here at all? Ainias and I are wall-builders—or rather fencers who are encircling Sparta with fortified free cities."

"To keep them in or out?" Mêlon was puzzled since he had only crossed the Isthmos once to fight at Nemea, and even then knew nothing of what was really down south.

"To keep them inside their own land and out of everyone else's. The days of the Spartan kings coming northward up here are over. Leuktra proved that. What happened in Boiotia will eddy into the Peloponnesos. Once more, we will crush the head of the serpent and leave free people to surround Sparta. There will be Leuktras all over the south." He was almost childlike in his ramblings, a real *nêpios*—and sounded suspiciously like Nêto in her zeal. But Proxenos went on still. "We didn't start all this. A free city in new Messenia and a free Mantineia and a free Megalopolis would be the locks that keep Sparta chained—forever."

Ainias broke in, "You see, Arkadians have plans for something even more grand still. They will build a second 'big city,' a *megalê polis* that will rise with walls higher than even those at Mantineia. Proxenos promises me he has drawings on those other newer scrolls wound tight in his pack." Ainias went on. "Mantineia is not more than five days, maybe six with the winter mud and rains, from this farm. We have no fear to get there. The Korinthians let us through at night. We started the tenth course of the city circuit last month. The people are also waiting all the days for news of Epaminondas, waiting for him to lead all these new men into Sparta itself. Mantineia will be the great way station for the armies of Epaminondas before they make the final descent into Sparta itself, the gateway to our new Hellas."

Proxenos interjected. "Mêlon, Mêlon. I don't understand it all myself. We are caught in a divine madness to mount ladders and hammer in the iron clamps. Thousands of free men, maybe fifty thousand and more, are at work south of the Isthmos. They bring their towns into one fortress, a walled circle in the plain, the greatest *synoikêsis* of our age. We are living in the great age of stone. Build a city on a grid and the people will at last think like right angles."

But Mêlon asked the two, "How can you bring your goddess Dêmokratia by force, if men there won't do it themselves as we did? And I doubt most of these bounders outside our walls here are following Epaminondas for democracy."

"Who cares what they think, only that they will march and they will free the unfree. And when has democracy not come from force, and with help from others? At Athens? At Thebes? Please. My friend, name one polis." The shed grew quiet as Proxenos finally calmed. Ainias took a quick glance to see if anyone was about, since the dogs had started up again. It was only Chiôn. He had seen the light and come down with his big knobbed stick in his good hand. He said nothing as he walked in and sat down. The two seemed to have feared his presence and worried that he had been listening outside to their talk of maps. Both ignored the blood that spattered his cloak and was smeared on his stick.

Chiôn murmured, but bolder now as the free man and lord of Helikon that he had become, "Was hunting. Go on. I came here to press. But don't you two waste our time. Not with your big cities and freedom and all that in the south. Just kill the Spartans. Then leave. Build nothing. Put away your maps. Kill the bad before they kill the good. Then go home. If southerners are worth being free, let the Peloponnesians get their *eleutheria* themselves."

Proxenos ignored him and backed out, facing Mêlon. "We are leaving tonight on the big road over the pass of Kithairon and then down to Eleusis. We came to part, not to drag you off again." Ainias interrupted Proxenos. "We have not seen Epaminondas in days. He was up in the north, where good men boast of a great march. For the better souls, the promise of this new attack is to free those from Sparta in the south. For the worse you already see them in the fields drifting in hopes of profit and plunder."

Ainias finished with, "Mêlon, send one of your boys to Thebes with our message to Epaminondas. Tell him as promised we are marking a winter trail for his army with tall stakes with red paint on the tops, all the way to Isthmos—among the friendly towns that set aside food and more when the army comes."

Mêlon turned to his guests. "Be careful as you hike out from Helikon, since there is some man-beast out there that took Dirkê's Thrakians, and maybe Hippias as well, the master who wanted back my Myron. Though at least this forest bear strangely kills the right men." Then he raised his voice in further warning. "Remember as you dream in this shed of cities and battles, the king, the better of the two kings, Agesilaos, is on the acropolis of Sparta. He remembers his dead weak partner Kleombrotos. He stalks. He limps. He knows who killed his favorite Kleonymos. And cut down Deinon. And ended Sphodrias. He plots to tear the work of Proxenos down, of outsmarting the next plans of Ainias. Always the hated Epaminondas must be on his lips—our Epaminondas that he must kill if he himself is to survive. To win a war you must always imagine how your *enemy* thinks to win it." Mêlon went back over to the press before the two left. "Remember the good warnings of Nêto. But enough—farewell and go safely."

"Farewell, hero of Leuktra. You are on the lips of Hellas—and yet sit in the wilds of Helikon, in filth at the press. But not for long, not for long." The two left down the trail with torches that Chiôn had provided. They trampled out heading to the south, despite the warnings of Mêlon and the prophecies of Nêto.

Chiôn looked at Mêlon. "I was a better hoplite than I am a husband—and a better killer than I will be a father. The fury of revenge Elektô flies above my head. She won't let me alone—ever. I saw one of the Kêres as well. The hag was perched up in the high orchard, waiting, waiting."

Mêlon caught the flash in his eye. "You cannot even hold your shield chest high—and you talk of walking to the end of Hellas to kill yet more Spartans and our Gorgos? No, stay here with your son to come and the boys of Lophis to finish the harvest. But I'll take your Xiphos if you will spare him for a few days. Tomorrow I ride to Thebes to learn news of this muster, and when these strangers will leave Thespiai and head south. I have half a mind that our crazy Epaminondas really does plan to march in the winter." Then Mêlon pressed on, "In the meantime, you hike over to the farm of dead Staphis. Learn from his Theanô when or even if Nêto left."

"I saw Theanô this morning," Chiôn sheepishly offered. "She says in two days there will be a word fight, a real *ôthismos logôn*, at Thebes. Bigger than we saw before Leuktra." Then he spoke more softly. "One last thing—did you know that months ago our Nêto left Boiotia? Not long after she left our farm. Gone to that city on the map of Proxenos. That new Mantineia. At least if it's really there. Theanô promised to keep silent about her leave. Now all word of her is lost."

"I feared as much," Mêlon said. He did not add that he had already decided to go southward to find her. "Don't pull so hard, Chiôn, it is a press, not a trireme." Mêlon shuddered as his friend with one hand yanked back ever farther on the lever of the windlass, in worry that either the lever or the stone itself would shatter before the strong arm of his friend gave out.

Chiôn stepped back. He had two long scars from Leuktra on his jaw to match the brand mark on his cheek. His forearms were all torn and creased. His good right arm was malformed from overwork, though stronger than ever from its stacking and terracing. His scars and wounds appeared more a storybook of the Boiotians' fate, both good and bad, past—and future. And now Chiôn pulled harder on the lever still to remind Mêlon that his one arm was stronger than two of most hoplites, and that he could break man or machine as he pleased.

# CHAPTER 17

# On the Road to Thebes

The next day Mêlon put a stouter lever on the machine for the one shattered the evening before. He was careful to tell Myron to keep Chiôn from it. His three grandsons were gleaning the trees for the last remnants of the olive harvest in the upper orchard. At last he made ready to ride over to Thebes—just for a day or so—to learn of the great march to the south. Perhaps if they could get to the south and kill Lichas, then would come real peace? Not likely, since Lichas was symptom of the Spartan malady, not its cause. Mêlon shrugged as he reflected that the iron laws on the farm are the same that govern men. Pride and honor are deathless and deep within the hearts of all men, who always find those to convince them that the taking of what is not theirs seems easy. Those who would stop them are few and weak. Even when Epaminondas freed the Mantineians, these friendly Arkadians would turn on their liberators in new worries that Thebes was too strong, and Sparta too frail. So often do good deeds earn bad ones. So often is magnanimity seen as weakness that earns contempt, rather than appreciation and gratitude.

Once again this moment marked another of Mêlon's great changes in his heart. Indeed, this desire to go to Thebes—and beyond to the south if that were to be the decision of the assembly and if he heard word of Nêto—was his third turn of mind and heart since Leuktra, from the recluse to the new Thespian busybody to now something in between. He worried whether that blow by Lichas had addled his wits and made him wander off the path of wise counsels of *to meson*—the constant, sober way of farming. Still, the worst thing for any man, the new Mêlon figured, was not dying at Leuktra or being spurred to the south in Lakonia with Epaminondas to burn out the nest of the Spartan wasps, but letting weaker others try what he could do far better.

No, he feared most to live idly, like the horse lords of Thespiai—risking nothing, enjoying their wine, bending over their flute girls and slave boys, watching their bellies fatten and their arms shrink as they aged and passed into oblivion, mere shadows of men that were forgotten by their sons. Instead, most good demanded risk; most bad was always without it. He wanted nothing of such a soft peace that wrecks as often as war the cities of men. After having talked with Ainias and Proxenos on their way southward, Mêlon was once again reminded that he could stomach the Pythagoreans and their talk of helot freedom—if they at least acted, and risked their all for some great thing. Mêlon cared not so much for what this great thing Epaminondas planned was in the south, even if it were as wild as freedom for the helots. Although a sort of Pythagorean himself, he had no real philosophical interest in freeing the Messenians—only that it should be great and big and lasting, something on a grand scale that Malgis had once attempted with the farm on the slopes of Helikon. Of course, he would now follow Epaminondas mostly because he wanted vengeance for the death of Lophis and the maiming of Chiôn. And Mêlon was convinced that he somehow alone could bring back—or save—Nêto when others would not. All that urged him to leave the farm a second time and in hopes of going southward to Sparta and to Nêto in Messenia. He would go to Thebes, not to enjoy the city, but only to endure the evil as a means to his end of finding Nêto and settling up with those in the south.

All this Mêlon mused over, as he led Xiphos down the hill to Thebes. He left at midmorning for the ride of eighty stadia. If he pressed, he would be at the hill of the Kadmeia in Thebes not long after noon. But Mêlon did not take the main road to the capital. Instead he went south on a detour for a while on the Thisbê way, the same wagon path he and the two slaves had taken to Leuktra. He didn't like passing on the busy path by the sanctuary of the Kabeirioi anyway—those eerie priestesses who floated about the roadway and sometimes shook down offerings from the lone wayfarers. Shrieking women with masks they were who came out of the brush and pointed their bony fingers in the face of the traveler. He had hit two before and didn't wish to strike a third when time was short. On the main road he used to shout as they came into the middle of the path. "Leave the road, foul harpies. Make way before I put fire to your masks and shrouds and ride you down." They parted, feebly throwing pebbles in his wake, screaming "You will all die with Epaminondas, you who forsake the old gods." No, he would miss the Kabeirioi and gaze instead at holy Leuktra.

After a bit, Mêlon took the next fork and the narrower trail south and eastward to the field of Leuktra. He trotted Xiphos over a low rise, where he could see the battlefield among the rolling hills. There he stopped at the new marble monolith of the Boiotians—planned by Proxenos of Plataia. Scaffolding and a winch stood alongside it. So did piles of pig bones and ash from the masons who had camped out by the battle trophy. The column was almost finished save for the moldings. A bronze statue of Epaminondas was planted on the plinth high above, sculpted by Xenon, the apprentice of Aristides himself.

This was foul country for Mêlon. Lophis must have fallen not far from where Mêlon sat at the base of the *tropê*. Yes, it was near the spot perhaps where the Spartans had first been turned. His body had been dumped not far away at Kreusis, where the road led on down the cliffs to the gulf and the shrine of foul Kallista. Mêlon walked over the ground where he had killed Kleombrotos and picked up relics that had been missed by plunderers well more than a year after the battle. Here was the butt-spike of a broken shaft, Spartan from the look of it. Had it gone into Chiôn, Lophis, or Staphis? Mêlon sat for a bit. He drank some vinegar water, with sharp garlic and white cheese that Damô had packed. Then, feeling sleepy, he lay down near the monument's base and drew his fleece cloak over him for a brief nap out of the winter wind. Closing his eyes, the farmer immediately was on that mountain again, in that now familiar stone cottage. More dreams came of bowls of hot food on the table. But the diners with him were huddling by the wall or in the corner and the soups were foul to the smell. All were ready with raised weapons as shadows came to the door. He never seemed to find out what followed from all that. Then suddenly a voice, one he should know, jeered him.

"*Euia, euia*, there."

A jolt or something loud woke him. But it was a shrill, raspy, and unfamiliar voice in the world of sun, not dreams, "Wake up, sleepy man. We hear you snoring even from here."

Mêlon jumped up at the sound of what he took to be Lichas. He had his hand on his spear, grabbing his sword scabbard with his left hand on his shoulder should he need to throw first and then close with the blade. He would hit the first of them, then stab the second in the hand-to-hand.

But the two figures that approached him could not have been sadder to the eye. They halted as they saw the Thespian hoplite plant his feet for battle. The caller proved to be an older man, far more wrinkled than Mêlon. He hobbled up on a walking stick. He was helped by a young boy. If the elder one had once been broad at the shoulders and showed that in his youth he might have been a stalwart fighter in the first rank, the younger other gave no sign that he ever could do such a thing, so thin he appeared as he neared. And he was a bit audacious as he spoke first: "We found you at last, the hero of Leuktra. You must tell us how the Thebans won here at Leuktra. They say the Stymphalian Ainias fooled the Spartans with his *loksên* attack and left wing and fifty shields and all that. And did Epaminondas really spare the allies of Kleombrotos so that they would join him in the south? Is it true that the Pythagoreans always attack from the left, or was that again the smart work of Ainias, the drill master from Stymphalos? Tell us, please. We are all ears now. But first, how can Epaminondas plan a march this last month when his tenure ends at the first of the year? Is he a renegade? An outlaw? How will he come back in time or does he not fear the noose? Oh, and how many bushels of grain will it take his army to get to Sparta, and how fast do you Hellenes march, and do the Boiotians spear as well as the men of Arkadia? And do . . ."

He would have continued, had not his old master slapped him twice to silence him. "Keep still, my little barbarian, before strangers. Quiet unless you want three welts on your cheek. We have not yet introduced ourselves to our sleeping lord. And down here in the civilized south we do not speak so rudely without a warning first of who we are." Then the old man continued. "Stranger, he tries, this Melissos does. But be careful. As I now warn, and as you just heard, he may not be as dull as he seems; his bad eyes dart about even if his mouth stays shut, and see more than mine or perhaps yours as well." Then the man finally extended his arm, "But my apologies. I am Alkidamas, student of Gorgias, born in Elaia, a man of Asia. I need no introduction to you or to your clan. I hear that you are to stay in Thebes during your trip, which I don't think is as sudden as you thought." He paused, as if he had said too much, but then went on, far more slowly. "I am often a Theban, it seems. Though Athens is now my home, and, as I said, I claim Ionia as my birthplace as you can tell from my speech—so I am an itinerant."

Mêlon was relieved they were not robbers. He found the old man a good sort and was struck by the boy's spirit, even as he kept noticing that the boy's dark arms and legs were like the thin reeds of the lowlands by the Euripos. His long nose was sharp and bony even without much flesh. All that was made even funnier by being stuck between squinting eyes that were not so much crossed as half-closed and bleary. This boy seemed to have suffered from the blurs. That was the curse of Zeus that made men squint with their weak eyes that could see little more than the palm before their face. He had some fuzz on his chin as sign of his age. But it gave no sign that it would ever be any more than that. He didn't look quite Hellene at all. Instead the youth had a darker, barbarian look to him, with low bushy brows, like a northerner, maybe Epiriot or even a Makedonian with the short forehead. Before he replied to this strange boy, Mêlon paused in his approach. For a bit he was thinking how the gods sometimes bedevil men. They put into one Thersites like this, Homer's ugliest man at Troy, all the physical lapses that others abhor. Only with difficulty are these eyesores to be endured if such ugliness can be trumped by cunning, or at least by spirit. The more Mêlon stared at him, the more it seemed that a strong wind off Helikon would have blown this boy into the marshes. His hair was like chaff in the wind, sticking in all directions and not to be combed. How could such a fellow ever amount to a man of any worth? Through audacity? Luck? Cruelty?

The older man Alkidamas had seen Mêlon smile at Melissos. So he now saw an opening and continued nonstop, "As I said, please excuse the boy, you won't see northerners like him here in the south. He is young and not one of us, and knows too much for his own good. But now I will tell you more about him—a barbarian, as you have guessed. Maybe ten and three. Or at least between fourteen and fifteen years, though he claims he knows less about how old he is than we do." The man went on still more, as Mêlon listened to his word-flood dumbfounded. "Our Pammenes got him as a hostage for Thebes to ensure those lying kings of

Makedon up above Tempê keep their oaths about the peace. This boy Melissos is a pledge: If they invade, he dies; if they keep north, then after his year he goes back untouched. They say he is of royal blood. But who knows? Even if he is as important as they think, he still looks more like a Thrakian beggar than a Makedonian royal to me. He has a name I suppose. But I forgot it long ago and so call him Melissos—a honey gift from the general Pammenes to carry my bags, at least for the rest of his year. Those sticks he has for legs and arms, I've also learned, are of solid oak. Stronger than yours, old man, I wager. But then he is not quite what he stutters he is. I'll be sad to give him back when the hostages are returned in the spring. Yes, he says little, watches everything, cares for nothing. I'd say he was a spy, but the blockhead has nothing to spy for. But enough of me. I know you are Mêlon, son of Malgis, of the line of Antander on Helikon, killer of King Kleombrotos. How fine finally to catch you here at the scene of your *aristeia* of last year."

Mêlon at first did not like the sophist in him, and thought, *rhêtôr.* Another wind bladder. He earns his silver by not working. Then he made plans to leave them both, or so he thought. "Old man. I was just leaving this ghost field. I have another half-day or so on the road. I've decided for the rest of the way to lead my Xiphos. The pony has not been off my farm on the hard stone for a year or more. So forgive me for leaving now, but I don't go in with strangers on the road, whether old men or the infernal Kabeirioi."

"No bother at all," the sage cast back with his wide smile as he pointed to Melissos to follow. "We are going your way to Thebes. No doubt Thebes you head for—even by your roundabout way? Your Zeus on Olympos apparently guides us where we should go, since we saw your servant Chiôn this morning in Thespiai, not far from the house of Phrynê. We were going to walk up to your farm until he told us to head you off on this detour." Mêlon had not yet said a word in answer, and the man continued. "I've wanted a word with you for some time. But some such thing always bars my path to your vineyards—whether that cold wind on Helikon or these bony legs that tire from the hike. The battlefield is so much nicer for talking than catching you on the main road to Thebes by those dreadful Kabeirioi that even we Pythagoreans fear. And with all these bounders in the countryside it will be safer for three of us than one."

Mêlon paused and at last said his first word of greeting. "Did my

Chiôn talk to you now? But he—like my Nêto—was freed by decree of the people of Thespiaí, and so can say what he pleases. After Leuktra I have no slaves. But you, our architect of liberation, apparently do? Your boy here has a pack on his back large enough for the two of you."

Melissos backed off out of slapping distance, and then interjected, "His son fell at Leuktra, not far from the Spartan king. Lichas killed him. Where is this Lichas? Will we ever meet him? I have no fear of this man. We in Makedon have no fear of the Spartans."

"Enough, Melissos, before you become too familiar with my right arm." Alkidamas was encouraged by all the free talk, and pointed his finger at Mêlon's chest. "Ignore his babble. Just three days ago we came through the Oropia from Athens. The boy and I sat on the Pnyx beneath Athena's temple. The Athenians sent an embassy that should be in Thebes ahead of us—to stop Epaminondas from marching south any way they can, to save their dear Sparta. Old silver-bags Kallias will come. I know these Athenian folk. Some of them are my pupils. I had better be there with you to counter their lies. I saw windy Platôn himself and his long-hairs as they went out on the Panathenaic Way toward Thebes. In any case, a word-fight will come tomorrow in the assembly of the Boiotians. Remember, Mêlon, that the Athenians are a tired folk. They have no belly to fight Sparta, much less to worry about Persia and Makedonia. They are exhausted from their long war of the past with Sparta, and simply wish to curry favor with whoever they believe is strongest. Athens is a dead city that believes in nothing other than finding the foe of its foe useful. Do not believe they are now a democracy, if they ever were. They are a mob, an ochlocracy that votes themselves free this and free that that they have not earned. As the orators dress up their greed with purple words once again, they seek to shake down their allies abroad to pay for their sloth at home. They damn the Spartans for their helots, but once in the days of empire had far more helots of their own that they called 'allies.' And the beauty of it all is that they still call themselves 'the school of Hellas,' as if wiping out the Melians or the men of Skionê, or trying to enslave the polis of Syracuse, is a fine and noble deed because it was done on a vote of the 'people.' No wonder they drove out the good men like Euripides and Sokrates and welcomed back the bad like Alkibiades."

Mêlon had begun to like this rant, for he hated the Athenians as much as did any Boiotian, and Alkidamas put all that venom in much better speech than he ever could. So, Mêlon thought, at last, here was the great speaker Alkidamas in the flesh. The clever teacher of his Nêto, who had put thoughts enough into her chest for her to leave Helikon altogether. The more he examined the *rhêtôr*, the more Mêlon had no bile at this man. The stranger, by a second look at his hands and shoulders and the wear on his frame, seemed that he'd been behind the ox perhaps, or maybe stood his time in battle as well. When the winter sun hit Alkidamas's worn face at odd angles, Mêlon could see beneath the wrinkles and creases a fighting man of stout nose and broad chin. And best of all, this man of Asia hated both Athenians and Spartans as if he had been born on Helikon.

So as the probing eye had seen, this Alkidamas had once been a grand man of action. That he said nothing to Mêlon about his own high station made their first meeting seem even more remarkable. For indeed this was Alkidamas, the most eloquent of the sophists of Hellas and a man known in Thebes as the student also of Lysis and Philolaios, the inheritor of the rhetorical style of Pythagoras himself, whom the best men at Thebes and Athens asked for advice, the sole philosopher of Hellas who had called for the serfs of Messenia to be freed and all men of Hellas to be judged on their talents rather than their birth. Mêlon was speaking to the greatest persuader in all the city-states, right here on the road to Thebes. Yet he did not quite fathom that this meeting was by design rather than chance, and that it could prove to be of more consequence than it now seemed.

Alkidamas had won a companion for the short journey to Thebes. "Well, can we join you then, Mêlon, on our way back to the main road? We have some things to talk about. Boiotia is a free country for wayfarers. Or so they say of our new democracy of hoplites, so unlike the mob who votes in Athens. The three of us will find the walk quicker with company." Mêlon was surprised by his own new friendliness to strangers, but he seemed to be at home with both. Better to hear news than the snorting of Xiphos. He grabbed the reins and led Xiphos on. The three made their way back onto the road and headed to the hills of high Thebes in the distance. "I know your Nêto as well. She told me much of you, Mêlon. Or I should say much of your doubts. This day I don't find you the legendary *misanthrôpos* at all. But they say after Leuktra you began to revisit the world of men, or rather so Phrynê has told me."

Melissos was squinting and followed the two as they kept talking. Mêlon had slung their packs over the horse and passed the reins to the boy, who was chewing some dried figs in bliss at being relieved of the weight. The three were moving at a brisk walk. The road was quick after they had hiked across some green barley fields on a shortcut back to the main Theban way. They had about fifty or so stadia to go. The winter clouds parted over Parnassos and the sun shone through. For all the good winter weather, Mêlon had at first frowned at mention of Nêto. He had remembered back on Helikon that Nêto had talked of meeting with this great *rhêtôr*. It had pained him, her devotion to a stranger, and a sophist at that. But now that he had met this Alkidamas it no longer quite did, since he seemed a different sort from most of the sophists at Thebes. He certainly was not young nor rich nor handsome, like Proxenos.

Alkidamas turned to his new friend. "Well, Mêlon, master of Nêto who learned much from you before she left us—from the look of your pack and the shield on top, you are preparing for a longer march than today's hike to Thebes."

"Perhaps, but I am ready for robbers all the same, and strange folk who accost me on the road," he replied.

Melissos quickened his pace. With a shrill accent, he broke in, "Oh, no, Mêlon of Helikon. We are not to hurt you, but to learn from you. Or at least my master says we are. We are not robbers at all—we are students, watchers. No one more than I."

His northern speech grated on the ear. Mêlon immediately had been uneasy that the servant with them was a Makedonian. Behind all this Boiotian talk of helots and Sparta and Lichas, he had heard rumblings of far worse tribes to the north. He used to talk with his Gorgos of this Theban folly, this silliness of Epaminondas of fighting Spartans when they were needed to unite to stop the horse-lords from the north who were half-Hellenes at best and wanted to enslave all those to the south of Thermopylai. Yes, the boy was a Makedonian. Still, Mêlon laughed back, "Learn? But I am going to Thebes to listen. Strange people like you come in from the islands and the north. What this is all about, I suspect. For in battle I have sized up this Epaminondas well enough. I have heard his plans for his own *katabasis* to the south."

"If he can march," Alkidamas sighed, "if he can march. For three of the seven Boiotarchs want no part of it, no part of dying outside Boiotia for the freedom of others, especially the helots of Messenia. They cannot see that they are safer when Messenia is freed and Spartans are reduced to being farmers rather than warriors. Boiotians like the foul *rhêtôr* Backwash are not the sort to be taken lightly. I reckon the Athenians may bar the way as well. Who knows what the Korinthians will do at the Isthmos? I can conjure up all sorts of problems that Epaminondas must overcome. So I do my tiny part in trying to ease his burdens. That's why I sought you out today, since your name alone will be worth a muster of one thousand for the way south."

The man continued nonstop in a funny sort of Ionic speech and now and then with high Attic mixed, along with the wayfarer talk of Boiotia. "We will see tomorrow whether a council is held." Alkidamas was turning to Mêlon and shaking his finger in his face. "I don't wish to leave these folk for our boys up here to clean up. Not now when we are so close to finishing the business for good. But I wished to see you for another reason as well, Mêlon—a small one beside the great one of seeing Mêlon, son of Malgis, hero of Leuktra, blessed of prophecy and fate, once more at the side of Epaminondas as he sweeps into Lakonia and on over to Messenia."

Alkidamas then quite surprised Mêlon and stopped for a moment in the road. "You have no slaves now, and that is altogether fine and good that you do not after your servants at Leuktra proved themselves better than the free men of Thespiai. But all that does not change the fact you are old, without hair on your head, and with a stagger in your walk—and in need of a servant to carry your bags, a boy like my Melissos here. For all his wild look, he has an air about him of loyalty and duty and could serve you well. And we will call him a hostage rather than your slave if some think liberators should not own others. You would, of course, give him back in the spring, as we promised the Makedonians."

To convince Mêlon further, Alkidamas finished the story of his own son Kalliphon, who had fallen at Leuktra. "I saw you at Leuktra, Mêlon, as I bore my Kalliphon out. Lichas chopped off his arm. But my Kalliphon was a talker, not a killer. At Leuktra he learned that difference well enough. Lichas and Antikrates cut him down not far from you at the moment the Spartans broke, took his arm right off. So you see we had our own reasons to come to the monument this morning besides the chance of meeting up with you." Alkidamas lifted his voice a little after he had recalled the ordeal of the Boiotians at Leuktra. "I kept Kalliphon in the symposia and schoolhouse. Kept him away from the muster yard. For that, later he paid quite a price. His hands were polished with scrolls, without the blisters of the plow and spear—learning to counter slurs, never iron. This here Melissos, for all his squinty eyes, knows how to wield a spear in his hands, although I coach him how to master *hyperbaton* and *asyndeton*. He is not my flesh. But I want to do him right and make him the man that my son was not, barbarian though he is. I am training him this year to argue some, but to watch more than talk. And if he goes back to Makedon and tells those wild folk that he apprenticed with Mêlon, son of Malgis of Helikon, and was well treated for his work, then all the better will the Makedonians be pleased with the cities of Hellas."

Mêlon answered back, "I raised my son Lophis to plow and prune, but Lichas killed him as well—and my father Malgis, and nearly me twice. So I think, Alkidamas, the problem was not in our sons or in us, but in Lichas, whom few who breathe and walk can kill. As for the education of your Melissos, perhaps let him ape the Sacred Band. They drill, they say, and take kindly to boys in their midst. Though, to be frank, your spindly barbarian Melissos with his bony nose and foreign tongue might not stir up Erôs in those boy-lovers."

"The note of contempt in your voice I share, Mêlon, for such folk. I grant Melissos has not yet a look of a hoplite. He is not the horseman that we expect from such northern tribes. But in the year I've had him, I wanted his muscles to grow behind the plow in a way Kalliphon's did not. You, like me, have no son now, you the far better father than I ever was. Why not a young boy to teach as your own, at least until the next grain harvest comes and these northern hostages go back to Pella? I wager as you watch this sapling grow up—for I can see it myself—you too will grow in a sense."

Mêlon laughed at that prophecy, but warmed even more to this man—a sophist to be sure of smooth talk, but one who, like himself, had already given his only son to Boiotia. But there was something also about this Melissos that gave him a second stare: He had a hard look for all his ugliness and listened more than he should to each word spoken. On occasion the gawky boy blurted out *ti*'s in his half Hellenic: "What's that, what's that? Tell me what that means." Yes, he was a spy of some sort—but for whom and for what, Mêlon could not guess.

Alkidamas with a wink added, "But of course, as I said, he can carry armor as well as haul out olive limbs. Melissos might prove as good a groom to you and make you into something else as you do the same to him."

Mêlon laughed. "My manservant Gorgos is gone. But I don't miss him since there are only vine props in my hands, and I don't need a shield carrier. Your Melissos will learn all that well enough if he works with me high above Thespiai on Helikon—or if the Boiotians decide to march to the south and I join them to find my Nêto in the south. It is already cold and the season of battle is over. The new year is upon us. Orion and the Pleiades and the Hyades have all long ago set and hid from the sky. I doubt anyone will vote to march anywhere in the coming winter. There is not a stalk of wheat in the fields."

"Listen, as I said, you may learn as well, old Mêlon, from young Melissos—though in ways you'd rather not."

Mêlon sensed what Alkidamas meant and now knew not merely that he would take in this Melissos but that something good would come of it as well. For a second Mêlon saw all this in the thistle Melissos, who looked and took in everything and boldly poked his nose into the talk of his masters—this young weed in the field that might just keep growing despite the Spartan scythes to come in the days ahead. He was sharp, as thistles sometimes are. Sometimes the young, the ugly, the outsider— they can see through the smoke and dust far better than those who make it, and so teach their would-be teacher the lessons that the masters had mouthed but forgotten. Besides, even if the army stayed home Mêlon would go on alone and be entering enemy ground soon, in search of his Nêto and without his Chiôn, and so he could not be choosy in his helpers.

Meanwhile Melissos fell about a stade behind the two, looking at the terrain of Boiotia as if he were forty and a general on a horse, scouting a camp outside Thebes for his army of thousands. After the two ahead ceased speaking, Melissos caught up, muttering that the Thebans' walls did not look so high after all.

The great polis was now before them. At last, all of them quieted as they turned the final corner of the rising road. They passed through the gate of Kadmos and entered the seven-gated city of Oidipous and the heroes of legend.

# CHAPTER 18

# The Great Debate

The three had taken most of a day of steady walking to reach the high ground of the Kadmeia from the monument at Leuktra. The Thespian had been to Thebes only once before, in the year of the twin musters before the battles at Nemea and Koroneia. But that was more than twenty seasons prior. Mêlon now was bewildered by the unfamiliar sights in the capital of the Boiotians. The Thebans, with the sales from the spoils of Leuktra, were rebuilding the great temple of Apollo Ismenios. Twelve new columns rose along the temple's long side. Forty men, with scaffolds and block and tackle, levered a huge marble capital on the nearest, a scroll of the Ionian type. This was the great gated city of Kadmos and Oidipous and Kreon, now to be remade as the democratic capital of a new Theban hegemony of equal poleis. Mêlon stared like a country ephebe at the seven arches and hills, as the travelers went over the bridge and through the Onkan Gate and on past the walls.

They made their way to a hut that Alkidamas owned near the Borean Gate. There they spread out three cots. Melissos led Xiphos down to the public stalls on the nearby hill of Ampheion, then went quickly back to join the two in this hovel near the tomb of Herakles. The place was more a sty than a house. It was not long until early dusk. The room was already cold and damp and offered little shelter from the winter sleet that was pelting the city. Shouts rose amid the storm. Outside the shuttered window, Thebes was in a frenzy. Strange-sounding foreigners from all over Hellas were yelling and scuffling in their drink. What had Epaminondas wrought? Thousands of hoplites were sleeping in the cold sheds and icy stalls of the agora. More were perched on the turrets and walkways on the city walls. How many were camped beyond the walls all the way to the coast? All boasted they were ready to march against the men of Sparta in midwinter for plunder. As Mêlon fell into sleep, he could almost hear the voices in the assembly.

Mêlon guessed that the Boiotians had no stomach for any more war, despite the cutthroats who were flocking into Boiotia and the muster in progress, and despite the victory at Leuktra. At the debate tomorrow, there would be more of the same rabble-rousing as there had been the previous year on the eve of Leuktra—the usual shouting mess of democracy. That was both the beauty and horror of *dêmokratia*: No one gave the wealthy or sober or educated his due, but the crowd in a moment could judge what seemed best to most of them and then act on it without pause, even if a scoundrel had proposed the measure. Did Epaminondas hate Sparta and wish it gone? Or was he a more practical sort who wanted to ring in Lakonia, surround the Spartans with the walled cities of Arkadia and Messenia? How better to cut off the murderous lords of Sparta from their helot servants? Isn't that what the new cities of Proxenos were for?

Of course, if he marched in winter, he might spare his men the heat of the hard summer in the month of Panamos. It was smart, too, to leave right at the end of his tenure. That way the Boiotian high-talkers could not call the army back. And Epaminondas surely knew that should he not preempt now, King Agesilaos next spring would come northward back into Boiotia anyway, as he had so many times before, and make the Boiotians once again the subjects of Sparta. Then again, it was possible that the wild stories of Nêto and Lophis—and Damô's warnings—were all true: that this Pythagorean Epaminondas really did believe in a wild idea of the "freedom of the Hellenes"; that he wished all of Messenia to be liberated, the very idea of helots—or even slaves as well—to be a thing of the past, for the security of Boiotia and the justice of Hellas and the salvation of their souls.

The hovel was not far from the assembly on the Kadmeia. The next morning Mêlon got up before the snoring Alkidamas and went on ahead to beat the crowd to the assembly hall. But on his way to the *ekklêsia*, a tall, broad-shouldered stranger greeted Mêlon in the street, a stadium from the assembly seats below. He was somewhere past his fifth decade, with a gray beard, a strange stiff one that tapered into a cone, and he addressed Mêlon in a High Attic that the farmer could scarcely follow. An Athenian no less, he was followed by four ephebes, no more than twenty years each, rich ones, with rabbit-fur collars, bright green wool cloaks, and hob-nailed tall boots, and soft faces with eyes darting side to side. They had all come over the pass with their master to warn the Boiotians of the idiocy of Epaminondas.

"A waste of time, that assembly of yours." The stranger laughed as if he knew Mêlon well and could start in with him in mid-sentence. He now stopped and pointed his finger. "I came north to learn of these Py-thagoreans, to see whether their *logos* would set them apart from the mob. But from my talks with these Epaminondians, as I call them, Pythagoras has only made them worse. Imagine: our One God of numbers and good Pythagoras twisted up here to serve the Boiotian rabble. Enough, enough of them all. I am on my way home. Why wait for the assembly, when not one of these Theban rustics would even be allowed on the *bêma* at Sparta?"

Mêlon laughed. He had a sense of who this odd squeak-voiced fellow was. "You're going to miss a good speech from General Epaminondas, who will rip and chew your Athenians to pieces."

Now this fellow closed in and put his finger on the nose of Mêlon. "Most know me as broad shoulders, Platôn as they call me at Athens. I have no stomach to see the big fight between my Athenians and your Al-kidamas. This is what it is all about anyway, isn't it—a war of the philos-ophers, as each plots to get the farmers to march for his idea of a new Hellas? None of that for me." So this Platôn railed. "Far better to get back over the pass at Kithairon anyway and to civilization at Athens again, before these cutthroats in the hills sidetrack an Athenian. Stranger, your *ochlos* up here is as bad as ours. Your cobblers and tanners are doing to your good Pythagoreans what ours once did to our Sokrates. That Epaminondas of yours, he demagogues to march southward and destroy a great polis—a city of heroes, one far greater than any of the Hellenes, yours and mine included."

Then he stopped and looked down on Mêlon, for Platôn was taller and broader than most, for all his scroll reading. "Be careful what you tear down, hero of Leuktra, when you would promote the helots and such rabble. You think that you are torching the limp-wristed aristocrats at Athens or maybe the Spartan lords, with their scarlet cloaks and oiled locks. But you are not doing just that. Turn Hellas upside down, and you scatter to the winds all the good that oligarchy ensures—from the table manners of the refined who don't soil their hands as they eat their greasy pork, to the *Orestia* of our dear Aeschylus or the hymns of Dorian Alkman—all that is the cultivation of refinement that the poor have no taste for. Do not imagine your Epaminondas can make the potter in the Kerameikos the equal to the sculptor of the Panathenaic stones on our temple to Athena Parthenos, or that there are thousands of singing Hesiods plodding behind the plows, their geniuses undiscovered only because there is not enough democracy for them."

Mêlon was no philosopher, but he had these worries as well, and so wanted no word-fight with Platôn of Athens. "Farewell, Athenian. We mean you no evil, none at all—unless of course you block the passes on the way south."

Platôn laughed at that and muttered as he left, "Oh, they all say that as the tanners and tile-makers take over the assemblies and kill their betters. Pray for some elite guardians to guide you. Put the no-goods to work stacking stones, or mixing clay, anything but letting them loose to vote in an assembly against their betters. The Spartans do us a favor—those good guardians who watch over the helot animals below the Isthmos. So just remember, Thespian, that Platôn, son of Aristôn, an Athenian, and lover of wisdom like his master Sokrates, warns you about turning the Peloponnesos upside down and making the bad good, and the good bad. I hope I'm not here to see the mess that will follow from your march southward."

With this, the philosopher Platôn turned toward the southern gate and the road to Athens shouting without looking back. "Mêlon, son of Malgis," he called out, "guardians of *hoi polloi* you need. Laws in stone. *Phulakes* and *Nomoi*." Then he and his attendants were gone around the corner.

Mêlon soon arrived at the assembly and elbowed his way to the front. The meeting was already filling. Guards were roping off hundreds of attendants, those milling about, eager for a silver coin in pay to attend the voting. Epaminondas had heard of Mêlon's coming. So his men now, just as on the night before Leuktra, escorted the Thespian through the mob to the front row of the stone theater, open and cold under the gray, wet winter sky.

Pelopidas, wearing his shiny breastplate and flanked by the officers of the Sacred Band, spoke first. Despite his pride, he proved sober in advice, without ever raising his voice. Indeed he talked in near whispers in a deep Boiotian manner, on the cue of Alkidamas, quieting the roar with his hands upraised. His men went among the front rows and smacked down the hecklers. Pelopidas then gave the delegates of the Confederation the story of the events since Leuktra. The mob stopped for a moment throwing crusts and pine cones. Most in the crowd grew still to hear of the long work of Epaminondas to the north in Lokris and Thessaly that had brought allies down into Boiotia on promises of pay and plunder to the south at Sparta. Pelopidas warned—and his voice grew a bit louder—that King Agesilaos had sent his Spartans into the new city of Mantineia. The lame king wanted to stop the fortifications of the Arkadians, who wished to live in grand cities of stone rather than be terrorized and picked off one by one in their many hamlets by the marauding Spartans.

"We, the victors of Leuktra," Pelopidas then continued, "are worrying whether we can march a mere five days to protect the new polis of Mantineia. Meanwhile, the king of the defeated, why, the aged Agesilaos himself, marches as we speak, wherever he pleases. Winners of Leuktra cower—while losers boast." Pelopidas had other news of the south as well. The same zeal for this new democracy at Mantineia had spread also in other Arkadian towns. The friends of Ainias had sent word that there was already a friendly rivalry in the south between Mantineia and the western Arkadians laying the stones of an even bigger city, the *Megalê Polis*—sixty, maybe seventy stadia to the west in hills along the river Helisson. They were to be the twin pillars of a free Arkadia. "They ask," Pelopidas reported of the leaders of the new democratic Confederation, "only that we join them to keep the Spartan thieves busy until they raise their walls head-high to keep them out." But grumbles followed him from the crowd. There was already snow on Parnassos. The Megarid was muddy. No crops in the field anywhere along the route. How were they to get through the Athenian guards at the Isthmos? How were they to eat?

Pelopidas waved down the hissing and batted away some hard dried apricots—the mob was unruly, just as Platôn had warned. He was soon reminding his audience that there were already ten thousand foreigners, a myriad of *xenoi*, outside their gates. Another seven thousand Boiotians would march if the *dêmos* so voted. All could be ready in a day, maybe two, to break camp. They'd be back home in twenty-five days—with a good ten or fifteen days to crush the Spartans and break their power in Lakonia. If they quit throwing their food at him, the Boiotians would have enough road rations for five days. Pelopidas reminded them that winter granaries near Megara were already secured for the army. Who knew how many friendly Peloponnesians would join in, once they saw a proud horde of twenty thousand marching across the Isthmos to Sparta?

The Boiotian crowd finally calmed, eager to learn whether there was money or fame to be had in all this. Pelopidas raised his voice and provided newer bits that left most stunned: "Yesterday, ambassadors from Elis arrived from the south. These are the oak men, with roots in stone from the coastal villages around Olympia, and they have an offer. Should we Boiotians muster to help Mantineia, should we lift the Spartan boot off their own necks, then they pledge us ten talents—sixty thousand drachmas—or enough to pay the army of the Boiotians for ten days of campaigning. The sacks of silver are under guard on the Kadmeia as I speak."

"This coin," Pelopidas finished, as he pointed to the temples and lowered his arms once again to calm the noise, "is in addition to what our Mantineian and Arkadian friends have promised. Of course it comes on top of our funds that the council last summer had allotted. Who will object when war is right—and profitable? I say nothing about the booty. But no one has plundered Lakonia in twenty generations, and it is ripe for the picking." The crowd roared its readiness to march. They were drowning out the few gossips and whinings of the knights and rich long-hairs, who were saying that Pelopidas had no intention of marching five days down and five days back and then staying a mere twenty in the Peloponnesos. It sounded instead to these few rich men as if the army of the Boiotians would not be back until threshing time the next year. Still, the general of the Sacred Band strutted off the *bêma* to wide applause—such an astute diplomat, this Pelopidas, to have managed to grab ten talents from the wily Eleans for the farmers of Boiotia.

As Alkidamas had warned, the Athenian visitors were present in force. Perhaps twenty or so in their delegation had come over Kithairon two days earlier, in their long cloaks and costly leather boots, even if their Platôn in disgust had gone home to Athens. Mêlon noticed that the allies were all sitting by a stone column of the arch that led into the theater.

Now and then they hid or came out in full view, depending on how they judged the pulse of the mob. The Athenians had already spent a day working the symposia and gymnasia among the Theban rich soft-hands, lobbying for neutrality.

A few of the older ones were murmuring now, following the words of Pelopidas and perhaps worried that the crowd was beginning to eye them and mutter its threats. No wonder Platôn had left before all this started— just as he had once conveniently said he was sick during Sokrates's trial, and then disappeared after his teacher's death. The smiling Athenian general Iphikrates, no friend to the Thebans, came out from behind the column wearing his breastplate. He paraded in with his guard of light-armed skirmishers and *peltast*, javelin men. Iphikrates was clean-shaven and was as bald on top as his face was hairless. A wrinkled vulture with his long chin and beak nose, he began squawking as if he'd found his dinner in some half-eaten rotting carcass on the byway. Iphikrates yelled out to the crowd, "*Siga. Sigate.* Let our Kallistratos speak; it is his right as a guest. He'll set right the lies of your Pelopidas. Listen to your friends from Athens. Give us our due as guest-friends. We are envoys—protected by the *nomima* of the Hellenes."

Alkidamas was sitting behind Mêlon. He leaned forward to whisper in his ear as he identified the Athenian strangers. "There is Kallias. With the bun of hair tied on top, the money chest next to Iphikrates. He has more coins in his mouth than even you do in your strongbox." Alkidamas went on. "Kallistratos is a follower of Isokrates. He loves the Spartans dearly. His name may imply "a fine army," but he is a weaver of intrigue, not a fighter. Even at Athens these two know more about us and our Epaminondas than we do ourselves—thanks to the nighttime visits north and south by Phrynê and her agents, that spy whom you dub Sphêx. Even I have not fleshed out all her plots, both with Lichas and with the Korinthians who so often bar the Isthmos."

It was just this Kallistratos who finally mounted the *bêma*. He began the Athenian attack. "Men of Boiotia and friends of Athens. What is all this fiery air that this lackey of Pythagoras has breathed into this hallowed assembly of yours?" With that start, he bore down on the friends of Epaminondas in the front row in their broad-rimmed leather hats. "Do you have the noble dragons of old on your Kadmeia? If so, who let in this serpent Pelopidas who for no reason would scorch Hellas with his sparks and embers of hate, trading in peace for hateful war?" Kallistratos was pointing back at Pelopidas and Epaminondas. "Bloody Ares has left us. Peace with all her gifts is at hand. Yes, beautiful Eirênê has flown in; peace sits atop us all. Yet these men alone spurn her soft, feathered wings and downy breast, and instead yearn for the black-taloned Kêres, whose beaks drip with the meat of corpses rotting in our fields. By the gods, man, at least give this peace a moment. You Boiotians, the summer before last, won a great victory. All Hellas acknowledges the achievement of Leuktra. This turnabout was not unwelcome in my own city of Athens. But do not spoil the triumph with greed. Why would you drop the firm shiny apple in your hand by now grasping for the rotting one on the limb so far above your reach?"

Jeers followed from the crowd with a hail of flying nuts and raisins. Nonetheless, the Athenian pressed on, still striving to undo the work of Pelopidas. "We men of Athens have no love for the Spartan. Indeed, for thirty years we fought him." Kallistratos spoke carefully now. "Then your own grandfathers were not so friendly and indeed as enemies were heartened by our grief. Thebans, not Spartans, stripped our houses on the border. Thebans sent men to Sikily to spear our Athenian sons. Thebans clamored to tear down Athena's city when Lysander sailed into the Piraeus in his pride. All this we paid you back not with invasion. No, we gave safe haven for your radical exiles—when the Spartan occupiers then turned their attention to you and sat atop the Kadmeia right over there."

Kallistratos once again lowered his voice, and he extended his arms with his palms open to the audience, now and then grabbing the folds of his outer cloak. It was easy for the crowd to say they hated Athenians, but more difficult to jeer at such mellifluous Attic speakers who sounded far better than their own, and were offering peace rather than war. A few Thebans now rose and cheered him on. "He makes more sense than our own warmongers. Give him more time, tell us more."

In response, Kallistratos now threw out his enormous belly. He cared little that he was already bathed in sweat in midwinter. He wanted these enraptured Boiotian pigs to see just how rich was his table, and how much high-priced food from Attika went into his gut that alone could fuel such deep cadences. "There are many faces in this crowd—not the least this tame Pelopidas himself—that I recognize from their sanctuary in Athens. We the men of Athens once took them in, all so hungry and all on the run. Then no one else would—we did so at great danger to ourselves from our newfound Spartan friends. But these renegades would turn their flames on their benefactors by scorching friend and enemy alike. Gratitude and—magnanimity—*xenia*, I would have thought, are attributes not lightly thrown away by the Hellenes."

To scattered applause, Kallistratos now frowned and took on a melancholy tone. "We Athenians are magnanimous folk. From the time of Theseus the men of Athens have come to the aid of you Thebans. Learn from us. War, after all, has proven a great leveler. We have had our fall. So has Sparta its own *ptôsis*. Beware that you of Boiotia do not trip up as well." Slowly the sadness began to leave Kallistratos, and then with an increasingly contorted look, as if he had a bone in his throat, or had a stinky tooth, he began to raise his voice a notch. "We should patch our tears, and pull up over our heads our shared stitched Hellenic cloak to fend off the harsh wind from Persia. A new order has emerged after the war: No one city of Hellas, in this balanced world, dictates to another. My Theban friends, stay within your borders. Do not put the democracy at Athens in the unenviable position of having to censure its cousins across the mountain." Kallistratos felt the crowd hush. Only one Theban, no more, yelled out, "When did Athens ever stay within its borders—or is our Delion in your Attika now?"

Kallistratos ignored him, but began to worry that the fickle farmers five rows back were tiring of his Athenian oration, as they groaned, then clapped, then hissed, then laughed, depending on the skill of his performance. "Now I address men of substance and prudence and dispense with you of the mob. My dear Boiotarchs, men of moderation and sobriety, ponder this wise counsel and put off action until after the new year. Then once more when the weather warms and the buds break can we bring matters to the council of all the Hellenes in peace, without the disruption of firebrands who as infants soil their diapers and crawl out of councils when they do not get their way." At the end, Kallistratos's voice had once again turned soft, as soft as Pelopidas's, but by far the more polished. Had he not been an Athenian, the Boiotians would have perhaps preferred his mellifluous speech to that of any of their own. As Kallistratos began to slowly walk away, he stopped in the aisle amid the shouting. "A final warning. You are not talking of war thrust on you, as happened on that dark day of Leuktra when a red-caped king crossed your borders."

He pointed his finger at the front row where sat the long-haired estate owners who owned the horses of Boiotia. "No, lordly men of Boiotia, you are pondering a war of choice. This is a preemptive act. Why an optional war? Why lose the goodwill of the victim to earn the antipathy of the aggressor?"

Kallistratos went on even louder, eager to win back the crowd. "Epaminondas will just say he wants to go to Arkadia. When he gets there, he will just say he wishes to go on to Sparta. Then once there, that he wishes yet again just to cross Taygetos into Messenia—and there he gets killed any still alive. We supported your first good war at Leuktra. But not this second, unprovoked, bad war against the Spartans, this we cannot stomach. Preemption and unilateral aggression—these provocations are not in our Athenian natures."

The assembly grew silent at that, after having laughed at his girth and been entranced by his oratory. Now they were simply confused by his warning that they might die in an unnecessary war that would have no end. Mêlon, however, saw that the real message, the only constant, from this rogue was whatever the men of Thebes did, the Athenians were against. The former was a young, a fresh democracy of farmers, the latter an old democracy of the jobless and those who looked to the dole. The one was as confident as the other was fearful. Perhaps what wily Kallistratos really had meant to say—or so Mêlon barked to Alkidamas above the shouting—was that Sparta once in the great war had beaten Athens badly. Now Athens feared that Thebes might do the same to Sparta. After all, it would be a bitter blow indeed to Athens, the self-proclaimed school of Hellas, if Epaminondas could do to Sparta in a single season what Athens had not been able to in twenty-seven.

# CHAPTER 19

# No Man a Slave

S uddenly there was a commotion as a Boiotian loudmouth stood up in the crowd and demanded his say. It was Menekleidas of Aulis again, old Backwash, who had tried to stop the fight the night before Leuktra. After the battle he had appeared on the battlefield, amid the wreckage and corpses, covered with his rubbed-on blood and screaming in pain, he said, from a blow by Lichas himself. How he had been nicked in the fiftieth row from the front, no one quite knew. But that had been more than a year ago, and in the interim Backwash had repeated so often the lie that Leuktra had been his plan all along that the wearied listeners came to half-believe it—and his false wound as well.

He did not believe that Epaminondas could take an army into the vale of Lakonia in midwinter—and moreover the Athenians had given him five pouches of silver to say so. He was as firmly set against fighting now as he had been in the tents of the generals on the eve of Leuktra. Quickly Backwash brawled his way through the crowd in the assembly, turning his head from Mêlon when he got to the front, already chanting "*Eirênê, eirênê*—peace" before he had even reached the dais. Backwash announced that it was past time for a real Boiotian to speak. Yes—a real Boiotian like himself, one born in the black cow-soil nearby, a man of the people to address his own people. Mêlon remembered why a year and more ago he had kicked the scoundrel into the trash heap outside the tent of the generals. But now there was no Chiôn to be seen, nor a man quick to temper like Philliadas of Tanagra. So Backwash felt safe amid the mob with Athenian mercenaries on his flanks. He ran back and forth at the *bêma* like a wobbly, webfooted drake who has just lost his head to the butcher.

Despite his smell and his pear-shaped bald head and jowls, Menekleidas was well liked by the Theban town-dwellers to whom he helped spread the obol dole. Now he sought to take up the hammer of his Athenian paymaster Kallistratos and pound down Pelopidas's peg a bit farther. After Leuktra, the farmers of Aulis had driven Backwash out to Thebes, for they knew his lies and had tired of his tongue. He left his toll taking and took up his kiln work full time. His clothes were usually stained with clay, for this Backwash spun pots in the agora, when the law courts were slow and few paid for his arguments. But he had turned his cloak inside out and felt he was as lordly looking as any horse-owner.

"As a spear-wounded veteran of Holy Leuktra, let me speak not of what is right—for who knows what's right in a difficult matter such as this? Is not 'right' anyway a relative thing, and always dressed up as the 'good' by the man with the heaviest fist? So instead, let us of the poorer kind ponder what is expedient for all of Boiotia." He pointed over to Pelopidas, and he began to shake his body and twist his head in agitation. "Did you listen, men of Boiotia, fellow veterans of the hard fight at Leuktra, to your own Pelopidas—to his appalling madness that will engulf us all and take our sons from the vineyards so that they can rot in the mud of Sparta? For that is where this Arkadian gambit will end up." None challenged him, so Backwash went on. "Look—men are in armor outside our walls, before our vote. They put a dagger to our throat and then ask if we dare sheath it. Consider the logic of it all. Does this Pelopidas or Epaminondas, does either have a son in the front ranks among the *prostatai*? Or do they instead talk of war but send your kin to the sound of Spartan pipes, like they did to us at Leuktra? Is not this childless drone, like his master Epaminondas, always buzzing about wars for the children of others to fight in?" He hurried now, just as if he were spinning out a smooth calyx or hydra for his clay kiln.

"What business do our folk have in Arkadia, in Sparta, and in Messenia on the slopes of Mt. Ithômê, in shadowy cold Messenia, far after the Pleiades have set? That's just where such an expedition of these mad Pythagoreans will all too soon end up, mark my words—with our red blood on their white snow." He paused again, and was ready to duck. But when no fruit was thrown, he continued. "I have heard that the Peloponnesians wish to have walls; fine, let them build walls. So the Messenians wish for their freedom; fine, let them earn it as we did at Leuktra. I have heard hoplites are needed to surround the Spartan acropolis; fine. But let Pelopidas and his Sacred Band—not us hoplites of Boiotia—leave tonight." Then his face twitched more and he became louder: "Let us spend money on Boiotians, not helots. We could have a new drain to the agora, some plaster for the columns of the Herakleion, or an extra obol for the dole, for the price of a day fighting down there."

A few shouted in unison, "No, to war! No to money for the helots! Yes, yes, yes to peace. Stay home. Spend our coins on ourselves. Keep spinning, pothead." The argument that neither a free Messenia nor a defeated Sparta was worth one more dead Boiotian was good Nemean red wine for many in the crowd, who had already had enough of someone else's glorious war. That there was a free council of the Boiotians without a Spartan guard on the acropolis—and thanks only to Epaminondas—was forgotten by all.

"The truth," Backwash said, finally slowing down and walking in tighter circles, "is that Messenians, our so-called allies, are by nature servile folk—every one of those helots fitted for their proper task as serfs to their betters." He was pointing to the Boiotians in the first row and speaking in the drawl of the Euripos, accented with lisps and nasal drones. "By the gods, the helots are a rural and backward race of tribes and sects who quarrel and kill like savages. They are no better than Homer's wild Cyclopes."

"Few of them can read letters. Fewer still know anything of mastery of the sea or the polis. Do they know of anything other than tilling for Sparta in their black soil of the Peloponnesians? They don't even have their own language or race. Any other people would long ago have built cities and harbors and at least a trireme or two. So let us stay put and far away from such folk. Let us, the heroes of Leuktra, start finishing our own walls in our own cities, and rebuilding our ties with Athens whose friendship Kallistratos here has so ably outlined." Kallistratos stood up and waved to the crowd. But Menekleidas ignored him and went on, not about to let even his benefactor cloud his moment. He was laughing, and chuckling at his own jest. "As I warned all of us on the night before Leuktra, is Ainias the killer not that fair-weather crane from the shoreline of Stymphalos? Has he not flown back home, cawing and cackling, when his feathers were ruffled that he could not muster our folk to do his own dirty business down south? No, men of Boiotia, let us accept the world as it is—not as we dream it might be. Enough of this mad democracy-spreading."

Mêlon shrugged. He had come to Thebes to learn what the army of the Boiotians would do. Maybe he would get a word about his Nêto to guide him when he went south to find her soon. But as he heard more slurs from such folk, it had the unintended effect of making Epaminondas, for all his talk of freeing helots a thousand stadia away, only wiser in his own eyes—especially as he contrasted these sophists and windbags with the quiet general facing down Lichas in those moments on the left at Leuktra.

Backwash turned to end his case against the march south. He leaned against the *bêma* and took the corner of his cloak to wipe sweat from his dry forehead. "Then there is our acquaintance, the ghost of Pythagor—aaaas, who, it seems, is floating always right above this madness. Why all these strange -*as* names. I am sick of -*as* this, -*as* that—these plotters like Pelopid*aaas*, Epaminond*aaas*, Alkidam*aaas*. Yes, this new *Pythagoreaaas* cabal who have taken over our democracy. They taught not merely the secrets of triangles and the patterns of numbers, but apparently, in between their frolicking with our women, they schemed to take good men from Boiotia and get them killed for the nonsense of Messenian freedom."

Backwash was using his hands to bring on the hoots, working his fingers, even, almost as if he were at the wheel turning out a grand wine bowl to be painted with red-figured dancers around its base. "So let us next spring find it to our advantage to march when the grain is in ear and food on the march is aplenty. Let us wait until there are strong walls and proven allies to cover our retreat. We should cultivate our alliance at home in soft familiar ground rather than in vain break our plows over barren and rocky soil abroad." While no one was ready to abandon entirely Epaminondas's notion of invading Sparta—given their prior sanction for a winter muster—the rough sanding done by Kallistratos was now polished fine by this Menekleidas.

Still, there was always that hope and doom of democracy—what the majority wanted, anytime, about anything, they got in a moment's notice. The mob cared little for the yoke of the law or the time-wasting of the overseers in the council or the shame of turning a previous day's vote upside down. Old Herodotus had it right: It is easier to get thousands of hotheads in a democracy to muster than to win over a few stern-faced oligarchs. So Mêlon looked over and watched a grim Epaminondas in his armor and tattered cape slowly stand up, smile, and carefully make his way onto the *bêma*. As the general passed, Mêlon saw him slap Backwash on his temple, "*Phugete, phugete.* Foul mouth of the channel, flee, before you get a fist as well. Get back to your clay."

The small Theban began in a slow style and without anger for the hostile crowd he addressed—since he knew that outside the walls was an army mustering far larger. "Men of Boiotia. These two who have spoken to you can always give a hundred reasons not to act. But never a single reason for taking action." Epaminondas pointed over to the Athenians and Backwash. "Wait, stop, relax, ponder, consider. What is new about all this throat-clearing and back-stepping? Are you really to be persuaded by a channel bottom-feeder named Backwash? You know all this is only the coddling of Sparta. The man who bows and does the Persian kow-tow, the ground-kisser, always dresses up his cowardice and unconcern for others—in appeals either to collective self-interest or to neutrality."

Epaminondas went on with a voice louder than any before. "You all have forgotten the battle of Koroneia. You know nothing of Tegyra. Even Leuktra of year last is as old as Troy." He was pointing his finger at Menekleidas and Kallistratos and the others. "These bought sycophants up here are the foul carrion of hindsight. Their beaks always try to peck away the great deed of Leuktra. No one seems to remember the ancient rule: The more the Spartan army has marched into Boiotia, the more the next year it comes back into Boiotia. Lichas and his sons crow that their dead are always buried in someone else's earth."

The general then abruptly grew restless as he reached the end of his address, as animated now as he had been lackadaisical when he began. "As for the sluts, I plead guilty to all the charges brought by Kallistratos. Yes, forty thousand more Arkadians are waiting for us. More in the new cities of Mantineia and Megalopolis that rise. Yes, we will finish their walls in the south. Yes, in the middle of winter we will enter Lakonia. There are twenty thousand of us ready tonight to march out of this city. Look out below. If all this is a conspiracy, then I plead guilty for wishing it and I will bleed for it." Epaminondas had no ability to out-talk either Kallistratos or Menekleidas. The man in the weatherbeaten thin cloak with his cracked and broken helmet pushed back on his head was appealing not to the heads but the spirits of what he hoped were his unbroken Boiotians.

His shield and spear lay at his feet, and he was pointing with his dagger. "The Boiotarchs and the *Boulê* already voted for a muster days ago. So I went north and did just that—signed up thousands as you can see from the sea of tents below here. Your coffers are full of silver from allies. The army of our coalition, Phokians, Euboians, exiles from the south, and Lokrians—you know them all—is outside our walls. Eleans and Arkadians wait on us in the south. They are ready to cut the head off the Spartan snake. Unlike us, they care little that it is cold and wet. Those without freedom don't worry whether the season for campaigning is over. Their eyes instead are on the Spartan acropolis alone. They want to share in the freedom you have—what you shrug at as your tired birthright."

The Boiotians were murmuring that the angry general seemed like the beggar Odysseus about to throw off his rags and take revenge against the suitors. Indeed just then Epaminondas took off his helmet and began waving it around with his left hand. "Our purpose, you ask? Why, it is to help the men of Mantineia and that means kill Spartans, of course. The more the better until there are no more—or for their part they kill us all. Some talk grandly of war. But war, my Boiotians, is killing all of the enemy who need killing—and there remain thousands in Sparta who do need killing."

The tiny general then paused. "I swear a great oath to you, men of Boiotia. The Boiotians will march out tomorrow following this vote today to give me command. But I care little whether it is the month of winter Boukatios or summer Hippodromios. Or whether I have thirty days or three hundred days left of my tenure. No, we march at dawn. We will cross the Isthmos. Then if the One God wills it, we keep safe the Mantineians and then go over the pass with the Argives to the heart of Lakedaimon. We Boiotians will hit the Spartans in their own courtyard, the first foreigners to take arms into Lakonia in five hundred seasons."

Some, maybe half of the Boiotians of the assembly, were beginning to stand and clap in approbation. Epaminondas jumped down from the

*bêma* and walked out. Just then he caught the eye of the Athenian delegation. Then he made a sudden detour in their direction at the front column. The Theban stood not more than a cubit from their noses and stuck
his blade in their faces for the Boiotarchs to see. At least he was not clubbing them with his helmet. "As for this Kallistratos and his Athenians
here, listen well, Boiotians—especially this Iphikrates that I am nose-to-
nose with and his Athenian thugs. At sunrise, I take this army out over
Kithairon. On the next day right across your border over Kithairon to
Megara." With that, far more of the crowd was on its feet, hooting and
clapping, as they strained their necks to see the hapless Athenians—for
they knew their Epaminondas was at times a sort of brute himself, who
would beat a man in assembly as easy as salute him. "Join me, fight me,
ignore me—that is yours to decide. But should I see a single Athenian
hoplite barring the border pass on high Skourta tomorrow, this army of
free Hellenes will first turn south to Athens. We will climb up your
Acropolis and march right through your white marble Propylaia, Perikles's
unfinished gateway to your city of Athena. We, the pigs of Boiotia, will
tear it down, block by block, and cart it back in our wagons back over to
Thebes."

Epaminondas's voice rang out above the crowd. "We will rebuild the
Athenian marble on our own Kadmeia—proof that we are deserving of
such a gate to our city. We are the real democrats, you the ghosts who live
in a city built by those far better than you. As for you Boiotians, listen to
Kallistratos and his lackey potter Menekleidas until dusk tomorrow if it is
your wish. But I have an army to muster at dawn and a date to keep in the
Peloponnesos."

"A date to keep in the Peloponnesos!" Mêlon too found himself standing and roaring approval, the first time in his life he had ever clapped for
anyone or anything. As the philosophers of old said, it was easy to moral-
ize in your sleep. But he saw that performance, not intent, judges a man
good or bad. All this the brawler Epaminondas had taught him at last in
his old age—or perhaps retaught him when he came down the mountain.
You didn't have to be perfect—a god on Olympos—to be good, to be a
mortal better than others. So here he was like a witless democrat alongside the illiterate stall-sellers and rope-makers. He had been carried away
with the current for war by the single speech of a single man—in the

manner at which he used to scowl in others. He was headed for the vale of Sparta for Epaminondas and then over Taygetos to help free the helots and bring home his Nêto.

Mêlon found himself almost hoarse. He was the last to stand in sounding his approval, possessed by the wild rush to march out with this army, for Lophis and dead Staphis, and for the safety of Damô and the boys, and maimed Chiôn, too, and always for the dreams of his missing Nêto. For all this and more he yelled out until his lungs nearly were raw to follow Epaminondas. He could not care less whether a wintry *katabasis* into Lakonia was possible. He only knew that he would rather be on the wrong side with Epaminondas than right with these buskins of the assembly. In a wild mood such as this, he might well go back on the left wing again, even if Epaminondas asked him to cross the Eurotas and storm the acropolis of Agesilaos himself. The cure of Mêlon—the old misanthrope and cynic on Helikon who after the battles of Nemea and Koroneia had hid from the affairs of the Boiotians—was at last complete. Epaminondas had brought him back into the world of men and ideas and belief and off the mountain of his isolation, and the search for Nêto would take him the rest of the way southward.

The applause quieted down, as if the crowd itself had been stunned by their own spontaneous roaring. But what now? Did they know where the ripples of their wild assent would lap? Would harsh Reason goad them back to quiet? Then Mêlon for the first time noticed that the sophist Alkidamas, of all people, not the other Boiotarchs or once again Pelopidas, or the Athenians, was approaching the *bêma,* both arms upraised with his big open palms to calm the crowd—as if this were his plan, as if it had been his army all along. The Athenians were murmuring and starting to become nervous; they were surrounded by now frenzied Boiotians.

Then Alkidamas spoke: "I take this thunder as a voice vote that we are to march under General Epaminondas in the morning before the frost melts. Pelopidas as his habit will be in charge of the marching order. Look out in the plain below; the muster is nearly complete and only awaits our nod. Let the Boiotarchs sort out the details. The seven generals who had doubts have already ceded their command over to our two leaders. I have nothing to add to the promises of Epaminondas—other than this." Now Alkidamas himself also grew quiet, not quite sure what he would say next. But speak he did. For the great sophist of the Hellenes was possessed, he would say later, by an inexplicable fire, one from the mouth of Pythagoras himself. So the words came out not entirely his own. "No man is born by nature a slave—this curse that so often makes the strong and wise unfree and the weak and dull their master."

The crowd was bewildered at these lofty thoughts so out of place in a sermon to march to war, but stayed quiet for more. "Beware of those who say the Messenian helots know nothing of letters as if they were man-footed beasts of dim wits and animal grunts. They are unfree because they live next to the Spartans. So we the Boiotians, and Kallistratos and his fancy Athenians, might well have been as well, had our borders butted such a race of granite as those who wear the red capes. The Messenians will be free thanks to the strong right arms of the Boiotians." Now Alkidamas waved his arms and yelled to the crowd in far louder fashion than had Epaminondas. "Yes, they will have their free city of Messenê."

With that, Alkidamas stepped down and abandoned the politics of Boiotia for good, for this man of action also had business himself in the Peloponnesos. As the assembly of the Boiotians broke up, the white-haired sophist lumbered over to Mêlon, who put his hands on the shoulders of the old man and raised his voice over the din, "I hope to be alive to hear all that again, your defense of the Messenians, this *no man a slave*. I think you have the beginning of a real speech some day from these embers that flared up in your chest as if the One God of ours was working your bellows." Then he pointed where the general had stalked out of the assembly. "This winter Epaminondas will go beyond his tenure that expires at the new year. Then I wager that we will all be renegades. It will be our choice to be right and dead with Epaminondas or wrong, alive—and growing old—with Backwash. We all go out under the command of Epaminondas who soon will find himself an outlaw general. There will be a death sentence when—or if—we return, earned for the freedom of distant slaves."

Alkidamas then barked to Mêlon over the noise, "When the law is in service to servitude, and its violation means freedom, then the choice for a good man is not hard. If the helots are freed and we tramp back alive, then our faces will be chiseled in marble on the high temples at Delphi. But if we trip, well, then you know the fate of Epaminondas and all of us who follow. There won't be a gorge—not even the Apothetai of the Spartans—big enough to hide all our corpses."

Together they made ready to walk out. Alkidamas turned to Mêlon. "So, are you, ready? To leave your fine press on Helikon? Your newly acquired Makedonian hostage, Melissos, is waiting down by the square. He is already here with your horse Xiphos and two packs. The boy has been walking the entire circuit of the wall, bored to get going. I suppose that he will be not be behind the ox, after all, but at your side with a spear—as I confess I wagered to myself when I so graciously put him into your service. Still, you will be lucky to have him at your side. One more thing. I sensed our general would win over the crowd, and so I asked Chiôn to meet you for a last farewell at Plataia at tomorrow lamp-lighting time—just as you and the army all will enter the borderland of the Athenians. As for your new friend Alkidamas, look for me in the spring down south, four new moons from now at vine bud time when you arrive. I will wait for you under the slopes of a liberated Ithômê, with a board of free helot officials to meet you. Perhaps some of us will find your Nêto. She is a holy woman, or more than that, they say. News has reached me that in the past half-year she has let loose lightning above Ithômê and soon we will hear its thunder. I think you had better go southward to find her." He stepped away, then almost as an afterthought, Alkidamas turned again.

"The army marches at sunup. But I leave tonight on the road by the sea. There is a young man, though a frail sort at that, I must see on the way. A writer of history, Ephoros, an Athenian born in Kymê, and of some use to us, he may be soon enough. Who knows, perhaps this fellow and I will boat to the Peloponnesos and be in Messenia before you. In any case, as I told your Chiôn two days ago, I go to Aigosthena to meet a ship full of Athenian helots, and a fat one-armed captain."

CHAPTER 20

# The New Mantineia

After leaving Helikon and Mêlon at his press, Proxenos and Ainias had climbed out of the plain of Korinth. They had continued to the south, with the massive rock of forebidding Akrokorinthos on their right. The peaks of the hazy mountains of the Argolis rose on the left. They were going to Mantineia to prepare the way for the army of Epaminondas to follow. The Korinthian farmers in the fields paid the odd travelers no heed. The two had kept away from the Long Walls of Korinthos and crossed the road to Kenchreai at night. The Doric speech of the Arkadian Ainias and their broad leather hats and wool cloaks made them appear to be two mere rustics of the Peloponnesos doing their business with ships on the *diolkos*. Along the way, with the gold of the Eleans, they had hired villagers to organize depots for the huge army to come behind. Now at a slow walk, the two were already on the fourth day out from the farm of Mêlon. As they climbed up the gentle vale that marked the approach to the valley of Nemea, Ainias looked back to see both the gulf and the Aegean, and off in shadows some of the Megarid north of the Isthmos, with the neck of Perachora beyond.

At last the sun broke out of the clouds and the beauty of Hellas, north and south, was before them. The winter sea had turned deep blue. All day long Ainias had his hand on his sword hilt. He assumed that to get to the south, they would have to kill a man or two, whether bandits or Korinthian rangers. Ainias followed Proxenos, who was singing ahead as he climbed fast toward the hills above Nemea. The Plataian had never liked the south, where he had done most of his stone work, but he thought his melodies would at least lift his melancholy. The next day the two had the brisk northern breeze at their backs as they continued southward. They had stopped at Zeus's high temple at Nemea for the night, and paid well for two sacks of food. The townspeople were advised to look for Epaminondas and his horde ten days before the new year—and that they would be well paid for their flocks and granaries by Theban agents four days before the army's arrival. Finally the two zigzagged down the steep road, and on their sixth day from Kithairon could see fog blowing out from the great swampy plain of Mantineia clearly below them. Ainias was confident that Epaminondas could make this same march this winter, at least this far, and the return home back north across the Isthmos. He had put out more than a hundred stakes to mark the way for the army where food was plenty and local folk were eager to sell the Boiotians supplies.

The two slowed as they made their way down through the mud and past the junction at the Tripolis road. Then in silence Ainias pointed to the left jaw of the mouth of the plain. He had decided first to climb to a low spur of hills overlooking the rising city of Mantineia to scout and ensure the city below was safe to enter. Perhaps from the hillock they could get a good view of the first stronghold of the Boiotians' grand plans to close off Sparta with cities of free people. From this small lookout mountain—Skopê, the locals knew it as—both would be able to gaze out at the borders of Arkadia and see land that months ago in summer had been rich with cherries and grapes and thigh-high wheat between the ranges of Maenalos and Ktenias.

Here and there on the fields of the plain barley sprouted, though there were few farmers in the field in the winter cold. The sprouts of next spring's grain had already come up green and were a palm's width from the ground. But there were no ripe crops of any sort in the countryside. The dirt paths below long ago had turned muddy with streams from the storms raging down from the mountains. Yet the two travelers, who had a good eye for farmland, were struck nonetheless at the layout of this new city in the rich bottomland below—especially Ainias, who stomped and kicked the ground of his native Arkadia, as he climbed up the small lookout. Suddenly a laborer, a dirty-looking stranger in patched leather, came down the path and muttered to a surprised Ainias, "*Daimones kakoi, pantes kakoi.* "Demons, bad ones, all bad ones." Then he disappeared into the low underbrush. "*Ide. Ide.*" "Watch the foul wind, watch the stink up here. The bad hill—*lophos kakos, pas kakos.*"

Proxenos was atop first, and calling out over the breezes as he gazed from the low summit of Skopê at the city below in the distance. "Forget that rustic. Ignore his superstitions. Look down instead at my Mantineia, and how your Arkadia has a polis bigger than Athens, the tired democracy. Thirty stadia and more it goes off into the horizon. Look at my *Nea Mantineia*. They have followed my drawings. We can see at least a hundred towers and tall gates, ten and more, with walls as thick as six or seven men."

Ainias snapped back, "I see, I see. I know who planned it and who built it. But who was that leather-clad fellow coming down off Skopê—the one scared out of his wits?" He was full of bile, and angry at his own detour. On the way up, they had had to fight through dead thistle and the branches of tamarisk, slipping in the mud and ash on the slope. The view from the top was not worth the climb. "From boyhood I knew this valley," lectured Ainias. "But I never liked the scent up here on Skopê. Now something about this perch riles me even more, more than the terrified stranger who just warned me. A bad wind blows across the crest. Nêto could tell us why. Had we her gift, we could make something of that circling black hawk up there, warning us what plans Zeus has. I wager that black bird above is really a Kêr, and not a hawk after all. I can keep you alive to finish Megalopolis, but only against those who bleed, and not the shades who feed on them." With that Ainias grabbed the arm of his friend. "Proxenos, come down from this place. I don't want to ever come back here. Voices of the dead waft in."

Proxenos laughed. "Ainias, you sound like the bitch Hekuba barking at the crossroads. Skopê is no more than rocks and dirt, not the home of the goblin Empousa to scare little boys. But we go down now. There are four towers unfinished down there in Mantineia that I can see from up here. Another bridge over the water is no farther along than when I was here a month ago—and in the wrong place." The two began to lumber down and headed back along the road from Tegea to the new city. Ainias immediately felt better to be off. He was home at Mantineia and the two were safe. Now as they walked on flat ground he felt embarrassed about his fears of the hill and tried to praise the genius of his friend, who was somehow growing fainter in voice and slower in his walk.

"Proxenos, you have your immortality. These three cities—if later Megalopolis and Messenê on Ithômê grow as Epaminondas promises— are your legacy. If your scrolls burn tomorrow, it doesn't matter anymore. Our ideas are already set in stone. For a thousand seasons and more they will be known—or at least until the stones of these cities themselves are carried away by folk whose names are not yet even known. Men not yet here will praise your work. They will wonder how the style of Epaminondas's cities—your *emplekton* way—found their way deep into the Peloponnesos."

"Perhaps, Ainias," Proxenos said as they walked on. "But we have no idea of the way we shape others, or what word or small act sparks another to do good or evil. Some of us were noble by our disposition and our voice and did good, but that won't be known until we are long on the other side. Others are foul sorts. But for a moment, a beam of goodness, of *to kalon*, comes out from them. It hits the bystander more than even do the soft words of the far better. But enough." He plucked a blade of green barley and stuck it in his mouth. Pointing at his friend, he continued. "No man alive knows more of war than you, Ainias—how to organize the defense of cities and bring in supplies, to spot traitors inside the gates, to discover tunnels and signal with fire, and create passwords and open locked gates. You Stymphalian, better than any, know how to marshal an army on the plain to battle. So I will call you *taktikos*. Yes, you are to be our Ainias Taktikos—the tactician." Proxenos was pleased at that new title and was on to something. "Leave something behind of this skill. I have scrolls aplenty in that sack. So scribble down your thoughts. He who doesn't write, dies. Leave a little behind at least of the mind of General Ainias Taktikos of Stymphalos and his skill that defeated the Spartans and kept the Arkadians free." Proxenos then grew serious. As the good aristocrat, he was without much envy of the gifts in other men. He had taken stock of Nêto's warning against crossing south of Isthmos, and he felt now, after the smell and bad air of Skopê, that his life rope had fewer strands here in the south where he should not be; and this oddly gave him relief rather than worry, despite his money and fame.

Why, Proxenos the Plataian wondered, had he once more ended up so far south, in a once familiar country, headed even farther southward? The rich like he who owned green fields on the Asopos had no business down here in the barren crags of the Peloponnesos. But then did the Spartans, men like Agesilaos or Lichas, have any reason to be in Messenia? How would Sparta ever let men live freely if the Proxenoi of the north counted their trees and talked in the *stoas* of the freedom of Pythagoras and yet did not put a spear under their chin, when ten myriads of helots were but a quarter moon away? At any rate, his legs became heavy and the ash and the blowing seeds of the dead grass on Skopê had clogged his nose and swelled his cheeks. He began to like the idea that he might not need to come back along this long road south when the war was at last over, as most wish to take a different road home than the long one out.

Proxenos then tried to talk his way out of his sluggishness. "I have heard your war talk, Ainias—how warfare has changed, and your rants that fighting is no longer battle between gaudy-crested spearmen on fair and level ground. No more spears and shields. As you say, it is a war to the death of all against all, *pantes pros pantas* with the slaves and poor and sieges and ambushes and betrayal. We for our part cannot win such a war without the helots of Messenia. Yet you have mastered this new hateful war. Write down how we are to survive, so that we Hellenes don't relive all the mistakes again and again. You will be a writer of war, you Ainias Taktikos."

With that, the two forgot their grand talk of tactics, scrolls, immortality, and all that and in no time had left the gloomy hillock of Skopê far behind them. Once they were distant, their spirits lifted for good. As they neared the new walls of Mantineia and crossed a stone bridge over the river, both looked up at the main gate that had been hung since the last visit of Proxenos. It was built of mountain oak wood, twenty feet high, with black iron on its borders. A massive beam hung to lock the doors at night. The gate was ringed by towers—each forty cubits and more above the plain, about every half stade on the walls.

Proxenos was counting. "Ten gates, one hundred twenty towers. Like nothing in Hellas, this city. Yet had I my way, my towers would have been round rather than square. A round one pleases the eye. It is harder to knock down, and the stones and iron of the enemy glance off it better. But it takes a builder with a keen eye, and a mason who knows something of art and beauty." Mantineia was the largest city to have been built in Hellas in five hundred years and more. Unlike all other walled cities in Hellas, it had not been laid out around an acropolis in the hills or on the slopes, but spread out in a large oval on flat farmland, in a valley ringed by tall mountains. Proxenos's proud citadel had no need of the high ground to survive, and there was not the bother of the long walk up to an acropolis. He had planned an entire city like the rich houses of the *aristoi*—with running water piped into the fountains, and with sewers beneath the floors and streets to carry out the waste—all to tower over the hovels of the Spartans. The men of Mantineia would find no help for their security from rocks and heights of nature, but instead their polis grew out of the mud of the valley. Yes, this new city of the Mantineians proclaimed to the Spartans: "We new men of Arkadia can build something in a season better than anything over a lifetime at Sparta—and we dare you, who need an acropolis, to take down our walls in the plain. Come, take them if you can."

The stone work of the new Mantineia was unlike that of other poleis. It incorporated strange ideas of regular courses, a moat, and a grid of square city blocks inside with streets that made sharp right angles, with the names of the ways chiseled on the building corners. Its dressed stones had the cut of Boiotia with their trademark corner drafts, as if to proclaim also that Epaminondas was on his way and the Arkadians were more Boiotians than Peloponnesians. Proxenos thought that the order and symmetry of his Pythagoras would grow into the minds of these new dwellers. Men foul and low by birth were to be given a new city, and a new democracy, and then they would act with reserve and show taste like those born into the great houses of Boiotia, once their material surroundings uplifted their spirits.

Why were men poor? Because of accident or hurt, or was it rather due to their sloth—poor because they were no good by nature inside? Or drank the unmixed wine? Or stole, and killed and maimed when they should have been pruning the high olive trees? To find that answer Proxenos had followed Epaminondas down here in the first place. So would these freed Mantineians, and better yet, the helot Messenians next, turn away from superstitions of the Olympians to worship the deity Reason that had so ordered their own lives? Or would they loot in their new city as the serfs and helots they innately were, and prove the Spartans right that they were inferiors by nature and would make their new city as foul as they? A voice of the master answered in the head of Proxenos, "No, one day they will think as they live in their new grids. Square corners make square thoughts."

A storm was blowing in from faraway Thrace. Winds and sleet

headed down the pass to the Peloponnesos. The drenched hoplites ran under the arch, happy to be alive and off Skopê when the lightning hit. Mantineia was the first city of this new Peloponnesos where rank was gone, a *dêmokratia* that made Athens tame in comparison. Owning big orchards or bottomland wheat fields meant nothing. With the promised end of Sparta, bulwark of oligarchy, the idea of the polis of privileged property owners, alone fighting in the phalanx on behalf of the lesser community, was to be over. Instead, here in Mantineia the *dêmos* would tax the rich horsemen and the orchard growers to pay for the walls to protect the landless. The world of Hellas was to be upside down. The poorer the man was, the more qualified he was to run the polis. Squeeze the soft rich until their juices ran, and then go after the pulp as well—or so the new democrats of Mantineia bragged.

Many *plethra* of wheat fields were walled inside this strange city's fortifications, and newly transplanted olives lined the streets. Wooden grape arbors with bare winter canes covered the city squares, as Proxenos's walled Mantineia was to be both city and country. How could Agesilaos and his Spartan raiders ever starve out a town that grew its own food year-round inside its ramparts? The snake river Ophis had been diverted to run around the oval city's foundation to serve as a great moat, dug thirty feet deep and lined with paving stones. But far below the foundations of the city, clay pipes brought the water into the fountains and cisterns and fed small ponds around which the city dwellers grew their own gardens, and that they stocked with fish and water fowl as well. In the previous wars, the Spartan army once had turned the river to flood towns in the valley and wash away their mud bricks. Now the waters were to be the bulwark, not betrayers of a far larger polis.

The engineers of Proxenos ensured that no machine of the Hellenes could tear down his stacked blocks, not even the new belly-bows from Sikily that sent iron shafts of twenty palms and more in length—and faster and heavier than any arrow—for two stadia. Double iron clamps, in the shape of axes, joined his blocks, and heavy lead sealed them from rust. The walls were half as deep into the ground as they were tall. Far beneath the earth they were anchored to hold the weight. Subterranean stones stopped the burrower and the miner from pulling out earth from beneath. King Agesilaos could not go over, under, or through these stones, or flood or starve out those inside, either.

Scaffolds still rose above the street. Ainias pointed to them in every direction. Thousands of Arkadians were hoisting cut stones and trays of mud bricks on ropes and pulleys up from booms for the final courses, even as the wind blew ice over the works. Wagons made a continuous trek into the circuit's gates from the farms beyond, full of household rural folk moving into the still unfinished fortress. Ainias tried to make sense of it all as the sleet began. "Walls reveal a people. You are a Zeus who has taught these Mantineians that they are better than Spartans and can do things because they think they can do things. Yet something more even than Mantineia will soon be rising to the south at Megalopolis, and perhaps in Messenia something greater than Megalopolis. You have turned the men of the Peloponnessos into hemi-gods, and from the barren earth they are building a new Olympos."

Proxenos stayed quiet and at the boast of Ainias hoped only that the Spartans were wrong who charged that Epaminondas instead was intent on a Hades above the earth, with an Acheron and Styx in the light of day, inhabited with thousands of anonymous and identical empty souls who only looked alive but had long been dead inside. As the two passed through the gate and into the bustling city, a wealthy-looking archon in a clean white tunic, fat and loud, met them. This was Lykomedes, the son of Aristoteles, democratic leader for the ages—barker of the agora. He was the head of the new Arkadian league, the democracy of allied poleis that was to follow the example of Boiotia and turn itself into a federated empire of the city-states. What had struck the careful architect Proxenos—who had seen him first three summers earlier—was not the ambition of Lykomedes, nor even his belly or his clean new long shirt, but his nose. It was Olympian, and worse, out of plumb, in need of saw or hammer work, its boar-like snout nearly resting on his lower lip, with his two bottom teeth like tusks protruding out.

Such a blemish, he thought, would have earned Lykomedes a date with the deep *Kaiadas* from the Spartans. Even at Athens such defects of birth were seen as a window into a flawed soul. Proxenos frowned, since he certainly did not think his new perfect city should have rabble like this in power—men that did not deserve the proud stones he was building for them. And he only worried more that the Spartans were right, after all.

Ainias remembered that it was also a mythic Lykomedes who the

poets said had murdered the good Theseus, and he expected no less from this reincarnated, fouler version. Still, Lykomedes's success was visible in the looming stones about them. Who could argue with that, since the final end always trumps the messy beginning and middle? In any case Lykomedes was aptly named "cunning of the wolf" for his plots and conspiracies. Because his nose muffled his speech, he had a boy crier with a screeching voice that met the two well before they could greet the man properly and get much beyond the gates. When they neared, Lykomedes's low murmur and hissing took over. "How do you like Homer's 'Mantineia of the many grapes'? Better than your Thebes of dragon-born legend? We have ten gates, not your mere seven. Now Arkadia prepares to build a grand monument, right on the Sacred Way at Delphi. We will buy our spot right in front of the Spartans." Then, turning to Ainias, he coughed and whispered, "My, my, our famous mercenary. I heard you were back among us."

Ainias said little but nodded to Proxenos. On the journey over the pass, they had talked of meeting this Lykomedes. The Arkadian had prophesied to Proxenos, "Before this is all over, this boar will rut at the Thebans his benefactors, as much as he grumbles about his hatred for the Spartans. He will do all that for the people, as he puts it." Ainias boasted that he could read men the way he separated out the fat and thin hoplites in his files and lines of the phalanx, and the cowards as well. His gaze centered on the eyes and the carriage of the head, the steadiness of the hand, and the direction of the toes, to learn who would drop his shield, foul himself, turn tail—or plant himself firm and stab ahead. He knew as well that Phrynê was passing messages all over the Peloponnesos, encouraging the Dorians south of the Isthmos not to expect the arrival of Epaminondas, so confident were she and her cadre in persuading her customers to stop the muster of Epaminondas. And barring that, she would at least provide the Spartans with the numbers and the nature of the Boiotian alliance. All that and more he now read in the face and bearing of Lykomedes.

Ainias's hard look, his scars, his wide-gapped teeth and stubble beard made his speech even more forbidding and bleak. He also had something of Mêlon in him—with taller ears for the bad than the good, a curse that made him moody with the black bile though seldom wrong. So he warned all to keep their distance from this Mantineian demagogue. Yes, he knew

Lykomedes as a two-shoe who would have his new Mantineia turn to either Thebes or Sparta as the iron vane on the tower of the seasons spins to follow the wind.

Lykomedes grabbed them by the arms. He led them up the stairs of one of the towers, about a stade from the gate, as they sought shelter from the sleet. For all his ugliness and age, he was spry and stopped to point out a step too high, or a gate that scraped its threshold as if the Boiotian should fix it. Then he hammered with his staff the stones at their feet, as if he could teach the architect anything about the city Proxenos had planned. "For the mud brick we have stone. For the river we have a moat. For the villages we have a fortress—all built in a year by my plans and the sweat of the men of Mantineia. This is *dēmokratia*, the power of people. This is what the Dorian spear so rightly fears. I am a *dēmokratikos*."

Ainias said little. But he reminded Lykomedes how their Mantineia had been reborn—and how others were at the heart of it all. "Our fortress, Lykomedes, here at Mantineia is the child of Epaminondas. It came from the mind of Proxenos here. Thebes is written over your walls. The city is not mere stone, but formed of free men. For the walls of a democracy are only as strong as the right arms of its hoplites. You can prove that soon at the Eurotas, down among the Spartans."

Proxenos cut in, "I wish it were so. But we will have a hard time in the days ahead to storm Sparta—if Epaminondas decides to go south once he arrives here." He pointed to the high passes farther to the south that cut off Lakonia from the center of the Peloponnesos. "The roads are deep in winter mud. There is nothing but cold there beneath Taygetos. Colder still in the shadows of Parnon. Their barrier to the city, the river Eurotas, is ice. I feel it even from here in my bones."

Lykomedes bellowed out in laughter. "Spartans? They hide inside their borders. Last month they came out to test our mettle, and we hit them hard, even though our walls were not as tall as you see them now." The three were drenched by the light rain but kept talking in their confidence of the imposing heights of Mantineia, until Lykomedes advised to go over to the city center called *ptolis*, to see the theater and new temple to Hera, the patron goddess that watched over the growing city. He talked as they walked. "We need only more roof-tiles for our new homes. Sparta has roof-tiles. So we will join your Epaminondas at month's end and go down to get our tiles from the Spartans. How's that?"

Both nodded, since the thief would be on their side to steal from the common enemy. The cold drizzle turned to a harder rain, and then promptly abated and left a wet fog. Proxenos held his nose from the over-flowing sewer. In anger he reminded Lykomedes that his plans had called for the tile drains beneath the walls to dump into the downstream of the Ophis, not into these pools inside the walls. Surely if these lowly sorts would not work for clean streets, they could at least hold their bowels and empty them only outside the city walls.

"A minor problem, stone doctor," Lykomedes laughed. "We piled the clay pipe outside the walls, but thieves made off with it all. We need more clay, as I said. Until then, these ditches will have to do. As you heard, we had a bit of looting. Some stealing, too—until my archers emptied their quivers. Things are settling down. You'll see. Hang up a few thieves for the birds. Toss their corpses to the dogs. Just a few is all that's needed. We'll get the crap out and the fresh water flowing soon enough." As they passed the cesspools, Proxenos saw that the stench came from the two half-eaten corpses hung above the sewers. "To teach the others," Lyko-medes pointed at them. "All executed fairly on the order of my assembly, the will of the *dêmos*. But first, tell me about the muster of the Boiotians. The year wanes. Rumors spread. We hear Epaminondas will not come in his tenure, that he will not be reelected Boiotarch in the year to come. Hoplites don't march at the winter solstice, right?"

The three were descending the ramparts and made their way down a colonnaded arch to the *ptolis* and the central city with its wide agora and broad stoas, the stones clean and shiny from the shower. Proxenos replied that the vote at Thebes probably was being held far to the north amid the cold as they spoke. "Boiotia was full of foreigners when we left. *Xenoi*, some from far above Phokis and Lokris, no less. Islanders too are camped beneath the seven gates. For good or ill, all say they have come to march. At least as far as Arkadia. Thousands of them, even as the summer is gone and the autumn wanes along with the annual tenure of General Epami-nondas. Yet I wager the spirit of Epaminondas and the hard reason of Alkidamas will make it difficult for the delegates of Boiotia to stop the army. But make sure your Mantineia has enough food this cold winter to feed them all. Mêlon, the killer of Kleombrotos, may end up here in the front rank himself. They are coming, coming in just a few days."

"Count on that," Ainias broke in. Lykomedes listened more to his fellow Arkadian. "The Thespian killer will tire of his olive press and his protest that he is a *misanthrôpos* who just wishes to be let alone. We saw that before we left. His man-hatred was cured by Epaminondas. Yes, he of prophecy will come, limp or not—as long as he knows that his Epaminondas can leave Thebes still as Boiotarch with a right to lead out an army, even if it be a winter one that is not even across the Isthmos when his tenure ends."

Lykomedes spat out between his teeth. "He might, but I hear the gods are finished with your Mêlon, son of Malgis, and from now on he will kill no more kings. Tell him to keep far from our Skopê, as they say it bodes badly for you northerners. Nonetheless, even cripples are needed. We turn none away. We have filled the city's granaries since late summer's good harvest. I had to stretch a few fingers of the wealthier ones, and even brand a few, to find their buried grain stashes. But they all coughed up in the end, all legal on the order of the *dêmos*. A thousand sheep and goats graze inside the walls. Another thousand are along the tall river grass outside near the walls."

Proxenos wanted to know something else, something he had promised Mêlon to find out back at the press on Helikon. "Now tell us Lykomedes, have you seen Mêlon's freedwoman Nêto, the prophetess from Helikon? She listens to the priestess of Pasiphai for the things that will happen before they do. Well before last high summer she was down here, scurrying around to find exiles of Messenia to stir the helots on. She might have had this poetess, Erinna, they say with her? They would have stopped here on the way west to Ithômê."

"Yes, yes, Nêto who babbled about, but a fine tight sort nonetheless she was. But without the *erôs* of men in her eye, as I learned." Lykomedes looked sideways and kept on. "The other girl, well now, the fiery one Erinna was even crazier with her talk about a new Athens on the slopes of Ithômê. I know of her songs. That is one reason why she walked freely in my city. But while I have long heard her hexameters—both the laments for her lost girlfriend Baukis, and the dirge on spinning—many have gone by that name Erinna, and all claimed that they were the one poetess of myth. I had never met any of them, so I was surprised that this latest Erinna seemed like one of Queen Hippolyta's she-men from Pontos with that wicked bow on her shoulder. But maybe she's more a woman than she let on. Both left—and with raggedy helots, no less. Your Nêto almost took my little Aristôn with them. Yes, the troublemakers left Mantineia thirty days or maybe forty or more ago, and with a full pouch of coins, headed toward the great mountains of Taygetos. Both will draw men, good and bad, on the road—if they are lucky enough to avoid the man-bear or wolf-men on the high passes. Look for that dirty Nikôn; he followed the two women. He's that helot upstart that I'd rather kill than let run free in my city. All of them found too few Messenian helots here for their liking. They said they were going south. To the new city, no doubt. Nêto fell under the spell of your Alkidamas. Most who do don't end nicely."

Lykomedes went on. "This summer Nêto fired up our helot exiles here in Mantineia with visions of a free Messenia—all twenty of them. And that helot mob leader Nikôn, who stinks of leather and lye? Well, he was worst of all the helot brigands, the killer who ambushed and waylaid and had no parley with the Spartans. Still, helots were no concern of ours. She gathered a few of these loiterers off our streets. If they kill Spartans, why, all the better. So she came here, poked around, and left." Something about Nêto had set the boar's mouth flapping and he couldn't stop spitting. "That pale poetess Erinna performed here, as I said, and breathed hard on your Nêto. Nêto thinks that they will lead an army of helots from the highlands of Arkadia. She plans on killing Spartans and freeing her people. I tried to talk some sense into the pair, but who can when these half-helots and crazed poets think they're gods?"

Proxenos laughed. "You mean you tried to talk *erôs* into Nêto, goat, and got beat by a poetess no less."

"That too," Lykomedes chuckled, "that too, for I like a tall woman with ribs that I can see and yet with breasts that flop and the rear of a wide sort as well. But your philosopher Alkidamas already won Nêto over. Why, I don't know. He has no fun in him, only serious stuff. For all that Erinna's short hair, I imagine she had some love of men left in her yet. If not, she's as good as my pretty little Aristôn all the same."

Proxenos wanted to have his leave of foul Lykomedes and start on the way to Megalopolis to muster more men for Epaminondas. "But she is among her own folk. And Nêto is far wiser from her long walks with Alkidamas, who, to be frank, is a different sort than you, Lykomedes. I hiked with this woman to Leuktra. It was her prayers that brought the gods out of the temples and her portents that the simple folk cheered.

Had she not been with me, Epaminondas would have had only half the number needed to stop Kleombrotos."

The three walked out of the theater. They kept bantering along the grand porticoes of Lykomedes, planning the provisions for the army they all hoped was already marching. It was decided that Ainias and Proxenos would head immediately westward into Arkadia and the new site of Megalopolis. There they would prepare another army of liberators of the south and join the Eleans marching as well. Perhaps Ainias and Proxenos would be back in half a month with a new army to meet the horde descending from Thebes, as well as the Mantineians under Lykomedes. The three armies would meet up for the final descent into the vale of Lakonia itself—if the generals voted to go on.

Proxenos finished with a warning to the plotter at their side. "Be careful, Lykomedes, when you soon meet Epaminondas. He has gotten word that you are to march with us. His spies have told him you have food that he will need. Don't deceive him. He is not of the sort as we, but has become something far different, far more dangerous. This is a man, after all, who when he kills his sleeping sentries on his nighttime inspections, only shrugs and says, 'I left them as I found them.'"

# CHAPTER 21

# Two Women

Not long after her summer parting with Mêlon, Nêto had visited Theanô, the widow of Staphis, and prepared to head south across the Isthmos. She thought that she might have a half-year, maybe more, to rally the helots and prepare the way for Epaminondas at the end of the year. Yet Nêto had never been beyond the confines of Boiotia. At least not since her childhood kidnapping and sale to Mêlon at the port of Kreusis. But she was glad to leave the north after her words with Mêlon. Alkidamas had told her the way and arranged for a guide to get her to Mantineia—and then, when near the borders of Messenia, for the helot Nikôn to lead her up to Ithômê. Still, Nêto wondered, how do northerners find a path over the peaks near Korinthos and then catch the trail that leads deep into the Peloponnesos beyond? Then do they go down farther south into Ithômê, and if so, on what road? She needed her Porpax—now no doubt in the belly of the man-bear on Kithairon.

After Leuktra, Nêto had slowly made herself believe that as a freedwoman she was no longer needed in Boiotia, much less on the home estate with the Malgidai. Chiôn with the boys could handle the chores for Mêlon as the master idled in town with Phrynê—while his terraces caved and the bindweed and thistle dotted his barley fields. Instead her new mentor Alkidamas had urged her to go south. "You speak of messages in your head from this Nikôn, whom I know as well from my travels in the Peloponnesos when I was still not considered an enemy of Sparta and walked freely beneath Ithômê. I think you will find him in the new

Mantineia, or so he says he will find you should you go there. There are now twenty of you Messenians for each citizen of Sparta, yet no common voice, no plan of revolt. Our Nikôn sounds as if he has the spirit, but not yet the sense, to free his kindred. Use your prophecies and miracles in the temples to aid his cause, and tell him visions, if you have them, of things to come. Hundreds of wayfarers won't all wait on Epaminondas and the muster of the Thebans. Already in twos and threes these men, our allies, make their way to join the new cities of the Arkadians, and soon you will find me in Messenia as well, and maybe well before the arrival of the army of Epaminondas. Still, be careful in the south. A woman without the black shroud and the toothless mouth is in as much danger on the road with men as she is alone with the man-bear on Parnassos or Taygetos to the south."

Nêto remembered that Alkidamas had added, "About that guide for you. Well, she is a strange sort, a misfit they say, like you, maybe. I have asked her to join you when the clusters redden and the grapes sweeten. She is a poetess, by name Erinna, a follower of the Muses at Athens, born out at Tenos, where the afternoon waves swamp the fishing boats. Many would-be poets, now and in the past, have gone by that name, both good and bad students of the Muses. But she is the true one who sang of her lament for the dead Baukis, that tale which is now played in the symposia of Athens and Thebes. And she is tired of Athens and its shouting democracy and its descent into chaos. Like you, she is a restless sort, in search of a great deed, and like you she hears songs in her head of Ithômê and the great awakening to come. She claims visions of tall ramparts to rise, and is a devotee of Epaminondas, though I doubt the woman has ever met our general. Men know of her songs and perhaps her name alone will open gates otherwise shut tight. You two women will hike to Ithômê, the blind with a hand on the shoulder of the blind. Both of you will be heading to war ahead of the great throng of Epaminondas."

All that was after Nêto had left Helikon, and Mêlon had sent no word for her to return to the farm. Now in the Dog Star days and a full year after Leuktra, the young Erinna of Tenos had left Athens to find Nêto. She waited for her for three days at the pass inn near Eleutheria as she hiked up from Athens on the high border road. Soon they were on the summer road to the south, a half-year before the Boiotians would even vote to march.

Nevertheless, the plan of Alkidamas for the two women was to head
to Mantineia in seven days, and find a Lykomedes. "A trickster of sorts,"
the sophist had warned, "with tusks instead of teeth in his ugly head."
Once there, they were to round up helots and head westward and to send
a runner back with news of the preparation for the revolt of the Mantineians. Alkidamas reminded Nêto that she was not alone, but if she and
this Erinna could rouse the helots, if Epaminondas and Mêlon could stir
the Boiotians, if Proxenos and Ainias could rally the Arkadians, they all
might descend like a horde of locusts, converging on the pastures of Lakonia. "Lykomedes may find you useful and so will not have his thugs slit
your throat and throw you in his proud new moat. That is the custom for
them when they catch a helot on the road—and a pretty one at that. So I
gave him some silver Athenian coins. He promises that he has food and a
room for you two under the third tower from the main gate. But be out of
Mantineia by a day or so with your helots. Prick your ears up to hear
word of Proxenos or Ainias, who may be crossing back and forth all year
at the Isthmos, though both may not get to Mantineia until you leave.
On some winter day the two will be leading an army back from Megalopolis—or so we hope."

As the month of Theilouthios waned, Nêto and Erinna slept most
of the late afternoons. They walked at sunset before nightfall when the
Aegean wind came up and the stars and early moon give softer light than
did the glare of Helios. In the beginning of their trek southward, it
was not hard to find the road out from the border at Boiotia. All Hellas was
afire this late summer, even though the congress of Boiotia would not
take up the march for months more. Then the army might not set out
until the cold and the year was well over. For now, the two could always
tail along the mercenaries who headed for the new city of Mantineia, the
rumored meeting winter place of the armies. Small parties were camping
on the paths to the Isthmos, some in wagons, a few with horses. At daybreak Nêto and Erinna sought out the resting shade of the orchards and
groves on the slopes of the Megarid opposite the sea.

From there they peered out at hundreds more on foot, with servants
trailing laden with panoplies, all these zealots convinced that Epaminondas would soon be going south and they should wait the summer out for
him down in Arkadia. Alkidamas was right. It was good that she had a
companion to share the road—especially one like Erinna. From the looks

of the warrior poet, she guessed that they could beat away even a determined throat-cutter. The two women made their way south on the Peloponnesos road that Proxenos and Ainias had trod so many times in the year after Leuktra, in their journeys to oversee the building of Mantineia and Megalopolis—and would make one last time after the women, marking out the grand route for the *katabasis* of Epaminondas to come.

As they made their way farther southward, Erinna explained her devotion to the Muses and her worship of the goddess Artemis. She gave Nêto bits and pieces of her long song on spinning and the loom. She was composing as they hiked, and by the second day the two were back walking in the light and returned to sleeping at early night. Her day speech was made with a high Attic pitch that so many of the islanders aped after living in Athens, though she had left Athens for the Boiotians because she wished to believe that men—men like Epaminondas—sought to serve their democracy rather than be served by it. But when she sang at night her song was more Doric, though more often a south Asian strain than from the Peloponnesos. "Hymen! O Hymenaeus, while the dark night in silence whirls about, darkness covers my eyes . . ." Nêto looked about, worried that robbers might hear Erinna's strains, and grabbed her knife as the poetess let out loud lines in the night. As they passed the islands below in the gulf, she sang more softly how Nêto was bathed in the scarlet of the huge sun that rose over Salamis out to the east. She went on about a prophecy that a new Themistokles was coming to defeat tyranny— and other such visions that came to her on the road. Nêto dubbed her "Epaminondas" because every third word seemed to be "Epaminondas will . . ." or "Epaminondas can . . ."

They stopped at the sanctuary at Eleusis, and then slept at the fountain house at Megara before heading over the pass of Geraneia at the Isthmos. But Nêto would later remember little of the trees and mountains and sea below on their hike to the Isthmos, only that Erinna knew of an entire new universe, of Praxilla, Korinna, and moons, plants, and birds, rather than the serried ranks of men at war. She often avoided the heavy hexameters of Homer and Hesiod, and instead preferred the lighter five-footed elegies of the love poets. Erinna was no longer young but nearly thirty winters, smooth-skinned yet untouched, or so she boasted.

Nêto had heard that the poetess was a Sapphic and avoided the world of men and so was a virgin only of a certain sort. At least it seemed that way, since her songs were often threnodies about her dead friend Baukis, who had married too early and died in childbirth in service to a man not worth the birth pangs. Now as they descended above the flatlands of the Isthmos, Erinna changed her themes and began to sing even more often of the life of Epaminondas, whom she had heard debate just one time in the agora at Thebes. Her Epaminondas, like Erinna, had married no mortal. He sired no children. He left *erôs* to lesser mortals, as he had pledged his years left for the greater good of *eleutheria* and the One God of order and calm. Or so Erinna imagined he did.

At day's end, when Nêto worried to her as the campfire roared that the Boiotians were only in a war of words, that the great army might not march until days before the tenure of Epaminondas expired, leaving him an outlaw in winter, Erinna began to chant a new refrain of Epaminondas, who would "shear Sparta of her glory" and leave "all Hellas independent and free," as if the cities of Mantineia, Megalopolis, and Messenê were already finished, the helots beyond Taygetos freed, and the farms of Lakonia on fire, a mounted Epaminondas galloping freely over the Peloponnesos supervising the upheaval.

"I like your 'all Hellas independent and free,'" Nêto answered as she heard the chorus for the fiftieth time. "But I worry that when you meet him, he will not have wings on his heels and golden locks down his shoulders, and so you may find your god merely half-divine, if even that."

"Well, Epaminondas may need my song as his defense, if he lives and returns an outlaw to Thebes. He will need that answer when he is in the dock before the jurymen of Boiotia, the ingrates who are angry that he has saved them." When the two could see the looming massif of Akrokorinthos in the evening sky, Nêto finally asked Erinna how they were to cross the Korinthians' narrow land. Alkidamas has warned her that it was hard for any of the northerners to pass into the Peloponnesos. Erinna only shrugged, without worry as they had hiked up a bit along the mountains away from the Aegean to avoid robbers. There they stopped with a nice fire of dried tamarisk, and heated up a broth of leeks and barley and dried lamb.

As Erinna took off her long cloak, Nêto noticed for the first time in their three days of walking that underneath she wore a heavy leather chiton. There were leather wraps up her legs, and broader hide bands with bronze studs on her arms. Nêto had seen some leather before on a woman, but not this close and with these odd designs of stars around a crescent moon. Strangest of all, she examined in detail a small bow on Erinna's shoulder, a Scythian type. That explained at least the hide on her arms and fingers. Erinna finally answered, "I have friends who will get us across. But I am more worried that your helots will not lead us into Messenia when the time comes and we cross from Arkadia. You talk of this Nikôn as your guide and yet confess you have never met the rebel; and yet you assure me you speak to him in your dreams. I wager I know more about him than you do. Is that how you convince me that you are not crazy as the Boiotians say, or fleeing Helikon in lovesickness? As for me, I promised your mentor, Alkidamas, I would see you safely to Mantineia, Nikôn or not. If he joins us, fine; if not, I head west anyway. I would start a school on Ithômê. I plan to train young helots to read their letters and know their Sappho, and their Korinna and Myrtis. And yes, Alkidamas gave me some silver Athenian owls to escort you safe to the south—but only half what Phrynê offered me to slit your throat here on this side of the Isthmos." Nêto looked baffled at that last confession: Should she be angry that Erinna had come along only as a bought guide, or happy that she had refused to be a bought assassin?

Then Erinna noticed Nêto's stare and scoffed. "The bow is not for you, so let down your guard. Leather is not for men alone. Not for a woman's show, but to protect my arms. How else can I string and fling the arrows? Don't raise your nose too high about my tools. At least not if you want a fresh rabbit or two for our dinner—and maybe a stag as well before we reach Messenia." This Erinna was supposed to be, Alkidamas also had warned Nêto, something more than a poet, a woman who could strike verse or strike down a good-size man with equal skill. Nêto prided herself that she had stacked too many stones with Chiôn ever to have gone soft, and that her arms were taut after plowing and seeding the fields of the dead Staphis. But Erinna was more manlike, yet not mannish altogether. As she got up to throw some wood on the fire, Nêto noticed that Erinna's limbs were like those of Lophis, lean and stringy, and yet her breasts and backside were full.

Erinna sensed all this, and turned back to Nêto. "Don't believe the poets like Hipponax or Euripides of Athens that we are a helpless sort. Women are not mad like Medea or Kassandra, or bloody bitches like Klytemnestra, or eager to die as was Antigone. Only men like your Hesiod on

Helikon or Sophocles and Euripides sing of such nonsense." She laughed and cupped her hands under her large breasts. "What do I care that men line up in the phalanx or have the rudder of the ship in their hands. While they boast and babble, there are plenty of cracks in their granite for women like me to flow through. They can no more stop me than dam off the streams that cascade down the mountain."

She restrung her bow and pulled out a feather arrow. "So, yes, we women of spirit do almost anything we want. No children, no man, no vote? Sad perhaps, but do menfolk take this quiver from me, or tear up my scrolls? Hardly. Or tell me what I can sing or when? No, while they scurry around in their men's *kosmos*, and mount their wives and whores, they leave us alone. The smart ones like us, why, we simply live in a parallel world—right under their noses. Yes, just as two lines that don't cross or the wandering planets that march across the sky side-by-side never meet. So no pity for me. I am as free as the cranes on the shore that the duck hunters will neither eat nor trap as they strut by in their beauty."

Before Nêto could stop her, she finished with a final outburst. "Maybe we women don't even need our one Pythagoras. I think he's just a name for the world of numbers and order that we discovered on our own. But no mind—I told Alkidamas I would do three great things. Get his Nêt-ikê to Mantineia and perhaps to Ithômê as well. Start my school. And if this Nikôn kills Spartans, help raise the countryside against the Spartans. So are an odyssey, a war, and poetry enough, my Nêto—or is there to be more still from your Amazon Erinna?"

Nêto laughed, "And fourth—kill Gorgos, whom the helots fear as Kuniskos. Do that and I'm happy."

Erinna shook her head at that command, for she had heard this past year of a Kuniskos, who put fear into the children of Messenia and had an eye for helot women for his sport and worse. Now she moved quickly around their small camp with her bow on her shoulder to patrol its edge, bringing her small sword out of her pack. "Don't utter the name Gorgos. It is bad omen. Look, I fear demons and worse will come to the call of the evil sound. Maybe wolves or a man-bear, Nêto. We will watch for them all. I am happy to see your hilt at last peek out from your own bundle."

What an odd woman, this Erinna, at the same time looking to kill, talking of helots, singing her poetry, serving the world of men, idolizing the general Epaminondas—all as she cooked and paced and broke into song, and went out beyond their fire to find a rabbit. She was a Prometheus who in two blinks came back with a skinny hare, hit with a shaft through its shoulders. As Erinna skinned the animal, Nêto moved a little more distant from the fire to watch her from the far side of the camp. She remembered Alkidamas's final warning at their parting: "You may find Erinna not of your taste, but strangers will want their way with you, to rob and kill you both, to mount you on your march down. And your new protector can seduce or slit a throat with equal measure. You are too dour, Nêto, as well, and think only in lines and angles, while Erinna sings of things of the other world that do not follow your *logos* of numbers."

They looked for shadows beyond the fire as they sipped their broth. In her brief quiet Nêto thought it better to blurt it out and ask her strange companion whether she was widowed, even though she knew she had never married. Erinna flashed back. "Will I bite you, Nêto? Is that your worry, that I am the mate of the man-bear? Or do you wish to see whether I have burned off a breast like the Amazons? Or do you think I have no private parts like the statues of women in the houses of the rich? Why hide what you already know—that I taste no man's flesh, and find my *erôs* with those like you and me? Why not? What higher form is there for a woman than the love of the like kind, whose bodies are really our own?"

She then laughed out loud. "Did not gruff Platôn—or was it foulmouthed Aristophanes—say it was a search for our second half? Men anyway are a nasty brood. They come stinking of the hunt, with blood and entrails on their cloaks. They use us as the playthings that we are, only when finished to turn over to snore, to fart and grunt. No, none of that was for me." The she smiled, "Most are not like our Epaminondas. So why not sleep with whiter, softer flesh than with cuts and scars and worse among the burnt and rough? But no worry, my Nêtikê. Baukis is gone. I have no time any more for *erôs*. If you worry about those unwed, go ask our Epaminondas why he too has not married—and why he has not heard of Erinna, his devotee, who sings his praises and would kill or die to see his dreams as fact among men. Or better yet, look in the mirror glass and ponder why you too have no partner."

At that, a barking erupted in the brush beyond the firelight. Nêto got up. She pulled out her blade and scouted out the source of the sound. A dark shape, with a tail shaped like a wolf's, appeared, moving in and out of the rocks. Had Erinna seen the wild thing when she hit her rabbit? Or was it a trick the god was playing on Nêto's eyes? Erinna ignored her friend's restlessness. "But don't worry, Nêto. When I saw you, I knew you weren't one of us. I first thought your long legs and those man muscles made you an Amazon. I believed Alkidamas that you are still a virgin. But I see it not for the dislike of men—but perhaps for the like, or maybe worship, of one man you hold back." She followed the girl and then gave Nêto a pat on her rump.

"I am going to the new Messenê with you, Nêto. As Alkidamas says, to start a thinking-place, what they laugh at in Athens as a schoolhouse, one for women who need no men, or at least need to do their own chores on the farm and hear within themselves the voices of the Muses. New Messenê will need us." She stared beyond the fire in search of the night beast as she talked. "But all this you will see. For five days more we will be partners in our phalanx of two. I won't press myself on you—as if your false protector would become the very thing I was to protect you against. But yes, I will put an arrow through your Gorgos—whoever or whatever or wherever this gorgon of yours is."

Nêto turned back to the fire to slice off some of Erinna's rabbit. "I need shielding from no man or woman. But there is a night-wolf out there and maybe my Gorgos as well, and it will take us both to cut him down. Yes, on this trip the two of us will need each other. For food and water, at least."

Much of the way they had kept to the scrub oak of the low hills and dared not go into the long walls of Megara. Islanders were coming into the port there—and at Aigosthena and up to Perachora on the gulf. A few northerners going south tried to get the two to join their camps, but most backed off when they saw the blades on the shoulders of the two women, unsure whether the two might be two beardless ephebes eager to mix it up. Erinna flung a couple of arrows at three wayfarers with sticks and packs who were closing the distance behind them and full of threats and taunts. When the shafts whizzed over their heads, they tailed off into the scrub. "Thieves and worse," she laughed, as she hung her bow back over her shoulder.

After another day of hiking, now with the Isthmos in their faces, the shadowy night-beast grew closer to the scent of the women. The four-leg had trailed them for three or four stadia, on a parallel course on the higher ridges where the olive groves ended. Both had seen it, or at least its outline, and had taken turns on the watch this night. Erinna warned of their danger. Was it the man-bear of Kithairon or a worse monster from Helikon? "Nêto, I think it is no bear, but a dappled wolf. My eyes are better than yours and I can see the big wolf has left his pack. Tonight he comes by the fire. He's either a man-wolf or a wild dog that has the thirst madness. He will only get bolder when he scampers to Arkadia and he meets his own kind in the packs up on Lykaion, the mountain of the man-wolves. This follower of ours is as bad as the man-bear, if not his brother in evil. Draw that long knife. I string my bow. It has the man-wolf mania and his fangs will turn us into something like himself. Lichas no doubt sent it. Or your Gorgos."

No sooner had Erinna pointed out the shadow than the wolf circled at the edge of their camp. Suddenly the wild thing broke out of the dark, changed course, and ran, heading right toward their fire with teeth bared. Nêto froze. She could not lift her knife in time. But then as the animal neared, she pointed to Erinna, "Put down the bow. Stop. Stop!"—just as the large dirty hound charged her at full run and jumped up to her bosom and knocked her flat.

"Porpax, Porpax. No wolf. No wolf. My Porpax, Porpax of Helikon." Nêto wrestled with her dog with the bared fangs. Nêto laughed. "Living in the high caves on rabbits? Or on worse up on Kithairon? But you're home with me, your Nêto—and ready for our long march." The dog was growling but at least put his head down, as Erinna kept her bow taut.

"He may well have been your dog. But who knows what sort of flesh this Kerberos has tasted? He's changed to man-shape and back many times, I wager. We could cook a meal from the ticks and fleas on his raggedy fur. Nêto, Nêto—let this hound rejoin his new kind. He's gone over to the other side, either a wolf or worse. Or let me put an arrow through his head and kill off the demons in his black heart."

"Oh, no, he is my Porpax all right," Nêto laughed. "We will find no better guard than his long fangs." She patted the monstrous hound. "You'll see. He can smell Lichas ten stadia away and has Gorgos in his nose already." The aged hound had hard sinews and plenty of scars on his legs and back—and a taste of the wild that put him on the edge between feral and tame. His wandering on Kithairon had suited him since he left Nêto that night when she bore home Lophis. A year on the mountain had taken three off his frame. In his growling after the loss of Sturax, he killed a wolf, a young one with sharper fangs but half a head smaller. Then the farm dog took over the wolf brood that feasted on the goats of the highland shepherds. With his age and a near year in the pack, Porpax had lost his paunch and the jowls beneath his fangs.

Still, Porpax was not quite gone over to the way of the wolf. And in the morning this unlikely three—aged hound, helot virgin, and Amazon poetess—trotted along between the gulf and the Aegean. Erinna had planned to meet a few girls from Sikyon. Her friends were to hike them through the harbors of Lechaion on their right and Kenchreai to the left, all the way to sanctuary at Nemea. There the two would head due south to Argos—the same trail that Ainias and Proxenos would follow in the winter to come with their red stakes. As they all headed toward Akrokorinthos, Nêto was spinning long tales to the mute hound. She went on about how often he must have tried to leave his wolves to reach Helikon, about how Zeus had once turned King Lykaion into a wolf and the guard dog Kerberos in Hades, and how Charôn on the Styx would meet them all with his wolf ears.

Erinna put all her silliness to verse—"Nêtikôn and her talking dog"—in her low singing. Then Nêto announced, "Our dog is reborn and I name him Kerberos. Yes, he is guard dog of the underworld now. Our Porpax has become Kerberos of the three heads. If Gorgos can become Kuniskos, why cannot my Porpax be renamed Kerberos? When the two meet—and I am told at night in visions that they will—may the best dog win."

Soon the two women and the new Kerberos met the friends of Erinna. Three of them approached in cloaks, carrying two more cloaks for Nêto and Erinna, the women now all dressed out in deep green hoods, in the garb of pilgrims of the goddess Hera. The throng told strangers and the toll-men of Korinthos on the Nemea road that they were escorting the granddaughter of Chrysies, a new priestess for Hera at the sanctuary of the Argives near the sea. Most let the women be, once they saw Kerberos and feared the wrath of the goddess should her servants be touched. At the sanctuary of Zeus, the three guides left Nêto and Erinna at the guesthouse in Nemea, with a map of the road carved into an *ostrakon*, leading south into the valley of the Argives and then west over Mt. Parthenion to the three poleis and the valley of Mantineia.

Nêto reminded the innkeeper to be on watch for Proxenos the Plataian and a Stymphalian in the late autumn who would warn them all of a vast army to follow before the new year. The two set out southward over the pass into the Argolis, keeping the Heraion on their left and the *aspis* of the Argives on the right. They passed into the long walls and then beyond to the pyramid at Kenchreai, where they slept. "Keep away from Lerna and the Hydra," the Argive guards at the garrison laughed. "The air is bad over there on the swamps and their monsters bring fever to all who get near."

"Oh, don't worry," Erinna countered. "We believe in no tall stories of Herakles and his hydras and whatnot. We know that the sickness comes from bad air that hangs over the stagnant water there, not the bite of monsters in the night. Anyway we have no wish to head to the sea but instead to the high peaks of Parthenion, even with Pan and his Satyrs. The mountain protects virgins and there is no sickness on its heights. Even the hoofed god up there will leave us be. Once we reach the summit, then even we can't get lost since Tripolis and the valley of the Mantineians soon will be in sight below."

At the end of the fourth day from the shadows of Akrokorinthos, Erinna and Nêto entered the walls of the new city of Mantineia, though there was as yet no gate and only a few makeshift timbers to bar the way. Nêto had steered them far from misty Skopê on their left, and whispered to Erinna to turn her head from the hill where in her visions told that one day too many good men of the north would perish in yet another battle. The towers of Lykomedes this summer were only half built and the channel of the new Ophis still dry. There was no word of Proxenos or Ainias, who had gone to Thespiai to finish the town's walls and would not return south until the summer was spent. Still, the three were given a wide opening. None of the lords of Mantineia wished to test the fangs of the huge wolfhound on Nêto's leash.

On their fourth day in his city, the long-toothed Lykomedes, chief archon of Mantineia, finally gave them an audience, with a booming shout, "Alkidamas warned me of you two." They now spoke with him near the Arkadian gate in a small stoa where his archers lowered their bows, despite the growls of Kerberos. He had it in his mind to kill both women—whether out of spite as their cold stares met his probing eyes or out of worry that the Spartans might win still and blame him for intriguing with the helots—despite the money Alkidamas had sent him for their safe passage. But first Lykomedes was curious to find out whether they

knew anything about the number of men that might come with Epaminondas and his winter army. Such an army might make even more dangerous his own ongoing secret talks with King Agesilaos and the Spartans,
a way to earn Lykomedes some silver and an escape should the Boiotians
not come southward after all. Because Mantineia was close to Sparta and
far from Thebes, Lykomedes was not quite ready to join Epaminondas
unless he might show up at the city with thousands at his back. And even
then it seemed a wiser course only to plunder Sparta to strengthen Mantineia, but not to go farther west in some mad pursuit of the freedom of
the helots. Better for both Sparta and the helots to stay weak, since Lykomedes figured that after Epaminondas was dead or exiled, he would himself have to deal with those on both sides of Taygetos. So he now spoke to
the women carefully.

"Alkidamas urged me to help you. But I can see that you are queer
folk, both of you. Why, look, you carry men's weapons, and have a man-
dog with you and are looking for phantoms in some mythical city of Messenê to come. Still, I give you leave of our polis to find your helots—for
a day."

Then the boar-tooth stuck his finger into Erinna's breast. "But you
are only to find the visiting helot Nikôn—then leave. Stymphalian Ainias
for all his promises may not come back here to new Mantineia. I believe
our builder Proxenos will abandon us before the walls are finished. Neither has returned of late. So we want no charge brought on us by the
Lakedaimonians that we are stirring up their runaway helots. Find your
troublemaker Nikôn before I do. Just follow your nose to that tanner.
Then leave. Cleanse all the helots from the city. I do not trust your Alkidamas and all his wild talk of revolt and helots and a huge army from the
north—not while my walls are half-done and our Proxenos is missing,
and the Spartans on my borders are restless."

The women nodded, smiling that the silver of Alkidamas had bought
them safety, or at least time to round up the helots for the trek into Messenia. So they left Lykomedes. Nêto and Erinna covered their noses. It
was the black pond, where open ditches dumped the public toilets and the
butchers threw in the carcasses of their sheep and goats, among them an
occasional corpse of a hanged thief. By early evening the two women had
returned to the straw of the public stalls, and they talked late into the
night about how to scour the city to find the Messenians. But before

dawn they woke to an image at the doors. A tiny man in a rough cloak of wool riled the horses. Then he burst into the barn. Neither had time to reach for a blade. Nêto grabbed her cloak and covered up. Erinna jumped out of the straw and faced the intruder naked, ready to jump at his throat. Both then heard a husky voice in thick Doric yell "*lykos,*" and without warning Nêto answered in turn "*lykos.*"

"Calm down and get your cloak on, woman. Your Alkidamas sent me. So Nêto here knows our password "wolf." Then the shadow man hesitated and stepped into the torchlight. "We are to take you to Ithômê, Nêto. We leave this morning. Pack. We have twelve from free Messenia here. Another eight helots will join us on the trail. We march due west, with the warm sun at our back. I say I am Nikôn. But you knew that from your night dreams long ago."

"We do know you, Nikôn—from our dreams." Nêto nodded to Erinna. "I heard you from the hill in far-off Messenia calling me. I even hear you on your cliff in my sleep. I don't believe you're the killer they say you are. I learned that in my visions."

Erinna glared at him and scoffed, once her hawk eyes saw a small band at the barn door. "This is your army of freedom, Nêto? I mean you no ill will, helot Nikôn. But I had heard your band is the fiercest of the rebels, and yet I see just a handful of men in rags and with the smell of cow hide and pig fat. And when we two women are taller than any of your army, well . . . well. I worry that the Spartans will not worry." She kicked the straw and pulled her cloak over her head and finally picked up her bow.

Nikôn frowned. "No tall Spartan helmet crests here to scare you women. No tricking your eye with our false height. We're not Spartans. But laugh at us, and then see if we can't hit a cow's eye at thirty steps with the javelin, or follow that throw with the knife to split the shaft. Ask Antikrates. Ask even black Kuniskos just how many hoplites of Sparta they have found rotting in the passes from Ithômê. Ask him why they all stay barricaded in Ithômê, and why he fears us."

Erinna put down her bow. Good. This Nikôn was a bit mad himself— and armed, and might show her why his name brought terror even to the *kryptes,* the helot killers, of Kuniskos. The growing light showed that at second look these helots seemed a tough lot, with blades and worn quivers, and cornel javelins as well. Most had a savage look about them. Some

of the men were pointing at the big breasts of the poet herself and beginning to smile.

Erinna laughed as she took two steps back. "We will go safer for your
company—at least until we can see the peak of Ithômê."

Nikôn turned and pointed his sword at Erinna. "Our trip is for us,
woman, to decide—since we hear only a trace of bad Doric in your talk.
Nêto we know of. She knew the password. But as for you, Amazon, only
Alkidamas pledges his word. Where is he now? We watch—so you don't
earn silver from a Spartan *krypt,* or any other helot hunter. Don't bristle;
plenty of Messenians have done just that. Kuniskos was once a helot, we
hear. We have been killing Spartans, lots of them, while you sing of our
fights from a distance. Our fifty have become five hundred. And then
again five thousand. Soon ten times that."

Nikôn, as the light confirmed, was a dark sort, with an eye that gave
off bad intent to anyone it caught. Still, once he started, it was hard to
quiet him down. He was a runner as well as a cutthroat, who flitted about
Taygetos with messages for plotters and firebrands. Nikôn went always
with this short fellow Hêlos, who carried a long scroll and wrote down
orders and messages, one of the few of the helots who could write the
block letters and yet believed his illiterate master was far smarter than
any of the bastard helot leaders who in private boasted of red-caped fathers. Nikôn wore no helot leather, no fur cap. But he had a black wool
cape on his shoulders—and a looted Spartan breastplate beneath.

In silence Nikôn and his helots at last set out of the main road from
Mantineia with the two women. As they neared the western gate of the
city, Nêto was already staring at the cut square stones and bull-nose-
edged corners of the foundations, and at a new course of rectangular
stones that had been freshly laid. They were just like those at new
Thespiai—and what she had seen at Plataia. So the proud aristocrat Proxenos had not heeded her warnings but had long been down in Arkadia
supervising the finishing of the ramparts, even after her visions at the
generals' tent before Leuktra. The scent of the stone-man Proxenos was
already spreading all over the Peloponnesos, as if he had stamped a beta
for the Boiotians on every wall that rose. Without Proxenos, Nêto reminded her travelers, there would be no freedom here in the south.

In another day on the trail westward, Nikôn's band passed through
the stones of the sprawling Megalopolis farther down the Arkadian road,

heading south over the low mountains to ford the Alpheios. They re-freshed at Lykosoura. Then they all went up the side of Lykaion to the cave of Pan for the night. Soon Nêto could see the dark, gloomy shape of Ithômê, the mountain of myth, home to the gods of Messenia. At dusk on the fourth day from Mantineia they crossed into Messenia toward Andania, with a larger throng of armed helots of Nikôn's band—maybe a hundred now, the first invaders of the great war to come. "Look at it, Er-inna. Black Ithômê at last, home to Aristomenes of legend, the great ref-uge of the helots. The mountain rises as the beacon to all Messenians, of all helots for a thousand stadia in every direction." Nêto had not noticed the bands of helot rangers who had been shadowing them from the woods.

These new companies of Messenians were wearing Spartan breast-plates and carrying heavy willow hoplite shields with double grips. The helots had come to welcome the newcomers and escort them to the ruins of Thouria. They had often trailed the Spartan *kryptes* to harvest the stragglers and strip their panoplies up on the higher passes. The El-eans had sent breastplates and shields as well, so this was no *ochlos* but a well-outfitted phalanx of hoplites. Finally Erinna, as she neared the slopes, found her voice and began chanting her own new poem of her Epaminondas. She had added a new line about this second great city, holy Megalopolis that they left behind as they headed farther west still: "By the arms of Thebes, Megalopolis was girded with walls."

Nêto asked, "Sing of Messenê, my Erinna. It is past time to look for the third, the greatest, the tallest of all the fetters of Sparta to rise."

Erinna smiled. "Not yet; not until the city of our helots is free."

PART THREE

# *The March Down Country*

# CHAPTER 22

# The Great Muster

With the vote to go south before the new year, and the breakup of the Theban winter assembly, Mêlon made his way through the noise and elbows to a small shrine on the Theban Kadmeia. Still in the high city he stopped by two laurel trees that grew out of a stone outcropping, a viewing place with benches and a fountain. For the first time as he gazed below he understood just how many thousands of winter fighters were camped outside the walls of Thebes. A myriad? Or were there two and more ten-thousands?

How could Menekleidas with his two-pointed shoes prance around the hall as if he could stop what already was started? As the rhetoricians had been warning that very morning, thousands below were sharpening their blades and oiling their shield blazons a stone's throw from Iphikrates and his thugs in the assembly—and all this at the onset of winter. They looked more like mercenaries than liberationists, scarred with blade nicks, lame from spear jabs, clad in leather and bronze, eager for pay, more eager still for Spartan booty, with not a worry about their icy breath and sleeping on snow. These islanders and northerners cared little whether the Boiotarchs voted for their war, only whether Epaminondas was to be at their head with plunder promised. All had their grudges with Spartans. All could claim that a harmost or a Spartan admiral had ravaged their land or killed a cousin or friend in battle.

The law of Boiotia or the freedom of the helots meant not so much to them; the hatred and loot of Sparta everything. Mêlon saw tents and midday smoke rising all the way to Kithairon to the south and then even more camps northward up to the spurs of Parnassos and even toward the gap at Chaironeia. As he left his lookout point, the Thespian fought his way through the crowd. Then Melissos finally caught him on the back of his cloak. The boy had just tied Xiphos nearby to a plane tree. He was in high spirits due to the wild eyes of the delegates that had filed into the assembly—and what he had heard from the grove above the theater, where the poor and slaves listened in.

For all Melissos's bad sight, the boy was counting tents below and already numbering loudly the size of the army to be. "Two myriads," he gasped, "maybe more still if we could see all on the foothills to the south. Even our armies to the north are not this size." Suddenly the two were called over by Pelopidas. The general had a bright green cloak on, and a heavy leather tunic beneath. He was allotting scrolls in leather pouches to a group of young ephebes. By prearranged signals, well before the actual voting, the Theban already had sent out runners throughout Boiotia. The general was ordering more messengers to the marshes to ensure that the tardy and stubborn Boiotians of Orchomenos and Helikon showed up in the morning as they had promised. The eleven districts had had less than two days to send in their allotted *lochoi*—five hundred hoplites each and as many light-armed were the orders. The tribes in all the districts were to fill their quotas by daybreak, as the army would be on the passes outward within two days.

Pelopidas turned to Mêlon. "If we can get even a half-myriad of those Boiotians who stood firm at Leuktra, we will be doing well enough. That would give us altogether on the morrow almost two ten-thousands, with these volunteers from Euboia, Thessaly, Lokris, the islands, and even the men of Phokis who are still trailing in. And, of course, there are mobs in the south that will join us. So your Thespiai will send troops this time, even if they are not like those of the Malgidai or Chiôn?"

"Yes, some Thespians may march in. I am a Thespian, and pledge I will go south with you, and then over to Messenia to find my servant girl, whether alone or once again at the van of the army of Epaminondas. The fame of Chiôn and the big talk after Leuktra count. But mostly they will be the hill folk on Helikon, those in the backcountry all the way to Parnassos. Together with all these foreigners, I reckon that we may set out from Boiotia with more than Kleombrotos had when he came up here, at least."

Then Pelopidas continued. "You know that the larger the army is, the larger it will become. That's why you see out there wagons pulling in from over the pass. The mob has decided it is a fine thing to march southward. But that's not the half of it. We will need more than even these two myriads. If Proxenos and Ainias have done their work, if they keep that slippery Mantineian Lykomedes in line, maybe more than two ten-thousands are already mustering to the south at Arkadia." He paused and spoke slowly, as if Pelopidas himself could not quite believe the numbers of Hellenes on the move toward Sparta. "Altogether I'd wager sixty thousand and more will pour into Lakedaimon, with us and them combined. Don't forget the firebrand Epitêles and his Argives. There is no better friend of the *dêmos*. He will bring Dorian hoplites with him. These are the sorts that will continue over Taygetos into Messenia if they have to. King Agesilaos can't thwart us. We know Alkidamas with his Nêto has stirred up the helots. So the Spartans will have enemies in every direction."

Pelopidas waved at the throng below. "Ainias promised me that thousands of Arkadians will join us in the south, all with the club of our Herakles—the *ropalon* of Thebes—painted on their shields. I think before we're through, all of Hellas will be on the road. Ten myriads, and from every polis in Hellas."

Mêlon wondered how many Spartans would meet them. Maybe a myriad red-capes, from the allies and the Spartiates who had survived Leuktra, together with some more in the south and the home guard. Some Lakonian helots who wouldn't bolt over—be sure to count on those. Then there were the loyal *perioikoi* and the other half-citizens of Lakedaimon. Put them all together and Agesilaos might have thirty thousand with spears to guard his acropolis. If Epaminondas and his invaders had twice that number, or three times the army, the odds still were with the Spartan defenders, who only need not lose, not ford the icy waters of the Eurotas and break into the city.

Mêlon thought that even if they did not storm into the streets of Sparta, at least they could claim this horde might make it alive into the borders of Lakonia. That would make them the first invaders to have done so in nearly twenty generations of the Hellenes—not since the sons of Herakles of the myths and stories depicted on the pots and temple stones. Then Mêlon quit his dreaming and checked his pack. If the army were to leave in less than two days, he would have to send Melissos over to the farm for provisions. As an afterthought Mêlon had roped his own battle gear on Xiphos for the trip from the farm to Thebes, so it was just a question of food, not armor, and to let Damô know that he was marching south.

Melissos came up closer. "Master, I've already fetched Xiphos, fed from the stables. There's food right now. On the back of our stallion I've got dried fish, cheese, and wine—and our bronze breastplates and helmets. Last night Alkidamas had me empty his house of provisions. He has already left."

Mêlon laughed, *"Our* armor?"

"That's right. I have my breastplate, and the shield of Kalliphon, that dead son of Alkidamas. I fetched that with the food from the house of Alkidamas. So we are ready to march? I'm eager to see what you Hellenes can do in a day."

"So we will, boy, first to Sparta with Epaminondas and then on to Messenia, alone, if need be, to find my Nêto." With that, Mêlon patted the northerner's head, as he led Xiphos behind them.

The two of them walked the horse out through the gate to find the field camps of Epaminondas, a half-morning march to the south, where they would spend the first night. As they walked, Mêlon repeated what his father Malgis had once taught him before his own first outing at Haliartos. "There is an art, Melissos, to a muster. It's not like a pack of dogs that snarl and sprint out after the first hare that crosses their paths. Epaminondas is already forming up the columns, right over there under the clouds of Kithairon. The first thousands will leave in the morning, over the pass with us at the van. Then the hamlets from the eleven districts drift into Thebes. Their officers will have these late-coming regiments fall into line by companies, six men wide along the road—all the baggage in the middle of their column. We at the head will be over the mountain and halfway to Megara by nightfall tomorrow."

"Or by midday, master," piped up Melissos. He went on as he gazed at the long columns behind. "We are a snake then, Master Mêlon. A long snake, always ahead as its coils unwind to the rear. We're getting longer even as we get farther from Thebes?"

"Longer? I'd say when we head down the pass our tail will just be leaving Thebes, seventy stadia back. Who knows, Melissos, it may be snowing on us on the pass yet sunny on those behind in the plain—and all in this same winter army." Later, near the foothills of Erithryrai, Mêlon got word that Epaminondas was waiting for him at the head of the column. The generals were already high on the Plataian road, camped outside the walls of the city that Proxenos had rebuilt years earlier. This was where Mêlon wished to go anyway, since Alkidamas had told him that one of his agents would be meeting him there by nightfall. Before sunset the two slipped into camp. They tethered Xiphos beside a fire. Maybe a half-myriad of northerners were busy around them, and at least that many Thebans all along the road back to the Kadmeia. Officers kept the road clear. The winter rains were late here. The road was free of the deep red winter mud of the valleys of northern Boiotia.

Mêlon grabbed Melissos by the shoulder. "Stay close. These northerners, folk like your own, can't be trusted, especially the riders. The Lokrians would run us down for play. The Phokians, well, the Phokians, they're worse than any Spartans I know. I've seen some outlaws from Thessaly, too. Temple robbers and shrine looters, all of them, neighbors of yours. Still, our Epaminondas can't be choosy in his allies. And he wasn't." The two got directions. They were soon in among the tents of Epaminondas, on a rise with a view of the distant hills above the battlefield at Leuktra. Mêlon noted that from the slopes above the river Asopos they could see the last light of the short winter day flickering off the white marble monument where he had met Alkidamas only two days earlier, not far from where Lichas had taken Lophis down. To the west along a bank three stadia away they could see the majestic hilltop estate of Proxenos, son of Proxenos of Plataia. Its torches on the portico above the river were blazing before the sun even fell, perhaps the household's eager beacon to guide their master home—as if he were not somewhere already far distant, wandering down in the Peloponnesos.

Mêlon helped Melissos unload their packs. "Sleep, Makedonian. Tomorrow we talk as we march. This twilight let the young bloods put our *lochoi* in their order. The *peripoloi* and the rangers rouse the countryside, as they search for the stay in beds and the hide-a-ways. Anyone is fair game that the muster officers can't find on the first go-around. We strike out at dawn. They say we will be at the flatlands of Mantineia in five days or six. Then two more on to Sparta."

Then from his back a familiar voice took over from Mêlon. "Maybe seven days for our tail end. The full muster won't even pass out of Thebes until tomorrow night." It was Epaminondas. He had no helmet but wore a leather broad-brimmed hat that nearly covered his face. "A bad habit of walking up behind you, Mêlon. No worry. You are no snoring sentry. So in peace sleep, Thespian. All is planned." With that Epaminondas passed on by their camp with four or five hoplites. "Come to the head of the march at daybreak. We will be waiting for you."

Mêlon and Melissos were drifting off to sleep even before full darkness and the Great Bear had yet taken over the sky. How had he ended up here on the ground at Plataia? Just three days earlier, he had been at work at his olive press, promising Proxenos only that he might ride over to see things at Thebes. From that sudden urge, he had fallen in with the stranger Alkidamas, taken on a new servant, watched the great debate in the council hall of the Boiotians, and been called to the head of an army on its way into the frontier of Sparta. Suddenly Mêlon jolted up. Someone had kicked him. The voice was Boiotian. He recognized the tongue as well. "Sleeping so soon? But it is not even full dark—the moon is still in hiding."

Chiôn was standing over him.

"This sapling next to you, what is it? A slave boy? A helot? You were never a boy-lover, Mêlon. How did this mushroom clamp onto your trunk?"

"Careful to kick the sleeping dog, Chiôn, he may bite yet."

Mêlon rose to greet Chiôn. "This Melissos comes as the hostage servant of Alkidamas. That man's own son Kalliphon was cut down near us on the left at Leuktra. So he lent me a spare Makedonian hostage that General Pammenes brought back to the men of Boiotia. He is a truce pledge from the Makedonians of the north. If the peace holds, he goes back to the north after the barley harvest. Then we get our own captives back in the bargain. He claims he's royal. But he won't tell us more. In the north there every tribe boasts they have queens and kings. He watches more than he talks."

Chiôn nodded. "I know, I know of those two. I met both in Thespiai and sent them after you. But so they found you. I had Eudoros and Neander show them the road, and where to find you at the trophy of Leuktra."

Mêlon was puzzled. "Chiôn, are you here from Alkidamas? He was supposed to send me a messenger. Why you? Why leave Damô, even if she's with the dogs and the boys? She's with your child. The country is swarming with bad sorts."

"But Master, forgive me. I come for a reason you won't like. Your coins in the well are yours. I've never drawn the boxes up without you. You know that." Now Chiôn looked up and talked bolder to his former master. "But a strange helot from the south met me when I was pruning in the red grape vines two days ago. A Nikôn, he said his name was, as he ran up. A proud label for a slave, this man called "Victory." But Nikôn could hardly stand. His sandals were worn to the soles, and he was about through and shaking. Even if he had been fresh, he was a scarred and leathery sort, an ugly one with whip scars on his neck and back, and with a stink of hides on him. Begging for money, he claimed, so that he could ransom our Nêto. In chains to the south, he swears, she was. A prisoner in the log fort of Lord Kuniskos, he swears. He hands me a note, with the block letters scratched on bark from a woman who wrote the Attic way— why in the south I don't know. At least that's what he said. He looked like he'd run the whole way. But he was at least a Pheidippes, an iron legs."

Mêlon grabbed his forearm as Chiôn continued. "I needed a thousand good silver pieces, Master. I only skimmed the top of the iron boxes, and didn't touch the gold below. So I told this Nikôn the ransom money would follow in five days. I will take it myself to free our Nêto to keep her alive. I promised Nikôn the helot that. We gave pledges. I sent word to Alkidamas, who is on the side of Kithairon by the sea waiting for a ship. But Nikôn took off back southward out to the harbor town Kirrha on the gulf like he was running the race in armor at Olympia. Here is the letter that Damô read better than I. I memorized what she said was scratched on the bark:

Erinna tês Ithômês tô Mêloni. O Mêlon Malgidos. Pempe nun chrêmata pros tên Erinnan en tê gê tê tôn Messêniôn. Autên apoagorazein dei tina Nêtona apo tôn Spartiatôn. Pempete auta meta toude Nikonos, andros men agathou, agrammatou de.

"Erinna of Ithômê to Mêlon, son of Malgis: Send money to Erinna in the land of the Messenians. She must buy back Nêto from the Spartans. Send it with this here Nikôn, a good man, but an illiterate."

Chiôn remembered more or less the way Damô had read it, but half the words on the bark were unclear to him. So he handed it over to Mêlon and kept talking. "What do these scratches mean? That stringy helot

Nikôn went to his knees in begging, an odd thing for a tanner by his smell who says he will set all of Messenia on fire. So our Damô had me pull up the coin box. I had no wish to trust this helot, even if Nêto had long said that she spoke to him while asleep. But Nikôn told Damô well enough what our Nêto looks like. So he does not lie, at least not completely. But who is this Erinna? When I asked Nikon, he said, 'Ask Alkidamas.'"

Mêlon at least knew as much as Chiôn. "I am sworn to march with Epaminondas, but it is southward all the same, and I will be over Taygetos perhaps before any of you. I see that you know that Alkidamas is not here. He left the assembly for the bay at Aigosthena and has some grand plan to sail into the port of Messenia with helot rowers, no less, that he rounded up at Athens. He was supposed to send me word when he was to leave and where we were to meet in the south. Maybe he had wind of your Nikôn last night. But I see you planned to row with him all along or at least the two of you cobbled together some sort of plan on your chance meeting when I had set out with Xiphos to Thebes. Chiôn, you did well enough. Don't worry about the silver. But now there is no need to go yourself. We can send the pay-off with Alkidamas, who as it works out is going south anyway, even if you were his agent after all. I see that now. Trust this Erinna. I've heard from Alkidamas at Thebes she is with Nêto. Stay on the farm. I am marching at sunrise. As I said, I hope to beat all of you to Messenia and still keep my vow to march with Epaminondas into the vale of Lakonia. I may get there first anyway."

"If Gorgos is this Kuniskos," Mêlon went on, "then he will not kill her, at least not yet. He knows us, that we will send ransom money. You or I will even up with him. The man Alkidamas, I saw just these last two days in the assembly at Thebes. He is on his way. He must know this Nikôn and is close with Nêto and what she was up to. She never said anything much of her plans to me before she left." Mêlon finished slowly. "So take the money from the farm to him at the port. Do it this day. Then it will go by sea to Ithômê, while I try to get south first. Yes, go to the port and find your Alkidamas."

Chiôn looked troubled. So Mêlon warned him a last time. "Chiôn. This is not your fight. Your one arm, wife, your son to come, and the farm, too—all that means you stay on Helikon. You give the money to Alkidamas at the port, and then go home. That is enough. I'll race the old man by land to Messenia, and see if I can beat his ship to deal with Gorgos wherever and whatever he is. That way one of us at least will get to Messenia, by land or sea."

Chiôn paused. "Maybe. But I fear I can do far better in hunting Nêto down than you, Master. Besides, I've only seen the Spartans twice. At Tegyra and Leuktra. Not in their home. I can even up with Lichas for my arm. I'll make him bow to Lophis in Hades—or worse still. No one knows Gorgos better than his fellow farm slave. I can figure out where he is before either you or Alkidamas. And we hear still of the boast of that Antikrates. We missed him at Leuktra. The tongues of your Olympians say he will do harm to our Epaminondas. So I will give the money to Alkidamas and come back and march with you to the Isthmos."

"No. No. All in good time, Chiôn. I let Nêto go off, and it is my debt to bring her back safely. I have waited far too long this autumn in my anger at her leaving. These other debts are on my ledger as well, along with seeking Nemesis for Lophis and Malgis. The reckoning is soon. Lichas, or so my *daimôn* tells me, is not long for this earth. Not with all of Boiotia heading south in the morning. But remember the words of Nêto," Mêlon ended with a laugh. "You are not to see the sea. So again head home, and keep our farm safe. Take our Xiphos here. You need him on the farm, and you can save me from having a Plataian ride him back over there. Either Alkidamas or I will find Nêto."

Chiôn frowned at that. "How silly. Proxenos was not to cross the Isthmos, and yet he is now a hero down there in the south. I will swim in the sea anyway if I give the silver to Alkidamas at Aigosthena late this night. But, yes, I go to the sea and then home to Helikon." With that he nodded, took the reins of their Xiphos, and led the horse away. Then he was gone as abruptly as he had appeared. Mêlon almost thought he saw Myron, or some brute, in torchlight waiting for his friend on a crest not far from camp.

As Chiôn headed toward Helikon, he seemed to see visions again in the starry night, as if, amid the stars and moon, there were bright outlines of a timber stockade. Then he paused and the trance was clearer and right before his eyes. Inside this fort he saw through the lamplight the head of Nêto shaved—was it on a pole? Nêto was either dead or close to it. Gorgos was near or at the center of this crime, though he seemed to go by different names and had altered his look, or so they said of the helot lord with the shaved head and fine cloaks. So Nêto spoke all this to him for a moment from across the Isthmos far to the south. His dreams had stayed with him in the waking hours, and now were even stronger enough to stop him in mid-stride. Myron shook him and the visions ended as the two picked up their pace.


After Chiôn left, Mêlon and Melissos slept for only half the night, and then arose well before sunrise. Mêlon was eager to press ahead to find Nêto, but he was still not sure whether this Nikôn was a scoundrel who had heard Nêto's master had coin, or was an agent of Alkidamas, or was a lover of Nêto. In any case, for now all Mêlon could do was send Chiôn with his money for Alkidamas at Aigosthena. He would march with the army into the Peloponnesos, and then hope by burning Lakonia that the helots on the other side of Taygetos would rise up and so free Nêto wherever she was—though he thought he would slip away at some point and arrive at Messenia before the army.

Others this morning were stirring even before Mêlon and Melissos. Soon they were waiting impatiently at the head of the column, nervous to move out. There was a growing noise of horse and leather and wood and bronze, with plenty of clatter and cursing in almost every dialect of the Hellenes. Everywhere arose the din of the heavy tread of thousands of feet milling about as they readied to march out. "Look back toward Thebes," Melissos yelled. "The torches, a myriad of them. Even more, below." Then they heard the voice of Epaminondas. "March out!"

With that the mob at the back of the hoplites let out, "On to Sparta. To Sparta." Then a roar of just "Sparta, Sparta . . ." The columns at the van moved out toward the mountain passes, in the gloom as the winter sun was behind the mountains. In quiet the army knew it was late in the year for war, on this the shortest day of the year—the great brooding solstice when all shuddered that the colder times were ahead. This northern horde was perhaps three or four times larger than the one mustered at Leuktra. All Hellas north of the Isthmos seemed to be on the move, either to fight or follow the throng peddling food and drink and women. Even more would join up in the south. Northerners had never marched in mass before, much less had they joined with islanders and the men of the Euboia to the west, soon to be alongside hoplites mustering at Elis, Argos, and Arkadia to the south. In the early darkness most appeared strange folk. Some had open-faced *piloi* without nose guards in the new style. Others wore cheap armor on their chests from the foundries of Euboia that were scarcely tempered or hammered. Most had painted the club of Thebes over their shield blazons—as if for the next few days they were Epaminondas's own Boiotians. A few had the heavy sheet-bronze breast-plates of their grandfathers, but far more wore glued fabric with small metal plates. Freedmen and the poor had neither the *thôrax* nor even greaves. Many, Mêlon noticed, were the hide men from the mountains on the north shore of the gulf. These carried small Thrakian leather crescent-shaped shields and long javelins or bows across their shoulders—the tribes of Aitolians, Akarnanians, and Ambrakions for whom ambush and outlawry in the hills alone won honor. Thessalonians and Lokrians rode on past atop shaggy ponies, with long fur capes and quivers and javelins strapped to their saddles. The looters of Delphi, the Phokians, came with good bronze armor—no doubt lifted at night from the votive racks in the temples.

"No worry, Master, about how they look. The uglier the better, yes?" Melissos stammered. He went on. "As for us, up in the north, we pay any who will fight. And Master, when they fall, we burn their corpses, with-out charge for the timber to their families, as promised. That's enough. These are men who have strong right arms; why worry why they fight? For now, aren't they on our side?" He went on with an eye on Mêlon to see whether his new master was ready with a slap to quiet down. "Who cares any more whether spear-men own land or meet your census? Our poor men from the hills, why, they can kill a lord with his five hundred *plethra* of wheat land just as easily as they can a snake. Watch when this army pours into Lakonia. One of our landless robbers from Ambrakia will jump on the back of a Spartan ephor. Cut his throat without any music or two-step or any of those other things the Spartans drill at. These are the wages of *dêmokratia* of your new Hellas, a real equality—in killing. Why dye your cape scarlet when it keeps you no warmer?"

Mêlon laughed at his new talkbox servant. For a blurry-eyed boy he knew too much about the darker nature of men—and how much better it is to use than be disappointed by it. Yes, this Melissos was hardly the gangly servant that he had dismissed in his mind just three days earlier. He had grown up royal in the rough north, it seemed. There the Makedonians

grunted rather than spoke the Hellenic tongue. They poked or killed anything that they wished to in their wine halls after battle. They fought for
women, or gold, or land, not for ideas, and much less for helots. So how
odd, Mêlon mused: These northerners like Melissos and his brood flocked
to civilization to enjoy the finer life that the law and justice would bring,
even though, like the flat worm in the gut, they would eat enough holes
to starve and kill their life-giving host. Odder still, the more the Hellenes
adorned their cities in marble and wore gold clasps and purple cloaks, the
more they lost their stomach to get into the muck and fight those like
Melissos who thrived here in the mess and would storm their gates. No
wonder Epaminondas dressed in rags and drank gruel and had no children—no concerns for the safety of kin that so blinds men, no worry
whether he would tire of ice baths in the river. To keep his soft Hellas
free, Epaminondas would shun its softness. When a man gives up gold
and land and family, he's halfway living in the other world anyway. But
then so were men like Proxenos, and Ainias—and Mêlon himself. Was
not that why they followed Epaminondas in the first place? Mêlon thought
of all that—and how this Melissos might be a good servant to have in the
days ahead.

The sun rose just as they trudged up the mountain, and they soon
passed through the forests of spruce and pine of Kithairon and the high
plains among the woods. The army was already moving at a brisk walk,
along the road that would lead them out of Boiotia through the mountains down into the Megarid and onto the Isthmos. Without the usual
August heat, a winter march was far easier on the men—at least if the
weather held and the ground stayed firm. Mêlon and Melissos were at the
van during the ascent to Kithairon's summit. So they fell in with Pelopidas and Epaminondas at the head. Both at intervals already were sending
out runners ahead to watch for Athenian archers and horse who might
try to waylay and whittle down the army in hopes that the war between
Thebes and Sparta might be more evenly matched and more lethal for
both. Some had already spotted the red stakes—the ones that Proxenos and
Ainias had set out a few days earlier to mark the way where the Megarian
tribes of the mountains had supplied food. The idea of the Boiotarchs was
to skirt the Athenian border. The army would take the mountain fork and
avoid the Eleusis road. That way they could get to the Megarid along the
Oinoi path between the watchtowers to the plain across Salamis, with the

summit of Mt. Pateras on their right. They could sleep up on the pass on this first night and be tented around Megara and its market on the afternoon of the second day.

At noon on the third day from Thebes, the army would cross the Isthmos—Korinthians and Athenian guards not withstanding. Then by noon on the fourth or fifth, Epaminondas would market outside the *aspis* of Argos. In two more days from there they would be coming down from the hills of Parthenion and spreading over Tripolis. On the seventh or maybe the eighth morning, when they joined the Argives, fifty thousand of them would be camped at new Mantineia. Or so was the plan that Epaminondas and Alkidamas had worked out when they sent Proxenos and Ainias ahead.

Lykomedes had promised good stocks in his new city, and they had pledges of twenty thousand to join them from Elis and Arkadia, all to meet at Mantineia. Ainias and Proxenos along the way had bought in advance a thousand goats, five hundred cattle, and two thousand sheep to be picked up by the army as it moved, some of them paid in Elean silver in advance to the Megarians and Nemeans. The two already had purchased five hundred *medimnoi* of barley and five hundred of wheat in measures of a hundred stored in dry cisterns every other day past the Isthmos. Ainias had posted a warning to the plainsmen of the Megarid and those beyond the Isthmos that Epaminondas would take what he had paid for, should the towns not produce what was bought, especially since Ainias had agreed to the high winter prices and put down two talents for the grain stores.

Before the high noon of this first day of the march, the generals parleyed over the food and route—snow in the shady ravines, with some ice in the low spots under gray skies. Even with the sun out, the morning was windy and cold, and the oncoming low clouds from the north made Mêlon worry that this huge muster was star-crossed or cursed by barren winter. He had marched for thirty years but never in winter, and never under *stratêgoi* with less than a month left on their tenure. Yet his farming sense told him the wind would let up and they would see the sun before they crossed the

Isthmos. Epaminondas noticed the Thespian's silence. "Worried about becoming an outlaw, son of Malgis—a hungry *phugas* or an *adikôn* even? Don't. Don't give in to your fears. The army will march at the pace of your limp. If we don't make it by the new season but decide there are other things to clean up in the Peloponnesos, well then I will gladly stand trial, not the men who follow. But I doubt the talkers in the agora wish to execute ten thousand of their own Boiotians in armor for the crime of humiliating Agesilaos."

Suddenly, at the summit, the sky in the distance became blue and clear, and the storm clouds blew on by out to the Aegean. Looking back they had a clear view of the horde following them. Epaminondas resumed his own talk. "Take in all these men tramping in the cold of winter. Think of it all, Mêlon." Even on this eve of winter the land looked lush with month-old green barley and some sprouting wheat stands. It all prompted a gasp from Epaminondas as they headed into a dark bend in the pines. "Farmland like no other, ours is. No wonder Kleombrotos tried to take all he could of it from us. I would too, if I were from parched La-konia."

Without warning Mêlon grabbed his arm as they marched, worried that his general did not know war for all of his years of bleeding in it. "Did he really only want that, my general? Doesn't the king have green land enough from the water that runs down from the ridges of Taygetos? Or do you think Spartans starve and are without the twenty thousand *plethra* of bottomland in Lakonia and Messenia?" The farmer, who knew something about land and the fight over it, wanted to let these generals know what they were about to march into. "Is this what we are marching about? Who will own the great plain of Boiotia? Is that all you think wars are about? Taking what you are in need of from someone else? This greed, real or imagined—this *pleonexia*?" Suddenly Mêlon felt a *daimôn* had in-fused his thoughts. He could not stop. His tongue ran on. He even forgot where his feet took him over the pass. Now his stiff leg eased, and the words poured out. It was as if for those last ten years of thought in his vineyard alone, he could claim his due to speak with a hundred captains about him as recompense.

"But why do the Athenians fight us over the salty marsh at Oropia or the scrub oak of Panakton when they had a vast rich empire in the Ae-gean? Why do men die for such trifles?" He was warming in the winter midmorning sun. For the first time in his life he thought he felt a larger truth coming out of his mouth that powerful men knew less than he and would listen to his logic—if only he talked even more. Mêlon was in the world of leaders now, not alone in his orchards, so his ideas grew sharper as they met frowns and nods among those who heard him. "O yes, tell me, my general, why do the Spartans mow down the Argives over that worthless *methoria* of high rocks and thistle? Why, when all the black soil of Messenia is already theirs? Or do you really think we Hellenes—or for that matter the Persians or Skythians up north—go to war only when hungry for food or land or for such good or bad reasons?"

Pelopidas stepped up and sighed, amused that a farmer of vines was lecturing generals on the subject they knew best. "Well, then, tell us what else, our Thespian wise man, causes war."

"How about our pride? Isn't there our honor—and our fears?" Mêlon pressed on. "Of course a sort of greed of the Spartans—the sheer desire of taking something from the Boiotians to add to what they already don't need in the Peloponnesos." Mêlon took Pelopidas's silence as a goad to go on, as Epaminondas marched a bit quicker on ahead. "Maybe we insulted Kleombrotos and the king Agesilaos, we rustics, the *agrikoi* of Hellas, marching when and where we pleased. Remember, Epaminondas stared the king down at Sparta. They needed the farms of Boiotia like they needed our eels or ducks—relish, dip, a side dish, no more. No, the thistle in their sandals was the very idea that we thought we were better than they—and most of Hellas was beginning to agree."

"So, Mêlon, do you really believe our Epaminondas should have settled up with the king? Do you think his harsh words caused a war?"

Mêlon frowned and went on, though he sensed his general was not serious, was teasing rather than learning from him. "Of course not, my general. Name a war, Pelopidas, that was an accident—just one that broke out over a wrong word." He was soon stammering, worried that a big man like Pelopidas, leading an army to war, had little idea why they were at war at all. So Mêlon pressed him further. "Listen, my commander. The men of the Peloponnesos invaded our land because they thought they could. And, by the gods, we had done nothing to persuade them otherwise. Why not? We lost Koroneia. We stumbled at Nemea. Tegyra was only a small victory. For years when you build women's barricades rather than raise shields chest-high, you send a message: that lesser men either cannot or will not keep the Spartans out." Mêlon found his words were clearing his own head, putting into some sort of order what he knew in his breast. He could not have stopped if he had wished to. "So for our part, why do you think Boiotians march this morning? Only because Leuktra taught us that we could—and these red-capes to the south cannot keep their enemies out like they have the past seven hundred years. Had we lost at Leuktra, not a northerner would be in the ranks with us this day."

Mêlon, the lone vine pruner on Helikon, had an audience and so he lectured the general on why his army was following him. He thought states were like people, and knew people well enough up on Helikon—both how to keep the bad off his land and to enlist the good to help him. "Most men have no belief, either for good or bad. They follow only the winners. So they claim we are liberators and follow you, Pelopidas, because they think you can do what you promise. If you cannot make them rich, then at least make them proud to lord it over the losers. But stumble and most will damn you not just as weak, but as bad also. Remember Backwash in the assembly. Just like at Leuktra, if we win, he'll claim us as disciples. Lose—and he will put the nooses around our necks. Back home, right now he's waiting and tapping his foot as we march here. Most men are like that: They pass on risks to be safe and liked."

Mêlon forgot that they were making good progress toward the junction to the road through the watchtowers of Megara, along the very trail where Erinna and Nêto had first met so many months earlier. Melissos was right behind him, listening as Mêlon talked nonstop as if he were a Theban general leading the ranks. Mêlon at last noticed his tall ears. "So are you listening to this, Makedonian? Or do you tire from the banter of Hellenes?"

"Master, I live and sleep war. I may be a hostage. But for four months longer, I am pledged as proof of the truce to the Boiotarchs with the Makedonians—and with Alkidamas and now you, Mêlon, son of Malgis. Please tell us more; the march is no march when you talk."

Meanwhile Epaminondas gave orders to his scouts and messengers to go back up the pass and hurry up the tail of the column. "But my Pelopidas," Epaminondas for a blink turned and took over from Mêlon. "If we all agree wars make no sense, if they start out over pretexts, these *pro-*

*phases* as the philosophers call them, what exactly allows them come to pass? Why do these shoves end up with spears and shields? What is the *aitia*, the real cause of what we are doing this day?"

"Mêlon just told us," Pelopidas laughed, but he then paused before going on. They were climbing and he needed a deeper breath. The general was light-headed, but finished up his thought. "Aren't we trying to restore our pride, the reputation we lost when we let the Spartans prance through our fields each spring?"

Mêlon nodded and was almost finished with his lesson. "We must with a state like Sparta. When I saw you Thebans below me hide every time Agesilaos came into Boiotia with his army, I had no stomach to go down from Helikon and join you. We are going into Sparta because we have to, because in the past you let them come to you too many times. Yes, some of you want democracy for the helots, but you march now only because Leuktra gave you honor and pride, and took both from the defeated brood of Lichas."

The army began slowly to go downhill, bypassing the high plain of Skourta. It was veering right at the crossroads, over the road of the high watchtowers that would wind down east and south to sea and along the coast to Megara. Epaminondas hurried forward and left them with an order: "Tell me how this all ends at camp tonight." With that he was gone, happy to be back alone out in front of the column.

Pelopidas was nearly as old as Mêlon of the one good leg, but was not used to the hard climbing in armor, since he rarely dug vines or scythed grain and his belly hung down at the bottom rim of his breastplate. He was wheezing. "Well, if Spartan fear and pride brought them northward, and the hunch they would walk over us at little cost, what will make them quit? We won at Leuktra. So why does this unending war go on?"

"Don't play with me, Pelopidas," Mêlon warned as they too made the turn onto the Megara road and by its first tower of many to come. He noticed that thirty or so of the Sacred Band were still marching bunched next to them, eager to hear the exchange. "Wasn't it you, Pelopidas, in the moments after Leuktra, who called to bring the war home to the Lakedaimonians?"

Pelopidas frowned. "Yes, but I confess I like to fight—anyone and all the time. Just like your Chiôn or our Ainias, a bloody Ares that gets fat on the gore of war. So I am not a good touchstone of what others do. Much less our poleis. So how do you think wars, especially ours, will end? When we are all in Hades, a peace of the dead?"

Mêlon didn't even look at him as he answered back, as the sun began to warm his face. "I'll be blunter still: One side wins, the other loses. Only that way does the reason the troublemaker fights vanish, and do his big ideas get smaller. Talk never stopped any war for good; talk only passes it on to grandchildren not born." Mêlon grimaced, thinking that all the spearing of Malgis at Nemea and Koroneia had only left it to Lophis to fall at Leuktra. Leuktra? The battle to end at last the war with Sparta? Hardly. As long as the Spartans had the serfs of Messenia feeding them, they would keep marching up here. He went on. "As for the truces of the Hellenes, they are not worth the stone they are cut on. The more some of the Hellenes swear to others before the gods that they will both have the same friends and enemies for fifty years, the more likely such a peace will not last for one."

The two talked and were interrupted often by the Sacred Band, especially the younger of the three hundred. But they tired of the chatter and wanted to know only when they would arrive in Lakonia. Surely it must be over the next mountain as they looked down at the great plain of Megara before them and imagined they saw the Spartan Eurotas instead of a thousand stadia of walking ahead. Not a Boiotian in this army seemed to have been to the Peloponnesos. Mêlon ignored them all. "You see, we will change Sparta from what it was—take its claws away and cage it—if we can, that is. Do that, and it will never be able to make war north of the Isthmos. That is, I think, the plan of our general. So he preempts and starts this war to be the last."

Pelopidas sighed. "I fear even with war in Lakonia, and even with the Messenians free, we will leave this war to our children unless we level Sparta and kill her kings. Our Epaminondas must make war so terrible that the Spartans can never fight us again."

Mêlon slapped Pelopidas. "So this was a game all along, Pelopidas. You are no honest philosopher. No, you simply wished me to give back your own answers. I say that you are more the fire breather than iron-gut Epaminondas himself."

"I suppose," Pelopidas quietly offered, but then he stuck his head closer to Mêlon's and in a softer voice went on. "But sometimes others can give voice to the dark truth we prefer ourselves not to utter or even hear, but wish to be aired all the same. Because you know war better even than I, and not so long ago no doubt had no appetite for this great march, Mêlon, you have taken a great worry off my heart." Pelopidas stopped in the road to finish. "I know there is no other way. I am not just a war lover. There is really no other way to end this, but in the direction we are marching. Yes, we must cut off the head of the serpent and watch his slithering trunk die in pain."

"No. No, there is no other way," Mêlon answered.

"We will either end this war our way—or they will end it theirs."

Now even Melissos echoed. "No other way, no other way—no other way than to head south and cut them all down—or have no war and no peace, as it is now."

With that outburst, the talkers heard the trumpeters' order to halt and pitch camp and to wait for the twenty thousand men at their backs. Mêlon could already see well the Megarid below. They figured that they had gone some one hundred twenty stadia while they had talked the first day's march away. Still Mêlon thought on in silence. This new power of Thebes—would there come also in time the end of its own democracy? Of course it would. Sparta had once dethroned Athens. Now Thebes was doing the same to Sparta. He knew well an end-day would arrive in turn for these Boiotians. That was the nature of states. In their wealth and pride, they forgot the harder ways of earlier men who had given them plenty. Maybe the Boiotians would muster a year or even ten of such marches at his back. But even now as he looked around the front ranks of the column, he saw few such as Pelopidas and Epaminondas to lead such men again—and far too many men like Backwash to throw away what others had given them.

Victory, the wealth of peace, proves as deadly to states as does defeat. Is that man's doom? That as we struggle to plane down the edges for the young, old men forget that their own blisters and cuts from these knots and burls made us the savvy carpenters we are? That smoothing the splintery grain for our own children only ends up smoothing them, so that they know nothing of the rough to come? That in our wish to be good we ruin those who we wish to help, because we cannot let them suffer as we did when we have the power or the wealth to stop it? That law of iron explains the fall of families and the poleis as well. Did their Pythagoras have any answers for all this, since—Mêlon knew—his vanishing Zeus did not?

Only Chiôn and Nêto and Gorgos, even—the slaves born poor and with the coarse edge of life sharp in them still—showed the stuff of the older breed, and only for a while until they would become soft lords of an aging Ithômê of soft citizens who forgot that they had been helots. That was Chiôn's fear, Mêlon knew, and what made the freed slave stay feral and far from the appetites of the city. The key, he also saw, for polis man was to match word and deed, body and mind, the work of the hoe with the papyrus, avoid the lounge of Phrynê as much as did the shaggy hill men of Aitolia. Without the mean, *to meson*, the laborer becomes a thug, the sophist an effete. No, Chiôn would stay in the wild where he could do more for the tame in the town by almost alone of men not being tame. For his part, Mêlon consoled himself that at least for now the new Messenê to come, the city of the soon-to-be-freed helots, might yet remind Hellas, even in its dotage, of the original ways of the polis—once the low rough stones were placed on the polished top. Freeing the helots would end Sparta, Mêlon knew. But he guessed that Epaminondas thought their liberation would give Hellas itself a reprieve, both by the struggle needed to free them and the infusion of new blood into the city-states of Hellas.

# CHAPTER 23

## *Chiôn Goes South*

Meanwhile, halfway to the farm, Chiôn had stopped. He grabbed the wrist of Myron. He spoke slowly, and then Chiôn began to make the freedman repeat what he said, so that Myron could say it all to Damô when he got back to Helikon—just as Chiôn ordered. At the fork, Chiôn took from Myron's pack the sack of silver that they had promised Nikôn and sent Myron back to Helikon on the horse. He alone headed south and east over the spurs of Kithairon, running to the port at Aigosthena and the windy winter gulf. He prayed to the One God to forgive his lie to Mêlon that he would stay on Helikon; in truth, he had already promised Alkidamas that he would meet him at the dock. If Chiôn went all the way back to the farm, he would surely miss the ship of Alkidamas and his promise to Alkidamas to go southward with him and keep him safe. He had promised the old man to be on the shore by midnight and to come armed to guard them should the captain—and their money—need watching. Perhaps if he brought news of Nêto, Mêlon would grant him a pardon when they met again. Swinging the silver across his shoulder, Chiôn continued across the hills. The day gave way to dusk, then to black night, as Chiôn's shadow moved among the trees, like a night-hunting creature in the forest, whose byways he had long ago mastered on his solitary hikes.

Down at the shore, the dockers on the quays at the port of Aigosthena were calling out at the lights that were visible on the waves—*Thauma!*

*Lampades, ide lampadas. Lampades en thallassê*—A wonder! Lights, look, lights. Lights on the sea. Soon even the eyes of Alkidamas saw them, the twinkling flames over the water. Well after midnight at last the torches bobbed over the swells, without a sound of the approach. The clouds parted, and in the cold moonlight they could see the far peaks of Arkadia across the gulf, but nothing else. Then, late but safe, the long-expected ship quietly swished into port, oars up.

Alkidamas could smell it, as the wind swirled near shore, before he made out the trireme's silhouette. All that was missing was his bodyguard Chiôn and the ransom money for Nêto, and he hoped either the crew was honest or Chiôn would be soon here to ensure they were. He had plans— all at the mercy of the winter seas, a leaky boat, and a brawling captain— to take these helot-born Athenians to Messenia to organize the people before the arrival of Epaminondas. If he left now on the water, he would be in Messenia before the army would even reach Sparta—and so have a precious month or so to rid Messenia of its Spartans. The unlettered helots would need a few of their more polished about who knew the ways of democracy. He had received word of Nikôn and his news of Nêto, so Alkidamas was glad not only to have Chiôn watch the captain Gastêr, but also to have his bodyguard when the two would search for Nêto in Messenia.

Quickly the shivering, wet stewards roped the long boat into the dock house. Porters in wool cloaks and hoods tramped off for food and water. It looked like a trireme, but one of the older brands—smaller than most, with the paint faded and the timber warped. The sea-snake's eye painted on the side was half peeled away by the brine. Usually these warships came out of the water like serpents, with their sleek lines and bright colors. But this old thing was more like a smashed jellyfish washed up on the shoreline.

Once the creaky ship touched shore, a one-armed captain stood balancing himself with his good left arm on the outrigging in torchlight. Someone yelled, "There's Gastêr, our fat friend. Hey Alkidama. He's here."

The dark figure of the captain himself called back from his bobbing boat. "Hoa, Alkidama. I'm late. Fighting the damned crosswind out of the Piraeus all the way to the Isthmos. But this water is nothing compared to the straits off Asia, or the high waves off Rhodos. But then you're no Alkibiades either, not by far. Why that master, he knew more in his thumb than you folks today. Hey. Your crew of land boys you hired me can't row, and instead think that talking will push the ship along. I spent too much silver at the *diolkos*, getting this boat dragged across the Isthmos. But don't worry, I'll have all of us at your Messenia well before your friends by land."

He jumped down off the planks to the draw board. "Those Korinthian draggers are worse than Thrakians, always with one begging hand out as they work. The buggers will doze off right in the middle of their rope pull, unless we throw more silver into their general's chest—and a *pithos* of unmixed red wine for their tug work. But here we are, pulling hard the oars, hard all the way from the port at Korinthos. With a boat full of your helot captains with splinters in their butts—just as ordered, ready to get things ready for your Epaminondas. They hit each other with their wood as much as they did the water."

Gastêr then stalked back up along the top planks, swinging a torch in the dark like a sword, ordering the lower oarsmen to get out, to stretch their legs, to empty their bowels and be back before dawn. He had a long beard, but the ugly kind that was scraggly and showed his chin beneath, and caught food and worse in its thin folds. Once his cap came off, he was all bald and might have taken a razor to his head, since his dome was shiny in the torchlight. Unlucky he was that his only arm was his left arm. He looked all belly. But he had thick blubber on his arm and his shoulders, blubber everywhere, so that he was more a mountain than even were stronger men. His legs were sturdy. It would take a hard blow, maybe two for him even to feel the hit.

"No one pissing in my dirty ship and no slopping. I won't have stink on my water. We won't stop till well out of the mouth of the gulf. Not until we get an out wind with ice from Epiros. Then we turn to the left and my what a breeze will push us to Messenia. So eat and crap now, Alkidama. What a nice night—cold, and black and windy—what more could we ask of Lord Poseidon? Get on board, get out to my sea."

When one of the thalamians lingered and began to vomit, Gastêr grabbed his hair and pulled him on up. "Out now, my pretty helot boy. Puke on the beach, not my ship—or you'll row in chains to the gulf." With that he broke off a half-loaf of stale bread. In the torchlight he seemed an older sort, without any age, given that his fat filled out his wrinkles. But Gastêr was a scarred veteran of the fighting in Asia; his left arm was a road map of tears and healed wounds. A seashell, hard and crusty, Gastêr was, but his insides? They were long eaten away with drink and stab wounds, and bad food from Asia. He cared little when he crossed the Styx, since four or five times he should have already been across. So he was ready to stab or torch anything he wished on the shore, and pay whatever price he must. Near-dead men who come back to life think everything after is dessert. Gastêrs of the world live blink-to-blink only—always eager to test what kind of man can put them on the other side where there is only relief from the present ordeal. Such rough and loud sorts do well, until they meet a Chiôn, a like but stronger and more desperate kind still.

Alkidamas had met Gastêr twice before hiring him—and so had heard all the stories of his missing arm. How Gastêr and Alkibiades had warned the Athenians not to beach their ships on the sands at Aigospotami. How Gastêr alone saw the warships of the Spartan admiral Lysander on the horizon. How Gastêr was the first to get his trireme, the *Parrhêsia*, into the surf. How Gastêr took down five Spartan hoplites in the knee-high surf of the channel, until they swarmed him, spearing and stomping on his arm, and left him for dead in the tides. Finally how he had crawled in the water all the way to the tower of Alkibiades, who gave him shelter and whose doctor cut off his worthless stinky and green right limb and seared his stump with hot iron. None of these stories was of interest to Alkidamas, since Gastêr was hardly a Spartan spy, and in any case soon Chiôn would be here to ensure their money was safe.

Alkidamas finally found the writer whom he had sent for, the young Ephoros, alone and quiet on the outrigging of the trireme. He was silhouetted in the moonlight and under a torch, the only one sitting still on an empty ship, oblivious and cross-legged. The frail historian had made it from his home in Athens with his cloak and papers untouched. The entire way from Athens to the Isthmos, Ephoros had sat there mute—and now still in the gulf, well after the mob of rowers had cursed and shoved and elbowed each other off the smelly boat. This other Athenian at last in a soft voice tried to speak over the tumult, but without looking up from his scrolls that he was busy writing on. He talked too softly to be heard clearly. "Don't worry. We're here. About one hundred thirty of us, my Alkidama, if that. One or two died or fell overboard in the tempest off Megaris, or maybe they were pushed. All in all, a short crew by many tens at least. Yes, short some rowers, but foul all the same. I don't know how you are going to use these Messenians for much other than stone masons. I wouldn't turn anything over to these thugs, much less an entire city. Compared to them, Gastêr is an Athenian lord."

Then Ephoros slowly got up. He was careful not to trip in the dark or rock the deck and began to stretch his slight frame and toss his golden hair back down his neck. Alkidamas saw why this thin wisp had won fame for his writing on Kretan boy-love. He had argued in his books that the rite had supposedly made the islanders more virtuous, but those pampered boys in his books were a different sort from the crew now of the *Theôris*. "Some of these scum rowers tried to pull my locks and pat my backside, as if I were some street whore. But the Messenian hoplites, the bigger sorts up here on top, have their armor and gave me a hand. You now give me a hand, man. We have till dawn to plot and plan. But I warn you that Gastêr may well jump the starting blocks. He is a restless sort. He hates having his feet on land, where any can see his one arm, his woman's thin beard, and his big belly. No wonder he likes the sea, where fish and gulls think he's Adonis. He's a sly fart, who stares into the water like a made-up woman with her mirror."

Alkidamas waved him to stay put. He walked up the springy board to the outrigging. Ephoros was, as he remembered him from the previous year, of an age that was hard to gauge, with his baby face that wrinkled slowly. He was pale from his long nights with the stylus. But at least he had a strong nose and everything seemed to fit on him, except his floppy ears, which looked like the monkey's saucers on the pots from Egypt. But why not the tall ears, when the writer must listen and sift the wind for gossip and rumor, for the purposes of Alkidamas's war were in fact twofold: one to free the helots, and quite another to ensure that the truth of what they did reached the Hellenes. At least, that is what Alkidamas told Ephoros, who knew that Platôn and Xenophon, older, wealthier, and aristocrats both, would either damn Epaminondas or ignore him—and that far more of the literate would read their scrolls than his own. But he was here nonetheless and would have come even without the urging of Alkidamas, who feared greatly the fame—and influence—of Xenophon in particular. For Ephoros knew this march would be a great thing and he thought he could write the truth of what would unfold, and that in itself would finally win the day against his better-connected and wealthier rivals. And he was pledged to follow these Athenians of helot birth all the way to

Ithômê and with Alkidamas teach them the ways of democracy. He had been writing furiously since the moment the *Theôris* had left the Piraeus. Ephoros had finished the battle of Leuktra, and now was working on the anabasis of Epaminondas as it unfolded.

This warship *Theôris* that Gastêr had bought was leaky. Mice scurried in the hold, feeding on crumbs and excrement. For all Gastêr's talk, it was a foul mix down there, a bilge mess of moss and stink, as the sea seeped into bad planks of the hull. "Help us, Pythagoras," Alkidamas yelled. "I said bring me a small trireme, not a floating sewer. Good Messenian rowers, not thugs and freed slaves. We'll be lucky to make it halfway to the mouth of the gulf. I'd rather face Lichas than try my luck in this raft."

"Maybe, old man," Gastêr barked in reply. "You'll get your chance with Lichas soon enough. But when you drown it won't be the fault of my ship. I've captained far worse and never lost a hull. These Messenian cutthroats row hard, even if they don't quite know what they're doing with their oars. All of them would give me a golden Zeus to get a chance to get back home to their Ithômê. Next time you want me to row up in a new cruiser, pay with a pile of Athenian gold, not a few silver Theban shields. This *Theôris* of yours, or whatever it was once called, was ramming Korinthian triremes under Phormio before we were born."

Lopsided Gastêr then turned from Alkidamas and was strutting along the beach, calling at his porters in the black of night. "Where's my fish sauce? Where's my water? Three hundred hard loaves I paid for from these thieves at Aigosthena. Where are the bread baskets? Hurry now—or you'll get none of Alkidamas's silver from me. I want the ship stocked now. Get to it, lazy boys; this winter night won't last forever." Gastêr with his one claw pulled his wool fleece tighter over his shoulders as the wind picked up. The captain waved a torch over his head that nearly went out against the icy blasts. He was proud that he had picked up this ancient *trires* among the wrecks at the Piraeus. He put in a few ribs and planks, and caulked the leaks. He bought oars cheaply and then resold them at a profit to the crew as they boarded. And he had no problem rounding up men, once Alkidamas spread stories to the Messenians of Athens who lived outside the Dipylon Gate of a new and free Messenia to the south. They were to get passage to Ithômê for rowing and listening to Alkidamas prep them on the new constitution of the free polis of Messenê. But on the sly Gastêr had charged the helots another ten owls fare once they climbed aboard—and had knocked one into the harbor who had no coin. He hoped to make a quarter talent in fare and bribes on the voyage charging helots for what Alkidamas had already purchased. His *Theôris* was an Athenian brand, a small one, rumored to have been towed in after Conon's victory, then beached when the shipwrights thought it too leaky and broken to fix.

Despite the crusty surface, Gastêr had painted over the faded colors its new name, meaning "Sacred Mission," on its bow in a fancy block script. Now he and Ephoros sat onboard while the crew foraged, waiting until their bodyguard Chiôn appeared from Plataia with Mêlon's money for Nêto and some bonus coins for Gastêr. Finally before sunrise, the porters brought in bread and water. Gastêr barked out orders. The crew lined up and began counting off. He sent the bottom rowers, thalamians, to the lower benches first. Maybe forty or so climbed in. Then another forty of the zygians. These were the middle rowers squeezed in on top of the lower set. Much later the elite thranites sat up on top, thirty at most who had some oaring in their past, or who had paid Gastêr the most coin. Ten hoplites, swearing in their Messenian Doric, carried on their gear and were sitting flat on the outrigging, arms out to roll with the swells that came in, even at dock. Most below were soon pushing each other. They fell on the slippery planks and fought over their rowing pads, blaming each other for the farting and smell.

Gastêr yelled as he balanced on the top deck. "Alkidama, it's a small ship, not a fleet trireme. With you fatties up here and these heavy breast-plate boys, we'll have a slow go out against the wind this morning. Can't any of you slobber-mouths row, or is it to be talk all the way out the gulf? Cold, are you? I'm sweating and need a breeze." Alkidamas had never been on a trireme, and only once on a rolling ferry boat to Aegina. When he and Ephoros lumbered on top with the *epibatai*, the entire boat nearly keeled over.

"Careful, clumsy fools." Gastêr came up and slapped them down. "Sit with your knees crossed and don't move. Do you want to beach us before we leave the dock? A ship's not a dance floor. Hoa. Look over there at who's coming. He's late. If that's your big man, O Alkidama. We have to put that slave—or is he a freedman now?—somewhere. I was hoping we'd swish out before he came."

No one had heard the bellowing of the approaching stranger. Now

Chiôn was upon them, at the beach waving a torch with his good right hand, and then running up the plank out of breath. He seemed clumsy without two good arms, more so than Gastêr, and he stumbled as he approached, but he had a huge iron sword strapped to his back and a travel sack hanging from the leather belt. Finally he coughed out his story on deck—and more than his usual word or two. "I came, Alkidama. On the third day as promised from last we met at Thespiai. I made my Marathon, running the whole way. All the way, from the army camp on Kithairon, all the way and with Mêlon's money. But Nêto—she's been taken from the helots in the south, or so that Nikôn says. Into the hands of the Spartans, into the jail of Kuniskos with a ransom on her head. For Nêto, I ran. I saw Mêlon, outside Plataia. He let me take his money I pulled out of his well. Here, take it." Chiôn threw down the sack of silver and collapsed on the deck, his cloak wet and his breathing heavy. "Oar. Where's an oar? Give me a butt pad. I'll row. Where's the captain? I will watch him as promised."

"Right here, one arm, right here. So you decided to come after all." Gastêr laughed at the idea of a clumsy crippled freedman pulling, and instead turned to his drummer and pointed to the sea. "Hey you, *Keleuste*, hit your drum. A beat, one not too fast. I'll take us right up the middle of the gulf and then out westward." Then Gastêr broke off a half-loaf and handed it to Chiôn. "How do you like your one arm, brand face?"

"Like this." Chiôn jumped up, grabbed Gastêr's chin beard, and pulled the enormous man down to the deck. He would have torn off his scraggly whiskers had not Alkidamas waved him off. Chiôn had already tired of Gastêr's brag and let him up slowly with a warning, "I came to watch you, fat man. Trick us, or talk like tricking us, and I'll throw your head overboard. I would rather run to Messenia, so if I have to bleed you, it's better for me anyway."

Gastêr gave Chiôn ten feet of room for the rest of the voyage and turned his back to him when he yelled. And with that, the *Theôris* at last went out into the black gulf to the sound of beating and fell heavy into the surf, bound due west out of the great gulf of Korinthos toward the sea of Sikily five hundred stadia away. For all the weight of the hoplites and the short crew and the leaky hull, this *Sacred Mission* made good headway over the black waves as the rowers began to chant and sing, happy returnees now on their last leg to Holy Messenia. Like the wings of some old bird of the sea that limbers up when it leaves the shore, the oars of the

*Theôris* dipped and swung outward as the boat picked up speed through the gulf.

Gastêr was calling out over the sea's roar to Alkidamas. "I like this ship, Alkidama, like it a lot. Built with good seasoned fir from Makedon. Better than what they slap together these days. It has Phormio's smell all over it. Let's sell it in Koronê and split the coins. Or don't you want to give me a little extra for getting it here in one piece?"

Alkidamas ignored him, deep in thinking how best to find Nêto and deal with Gorgos, if Nikôn were right that he was the kidnapper.

All the oars were the same length, but only half the helots hit the waves in unison—even though they pulled from different banks. Too many of these beginners fouled their wood. The oars echoed as they hit each other. "So we row, Chiôn," Alkidamas patted the freedman as the two sat up. Then he went himself to a top bench below the outrigging and began to pull in front of the slave. "You came as promised, as you always do, Chiôn. As for this new report, don't worry, we will save our Nêto yet—if as you think your Nikôn is true in his messages, and Nêto still lives and if she can be bartered for in the house of our Kuniskos at Ithômê, wherever that is. A helot like Nikôn does not run a thousand stadia into Boiotia for nothing."

Chiôn nodded. He had not told Mêlon at the camp the prior night that he had met Alkidamas in Thespiai on the day Mêlon left for Thebes, and had been promised passage on his ship. That this Nikôn showed up on Helikon just before Chiôn's planned meet-up with Alkidamas made it even easier to go south. Indeed, Damô had told him to rescue Nêto and to hurry with money to Aigosthena, and to draw on the wisdom of Alkidamas. Chiôn fell into his new pulling. He had given the horse to Myron, and covered a hundred stadia on foot over the mountain from Plataia to the shore, all that late day and night, and reached the ship well before dawn as promised. But he could not sleep. Not yet, not with the chance that Nikôn spoke truly, and that Nêto was caught in the hands of Gorgos. So he was still yanking on the oar with his good right arm until the sun came out, when all could see Helikon on their right and off in the distance Parnassos and the waters not far from Kirrha, as the *Theôris* continued westward out of the gulf. He pulled for Nêto.

This rowing was far easier than pressing the lever of the olive-crushing stone on Helikon. These waves gave way to his strength in a way the stone smasher never did. Even with the sunrise, the hoplites were asleep on the outrigging, but just one or two were waking to the gentle surge of the ship. Chiôn could see tall forests close by on the northern shore of the gulf—good places for a man to live in the wild over there, with plenty to kill to eat. Soon the winter morning sun finally came out full, cold and bright. The sea calmed. Gastêr turned into the light wind a little more and in caution began to hug the coast of Boiotia. "A good night and a calmer morning, and already halfway out. We soon make a sharp turn out of the gulf at the mouth and catch the tail wind to Messenia."

Then something on the horizon caught his eye, and he turned to his tiller. "Hard to the coast! Turn full into Boreas. Take in the wind at our faces. Head right to Boiotia. Look at them, damned Korinthians. Six at least. Not pirates. But warships, faster than ours—and in Spartan pay. They're pulling our way from all sides. Look, look at them, all good long ships with full crews. Right, right, we go right. Head for the north shore. Cut into the wind. Outrun them. To holy Delphi. Pray to Apollo. Row to the peaks of Parnassos. Ten hecatombs to Poseidon for our safety."

The *Theôris* made a hard turn and had a lead of twenty lengths, and maybe five more. Ephoros in his trance about the great march kept on writing on the outrigging. But despite a sudden haze on the water and the morning glare, Chiôn already could see on the shore Phokians watching their race. The six triremes behind were closing the distance. Would they catch the *Theôris* before shore? Gastêr went up and down the top deck, grabbed the backs of the necks of the hoplites, and pushed them onto the top benches right below. He took their breastplates and shields and began tossing them over the side.

"Row, fools. You down there, hand them up spare oars. All of you row. Row you boy-butt Ephoros and white-head Alkidamas. Row *proktoi* or you won't have any scrolls left to write on. Give me an oar and I'll balance out your slave. Between Chiôn and me, we one-arms will have two arms still, a good left and right each." The *epibatai* climbed down among the *thranitai* and pulled with the rest. Ever so slowly the *Theôris* surged toward land on the northern shore of the gulf. There was a mob already forming at Kirrha, the port of Delphi, all waving for the helot ship to speed up. About a hundred or so rushed into the surf. These were Phokians who hated the men of the Peloponnesos somewhat more than they hated the Thebans—and they had been paid to harbor Boiotian ships if they came to shore in need. Some bent on one knee with shields and spears, waiting for the Korinthians to beach. Bowmen took aim to pick off the Korinthians if they neared the *Theôris*. Suddenly the pursuers veered off, about three stadia from shore.

The crowd waved in the *Theôris* that slid onto the shore. The helots climbed out and dragged the boat out of the water. They stacked their oars against the keel. Gastêr had them carry their food up the path to the crowd that swarmed them, hawking dry cloaks and for a few drachmas offering them wood for campfires. "Look. *Ide, philoi mou, ide,*" Gastêr yelled as he turned back to the sea. Another four triremes were joining the six, even as the friendly shore crowd of gawkers swelled and more Phokians came up in arms. Ten enemy ships were circling well out of bowshot, crisscrossing the rising early-morning whitecaps to keep the *Theôris* beached and off the gulf, as they relayed in and out from the bay far away at Perachora.

Phrynê had sent Lichas the time and route of Alkidamas. And in turn Lichas had sent the Korinthians money. In return the Korinthian captains promised to keep ships from the northern shore from leaving the gulf. When the wind died, those on the shore could hear the taunts of the enemy rowers over the morning surf. "Cowards. Wide-butts, come out to fight. We'll kill you for sport. We kill you still." Gastêr laughed and yelled back to the trireme that darted parallel to the coast. "Whoa. Maybe so. But we're dry and on ground. You Korinthians. You can stay out there until you freeze. Drink your bilge."

Then he turned to Alkidamas. "Well, man, we made it halfway, almost. Though I bet we could have hiked as fast on land as we made by the oars. This may be the end of our voyage, if these damned Korinthians decide to patrol in turn, five or so at sea, five or so replaced by fresh ships from over there to the south on the Peloponnesos. For now, we stay put here. We eat—until our Poseidon gives us a winter storm that sinks them. Remember I get paid whether you walk or ride the waves the rest of the way."

Alkidamas tried to reply over the roar of the surf. "Yes, safe for now—but trapped and still far from Ithômê."

# CHAPTER 24

# *A Free Messenia*

The two women had better sense than to board a winter trireme when Alkidamas had talked grandly of one day taking a boatload of free helots into Messenia to craft a constitution. Instead, months earlier, when Gastêr was still mending the *Theôris*, Erinna and Nêto had crossed the Isthmos as easily as the philosopher and the historian had later not even made it out of the gulf.

But once inside Spartan-held Messenia, Nêto saw that she should have listened to her hide-clad Erinna, who had known the woods and the mind of those like Kuniskos. For all Nêto's talk of helots and Messenia and the visions of Nikôn, it turned out she understood very little about life in the south, or indeed life outside the protection of the farm of the Malgidai— and nothing about how to live in the wilds of Ithômê. The priestesses of Artemis had offered their precinct to Nêto; but she too often was forced to sleep in the light rains and snow of the forests, given the constant Spartan patrols that crisscrossed Messenia on orders of Lord Kuniskos. It seemed odd to Nêto that the Athenian Erinna, with no trace of Messenian in her speech, might have turned out to be the better friend to the revolt. Or not so odd, since the poetess had lived up on the mountains of Parnes and Hymettos and knew more of the wilds, how to live on the red berries, skin the rabbit, and drink the cleaner brook water, than did even the helots themselves—and how to put an arrow in a mountain thief and yet be five stadia away in the brush by the time his gang found the dying corpse.

When Nikôn's party finally had climbed over the summit of Taygetos and crossed the borders in the late summer, Erinna went straight up to the highlands along the long spine of Ithômê. Her new spot was not far from the holy ground of wild Artemis Laphria and its priestesses of the sanctuary in their hunting garb. Erinna sang out to Nêto that the two were finally in holy Messenia and at last insurgents in the war against the Spartans that they so long had advocated from a distance. "Stay here where you are safe, Nêto. We are not like foolish men. They blindly walk by the food that can feed us—greens and herbs and berries under their noses. They stalk the bear and deer and are blind as bats to the rabbits and birds that fall into my snares. Up here learn to eat meat again. Pythagoras will forgive the eating of meat for the greater good of Messenia. Take in the peaks around Ithômê. Relearn your Doric tongue. Then, and only then, go down to raid the Spartans below. We cannot yet meet their hoplites in battle, and must kill them at night or through ambushes in the woods—where a stealthy woman can fare better than these loud helot men."

But Nêto was driven and would have none of it. "I walked a thousand stadia to fight, Erinna. Not paw the backsides and fondle the *titthoi* of your girls. There's not a *krypt* that can outrun me. Ask Nikôn who knows these helot-killing Spartan patrols. We will go in packs and swarm the Spartans, even on the daylight roads if need be."

"But Spartan hoplites, Nêto, still control the lowlands, far better men than your friend's ragtag tribe of insurgents. Better to organize up here until all the Messenians have armor and a good general to storm the fort of Kuniskos—otherwise you will end up either tossed into the Kaiadas or nailed up on one of Kuniskos's poles." With that Erinna turned and headed to the far side of Ithômê with Nikôn, while Nêto descended to the sanctuary of Artemis below to meet the priestesses.

At the small hamlet of Aitos, there in the woods Erinna set to organizing her school—to teach the orphaned helot girls the rhetoric of Isokrates and the way of Pythagoras, and for relish the poetry of her dear Sappho and the Boiotian Korinna, and as a treat Pindar as well. She would take her rhapsodists up to Olympia and then down to Pylos and thereby learn the news of Antikrates and his new henchman Kuniskos. If Alkidamas were to bring in his Athenian-raised helots to teach the liberated Messenians of good government, she would do better still and ensure that they had tragedy and lyric and epic poetry as well. Erinna's new

Messenê would not merely be Proxenos's walled citadel forever safe from Sparta, but a polis of the Muses as well—a new Athens that would ascend in the Peloponnesos as the old one in Attika faded away.

On a rocky face on the backside of the ridges behind Ithômê above a deep gorge, she pitched at first an oiled leather tent. Then word got out that the strange Athenian had silver owls. Soon the rustics were on their way up to sell her pans and shovels and anything bronze or iron they could steal from the Spartans. After Nikôn had left her to return to camp on the saddle of Ithômê, Erinna had set about with ten or so women, mixing clays and drying them into bricks in the late-summer sun. Then with a donkey and cart they carried in stones for the floor and built the school as a fortified compound. At night they were taught by Erinna to sing and memorize the words of the lyric and melic poets—before going on to Homer, in reverse fashion of the way the rhapsodists did it at Athens. By the end of the fourth month, their baked tiles were on the roof, held up by stout mud-brick walls whitewashed inside and out, with a good stone floor within. The girls were singing the new war song of Epaminondas on wooden benches in her schoolhouse—still more worship of the man she had seen only once. Erinna had put targets—old Spartan helmets that the helots brought her for barter—on rock outcroppings outside the courtyard, so that her helot girls could learn the bow, and how to put an arrow in an eye-slit at fifty paces. She had them wrestling and lifting small stones, so that their arms were as hard as Erinna's. Most wore small daggers in scabbards that were cinched over their breasts, and their teacher showed them how to seduce a Spartan as they put a blade in his backside. Erinna gave them all felt *piloi*, cone-shaped hats, with long red feathers tucked at the sides.

These were to be her *peripoloi*, her own rangers in brown felt and green cloaks who chanted their songs and yet could still kill as they sang. Her rangers would come down to lead the Messenians both to victory and to the Muses. No one got within ten stadia of her outpost without the entire school up in the trees and amid the rocks with their bows. But soon this upland sanctuary of Erinna—there was a spring here as well as terraced fields of barley and grain—was doubling as a camp, housing helots of the highlands on their way to Nêto and the sacred precinct of the other lowland Artemis below. Some nights a hundred and more helots came in through the thickets for the water and food and shelter in winter.

Poor Nêto. Erinna knew more of her danger up here through these spies than Nêto herself knew down below.

She wrote just that and often in letters like this.

> Erinna to Nêto. Listen. You learn from me.
> They know you, Nêto. Spartans do. Antikrates and Kuniskos himself. They follow you. You and the priestesses at the low temple in the marshes are easy game. Targets for that helot traitor. His packs of Spartan killers hunt you. He knows the paths of your helots. So come up here for a spell, out of sight. Here you will be in school, safe with my girls. The Spartans fear to come up our slopes, fear the wild and the wolves. Be in good spirits. Erinna of Ithômê.

From this new mud-brick school Erinna sent down agents to Nêto, who returned each evening from her to the safety of the sanctuary. Always Erinna's helots went back up to her with stories of the revolt, of Spartan killing, and of a countryside in rebellion—waiting for news of the great army of Epaminondas and the Boiotians' promised turn to the west, as had been ordained for the first month of the year, Theban Boukatios. The helots sang that this Boiotian first month would see the Thebans finally on Ithômê and their Spartan taskmasters gone. Meanwhile in the days of waiting from the first of the year, they kept killing Spartans in ambushes. They hid their wine and grain from the food collectors of Sparta and in threes and fours left the farms to hide in the highlands.

These helot marauders—maybe five thousand were loose, a thousand or more with Nêto and Nikôn—were fed and kept safe by the temple priestesses, in the shrines and sanctuaries from Pylos up to the falls of the Alpheios. Each night the holy women sheltered the helot Spartan hunters, ever hot after Antikrates and his killer henchman known as Puppy Dog. Meanwhile Erinna far above had taught the girls at her school that the prophecy was nearly fulfilled—the apple would fall again, and seven myriads of hoplites would sweep down from the mountains of Taygetos, all led by her Epaminondas, and Mêlon, and the blood-crazed Chiôn, all taught by Alkidamas and the deadly Ainias and the great-hearted Proxenos. Soon these names were in songs and chanted by the girls as they went back down to the markets of the Messenians.

Below, Nêto was seeing visions almost nightly of Epaminondas on the pass in Sparta. There he was addressing his men, staring down at Lakonia with seventy thousand soldiers at his back. Eight or ten days after the winter solstice, runaways from Lakonia came over Taygetos with more stories like Nêto's dream warning that a tide of grasshoppers would some winter day sweep over the passes north of Sparta, stripping everything in its path, and on the way south growing larger still. So Nêto, convinced that Mêlon and the army would be in Messenia within the month, took more risks, attacking with Nikôn's men the Spartans in broad day, and closer always to the Spartan base at the foot of Ithômê.

Finally as the days neared to the middle of Theban Boukatios more rumors spread over Taygetos with the high shepherds that the Thebans had already left Boiotia, determined to reach Lakonia before the new year. They might even have reached Mantineia. There they would join Lykomedes to burn all the farms and towers of the Spartans, turning their whitewashed homes black with soot. Soon Spartans, either in fear of the Boiotians to come or answering the call of King Agesilaos to hurry home to defend the city from Epaminondas, began leaving Messenia, swarming the short high road atop Taygetos. A few Spartans left behind in Messenia stayed in their compound under orders from Antikrates; otherwise they would be ambushed by the growing mob of helot fighters who fought at night and from thickets, and with missiles and arrows, rather than lining up in the phalanx. The Spartan rearguard under Antikrates had built a final redoubt, a log stockade on the spur of Eva on a lower hill beside Ithômê. It had a timber wall, two men high, with half a thousand Spartan hoplites trapped inside who could not stomach the notion that helots had driven them out of their Messenia.

Their captain was the renegade Kuniskos. Even in the twilight of Spartan power, he sallied out at night with two hundred horsemen to burn and level the helot hamlets on the northern borders, before riding in at dawn to hunker down at his compound. Finally even Antikrates had fled back to Sparta to join his king. He had left Messenia to his helot Kuniskos because the black soil, he knew, was lost, and his Spartans were to be better used defending their women in Lakonia in the battle to come. "Leave Antikrates," Kuniskos told him, "leave and let the real lord of Messenia at last be the better Spartan that he always was. For you, Messenia has fallen and so is better abandoned; but for me it is rising—at last in the hands of a child of its soil, a man better than both the whipped helots and the Spartans who lashed them."


Then Erinna heard no more about Nêto and her band of raiders. Had she disappeared? Even Nikôn had lost her. The temple of Artemis of the lowlands was razed and the priestesses scattered or killed—or sent to the gorge on Taygetos. Nêto might be dead or worse. Kuniskos had warned the helots that he would never flee like Antikrates had. Not he, the last good helot, who would kill all on sight who were not in the fields weeding the barley and wheat—would kill and kill before his stockade was overwhelmed. Even on Ithômê, Erinna heard reports of these final boasts from the last of the helots, all the bolder as his last band shrank and his enemies increased.

A *phoinix,* that was what Kuniskos proclaimed he would be, the war bird that would rise up on the ashes of Sparta to rule over Messenia himself, with his die-hard last *lochos* of Spartans, as lord of the Helots. If his compound were stormed, Kuniskos boasted, he would flee, but not to Sparta. No, if he must leave for a time, Kuniskos would go up to high Taygetos. "I, Lord Kuniskos," he would rail in his drunken fits to his retainers, "I will ride back down in triumph once these Messenians one day beg me to rule them again. Who else would put an end to this looting and raping—this mad idea that unlettered serfs could ever be democrats?"

It was Nikôn who brought word that Nêto was now five days a captive with Kuniskos—with an offer of a ransom. "No surprise that these Spartan gold-lovers wish to be bought off. He knows there is silver on Helikon, so he won't kill her just yet. He wants ransom and perhaps more. Klôpis his henchman left a scroll at the first column of the ruined Artemision, and my Hêlos read it and told me the threat of Kuniskos:

"You robbers of Messenia—listen! The rebel Nêto, she remains inside the fort of Lord Kuniskos, first man of Spartan Messenia. He says to the rebels and to the Malgidai in the north to fetch her with their silver. A talent wins her freedom, but only before the northerners come over Taygetos. If no silver, no Nêto and she dines in the Kaiadas."

Nikôn was desperate now, trying to get Erinna to bring her girls down the hill. "Get all these holdouts under Ithômê to collect silver to keep her alive. But better still, tell me, woman—how goes the road to Helikon in the far north? Which way? How many days away is this farm of Mêlon, the home of our Nêtikê? Those she left behind have money. So I run, Erinna, to the north and to this Helikon across the gulf. Maybe in ten days I am on this Helikon and then back on Ithômê with money for Nêto—if she lives, if she lives. Ten days, no more. I run hundred stadia, maybe more, each day. Maybe I'll know the way, at least from the dreams that come at night."

Erinna now told the helot how best to go north to the farm of the Malgidai. "No, no, Nikôn—don't go north in the way of the army. That is the long way." Erinna with a long knife drew a map in the dirt at their feet. "We are already far to the west, far closer from here to Helikon. Run up the Alpheios road, up to the long walls of Patrai, and across the gulf—not the way Nêto and I came to Mantineia. Cross the gulf here in the west. Then the helots of Naupaktos will show you the sea-cliff path to Parnassos and then over by Sphinx Hill to the backside of Helikon. Go now. See me here in your ten days. By then I'll know where our Nêto is, and where Kuniskos is to pay—again, if she lives." Then she wrote on tree bark more directions with lines and arrows for the letterless helot once he arrived on Helikon.

So it was that Nikôn, the nimble-foot, found Chiôn just before he was to leave by sea with Alkidamas, and in time for him to warn Mêlon. Both were on their way southward, by both land and sea, and with heavy sacks of silver, to free their Nêto if she lived. Nikôn was back to Ithômê in seven days with the news that the army of the Boiotians had already left. Nikôn had wanted the money, to take it back with himself, the swifter runner. But Chiôn reminded the stranger that the coin was his master's and that he himself must find Mêlon at Plataia, before Epaminondas and Mêlon got over Kithairon. Better yet, the Spartan-killer Chiôn promised Nikôn that he himself would be coming with his sack of silver by sea to ransom his Nêto and settle up with Kuniskos, and he would be there well before the army of Epaminondas.

But now where were any of them? No army yet. No Alkidamas and his boat. No Chiôn—who sat on the *Theôris*, beached with the Phokians. The Korinthian warships circled offshore watch after watch. Meanwhile, Nikôn had a long run ahead of him—to spread the word that Chiôn, along with the silver for Nêto, was not far behind him. But Chiôn was not—not for a while.

# CHAPTER 25

# The Night of the Three Armies

T he army of the Boiotians was already crossing atop the mountain ridges between Argos and Mantineia. In the middle of the month of Boukatios, as Erinna sent more scouts to find the imprisoned Nêto, and as Nikôn returned with news of Chiôn and the silver to come, and even as Chiôn argued with Alkidamas on the beach near Delphi, two haggard Arkadian scouts ran into the north gate of Mantineia far to the south in the Peloponnesos. "He's here—Epaminondas is well across the Isthmos. Break open your stores. The northerners—with others too to join—already are over the pass. A mob, an entire city from the north is coming down here."

As the crowd swarmed, the taller ranger, Lykander, went on. "We heard singing, and men marching in their strange sounds of the sort they speak above the Isthmos. Two myriads and maybe more. Yes, yes, with the sound of Thebes in their voice, but almost as if they were Bacchants in their song and zeal rather than an army on the march to war. Now on the downward slopes of Parthenion, covering all the trails, they come—and their tramping is heard three stadia and more before they appear on the passes. Already the men of Tegea are out of grain from feeding that horde. We will need even bigger ramparts to house them all. Thousands of them are heading this way."

But even these Mantineian scouts of crafty Lykomedes were not the first to hear of the arrival of the Boiotians into the south. The Arkadian shepherds of the high *methoria* had already seen an army far above on the ridges of Parthenion. Dim specks against the sky, distant thousands of shadows moving along the crests were enough for them—along with the butchering of their high flocks as hungry Boiotians took what they could. So with news of an entire polis on the move, the herders ran down from the *eschatia* with their wild stories to the homesteaders below. And these shouts of aroused farmers in turn warned the horse-owners farther below on the bottomlands that a *phantasma* of some sort, a fog of voices—with the clatter of bronze and wood—was coming off the high pass from Argos way.

Epaminondas had come after all—late, through the winter mists and with thousands more than promised. But there were more behind his army on the passes. No sooner had the high hill folk heard the clattering of the arms of thousands, than a half-day later another apparition rose behind them, on the *sterna* where the road crested on the high pass. This was the advance of another army, the Argives under their general Epitêles, that would spill likewise into the plain of Mantineia. A myriad of Argive hoplites were coming in on the coastal road, in shiny armor and with white clubs freshly painted on their shields.

These Argives were darker folk, with Spartan-sounding speech and old Korinthian helmets pulled over their faces. They wore the tall black-and-white horsehair crests in their fathers' fashion, swarming into Mantineia, democrats all who looked like Spartans, but also looked far deadlier than Spartans. The Argives worshipped Artemis and marched in perfect step, but they wore no red capes and had full hair above their lips. Their great captain Epitêles at the fore was wilder looking than any scarred veteran of the peers. He was stalking, rather than limping as did the Spartan king. So on the night of the same day of Epitêles's descent, after thousands of northerners had come in on the same road from Argos, there were two armies at Mantineia. But the sky was alight yet with torches, and more Hellenes of yet a third force were promised to come before sunup, still more from the west, the herdsmen and hunters swore.

Ainias and Proxenos had not been idle after they left Lykomedes at Mantineia, but at Megalopolis had found more Arkadian hoplites who hated Spartans enough to gamble on entering the vale of the Lakonia should thousands of Boiotians lead the way. The pair had promised to guide the Arkadians into Lakonia to join Epaminondas and end the threat from Sparta for good. This third and last army was larger, far larger than the muster of the Argives and maybe as big as the Boiotians' as well. These folk led by Ainias were the Eleans and Arkadians, and those who dwelled along the coast of the Peloponnesos from north of Messenia to western Achaia, hoplites all who had followed the Alpheios River to the south. They had snaked all night over the pass from Megalopolis, and emptied that half-built city as they passed by. Now they chanted as they marched, "On to Lakonia! Death to the Spartans! Death to Agesilaos! On to the Eurotas!"

At sunrise these westerners poured into the great plain of new Mantineia. Finally Epaminondas and Mêlon ran up to meet the third army whose arrival baffled all, since the Eleans previously had sent only money, with no promise that an army from the western Peloponnesos would follow that gift. Only Epaminondas or perhaps Ainias as well knew that soon Tripolis, the so-called three-city polis, would see three armies, not just one, come filling the plain of Mantineia. Mêlon yelled to Melissos and Pelopidas as he saw this night cloud of shapes drift into their new camp outside the walls. "Whoa. I know these men. How did our friends become generals greater than our own?" Then a familiar voice yelled out.

"*Ide. Thauma idesthai—hêde stratia, thauma mega*. Look at it. A great wonder this army, a great wonder. Here is the one army at last, all three into one. We here are the men of Arkadia. Of the new Megalopolis, with the Eleans behind us. And more of the Achaians. All of the free Peloponnesos is on the move. We are the death sentence of Sparta." It was Proxenos. He tramped in at the head of a column of thousands that now were scattering over the winter mud of Mantineia and filing into the city. With him came the Arkadian generals Archias and Philoxenos, and then Talos, *stratêgos* of Elis. Ainias started his own banter as he came into hearing range. "Hoa. Epaminondas. So you have three myriads? Well, we claim as many—no, more—from Elis and from the cities of western Arkadia. Keep your men back, for these bronze men of the Peloponnesos are snapping dogs, hungry for battle, and they might whet their fangs on your Boiotians, if you don't let us head south right away. Be careful of our folk—we might taste the flesh of Epitêles and his men of Argos, if we don't keep the leash tight and calm the men before the march into Sparta."

Ainias was hoarse from his winter hectoring but went on even louder. "Well, then, we march southward to find Lichas and his brood. Yes, we have been working in the new city, this *Megalê Polis*—not idle at all with the musters of the Arkadians. You and your Pelopidas will have to figure out how to feed all of us. I reckon now that sixty thousands is your total, or are there more yet? Or is my numbering off?"

"No man has seen anything like this. I never have," answered Epaminondas. "We are like Homer's Achaians on the plain of Troy, as ships pulled in on the beach unloading even more. The entire flatland of Mantineia is already full and they are sleeping on the ramparts of the city. Go camp on the wheat land inside the walls, and outside too if you must. And remember our hosts, the Mantineians, have not yet shown us their muster. All of Hellas is afire and soon I see seventy thousands pouring into the Spartan plain."

Mêlon tapped Ainias on his breastplate with the tip of his sword. "You will see the snout of Lykomedes shaking. Even his Phrynê could not warn him that his neighbors down here were massing to strike Sparta. His little boyfriend Aristôn is in tears. The boar-mouth walks around the camps with water running down his leg, mumbling, How to feed these? Where the wine? Like the tree caterpillars they'll strip our *chôra* of even the leaves of the olives."

"Lykomedes is nothing." It was Proxenos who came up with an enormous pack on his back with his scrolls sticking out the side. "No worry. Our Arkadians already have three-day rations in our packs. They plan to march out at noon tomorrow to the south, if only Epaminondas promises to lead. We have plenty of food to get us into Lakonia. Once there the king will have to set our tables."

Pelopidas broke in. "Well, then, you and your Arkadians will have to fight us for the road. We and the Argives claim the first right of way and leave earlier at daybreak. Why not? On our way we herded cattle and sheep and goats from the Nemeans and Korinthians and have eaten beef, no less—beef. And the whole way from Argos, with more on the hoof as we speak."

Epaminondas stopped them. "No need for a *stasis*. Plenty of Spartans for all. There are many roads into Lakonia and we will use all of them. The generals meet tonight to debate the way in. They are angry that the Spartans left the plain of Mantineia in the fall and scampered back home across their river, Eurotas out of our reach. But nonetheless they will all vote to go south to follow them rather than disband. Ainias knows that. The Argives go in head-on through Sellasia, the narrow direct route. That honor of the first army goes to Epitêles. His Argives will have a flat walk on the plain of the Tegeans and keep Parnon and Taygetos on either side with a good view of the Eurotas. But from the west, these men of Elis and Megalopolis will swarm behind you. Yes, the second army of the Peloponnesians will hug the foothills of Taygetos, close to the river Nedôn. You Arkadians here in Mantineia will join them. We Boiotians, the third fist, will march on the west side of Parnon, with the tributaries of the Eurotas, and meet down around Sellasia. The gods will decide who gets into Lakonia first. The best plunder goes to the fastest foot. We will never be more than sixty stadia distant from each other."

Ainias seconded that. "May the quickest army win."

Mêlon kept quiet. The generals had already voted to enter Lakonia, and sent messengers home to their poleis that Agesilaos was no longer at Mantineia, so the armies would soon invade. Mêlon could not yet leave to the west to find Nêto when they all must fight in the plain of Lakonia, before they could do anything for the helots of Messenia. For now the best he could do was to kill Spartans in hopes the guards of Messenia to the west would flee back home to help their king and empty the prisons as they left—and, of course, hope that Chiôn and Alkidamas were already in Messenia.

In the morning, almost seventy thousand set out on the march in the bright winter sun of the Peloponnesos. It took past noon for the armies just to leave the plain of Tegea and hit the passes. Not until the dark of the next day were they above Lakonia. At early sunset on this second day from Mantineia, the Boiotians looked down from the last rocky outcroppings past Sellasia and readied themselves for a morning war with the men of Sparta. The Boiotians had come a thousand stadia from Helikon. Pelopidas climbed up a boulder along the road and looked down to Epaminondas. "Look. Look at Lakonia—*Aporthêtos, aporthêtos*—unplundered, untouched, for five hundred years and more. Free from attack, not a foreigner, not a stranger buried in their fatherland, never a Spartan killed in battle in all Lakonia. But not now, not now. These plains will be their cemeteries tomorrow. The Argives below are already coming down on the plain. Look, it is already burning."

Then Epaminondas in response lifted his helmet off and turned to the officers of the *lochoi*: "It's yours, Boiotians—farmers of Hellas. The valley of the Spartan overseer is all ours. *Idete, stratiôtai mou, idete.* Look—there is no phalanx, there are no pipes to meet us. The villagers, the half-helots,

THE INVASION OF SPARTA

the neighbors have all fled or joined us. We will kill as many of the red-shirts as the number of their farms you torch. No Spartan, no Athenian—no Hellene—has ever seen the like of this army, and none will ever see such a thing again." Epaminondas mounted his small red pony and rode among the ranks. He ordered his commanders to column his Boiotians four abreast as his third and last army headed down the final pass. It was easy following the lead army of the Argives under Epitêles, who was a master of *taxis* and showed all how to squeeze columns over the narrow road and out of bowshot of the Spartan garrisons.

Below, the advanced columns poured out onto the green winter fields of the Eurotas, like a herd of sheep that makes not even a grunt as it stuffs its mouth—and leaves behind stubble, and holes, and vomit and dung where there was once fresh tall grass. Soon smoke covered the vale. Later that day, the last of the Boiotians to descend saw nothing but a cloud of haze drifting toward the acropolis, the smoke of a thousand fires and more, as the army of Epaminondas did their work, tearing apart the farms and sheds in the plain to fuel their winter bonfires.

Where were the Spartans, Epaminondas wondered? Where was the dreaded Lichas? Where the lame Agesilaos? None was at the head of a phalanx on the field of battle. His great fight with the tall hoplites of Lichas was now a fantasy. What followed, Epaminondas shouted to his generals, was the greatest surprise in all the stories of the Hellenes. The invaders walked in unopposed to the supposedly impregnable vale of Lakonia. The *perioikoi*, the villagers who lived in subservience around the city of Spartans, either had drifted into the army of Epaminondas or had fled into the hills of Parnon. Either way, more than half the helots of Lakonia had left their farms. The rest ran to safety of the city across the Eurotas with their masters, all to the cries of the Spartan women in town.

Lichas had chosen not to send out his phalanx—not with the memory of the piles of dead at Leuktra still fresh. Myriads of these invaders, without fear of a Spartan spear or a sword, were burning even more houses and fencing, rounding up stock, killing—and always lapping up to the banks on the icy river. Finally King Agesilaos hobbled out to the banks of his side of the Eurotas and sent his guards to line the river and bar the way into the city for any of his latecomer refugees. Helot-lovers he called them—better to let them die than to let them slink as spies into the city. No more Spartans were to come across the river into the city. The peers were to kill anyone who neared the Eurotas once the bridges had been torched.

When the Boiotians at last reached flat ground a day after the allies of the Peloponnesos, Epaminondas pointed out to Mêlon the hillock, just six stadia from the the high shrines of the Menalaion, where the generals would camp. "We sleep there on that rise, not far from the Eurotas—there in the middle of this new sea of ravagers. Look, Mêlon, look how we cover the spurs of Taygetos to the west. We're already lapping on Parnon far eastward."

Mêlon could see that the countryside of Sparta was scarcely big enough for the thousands of men in the three armies. The next day they were plundering again, without the fog or even much dew to dampen their fires.

Epaminondas came up with Proxenos, all in heavy woolen cloaks against the cold wind. Mêlon and Melissos fell in at the van with Epaminondas to head toward the city proper and the Eurotas, to scout the fords and plan the final assault. Mêlon shouted to Melissos above the yelling, "Epaminondas, dear boy, is an artist, you see, one better than Exekias himself; but his work is not to be found in painting clay, but in the wholesale destruction of his enemies—and the end of Sparta is his masterpiece, his *ariston ergon*."

None of the Thebans around Epaminondas cared for the booty that drove on most of the coalition that had poured over the plain of Lakonia. Instead, battle was their desire, and so always they eyed the Spartans on the other side of the river. Red-capes were running about there, taunting and overturning wagons as they threw up a makeshift rampart at the fords and shook their spears. Their women on the rooftops yelled at the sight of the fires of Epaminondas—as angry at their own men who had let the unthinkable happen as they were at the Boiotian pigs across the water. A few of the younger girls had climbed the peaks of the roofs. They were prying up the roof-tiles with iron bars and handing them down to their mothers on the balconies, who stockpiled their weapons for the street-fighting to come.

"Hoa. You three. Hold up."

It was Ainias again, marching in at dusk to the camp of Epaminondas. He was waving his hands in a way unlike the somber killer who usually stabbed first and spoke only later. "Come. Now get over here. Look at this. A Spartan party, a half *lochos*, maybe more. Look. They're trapped on that farm over here just as the early sun sets. Some slow-coach Spartans are caught on our side on the river, the wrong side of the Eurotas. They will either go up in smoke with their shed or fight their way through us to their king across the water."

Without waiting for a reply from his friends, Ainias pulled his helmet down over his face and headed back toward the Spartan holdouts.

CHAPTER 26

# *The Plains Afire*

E paminondas followed. As they neared the besieged farm, Ainias
called over the Elean lords Talos and Philoxenos and the captains
of their mounted rangers who had trapped the orphaned band of
Spartans out in the plain of Lakonia. Talos broke in, "We've cornered
something over here on this estate. Something big. A *phantasma,* a ghost
from their Zeus is holed up there. My Eleans have plundered the field
vats. But there is a hoplite bunch still in the house. And another hundred
or more Spartans milling about in the courtyard. There is a big man with
them that brings piss to our boys' legs who won't go near the tower. We
were too busy with the booty in the sheds to notice this enemy island.
Now we discover that we've surrounded a whole company of killers. They
say it is the clan of Lichas—or even worse—inside."

"Hold up. Stop your men. I know this place," Epaminondas yelled.
"I know this foul farm." The general then sent a runner to Pelopidas and
ordered after him, "Send in the Sacred Band. Send for another *lochos* or
more if you can. Get Philliadas and his hard men from Tanagra over here.
All of them before midnight." Then he turned to Mêlon and pointed to
the tower, still looming white as darkness fell. "Lichas may be here, or at
least some of his own. This is the farm of his dead brother Leôn. His
*klêros* is somewhere close by. I passed right by here on the embassy last
year to the taunts of Antikrates and his *kryptes.* I wager that either Lichas
or his son, or maybe both are in there, or at least nearby. So maybe we
have torched the grand estate of Leôn."

But it was far more than that. For the Boiotians had, in their ignorance, stumbled onto the compound of all the Lichades, all five farms, a thousand *plethra* of orchard and vineyard altogether near the Eurotas, with six tall towers, all built by their own hands, without the labor of slaves or helots, five of them by the grandfathers of Lichas—Xanthos and Prytanis—whitewashed *purgoi* all in shouting distance of each other. Little did they guess that Gorgos on his arrival from Leuktra had spent a half-year here himself, although Mêlon looked out among the bonfires and thought that one of the towers seemed strangely new with its fresh whitewash and a red border—and in the fashion of his own back on Helikon. Its roof and stones might easily have been built by the Malgidai.

Now Mêlon and Proxenos leveled their spears and advanced toward the fires and the hoplites who ringed the estate. Ainias headed to the outer field wall. It ran about twenty palms high around all the farms and had various gates, as paths from each farm led out of the family grounds. As they neared the path to the southernmost farm, maybe two hundred Eleans under their general, Talos, were throwing stones and javelins at Spartans behind the tower's courtyard wall—a man's height, its gate closed fast. A few were torching the door jambs of one of the abandoned towers. Talos was waving them forward. "They're in there. No worry about that. Lichas must have an iron gut to dare to be on our side of the river."

"Lichas has no gut, Talos. He feels nothing, but won't give up his own estates without blood—our blood he thinks," Mêlon said grimly.

"So let's storm it and get the killing over." Ainias pulled out his blade and put down his spear. "It will be too crowded for spear work in there, only sword killing. Man-to-man, hand-to-hand, a real blood feast for your night-loving Kêres, Mêlon, that you so often warn us about."

"No, no," Proxenos broke in. "Better to let them die on the vine. They're like a rotten grape cluster with the gnats once its stem has been nicked. Why go in there? It's too dark. We have thousands in this plain. They are a good stade or two from the safety of the Eurotas. We have them trapped on the wrong side of the water. They'll starve while we tighten the nets. All of them are not worth one of our dead. Let them be."

Mêlon agreed. "Proxenos is right, Ainias. Talos—you back step a bit. Well before morning we'll have enough men to surround the entire farm five deep. We can throw embers through the windows. So for now let the

Spartans be." Mêlon planned to keep his shield all night on his arm, as he sat against a plane tree that had grown into the stones. He watched the shadows of hoplites run up as the call went out that Lichas or at least his kin was trapped. "But don't think they'll starve. Hardly. They'll charge a little after daybreak. We need more guards here, but the army is scattered for thirty miles plundering and burning. Our men are looking for cattle and sheep, not the spears of Spartan hoplites."

Ainias nodded and looked over at the Spartan enclave. "Remember Leuktra. They'll fight their way out through our circle. Break out with Antikrates or someone like him at the front. They'll march out to the sound of pipes, with torches blazing. Maybe Lichas, maybe his son will lead. But they'll come out that gate before dawn and head for the river. These men won't die without killing some of our own. Still, there is enough of us to slaughter the whole herd."

The hoplites and their generals were crouched behind the long low field and cross walls, as sentries slung lead bullets and cast javelins over the high courtyard into the Spartans, sure they could wear down Lichas and his men. For the present there were at least stout walls between the red-capes and the Boiotians. Proxenos was sitting quietly. Some around him were sleeping by the campfires; others were drowsy but waiting for the men of Tanagra to come up, half-convinced these Spartans were already dead or would give up. Then Proxenos himself dozed off only to awake to the sounds of Doric shouting.

"To me. Spartans to me. Rally to me." It was not even dawn light yet. The Spartans had surprised them in their breakout by beating the sunrise. The waking Boiotians jumped up just as the Elean guards ran past them in terror. Ainias, who was on the front watch at the courtyard, flew frantically behind the Eleans. Then he ducked behind the road wall when he saw his Boiotians. "We were wrong. There's not fifty there, not by a long way, but three hundred hoplites, maybe even more—peers all by the look of their armor. Maybe even five hundred coming down the lane, keeping the walls on each side, and nothing to stop them in front, like a bull with his horns lowered trapped in town. All royal guard I reckon. They march in their capes as on parade. Here they come in a phalanx. They broke right through our ring. Get out from this road, up over the field wall, before they roll us over."

No sooner had the Stymphalian yelled than he saw that even the

Boiotian guards had fled as well. So Ainias looked at Mêlon as they struggled to get over the waist-high wall and hide behind the stones, whispering, "They're passing right beside us, over there. Now. Stay down. Flat on our bellies, even in our armor under the wall where they can't see us. Quiet." Just as Ainias finished, the Spartan Antikrates strode through the courtyard gate into the narrow walled lane. He led more than three hundred men behind him, four abreast, the front three ranks with spears out, more than eighty men deep, all in perfect column. His nephew, the piper Dôron, was hitting the war notes as they kept in time. Twice-widowed Elektra, the daughter of the daughter of Agesilaos himself, marched in the front rank. She wore no helmet but let her black hair wave over her breastplate. It was thick and wavy although Elektra herself looked like a skull with wrinkled skin pulled over. She was shaking a spear like a Harpy to her third husband, bald Lichas himself, beside her, laughing and chanting to her mate, "To the river and the city across. Kill the pigs in our way. My Lichas, lead us, my Lichas, lead us to Epaminondas."

The front three ranks also had their shields out. The Spartans behind them put theirs above their heads, as bolts and stones rained on the little army from the flanks as it headed for the Eurotas. The fleeing Thebans had raised the shout and called for help. In reply, hundreds of Boiotians who had drifted off to ravage the nearby farms now answered back and in small bands headed for the sounds of the Spartan pipers. Some of the allies who had not fled ran alongside the road, on the other side of the field wall, parallel to the slow-marching army of Antikrates. They hoped at some point to leap over its walls, form a line, and block the passage of this two-stepping Spartan phalanx. But still they had no idea of the size or fury of the breakout, or that it was led by the entire savage clan of Lichas.

Most of these northerners did not know they were inside the compound of the Lichades, with the tower of Elektra herself opening to the walled lane, and that of slain Thôrax, the son of Lichas, close by, beyond the apple orchard. This is where Lichas had raised his four boys. He had sent all of them to the *agôgê* at seven. With his new wife, the widow Elektra, he had sired another three. All of this second litter was alive—Charillos, Thibrachos, and Polydektes. At thirty each had returned and built higher their towers and taken their farms as inheritance from their mothers. Here Lichas worked bare-chested and with a wide hat in summer, drilling his boys and sending them up to Taygetos to bring back a deer, protecting his later brood of royal sons from his first-born Anti-krates, who shield-bashed his half-brothers for sport.

By the time the Spartans had passed out of the tower compound and headed down the lane toward the Eurotas, they found a mob of ravagers and archers waiting right at the start of the public road, with torches and iron bars, behind a barricade of a cart and some goats. Fools. The Spartans went through all of them in laughter. Behind Lichas and Antikrates, they tore through the Elean plunderers like the fisherman's blade tears up the soft belly of the bluefish. Most of the ravagers blocking the way weren't hoplites but light-armed thieves who hoped their numbers would turn aside Antikrates, or that the herd of goats might break through the red-capes better than they. Elektra herself cleaved the hand of an Elean who ran alongside and tried to pull her down.

"Proxenos, where's Proxenos"? Mêlon looked along the lane wall where he thought the Plataian had hugged the dirt next to Ainias. Then the Stymphalian leapt up, "Look. He went after Antikrates's flank." Proxenos had run down alongside the lane. He jumped over the cross walls ahead to hit them at an angle. "Look, the madman charged them, way over there, by himself, as they passed by." Ainias ran after the rear of the Spartan phalanx, which was at least four hundred paces ahead, spearing its way through the Elean ravagers—who threw their torches into the middle of Antikrates's small company and fled in terror back into the orchards.

"No worry. No worry. Mêlon, there he is, down by that plane tree." Mêlon saw something by the side of Ainias ahead, as he was limping at a wild pace toward another large bay tree, also grown into the farm's wall, at the main crossroad to the Eurotas. Mêlon stopped when he saw the two of them, Proxenos with his hand on his belly. He yelled back to the others. "Over here for Proxenos." The Spartans had passed by and were spearing their way onward to the Eurotas, still to the beat of their pipers.

Proxenos had a smile on his face, as he staggered up and leaned on the bay trunk, with his hand on his side. "I'm fine, Mêlon. Just pushed aside by that brute Antikrates with his spear. He swatted me without even a look. I gave him a stab and he turned and laughed at my sting. He nicked me as he marched on, and I managed to fall over this low wall as they passed by. No doubt he went away boasting that a tiny swat from Antikrates has killed a Boiotian hoplite." They could hear the shrieks of

Elektra echoing in the distance as the Spartans neared the last open bridge over the river. Proxenos fell back under the tree. Ainias grabbed at his tunic and tried to look at the wound. "More than a nick, Proxenos, you've got blood on your *chitôn*, red and thick. I wager it flows from deep inside—all the way down your shin. Some of it has a black look to it. Bile is in it. Let me have a look at the skin."

Proxenos pushed him away and leaned against the wall. "No, no, it's only red. Keep away. The breastplate stays on. Maybe a slice, but it is already drying, and two of those Eleans went to get wool, and if they can find it, some oil and honey. I'm fine. The blood stopped as soon as it ran. A hoplite keeps his armor on. Go look after that other fellow that the Spartan woman cut. He's lying somewhere back along the wall, without a hand."

Ainias was relieved as Proxenos kept talking, and wondered at what he had done. "Antikrates. Did you see him? You charged Antikrates as he marched at the head of the royal guard? Did you learn nothing from their final breakout at Leuktra? Look at their torches over there by the Eurotas—they are plowing a furrow through that mob of thieves. You thought one hoplite from Plataia could take down the son of Lichas? As they head over the Eurotas, they'll kill a hundred of our own for their ticket across, and before the sun is even fully up."

"But I almost did stop him," Proxenos sighed. "At least I stabbed someone before he slapped his spear across my belly and gave me this scratch. Nêto was right: There is a foul smell about this Antikrates. I caught it as he nicked me. Either we kill him or he'll spear more of our own before this is all over. He's a *daimôn*, more evil even than his father Lichas. That Spartan has some secret hole he crawls out of each morning, a cave right out of Hades, and then back at night. None of us here can kill him, not even you, Ainias, or Mêlon. But no mind. Let's go inside this farm that it is daylight and see how Lichas and his kin lived. Ah, Lichas has a tower now, in our style. Look at this, Mêlon, from here it looks better than any in Boiotia. Fresh and with new plaster. It's a copy of your own on Helikon, only taller." He was now walking about as he talked and proving to them that his cut was not too deep after all.

Mêlon's leg was sore and his foot blistered. This latest escape of Antikrates was the second time the killer had eluded the Boiotians. Was there a god's reason for it? Who, what could kill this man? The life of Antikrates and his father, Mêlon understood, hung by a thick rope, not a thin thread. Even the Fates couldn't cut through them with a sword. "Go ahead, you two. Burn the house of Leôn. Or maybe it is that of the woman Elektra, the wife of Lichas. But set foot in it without sulfur and flame? No, I Mêlon, son of Malgis, will not. I have too many dreams of farmhouses to come with the brood of Lichas, and flames in them as well."

So the Spartans under Antikrates and Elektra made their way at dawn from their compound and escaped across the Eurotas into the city of Sparta proper. Nevertheless in the next five days the invaders' ravaging continued right on into the new year and past the end of the tenure of general Epaminondas. The Thebans mostly kept apart from their allies, especially the men of Mantineia, the self-proclaimed liberators who were busy rounding up Spartan helots and *perioikoi* for their own slaves. Gangs from the potters' quarters of Mantineia had already foolishly crossed spears with Philliadas and his men of Tanagra. The Boiotian plunderers had killed their rival allies for sport—and warned Lykomedes they would as easily butcher all the Mantineians just as if they were Spartans. With the Spartans safe beyond the river, the three armies without a common enemy would soon battle each other for the plunder. Finally Epaminondas headed the Thebans out in the phalanx for the river and sought a way to cross it and enter the unwalled city of the Spartans. Thousands of plunderers began to follow behind the columns of Boiotians who had assembled under Epaminondas at last for this final assault on the citadel of Sparta. Even the looters figured that should the mad general get across, then the city would be theirs for the robbing. But the Peloponnesian allies in arms—except the Argives—were already scattering over the countryside as snow came in from the north. True, the Spartans were trapped inside their city. But the charge of Antikrates and Elektra from his farm had frightened the Mantineians. Few had any stomach to face him again.

Among the allies chaos reigned. Plunder, not the freedom of the helots, was what most of the allied armies had joined up for—cattle, and weapons, and bronze pots, even the oak doors and pine sills of the houses of the Spartans. Now in the icy wind, thousands of the Arkadians had already moved into the abandoned farmhouses of the Spartans and were camping in their barns and sheds as well, burning their fences and pens to keep warm. "Boiotian folly" and worse they called the plan of Epaminondas to storm the citadel of Sparta in the dead of winter. The green plain was smoky from thousands of campfires and burned towers. But amid the haze, all could see the acropolis opposite and the untouched roofs of the Spartan homes. All around Sparta was burning, but so far the city itself across the river was untouched.

Mêlon had just armed again. He formed up in the columns of Epaminondas with Ainias and Proxenos, and made sure that Melissos stayed clear of the looting. As the Boiotians broke camp for the final reckoning with King Agesilaos, their ranks passed some Mantineians swarming another grand estate that must have belonged to an ephor. Its tower and long whitewashed wall were as grand as those of the Lichades. "Here, over here," a Peloponnesian lord on a horse yelled out at the passing column. "You Thebans, here, right here, they say, this is the farm of lame Agesilaos, the king no less. Not Leôn's, but the king's himself. You know Agesilaos, the lame killer? The place is full of plunder from your Boiotia— even the man's clay pots are Theban. We even found the gold and silver from your temples. He stripped your land for years. Here, take your share."

Melissos and Mêlon paused to look at the estate of King Agesilaos. But this was all, just some simple stones and a few wooden columns? In this new Hellas upside down, a hoplite just walked into the house of the great king of the Spartans and did what he pleased? Was this the power of Epaminondas to make the make-believe ordinary? But then, Mêlon thought further, how small an estate for a king? This was all they were to burn? Were there still leaders enough in Hellas like Agesilaos who lived as simply as did their hoplites? Mêlon knew Agesilaos fought alongside his men, but now he saw that he lived like them as well.

Suddenly about ten or so Mantineians with iron bars pried the roof off, sending it down between the mud brick walls. Others were gathering the roof-beams and throwing any of the debris they didn't burn into wagons. Few knew that they had destroyed a royal house of the Spartans— built ten generations of men earlier and never a footprint of the enemy in its courtyard. Fewer cared. One cart was full of *pithoi* of oil, another of spades, rakes, and scythes. There were even some breastplates—the bell types that the Spartan elders wore a hundred years earlier and more when they had stopped the Medes at Plataia. Some Mantineians in their drink danced on top of the field wall. They were tossing like balls the light bronze helmets of the Persians, taken as booty long ago in the great days by the Spartan breed who broke the Persian general Mardonios. The livestock of the king's farm, cows and goats, had been driven off. Any that had been left behind had been butchered. Their carcasses had been piled before the entrance that was covered in smoke as the looters torched rafters and poured a vat of olive oil over some loose wood to light the mess. A few were already cooking rotten meat on spits over a bonfire in the courtyard.

Mêlon had thought he would never tire of the flames devouring all things Spartan, especially that of the royals. But now? The burning sheds and dead cattle were not so much Spartan, but the works and efforts of farmers like him—and the destruction was therefore senseless. His own strongbox in the well at home was full of silver that Malgis had earned doing just what these Mantineians were busy with. Yet Mêlon, son on Malgis, wanted no more of any of it. These were farms, not farmers, that they were destroying. He cared little who worked them, only that it was wrong to burn the holy olive, to cut the gnarly vine, to torch the well-oiled roof-beams that exist beyond the owner.

Meanwhile, Mêlon stared at some loud Arkadians holding a rope. On it a helot boy was lowered down a well. Already drunk on their wine, they were scuffling over a treasure not yet found and cursing each other for slacking—as the dangling youth below banged against the stone sides of the well. The more hardy beyond the house were trying to ax down a few olive trees. But most had given up after lopping off the low-lying limbs, and were content with scrounging moldy nuts from a nearby ancient almond. Lykomedes himself rode up and pointed to the passing Boiotians. He was happy enough, since his wagons were already full of plunder, he had met few Spartans, and his Mantineians saw no need either to cross the Eurotas or the spine of Taygetos. "Tell your madman Epaminondas to forget Agesilaos. Forget his acropolis across the river. Forget battle and fighting Spartans. There's sport enough with us. First the house of Elektra. Then Lichas's, and now the king's." He shook a fine silver pitcher at them. "The closer we get to the river, the richer the plunder. Every now and then we find a Lakonian holdout with a scythe—a wild one who thinks he can keep Arkadians out of his garden. But why go get yourself killed when there is more profit in plunder here? We can do the Spartan just as much bad, worse even, by carrying off everything he has. Get near the river to give us cover. But no need to cross, no need for battle, no need to get us killed when we can get rich." So Lykomedes laughed and rode by. A Lakonian wagon creaked behind him, filled with Spartan red tunics, plumed helmets, a set of armor, three helots shackled, and a horse and mule tethered to the back. The Arkadian driver yelled out, "For a Dorian race that has no money, these Spartan thieves have more than we do."

It was to be mostly a Boiotian army that Mêlon and Melissos rejoined, one prepared to cross the Eurotas and face Agesilaos in the streets of Sparta to try to end the king's power. Only the hoplites with Epaminondas were willing to head for the citadel and battle the Spartans beyond the river. Over there the eye of Agesilaos was everywhere. Spartans ran back and forth at each planned ford. As the army of Epaminondas pressed on, Proxenos and Ainias fell farther back in the ranks with Mêlon, at a slower pace than even the fat and lame hoplites. Ainias knew that if he questioned his friend about his stab wound, he would once again be met with furor at the thought of stopping, or even of touching his armor.

Proxenos finally himself grabbed his flank near his wound and whispered to the Arkadian, "Then it is to be crossing the river for us, after all?"

CHAPTER 27

# The Visions of Proxenos

D oes that bother you, Proxenos?" Ainias had an eye for small
things when his men marched. This day of assault he had found
his Proxenos a little slow and quiet, even for his aloof nature.
Ainias had tried to look at his wound, even as his friend had pushed him
away. So he was not so puzzled now that the Plataian lingered in the moments before the great fording. Proxenos had begun to walk even behind
the lame Mêlon and the slow-cart servant Melissos who carried a shield
and pole and pack. Ainias hoped that Proxenos's sloth meant, as his
friend had once laughed, that the lack of stone here no doubt bored the
architect of ramparts. The plains of Sparta were aflame, and its hoplites
were running or hiding. Did that mean Proxenos was not so much hurt as
bored, since here were no stones to set or tear down? Ainias asked again,
"Why do you fear the River Eurotas, man? Stop here for a blink and let
me see whether your bandage is bloody."

Proxenos ignored him and whispered again, "Did you hear me—are
we to the river?" He waited for no answer. "Is it really to be the water, the
black Eurotas?"

Ainias was relieved that his friend was at least talking and still walking, though he did not like the sound of the "black Eurotas," since the
river ahead was icy and white but not dark. Still, Ainias went on to try to
cheer his friend as they slowed and brought up the rear of the column.
"Let them go ahead, Proxenos. We will stop up ahead, since your brow is
wet and your face flushed. I'll wash the wound and salve it with the honey

in my pouch. But I also wish we'd leave the crippled king alone over there. Since there are no bridges left over the river, and the fords are all guarded. Even Megas Epaminondas cannot cross what you call the black Eurotas in this weather." Ainias mistook the silence of his friend as a friendly nod to go on. "Now I see that even without Spartans on the other shore, we couldn't ford this icy water. Then climb the mud of the banks? Impossible. I agree. But do not tell our Iron Gut that. Oh, no. Many will die trying. Many who shouldn't. Instead we should be marching westward to free right now the helot folk—or better yet just go back to camp and let me at last take a look where Antikrates nicked you."

Proxenos smiled at the thought of going home to the Asopos and his own orchards and vineyards near Plataia. Then when they were close enough to hear the roar of the swollen river, he finally spoke a bit more to his friend Ainias. "Oh, no bother. The wound closed. My breastplate keeps it warm. I slow you down, because I'm not sure why we are heading to the river, or why it is so cold so far south. You know that our strings are measured. A man can no more extend his own than he can stretch dry rope."

Ainias at first ignored his babble, and planned to force him to stop near the bank ahead, even if it meant holding him down and, with Melissos, tearing off his heavy breastplate. Proxenos talked more now as if they were lounging at the symposion than marching to battle the Spartans. Had the Spartan Antikrates knocked the sense out of Proxenos when he nicked him earlier at the farmhouse of the Lichades? Gone was the boasting of the wall builder of the past year that men are the measures of things and live or die according to their own merits. So Ainias countered him with a frown as they waited for a column of northerners that had joined their own phalanx at the crossroads to Gytheion. "If your wound does not bleed, and there is no fire on your brow, then at least clear your head. This black bile does not suit you, Plataian. We have men of bronze and iron to cut down. You have a city to found. A third one for the helots. Raise your shield. Show us what Plataia can do."

A sense of finality had come over Proxenos after his run-in with Antikrates. As he staggered along, Proxenos was measuring a life up before the black clouds above his brow closed in. His children were near grown. His Aretê had a good dowry of a house, one with three stories inside the very walls that he had rebuilt. Their two hundred *plethra* above the banks of the Kephissos made good oil and wine, all with a view of the wide bend below. Yes, he had three hundred more olive trees on the rolling slopes nearby. His wife lacked for nothing with a strongbox of ten thousand Athenian owls, good silver that his father had earned with the Ten Thousand, and the booty share given to him by Xenophon and the Spartans. His grandfather Ladôn had left behind a strongbox that was buried deep under the floor of the tower.

At somewhere more than thirty seasons, his wife, Aretê, Proxenos figured, if she avoided the summer riverbank fevers, the Egyptian pox, and hot-face Helios that blisters the face and arms and spins the head, had a good ten years left. He had made Ainias, when they set out southward, promise to visit her in Plataia, as they joked over the rantings of Nêto and her warning that Proxenos was not to cross the Isthmos. The breasts of his Aretê were deep, her hips firm—as Ainias, he wished, would soon learn. And himself? His teeth were still white and all there, his beard black as the raven's wing. His muscles were firm without the sagging of flesh in men half his age. But there was no life force. Proxenos felt no different from the collapsed puppets in the agora once the strings of their masters had been put away.

All his land, the height of his tower, the beauty of his wife—all that meant nothing in the snow of Lakonia. Or perhaps less than nothing here in the mud of the Eurotas far to the south where he was soon to be just another rotting spearman too far from home. Proxenos, although he had volunteered to come south despite the fears of Nêto, still thought it unjust—no, a real madness—that he, the man who had crafted the three great cities of the Peloponnesos, was a mere soldier in the ranks, for whom a single spear-jab to his gut meant no walls of Messenê or a wrong tower in Megalopolis. So in his delirium he thought Epaminondas or at least his friends should have kept their holy Proxenos in camp, a man of genius like Daidalos of old not to be wasted in cheap battle. But he also knew that often we are hardest on those we love most, and treat the friend roughly either because we demand his company in shared danger, or out of friendly envy want him to remember in our shared risk that he is no better than us. So Proxenos, the architect of the greatest cities of new Hellas, was but a common hoplite at the Eurotas. If here was where they wanted him, so here he would stay.

The two hoplites were soon standing at the rear of the column. They had kept falling farther behind the Thebans as the phalanx was nearing

the banks of the Eurotas. Ainias tapped his silent friend with a light blow
to his helmet to see whether he flinched from his stupor, and took off his
pack. He wanted to force him down and probe his cut, but Proxenos was
still standing and slapped away his hand. Ainias now sensed his friend
was waning, and that he could do little to cure either his body or his soul,
and perhaps should play this final act out until the end of the drama.
Nonetheless, he wanted Proxenos of Plataia to show the army that he was
a hoplite of the first rank who took his wounds in front and fell in the first
rank. "Wake up, man. Even lame Mêlon has passed us up and waits at the
fore with Epaminondas. Pelopidas needs our counsel at the spear tip. He
has no spirit to fight ice and Spartans together. Hey, Proxenos. *Hypnos* has
you again, man. Your eyes—they're rolling, ever since that farm. Shake it
off, this black bile. Spit out the lotus-eater in you. Come back from the
other shore."

Proxenos paid him no heed. Instead he continued to limp in the direction of the Sacred Band. But now his head sagged and he felt a strange
urge to fall asleep, armor and all. At some point failure became pleasure.
Resistance to the creeping ice inside him meant only pain. He felt a funny
kinship with thousands gone—with tens of thousands unseen—but less
affinity with the hundreds he could make out at his side. Where to find
his knot of strength? It had vanished out of his mouth, left him unstrung.
Cold voices of the dead began to whisper in his ears. The warm talk of
Nêto was not among them to drive these furies out.

Proxenos, Ainias knew at last as he glanced at his friend, was doing
the arithmetic of death. This starts when a man of the middle age begins
to add up what he has done and what lies ahead—and sees that the climb
up was far better than the trudge back down. He saw the Plataian gasping, breathing out steam that rose from his sagging helmet, and noticed
there was blood at the corner of his lower lip and foam as well. For those
who dare to do such summing up, even without a wound, the life force
itself can sometimes vanish and leave nothing but empty flesh in its
wake—a lyre fallen silent without a song or player. He wanted to throw
Proxenos down and cleanse his wound, but he also wished for his friend
to stand tall with his spear at the Eurotas rather than drift into sleep here
on the march.

Proxenos sensed his wound was behind all this mad thinking, but its
full malignancy was still not quite clear to either him or his friends. So

the Plataian was unsure whether this sudden waning of his strength was not a failure of his own will. Had he any courage left, he could have been at the forefront with Epaminondas, despite the spear poke that Antikrates had given him. Chiôn and Mêlon had suffered worse wounds and yet were always at the van. Had he incurred a bad *daimôn*? Perhaps there were Olympian gods, after all. Had his impious neglect of Zeus and Apollo on Parnassos and the earth-shaker Poseidon at the Isthmos in favor of the one deity of Pythagoras—had all that come back to haunt him in his final time of need? The gods, not Antikrates, had done all this to him?

Nêto had no power against the deathless ones to change or honey-coat her pronouncement of the doom he would face after crossing the Isthmos. The Plataian, through strange voices along the river's edge, was given a final gift of visions of things to come, majestic sights in hues of purple and soft yellow, all to the music of the pipes of Thisbê. Now pictures came to him of the finished Megalopolis, and of Epaminondas standing guard as the new gates of Messenê rose, then leading the army back home in triumph across the Isthmos.

Yes, his eyes were full of color and his ears of flute music. Proxenos could hear the voices to come of the demogogues at the trial of Epaminondas back home, swaying the judges to kill the general as he sat in the dock on the Theban Kadmeia. Did Ainias not see this—their general dragged into the *bêma* to be jeered before being hanged? Yes, there would be the bickering on their return; but then, as the envy and jealousy cooled, maybe also would come applause for the magnitude of the Theban achievement when fully grasped, no doubt only after they were all dead. He, Proxenos, the lord of a vast estate overlooking the Asopos, would have to stand in a Theban court while the rabble cobblers and tanners pelted him with fruit and jeered at his half-Attic speech and damned him for joining Epaminondas—only to be found guilty of designing the three greatest cities of Hellas and freeing the men of the Peloponnesos and making the Boiotians all safe.

Such is the way of men, Proxenos reckoned in these final moments, when given a great gift, to complain about the quality of the present or the motive of the giver or the circumstances of the largesse, all to lessen the need for gratitude and indebtedness—and fouler dependence. Proxenos in his delirium saw that there would be a need for more invasions to the south to come. Sparta was hard to break and helots were harder to free. Allies would switch and join the enemy if their deliverer became too powerful, or if he seemed too weak. He knew Lykomedes was already half with the Spartans, half with Epaminondas, unsure which side in the end would win and thus he should join. It is a human habit to relax in triumph and take the boot off the neck of the wounded foe who has not quite expired. Soon Epaminondas would have to lead out the army to finish what he could not quite this morning.

Would he, Proxenos, wish to spend the rest of his life trudging down here on the tail of Epaminondas, to end Sparta? Leave all that marching each summer to Mêlon and all the other zealots who had made the conversion to the cause of the helots. A Plataian, as Nêto warned, had no business in the ice of Lakonia. All this was too much, this monotony, this predictability. Now no matter how Proxenos tried to keep in step with the hoplites, he could not fight off a new tightness that was rising into his chest and neck at the same rate it had crept down his thighs. Since he knew all that was ahead, why the need to put off what was foreordained?

Ainias gave up trying to stop Proxenos and so instead hit his breastplate again. "Wake, do not let the ghosts take you, man. Not now, not when we are to burn the wasps in their very nests."

Proxenos, through his helmet that had fallen back down over his face, mumbled to Ainias, who heard him clearly—strangely so, as if the gods had stopped the river roar and muzzled the grunts of the hoplites and the clatter of their bronze, "Do you like Sophokles, Ainias?"

"This is no time for that, man. But if you must know—no. He was a pompous old man. But keep to the river, not the words of the dead poets." Ainias thought that if he kept Proxenos talking, the Kêres would stay away.

"Do you know his *Aias*, Ainias, his *Philoktêtes*? I never cared to watch *Oidipous* or *Antigonê*, especially to see us Boiotians on stage as eye-stabbers and woman-killers."

"Yes, once, at the big theater in Korinthos. But Aias was a suicide. I never put much faith in his 'Live nobly or nobly die,' not when it was by his own hand."

"But you do, Ainias! That is why you march with Mêlon and me—because so do we. All three of us are Aiases of sorts—here far from our homes, no friends of the Thebans or the Messenians, but merely for the idea of it all, the last breed of the Hellenes, with no expectation that we are to live through it. We live for a code that sets us apart, and now the toll comes due as it must. Why else would a Stymphalian, a man of Thespiai, and a Plataian all be near this accursed river in winter—for the helots?"

"It helps to hate the Spartans. Or have you forgotten that, my dear Pentheus who rages as he sees two suns and the sky in a swirl."

Ainias stopped the mad Sophokles talk because he knew where it led—as if a Proxenos were an Aias without a future or a Philoktêtês who with wound was exiled by those who needed his skill. As the two argued, the mist was lifting. Most of the army had stopped and was drawing back up on the riverbank. All were stunned at last by the sight of Sparta itself, the city that they had heard of only in widows' tales to frighten young Boiotians to come inside from the courtyard. Not a wall to be seen, just countless hoplites on the banks opposite to provide ramparts of flesh against the invader. Some of the faces of their own hoplites at the head of the Boiotian snake were white, but not just from the cold. It was a terrible thing to look across the icy Eurotas at a long line of red-caped hoplites kneeling with spear and shield. Epaminondas saw this terror and worried it had already ruined his army this day.

So he threw off his green cape and mounted his red Boiotian pony. The general galloped up and down the column and ordered his men as he reined his mount and for a moment pranced it on two legs. "No fear. No *phobos*. To me. Ford into Sparta with me." Five thousand of his hoplites thronged the banks and hit their raised shields with their spears. "Shields high, men, as we get wet. Hold them over our heads as these Spartan cowards try to hit us in the water. The water will touch our waists but not our chins. There are no stone walls over there. Cross the river here at the ford. The Eurotas is cold, but not deep. Wade it—and we are inside Sparta. She is ours for the torching. Who is afraid of a little water, a little wet?"

But as Epaminondas charged back and forth along the high banks of the river, the lame Spartan king yonder across the water was also visible to the Thebans through the whirling mists. Agesilaos limped along the Eurotas, always shadowing Epaminondas, pointing this way and that with his spear, sending companies of spearmen anywhere he saw a possible ford. What a small man he was, Mêlon saw—half the size of the Agiad king Kleombrotos at Leuktra. Smaller even than short Epaminondas. Were these Eurypontid kings dwarves? The king limped far worse than

Mêlon did himself. So this lame-foot man was all that kept Epaminondas from storming Sparta? Not quite all—for there was something else on the far bank, a figure standing next to Agesilaos. Mêlon, who was at the side of Proxenos, yelled out to his aide Melissos, "There, look. There, boy, there is the killer, Lichas. Look at that foul spearman. Bare-headed, with his white braids. No helmet."

The bleary eyes of Melissos thought he saw nothing other than the fuzzy shapes across the water. But he sensed the furor in Mêlon, who faced Epaminondas and called out again, "He's there, our Lichas, near the king Agesilaos. He is the one who dares us."

Then the king was gone, as quickly as he had appeared, into the hedges across the river. In his place ran his granddaughter, hair in the winter wind, with a black sword in her right hand. Now there was no mistaking her. She darted across the line of crouching Spartan spearmen, her *klôpis* hitting their wooden shafts as she reminded them, "Your king and my Lichas are with you. Stand fast and spear the pigs from the north. Leave Epaminondas to me." Her voice easily carried across the water.

Melissos cried out to his master, "I can hear them, Thespian, I can hear your Lichas and the king in their fury on the other side, and his demon bitch, all cursing our Epaminondas. Can they see us as well? Why not cross and kill them? I can help, I can do that." But Mêlon grabbed the Makedonian by the neck and drew him back from the water where the arrows were beginning to hit near their shins. The last bridge had been destroyed by the king, enraged that a Theban had shut his men inside his city when they were used to marching a thousand stadia abroad into the lands of others. Still, this Melissos was proving to be as brave as any in the phalanx.

Agesilaos came back out of the bushes and bellowed to the Thebans when he caught sight of the mounted Epaminondas. A wind came up and all the Thebans could hear his slurs from across the river. "O wild man" the king pointed at Epaminondas, shaking his spear, "you will not cross this ford, fool, you cannot without a bridge. Never touch the polis of Leônidas. You can't cross, not now, not ever. We are the better men. Our Elektra is a man, and you are women." For once the aged royal spoke true, as the army froze at the water's edge, stopped there by the fog and sleet and ice combined with arrows and javelins hurled from the Spartan side.

Mêlon spoke to the boy Melissos, as if he were a general like Epaminondas, as they both watched the throng across the wide cold river. "This morning is not our day. It is not fated, Melissos. I see that now. We are not to kill Agesilaos and Lichas today. Too high the water, too cold, too many Spartans on the banks." Even if they got across the current, the Thebans would be inside the hornets' nest. To fight in the streets of Sparta was a battle few welcomed. No wonder the Arkadians, the Eleans, the Northerners, even the Argives wanted no part of this. It would mean being pelted by roof-tiles and hit by the pots tossed down by frenzied women, as the Boiotians got caught in winding and dead-end streets and trapped in courtyards. Lampito, younger sister of Lichas, along with Elektra, his wife, had organized the women into *lochoi*, ten to a roof, sixty houses among them each. The Boiotians remembered the stories of their grandfathers. They had told of the Thebans who had once stormed into the streets of nearby Plataia. Few had made it out alive as the women and boys of the town had buried them with hard clay from the rooftops.

Until the sun broke through the heavy fog around noon, each time Pelopidas and the Sacred Band reached a new sandbar of the river, hundreds across the water ran up to the banks. The Spartans knelt down with spears on their shields to meet them, then lowered their heads as their archers and javelin throwers at the rear targeted the throng of Thebans with a volley of missiles. The Spartans had mocked that arrows were the work of women. But now they flung anything they could to stop Epaminondas at the Eurotas.

A few of the foolish among the Boiotians who had reached halfway into the current were already floating downstream, with javelins stuck in their necks and thighs. In vain, Epaminondas had ignored the advice of the veteran Ainias and Pelopidas, and of Mêlon as well. They had all warned him to avoid the city. Instead, why not burn the dockyards at Gytheion to the south? For this day leave Agesilaos alone. Once more, let Lichas be. Mêlon was at the general's side, trying to grab his reins and get Epaminondas off his red horse. He tried to talk over the shouting of battle. "Mad Theban. Don't ruin our army in the water when twenty myriads await us in Messenia. Join the Arkadians as they burn the countryside. This Lichas, he baits us. He's your nemesis. Wants us to climb out soaked on his side. Don't. Stay here. Burn and loot and overturn their farms. The Eurotas will be our warden and bars." Mêlon had remembered

Malgis's stories of the Athenian slaughter at the River Assinaros in Sikily, and he began to see that even Lykomedes and his looters had the better advice this morning. So he kept on with his early-morning warning to the mounted Epaminondas to avoid the water. "They will slaughter us. As if we were the Athenians in Sikily. Water is their helper. Back off, Theban. Today is not our day. Not this day."

Ainias saw in the lifting fog that his friend Proxenos had drifted off and was standing on the bank—deliberately in range of the Spartan archers. The Stymphalian damned himself again that he had allowed his friend to arm that morning when Proxenos should have stayed inside the warm tents of Pelopidas and finally had his wound cleaned and oiled.

Proxenos was the first to plunge in the icy waters and the last to lumber out as the rising waist-high current barred the way. Did he wish to be hit or to drown? Now on this last attempt, the Plataian had to be pulled out. He fell down, shivering on the bank, but had at least shown the Boiotians how a Plataian braves the missiles of the Spartans and cares little for the cold of the Eurotas. Ainias at last could treat his friend, still breathing on the bank, nearly blue in his wet armor, muttering of his visions of white women with barbed wings and bloody fangs. His eyes closed. With a whisper he touched Ainias's hand. "No man a slave. None really are. Where is my Nêto?"

"Eyes open, man, before you freeze." Ainias pulled Proxenos up at the arm. He ordered the hoplites to bring oil and woolen cloaks. Melissos ran up with his pack, a blanket, and a flask. He had seen Proxenos stagger into the Eurotas, shield high, and wanted rare men like this to live; he tore open his pack and tossed oil, honey, and cloth to Ainias.

The river, Proxenos knew, was no longer fast and cold, but strangely warm and slow. He wanted to crawl back into it. He still heard his friends jabbering; too loud, harsh, and grating, they were like the harsh crows fighting each other to pick apart the rotting sucker-fish on the quay. Were they Kêres now? So he looked instead across the river, and now found the floating shades far more to his liking with their soothing calls to ford the warm river. There were heroes, not Kêres, across the Eurotas. Scarlet and purple, these images sang from across the water, "Come across, Proxenos, son of Proxenos, hero of Plataia, guest-friend of Sparta. The water is warm here, my son, where you belong."

The rough, hard figures of his friends standing above him were of a tired world, one he was leaving behind. Across the Eurotas, there he saw the outline of his long-dead father Proxenos, friend of Sparta, in his armor at Kunaxa, waving for him to join him. Across the water there were not Agesilaos and Lichas, and Elektra with her bare breasts, but there now appeared in the mist Spartans enough, or at least a red-caped mob of shades milling around the angry spear-pierced King Kleombrotos. The ghosts were torn with the terrible wounds from the blows of Mêlon and Chiôn at Leuktra. Even Kleonymos and his companions who drifted to the banks and rattled their spears at him could do him no real harm—or so the voices in his head assured him.

The shade of Sphodrias was shaking his fist at Proxenos. The dead Deinon was screeching as well. There was Klearchos drifting up, who at Leuktra had at least taken down Staphis before being brained by Chiôn. Then Proxenos saw in the distance the ghost of a smiling warrior. He spoke the Thespian brand of Boiotian, and sang to him in the formal tongue, "I am Malgis, O Proxenos, son of Proxenos, friend of your father. Join us over here, O weary man. Come for the laurels you deserve. You served my son so well and brought the Boiotians out of their infamy— enough for any, all that. Join us, bask in the rising of your three cities; we can see them all from here. My grandson Lophis is here with me—and is a hero of the Boiotians, greater than Pagondas, greater than Ismenias, greater than any since Oidipous. Our farms are fine. Your work is finished. Now it is our time to rest. There is no more strife on this side of the river, on our sweeter side. Pay no attention to these red-caped men. These Spartans will float apart for you when you cross Styx. None of us endures the burdens and pains of the flesh here in Elysion. Over here there is order and law, just like among the good men of Plataia. There is no rabble and shoving and jeering along the upper banks of the Acheron, here in the green meadows with the nobles of Elysion."

Proxenos forgot the melancholy and felt warm with recognition of years well lived. How fortunate he was to be cresting before his wave broke and turned to tiny eddies and stagnant backwash of old age. He could feel for a while longer two men bent over him and saw the faces of Mêlon and Ainias barking and shaking him, as the Makedonian Melissos spread the blanket over his midriff. It was a gift to go in his glory as Proxenos of the dark hair and with beard black and thick, and full in his armor, the greatest builder in Hellas in its greatest age of stone. No more worries about hunting down Lichas or the traitor Gorgos or fears of the turncoat Lykomedes. As in sickness, the approach of death severs one from the world of cares, or the people that scurry about without a hint that they too live on mortgaged time, with bodies no more than Korinthian glass, a small break away from a mess of shards. Even for the healthy and young, death is not always unwelcome. No, Proxenos would exit the stage before the crowd tired of his voice.

And so he did.

In a blink the man of stone, the aristocrat from Plataia, Proxenos son of Proxenos went cold—only to skim over the black waters and reach a far different shore where weight and worry were only faint burdens of the memory.

"Wake man, wake, wake!" Ainias shook his friend, who was cold. "More oil, Melissos, more oil." He turned in disgust to Pelopidas, who had also reached him with a dozen of the Band. "He has left us, he left us. He simply gave up when we, when I, needed him most. He went into the river and caught a chill. His unknowing Aretê, even now a thousand stadia to the north in Plataia, sings of his safe return as she coddles his sons with stories of his high ramparts—and of his fame to come."

But Pelopidas was the cooler head and paid the grief-stricken Stymphalian no matter. Instead he had the breastplate of Proxenos taken off, and was wrapping him in a cloak. Mêlon scolded Ainias, "That was not his way. His ticket on Charôn's ferry was not of his own buying." Then Mêlon took over from Pelopidas and gently probed that slash below the dead man's navel. Two palms in width it had grown in the last day, right across the gut where the breastplate ended, the naked zone of flesh above his leather skirt. The jagged tear was now black and yet oozing foul pus, yellow and black. "This is no bile, but old rot. His gut is seeping through as well. How he walked these last days, only Zeus knows. I reckon the wound rotted him from within. He has had his finger on it to keep the mess inside since Antikrates cut his insides nearly in two."

Ainias wept, in loss and in embarrassment of his momentary anger at the departure of his friend—and the greater anger that he had not thrown his friend down and treated his wound before they had set out that morning.

Mêlon ignored him, "So ends Proxenos. This is a man who achieved rather than suffered death."

Ainias interrupted the silence as he stared down at the white face of what once was Proxenos and his black beard already spotted with ice. "The stones of the free cities of the Peloponnesos are his markers. He lies here dead cold for the helots. Pray to the One God that they were worth it. Dead for the damned helots."

"No," Mêlon answered, "for his pleasure. It was his pleasure to come south. That is enough for me. You can figure out the rest."

Meanwhile, Epaminondas had drawn the column back from the river. The army began its retreat to camp, cold and tired and disheartened that they would never cross the Eurotas. While the four had worked to keep Proxenos warm and breathing, the last fording had failed. Epaminondas was waving all back as arrows whizzed by his head. This was the first time Epaminondas had tripped—and yet it would be his last mistake. King Agesilaos had been right after all: No man of Boiotia would ever bring fire to the very heart of a defeated Sparta. The women were braver on the banks, and hurling insults at the Thebans, baring their icy breasts in mockery and throwing rocks into the river in disdain. In front of them always was shrill Elektra, like Medea of old, holding up one bare shriveled breast, waving her left hand above her head, spitting and ululating all the while. "You all need this teat like the babes you are!" she cried.

Nêto also had been right in her visions when she had long ago warned that none born in the countryside of Thebes would kill Lichas or his son Antikrates. Dozens were wounded and sixty Theban hoplites dead for this failed mad gambit to defy the prophecy. Proxenos was borne on a bier back to camp, with Pelopidas and Melissos carrying the front corners of his litter. Mêlon and Ainias did the same at the rear.


Yet none saw behind them the new Proxenos swimming across the eddies of the hot Eurotas. He waved to them all as they turned out of sight on the main road and headed to the camp north of town. He ascended the bank opposite. The Spartan shades, as promised, did the Plataian no harm. So the Olympian gods with their heaven and Hades were real after all? Now too late the Pythagorean Proxenos must concede that—even as he flitted as an empty ghost among the heroes of old who drifted about just as Homer had sung? Proxenos looked in vain for his Nêto for help, as if he felt she too were somewhere near or maybe already across the Styx at this very moment. Instead here were the Elysion fields of deep green and the marble homes of the hemi-gods.

So all the fables of the ignorant were true. Where would his soul end up in such a place as an unbeliever in Olympos, as an apostate follower of Pythagoras—down lower next to Sisyphos or Tantalos or in the depths of Tartaros? But then came noise and light. In another eye blink all these fantasies of his first twenty years of life disappeared. The false shades of Kleombrotos and Kleonymos dissipated. Proxenos felt himself in a vortex. He was whirling upward toward a bright sun. There was certainly no Zeus here.

Heat, heat of all things amid the ice, came over him, and in an instant Proxenos was given knowledge of how the plan of it all worked: that the good man alone finds peace and that the end of all things was, as his One God of Pythagoras had promised, not Hades at all, but a return to his very beginning. So Epaminondas had saved him, after all, as he knew he might. He was not in Persia like his father with Xenophon, on the royal wage, drenching his spear arm in blood for Spartans and for gold and land as well. He was not scheming to keep his olives free from the tramp of armies, but down here on the Eurotas for nothing other than his pleasure and the visions of Epaminondas for something called Hellas. For all that his soul had been made deathless a year earlier, and now he would learn that, as he would come no more again to the physical world, even as the crow or dog, but had won the battle for his soul in his brief life as the *aristos* of Plataia. The last thing he remembered as Proxenos of old was the soft murmur of Pythagoras's warning, "When you are traveling abroad, look not back at your own borders." Proxenos searched no longer for Ainias and his funeral march. Not now as he reached the light and became something better than he had been.

Ainias shuddered and almost dropped the corner of the bier. His breath stopped when a warm—hot even—draft from the south swept across his ice-bitten neck. Then he caught himself and whispered, "So it is. So as our holy one promised, my Proxenos."

But at that moment far away on the other side of snowy Taygetos, Nêto shuddered as if an icy breeze had reached her.

She wept. "Our Proxenos crossed the Isthmos, but not the Eurotas."

# CHAPTER 28

# Lord Kuniskos of the Helots

G orgos had not done too badly for himself this past year in the valley between the mountains of Taygetos and Parnon, back home near his gloomy Eurotas. There, as a young man and a freed helot, more than fifty summers earlier, he had once mustered in with the Spartan general Brasidas to join the long marches against the Athenians. He remembered the farmhouses of the Spartan clans of his childhood. Lichas even had given him back his name "Puppy Dog"—Kuniskos. The helot came faster at the sound of it.

Lichas feared that his Sparta suffered the curse of *oliganthrôpeia*, an insidious depopulation that was the wage of sending boys into the *agôgê*, separated from women until they were thirty, and deploying the army out on patrol for months at a time—his red-capes training and fighting when they should be sowing the seeds of the Spartan state. That the peers were defined by pure Spartan blood from both parents only made the hoplites shrink farther, as those of mixed and foreign blood began to act as if they were Spartiates themselves. The army had been large at Leuktra, but only because those left at home to defend Sparta itself were now few. So here in a shrinking Sparta a talented freedman like Gorgos found opportunity to reclaim his lost status, not just because he was gifted in the arts of guile and double-cross, but also because there were now few Spartiates in a state desperate for men of his caliber.

At Leuktra Gorgos had not really meant to take the wounded Lophis to Lichas at all—at least not at first. Or so he swore to himself and to others later. Instead, he had wanted to risk his bones to carry the broken body of the son of his master from the fray—back up, as promised, to Nêto and their wagon on the hill above the battle. Yet when he found himself near the red-capes and saw Lichas trapped amid a sea of dead hoplites, his Spartan blood warmed and drew him to the *lochos* of the old guard. Just as it had fifty seasons earlier and more when he had stormed Amphipolis with Brasidas. Most leave a losing cause; Gorgos had just joined one.

After Leuktra, and a third of the way home, the Megarians, as a sign of goodwill, had offered the royal wagon some honey to pack the dead Kleombrotos for the way across the Isthmos and then over the Argive passes back home. Gorgos poured it into the cask and smeared his king, just in the manner he had seen it done as a youth. It was Kuniskos alone who drove the fallen royal home. Kuniskos tended with wool, oil, and honey to the torn ear and bloody thigh of the lame Lichas, as he took back his proper place once again in the service of the high Lakedaimonians. It was as if for the past twenty years and more he had lived in a bad trance, trapped on Mêlon's Helikon with rustics, when he should have been serving his betters in Lakonia. As the army made its way back, Lichas in his wounds bellowed from his wagon for help. "Where is my Kuniskos? Kuniskos, how many stadia have we to home?"

After Leuktra, had Lichas not lived, the young regent Archidamos, who met the retreating Spartans with a relief force of old men and the young, would have lost both armies—if not at the Isthmos, then on the road through Mantineia on the way to the slopes before Lakonia. News of Spartan blood at Leuktra was then in the air. But it was Lichas who kept what was left of the army together, sending out patrols, bullying townsmen to offer up food and water, and promising the Argives an invasion should they attack his bloodied rearguard. Hellas needed a man such as that, a copy of Leônidas, a Lichas who had fought the Athenian hegemons and fought the Persians with Xenophon and fought them with Agesilaos; who had fought any who threatened the freedom of the city-states; the true Hellene, the only one left alive who would die for and save Hellas—a far better man to serve than the bent-leg Mêlon and the rustics on Helikon. Name a battle of the past fifty summers and Lichas had been there, fighting always for Hellas. Or thus now Kuniskos justified his treason.

As the disheartened and stunned men of Lakonia trudged home those long days of retreat, it was also the lowly Kuniskos who assured all that another Spartan army, born from the ashes of defeat, would soon rise. This was not to be a beaten force, but a victorious one with revenge and destruction its creed. "I marched with your fathers. You are the better men, my Spartans. After your Thermopylai will come another Plataia. I know the Theban pig. You will stick him next season." In these days, Gorgos was more Spartan than the Spartans. He put the wounded Lichas on his back and shoulders and marched through the retreating army, the two chanting as they went.

Kuniskos wrapped his master's festering wounds and gave him soup and bread when they returned to the wagon to rest. In turn, as the slow-moving army of the defeated reached Sellasia, the wounded Lichas limped out among the demoralized and hit their backsides with his cleaver and slapped the faces of the slackers. At dusk Lichas poked the slow with his spear, sitting in the cart of Kuniskos with the dead king as it wheeled into camp. When most slept, the wounded Lichas stumbled about the camp checking on the sentries, putting the fires out, and always calling out, "Kuniskos, Kuniskos, where is my Kuniskos?"

Lichas no longer called for his son Antikrates. Instead, it was Kuniskos who, Lichas boasted, had saved the army and the body of the king as the helot traitor now charmed the mind of the Spartan's father. Once the army reached home, Lichas kept this aged servant close by his side, for Kuniskos had proved his fealty on that bitter retreat after Leuktra. Lichas was reminded as never before that few Spartans were as loyal as this Messenian—and none, for all their woven braids or bobbing horsehair crests, as clever. Lichas gave Kuniskos a plot of ground and helpers to build a tower for himself on the many-towered estates of the Lichades. Soon Lichas made the Gorgos overseer of the flocks and buildings of the Lichades. Lichas himself, the regent of Messenia, knew that it was a lie that Messenians were natural slaves, by birth inferior man-footed beasts. They were as good as Spartans, or—as his Kuniskos proved—often better. Lichas knew all this better than any Pythagorean, better than any Theban liberator, but he was not concerned that it meant anything at all. So what does it matter that some good men are slaves, some free men are bad? That men who were by nature equal, yet were slave and master, spoke nothing to him more than the clever fox who was eaten by the savage wolf, or the cowardly knight who rode atop the brave horse. "Nature's unfair way is sometimes nature's way."

If Kuniskos, Lichas thought, was a better man than any in the *krypteia*, why should that mean he must be free? All the Hellenes were all a day from slavery. That's what Herakleitos had sung: War makes us free or slaves. War is our father. What was unfair about that? Who cared whether the slave were smart, the master stupid? It meant nothing that the unlucky man inside the citadel ended in chains, and the lucky attacker outsider the walls led him away. That was man's lot and a good one at that—that we are all a blink from having a chain around our necks. Why, that made us honest and eager not to fail. For all the talk of Spartan oppression, Lichas nightly reminded his Kuniskos, the men of Sparta in the barracks looked alike, talked alike, and were equal—far more equal than the slave Gorgos's old rich masters on Helikon. Most in Sparta were judged only by their spear arms, not by their Doric or fathers' names. If for the outsiders it was the most unequal of the poleis, Sparta was also the most equal for those inside. Gorgos agreed with his new master and was treated as he deserved, or so the helot thought. And so he relearned the Spartan ways on his way home to Sparta after Leuktra. Did the Thebans, did the Athenians, ensure their citizens were equal at the end, not just in the beginning? Did any of them have kings, ephors, an assembly and an upper-body Gerousia—the *eunomia* the good order of the Spartan state that stopped the power of the demagogues and ensured the rabble-rouser was checked in his infancy? In Sparta, a fat-belly tanner could hardly shout down a hoplite in the assembly, and yet the man with one hundred *plethra* of black soil fought alongside the spearmen with five *plethra* of rocks.

Lichas and his ilk were as good as their word and judged a man on what he did, not by how many olive trees he inherited. Lichas, not Epaminondas, was the true democrat of the Hellenes—or so Kuniskos told all—the sole Hellene who let the merit of the battlefield decide a man's worth, his real *timê*. That's why Lichas always asked of Kuniskos about this Chiôn, the killer of Kleonymos at Leuktra, whom he admired above all of his enemies, and peers as well. A mere slave had wiped out his own royal guard? Had a slave proved better than free Boiotians on the battlefield? Yes, this Chiôn of Helikon was a spirit of Lichas's taste. Lichas told Kuniskos to fetch him there to Sparta and give the freed slave a red cape. Chiôn was an enemy better than most friends.

For the next spring after the battle, Kuniskos ran the household of the estate of Lichas near the banks of the Eurotas, beside the orchards of both Antikrates his son, and his dead brother Leôn. Kuniskos was a new son to take the place of the dead son Thôrax, and a better bargain in the trade as Lichas himself admitted to folk. It was Kuniskos who bossed a few young helot girls about how to cook and had his way with them. He kept the animals fed, and taught the helots of Lakonia how to manage the farms—mostly what Mêlon had taught him on Helikon. The new farm tower kept rising, under Kuniskos's orders, wider, taller than the one of Malgis on Helikon.

Since the Boiotians were far better farmers than any Spartan, by spring Lichas's new estate was to be the best in Sparta. "You are to be free in Sparta as in the glory days of our Brasidas and Lysander, my Boiotian-lover Kuniskos," Lichas had laughed when he saw the crews of the helot terracing the slopes in the manner learned from the terraces of Mêlon's farm. "For all the talk of the democrats of Boiotia, you never were such a free man on the farm of the Malgidai. What you see with your own eyes in Sparta, you receive. We don't talk of setting helots free in the south— while they send their chattels scurrying about cooking their meals and emptying their slop jars. Like us or not," Lichas bellowed, "we are what we are."

Gorgos agreed. In this year after Leuktra, before the arrival of Epaminondas in the south, Kuniskos was not just the manager of the estate of Lichas, but was sent on errands all over Lakonia—to the sea at Gytheion, to the foothills at Parnon and Taygetos, and back north to the border forts at Sellasia. Always he was given rein as the emissary of Lichas the ephor. He was seen on a wagon no less, standing tall at the reins of a bright red cart with yellow wheels, up and down the valley of the Eurotas, with messages and instructions from Lord Lichas. Gorgos went about mustering a helot army against the Mantineians and preparing to purge Messenia once more of the agents of Epaminondas—especially the band of wild priestesses above Ithômê said to be stirring up the helots from their precinct to Artemis. Others in Sparta, who had no memory that went back to when Kuniskos had marched with the Spartans under Brasidas, treated the man less well. Most had heard little how he had packed Kleombrotos in honey. They had no word that Gorgos had driven the king's caisson all the way to the Peloponnesos.

Instead the wives of the Spartan peers remembered well that his Theban masters in Boiotia, the hated Malgidai, had once stripped the grand
armor of the dead Lysander at Haliartos. Did not this traitor Kuniskos in
the past wait on that foul Mêlon and work alongside that man-killer
Chiôn—the branded slave of the north, who with his master had taken a
half-dozen of Sparta's best at Leuktra? Treachery of any sort, disloyalty,
always was looked down upon by the good Spartiates. Many rumors had
also reached the women of Sparta of the wounded Thespian Lophis, who
had been dumped into the camp of Kleombrotos by his own manservant.

"Look at the wretch strut," the sister of Lichas, Lampito, would say of
Kuniskos as he bustled about the acropolis to buy a lamb or goat for his
master. "This mangy dog of ours paid his Thespian owner back by dragging him into our camp half-dead. A helot is always a helot, a man-footed
beast. I can smell it on him. Shaving his upper lip can't hide it. This turnabout helot did not even have the good sense to leave the losers for the
winners. No, the fool came over to us as we stumbled, and left his own on
the eve of their victory." In the Spartan mind, perfidy was especially to be
despised when it was coupled with folly.

But Lichas would have none of Lampito's talk and soon his wife
Elektra sent his sister out of his house. This Lichas was no simple Spartan
who followed the code of Lykos or let the tribe trump talent. No, his
creed was his own, of the spear and the muster, where men must earn
their equality. He had once been for Lysander, another rogue who cared
nothing for birth and nothing for the old ways of Lykos. The upstart
bastard half-aristocrat Brasidas of old was his hero too, the outlaw who
had freed the helots and made them killers of the Athenians. So when a
resourceful man, even if in rags, appeared, then Lichas gave him what he
pleased.

Besides, he was happy with his new tower that Kuniskos had built,
round and taller even than those to the north. Now with his third wife,
Elektra, Lichas at last had killers as both his servant and spouse. Elektra
soon came to adore old Kuniskos and would not hear a slur against her
husband's helot. In the courtyard the two fought with wooden swords,
and soon Kuniskos showed her how to swing her father's battle-ax like the
heroes of old. In this house of Lichas, Kuniskos also spent most of his
time mentoring the young Antikrates, whose own nearby estate had a
walled pathway to his father's vineyard. The bald helot from Helikon

grew his white side braids long and forked his beard—in the style of his master Lichas. He scraped his skull's top completely bare, and assured the son of Lichas that he was as loyal to him as he was to his father.

Antikrates and Kuniskos soon proved inseparable, as the young man needed tutelage in the ways of the helots, and the older one an ally in the house of Lichas. Because they were alike wily sorts and equally hated Epaminondas, they both were drawn toward and distrusted each other. "No need of your whimpers and dog rollovers to me, Kuniskos," Antikrates laughed. "When this is all over, my new old brother, Kuniskos, I will kill you in some way," the son went on. "For you lived when your betters at Leuktra did not. That's all that matters. So you too will die. But not yet, not just yet—or so my father and his wrinkly wife protect you. But I warn you that I am a different sort than he. I have no helot love. I say instead we are what we are born into. The priestess of Pasiphai tells me I will see you lying dead, with your bald head off on the ground. So I suppose she means I will kill you. Or maybe you will die with me, but first. But I know this, that you will not live beyond me."

Kuniskos laughed. "I hope not, toddler. For I have already thirty and more summers more than you, and grandfathers rarely outlast their sons' sons. Still, let it be. I am old and in years have outlived you, and probably all who hate me, whether on Helikon or here. But I know this priestess as well as you. I have put up with her stink and vapors on the altar of Pasiphai for nights on end as the goddess came into my dreams, all the while the greedy woman was chanting as she took a gold coin from my palm. She tells me dreams and swears that the greatest warrior of the Boiotians will die in my house. So I, not you, must be his killer. The fame goes to me, young blood, so what does it matter if I die old but famous?"

Antikrates had followed his father out of the mess at Leuktra. On the flight from the battlefield he had killed two Boiotians from Kithairon, both stabbed in the throat for sport as the mountain men tried to block the passes. Then Antikrates had topped that boast by reminding all that he had sliced off the arm of Kalliphon, the son of the *rhētōr* Alkidamas. "I would have gnawed on it if it had tasted any good," he laughed. Antikrates added, "The Boiotian fool was a softie. I'll kill the father to keep company with his son in Hades. Yes, that blowhard sophist I'll gulp down as dessert the next time around."

Before Leuktra, Antikrates had just finished with his barracks life.

Now at three tens, at his acme, he was given a full *lochos* of *kryptes* and
told to cross the high pass and patrol Mt. Ithômê out in Messenia to rein
in the helots. Yet still over there rumors of war and killing grew: A firebrand helot named Nikôn was murdering red-capes at night, some as
they slept in camp. With him the priestesses of Artemis were harboring
the insurgents to hammer weapons in new forges on Ithômê—killers and
cutthroats who were afraid to face the tall men of Sparta in phalanx
battle. "I need a helot I trust," King Agesilaos told Lichas. "Send that
helot man of yours with your Antikrates. Plug this leak before it takes the
dam itself."

"Kuniskos," Antikrates said in turn, "you better than I know the
Spartan way—how our grandfathers put a lid on the helot kettle during
the great war with the Athenians. So we do the same. Come with me
across Taygetos to put down these thieves and murderers." So it was almost a year to the day before the great muster of the Thebans to come
that Kuniskos set out over the high pass of Taygetos in the snow. He followed Antikrates and the young *kryptes* all on their way to Messenia to
patrol the mountain of Ithômê where the word was that a free Messenia
was first to sprout.

In two days the new partners and their cadre were over Taygetos,
descending through olive orchards near the coast en route to the dark
Ithômê, the volcano mountain that loomed off in the distance. This peak
was the holy silhouette of song that every helot looked to in his moments
of hope—and so beneath it was the best place to build a new Spartan
camp that would put down the growing insurrection. There all could see
the looming peak. Gorgos planned well. He wanted walls of all timber,
with sharp stakes at the top. Antikrates talked at length with the helot
who had already told him much of the landscape of Taygetos and where the
best black soil of Messenia lay and the richest helots, and where the precincts of Artemis were, and the nature of this Nikôn and his brigands—
and later rumors of a Nêto and a poet Erinna who were hiding in some
tall mountain pass. The Spartan pressed Kuniskos for knowledge of the
hard methods of Brasidas. He wanted to know just how in the great war
of fifty years past the legend of the Spartans had armed the helots to fight
the Athenians and thereby gone northward in victory nearly to Makedonia on his wild marches of liberation. The lash? Women? Gold? Freedom
and more? "How did a Spartan get its helots to fight, to beat back and

then nearly destroy the democracy? Speak to your Antikrates, helot. How can we do that again?"

"We helots believed," Gorgos grunted, as he watched carefully the knife hand of Antikrates. Indeed Kuniskos had all sorts of ideas that the young Antikrates was all ears for—drawn from the wise ways of his youth, fifty years and more earlier when all those now dead had held their shields high for Sparta. In fact, Kuniskos walked straighter than he had ever in the vineyards of Helikon. Gone entirely was his stiff gait. Old sprains had already begun to fade on the hill above Leuktra. He spoke his old Doric again, the grunts and cadences that only the elder few had remembered hearing, but in long tirades and with words only the sophists knew. Rule, he knew, rather than service suited him—even though in the house of Mêlon he had worked far less than he did in traversing the countryside of the helots. Epaminondas once talked of how freedom could cure anything. Now Kuniskos agreed.

Soon he pranced in his fine robe, with a scarlet stripe and a rabbit-fur collar, and messed with the red-capes in his compound, spurning Spartan vinegar water and demanding unmixed wine as he passed on the black bread and barley gruel of the hoplites, for finer wheat fare and red-blooded lamb. Kuniskos kept barking promises and lies to the helots out on his travels from the coast near Pylos to the border with Arkadia far to the east. "Spartans freed the few deserving it," Kuniskos assured all. "We—and I a helot like you—fear no Dorians, our brother Dorians." Then he used his learning from Helikon to lecture to the assembled helots about how men born into Messenia all have a place in the empire of Sparta. Helots must feel that they are in debt to those who can guide them best—however unhappy they are to be told that they are not all by birth deserving of equal portion. If Nêto and Nikôn could lie to the Messenians about freedom, Lord Kuniskos would counter-talk to the helot unfree about why and how they were already free under Sparta.

Kuniskos reassured himself that an upstart of little talent like the empty-headed Nêto, who could wiggle her high-rigged ass in front of Mêlon and the hungry Chiôn, would never survive down there where men earned rather than whined about freedom. To hide her dullness, Nêto talked the high empty talk. But men of the stuff of Kuniskos put their lives into the service of the Spartan order. His was the natural way of men, the *phusis*, that let them find their station by will and talent and not mere *nomos* and convention and long speeches. But Nêto again, why did he always wander back to Nêto? Did he wish to kill her or take her for pleasure or both or neither? Why Nêto everywhere, always? Kuniskos was troubled that he saw the revolt caused by Nêto alone, although he knew a single woman could no more stir up twenty myriads in a half-year than could Zeus himself on Olympos.

Kuniskos would stamp out wild helot stories of a liberation to come, hunting down this Nikôn and Nêto and rooting out their prophecies of a philosopher in arms invading from Thebes. All this prattle and more after Leuktra, Kuniskos soon discovered, the Messenians had gathered, exaggerated, and spread. Epaminondas had caused this revolt, after decades of obedience and tranquility in Messenia. Women were said to have sown these lies about liberation. The priestesses of Artemis of the lowlands had given seers and poetesses the power to see the minds of the Spartans. Or so they said, as the insurrectionists went from precinct to precinct, begging bread and sanctuary in exchange for wild tales of a new Pythagoras to come down from the north, with freedom and money for all. By late summer, Kuniskos discovered that the enemy was not just helots, but also *xenoi*, strangers like the new priestesses of Artemis, and another even higher up in the hills—this Erinna and her Amazons who spread lies that Spartans were fleeing even before the arrival of Epaminondas.

Kuniskos often instructed Antikrates at night that he, the young son of Lichas, could be killed by no free man. Yes, Kuniskos had gotten that out of Nêto long ago back on Helikon and he knew it to be true. Once spoken, it would give this indomitable Antikrates even more strength to make it true. Kuniskos patted Antikrates on the side of the head and went on, "None of the Lichadai has the nod of the gods like you do, Master. That is worth all that they had and more still. No free man, no helot, no slave can fell you. Not one."

At first Kuniskos had limped into the hamlets disguised as an old Argive traveler. He walked about with a walking stick and heavy wool hood, asking for shelter and news of robbers and the safety of the roads. Sometimes he wanted a meeting of the elders, as if he were a runaway helot in his thick Doric speech. A few claimed Kuniskos was also a farmhand, stripped to the waist, with wide shoulders hoeing the olives and learning of the strongest of the helots. But once he learned the nature of the towns and farms, Kuniskos came back on a horse with a phalanx of mounted spearmen behind him. *"Kuniskos eimi, akouete pantes, akouete ê apothanete.* I am Kuniskos. You listen up or die." Two hundred young *kryptes* rode fifty steps behind him. On his ululation, they galloped to cut down any he pointed out. "Join me or die. Epaminondas and his murderers, his rapists, and his thieves will soon shear you. Your Spartans alone can save you. Join me or die—*proschôrêite moi ê apothanete.*"

As the weather grew hot in the next summer after Leuktra, Gorgos was looking for the troublemaker Erinna. He had reports of a she-man poetess who plotted with Nêto—always Nêto, always her—who had joined wild Nikôn and the other gang of Doreios in organizing the helots in tens and twenties. Yes, he must find Nikôn and this Erinna, who had borrowed his Nêto and never given her back, as the two helped expand the revolt. Two hundred and more Spartans under command of Antikrates were found every month rotting in the countryside. Most were gutted in the byways by these breakaways—many with black-feathered arrows in their necks, a red letter *mu* for Messenia swabbed on their backs with their own blood. Whole tribes of Messenians were living free in the mountains and had since abandoned their farms. They even had a forge and bellows to make blades of black iron and bronze breastplates. Nêto had taken Nikôn to her temple and had his scribe Hêlos draw on an enormous hide map of Messenia, showing where the Spartans had forts and guards. Then she parceled out regions to Nikôn's helpers and he in turn had given them killing quotas each month. These helots rarely fought in daylight, but instead swarmed the Spartans at night, throwing pitch torches on their timber stockades and flinging arrows as they bolted out from the flames, or they hid in the forests and picked the red-capes off on the narrow paths. Or sometimes they would lie in ditches all night and cut the throats of drunken Spartans who in their wine sang their war songs as they stumbled back home from evenings with their helot women—most of them informers of Nêto's circle.

Soon the Eleans were sending daily more copper and tin ingots and iron from down on the Alpheios, as the helots spread their forges and hammered out new swords and spearheads. Finally, most of the daylight Spartan patrols stopped altogether. As summer waned they were forced to stay mostly in Gorgos's stockade at Ithômê. Antikrates had built a second outer wall, to surround the inner one, with more pointed stakes to keep the horde of throat-cutters out. But for all his warcraft, he began drinking

more than commanding and had no stomach for fighting outside the phalanx in the ambushes where the helot renegades might kill their betters
indiscriminately from afar with arrows, sling bullets, and javelins. Kuniskos soon ran the stockade, and the son of Lichas went back over Taygetos, ceding Messenia to Lord Kuniskos. Antikrates was hoping at the
first of the year to fight as a spearman on the icy Eurotas, to cut down
those Boiotians whom he had missed at Leuktra. Better all the way
around this way. He would kill Mêlon and Epaminondas to fulfill his
prophecy. The loss of Messenia—well, it would be due to Kuniskos, the
old helot who would have proved unworthy as a Spartan overseer when
his master had left him in charge—until Lichas and son would return to
Messenia from their victory to reclaim what the treasonous helot had
lost. Or so Antikrates figured as he rode home over Taygetos and left
Messenia to Kuniskos.

As the last month of the year neared, just about the same time that
Epaminondas was promising to tear down the Propylaia of Athens as he
headed out over Kithairon, the Spartans under Kuniskos could neither
leave the stockade at night nor lure any more helots inside its walls with
promises of freedom. Kuniskos more often than not spent his days by the
fire in drink, as his guards grew soft on the timber ramparts and fearful
of the helots who no longer sent their wagons of food over Taygetos to
Agesilaos. On these gray days, Gorgos prepared for the worst, and yet he
often lamented to himself that life was far too short for a man of his genius, and how unfair it was that he had come into his own at the end of
his sixth decade, with talents that had been unrecognized both when he
served as the young lackey of Lichas and then for too many years on
Helikon when he worked as a farmhand. He reflected that his life had
started out well, a helot with Brasidas at ten and six. He had grown to be
a man with children and freedom to his name when the great war against
the Athenians had ended and been won. Then all had been lost later at the
Nemea, when Malgis had caught him and made him a slave again—even
as Lord Lichas before the battle at last had made him a king's servant and
with a green cape at that.

While enslaved on Helikon, Gorgos had lost all track of his wife
Elaia and his son Nabis to the south. His family was banished—hungry
and now dead, or so Lichas had told him. Lichas had said they all had
perished when their papa Gorgos, well over forty seasons old, had not re-

turned home to his freedman's plot among the *perioikoi* near the Eurotas. Long-gone Gorgos was slandered among the half-helots as a runaway and a trembler, a dirty shield-carrier of the dirtier Boiotians. His family died in shame, or so he was told by Lichas, who often treated those he liked, and his own family as well, more harshly than he did his enemies.

Kuniskos thought, as he stretched out his long legs on his low table in his compound, that he could have created a new Messenia, had he just started at his first beard rather than in his near dotage, had he been given an indentured people at rest rather than being ordered to put down a rebellion. His dead son Nabis could have worn a red cape. He might have been a peer of Sparta, and had a hundred *plethra* of red grapes. Yes, if only Gorgos had not been captured at Nemea, if only the Spartans had not lied that he had not served his king. Life really was not fair when a man who was more Spartan than the Spartans had seen his genius marooned in the vineyard of Mêlon. These present triumphs, then, made Kuniskos even angrier. He was not so much grateful for his current renown as furious that it had come so late. He had been betrayed by his Nêto, by Antikrates who had left him with the growing revolt, by his master Mêlon who would soon come to settle up, no doubt to unleash on him the killer Chiôn. Only his own genius was left.

For a bit longer Kuniskos, fired by wine, about every tenth day tried to go out with his horsemen for a few stadia, to at least make a show of force with his mounted spearmen. In his wake the Messenians later would see an occasional helot with throat slit and arms tied to a post along the road. The few who could read the block letters told others that the placards read—in high Hellenic, no less—"I killed a Spartan and so am dead myself—on orders of helot Kuniskos, lord of the Helots." *Tina Spartiatên apekteina, kai ôs apothnêskô autos. Touto keluei ho helotês helotetôn despotês ho Kuniskos."* Kuniskos was after the girl helot seer who was said to be promising a day of freedom for the helots—and who was arming them to fight. Kuniskos was sure that Nêto led the helot ambushers from her sanctuary in the temple of Artemis; but he found few who would confirm his suspicions, and he was now as often as not befuddled with drink. So perhaps the chief troublemaker might be this Sapphic Erinna, who, his spies related, was causing rebellion in her supposed school on the high cliff. Kuniskos decided to make his own night raids to catch them both. With his last hundred horsemen, all the cavalry he had there beneath Ithômê, he targeted the shrines and rural temples of Messenia and all the farmlands that belonged to the gods, sweeping down on moonless nights to plunder and burn them, and riding off with the priestesses back to his compound by dawn.

Inside the stockade, Kuniskos would have their heads shaved. Then they would be given fur caps and dressed in skins and hides, with leather ropes and long fox tails dangling from their naked waists to their bare buttocks. The guards would chain the captives to serve meals for the *kryptes*. Kuniskos would keep twenty or so of his "animals," then when he tired of them, he would send the batch over Taygetos to Lichas and seek more replacements. At banquets, Kuniskos and his peers soon were throwing raisins at the helot servant girls while they danced and sang bare-breasted under coercion. Then, full of wine, Kuniskos and his thugs took whoever they pleased, the more virgins, the better. Life could be good in the twilight of Spartan Messenia.

As the new year approached, all of Messenia was in open revolt, with helots even armored and marching about equipped as hoplites with heavy armor. Theban scouts were rumored to be in the hills around Ithômê. Kuniskos's final batch of captives was small, not more than a few Messenian girls that had hid out near the Alpheios. They were all from the precincts of Artemis of the lowlands, all would-be diviners in training, they said. In their final late-night sweep, the handful of *kryptes* in service of Kuniskos had brought in seven temple women, to be stripped and to be asked—as they were hung by their toes from the rafters of the great hall—when and where Epaminondas would arrive, and who among them had prepared his way.

Kuniskos did what he pleased with Antikrates gone. If he were to perish in Messenia, then he would do so in a way that lived on in song— and in the terrified hearts of the Messenians. So his men whittled down his stock of prisoners. They sent most over to Taygetos to be thrown into the gorge. A few they roped to the fence post outside the stockade for the crows and buzzards that circled in wait over the house of Kuniskos. *Korakôn oikos*, they began to call the compound of Kuniskos, "House of Crows." The ugly ones they lopped, sticking their heads on stakes and throwing their bodies in the fire pit.

Soon there were almost no captives left inside the compound and there was no way to bring any more from the outside. Among the last haul of the prisoners from the Alpheios was a woman taller than the rest, who covered her head and kept apart. Kuniskos had told his guards to bring this one in last, and claimed she spoke a half-helot tongue, as if she had learned her speech from others beside helots. His henchman Klôpis wanted her, but he drew back when Kuniskos stepped in between him and the helot. She had caught the eye of the drunken Kuniskos, who poked with his walking stick at her thick winter cloak; he wanted some sort of sport with her.

Beneath the folds and tucks of her inner chiton, the old man could see firm flesh and firmer breasts, or so he fancied in his drink. A body it seemed as perfect as he had seen and without scars of torture or the brands of slavery, much less the tears and sags of childbirth—and a priestess unspoiled for his lust. As was his custom with the women, he reminded his men that it was his right to first order anyone into his chambers before they were noosed and dangled on the trusses. There she would first talk and then endure the passion of Puppy Dog. If she gave the name of a rebel or the location of a house of resistance, she would be given back her life, but only after the fire of Kuniskos had been quenched and a hot brand had been burned into her cheek—and if her tales had proved true and had led to the killing of those she had betrayed. But now there were no more fresh captives, and this woman, as ordered, was the last to be brought to Kuniskos.

"Why have you come across the Alpheios?" Kuniskos laughed. "You seem to have the look of the huntress, with your long arms and legs. Are you a Sapphic? There are travelers, they say, from Arkadia, or is it that a few lost Boiotians came your way? Surely you can tell Grandfather Kuniskos something of their talk?" He stuck his hand into her hood and pinched lightly her covered neck. "Where is this foul Proxenos? I hear he has a plan for a new city on top of my house, right here on my mountain. Stranger, do you know a Nêto? Or this Amazon Erinna whom you must have heard is in the highlands? Or maybe you've mixed it up with this Doreios? Or are you the woman of Nikôn?"

The cloaked figure muttered only a word or two about "a horde from the north."

"A horde, now? Of Boiotians maybe? You know the Messenian prophecy?"

"And some Arkadians. I know no more news."

Kuniskos laughed again. "What does this horde want with this Kuniskos? To throw down Sparta and raise up Messenia?"

"Perhaps—though the god has not told me all that. They act only as fate wills. It's too late. Neither you nor your Spartans can ward off the great reckoning."

"Reckoning, is it? Come nearer, priestess, sit on your granddaddy's lap. Either you be a talker of the gods' minds, or some faker in the robes of a holy woman sent here to stir up our kind. But I say, come near, scoot over, cast off that hood. Do you remember who I am?"

The hooded girl spat back. "They know you as Kuniskos. The new killer of the helots, or so the travelers say Lichas mined you out of Tayge-tos, hammering you from stone to smash down your own kind. You kill the Messenians sometimes as the farmer, sometimes the mounted man, sometimes their friend and recruiter. They say you are alone and a drunk-ard and even your lord Antikrates has left you to swing on a Messenian gallows."

Kuniskos liked her sauciness and even more his own playacting. In his wine-craze he was close to confessing to her his charade, but wished the drama to play out a little longer. Kuniskos tugged a bit on a thick cord that was wrapped tight around her left foot. "What a nice little bitch on a leash to visit her Kuniskos. But when Klôpis brings me virgins from the helot temples, I send them back soiled and stamped—the lucky ones that do not go over Taygetos to the pits. With the seed and the brand of Kuniskos—my own kappa burned right into their cheeks and a puppy in their belly, if I'm lucky."

He yanked on her leg chain a bit more. "They learn to serve men's lust on the street corners. Or maybe they play flutes at the fine houses for a few coppers. For the goddess has nothing to do with them stained and polluting her sacred ground, especially if with child, the new litters of my puppies to come." Gorgos was pulling the chain ever harder, as he went on. "So Virgin, talk—unless you wish to feel the spike of Kuniskos inside you. Then the pictures and whispers in your head will disappear for good. An ugly gamma will mark your cheek just as your own Messenian killers smear their bloody letter *mus* on my innocent dead. You alone earn the gamma—for the sake of the ancient days on Helikon." With that end to his drama, Kuniskos, drunk and stumbling, with haze in his eyes and dizziness in his head, threw off the young woman's long cloak and veil.

Then he tore her chiton. But then even he, lord of the Helots, froze for a moment in his delight as the wine no longer clouded his vision.

His eyes flashed, and he yelled to Klôpis, "Bar the door, bar it and for the night!" Kuniskos calmed and laughed. "You now. We are a long way from that hill above Leuktra, are we not, my Nêtikê? Nêtikê. Oh, my lovely Nêtikê at last. So lovely after all, in your nakedness, as I dreamed. So much the better for all my waiting. Now in service to the lord of the helots, of your own kind. Now you leave the virgin world of Artemis and will join that of Erôs."

She spat at him. "Kuniskos, a new name for an old monster. You were never drunk. You knew me even in your feigned stupor, liar, dogface."

"And no doubt, you knew that I did, at first sight when they brought you in, for all your denials of your old lust. You enjoyed our little game as much as I did. No matter. Past is past. For you alone, my Nêtikê, it is Gorgos. Only you can call me that, my old name, in your *erôs* as you groan for your Gorgikos. As I promised, I will brand you not with a kappa for Kuniskos, but you alone with a little gamma no less—a gammikon for the Gorgikos of old and for the sake of the Helikon days and on that soft unspoiled cheek."

She let out a shriek as the toothless satyr dropped his bright robe. It was the *alalê, alalalê* of Helikon, the war cry of Nêto of the Malgidai— the paean to Alalê, daughter of Polemos. Nêto was caught in the lair of Gorgos—no longer the loyal servant of Mêlon but Kuniskos, the fading lord of the helots. He pulled hard on her roped leg and sent her sprawling to the floor, as he had wanted to for twenty summers on Helikon even under the deathless eye of Mêlon, who was now far away on the road to Mantineia.

# CHAPTER 29

# Erinna of Messenia

For days Chiôn had been stuck in this port of the Phokians. He was drinking the worst of Nemea's red wine and eating squid and cuttle-fish by the fire with the helot rowers, pledged to protect the effort of Alkidamas to arrive in Messenia before the army. Five Korinthian tri-remes still battled the white caps off shore, with ten more arriving as they left. All the time he thought of Nêto in the fort of Kuniskos.

"They think we carry gold, not helots," Gastêr swore as he clamored over the deck of the beached *Theôris*. "Why do these Korinthian pirates keep circling out there? Hey you, Alkidama. Our hull rots, and I'm sick of these shorebird Phokians, worse than thieves. We either break out or hike home and let the *Theôris* keep rotting."

Alkidamas scoffed at the fat man. "Settle down and keep eating your oysters. The arm of Agesilaos is not so long anymore. Just be patient. A few more days, a few more coins sent over the Isthmos, and the Korinthi-ans will smile and leave, and we'll be back out. With these helot rowers, we'll be there just in time to help with the building of new Messenê. These Phokians here are not such bad cooks, anyway."

Chiôn had had enough. He left the small hut and glanced back at Alkidamas. "No more wait. Nikôn can't wait. Nêto can't wait. No more sea legs. You meet me wherever this Ithômê of yours is. I'll find it. In five days I'm there before you with a live Nêto and the head of your Gorgos." Chiôn put a long pole on his shoulder with a bag of rations on the end and set out along the sea. He had little idea of the world outside Thespiai but knew enough to follow the north shore of the gulf for a half day, always west into the setting sun, until he could see the long walls of Patrai looming across the water.

This was real freedom—no wife, no farm to work, no children to raise, just one man in the wild against all others. No wonder men liked war. He knew he did. He forgot Damô, even their son to come, and the three sons of Lophis, with the assurance they'd all be better off after he killed those who needed killing. Yes, he'd take a ferry across the straits to the Peloponnesos, skirt the shoulders of Erymanthos until he reached Olympia, and from there, or so he heard, he'd just hike up the Alpheios. Then take the south fork down to the land of the Messenians. Five days he reckoned and he would be at this Ithômê, and before either Epaminondas or the *Theôris*. He'd put the dragon head of Gorgos in this bag and stuff it with honey to show Mêlon when he arrived. Maybe Chiôn would pull the tongue out between the teeth so Gorgos would look like the gorgon he was. As he ran he mumbled to himself, as if Alkidamas was at his side rather than stuck back on the shore of the gulf.

"Nêto warned me about the sea, Alkidama, and so I'm leaving the waves to you to find her. I'm a hoplite, a front-rank *prostatês*. I have no worries. I've lived too long as it is. No death wish. Better yet, no care. Live or die, freer than any free man. You won't see me again, only hear of my work. I go into the hills to kill those who would kill our own. Free to kill. You'll see the good I do you all without the bridle of your law." With that Chiôn stopped his talking to himself and went over the hill on his way to Naupaktos and the mouth of the gulf.

Chiôn went on foot west, and in a day and half saw the torchlights at the eastern gate of Naupaktos on the water. Once back on land and free from the *Theôris*, he felt better and moved even more quickly than he was accustomed, convinced he could do far better without the leaky boat and the helots of Alkidamas. Already he was at the neck of the gulf. But could he run fast enough to kill Gorgos before he cut off the head of Nêto? He would surely be across the water tonight at least, since there were helot boats aplenty down there for hire. He had a full pack of Mêlon's coins and hadn't left much with Alkidamas. No doubt Epaminondas was sweeping down from Sellasia into Lakonia—and here he was not yet into the Peloponnesos.

Then a blast of cold air nearly knocked Chiôn over as he turned the

last switchback of the mountain trail, on the downward slope to the city
gate of Naupaktos. The odd wind came in the wrong direction, hard, but
blowing from the south. It howled and it brought winter ice in the air.
The torches above on the walls of Naupaktos went out with sudden gusts.
Where did that come from? Cold blasts on the gulf—but something
colder from the south across the water. Was Epaminondas blowing into
Lakonia? Or was the gust from Ithômê? Chiôn pressed on and would run
for the rest of the night.

Back on Ithômê, Erinna was stacking tiles on the roof of her school. The
Thespian Chiôn from Helikon had not arrived as promised. So there was
no ransom money for Nêto. Only if they had the money, would they learn
of the fate of Nêto, though most of Erinna's girls assumed that she was
locked inside the compound of Kuniskos, or that her head already was
impaled on one of his many trophy stakes. "Nikôn—no Chiôn? No ransom. No silver, and no way inside the house of Kuniskos. And no Nêto.
We can't wait any longer." Erinna pulled a long dagger and slid it into a
cotton sheath inside her chiton that she tied close to her waist. "This
Chiôn of yours has gone off with his master's treasure. Six days after you
come and no money. You said he has one arm—but maybe the slow-cart
had one leg? Or did the *kryptes* catch him? Or was his boat sunk by pirates?
I go to this camp of Gorgos and free her or kill him—or both."

Erinna showed Nikôn a finely curved leg and picked up her bow—as
she looked over at Nikôn and said the one would lead Gorgos to the
other. Nikôn nodded and followed her down from the school, wondering
how the Amazon without any silver would get close enough to Kuniskos
to free Nêto and assuming his own rangers would have to storm in with
her. Their small band of four helots made their way over the crest of
Ithômê. Nikôn stopped and pointed to the tamarisks and limestone outcroppings. "Look, soon there will be the great theater. On that hill, there
is our Arkadian Gate to come. A stadium will rise down there in the low
ground. With stone seats far better than any found at Olympia or Pythia's
sanctuary at Delphi. I've heard what this Proxenos promises us and I have
his city laid out in my head. When he comes, the new council hall of a
free Messenê will sit atop the camp of the Spartans."

Erinna kept silent at the idea of anything rising from these dry scrub pines and ancient oaks but she did not laugh since they were the days of flux when everything was not as it was and would be. She was at a loss as to how to free Nêto once they reached the fort of Kuniskos. Poets like herself, she thought, are no saner than this wild Nikôn. Who knows what twenty myriads might do if organized and inspired by her Epaminondas? "We both see things as we hope rather than as they are. I call out to the Muses, you to the dead helots of the past. But enough. Hurry, Nikôn, if Nêto still has her own head, hurry."

It was not far to the compound of Kuniskos below, and Erinna led Nikôn and his four helots, running down the gentle slope. Soon they were at the low-lying saddle and reached the edge of the scrub pine. The fort was in clear view, and they stopped their talk. Yet there was no way to storm the double wall and get to Nêto, unless Erinna might be let in alone. But she had no ransom money, only the power of her voice. So Nikôn and his guards trailed off into the brush as Erinna approached the path toward the Spartan guardhouses. The helots had no chance against a hundred Spartan hoplites and waited in a gully above the camp and would stay there until they heard the sound from the wooden whistle around Erinna's neck. She first went into a small clump of bushes by the timber gate. There, despite the winter morning cold, the poetess pulled off her leather jerkin, leaving the soft linen that barely covered her arms and thighs. She left behind her quiver and pack. But Erinna pulled over a long wool cloak with a hood, rough and full of burrs and stickers, as if she had been on the road for days. Then she approached the guard up on the rampart.

"Hoa. You. Red-cape. Come here. Leônidas or Lykos may be your name? Or are you Lysander back from the dead? At least you have the look of a Spartan warrior man. I'm an Athenian bard, a *rhapsôdos*. You see that, hear that. Yes? An Athenian. I'm a traveling rhapsode and music girl who can read out loud block letters. I entertain to the lyre. Let me in and out of the cold. I want a talk with your Antikrates or at least his hench-man Kuniskos. I want help." Now she shouted even louder to the man on the rampart, "Did you hear? Who's in charge? I'm cold and numb and lost. I fear these mad helots and their damn cries of freedom." Then Erinna threw off her outer hood and put her hands on her hips, and louder still cried, "And I can sing in the high strain for you and more still."

The gate opened. Two Spartans approached. One was a young tooth-less sort, Klôpis, who had hacked down three Thebans at Leuktra and reminded Kuniskos nightly of his tally. Now this Klôpis grabbed Erinna and took her through the gateway and inside the double walls of the stockade and then all the way to the stone courtyard of Antikrates's house.

The camp was an elaborate maze. Two parallel walls, both topped with sharp stakes, made a square. It ran about half a stade in each direction, with towers and a gate on each side. In the middle inside was another square, four wooden halls joined together, separated by an arch entry into the courtyard. These were the barracks of the young *kryptes*, at least of the few who were alive and served Kuniskos or who had not fled back over Taygetos. A fire pit was in the middle and hoplites came out of the stoas on all sides to cook their dinner and warm themselves from the icy blasts. There were guards at the gates of the outside walls and more still at the entry to the courtyard—everything built from massive spruce logs hauled down from the mountains above. Erinna quickly saw that the stockade was far too big for the garrison and that it would not last a day should the army of Epaminondas storm down from Tagyetos.

Kuniskos himself sat beside a brazier, with spits of lamb on the grill. His chair stood near the fire and a nearby table on the largest porch. Six spearmen, shivering in the cold, sat on cots and straw mattresses. He'd lost half his guard to helot killers and carried a spiked club wherever he walked. Klôpis pushed Erinna forward. "Hey, Master, there's a woman here. No helot. I brought her in, a stitcher of tales who walked over the mountain, or so she claims. No worry—she's no Messenian from her speech. You can see that well enough. I think she's a softie from Athens, and beneath that wool cloak of hers I smell rose petals and linen. She will sing and more for us—if we feed her and keep her safe from the murderers of the brigands under Nikôn."

"A singer, is it, woman—or maybe one of these rebels with a false sound to her speech?" Then Kuniskos stood up, leaned on his club, and laughed. "I am the leader, the harmost. Antikrates is over the mountain dealing with Epaminondas and his Theban pigs. Before I throw this saucy Athenian in the cage with the other one, let me hear her out."

Erinna was already walking up to the porch of Kuniskos, then paused, hands waving about and head tilted back. "What do you want, my lord? Is it to be war songs from your Tyrtaios? Or do you want me to play some Alkman maiden sounds? Or then again, maybe a chorus of Euripides in more of your harsh Doric? Maybe Medea with her snakes up in her sun chariot? Oh, yes. I can give you all that to music, even the slow beat of Aeschylus and his Klytemnestra with her gory hands."

She stepped closer to Kuniskos. "I can do all three and more—even a girl song about the loom. But let me near that fire. Those damn helots came down the mountain and almost got me. I hid in the glen behind an icy rock till they passed. They killed all three of my *perioikoi* guards, paid in advance for six days of passage from Sparta, where I have sung Alkman and even some Tyrtaios as they ready to battle the incoming Boiotians. Yes, I sang for crippled Agesilaos himself. But, Master, I need this wool off to dry out. Let me inside your halls, my dear Spartan."

"Oh yes, yes, come here, strange woman. Certainly you will go in. But first, sit near Kuniskos, near my little fire on the porch. No need for my spearmen. I'm well equipped as it is, even though this poetess I see has muscles enough. No danger. She'll have to play for me and whatever else earns her a dry bed and a rabbit leg or two for dinner. But, woman, tell me, where is our Mêlon, our Chiôn in all this?" He laughed when Erinna blushed at that. "Where," Kuniskos pressed on, "is that faker we hear about, this Alkidamas? Surely you know all three, my pretty poetess? They all have a bad, bad way of letting friends like you dangle. They flee when they find no more use for them—and the tab for the sacrifices of others comes due. As you learn. Or did you not say your guard ran away at the first sign of a fight?"

Erinna said nothing back as if he spoke Persian or was a Scythian whose grunts gave no meaning. So Kuniskos jumped up, grabbed Erinna, and pulled her inside. As she was forced into the chambers of Kuniskos, she blurted out some Tyrtaios in rough hexameters, while the guards outside on the signal of their master retreated to the outer stockade. "Sit down, woman, and sing louder and have some broth before we dine and drink. Dance as well, yes? I have no flute girls so you'll have to be both guest and entertainer. We'll have the barley pulp they serve here, but some special bowls with a bit of hare's leg and a dried leek or two. Then more wine for us both. A *kratèr* or two just to keep us dry and warm and feisty. But keep singing. No one here now. Just us. Your name, woman? Did you give me your name? I hear there are lots of poets in these parts and on the hill up there as well. But perhaps I know it already?"

"Oh, I go by Attis. Yes, I claim to be Attis, daughter of the trader Athenaios from the Piraeus. My family owned ten long ships and we brought in grain and timber from Ionia. I speak a pure Attic, as you can hear, but know Ionic and Aeolic as well, as my father reminded all, and they say the same at the symposia among the longhairs with the gold grasshopper clasps." Erinna did not sit, but walked slowly around Kuniskos and took in his anteroom. He let her explore his chambers but watched as she neared an interior door with an iron lock.

"I sing by the Ilissos at Athens. Yes, I am at home with men or women or so they also say of those who have seen Lesbos. But no one is here? The helots say the lord of the helots has a stable of women in his house, another poet, a rival that I can battle in verse. Let me wager with you that I have the best song, and you'll send me along my way with an escort. But I bet you're young where it counts, my Kuniskios." With that Erinna finally took off her cloak and stretched. They went from the back further into the mess room. The front door was open and Erinna moved to the central hearth. She then edged slowly toward the kettle that was hanging over the flame. She had already caught a chill with her wool off. Kuniskos stared and grunted out some noises.

She had dark hair, short with a touch of lighter strands, maybe even some red; and firm large breasts that pointed up, and muscles on her arms and a pretty neck. Her lips were pink and eyes big. Already Kuniskos tired of his nightly play with tall Nêto—like having a doe that flitted around the room and, when caught, only bore her buck with fright and pain. She was not what his years of lust had imagined. Worse still, she was not even much of a helot rebel, not a worthy foe in his bed or in battle. And there was no money yet. Not even a sign of Mêlon or Chiôn, who had thought wiser of throwing good silver after dross, much less trying to burst into the fort of a Spartan lord. Yes, he was going to send her away, to trade her eastward on the next trip with Antikrates for a younger, rougher love—or pack her off with him to Taygetos if he could not find ransom from Helikon to free her. He now found her flesh hardly what he had thought it would be when he had eyed her on the farm in the past. Fool—as if a woman were a sow or heifer who had no care who mounted her.

But for Gorgos it seemed far better to have an old wide-hipped matron who knew more than he himself. Still no ransom money here for her from Helikon as Nêto promised? No reward at all? So much for the great-souled Damô, wife of Chiôn, and the big silver chest of Mêlon. No money ransom for their wasp-waist helot girl, after all, even as his men had sent word of Nêto's capture to the helots? But now, now, this other woman was different. For all her talk of song, she had a bit of the man-woman in her as well. Kuniskos liked this hard edge. She'd put up a better struggle, maybe a claw or two on his cheek before she was through—and then she would shriek in mad *erôs*—so unlike the victim Nêto, who was little more than a sacrificial carcass on his altar.

"Keep singing my Tyrtaios, woman, I'll be right back, back yes with a surprise." With that he left through the back interior door. The guards were strolling back and forth, three hundred paces distant outside. Erinna's whistle was around her neck. So she slowly pulled out her dagger, and put the blade in the rock cleft above the pot. Then she pulled up her chiton high on one leg and rolled up her right sleeve and with that exposed the side of her breast, appearing as big now as she had usually wished it small. He might find her inviting, but she was now girded for battle, with her limbs free and shivering.

Kuniskos came back in, pulling and whispering to a battered woman in a cloak. "My Nêtikê, look, another poet. And an Athenian at that. What sport we'll have the three of us, a real triangle even with your fetters on. She's man enough for you, Nêtikê, and more than woman enough for me. Hail this Attis of the two faces who blew in with the northern breeze. I wager you know this little ranger, though perhaps by a different name."

Erinna kept still. But her face was flushed as she saw Nêto shuffle in—at least what she thought was Nêto.

"Surprised? Or all along did you know our Nêtikê? Don't recognize your partner these days with her little bruises and tiny cuts? Ah, don't hide your own *erôs*, my stringy Attis. Why should you? My Nêto here is a bit scared as I can see."

Erinna clenched her fist and eyed the corners of the room. Nêto looked down and avoided her eye. Her once long tresses were gone, with tufts here and there on her bloody scalp from the clumsy haircuts of Kuniskos's blade. Long slashes and scratches oozed on her arms. Her right eye was swollen shut. She had a fresh brand—a gamma—burned right into her cheek, though it oozed pus and most of her right face was black. Was this her Nêto?

Kuniskos had tied a rough sack weave around her that left both legs from her knees down bare. A thick cord was tied to her right ankle and cut into the flesh, and was stretched about twenty palms distant to the hinge on the door, where it was tied. "Now we drink to the helots and their lord Epaminondas." Kuniskos laughed. "Somewhere at home in Thebes that Pythagorean faker snores in his halls, deep in drink and vomit. Then the fools of the Peloponnesos run around with lies that the fraud is really up here, near the Orthia and pulling into Sellasia, as if he would ever dare to come into Sparta. Believe not a word. He hasn't even left Thebes, the drunkard. Yes, I know that, a brothel woman in Thespiai sent word to me. Our Phrynê knows more of Boiotia than the drone Epaminondas himself. Poor Antikrates in his fear of a phantom fled back to Sparta."

"Who are you, helot?" Erinna ignored Kuniskos and stared at Nêto to play out to the end their deadly charade. Now she turned back to him. "Lord Kuniskos. Please scrub down that woman. I can smell her from here and who knows what's under those scabs. Lice too on her stubble, *phtheires* crawling everywhere, Master Kuniskos. She's a tramp and dirtier than any helot. She has worms in her belly and crawlers under her arms. Look at the ooze on her face—is she a man or beast?"

"No, no—look over here, my Attis. I have a pot of warm water, and sponges from Kalymnos no less. You can scrub her down and use all the oil you want. Give yourself a rub as well. You look the road almost as much as Nêtikê does."

"I am no Amazon, stranger," Nêto flashed. "I am a freewoman of Helikon. Priestess of Artemis of the Messenians."

"Perhaps once," Kuniskos answered. "But no longer, no more the dainty little *parthenos* who thought she could tease her way on Helikon to an orchard or vineyard with your Gorgos as doorman to your new tower." He had pulled on her rope. "No, no, no—soiled women. Those who serve my lusts make no priestesses and even worse wives. So drink up and soon we roll the dice for turns. All you have left are your long legs, and I mean to club one of those as well before I'm done. To slow down a bit those doe runs of yours leading lame Mêlon of the Malgidai in the high woods."

In these final days of winter calm, for all his loud bluster about a ter-rified Epaminondas hiding in Thebes, Gorgos had accepted his fate, the shared fate of Sparta that would soon end in Messenia. Yet the old man was strangely without much of a care, even though there were now hardly more than a hundred left, after Antikrates had taken a thousand home to

Lakonia to face Epaminondas. He had been a lord, and ridden at the head of Spartan Peers, more than any helot had done since the days of Brasidas and his wild band of freed helot marauders. Yes, he was satisfied. One day as Lord Kuniskos was well worth what would now follow.

He felt the warmth in the wine, and he drank it from the time he woke until he slept. It brought with it the creeping sense of good liberation from worry and nag—a peace of mind, the *hêsuchia* that comes when cares are all banished, and nothing as before matters—right before the fall. What did he care whether Epaminondas really did come and Mêlon and Chiôn as well, and overturned the world of the Spartans in Messenia? Let them come some day, but they surely would not arrive this day, his day. And they could hardly overturn all that he had wrought in Messenia. As for now—why, he was Lord Kuniskos, harmostês of Messenia, and couldn't worry about what a day ahead might bring. He grimaced a bit, as he knew he would either be high lord here, an *anax* of the Messenians, or dead—but never a house slave, a mere *oiketês* on Helikon.

But then Erinna tapped Kuniskos and woke him from his idle wine thought. He caught sight of her breast and thigh and put down his cup and turned from Nêto. Erinna eyed his club far off in the corner. "But play with her comes later, Lord Kuniskos. After we have done our own business. But first, I want you to promise me a boat ride from up the gulf to the Isthmos for our sport—anything to leave this frozen Hades and these dreadful unlettered helots. Remember I came into your fort looking for a ticket home." With that last talk, she at last reached for the dirk on the ledge behind him, placed above the fire between the stones with the handle out. She was freed of her sash and had plenty of sway in her arms. With her hem cinched up tight, Erinna kicked the old man in the groin and then swung around and stabbed down hard on his shoulder.

"Run Nêto. Out to Nikôn, out to Nikôn. Out to the gully. Now."

But Erinna pulled out the dagger too early from Kuniskos—before she could plunge and twist it—so that she could turn and slash Nêto's rope. "Run Nêto. Before . . ." Nêto leapt free, and Gorgos for a moment was stunned. Then Erinna picked up the heavy kettle with the long wooden handle and threw the broth onto the back of the neck of Kuniskos.

He staggered with wound and burn and wine, bellowing at the door to his henchmen. But they were on the other side of the square, used to their captain's noise and frolic, and far enough away to give Kuniskos his sport in private. The two doors to the house were unguarded, as the cold guards had built a fire far to the opposite side of the stockade. Kuniskos cursed the two women in his moment of blindness. "Helots, they've stabbed me! Klôpi. Klôpi. Bring Hekas. Bring Pharis and the band. Run. They're in the house here. Fools, get them!"

Then the raging Kuniskos dove at the ankles of Erinna, who kept ordering, "Run, Nêto. Out for us both. For us both."

But then Nêto paused and could not leave her would-be savior. She called back, "Fight him, Erinna—both of us, together." Then Nêto punched Kuniskos again and again as he placed his hands around the neck of Erinna. He was old, but stronger than any guardsman a third of his age, and tall and leathery with a grip as cold as winter's ice. Kuniskos freed one hand, and then slapped and punched Nêto back. She went out the window right through the open shutters and through the porch, rolling into the courtyard. Her sore leg hit sideways on the flat stones, and snapped at the ankle, as she fell back, got up, staggered and then fell again.

Nêto was alive and ready to limp back in. But she looked up and here was Klôpis with his rope and blade. Then a loud sound pierced the air behind her, as Erinna blew the whistle for help and then a final yell, "For Epaminondas, for Epaminondas." Nêto squirmed on the ground, but then Klôpis hit her with the flat of his sword handle, and she went limp and her world turned dark.

Erinna thought she could stun Kuniskos and maybe give Nêto enough time to reach the front gate and climb over, maybe even to reach Nikôn. She thrashed and scratched at the burned Kuniskos. For a moment she got her nails deep into his thigh as she struggled to break his grip. His hands were calloused and both again on her neck. She bit at his cheek, spat in his face, and tried to slam her knee into his belly as he lifted her off the stone floor.

Erinna got another nail into his backside and dug it deep into the flesh, searching for a vein and the burn on his neck and cut on his backside. Gorgos was burned, and stabbed and kicked, so why didn't he let her go? "Shhh, my poet girl. Quiet now. Your Kuniskos has only scorched his neck, and your toy blade has missed my insides. But your nails bring me joy, so go on with your scratches. Oh, but your pinprick hurts."

He shook Erinna around and raised her higher, face-to-face, a foot maybe off the ground, her nose touching his, both hands squeezing her tighter all the while. "Shhh. Don't fight it, my pretty little Pythagoras girl. Shhh. Quiet. Let your soul out. Let it fly quietly to Hades like the little poet you are. No pain, no pain, go limp. Take the sleep that takes all pain, little Erinna. No more worry any more, ward of your Pythagoras. Sleep in the hands of your Kuniskos. You keep your Erinna's soul—I your body."

As he squeezed Erinna ever so slowly, she whispered a last "Epaminondas will come, he will, my Epaminondas . . ."

Erinna's eyes bulged and her once red face was white, as more guards ran into the courtyard to help Klôpis pack off Nêto. Erinna sputtered and then made a loud gurgle and then she too went limp. Kuniskos had forgotten his cuts and burns and kept talking as he squeezed, listening to his own voice. Still he talked on. "Ah, my pretty Attis has gone to the majority. Without even a fart or two, as most of my girls do when I send them off with that last hug." With that Kuniskos threw what had been Erinna over his shoulder and went back into his chambers. "Bring a hot iron to close up my shoulder, and a sponge of oil for my eye and some grease for these scratches. And, oh yes, fetch her cloak to keep her warm. Carry back in that bald-haired Nêto. If she's alive, she may still bring us some silver. But if she's dead, we'll post the two heads out on both sides of the road. A nice twosome for us. Klôpi. Get in here. No one does knife work better than you."

He missed his wine and was soon roaring with pain from the burn and stab. But the idea of hanging them up or at least their heads, that notion got his blood even hotter. "Soon two beauties will smile on us, guarding the path of the camp of Antikrates. So Klôpi, bring me a tall pole, two men's height and more, and your cattle knife. We will have our little Attis mounted for all to see this Amazon. In this winter cold, the pretty head of Erinna-Attis will stay fresh enough up there for the season. Look at little Erinnikê, why she smiles—the smile won't leave. What does she know that we don't?"

Nikôn and his four helots were near at the first sound of Erinna's whistle but as he looked through the brush the ramparts were thick with Spartans running along the parapets and now the shrieks of the two women ceased. There was no chance to storm the Spartan fort with a hundred *kryptes* inside. So he sent his men back to Ithômê for help and then found a thicket of willows to sleep in until night. He whispered to the four helots as they left, "Maybe tonight at moonlight I will sneak in to fetch the bodies of Erinna or Nêto, at least if there is anything left of the two. Gorgos has chopped his last head—save one. The next will be his own. Or so even to me the god spoke that. I will bring the heads back and leave Spartan ones in their place."

Nikôn went alone back to the camp of Kuniskos at dusk. He crawled on his belly alone to the stockade, and shimmied up the back walls, like his helot hunters on Taygetos who went after bear cubs in the tall firs. He did as he had promised, as he always did, and by dawn had brought back the head and body of Erinna. But for all his night crawling through the compound of Kuniskos, Nêto was nowhere to be found.

Gorgos woke to two heads on his gate poles, but they were male and Spartan.

# PART FOUR

# *Freedom*

# CHAPTER 30

# The Shadows of Mt. Taygetos

I f Agesilaos won't come out, and we can't get in, then we will make the Spartans feel in just a few days what it is to be a helot forever." With that warning of destruction, a defiant Epaminondas led the armies into the Lakonian plain to ravage even what they had gone over once before. Yet not all in the huge army wished any more to follow his lead, given the failure at the Eurotas and the death of Proxenos—and beyond that, the growing cold and the end of their tenure in Boiotia that made them all outlaws. Still, Ainias, Pelopidas, and Mêlon roused the troops, and for the next seven days the Boiotians, alongside the men of Argos, the Eleans, and the wild Arkadians, tore and burned their way through all the remaining houses and sheds of Lakonia.

It rained, and fog hugged the ground, with evening snow near the foothills. The ravagers found fuel from the fences and the woodwork of the windows and doors. Fires continued all over the farms in every direction to the mountain ranges east and west. Despite the cold, the men of Epaminondas sang and chanted as they kept at it, piling on the roofbeams and torching all the Spartan farms they had once passed over in cold mists and fogs, cutting down the smaller trees and hacking the limbs of the larger. To destroy centuries of what was once Sparta was no easy thing. The carnage spread from the Spartan port at Gytheion back up to the mountains near Sellasia where the ravagers had entered in the north, and then across the plain from the slopes of Parnon to Taygetos. Three hundred stadia east to west, and another three hundred from the north to south, the ravagers scoured the countryside.

It was not Boiotia, but Lakonia that was the new treeless and barren sheep walk of the Hellenes. That was what Epaminondas promised when he told his Boiotarchs that in a Lakonia denuded of its trees the grasshoppers of Sparta would soon all sing from the ground. If there were any alive next spring, they surely would. For the funeral of Proxenos, the Thebans piled carts and any wood they could find on the banks of the Eurotas—a pile ten times as tall as any tall man, with the dead builder of walls at the very top, looking out over the houses of Sparta across the river. Then Epaminondas lit it. "O king Agesilaos. Look at the campfires of your enemies. Look right before your faces. Not a Spartan man among you can stop it."

All during the night Ainias stalked around the fire, adding logs as the Spartans looked back out from across the river at the coals of the pyre of Proxenos. Still, King Agesilaos would not come out to fight. The Boiotians had learned the enemy had horded months of food stores across the Eurotas and more than five thousand goats and sheep. The Thebans tried to incite the red-capes. Yet Agesilaos kept his men on the hills of the city, despite the shrieks of his women who saw their fathers' orchards shamed. Elektra in her wild tresses ran berserk along the opposite bank, begging her grandfather to cross the river and with her husband Lichas drive Epaminondas out of their farms. She was met by a backhand from the king, "Go inside, mad woman, before you kill off what was left of us after Leuktra."

Mêlon saw that the Boiotians could neither draw the Spartan across the Eurotas nor themselves wade through the river to torch the town—or stay much longer in the plundered countryside in the mid of winter. "There is a reason why he is king, that Agesilaos. He's no Kleombrotos. We're like the bloody-headed ram butting the shed walls when the she-goat won't come out." Mêlon finally warned Pelopidas about the ravaging of once-ravaged ground. "Put a stop to this madness of Epaminondas or soon we will destroy the land that must feed us. We either move on or go hungry or cross the river and take their food. But Epaminondas must do one of these and now, before the snows and the ice get worse."

Ainias gave Pelopidas a cold stare of approval of Mêlon's advice. "Yes, my general, leave this infernal place. Either head home or west over Taygetos. I will take the ashes of Proxenos either to new Messenê—or back home to Plataia." When the invaders at last were done with fire and ax, the wagons and most of the herds of Sparta were stolen or burned. A few thousands of the stranded helots of Lakonia were run off or fettered by the Mantineians, against the orders of Epaminondas, who wanted them freed outright instead and sent to the new Messenê to come.

Lykomedes now boasted that his Mantineians alone had the glutton's share of the loot, some four hundred wagons of oil and grain, and most of the windowsills and doors torn from the houses of Lakonia. His new city of Mantineia could be finished out with the ornaments of the Spartans. Ten more carts were loaded with iron ingots and chests of hidden gold that his men had pulled out of the wells of the Spartan peers who supposedly owned no gold. After unleashing his helot captives, Lykomedes bristled even more when Pelopidas and the Sacred Band confiscated half of his booty to pay for their march west over the pass into Messenia. So yes, Lykomedes thought, let us talk of war with Lord Epaminondas.

At first dark around the big campfires south of the city, the allied council met about the next march. The choice was either to head back with a half victory to their homes or west to Messenia. The weather was even colder and damper. The green olive limbs that were thrown into the fire sent smoke into the eyes of everyone and wrapped the speakers in a cloud of haze. Men coughed and sneezed and swore at each other over the allotment of booty. Some had the chest rattles and the leg aches, others the winter nose runs. Their leaders grumbled that too many slept on the winter ground. It was long past time to sit by the hearth in victory, not camp out in the fields and court defeat. Didn't the Spartans have it right to stay warm in their houses across the Eurotas, fed and rubbed by their women?

Lykomedes stood surrounded by his archons of Mantineia. As arranged, he spoke first, and wished only to play up to his hoplite kinsmen who were eager to report back all he said to the assembly of the Mantineians. "After our twenty days of hard work we have gone past the new year. Then all our tenures expire as the assemblies demand. That is the custom in our democratic cities here in the south." Then Lykomedes walked toward Epaminondas to shout at him directly in front of the camp crowd and for all to hear. "We have won. The war is over. No reason to stay. We are on their land, they are hiding with their women. Their Messenia is lost. Time to leave as victors before we get sick and piss it away." Little Aristôn was at the side of Lykomedes, clapping as his master's voice rose. "We have eaten ourselves out of our new winter home despite the generosity of the Spartans. But it is the time of the sick cold that grows much worse after the winter solstice, at the time you know of as Boiotian Boukatios. We Mantineians are leaving at sunrise back home to Arkadia, so that we won't find ourselves the besieged when you northerners leave us exposed and are safe far away. We wish you Boiotians well. It's your throw of the knucklebones—whether you take our good advice to go home, or as fools venture farther to the west to start yet another war in the dead of winter. Either way, tomorrow you will no longer see your friends here from Mantineia."

More than half the men who had descended into Lakonia earlier were to leave, maybe three or even four myriads packing for home—all the hoplites from Mantineia, Elis, the cities of Arkadia, and the northern tribes other than the Boiotians. They had sacks of bronze pots and tools. The flatlanders of Mantineia even had Spartan roof-tiles stacked high in their pilfered carts. It mattered little that it was Epaminondas and his Thebans who had sent architects—and that their Proxenos had fallen—to plan their cities Mantineia and Megalopolis. Or that the ingrates of the new Mantineia could be safe to finish such high stone walls only because Thebans had come south to keep the Spartans at bay or even that a free and fortified Messenê would keep the Spartans worried and away from the Arkadians.

Lykomedes finished. "So to stay friends we will part. Many of us supported this war against Sparta to end her rule over others. That is now over and won. But we are not so sure that we need press on in the snow to Messenia for this winter madness." In his cockiness he walked and stared at Pelopidas and Epaminondas and he tossed his head up and down, like the morning chicken free of the dog, who struts about the courtyard. Now he laughed in the generals' faces. "Yes, we can kill all the Spartans. But what, pray tell, would we do with thousands of their helots over the mountain in Messenia, all free? Who by Zeus would govern them? Who is to feed and house them all? Who wants to own fragile pots that will surely break and then become the burden of the owner to mend them, ugly though they will always thereby be." Lykomedes was speaking to hard hoplites in arms, not back home to Mantineians on the three-obol dole or with the young boys of the *palestrai*, so he was careful to blame only the Messenian helots and not Epaminondas and his generals. There were twenty thousand tough Boiotians and worse-looking Argives, with long spears upright in their gloved right hands and the club of Thebes painted on their shields. And this Argive general Epitêles? Why, he looked more a Thrakian cutthroat than a man of the polis.

So Lykomedes chose his words one by one and went slowly on. "Such helots over there below Ithômê are just tribes. They will go at each other with iron once their Spartan muzzle is ripped off. Yes, yes, I supported this war to end Sparta. But the second thoughts always run the wiser. Second thoughts I have plenty as I see my friends in their pride call for endless war and far-fetched ideas about democracy for savages, fueled by the theorems of my former master Pythagoras and a perennial war that allies cannot agree on."

Most hoplites from Arkadia backed off when they saw some of the Argives push forward, and went back to haggling over booty as they prepared to go home. But Lykomedes was oblivious to the growing throng of the Argive killers who shoved their way forward to the campfires, as if they were pushing their way in the phalanx to get at a Spartan king. The general of the Argive Epitêles had nodded to the well-born in his midst to press ahead, the aristocratic killers that were the sword's edge of his phalanx. They were the professional hoplites of the One Thousand of Argos, who were in armor in the front row of the crowd and began to jeer and spit as Lykomedes went on.

Lykomedes continued his shouting to the assembled captains of the alliance. "So do not let Epaminondas spoil our work in Sparta by turning our thoughts to Messenia. Just because he cannot storm the acropolis of the Spartans, that is no reason to try to regain our reputation in an accursed land—one that would soon be our graveyard."

Ainias sat in gloom among the *hopla* as Lykomedes droned on. He was leaning on a pile of shields and breastplates, murmuring to Mêlon— tiring of this war after the death of Proxenos. Not one dead Spartan, not one live helot was worth the life of his friend—even though he had long feared his aristocratic Proxenos was not quite up to the bloodletting, to what a Chiôn or Epitêles had to do to break the backs of the Spartans. Ainias had not washed or cut his hair or trimmed his beard or changed his clothes since the death of Proxenos. He promised that he would not until he neared his widow's estate on the Asopos far home to the north.

But he stood by his Theban friends. He leaned over to Mêlon. "Our boar-tooth Lykomedes is the perfect balance weight, neither with us nor against us. See how he charts out his distance, seven measures from Sparta and five from us." He had never liked Lykomedes, but Ainias had never wanted to go all the way to Messenia, either.

Mêlon nodded. His bad leg hurt, not surprisingly, for he had not marched this much since the time of his wound at Koroneia well more than twenty summers earlier. He got up nonetheless and tossed an empty scabbard over at the feet of Ainias in disgust. "I wish Lykomedes were such a clever sort. But yes, it is only about gold. His belly rules his head. His table costs more than his silver tongue can feed. I hear he has eaten himself the hindquarters of many a goat in the halls of his new Mantineia." But then Mêlon cheered up and pointed to the thousand Argives who had swarmed forward to the speakers silhouetted by the campfires. "Look, Ainias. I'd rather have one of those spearmen than ten Mantineians. We have a thousand by their look, and another myriad behind them, every one a match for a Spartan and nearly as good as ourselves."

The Theban Sacred Band joined the Argive Thousand. In fear, a groan rose among the elders of the Arkadians and Mantineians that the northerners would kill their Lykomedes this very night, as he slunk off into the shadows. Nonetheless, Sinon, the olive picker and demagogue of Mantineia, nodded at his master Lykomedes. He was the right fist after the left jab of Lykomedes and pointed at Pelopidas and also swung at Epaminondas. "Your work is done, Theban. Declare victory. Set up another trophy with another horse and rider in bronze. The great city of Megalopolis is about done. With Mantineia you have your two democratic fetters of Hellas to keep chained the defeated Spartan beast. After all, it is we the neighbor, not you the distant foreigner, who must keep the Spartan animal in our nets."

"I need three fetters, Sinon, not two," Epaminondas yelled out to the throng. "With chains, not webbing, for a monster like Agesilaos."

Sinon stood up again. It was clearer in the firelight that he was a plump sort, with soft hands and a shape like some shadow-tail squirrel whose back legs were twice the girth of his tiny claws in the front. He gestured nervously to the audience, as if he were gnawing on a winter nut. He was not as good a speaker as Backwash of Aulis but he was a braver sort who wished to humiliate Epaminondas, not just to abandon him.

"Lords of Boiotia, you can vote as well, either to face a stoning in Thebes, since the new year will be upon you in three days—or to face death with the helots when the Spartans break out of the blockade and go on to hit your backsides as you march to your west." A roar followed. But heads were already turned back from Sinon—who had six large bags of Spartan gold from the agents of Agesilaos in the bottom of his wagon beneath the tiles. The sudden noise was not approval for Lykomedes from the Mantineians or the Eleans on news of their departure in the morning but rather wonder at the shaggy man who entered the arena and stood next to Epaminondas.

Hundreds were pressing toward the center as the mob contracted and then surged around Lykomedes, who desperately tried to break out. This new intruder looked more like a wild Epiriot than a man of civilized Argos, with unkempt beard and hair—and a long, dirty leather underjerkin beneath his bronze that fell beneath his knees. The Argive Thousand in the front yelled out, "Kill him, Epitêles. Kill them all, Epitêles. Epitêles." He pushed aside Sinon as he entered and sent the wide-butt onto his backside. Lykomedes stepped back, but the wild man hit him, too, harder than he had Sinon. A black cape covered the heavy bronze armor of Epitêles, with full greaves, shoulder and arm guards, and a Korinthian helmet of the masters with a black sideways crest, officer style, slung back on his head. The brute, with a crossed eye, appeared a near twin to the Tanagran Philliadas. He was as ugly as Lichas himself, though evil was not quite in his look. No wonder the Argives called him "Torn Dog." Yet he spoke like a *rhêtôr*, not a brawler, and he was as careful in speech as he was rough in look.

"I am Epitêles of Argos. I claim myself *polemarchos* of the Argives for the year to come. We Argives, seven thousand strong and more, we have voted ourselves last night. We march west to finish the war. Go home in peace, you men of the middle Peloponnesos. We were never folk like you Arkadians or Eleans. We have always fought the Spartan, Dorians though we are. So, yes, we march tomorrow ourselves—with Epaminondas over the mountain to free the helots and finish Sparta. The fewer of us, the better the army. Let it be said that both Epaminondas and Epitêles have a final task under the slopes of Ithômê. The only problem I see is that there is no enemy to kill, none that wish to try us." Yes, this Epitêles sounded like even a better orator than Alkidamas himself. "Well, then, let us all part in friendship, the men of the Peloponnesos except for the Argives. It is decided they return home to the walls that our Proxenos built, with the booty we earned for them, and without the hoplites who protected them."

Small groups were scuffling even, until Epaminondas abruptly ended the council. "It is decided. We go west, Epitêles and I. You others go home. Friends we all remain who hate the men of Sparta, Lykomedes—at least for the year to come." At daybreak twenty thousand Boiotians and Argives headed up on their side of the Eurôtas northward. They were eager to sweep into Messenia from the topside as the pestle that would hammer the Spartans there against the mortar of Taygetos, and end what was started far to the north at Leuktra. The freed helots among them ran fast to the west to warn their own of the final approach of the men of the north, to ready food and to kill any Spartan on sight still under Ithômê.

As for this stranger Epitêles, Mêlon smiled that sometimes a single good man comes from the shadows for a single task for his own motives. He may have had no stomach for storming the Eurotas or building a city of stone for the Messenians, or for giving democracy to the mob. But for a few days of chaos, marching in the cold to free the helots and killing Spartans on the pathway up Mt. Taygetos? The very gods could not do it better themselves. Mêlon was now at the van, with Ainias and Melissos, marching once more with Pelopidas and the Sacred Band. All were happy to be on the move and out of the fog and mist of Lakonia, following Epaminondas across the barren orchards to the foot of Taygetos. The sounds of the chafing of wood and metal from thousands were deafening as the army headed for the ice of the high passes. But not a yell, not even a voice was raised, as the men shuddered at the black clouds on the mountain and met a growing hard wind with sleet from the north. Mêlon had had no word of Chiôn despite the mob of helots that was coming east from Messenia. He could only hope Chiôn had settled up by now with Gorgos and freed Nêto. Yet, he was not sure whether the freedman was making his way to Ithômê down the Alpheios, or had he been killed by *kryptes* along the way. And Alkidamas—was the old man shivering on the gulf, waiting for a ship to the south? Nor was there any report of Nêto after her imprisonment by Kuniskos, but at least Mêlon at last was heading west to find her and settle with Gorgos. No mention either of the reception ahead in Messenia. The fate of Erinna? Erinna herself was not even much known to Mêlon. Was his silver at the bottom of the gulf? Mêlon wondered; since Chiôn had left Plataia with plans to hand the money over to the trireme at Aigosthena, there had been only silence.

Ainias pointed out Epaminondas. He was riding a three-year-old black stallion, not his red pony, but one taken from the stables of Antikrates. Their general was again bridling it on its back legs in the wind, and waving them all to follow in the howling of ice rain—happy to be free of the Peloponnesians, and happier to have this shaggy Epitêles and his Argives at his side. The tiny Boiotian seemed to have a feel for the frisky horse. So he turned his mount around at the foot of Taygetos as they started to ascend the steep narrow road that wound to the west and northward toward the cloudy pass. Epaminondas called out to this army. It was icy and windy, but there were not yet the high snows blocking the pass, and so the shorter route over Taygetos was open to Messenia. "Follow your Epitêles. Follow Pelopidas. We lead you to the freedom of the Messenians and to freedom for us from Sparta forever. Make the strong weak, the weak strong—and a new Hellas like none other."

Thousands of Argives and Boiotians heard his message and answered back, "Freedom. Freedom. *Eleutheria. Eleutheria tôn Hellênôn.*" Now they left for good the valley of Eurôtas as their voices bounced off the rock walls above. Smoke from the fires of the valley blew across as they climbed and even now the Spartans still dared not cross back over the Eurotas. Mêlon felt his leg loosen up, the pain vanish, just as it had during the battle at Leuktra. Pelopidas was calling out in unison with the Sacred Band. Runaway helots had cut out a path ahead. The Messenians had cleared the road of the black ice and some light snow as they went up the summit, peeking out of the fir and cedar in twos and threes as the army passed on.

Only Ainias kept quiet, with his bloody cape on and his patches of wild hair and his beard mangy. He was full of black bile that this army had forgotten his Proxenos, whose scrolls were about to come alive in stone at Messenê, the greatest of the three fetters, on the other side of this dark Taygetos. Helots, Ainias cursed, had brought Proxenos southward across the Isthmos—and helots were not worth his death. Few among us, Ainias snarled to himself, are prisoners of memory and loyal to the past. There are too few of these faithful ones who have a bond with the dead, the sleeping majority who came and went. So, yes, the good few resent mightily that none praise their ancestors, the better, now forgotten men

who made their roads, tiled their roofs, and planted their orchards. Not a
man among the thousands marching here, not one cared that these cities
came from the hard work and thinking of Proxenos, son of Proxenos, forgotten even before the fires of his pyre had eaten away his flesh. Ainias
muttered to himself that this was silly to climb a mountain in winter when
there were clouds on its top and ice in the air. Better to go up the mountains in summer—or go to the north to the kinder passes around the
mountain. That they were passing the Kaiadas, the pits of Sparta where
the helots were thrown, meant nothing to the brooding Ainias.

Still, he always liked to fight, and he now was the sole Arkadian in
this new army of Boiotians and Argives. So Ainias said nothing ill about
fighting into the new year that would confirm Epaminondas a death sentence back at Thebes. Nonetheless, Ainias thought it useless when Spartans were alive at their rear—and the helots hardly worth any more
death. Most in the columns left him alone now, since he stank and would
not change his cape and jerkin with the blood of Proxenos on it. Rumors
spread that the ashes of Proxenos were in his leather bag on his belt,
which the Arkadian patted as he swore and slurred.

They marched up through the storm to the passes over the mountain. The army grew as more helots in furs and leather capes began to
come out of the snowy pines, and followed along at the rear of the columns. A few Spartans spied down at them from the tallest heights, but
quickly fled as some freed helots hiked up the cliffs after them. The red-
capes in threes and fours were too late heading home on rumors of the
enemies pouring into Messenia, and so gave Epaminondas and his army
their road below—terrified of the Boiotians and more scared of the rumored
man-bear loose the past month on Taygetos who hunted down Spartans
alone and left others be.

Few of the liberators knew what to expect when they crossed the
summit into Messenia and down to the Spartan fort beneath Ithômê.
Would there be a helot version of Lykomedes, or a Messenian Backwash,
to undermine their arrival?

# *All Roads to Messenia*

C hiôn was roaming on Taygetos—right now no more than a hundred stadia away from the army, camping alone in the tall icy firs with a bright fire, hunting for Gorgos and his guard. He had come too late to ransom Nêto, and heard only that Erinna had failed to rescue her as Gorgos fled into the highlands. Chiôn now followed Gorgos in his flight to the upper reaches of Taygetos, since there was of yet no trace of Nêto back in his abandoned compound nor word of her with him in the upland. He assumed that her corpse had been either burned or buried, but he kept quiet and again promised only that he would come down the mountain with the head of Gorgos and a live Nêto by the time Mêlon arrived with Epaminondas.

For Nêto's fate, Chiôn blamed Alkidamas, and Gastêr, and cursed the Korinthians for the foul ship and the delay with the Phokians. On arrival, he had given Nikôn all the ransom money of Malgis for his men, to keep them forging swords and fed as the helots left the farms in revolt in hopes of the arrival of Epaminondas. So now Chiôn was free of his obligations, and free to play out the finishing of Sparta to its end.

The Messenians had enough men in the valley to pursue the red-capes, but not enough mountain folk on high Taygetos, who knew the ways of woods and streams and how to live like the bear and the panther, to hunt down the packs of the fleeing Spartans and find the dead scent of Gorgos's hideout. So Chiôn was hunting on the mountain, always on the heels of Kuniskos and his band that had left Ithômê two days before his arrival. These Spartan *kryptes* boasted that they were scouts of the wild who could live on berries and game and slit the throat of the wayward helot. But they had never met a true wild man, never an animal like Chiôn who felt he at last had found his proper place—not a slave, not a free man, but a wild one now, beyond the rules of the polis, yet more free than any of the city-state. He was no politês, as he once dreamed but an *agrios*, an *ômos* who did not cook his food, but instead drank the milk of the wandering goats he strangled. He forgot Pythagoras and began eating meat again, raw, on the sly among the no-man pines. Soon all mention of Chiôn of Helikon ceased in these days as the Messenians figured he had perished among the wild animals on the mountain. Indeed, the shepherds told of a new nameless, half-human beast who broke the necks of Spartans and left them dangling by the heels from their trees, tied tight with their capes, and with a red beta smeared on their bare backs.

Finally the leaky *Theôris* of Gastêr pulled into Koronê, the port of the Messenians. Alkidamas and Ephoros headed to Ithômê with the helot crew, both the unarmed rowers and the ten marines. Gastêr followed from the docks a half day later, cursing that he had to put his feet on dry soil. He had expected to find dock men at the port, but now had to hike over to Messenê, in a war no less, to find a new cargo, and maybe a better ship and, of course, a new crew. He soon found Nikôn. "Who's in charge, helot? Who to deal with? I need outgoing rowers and I am the man to hire to fetch your helots from up north. Ten owls per head from anywhere along the gulf. Give me a cargo for the north, and I'll come back here in the south with more helots."

It was the work of the philosopher Alkidamas now to stop the killing of helot traitors who had served the Spartan. He was determined that with his Athenian helots sensible statesmen might stop the chaos and plan out the infant government of a new Messenia. "We came to find our Nêto, and Erinna, but it would have been better to stay with Epaminondas for all the good we slow-foots have done. Pitch our camp, and muster the helots here to start the building of Proxenos's third city. We can at least show Epaminondas when he arrives that we are Hellenes of the polis, not tribesmen in hides."

Meanwhile, Mêlon had kept quiet as the army snaked through the icy flat ground on the summit of Taygetos, going over his plans to find Nêto, or at least bury her. He hoped that Chiôn, if he lived, had found her scent, and maybe even done away with Gorgos if it had come to that, or at least paid him for her release. Finally, Mêlon turned to Epaminondas. "There will be few Spartans on this side of Taygetos, General. Our largest problem will be feeding the thousands joining here and convincing them to start on their walls as we arrive. This mob will be worse than the three armies that met up in Mantineia."

"No," Ainias broke in, "our task is reading the scrolls of Proxenos. He is Messenia, not the helots. Still, his plans for the city alone will not build Messenê. Somebody will have to stack the stones." As the army marched, the captains squabbled over what to expect when they came down off the other side of the mountain, whether they were to be fighters or builders, for after the ravaging of Lakonia no one knew whether the Spartans would flee before their entry or had red-capes ranging over Messenia to stop them. On the third noon from the Eurotas, the army descended through the olive groves on the gulf of Messenia, following the road that led on to sandy Pylos. But few in the army looked that way, since all had their eyes on the cone of Ithômê that now was thirty stadia to their right, as they still chanted their slogan *Eleutheria*, happy to be off Taygetos. Where was the enemy? Where the Spartans? Epaminondas ordered the army to strap on their breastplates and pull their helmets down. Why no Spartans?

The wagons and pack animals slowed and brought up the rear of the column. Mêlon felt the first pangs of his *aristeia* in battle returning as Melissos handed him his armor, heavier in the old style than that of most, long patched and hammered flat after the blows of Leuktra—the shield, spear, helmet, breastplate, greaves, and sword of Antander his grandfather. By dusk they were coming down to the plain before Ithômê, uncertain whether Lichas himself would be barring the way with the survivors of Leuktra who had beat them over the pass. But even on the rough plain below there were no Spartans. Instead the hills were covered with plain folk in leather and rags, all calling for the Boiotians, shouting out the names of Epaminondas and Epitêles—as if it were spring Dionysia and not the cruel, cold beginning of the new year. "Look and keep your silence," Epaminondas yelled out to his generals. "Look at the helot clan. There is not a Spartan to be seen. They did not face us in armor in Lakonia. Not now in Messenia either. The cowards over here have run home to the safe side of the Eurotas."

The sun fell and the army of the liberators paused, as they looked down at the plains of Messenia, bathed yellow in the winter sun's dying light. Helots dotted the spur of Ithômê. Some spilled out from Eva onto the lime-green valley below. There was the flotsam of a recent battle, corpses and weapons strewn over the ground. Ainias spotted the Spartan dead in twos and threes in the gullies and ditches beside the Lakonian road as it went up toward Taygetos. He spoke to Mêlon. "Who knows what happened? I doubt we ever get much word of it. But the end seems to have come quickly. When they heard we were on the crest of Taygetos, the Spartans just ran, and the rebellion fled after them. A house of straw, this Spartan colony of Messenia was. When Epaminondas blew, it simply collapsed in his wind."

"Thank the god in heaven," Pelopidas declared. "Look. Take in these hills and valleys of men, and old women, and children as well—ten tenthousands below. If we give them stones, they will have the biggest polis in Hellas."

Mêlon saw the same. "Not one Spartan, but likely twenty some thousands of armed helots. Where and how they came I don't know. But someone has not been idle. Someone has planned all this. I hope there is food for us. But these locusts may well have eaten the green leaves off the olives and be living now on snails and roots. Perhaps one of them knows where my Nêto is." He stared at every Messenian girl they passed to see if one might be his freedwoman and then called out her name in hopes strangers might know of her fate.

Nikôn had already mustered two myriads of helots to meet Alkidamas. They had begun their attacks when days earlier a runner from the east had arrived to cry out that seven ten-thousands under Epaminondas were just then burning Lakonia. At that news most of the Spartan garrisons fled. But then even more thousands of the southern helots rose up and boasted that they had cut down five hundred *kryptes* and had overrun Gorgos's timber garrison beneath Ithômê. Nikôn knew that, had it not been for Alkidamas's urging to let the Spartan jailers flee to the wilds of Taygetos, every oak in Messenia would have had a Spartan hanging upside down, tied by his heels with his cape. "We can't build a new city by killing prisoners, or hunting down Spartans like dogs, the way they themselves did the Messenians. We are not *kryptes*. We will have no abyss to toss in prisoners. Free Messenia will be not just better than Sparta, but better even than free Mantineia and free Megalopolis. So let the Spartan mice scatter. We have a city of stone to build."

The column of liberators was now surrounded on both sides by cheering helots. They threw the men bread, onions, and cheese as they passed by. Here and there they had a bound Spartan who was stripped, helot-style, shaved bald, and slapped as he was dragged through the two long lines of the beating crowd. On a few bare trees there were Spartans hanging—strung up by their own red capes and swaying in the hard north wind. Some had placards around their necks, declaring DOULOI TÔN MESSENIÔN—slaves of the Messenians. In the bedlam, Mêlon turned to Ainias and yelled over the din, "Begin the work of Proxenos. Remember, thousands to feed. Where is the genius of Alkidamas? Where is Chiôn? Time is short if we don't want riot and murder on our hands."

Ainias viewed all he saw with an icy heart, but he noticed far more than did his generals. "I see no starving helots, but plenty of food and markets. Someone again has been doing our work for us. Marshal these men as I did the workers at Thespiai. Tomorrow we will have Epaminondas parley with the officers and get the builders to organize the work brigades. We get the walls up—and then never have to come back."

The next day a group of Messenians made their way to Epaminondas, who was already this first day issuing orders to mark out a camp. Thousands of the army to the rear who were still on the foothills of Taygetos would find shelter and food when they arrived in the black cold night. A fat fellow in a dirty wool cloak and hood walked up to the head of the column, with a taller dark man at his side, who had neither beard nor hair. The heavier one started, "I am Lelex. My bald friend is Tisis. Messenians we claim to be, and leaders as well. We look for Epaminondas of the Thebans, and the Argive Epitêles. These generals sent word these last months to assemble here at Ithômê. We did that. Look, thousands of us wait. Nêto of Thespiai, whatever world she is in, said that only these two can found the new capital at Messenê. And that it must be on Ithômê, here where we have assembled to build our city. Ten days ago we rushed the Spartans. When Antikrates fled last month, much of his army did, too. Lord Kuniskos was left on his own to get out with the young and old hoplites. Most of them went nowhere. Whether Kuniskos escaped into the upper forests, no one knows. But a new man-eater roams on foul

Taygetos and may have him in his belly. The last few days fewer hike up the mountain as in the past—and even fewer return."

Epitêles was sent for, back with the Argive *lochoi* that had camped ten stadia or more away in the middle of the column. Epaminondas laughed to these two helots. "I sent word half a year ago, expecting one thousand might meet us on Ithômê after the first of the year. But Lelex here has brought the entire folk of the Peloponnesos to the shoulders of Ithômê."

Lelex slowly replied. "Nêto had told us there is an urn, a stash somewhere with the sacred books of the ancient hero Aristomenes who left directions how to build the city of his visions. Only she and you and Epitêles know the whereabouts of these plans. But we can't begin raising this polis until these written prophecies are found."

"Yes, I know," Epaminondas answered. "Epitêles tonight when the moon rises will walk the slopes and find this sign, as Artemis has told you. Your Nikôn and Doreios will help. Then look for us tomorrow at midmorning here where we will pitch our permanent camp."

The Argive generals under Epitêles joined Epaminondas for their late meal of garlic, dried apples, and, for the Dorians, some salted goat. As they parleyed, Ainias went out among the company commanders. "Women must cook. Make shelters as the men cut and drag the stone down the hill. We hear there are a thousand oxen and as many horse. I see they have wagons and rollers, all hidden away on the mountains and already coming down." The more Epaminondas noted the organization, the food, the quiet here, the more he puzzled how the man-foots had routed the Spartans and made themselves so ready to start to build. He turned to Pelopidas. "This is all the work of Alkidamas. For a sophist he seems to know something about stone. He plans to drag and roll the blocks down from the quarries, right up to the walls. Our Proxenos figured that we could cut our rock on Ithômê and have the downhill walls up in three months and be home before the grain heads droop."

Epitêles scoffed. "They'll all loot. So we better kill the first hundred to remind the others we're hoplites, not dancing girls. Do it the Argive way. Hang a few of 'em from that oak over there as a sign to the others. The Spartans left, and about ten thousand no-goods will come out of the shadows, wolves from the hills to butcher the sheep. They've been killing hoplites this year, and they won't stop just because we're freeing them. Whether they kill enemy Spartans, or their benefactors the Argives, they care little. Blood is blood to these waylayers. So we kill the worst of them, peace returns, and the city builds. Do it right at the very beginning and *nomos*, law, reigns. Else—we have another Kekyra of old, a war of everybody against everybody. Just watch. My Argives will go out tomorrow and kill the first helot they see who has a goat or pot not his own—and then a hundred more for good measure." With that he grunted, threw on his shaggy coat, and stormed out of the tent, ordering his officers, "Help the helots who work. Kill all who won't."

Epaminondas let him go. "We need more brutes like that. Our Ainias counts as only one, and he needs help to bang a few heads." Then a silence came over the meeting as all turned toward a procession of torches coming into the camp from Ithômê way. In walked priestesses, a half-dozen women in hoods, accompanied by ten or so Messenian hoplites and dancing in unison to the tune of pipes.

# CHAPTER 32

# The End of the Beginning

T he women then threw off their capes. They cried out that the Spartans had all been killed or scattered in fear of the arrival of Epaminondas. "Our thousands chased down their hundreds. Ask the priestesses of Artemis how many have been hunted down and gutted. The bodies of our masters are scattered all over Ithômê. Talk to Alkidamas. Look, our Alkidamas is here. We have the plans of the city and are ready to have the gods bless the founding—and start tomorrow."

Bedlam followed as the celebrants lit more torches. The drummers took up the strain. Thousands of Messenians came out of the shadows and mingled in with the Thebans and Argives. Then Alkidamas came forward with a sickly sort of fellow at his side. Ephoros waved as the man addressed the throng. "Patience, silence, my guests. We sleep now. Soon the high priestesses return from Ithômê and Eva with the gods' nod about our city's founding. So for now, sleep, our Argive and Theban guests. Lay out your camps and tents. Sleep in peace, we of Messenia have food and peace for you—and a city to build tomorrow." Then the tribal leaders of the Messenians went into the camp of Epaminondas and waited for his arrival.

On the next morning Epaminondas called Lelex back to the camp of the generals. Epitêles was at his side, and he was calmer now, since a thousand of his men had found the night quiet and most helots asleep around Ithômê and Eva. Lelex and Doreios, along with Nikôn and some others, sat down as Epaminondas threw down a bag of scrolls taken from the sack of Proxenos. By rote he claimed, "Here. We found them. Just as it was fated that the urn of old Aristomenes would be uncovered when the Spartans left. In it are the plans of the new Messenê, buried on the slopes of Ithômê since the time of the great ones. The priestess Nêto once told us where the goddess had hidden the plans of our city. We have brought the ancient scrolls back from the crypt on Ithômê."

Lelex went dumb. Before him on the ground of the tent was a pile of Proxenos's papers, with charts of towers, and four gates, and drawings of the mountain Ithômê and the saddle to Eva surrounded with walls running up the sides of Ithômê—which he believed had been unearthed from a crypt just dug from the ground of the mountain, written, he thought, hundreds of years earlier. "Artemis of Ithômê. We are where we should be. We are standing on the city walls of our grandchildren. So we will start today with the quarrying. Tisis here will organize the companies." For the rest of their second day in Messenia, the Boiotian generals divvied up the protection of the Messenians with the Argives. One myriad would guard the workers. The other ten thousand would join with the Messenians laying the foundation trenches, some thirty stadia of them. Fifty thousand Messenians were to stay up on Ithômê, cutting and dragging down the gray stone. Another twenty thousand would work the machines to hoist the blocks and guide the iron and lead mongers to fasten the stones. Half the women were to cook, as they hunted down the Spartan stores and the caches in the abandoned Spartan camps. The other half set up tents and shacks for the workers and hoplites. Nikôn's crews already had cut tall spruce timber, forty feet and more. With the help of Ainias, he was planning to build ten tall swiveling cranes, with pulleys and tackle, that would hoist the blocks some thirty feet high and more.

It was a good time to build. The winter of grain had been planted now for over two months and harvest was another five months away, so the oxen were free and could pull the cut stone down the mountain. Proxenos's craftsmen, a hundred or so in the army, who had worked at Thespiai and advised the builders of Mantineia and Megalopolis, brought from their packs drawings of arches and battlements—as if they had just inked them—and paired off with Messenians to ensure the walls went up straight according to their plumb lines. Now Ainias took up his dead friend's scrolls and with Epitêles and Epaminondas held parley with the leading helots. Beside the Athenian helots that had come with

Alkidamas, there were Doreios, Tisis, and Lelex, who spoke for all, though it was Nikôn who claimed preeminence by having done the most fighting against the Spartans. And, of course, he had made the long run to Helikon to fetch Chiôn and had rescued the corpse of Erinna. He now stepped forward. "We are the leaders of the Messenians. At least until we elect our archons. We'll vote once the walls are up. Our Athenian helots are drafting the laws. So we are ready to build our city. You, Ainias, tell us of our plans. We want to cut stone. The sooner new Messenê is up, the sooner you go home. We want you home by the end of the year's fifth month for your wheat harvest this spring as much as you do."

Ainias looked at Proxenos's master plans that he had gone over for a year, recently dirtied, wrinkled and torn a bit, as though Aritomenes had sketched them at the dawn of the polis. "Look here at these ancient worn scrolls. They say that the wall goes up thirty feet high at the towers, twenty high on the ramparts in between—the tallest in Hellas. It runs thirty stadia from the backside of Ithômê's crown. Then it takes in the crest of Eva to the valley. Look for the guide points. Right here on the mountain. That's where we put our northwest corner. All the holy ground to Asklepios and Artemis are set aside—and marked up here."

Then Ainias tried to remember more from all his long talks with Proxenos about this third and best of his citadels, and so went on. "My men are cutting out the traces of the walls with spades. Only a city this big can have your herds and crops inside the walls, along with your houses and temples. All will be out of the Spartans' reach, but with more inside your walls than either at Mantineia or Megalopolis. You can farm or vote or bathe inside, and care little whether ten or ten thousand Spartans are outside your walls. We put towers on every rise, like the scrolls of Aristomenes tell us, forty and more—and more of them square than round. Yes, four gates, one in each direction. But our busiest entry will be the east one, facing our sister-polis in Arkadia. There we will have a courtyard and swing doors higher than any at Mantineia. Its lintel—well, it will weigh far more than the Cyclopes' work at Mykenai. Just watch when we slide that stone down the mountain. It will take forty oxen to pull, five hundred men to hold tight the ropes behind."

Then Pelopidas walked up and warned the leader of the Messenians what to expect this spring. "You can say these plans were buried in sacred pots and come from your hero Aristomenes, or we can say they were the work of Proxenos who died on the Eurotas. It matters nothing to me. All we care is that ramparts go up and go up now. We have only three months for you to build the walls, and for us to keep out the Spartans before their spring campaign seasoning starts and maybe as late as Homôloios. Epitêles promises us a few more days for his Argives. He claims that he followed us to Messenia and will lead us out of here—the last to come and the first to leave. At night Alkidamas's Athenians give you the laws and constitution. Listen up. You have no choice. The Thebans did not come south to set up an oligarchy. But we don't want rule by the *ochlos* either. We kill the first looters we see, hang 'em up on the scaffolds we will. Epitêles has already done that. You bring Spartan hostages to us, no more killing of captives. Fix your own affairs by vote of the people—but only after we leave. Until then Epaminondas is your king. Don't forget it. If you wish to eat, you better have the walls up before the barley harvest—otherwise you can chose between eating or dying in the open field when Agesilaos brings his Spartans over the mountain."

For the next month, the helots cut stones at dawn with iron saws and then put them on carts to be guided down the mountain to the trenches. There, all night long, the forges turned out thousands of iron clamps for each day's work. The fire men kept molten lead in huge iron pots to seal the joints from rust. The Messenians on the rising walls quit only after the lighting of the torches, even as the days lengthened and the spring equinox approached. While the men cut and stacked and the women cooked and weeded the fields, Epaminondas and his Thebans patrolled the countryside. They killed another four hundred Spartan holdouts, making two thousand altogether now dead from among the Spartan overseers and half-helots. Epaminondas knew the number because Ainias wrote the count on a vast scroll and posted it each day on a wood pillar next to what would be the Arkadian gate. No one counted how many Messenians Epitêles executed, for he hung up outlaws and thieves well beyond Ithômê, down the Alpheios and all the way to the sea.

But Epaminondas himself had also strung by the heels another eight hundred Messenians, looters and cutthroats who would neither work nor let those be who did. Most were Spartan inside anyway, but not all. The bodies of the murderers and thieves swung in the winter cold afternoon breezes with placards around their necks APEKTENON or EKLEPSA—"I murdered" or "I stole"—followed by APETHANON and "I died." Some Messenians worried that they had exchanged the executions of Kuniskos for those of Epaminondas. Epitêles talked of his killing in camp at night while Epaminondas kept quiet. "It took us a hundred years and more at Argos, and we started as free, better men than these man-foots. Why do we think that those who were slaves will be masters of themselves and vote? Even if they vote, what's stopping these hide-wearers from stealing money from the rich and voting themselves all sorts of free this and free that—the way they do it in most of our democracies?" Then he turned gruff. "Let's find this Nikôn fellow, or maybe Lelex over there, give him some spearmen. Let him sit high in a castle on their new acropolis and like a good *tyrannos* run things until these people learn the rule of law. Before you have a Perikles—and I don't see any here—you need a Solon a hundred and more years earlier, or better yet a Peisistratos or Pheidon. You can't smooth a road without a hard rock bed underneath."

Epaminondas laughed at the brute, but sensed also that he was a keen judge of the polis, having survived the killer gangs at Argos to come out on top. "Maybe. But babies can't walk, yet at five they run faster than those in their seventh decade. Hellas has lots of democracies, my dear Epitêles. But they are old and tired, and need these toddlers and crawlers to keep us young and remind us what we once were. We gave them freedom, and they in turn have saved us from what we might have become, new barbarians of leisure and affluence who won't put a toe outside of our city gates if there is a cloud in the sky. Now freedom is theirs to keep or lose. Either way it does not detract from our gift."

Epitêles did not back down. "I and my Argives, we feel no better or worse from freeing them, and hardly think their freedom is a gift. Sparta is weak. Finished as we know it. She has no farmers to feed her phalanx, and won't march out of Lakonia, at least for a while. That is good enough for me and mine. These helots can do what they like." Epitêles laughed and for the next few days kept patrolling with his guard to hunt down more thieves who were stealing from the bread carts next to the scaffolds. He knew men by nature to be bad. They would kill and worse if they were not tired from work or scared of punishment. It was not in his nature to build, so he did what he knew best, he punished and hoped he killed more guilty than innocent—and worried little when he did not. "These Thebans can free anyone they please. But then who can't do that? But they have no idea how to knock heads and keep these half-tamed on their leashes. Zeus in heaven, I think these Boiotians want to be liked rather than feared." That the helots slacked off from the walls was of no real concern to Epitêles, other than as reason enough to kill those who were probably stealing rather than working. When enough were executed to discourage the no-goods, Epitêles would head home to Argos and the hard life among the murderous factions there. And so he did soon, and passed out of the history of the Hellenes.

Epaminondas thought he had Epitêles right when he had said of him, "Don't wonder that he will leave us soon, but instead ask why this man in fur has even come. He is a warrior, one who wakes up in the morning promising to cut down Spartans and goes to bed each night in lamentation that he has not killed enough of them. We won't see his like again in Hellas. He's the good coin side to Lichas, though both are at home killing and so more alike than we think. Maybe our Chiôn, if he lives, is a third who could join this cabal of Aiases. But for now thank our One God that Epitêles was on our side."

The friends of Erinna were also hunting down Spartans with Nikôn's old band, always on what they claimed was the scent of a live Kuniskos. Still, they kept their distance from the trails in the uplands of cloudy Taygetos in fear of the man-animal—wolf, bear, panther or whatever he was supposed to be—that killed wayfarers. As the walls reached their sixth course, and the buds swelled on the fruit trees, all gave up on the Spartan stragglers—except Nikôn, who would not believe that Gorgos, the killer of Erinna, was dead and so went out after his ghost each morning. Finally, when the grain stalks bent, and the night frosts quit as the top courses were laid on the northern sections of the walls, he came late into the camp of the Boiotians.

"Gone. I know that now. Nêto must be long dead. But her killer Kuniskos I wager lives in the wild. He's in the high pines, Mêlon. Your Gorgos—he has gone to the highlands. We hear that from some of those Spartans who are left on Taygetos, thinking Agesilaos will come back yet. But both banks of the Alpheios are now free and wide open and our boys are throwing their Spartans and their friends off our lands all the way to Elis in the north. Only a few grandees remain on their estates, lackeys of the Spartans, but we will get to them by the time the grain droops."

Mêlon scoffed at Nikôn. He thought all of his Helikon people were now dead—his Nêto, along with Gorgos and Chiôn. All were gone to join Lophis. "Gorgos? He's dead. Gone to the other shore, you mean, to meet the killers and robbers in the gloomy pools and pits of Tartaros where he belongs. How could he have escaped when his compound was said to be surrounded and his men hunted down? Nikôn, remember that the ghost you are hunting is only one man. Just one old Gorgos you run after. I wager he was surely run down amid the mob of fleeing Spartans—and forgotten in the carnage. I wish he were alive, so I could kill him five times over for his taking of Nêto."

Nikôn raised his tone. "No, no. I sense it, even if the Spartan rumors are false. The soul of Nêto speaks to me, warns me of our danger. Gorgos at least lives. He's alive but gone from here. He's with Antikrates. Both are fated to no good unless we kill them now. They will lead an army against new Messenê. Ask the souls of your Proxenos and our Erinna; they'd be alive now if those two were dead. Doreios and I will go back out, one last time, and scour the valleys from the altis at Olympia to the summit on Taygetos. We can smell him from here. I will come back before Epaminondas leaves with news of your Gorgos or the head of our Kuniskos." Nikôn went back up to Taygetos and all word of him went as well.

The builders from Thebes had taught the helots how to cut and dress stones, and how to swing their block and tackle over the walls' rise with cranes mounted on oak beams. After the bloody work of Epitêles, there was no need for patrolling any more for bandits as spring came on, and the blue lupin of the month of Agriônios began to bloom amid calm. The helots stacked their stones, and it was agreed that the Spartans were all either dead or on the other side of Taygetos. Ainias sat atop the first tower and with a clay-baked cone barked out orders to those below. Epaminondas was drilling Messenian hoplites and teaching them the spear work of the phalanx—just in case Agesilaos came before the seventh or eight circuit was finished.

Alkidamas had reclaimed his hostage servant Melissos. The boy, for all his tough talk of armies and killing, was quieter as he took in the rising walls of Messenê—as if the stones held him in a trance and were no longer ramparts to copy, but almost had voices that spoke to him about the power of democracy. He, like Ainias, had thought the helots would only kill and loot, but was learning that they were better wall builders than the men even of Mantineia and Megalopolis—and wondered why the Spartans themselves could never build a citadel like Messenê. Alki-

damas and Melissos took Mêlon and Ephoros up to the high perch of
Ainias, where the five could see the entire circuit of the new polis and the
terraced fields of the spring-green valleys beyond. Off in the distance they
could spot Epaminondas at dawn, coming back into the valley of Ithômê,
after a final march from Pylos by the sea with his new army of Messenian
hoplites. They saw the outline of an entire city—the people of Messenia
in constant motion, up and down Ithômê, as walls rose higher by the day,
the towers elegant with dressed stones and polished embrasures. Pelopidas's men were leading hundreds of teams of oxen, bringing down the
latest batch of gray blocks from the mountain crest. Alkidamas pointed in
every direction, as if he were charting the stars, in a slow methodical
circle. "What are we to call all this, my conspirators in democracy? Has
any in Hellas ever seen men working on through the dark—and yet back
sweaty as well by the sunrise? No wonder the men of Sparta ate well with
slaves like these. But how much harder they work when their fruits are
their own. They are Hellenes all along, better than any of the free Peloponnesians."

Ainias kept pacing around the parapet, unsure himself whether to be
proud over Proxenos's city or angry that in his mind it rose so slowly—or
madder that he was here at all. But for now, he was confident that the
helots would at last shackle the Spartans and keep them home for good.
"There is a natural law, Alkidamas, at work, that always winnows out the
chaff from wheat. So now with these fields and stones, all the Hellenes
can see cities of the Spartans and Messenians side-by-side, and determine
who are the better folk after all."

Alkidamas laughed. "So Ainias is now won over to our side? The
good cities are the work of the *dêmos*, just like when our Boiotians settled
all their own affairs. What has oligarchy ever brought Hellas? If we are in
the age of stone, it is because these vast new cities marshaled the people,
who alone decide how it will protect itself. It is the people, always the
people who both loot and yet alone create lasting cities of stone." Ainias
ignored him. But Mêlon was troubled hearing that praise of the *dêmos*,
inasmuch as he was in deep thought about Nêto and Chiôn, and wondered what his son Lophis had died for. In this new age of Hellas, where
walls and democracy made all alike, there were no longer to be men like
the son of Malgis, Epitêles, and Ainias—and, if the truth be known,
Lichas too, who had warned them all of what they had done at Leuktra in

the parley after the defeat of the Spartans. There would be no more Chiôns either? No, the age of the hoplites, of a few exceptional men in bronze, who would decide the fate of states in an afternoon of hard war, was now over—destroyed by a few exceptional men in bronze. Perhaps Alkidamas was right after all about the good future ahead for the helots, but in a fashion he hardly imagined. The people had their bellies full of war and the songs of battle, and the armored men who owned land and could alone afford bronze. So they had built themselves walls to avoid fighting, at least fighting in the fashion of hoplites and phalanxes. Perhaps the people would stay snug in their high stones, and settle their quarrels with the new machines that flung iron arrows over the ramparts, or draw on the book knowledge of Ainias and Proxenos how to mine, and countermine—how to do anything other than march to the sound of crashing wood and bronze. What would the stone-bound do if they met folk like Melissos and his Makedonians, his tribes from the north who were weaned on horses and carried on their belts bright badges that marked the number of men they had cut down in battle?

Mêlon woke up from his day trance and noticed that Alkidamas and the dour Ainias had been talking the entire time as they moved all over to the highest ramparts of a section of finished walls. Ainias now continued: "Come over here, Mêlon, we can talk and I can point to you the stones as they rise. You can see that by month's end all twenty towers are finished. Look at the streets of the city. They're all paved with flat stones and drains, and all in a grid, with corners square. Look at the city of Proxenos. He drew it from the mind of Hippodamos, who got his odd and even streets, his straight lines from the voice of the One God himself. And the childish Messenians followed his plans only on the silly myth they were not really Proxenos's ideas, but those of their ancient hero Aristomenes who supposedly three hundred years earlier had prophesied that his people would build a city far grander than the Spartan hill and then buried his plans in a jar. When a Spartan goes to battle, he leaves a mess, a labyrinth of clutter on his acropolis. When a Messenian rushes out to meet enemies, he now runs down a broad way to a square agora. His phalanx falls together in the manner in which his city was planned, his field surveyed, and the seats of his council hall divided up. Every hoplite, every house, every farm, every bench will be equal to another, none greater,

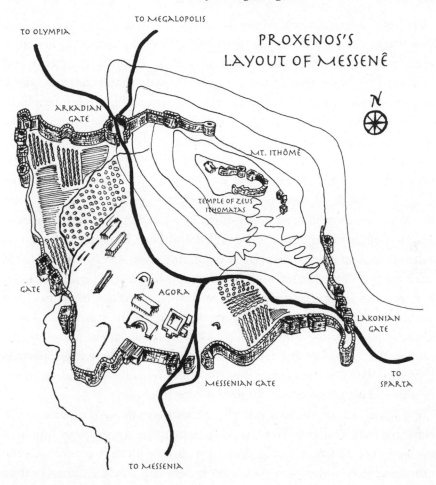

TO OLYMPIA

TO MEGALOPOLIS

PROXENOS'S
LAYOUT OF MESSENÊ

N

ARKADIAN
GATE

MT. ITHÔME

TEMPLE OF ZEUS
ITHOMATAS

GATE

AGORA

LAKONIAN
GATE

TO
SPARTA

MESSENIAN GATE

TO MESSENIA

none smaller—daily reminders that there are no more Spartans, no more harmosts, only the square corners of square thoughts."

By the fourth month of the new year, the capstones of more than half the walls of Messenê were nearly finished—even though the Argives and Boiotians had forced the Messenians to add ten stadia to ensure that the circuit ran up the slopes to the crests of Mt. Ithômê. Rumors of a Spartan army on the move against the new helot state proved fantasy—as did more stories about Nêto and Chiôn alive on Taygetos hunting down Gorgos. In truth, Agesilaos was still hobbling along the banks of the Eurotas and waiting for his Spartan stragglers to get back home safely over the high passes of Taygetos as the spring snow melted and with it the last

guard of the Spartan-held Messenia, never to return. When King Agesilaos finally drew up his muster lists, he discovered that few of his Spartans in the west had made it back alive from Ithômê. Shepherds had
brought him more news of the arrival of the wild shape-changer—not a
god, or even a half-god like Herakles, but a man-wolf, or mountain bear,
yes, more a man-bear—hunting down all winter long the Spartan packs
in the mountains, and hanging the *kryptes* by their capes. For some he
was surely some *daimôn* of legend. Perhaps he was wily Sinis, who tied his
prey between two bent pines and watched the trunk split the legs, now
come up from Epidauros to find new prey. Others swore they had seen
the killer Skirôn who tossed his victims over the gorges of high Taygetos.
Many thought the monster was grizzled and lame Korynetês of widows'
tales come back alive who smashed the brains of wayfarers and shepherds
with his iron club. The helots, however, knew him as the Great Deliverer,
the shape-changer that ensured no Spartan dare return home over the
passes of Taygetos. Nikôn, who alone went up to the summit and who
alone came back, knew the man-bear as the real bulwark of Messenia, the
demon that came late and from nowhere and had so scared the Spartans
that they dared not muster to stop the rising walls below. And yet as for
Nikôn and his rangers, the monster let all of them be.

Lichas, still on the east side of the mountain in Sparta, promised to
send his best of the Spartan royal guard up to Taygetos to find this
*daimôn*. The Spartans would drag him down—demon or not—to the
gorge and throw him onto the rocks. If he were some enormous bear or
freak wolf-dog, he would surely bleed; if a ghost they could get priestesses
to cast spells and incantations to send him back into the crevices below. If
a black god in human shape, Lichas would wrestle him down to Hades.
So he sent word for Antikrates and the sword man Klôpis, and tall Thibrachos as well, and the mother of Thibrachos, fiery Elektra his latest wife
whom he bedded in her tall tower despite her four decades and more—all
eager to kill helots and their friends and mount the severed head of this
man-bear monster among the trophies of the Menalaion at Sparta. The
best of the Spartans would kill the man-bear. Agesilaos would see that the
passes were open and the silly stories of old women about monsters and
demons were no more than the babbling of the unhinged. Then the way
back to Messenia would be open.

Even as the small band of Spartans plotted to find news of Kuniskos and scout a way for Agesilaos into Messenia, the time of departure for the army of Boiotians neared. The walls were finished, and there grew talk against Epaminondas, both among his own men who wanted to leave immediately and among the freed helots who almost had their circuit and wished the foreigner gone. A free people, their new demagogues proclaimed in the assembly, no longer wanted to feed three myriads of "friends." Anyway, the camp of Epaminondas stank and fouled the field near the Arkadian Gate. The Boiotians drank at night and sang of their spearing in Lakonia and took all credit for the end of Sparta, and laughed at the helots for their pretensions of being men of the polis. Too many of them spoiled the sanctuary of Asklepios and were bathing in the holy waters of Klepsydra.

As he readied to leave, Epaminondas wished to remind all of the good done, in this his first and last public address to the helots in the half-finished stadium of the Messenians. All the citizens of the new polis filed into the stade-long course at the south of the city, near the Messenian Gate. There were forty thousands on its earthen seats, and maybe as many more on the field and on the walls above. Epaminondas spoke in front of a new iron statue of himself near the entry to the stadium and an altar of thanks that the women of Messenia had raised for the Boiotians and Argives.

"A great plague has passed, men of Messenê. Those who crossed their borders to enslave others are themselves surrounded. The Spartan hunters have become the hunted. Yet I remind you only that freedom won after these hundreds of years can just as easily be lost again in one—should the nerve of your newfound democracy fail and you let your shields slack to your knees. It is the nature of all men in peace to become soft and scoff at the prior hard work of their fathers who gave them such bounty. Beware the real enemy is the smoother second thought that always mocks the rougher first. You tire of us, we of you. Such is also the way of peace. So be it. Enjoy these last days of spring. Soon when your hair is white or gone, the remembrance of these great days alone will give you comfort when all else is gone."

This was no audience of jaded Thebans who usually hooted and pelted their speakers with fruit, but one of recently freed men who slowly grew silent in renewed appreciation of their liberator as he finished and would soon depart. Now this Epaminondas took them all back to the first days when he and Epitêles came off the mountains, and the Spartans fled in terror at the mere rumors of their descent, and the helots and their liberators were one.

"We are seeing the new age of walls under holy Ithômê, worthy of Mykenai or Troy of old when only the Cyclopes could build such stout ramparts as these before us. But men of Messenê, do not trust solely in such rock or oak. It is not towers or the new machines that cast stone from afar that keep men free. Only the right arms of those willing to meet the enemy shield to shield and spear to spear will keep the Spartans out. Now the time comes for us to return to our families in the north below Helikon and Kithairon. Farewell, men of Messenia, and do not forget what those heroes of Hellas did on your behalf to make you the best men of the Peloponnesos."

A roar followed the general's finish. Even the dour Pelopidas and Ainias were struck by thousands of these folk who stood on the walls and towers shouting in their trust of Epaminondas—this tiny man who in a few days after all would be put on trial for his life when he arrived back at Thebes. The great war for Messenia was at an end. The great war to live in safety as free people had begun. All that was left was the cleanup, and the muster of the Boiotians as they broke camp. For one hundred and twenty days the men of Epaminondas had worked without a break, despite the furor of Epitêles and the whines of the Sacred Band. Vineyards and orchards were to be planted inside the walls, and two thousand *plethra* of barley and wheat. Five thousand head of stock roamed in open pastures beneath the walls. The grape land was black heavy land, watered by ten great springs on the slopes of the mountain—all taken from the Spartan clan of the royal Agiads whose helots had sent its harvests for four hundred years back to the royal family of Sparta.

In thanks for the health of the *dêmos*, the Messenians had laid out a temple to Asklepios, the healing god. In front was a marble statue of Nikê, the goddess of Victory, which they had erected to honor their Nikôn, now *stratêgos* of the Messenians, with his deputy Doreios, the first archon of the people. Inside the half-built temple was a model of clay that Ainias had made from the maps of Proxenos. At last the city and this model were one. There were thirty stadia of walls, ten feet thick, fifteen high, all faced with gray limestone and filled with rubble in between. The courses ran up and nearly encircled the crest of tall Ithômê. Thirty towers—two square for every round—rose thirty feet. They had put two stories in them with embrasures below their sloped roofs and, thanks to Ainias, the new belly bows aimed out the windows. Four gates, the tallest, the Arkadian in the north, shut the city tight. They left standing in the agora the hated log house of Kuniskos, a reminder to their children not born of their past bondage and the cost to free Ithômê from the likes of Antikrates and his Gorgos. His timber stakes were red with blood and gore and Nikôn had ordered the horrid poles stay up—until the head of Kuniskos could become their last trophy and they could be burned.

# CHAPTER 33

# The Reckoning

When Epaminondas finished his speech, he headed to his muster yard outside the city, between the walls and the hamlet of Andania, in the stony ground between the great olive groves of the city. Yet even before the crowd broke up, Nikôn at last appeared as promised. He had missed the words of Epaminondas and just come down his accustomed path from the summit on Taygetos. But this time the helot headed for the generals in a frenzy.

Nikôn pushed in among them and announced loud enough for the entire Sacred Band at their sides to hear, waving a walking crutch. "Kuniskos lives! The killer of our Erinna is alive. He's not dead. Not yet. I saw Nêto as a *daimôn* in a dream two nights past as I slept in Artemis's shrine and breathed her vapors. Her ghost told me of Kuniskos, just where on the vast mountain he was. Then last night up at the house of Zeus Ithomatas, I saw the hut in dreams. Just now, just this very morning on my return, one Scorpas, a half-breed uplander, came over the mountain and in through the east gate following a patrol. He said the same thing as what I had seen from the goddess. And then he handed me this crutch, Nêto's walking stick, he says. She once lived in the jail of Kuniskos on Taygetos, crippled and leaning on a stick, or so he swears."

Nikôn went on and retold his conversation with half-helot Scorpas. "His words, those of this trader and go-between Scorpas, went like this as I remember it: 'Your lost helot traitor—he is up there in the high mountain glen. A mad bear hunts him or something worse. The monster can't find Kuniskos—at least not yet. For he's safe enough in the high house in the deep woods. Up there I saw him. He was holed up in a hut. On the crest of Taygetos, the dark mountain of death. Fifty stadia and more he was from the high road. An upland trader I know saw him two nights ago. He brings him food for gold coins. Brought back this crutch, a woman's cane. Or so Kuniskos said it is and wanted those in Messenia to have it. Still, Kuniskos will not get far. Up high near the pass, he is cut off by the fear of the man-bear or the helot rangers amid the highest trees on Taygetos. Your Gorgos cannot get home to Sparta. Yes, I know his real name. He cannot go back to his eastern side of the mountain. He is holed up. Waiting for the bear-god to attack—or maybe to be rescued by Lichas. Or maybe in fright waiting to die.'"

So Nikôn finished relating the speech of Scorpas. "This time your Nikôn does not see ghosts, but has a live witness."

Mêlon scowled. "I knew he was alive. I know the helot speaks truly, for I have had visions of a hut well before Leuktra, though where it was I did not guess. And just as my dreams of the good city of Messenê trumped those of a polis in ruins, so too I know the ghosts tell the truth of our meeting with Gorgos in a hut on high Taygetos. Chiôn told me that he has also dreamt of a mountain house in flames, with Gorgos its master." Then he looked to Epaminondas. "I would have wished news that Chiôn and Nêto live, rather than that Gorgos is soon to die. I suppose some will follow me to find this man. I take care of my own—my way. I leave for Taygetos before dusk. Follow who wish. But none need to."

Epaminondas stepped up to face him. "Watch out, Melôn." He then turned and grabbed the helot. "Now wait, you Nikôn. This is just the latest of your many stories and false visions. Like those before, it too is but a phantom. It is the hatred of Gorgos that haunts you and the wish of us all that Nêto still lives and that Chiôn did not fall to the man-bear, who no doubt is some demon our grandfathers warned about. Sometimes the soul makes up pictures at night of what it wants us to believe. Or we make thoughts and then claim there are gods to be honored for giving them. Your dreams are as false as the reports of this two-shoe Scorpas. That liar whittles some wood into a cane and then calls it Nêto's—and you give him gold for his stories? Do you want Mêlon to tramp after ghosts up on the summit, to end up like Chiôn in the highlands—dead and forgotten as he goes chasing shades and half-men monsters of myth on Taygetos?

The mountain is a foul place, Nikôn. Maybe not fatal for four myriads, but lethal for four or five of you. Yes, the man-bear up there may have eaten your one-armed Chiôn, as well as the *kryptes* and soon you as well. If there was ever a Kuniskos up there, they are bones and ash now, though alive enough for fakers like your Scorpas to cheat a gold owl from you."

"Yes," Nikôn replied, "I hate the helot Kuniskos. And I know better than you of the man-bear. I've seen a lesser kind of that monster before even here on Ithômê. Unlike you, I have seen his victims swinging by their capes from the spruce limbs. Still, the voice in my dreams last night was Nêto's, as real now as in the past. Her voice lives and she whispers that Kuniskos did not die in the flight from Ithômê. Maybe this man-bear is finally dead and the mountain passes are open, and so the ghost of Nêto tells me it is at last time to come up. This Scorpas, he is a peddler, not a spy. He is dense and has no reason to lie."

"Oh? No reason other than to do the work of Lichas and get our best killed in an ambush on a high pass? I wouldn't be surprised to hear your trader once led Chiôn up to his death on the mountain with the same stories. Or maybe he works for this man-bear bandit who scares those at the loom with stories that he is a Sinis or Skirôn come alive. I imagine this bear scare may be a run-away Spartan lord or a pack of renegades that prey on shepherds and the lost."

Mêlon heard little of this good-sense warning of Epaminondas. He was too eager to clear the ledger with the killers of the dead Lophis and Proxenos and Staphis, too. Who could believe that anyone or anything could put down his Chiôn? More likely this shape-changer, if he were real, was already in the belly of Chiôn rather than the other way around. That might explain why Gorgos was suddenly free to call back in Lichas, free from the terror of the man-bear—free to carve a cane and claim it was Nêto's and get back to what he did best, lying and plotting. If Gorgos were alive, Mêlon at least would know the fate of Nêto, whether she was killed long ago in his compound or perished in the flight from Ithômê. Without a live Gorgos, no one would ever learn her fate. He turned to Melissos. "Bring a pony and our arms and plenty of rope. I want to take our Gorgos alive. I think he lives and I want to see whether he really is, as Nikôn says, the foul Kuniskos of the helots—or, before I kill him, still part of him the loyal servant who walked with me each morning on Helikon. If he has Spartans with him, the better to kill them all."

Suddenly Ainias, who had been listening to the back and forth, stepped up and grabbed Mêlon. "Son of Malgis. Something is not right about this Scorpas. A half-helot at best, maybe even a *perioikos* who trades with Spartans in the morning and sells his wares to helots at dusk. If Gorgos lives, why has he not sneaked back to his masters? How can he be trapped by our thin patrols on the summit? This story of Scorpas makes no sense. But all the same, I will go with you to ensure that we end up killing someone, maybe even Kuniskos or Scorpas or both."

Melissos was already packing their gear. Ainias said that he was going back up the mountain to learn the fate of Nêto. On Taygetos he would kill some of the Spartans who had killed Proxenos. Epaminondas finished with another warning. "We will see you back here in two days—with the camp cleaned up and the army mustering. If not, I will go up the mountain and follow your trail with Pelopidas and the Band."

So they parted. Ainias and Mêlon led toward the peaks of high cloudy Taygetos. Melissos behind followed, leading a small pony. All set out armed with spears and swords. Nikôn brought up the rear. They soon met Scorpas waiting for them on the trail ahead. Mêlon kept still and limped ahead as they went up the path to the low hills. Nikôn had unleashed Kerberos, now without his mistress Nêto. He growled more than ever, since the hound had picked up a wolf scent, one that brought back some memory of the lost Sturax; and he heard too many say "Nêto." The dog did not like the smell of this Scorpas and twice nipped the stranger's calf. He already had the smell of the dog-kicker Gorgos in his nostrils.

None knew much about these wilds, only that most of the snow was melted and the even spring high country was now passable. Twice they saw bones tied with red cloth, hanging from pine limbs over the trail—crow and buzzard meat, maybe a month old, maybe two, *kryptes*, or what was left of them, killed by whom and left as trophies for what? Scorpas had already seen bones like these and was terrified that there would be more ahead. Now he begged them to keep off to the side of the main trail that went into the high forest. The five headed for the crest of the lower peak of Taygetos, but it was soon dark and they were glad to find the huts of the woodcutters for the night at the timber's edge.

Little was said, though they noticed fresh coals in the hearth and half-eaten deer bones by the door. If they found their old Gorgos, he would not be alone. The small party was happier for that chance of revenge nonetheless, since men had been here in the past ten days. At first light they went up another small creek bed, amid stands of spruce and fir on the banks and a few upland poplars. It rained until midday. Ainias took charge on the route, and was content enough to keep the small band hidden and dry beneath the evergreens. Again they walked in gullies near the trail above to keep away from the sight of the man-bear. But Ainias thought it queer that this hillman Scorpas could discover a mountain hut, even with patches of snow on the ground hiding the trail and with a fresh scent of men, months after the flight of the Spartans. In fact, little was known of this mysterious trader Scorpas, before never named, never seen. Much less did Ainias believe that Gorgos, the flatlander, who had hated the high farm on Helikon, would hide in the up-country. Worse still, for most of the day Ainias saw few signs of goats and so turned back often to Scorpas to question the way and complain there were no longer traces of flocks or shepherds in the shadowy vale.

Most herds were down on flat land with the last of the spring grass and did not come up before Homôloios, so his story about goats and sheep and Gorgos in a shepherd's hut made even less sense. Proxenos was dead. Nêto too. The helots were freed. So there was nothing much left for Ainias to do down here in the south. What happened to him, he confessed, mattered little anymore, though he wanted to learn the fate of Nêto or to kill Gorgos before he left or at least find the bones of Chiôn, or kill Proxenos's killer. The list of his targets, he offered, was endless, after all, and gave him warmth in the spring air on high Taygetos.

The guide was bundled in fleece, with that rough wool hood over his head. Two gray braids hung through to his shoulders, Spartan-style. A man of sixty or so, slump-shouldered Scorpas said he packed in for the shepherds of Taygetos bronze pots and other goods each spring and led back a she-goat or an ewe for the barter. "I am your eyes back here," Scorpas finally called out, "to make sure we see any Spartan ambushers behind. We are near the crest. Be careful since we are ever closer to the border of Lakonia."

Ainias patted his hilt on his sword belt and gripped tighter his spear. Melissos said little, though he grunted under a pack on his back and the reins of a stubborn pony struggling with two shields that hit the brush and boughs of spruce. If there were to be spear work, he would be at the van and take a stab at Scorpas first of all. He knew that much. Melissos had started out the lackey of Mêlon but this day he would have come, slave or not, on his own accord, since the liberation disease had infected him as well—that notion that one kills for something other than money and fame, and someone far worse than oneself. Melissos had long ceased spying out the forts and landscape of the Hellenes and pondered only how the helots had revolted—and why his masters had come south to free them.

Finally in late afternoon of their second day, Scorpas came to the fore and grabbed the arm of Mêlon. The small band spread out in the trees. "There, over there, far in the distance, in the meadow by the outcropping, see the hut? And beware, behind it there is a small cave that ends up on the other side of the peak out to an opening among a stand of spruce. There my friend said your man Gorgos hides. He is afraid of the wild monster of the forest. He won't quite yet leave his cottage until he is forced out. There, there we go. I think dogs guard the house on the ridge. Though I don't see them as I once did."

Ainias was quiet at this. He signaled Melissos to put down the shields and tether the horse. He hadn't wanted to bring the Makedonian, but now he was glad that he had the boy's extra right arm. Nikôn also had been silent for most of the day. He whispered, "Strangers are in this vale. Not all of them enemies. I don't know whether I dreamed this or our dead Nêto told me or I only sense it now. And now I see Scorpas has already slipped off into the trees."

"No matter." Mêlon motioned to Ainias. "Gorgos, not that half-helot, is our business. Now if there is someone alive in that hut, and if he is really our old Gorgos, then we learn whether he is our friend with a shred of good. Or, as you say, he is really the killer Kuniskos of the helots and more still."

Ainias knew better and laughed out loud at that nonsense. "Learn what? Oh, my Mêlon, you always knew your Gorgos in the blink you set eyes on his no-good hide on Helikon. And I would feel better if I had killed our missing Scorpas long before now. All done quietly as well. Fouler still he is now at our backsides. Let me backtrack and grab this man. He can't be a step or two into the forest. Then at spear point he will lead us into the hut or die in his tracks. Better yet, wait till sundown. We can crawl on our bellies into that hut in the darkness and kill Gorgos or whoever is in there in his sleep or pile boughs on his walls and smoke him out."

Scorpas had run off the trail into the forest, since Nikôn in all the talking had lost thought of him as they spied the hut. Right now Mêlon needed every spear arm to confront Gorgos, and could hardly have Ainias chasing Scorpas down the mountain, Melissos drew his own long knife as they all quickened their pace ahead on the flat ground to the hut. He quietly spoke as he walked, "No Scorpas around here to be found. I see our Scorpas has no stomach for iron. He is nowhere to be seen. Maybe my eyes don't spot him, or he is running through the trees to collect his wage for leading us here."

"Yes," Nikôn sighed, "and I am worse. I too took my eye off him for only a moment. He is gone into the shadows. Nêto's Porpax, our Kerberos, is gone too, but on the scent of something else—something in these dark trees, since I haven't heard him bark like this since I found him in the woods near the camp of Kuniskos yelping at the gate. Listen to how he howls on the run. He is gone after the scent of Scorpas, who won't get far from that hound. So we four are alone. Careful now. Kerberos has let all inside the hut know we are here. There was more to this tale than I knew when I ordered you all to come."

The two hoplites approached with leveled spears. Behind them Melissos and Nikôn had blades, choppers with one edge. They all imagined that Scorpas was even now backtracking down Taygetos, perhaps on his way for the coast near Pylos or right down to the gulf. Ahead in the opening was more a stockade than a house. It was dreary and dark, in the shadows of the tall spruces that ringed the building. Flat stones piled as high as a man's shoulders were its sides that supported long beams. On them rested heavy stripped rafters of oak that held up a roof of broken tiles and flat stones. Sparks rose from a fire pit at the back of the house, and there was more smoke from a chimney inside. The light rain was unable to quench the burning in the pit. A small wooden stockade connected the shelter to what looked like a cave. A few goats and a steer were inside the fence.

The two hoplites were no longer crouching among the grass, but stood upright and began making their way on a path that led to the north side of the hut. As they neared, both raised their shields and leveled their spears. Nikôn was behind with Melissos and could see they were almost to the hut. In fact, the four were a hundred paces from the door. There were no windows in the hut but smoke proved someone or something was inside. Gorgos, they remembered, was good enough with a bow or javelin, and there was no proof yet that he was not in the dank hut, and if so no doubt hardly alone. The trees around offered good cover for an ambusher, and the cave even better.

Then a sharp, familiar sort of voice stopped the four who had long been seen and heard. "Hoa, you're late, my Mêlon. Ah yes, the son of Malgis returned. Are you so rich from your winnings in Lakonia that you forgot to fetch your slave who has loyally awaited you these long months?" It was Gorgos. Gorgos was alive, after all. And now he threw open the door and waved them in.

Mêlon wondered whether this was the Kuniskos of the fur collar and forked beard of the house of Antikrates who had cut down Erinna and killed his Nêto, or the aged helot Gorgos in rags, the harmless broke-back servant of Helikon that had stoked his fires and cooked his meat—or both. It was Gorgos, that much was sure. He was bare-chested, even in the spring mountain air despite the cold drizzle, with only a small tunic wrapped around his privates. "I was asleep. So I needed wakening and your dog did that well enough." At that he walked a few paces from the cabin toward them, palms out and open. Mêlon kept silent at his appearance, since he had not seen him in this year and a half after Leuktra, not since the day they had wagonned together to the battle.

Maybe this half-naked man was the killer Sinis whom the villagers in the foothills said had a dangerous voice and a new shape for each day to lull his victims to drop their swords. He wasn't the man-bear, since Gorgos loved his Spartans and did not hang them by the toes from the forests of Taygetos. True, in winter on the farm Mêlon had never seen much of the helot without his tattered long cape, and even in summer he had worn two tunics, and often a hood. The muscles on this man suggested someone half his helot's age. Yet his voice was surely that of the Gorgos he had known, though his words were longer and more delicate and with a Doric tinge. So was this an apparition?

Kuniskos turned around again, pointing to the hut. "Oh yes, the answer to your doubts is I am Kuniskos and I am also your Gorgos—or more than your Gorgos of old, I should say. You slave liberators should welcome a freed helot in his pride. Come in. Come in. There's a chill out here from the rain, at least I feel it on my bare back. Anyway before I napped I made sure to have a surprise for you, or maybe two or three of them. Do you remember our Nêto? Yes? Or have you gone helot-freeing without a thought of your old love back on Helikon, now that you build great cities and talk of democracy and no more the small folk like us."

Nêto?

"Oh yes, your Nêto. Well, she may not be quite dead, at least not yet. Or then again, she may be gone by now. Let me go on a bit about her. She is here, or at least something like her is. Inside, inside as I said. So come in, come in—look under the table when you enter and see if she breathes with that iron collar on her neck or maybe I replaced it with a rope. My, how age has clouded my memory. Yes, just a rope now. Or maybe the mind loses its edge up here in the high country. Dogs need leashes of some sort. I think she's better than any dog I have. Down here they called me the little dog, so I should know. I'm not so sure she breathes with her hood and limp, and that pretty branded cheek. She is copying our gimpy master these days and has been quiet the last two in her night trances and murmuring. Yes, Mêlon, if her heart still beats, her leg is worse than yours—and likewise the work of Sparta. But come in. Let's pull her out from under the table, take off her cape, and together see what's left. I'm heating up some black barley broth out back. Your servant has set a table like in the old days. Though my new house is less than what I enjoyed below on Ithômê. It surely isn't like our shed on Helikon where I slept in the dung with your animals out back. I want company. There are black rumors of a wolf-man or shape-changer out here. By Zeus, a monster in fur with an iron club who eats Spartans and tidies up his dinner plate by stringing up their bones. Or have you heard? Yes, beware you of the man-bear loose on Taygetos. How did you get by him to reach me?"

Melissos grabbed Mêlon's arm. "Don't go in. We have room out here to fight, Master, plenty of room to spear and stab, since this vagabond will have others like him lurking in the corners and rafters. He's lying about Nêto. She's dead, months ago he killed her. Or better yet, let me and Ainias go in first. Nikôn can guard our rear."

Mêlon would have praised this Makedonian boy for his growing sense, and taken his advice as well. But he had heard "Nêto," and wanted to find her or her body—and then kill all who had a hand in her torture or death. So he went in, spear ready, and all three followed. The room ahead was dark with a weak lamp light on a table. The four were not sure Gorgos was alone. The murmurs inside below the table were of a dying or sick dog, at least at first so they thought. But as they reached the long table, it leapt up. Alive? Or at least they thought this caped thing was something close to alive. Nêto? The four pulled it up.

It was Nêto and alive!

They could see their old Nêto beneath the dingy blanket, and the scabs and scars. Mêlon embraced her, as Ainias kept his eye on Gorgos. Melissos helped Mêlon quickly cut off her binds. Nikôn kept his blade in the face of Gorgos as they all stepped back to the wall. Mêlon grabbed some wine as he passed the table and soon had her talking and wide-eyed. She was a lot more alive than she looked, and was soon pointing to the door and crying at the same time. "No worry, Nêto, no worry ever again." Then he sat her down gently and put himself between her and Gorgos, alongside Ainias.

The Stymphalian called the old man out. "Gorgos, you speak well for a man about to be speared, for one who invited in four of his executioners." Ainias then lowered his spear as they all backed up to the corner of the hut and prepared to charge the helot. But first Ainias grazed Gorgos with his spear tip. "I never liked you, helot. We are here to fetch or kill you for what you have done to the Messenians and to our Nêto and to our Erinna. I prefer to end you here; the others down in new Messenê want to hang you, no doubt. Save us all much labor and come with us back to Ithômê so you can sit in the dock of the Messenians and hear their justice. They will swing you up for ten days above the Arkadian Gate until your bald head rots off."

Mêlon kept quiet at that. He slowly made his way around to the corner of the dank room behind Kuniskos, with Nêto up and shuffling at his rear next to the wall, her hands on his shoulders. Nikôn felt for his sword. Melissos stayed near the threshold with Ainias. Both had iron ready. Kuniskos had his eye on all of them, all the time. Nêto was shaky, but growing stronger from the wine and her hatred of Gorgos. She hissed over Mêlon's shoulder. "He's alone, though he wants you to think his army is outside. Kill him and we go home." Mêlon nodded and was ready to spear him.

Then the helot laughed at her. "Put those points away. Of course, I am alone. Your Gorgikos is tired of the slur of Kuniskos. I am no puppy dog, but a dragon man, a Gorgon of Helikon, watcher and protector of the farm of Malgis. The gods wish me back home on Helikon. You hate me because I killed your Erinna, yes, that red-headed Medusa sent to kill me. Was I supposed to stare at her and turn to stone? Gorgikos the loyal hound is to be killed because he bit first the master's son who wanted to kick open his head? Master, at least give thanks to me. I both kept your dear little Nêto alive and yet ensured you need worry no more that she might like other men far better than she did you in your dotage and lameness—especially with the passing of that faker Proxenos of Plataia. Let us eat, since I know you know your way around this hut. I wager you had the same dream about it that I and your late Chiôn once did—since we met here before in our sleep, as you know from the nighttime shades that Hypnos and his son Morpheus sent to us alike."

Mêlon ignored him and was wondering if he could stab this Kuniskos before Ainias the spear-tosser impaled him. The Thespian also noticed that, in fact, Gorgos was right. He thought that he had seen the table before in his night visions and even on the wagon ride to Leuktra. He also wondered whether, as in the apparitions, there were also two doors to the hut, not one, as it had seemed when they first entered. So he looked into the shadows at the back of the long dwelling, and in fact thought he saw some sort of a smaller rear door.

Then Kuniskos seemed hurt and wounded and so sat sunken back into his leather-woven chair. Then his voice lowered and he was almost once more what they remembered of the broken-down Gorgos nearing his seventh ten-years on Helikon. He pointed his fork at his friends and softly, slowly told them the way of their world to come. So there would be peace and a quiet descent with him as their prisoner back to Messenia after all. "The great game is over. My Spartans are broken, a race humbled by lesser folk by far. My helot people are free, as I suppose they should be. You have forgotten. I, whom you slur as Kuniskos, I too am a Messenian, born one, bred one, and so should be happy at their freedom. Even here I pick up things from my messenger, my dear Scorpidion. Yes, I heard that your Chiôn could not stop his killing on Helikon. Who else could have hung up Medios or drowned Thrattos, my friends and neighbors. So he died an outlaw now, a killer of the old and weak? Or was it all on your prompt, Master, who wishes me to face the law of bloodletting? Who is the killer and who in contrast pulls wounded boys out of battle at great risk to himself? And my, my, how everyone seems to have passed on."

This fluent Kuniskos was for a blink confusing his old friends with his long new way of talking as Lord Kuniskos. "Are you four alone? Just four? No more? So few to come so far? Three with good legs in your new band, and two sadly now with not? I thought I spied five of you as you came down the path. Or were there shadows in the woods? Were there not five or perhaps six of you? So many to fetch—or is it to kill—your Gorgikon. No Alkidamas here? I hear he is never far from you all but always safely distant when iron is drawn. Of course, Epaminondas stays warm back in my fort, too wise to tramp up here in the spring rain. And where is my Scorpas, always the loyal messenger to the end?"

Mêlon kept his spear pointed at his helot. "Ready your things. We have a night of walking down the mountain still. Epaminondas wants you to face the *diskastêria* of the Messenians. Down the mountain I will settle up with you for Nêto and Lophis, if the court of the Messenians leaves me a few scraps."

"Calm, calm down, Master, my master. Nêto no doubt will tell you soon enough that she lives due to me. I kept her safe in my fort. I tried to save Lophis, at Leuktra, though he was near dead when I picked him up from the gore of battle. How could I return to the Boiotians when your Chiôn swore he would kill me after the battle? I had no choice but to cross the battlefield, since for all my babble I loved your Lophis and you too in my way. I yelled in vain to my Lichas to let him live. I, no one else, dressed out his body. I, Gorgos, left my own good money on the road south for the priestess Kallista at Kreusis to keep him safe from the birds and dogs. I was the good servant, and you are angry only because I the lowly now am free. May Zeus bless Lichas who alone let me live free, the true, the only liberator among you."

Mêlon stopped for a moment, and thought he heard traces of the old Gorgos in the talk of Lord Kuniskos. Indeed the helot was slumped even further in his chair, and seemed wrinkled as he always had been. Yes, he was almost the helot of Helikon once more—tired, old, flabby even. He had a tear in his right eye and slobber at the side of his mouth. Maybe he had tried to save Lophis after all?

The myth floated away in a blink with a shout of "Liar!" Nêto shrieked again, "Liar!" She may not have looked any more like the helot maiden of Helikon, but her voice was the same and she dragged her foot and closed on Kuniskos. "Liar. Dogfaced liar. You killed Lophis as if with your own hand. I know your hands that snuffed the life out of Erinna in the house of Antikrates. You can tell the jurymen all that—even more when we get down the mountain, about the dead Messenians hung up on trees, and their women sent to the Kaiadas after your play. You will drink the hemlock poison or they will throw you into the pit alive, as you did to hundreds of our own—or you will hang for the buzzards. We will stone your poisoned corpse, then hang it from the new north gate before throwing it as *bora* to the dogs and crows."

Kuniskos now stared her down. "Jurymen? Trial? Aren't you talking of your own day in court to come in Thebes, you renegades who are this year outlaws, the real lawbreakers of Boiotia?" Kuniskos shouted and all the pretense of the old good Gorgos vanished now for good. "Such hypocrites you are. You slave-owning liberators of helots." Kuniskos could not stop. The spell was broken once his tears had not swayed any of his guests. "How do your helot folk govern themselves or keep the Spartans out without hiring Epaminondas each season? When you are through with your fun under Ithômê and all go home, who will clean up this mess, govern these wild tribes? Who gives you the power to free anyone, you who owned me, the better man, the helot who wants freedom from the likes of you and your kind? Do you plan to move down here to watch them, as if parents who must change the soiled clothes of their half-grown children?"

Nêto cut him off. "Liar, liar you are, old man. Liar on our Helikon. Traitor of your own kind, sell-out to the killers of Agesilaos." Then she stepped up and slapped the palm of Kuniskos, thinking how these hands had squeezed Erinna and tightened the bonds on her neck. The other four went silent as they watched instead the right arm of Kuniskos, who was now up and out of his chair. As Mêlon knew from the weak lamplight, the long narrow cottage was far larger than it seemed to the eye when outside. Maybe twenty or thirty paces to the rear, eyed again the second door of his dreams—now noticed in the dark shadows as well by the sharp eye of Ainias, who usually scanned all rooms on entry as if he were on a crest over the battlefield.

Suddenly three tall shapes appeared there at the back of this single room. They swung the rear door wide open. At the same time, before Melissos could yell out, a spear tip pushed him back off the front threshold as another two men and a woman came in from the front door. Mêlon's band had Gorgos in front of them and Spartans on both their right and left, altogether seven to their five.

Melissos grabbed the hand of Mêlon. "The cave, master, the cave, they came out of the cave." The rescuers were trapped. Both doorways were barred by tall men in armor—Spartans who were veterans of the *kryptes*, and raven-haired Elektra herself, who stood blocking the light without entering all the way into the hut.

"Meet, Master Mêlon, my Spartan friends." Kuniskos laughed and waved with each hand to the six Spartans at the two entries. "And you, my Lakonian friends, this is my master of the long whip, lame Mêlon. He is the killer of our king Kleombrotos. Over there is his new lackey Ainias, another rat in our trap who smelled some sweet cheese up here on Taygetos. They claim this mercenary thought up the ruse of attacking you from the left at Leuktra. That other wild boy from the far north does not matter. Forget the skinny helot—the one they call Nikôn. He will run when the blood flows, like all helots. Nêto over there who barked this winter under my table for a bone, whether rabbit or mine, why she prides herself the mouthpiece of the helots—yes, that brand-face in rags that stands there across the table. I doubt this time she will find a way out of my hands as before."

The Spartans ignored the big talk of their Kuniskos and watched instead the hands of Ainias and Mêlon. There was not much room to move. Mêlon clinched his spear. Ainias backed against the wall. All five bunched up. The two hoplites shielded Melissos and Nikôn behind them, who had only their blades. Nêto in the middle of the tiny phalanx picked up the walking stick of Kuniskos. Ainias also drew his cleaver, and quickly handed his spear to Mêlon, who had Bora in his other hand. Like the Stymphalian, Mêlon had dropped his shield outside on the path before the threshold—not because either one trusted Kuniskos, but thinking they would have no room in the hut for the wide swings of the willow shield that had brought so many low at Leuktra. There was a pause before the fighting. A gruff, harsh voice of a man in the shadows took over and stepped into the lamplight of the hut, speaking more like an Athenian than an ephor of Sparta. It was Lichas himself.

"Old Chôlopous. So we meet again, the half-dead Mêlon, son of the long-dead Malgis. You are the father of the dead boy at Leuktra? All has turned out as promised. Or do you remember me? We first met on your farm when you had your first set of teeth, when you ran under your arbors before I could cut off your tiny head—and at Koroneia, and yet once more at the fight at the Nemea. On that night at Leuktra, and then on your recent visit to burn my farm at Sparta. My, my, my friend, how we've grown old together."

This tall but stooped Spartan stepped even farther forward near Kuniskos while the others stayed put by the doors. Lichas was ageless like his Kuniskos, and likewise he felt no burdens of age or time. In similar fashion, Lichas felt freed by his long years and the end of Messenia and the idea he could do at last whatever he wished—which for Lichas always meant to kill without penalty whoever he wanted. Lichas continued. "I speak for a bit before you bleed. I wanted Pelopidas and Epaminondas to visit our hut and maybe Alkidamas as well, so with a clean cut today we could finish this Messenian mess once and for all and get our boys back down over there where they belong. Only the hungriest rats scampered up here, I see. Even the best trapper must put up with the rodents who clutter his nets. I brought today my son Antikrates, who killed so many of yours at Leuktra. More of our friends are here as well. You say you will take our helot back down the mountain? Oh no, no. Not this time, Master Mêlon. You will go down no mountain—not even a hill, not even dead. Where is your proud Epaminondas or Pelopidas—or even one of those brutes from the islands here to rescue you? We had soup here for both. Your islander, we hear, has gone feral. He flees the blood guilt on your Helikon. If he comes up here—and he won't because he's dead—by now he would have met our man-bear who bites the throat of all lone wanderers on Taygetos."

Then his wife Elektra stepped to his side, proud with her long hair, some tresses braided and some dangling out the sides of her helmet. She boasted, "Too much talk, my Lichas. Kill them before that branded helot over there puts a chant or spell on us. Let me cut her tongue out before this Nêto bewitches us all. Or let my boy Thibrachos have a taste of her first."

The Spartan had drawn his sword, a shiny *xiphos* with both edges gleaming in the candlelight. Elektra had a black *pelekus*, a battle-ax given to her by the king himself, and she swung if far better than did her son

Thibrachos. The outnumbered band crouched and made ready for the rush, Mêlon and Ainias still covering the flanks, Nikôn and Melissos between them three steps back with drawn long knives—and Nêto in reserve with an oak staff. She put both hands on the shaft and looked for an opening. The five had backed flush against the wall, as the Spartans by the two doors covered the escapes. They could at least take down Gorgos, and maybe even Elektra before their deaths. These were armored men, Sparta's best; and Mêlon's side was without bronze—and with boy and a lame woman.

"Come over here, Mêlon. I want you to join your father and son, so you can all boast in Hades that Lichas sent you there." Lichas talked more than a Spartan should, talked more than he ever had, as he shifted his weight from foot to foot to find the right moment to stab. "If you throw down your weapons, I promise a good enough burial. Antikrates over there, my best son, took out that fool of yours who built walls. What was his name, boy? Yes, yes, the soft Plataian rich man Proxenos? The grand thinker whose belly you cut open when that mob of northerners stormed our tower."

There was to be no parley with Lichas. He meant to cut them all down and wanted them to know it before they fell. No quarter. Elektra started her ululation. Still Mêlon called out, "If you have an ax, swing, Spartan woman, don't talk."

Lichas had a final word. "You have it wrong, all of you. God has made every man a slave. Only a man, if he's worth anything, makes himself free." Lichas wanted to get closer, to cut with the sword and taste the blood flying in the air as it dotted his face. Kuniskos pulled from the rafters a cleaver and backed aside to let his friend charge through. The blade had been hidden above the table right near his head. He had taken the idea of hiding it from the dead Erinna. He had hoped to place it at the throat of Nêto and drag her outside for some final sport—or to strangle her slowly and give her his death whisper.

At the back of the cottage, facing his father on the far side, Antikrates pointed his spear with the underhand grip. He and his two henchmen had been hiding in the cave when Mêlon arrived and had quietly sneaked out to block the rear door once the visitors were inside. Lichas, Elektra, and his retainer had come around through the forest path to plug the main entrance.

"That damn Scorpas and his phantom goat-man—and without a helot patrol to be found," Nikôn cried. "We are surrounded, with nowhere to go." Then Melissos pointed toward Lichas. "Spartans fight in the sun. Let us out. Duel in the open air. Kill or die face-to-face like men should." Melissos could have run, having no part in war against the tall Spartans. But no words of retreat or surrender came out. Instead, he decided to stand his ground, blade in hand, here with Mêlon, Ainias, Nêto, and Nikôn—and for something more than the love of gore or a Spartan scalp.

# CHAPTER 34

# The Old Breed

No way out, Melissos knew. Still, if the henchmen of Lichas thought to kill a royal of Makedon, a son no less of Amyntas, then they would at least learn it was no easy thing. Mêlon covered Melissos to keep the youth safe until the last. The five Spartan men wore full armor. The near-naked Kuniskos was more than a match for the staff of slow-foot Nêto. Elektra would have to fight him for her head, or, better yet, let her Thibrachos have first claim on her.

Lichas paused at the Makedonian boy's plea and scoffed, "Leave, foreigner. You are nothing to me. We kill the rest as they are, and burn them up. You go down the mountain and tell all of the funeral smoke you saw." Melissos stayed quiet and right by his master Mêlon, no longer the hostage but the loyal man of the Malgidai, as much a Boiotian as any in Thebes.

The long talk ended and finally Lichas raised his slashing blade of black iron, to cut down this Makedonian upstart first. "You, you . . ." Then came a loud crash, as if the rafters had been ripped off the house. Lichas was cut off before "*humeis*" fully left his lips. The Spartan tottered, blood spurted out his nose. Then only for a moment he let out a wild shriek as he vomited more blood. His helmet flew off his head as he fell face first to the stone floor, with a long spear stuck firm into the base of his skull, cast from twenty paces outside the door. Just like that, Lichas, of forty years in the first rank, killer of a hundred and more—he just fell over, a man, not a god, after all.

The spear throw had come from outside the threshold. Was Ares or Apollo in his armor roaming Taygetos? No mortal with mere blood in his veins could fell such a peer with a single throw, surely not tall Lichas, whom the prophets said was sacrosanct and immune from the blades of free men. There he lay in a growing pool of red, on the ground gurgling and twitching about, a spear point gone almost out through his mouth. A moment later his killer was at the threshold and leapt over the fallen Lichas. The Spartans were frozen in place, stunned as the stranger burst upon them. Then he stabbed the retainer of Lichas, tall Lakrates. That Spartan too toppled over. The sword stroke hit well above the shoulders and came out through the upper throat. Was the house under attack by Pelopidas and the Sacred Band?

No. A sole figure had come through the front doorway and stood over the two bodies. He was deliberate in his sword and spear work, and now almost motionless as he looked about. A wild dog barked behind him. The stranger still paused and then finally stomped on the corpses and let out a piercing war cry as he at last turned toward Elektra. He picked her up by the back of the neck with his good right arm, and then swung her head against the hut wall—three, four, and five times before she quit her pleas. "Lichas! Help, Lichas. My Lichas!" So ended the granddaughter of Agesilaos. She had come to kill the leashed Nêto and earn five hundred silver owls from the strongbox of Phrynê—and yet never got in a single swing of her grandfather's black ax. Chiôn of Taygetos finally stopped slamming Elektra into the mud brick, as he looked up at the three Spartans at the other end of the cabin turning to flee. Should he first deal with Kuniskos, and then go after the other assassins? He yelled to Nikôn to the side as he threw down the pulp of Elektra and carefully stepped ahead. "Kill Gorgos. Kill him now—and I'll get the others." As he stopped, Chiôn punched Gorgos in the gut and sent him stumbling backward.

So broke in Chiôn of the good right arm, long thought dead here in the south in the tumult of liberation, always on the scent of his Nêto whom at last he found to be alive in the remote hut of Gorgos. He for weeks had followed Gorgos's trail on Taygetos, waiting for this moment to finish what he had promised. Now Chiôn lumbered on through the room, half-crouching to avoid jabs to come if the three Spartans ahead should choose to turn back and fight. The wolf-dog followed to guard his

Nêto. Mêlon immediately turned to take on the Spartans at the rear door and kept himself between their spears and Nêto.

Behind Chiôn in the din, Kuniskos stood up again, still off balance from the blow to his midriff. "Get the slave one-arm. Where is my Lichas? Lichas. Lichas. Lich—." He too was cut off. Nikôn and Melissos in near unison slammed their blades—wide choppers that were hard to poke with, but made a larger hole if they got through flesh—into Kuniskos's lower gut. The man had been made dizzy by Chiôn's blow, and his head was still crackling with fire, when he had turned to his left to warn the Spartans on the other side and fell to the floor cursing them. Nikôn was then atop the dying helot even as he tumbled to the dirt. He plunged his knife five more times into the back of Gorgos to keep him silent. At the same time Nêto, weak, lame, and dizzy still, took up her stick with both hands and clubbed the bald head. Melissos jumped on him as well. He had no beard, but he had once learned in Makedon to kill with a careful jab to the big neck vein, and his thin arm was as strong as any ephebe's in Boiotia.

In a wild frenzy, her stick now broken, Nêto kept thrashing with her nails and fists at the backside of the dying Kuniskos. She was tearing his two braids right off the sides of his head. "Helot to helot, old man," she kept repeating as Nikôn rolled her off. "Helot to helot. For Erinna and all the rest. For Erinna. For Erinna. For Chiôn. For Lophis. For our Proxenos."

Here ended the helot Kuniskos, once the terror of the Messenians, who had taken off so many heads and was about to lose his own. He was once the good servant of the Malgidai, but now pierced by Nêto, the freed woman of Helikon, and by Nikôn and Melissos, he bled out his life force on the floor of a dirty hut where the goats and cows of Taygetos sought shelter. Nêto had known, even with rope and chain these many months, that he was to die by the hand of a Messenian, but the goddess had told her only that—not that Nikôn or she herself would strike. Gorgos had wanted his way one last time with Nêto, but she got hers with him instead.

Kerberos, splattered in the gore of Lichas, took over and tore at the neck of the Kuniskos whose scent Keberos he now remembered from Helikon, along with the kicks he had endured. The wolf-dog locked onto him hard and bit so hard on his neck that the hound ripped off the head of Kuniskos from his body. Nêto stumbled up and let out a shriek—or was it laughter? "Pull it off for your dead Sturax. Look. The head cutter has his own cut by a dog, by a dog like him." She let out her war cry and like a Bacchant grabbed the head of Gorgos and threw it over at the battered corpse of Elektra.

Amid the killing of the four Spartans, Ainias and Mêlon had turned to stab their way through the back entrance. They were eager to catch the three remaining Spartans who had backed out into the open pen and were turning to run through the stockade. Chiôn now was heading to the rear of the hut to join his friends for the final fight, but Mêlon first hit the backpedaling Spartan, a stab below his war belt into the groin. He was a youth of twenty seasons or so on his first patrol—Thibrachos by name, son of Elektra herself from her first marriage to the brother of Lichas.

This fool Thibrachos for a moment had turned back around to fight after all, once he saw the brains of his mother splattered over the flat stones of the opposite wall. He had his eye on the slashing sword of the approaching Chiôn in the distance and never saw in the shadows Mêlon's jab with Bora that went in above hip and brought out the black blood from his insides, along with his guts as well. Though the thrust was underhand, Mêlon sent the sharp iron right under the bronze, three palms deep into the Spartan's midriff. Thibrachos died too, not more than twenty paces from Kuniskos—the fifth of the ambushers to fall before any had a chance to strike back.

As Thibrachos crumpled, the last two Spartans had tried to turn and flee out to the courtyard beyond. Ainias was quick with his blade and stabbed the second Spartan from the side. The doomed hoplite had tripped over his cloak and for a moment only flashed his unarmored flank. That was enough for Ainias, who sent the iron right into his armpit, and the sword tip up toward the heart, lifting him off the ground. This second Spartan was a better man than young Thibrachos and was known as the chopper Klôpis, son of Deinon, and the enforcer to Lord Kuniskos in Messenia. As he fell back from the spear-thrust of Ainias, Mêlon came up behind and jabbed his spear butt through the back of his neck, and the Spartan hit the floor.

Chiôn for a second time halted in slow walk toward the back door, as his friends finished with his last two targets. Now in greater fury still, whether at his friends or enemies, the freedman suddenly headed through the back courtyard as he caught sight of Antikrates, the last Spartan alive. But Antikrates was a wiser sort than the two firebrands at his side. He had spied his planned way of escape the moment his father had fallen. Antikrates knew the perfidy of Gorgos—who had tolerated no rival to his return to Messenia—and so long ago had planned an exit should Kuniskos and his Klôpis try to kill him as well in their bloodlust. Antikrates had thirty paces at least on Chiôn, heading through the pen to the mouth of the cave and safety. A wiser Chiôn of two good arms and of earlier times in the high vineyard of Helikon would have stopped, and with raised shield defended himself from a spear toss.

But like all of the old breed in the hut, friend and enemy alike, Chiôn held life less dear here at the final reckoning—and more so for Chiôn with the loss of an arm, the deaths of Proxenos and Lophis, and the maiming of Nêto. Without breastplate and shield, Chiôn reckoned that he could catch the better-armored Spartan before he cleared the fences and was into the mountain. Why not? His legs and chest were tired but still stronger than most others'. And this Antikrates looked fat from his year after Leuktra, no longer the same man who had saved his father and the body of their king. Chiôn went right on past Ainias and Mêlon, who were finishing their iron work with the two henchmen of Antikrates. He began to trot with his sword in his good right arm stuck out in front of him for the final jab. Chiôn quickened his pace, and indeed closed much of the distance, but the running Antikrates was too far ahead, the mouth of the cave far too close.

Even Kerberos could not reach the Spartan. Just then at the entrance to the mountain Antikrates himself had a wild idea. This Chiôn was one-armed and slower than he thought—and no doubt spent. So the son of Lichas turned and for a moment saw that he would be safer, now and in years to come, to attack his nemesis than to keep fleeing into the cave. Antikrates raised his spear and cast at the onrushing Thespian. This was not a light willow javelin, but a heavy cornel for stabbing with its broad iron head, like the spear Chiôn had just flung into Lichas. It took a man of Antikrates's size to hurl the long shaft with any power. Still, his pursuer was an easy target, large and without armor, coming on without balance. Chiôn had no left arm for a shield—nor even a spear any longer to bat away the thrust. It was back inside the hut, buried deep into the head of Lichas.

Chiôn was using only the sword, an old blade that Mêlon had given him on Helikon that he had torn back out from the dead Lakrates. Chiôn saw the spear and swung at the incoming tip. Too late. Antikrates's throw hit him under the chin. The iron went deep right through Chiôn's neck above the left collarbone, not far from his old wound at Leuktra. The tip broke through on the other side, as the weight of the shaft itself brought Chiôn to a stumble.

Antikrates stopped for an instant and announced to the sky that he had killed Chiôn, the bane of the Spartans. Kerberos froze and then turned back to shield his downed master. With a wild yell of triumph at his felling of Chiôn, the better man, Antikrates ran through the cave on his way to Sparta and fame. He reckoned up his kill, bellowing *"Apektenon Chiôna, apektenon ton doulon, ton megan, ton doulon tôn Malgidôn."* Even as he yelled, he had bigger thoughts held quiet in his chest, for he was wild in his escape and his freedom. "I run free of Chiôn. Free of my father Lichas who had lived too long anyway. Free and richer with my orchards and vines from the snake Elektra. Better they're all dead and the old age of Sparta as well. I will live for better kills yet, kill better than this Chiôn. It will be sung a hundred years from now in new, better Sparta, that I Antikrates killed the best pigs that Boiotia offered. I kill today so I can kill more tomorrow. I killed Chiôn of Helikon. I will kill his master soon enough and then Epaminondas too."

Such were his mad unspoken thoughts, but those behind heard only one refrain echoing back out the mouth of the cave: *"Chiôna apektenon, Chiôna . . ."* I killed Chiôn. Chiôn was down amid the dung. He had tried to grab the fence rung before sinking back into the muck of the pigsty. Chiôn had been foretold to be a killer of the royal ones of Sparta. For his part Antikrates likewise, the gods said, was to live on to kill the best man of Boiotia. These two prophecies dueled. Chiôn lost out. Perhaps the goddess Artemis forsook this believer in Pythagoras, ruing his lack of good meat on her sacrifice table. Perhaps she figured the slave had already killed enough of the royal guard at Leuktra, as she had promised. So the Messenians later would argue to explain the death of the godlike Chiôn and the win of the coward Antikrates. Had Chiôn not sent his spear into Lichas and killed Lakrates, or had he not kept smashing Elektra long after she gave up the ghost, or had he chosen to rest on his laurels while Mêlon and Ainias finished all three of the Spartans off, he would have come back to the farm with his master, once more the heroic pair returning from their defeat of the Spartans.

Yet Antikrates was relish, no more. Chiôn had gone wild anyway on Taygetos and was no more Damô's farmer. He had long since finished with Helikon and would leave Mêlon with no enemies at his back, and Damô and the boys safe with Myron from the likes of Dirkê and her henchmen. In a moment Mêlon and Ainias rushed past the dying Chiôn and chased the Spartan into the mouth of the cave. Antikrates had peeled off his armor and was sprinting ever deeper into the mountain. All they heard was that distant echo off the walls: "Chiôn. I killed Chiôn."

By the time Ainias and Mêlon reemerged from the tunnel and ran back to the hut, Chiôn was white. Nêto was wobbly on her legs and now had come out of the hut. Fury had revived her, that and the blood of Gorgos. She had not dared pull the spearhead out of Chiôn, since it had an ugly barb that had barely broken through the skin on his backside. Ainias somehow broke the shaft off at the socket. This time no hot poker he knew could close such a hole. The wound was a half palm or more wide and showed a ripped vein and blood squirting over Chiôn's torso. Nêto tore off a strip of her cloak and stuffed all of it into the mess around the spear socket. At the sight of the old ugly lambda brand burned into the flesh of the poxy cheek of Chiôn, Nêto shrieked out at the hated Taygetos.

Chiôn whispered after her yells died down. "That damned ship. Five days lost. Our Nêto warned me of water. No fear of the sea." He caught a breath. "Gorgos, Lichas no more, Master. Antikrates won. Too late for Erinna. Up in the ice and snow, to pay back for Lophis, for Proxenos, for our Nêtikon. But Nêtikon, our Nêtikon lives. And Damô and the boys."

He was gasping. Then his eyes went shut, and he sputtered out, "Live on Mêlon. Last of the Malgidai, last of the way Hellas once was."

Chiôn went quiet. He smiled at his beaked Kêr who was on the corner on the hut's roof shrieking, ready to swoop. If she neared, he would strangle her as his last victim, even as the two tumbled into Hades. His chest heaved up and down with the deep, methodical breathing of death's embrace that not even he could escape. Chiôn slipped off with visions of the evening at the lever of the press and the reflection of his master's face in the pond above the farm.

Mêlon whispered an epitaph. "I will hunt this Antikrates. That I promise." But even in his furor Mêlon promised nothing about killing the fleeing Spartan, since no Boiotian had managed that yet. And now he was gone and headed down the slopes to Sparta.

Chiôn was far distant, with both good arms, skimming the moss out of the pond on the farm, as Damô called for him to go up to the tower and gaze with her down at the grids of their trees and vines of Helikon. Nêto was skipping on the farm path, her deer legs as long as they were hale. His lips froze at last in a smile that did not end. He could leave this forest after all, and at last go home to his high, his sunny vineyard.

Not far away, the young Klôpis stirred and staggered to get up, woken by the echoes of the wailing of victory from Lichas's son deep in the cave. Then his ragged cloak caught a fence rail. Ainias had stabbed the brute only with a single blow, deep, but not enough to drain his blood. So there was some beating for a while longer in the heart of the Spartan. The keen eye of Nikôn missed him. Hatred gave this Klôpis power still, even though he had been groaning in the dirt. Klôpis thought it enough to win some glory for his one son back home, perhaps soon to be made into song by his dead father's killing of Mêlon of Helikon. Half-dead Klôpis thought he could rise to spear one or two of the four as they crouched over Chiôn, or maybe tear out dead Chiôn's windpipe as a trophy.

Fool. He had hardly neared Chiôn, when Kerberos let out a howl and tore at his ankle, his jaws locked fast. Nêto rolled over to him, and she shrieked with her own war cry, shorter and louder "*Alalê. Alalê.*" Kerberos held the dying man fast. Nêto got to the side of the staggering Klôpis, and then plunged her long knife between his thigh and the back of his knee. Ainias finished him off with a wide slash to his neck that nearly took the head of the head-cutter Klôpis off altogether. "I cannot even kill a man right any more," he offered.

"Get him off, get him off. Get that dung off our Chiôn," Nêto shrieked back. "That filth won't touch our Chiôn." She hit the dead man with her stick. It was all the two could do to tear off Kerberos. He was again the wolf on Kithairon, eager to chew on this head and take it over near that of Gorgos. As Nêto's rage subsided, Ainias turned to Mêlon. "Are we so short of men that we need women and those with one good arm? Are we so sightless that we did not see what he planned all along—or did we wish Chiôn to do all along what we said we did not?"

Now that they were surrounded by dead Spartans, Mêlon relaxed and answered slowly. "Chiôn lived as he wished, with faith in his One

God. He could not—like you, Ainias, as well—live in peace, not a man like this, knowing that worse enemies walked free in Sparta and that Lichas and his son had paid no penalty for the good men they had killed at Leuktra and the more they planned to kill down here."

Nêto was crying. She leaned on the fence. Her cloak was soaked with the blood of Gorgos and Chiôn. "I saw him days ago on a ship, on the water near the Isthmos. His face was always hidden in the shore mist. Our Chiôn wandered cold and dirty on the mountain, always to our aid."

Ainias calmed. "We will take him back to Ithômê in the fashion of a king, and burn him as first citizen of a free Messenia. He saved us all at Leuktra and here on Taygetos. He killed the best of the Spartans even after he saw the Aegean." Mêlon could not speak any more, for Chiôn was his second self, a man he cared for more than any but Nêto, so he turned and readied a pyre. He dragged the twice-struck corpse of Klôpis back into the cottage, its head trailing in the dirt, hanging by a sliver of tendon attached still to the spine. Then in fury Mêlon shuffled back out of the hut and with Ainias carried Thibrachos back in as well and threw him on the table above Klôpis.

Nikôn groaned, "That's two and the worst are to come." Mêlon grabbed the heels of Lichas across the room and dragged him over, then bent, picked him up, and dumped him on Klôpis. His eyes were closed, but Lichas in his greed kept some of the life breath inside his chest, beat off a Kêr, and sputtered, "Hit only from the back I was. I killed that man at Leuktra. I killed the slave at Leuktra. A *daimôn*, not a slave." Then he spat out a final boast, "From the back I die—*tethnêka*. You all will miss me."

Mêlon scoffed at the dead Spartan. "Fool. Chiôn was no slave. Remember that as you are winged away to the other side, foul man." Then he put his hand around the throat of Lichas. The bane of the Thebans was already gone, gone with the truth that it was a free Chiôn who had sent him to his reckoning, gone with some choked-out noise that sounded like another faint "you miss me." Meanwhile Melissos was busy and had pulled Lakrates over by the helmet crest, his chin strap holding the drag well enough. There were two Spartans on the long low table, two below on the floor nearby with the body of Gorgos and his head. Ainias blurted out, "Antikrates is halfway to Sparta now with big talk of killing Chiôn, always to boast over the better man. The stink of Hades is on that Spartan. Or maybe he's no Spartan, but one of those *daimones* who have a secret door to go in and out of the darkness below with ease. Maybe he was the man-bear, since he knows the caves on this mountain better than any."

Nikôn answered. "Nêto warned of the son of Lichas who lapped up the poisonous milk of Kuniskos. I fear he will do far worse than boast of killing our Chiôn. He has a bad date with one of us, or maybe many to come."

The trunk of Gorgos was lying face down in two large puddles of blood. "He bled red," Ainias offered. "I thought he would leak black like what has dribbled down his legs."

Mêlon was already dragging over Elektra by the braids and stopped to grab a wider grip of hair from the backside of her head. The weight vanished from his hand, as he pulled off a thick black horse-hair wig. Below him fell the bald Amazon, old and wrinkled, her hairless skull hitting the stones, with its teeth all knocked out. Mêlon picked her up and tossed her on top of her husband Lichas, royal granddaughter of Agesilaos, as if the hag were no more than a sack of barnyard waste. "Yoked to the last, they can say of these bald Spartans." All of the Spartans were finally on or under the table in Nêto's old haunt. Gorgos's bowls were still set for his victory feast.

Mêlon then put the mangled head of Kuniskos on the table, on top of the torso of Thibrachos, and passed his own right hand over the man's bald and partly crushed pate. The braids were torn off, and Nêto's nails had shredded his skin. Gorgos's right temple was caved in from her clubbing. "He was a good man with a pruning hook. Some evil that was sired in him in his youth ate away at his heart. So it often is that when the good go bad, they prove the worst of all. He was a cursed helot, then free, and perhaps got too many of my foul looks when he got up late or pruned the wrong canes. The Spartan brand burned him all the same. I hate this man and can only think of my Homer to say how much: "I only wish that my spirit and fury would drive me to hack your meat away and eat it raw for the things you have done to me."

Then Ainias paused and barked out, "Melissos, bring in the wood of Gorgos. The burners will be burned. And we will tear apart the fence out back to pile even more fuel over these vermin. Yes, torch them as they lie. That's far better than how they would have left us. The Spartans will call it a hero's pyre—we a purification."

Nêto was still weeping as she sat in the dirt outside, propping Chiôn in her lap and wiping away the oozing blood of his wound with her tunic. "Had I killed Gorgos above Leuktra near the wagon. Had I had the courage even in the fort of Antikrates to end him, our Chiôn would now live. Instead I polluted our Chiôn, I let that foul killer's blood drip on him from my tunic."

Ainias was back outside and shrugged. "So we all could have done our part to avoid this. I froze when our hemi-god crashed through that door. No mortal kills Lichas with a single blow. No man takes down two of the royal peers as he rushes after three more. We were all a step behind him. Just as at Leuktra. We thought some god was upon us. But then Chiôn was a god of sorts."

Mêlon answered Ainias. "Put him on the pony, just as Nêto once bore Lophis home. Wrap and tie him in these red Spartan capes that will hide his blood. Take him to Ithômê where he will be honored and burned as the hero he was. So ends the Fury who evened the score on Taygetos, so ends the man-bear of the high mountain. And when we return to Helikon I imagine we will see none who once bothered us. Yes, he had cleaned the field of thistles and burrs, but Chiôn had too many cuts and splinters on his hands to show for his thinning."

Ainias walked away mumbling. "The end of the man-bear? Maybe— and then maybe not."

The victors had piled the dry limbs and brush over the corpses, along with the posts and rails of the pinewood fence. A fire was soon licking the roof-beams, as the burning hut crashed down on the dead killers. The five watched it transfixed. "Do not breathe the smoke of Kuniskos or Lichas, master, or even that of Elektra," Nêto whispered. "It is poison, and may draw the dark spirits who feed off such evil."

Mêlon grimaced as the bodies crackled. He knew that laxity is the evil of the world—that the real barbarians were the refined and double-thoughters who think their hands are too smooth to put around the necks of the accursed. Too many times on Helikon Mêlon had let the killer Gorgos live. He knew now that the good, *to kalon*, comes alive only with action—the hard willingness to kill the bad and end the false sense of good that prompts us to lord ourselves over others that we are pure and free of blood guilt. Worse men worry whether the Gorgones of the world are given a good burial, the better only that they are dead. Terrible souls fret that Gorgos might have been a bit good, better ones know that it mattered little since he was mostly bad. And Mêlon did not know quite where he himself fit in all of that. He turned back as the flames devoured the head of Gorgos. Then loud sounds came from the pyre—either the juices and bones of his head frying in the heat, or maybe yet another gasp from a reawakening Lichas. Mêlon mumbled, "Even in death Lichas and Gorgos have the last words. Even the fire recoils from its foul fuel."

"No, flame conquers all. *Pur panta nikâ.*" Ainias at last smiled and for just a moment the smoke intoxicated him. He now spoke, but just for a moment, as the Ainias of old, as he had before the death of Proxenos. "This time they have found fire, something stronger than their lies and evil. They will be ash on the needles of these trees by today's breeze. They have all died poorly, these fakers of Lichas who claimed to be the true Hellenes because they so long and so eagerly put down the weaker—until we proved that they, not the helots, were the frail ones, the dregs of a new, a better Hellas." The five in their fury had burned the hut, the fences— everything they could find that would ignite in the light drizzle. Sparks lit up the cold late-afternoon spring sky. Then carefully, with two red Spartan capes, Nêto wrapped and tied Chiôn. They cinched him over their small Messenian pony and headed back down the trail under the stands of wet spruce and fir. Kerberos led the way, howling at shapes on the crest above.

After about five stadia from the pyre, the dog sprang ahead. The five turned from the bend of the path back into an open meadow. The trail was muddy with stagnant pools. It was late afternoon. Kerberos howled and stopped. At last they found their guide Scorpas just as Chiôn had left him. His big idea to reach the old port of Pylos in the west had gotten no farther than a short walk from the hut of Gorgos, where the wolf-dog of Kithairon had cornered him. Chiôn had found him shuddering above Porpax, on the lower branch of a mountain oak, whimpering for his life and offering to lead the way back to the hut of Gorgos. Chiôn, the man-bear of Taygetos, had dealt with Scorpas as he had with the wild bears that he and Porpax had once run down above the farm on Helikon. The throat of Scorpas was slit from ear to ear. He was hung by the heels—and with his own tunic—from a limb. A pool of blood soaked the pine needles. A red beta was swabbed on his back. Kerberos now pulled on his dangling braids, furious to bring the corpse down.

"His end is a small nemesis," Mêlon whispered as he gave the hanging corpse a push. They went on by and shooed Kerberos off, leaving Scorpas to swing as an offering to Chiôn. The wolves yelled as they went down the trail, in answer to the greeting of Kerberos, who knew their way well. The five hiked all night on the downhill path. It was right before dawn when the night walkers with Chiôn draped over the pony reached the low foothills beneath the west slopes of Taygetos. They had not bothered staying at the upland huts.

Nêto wept. Where was Alkidamas? Why had he let Chiôn go on from the coast? Then she sighed that it was hard to save a man who had begun living to die, rather than dying to live. Then Nêto—always the good bearer of corpses—leaned with her side on the horse to lay her arm on the wrapped Chiôn and secure his corpse, her Chiôn, bought slave of the Malgidai—free citizen of Thespiai, hero of Boiotia, and the great nemesis of the Spartans.

# CHAPTER 35

# The Way Back

There were more guards on the streets when the five reached the torches of the new city. They brought in Chiôn to the houses of the dead, put him on a table, and then went to sleep in the tent by the Arkadian Gate. Mêlon kept his distance from this Nikôn, and wondered once more whether his city was the calm or nightmare of his nightly dreams on Helikon. The helot in turn was babbling about more bad helots to hang. Epaminondas turned. "Quiet, Nikôn, we have a better dead man than all your men alive. We mourn Chiôn as he burns. At least torch those you hang. Don't leave them for the dogs. We are better than the men of Sparta. Kill the looters if you must. Hang the traitors. Hunt down the Spartans left, though I wager there are no more than a handful alive and none on Taygetos. But do it on the vote of your *dêmos*. Burn them outside the gates and let their womenfolk collect the ashes."

In the days after the deaths of Lichas and Gorgos up on Taygetos, Mêlon and Ainias said little. They kept busy on a hero shrine outside the Arkadian Gate where their hired Messenians had erected two gray limestone lions. Proud heads roared in stone over the ashes of Proxenos and Chiôn. Each sat on his haunches and seemed to be bellowing out to the southeast, "The end of Sparta." Ainias took up the chisel himself, and wondered again as he cut the stone what had driven two northerners to come so far south to die for those who had never known them. When he was done, something of the faces of Proxenos and Chiôn stared out from the lions' manes and whiskers. For a bit he was angry again for the end of his friend, the death of Chiôn and the laming of Nêto, angry at the once-grand idea to free the Messenians, and so he could not keep quiet even among the helots around him. "Look at us, Mêlon. Making stone beasts roar like our Chiôn and Proxenos. Look at what they died for—a city of crooked towers, of thieves, of looters and worse. Proxenos planned their city and we cannot even give him credit, so we lie about some faker Aristomenes who envisioned it so that these child helots won't have hurt feelings that they could not even plan their own city. Now look at them, drunk on the freedom we gave, all in need of the Spartan lash. Killing each other when they can't find Spartans. Next they'll turn on us, their liberators. I helped do this. No polis here at all—there never will be. Why, most city-states wouldn't even let that thug Nikôn in the city gate. Here he is an archon. I would burn him up before I would Lichas."

Mêlon ignored the rantings from the dirty and unkempt Ainias. He smelled of wine and sweat and wore the blood of Proxenos on his cloak like the victor does the laurel, and went from the middle way to unhinged in a blink—and would yet return to his senses soon enough. Mêlon the farmer saw something quite different from Ainias. With new eyes he began to perceive a stirring amid the mess, and larger walls than either at Megalopolis or Mantineia. For the farmer who brings the wheat field out of thistle and bramble, his eye is always not on the natural chaos, but on what order can emerge from it. Amid the gallows, and the sewers, and the corpses, he saw majestic stone temples, and houses—and the skeleton of a great polis to come, one that grew flesh each day. And the clouds above it all, this day they seemed now to be as faces, yes faces of Chiôn and Proxenos both, as if they had become Olympians who smiled down on their subjects.

His mind took in Messenians torching the corpses of the executed and arguing to stop the killing, and young men racing in the half-built stadium, throwing the discus and hitting targets with their javelins, in preparation for the great games of the founding of holy Messenê. "Freedom is not so clean. The Athenians have had their democracy maybe a hundred and a half-hundred years, they say. It still is, well, you know, chaos, Ainias; these Athenians who started wars each season and killed Sokrates and slit the throats of the Melians, and all the rest. And us? Has it even been ten years since Pelopidas and his gang dressed up as women and assassinated our oligarchs in their drinking parties? So we are to demand of these helots perfection, our beautiful virgin *Dêmokratia*, all in Parian white, without a blemish or chisel mark on her bosom?"

In their grief the two hoplites were largely left alone by Epaminondas, who had mustered the army only then to camp it three times and more, reluctant to leave Messenia and face his trial at home. The general instead walked all night, paced the ramparts of the nearly finished walls of Messenê, wondering whether his victory would draw out Agesilaos—and whether he should head back east over Taygetos for the summer to attack the lame king.

Pelopidas laughed at his fantasies. "You'll be lucky, Theban, to get this army home as it is. One hundred and twenty days and more I reckon our men have slept outside and fought the Spartan. Half are sick from the cold. The rest vomit from the bad water. They feel the foul air and the fever it brings. If we don't leave soon before the summer, they'll hate the helots more than the Spartans—if they avoid the fevers of these lowlands by the coast." Pelopidas then pointed to the Boiotians in the camps below the finished ramparts. "They need do no more. You promised a march home thirty days ago. Not even Zeus with his thunder on Taygetos could get them to go back east. They will not go back into the lair of Agesilaos. No, they are tiring of founding cities for ingrates."

"If you want your Messenians to enforce their laws and finish their walls, then it is time for us to dry up the teat and wean these infants who have grown teeth aplenty. The spring star Arktouros has long ago arisen with our month of Agriônios and winter is past. Even Epitêles knew that and took his Argives home last month—and no less on the advice of Lelex and Nikôn, who want their polis to be their own. Do you like your uncle sleeping in your tower bedroom a hundred days after his promise of a short visit?"

Nêto had drifted back to the empty schoolhouse of Erinna far above the city, and was said to have gone quiet in the night as the vapors of the goddess had set the other virgin priestesses afire. She could tend the outer sanctuary, and plant her garden, but was not allowed into the temple proper or precinct, not after her stay with Kuniskos. She wished to avoid Mêlon, ashamed that he would spurn her, for she was soiled and ugly and she walked slower than did her master. She instead talked to Erinna in her sleep, but out of make-believe since the visions of what was to come were gone. Even Doreios, who before her capture had claimed he would make her his own, let her alone now, since he saw that she drew men's eye for her scars rather than her beauty. The more he had once talked of yoking his Nêto, the less he saw of her, for her deer legs were a faint memory and her gait was not a pretty thing to watch.

Nêto at last had her free Messenia, but the deaths of Chiôn, Proxenos, and Lophis, and the looming date of departure of the northerners, Mêlon especially, bore hard on her—as did the truth that her dream talk to Nikôn had almost gotten them all killed on Taygetos. That lamentation turned Nêto away from the world of reasoned men and for a time back to the gods of Olympos who alone, it seemed, a day or two each month spoke to her. If a year earlier she had turned all the heads in the agora at Thespiai, now few in Messenia gave her a look, and then only to gaze at her slumped walk and her scarred cheek. Her leg had healed with a bad bow and she favored it like the old women in black shawls with the hump-backs and staffs.

Gorgos had left her a bitter look, as he promised, with her branded scar. Nêto for her part wanted no man. Kerberos would not leave her side anyway and she in turn kept him from going back to the wolves. Nêto in her shame soon limped more into the deeper hills, even far above the house of Erinna and was seen with the deathless naiads of the glens, now more a phantom than a fleshy mortal. Mêlon had tried to track her down, but the mountain helots were ignorant of her wanderings, and he had lost his tracker Chiôn. Finally, he sent out messengers with word to her to come home. But no ranger could find her, not even the hounds found a scent of her Kerberos. Both vanished from the thoughts of the Messenians. Mêlon remembered her harsh talk to him the previous summer on Helikon and at least figured she was happier in her free Messenia than back in his Boiotia. Or so he told himself.

Finally, not just the hoplites, but their officers also, told Epaminondas to leave. They demanded of Epaminondas that they reach home before the green stalks of the wheat fields of Boiotia turned yellow and heavy. The army took inventory and prepared provisions for the march across the Isthmos. Then Alkidamas appeared again. He had gone north to Olympia, and had news as he returned southward to the new city. "I have called on you too much, Thespian. You have given too much of the earth and water of Helikon for the cause of the Messenians. I ask a final favor, a homecoming gift. I think that when you go north with the new month, we will not see each other again—at least until the trial of us all. So our tiny band of liberators should go homeward toward the gulf, ahead of the army, together as part of one final good deed, to smooth the rocks from the road before Epaminondas arrives with a bounty on his head. Let us get to Thebes first, before Epaminondas arrives, and make sure he sees flowers, not a rope, around his neck."

So five left ahead of Epaminondas. Alkidamas led with Ephoros, the writer of history. Melissos followed at the rear. Ainias and Mêlon walked in between, both silent in their hatred of the Spartans who had killed Proxenos and turned Nêto feral. After a two days' walk, the five reached the coast of the gulf of Korinthos. From there they could see the wave-crested sea of Megalê Hellas to the west, and the dark cliffs of Aeolis directly across the water where men of the polis seldom went. Soon on their way to the docks, they passed the first huts outside the great walled city of Patrai, city on the gulf, friend to Athens and home to the Achaians of old.

Ainias had grown tired already of the south, of his own Peloponnesos, and was ashamed of his Doric—and now even of himself as well. As promised, he would tend to the farm of Proxenos up on the Asopos River, at least for a while. The sooner he got to Plataia, and away from this southland, the better for himself and his companions condemned to see him in his madness. He would find his cure in the olives and vines of Proxenos. There he would swear off Dionysos, and bathe in the cold Asopos each morning to cleanse his stains. He would teach the sons of his friend to bend the bow and dig the vineyard. Or so he promised once he was north of the gulf and free of his homeland.

The joints of Alkidamas were stiff, and Mêlon himself was quite lame from his bad leg. His knee was nearly twice its normal size. His foot was blistered and torn from walking on its side. Lame and tired, they were all glad to go inside the city gate of these men from Achaia and walk down between the Long Walls to the port on the gulf rather than continue east to the Isthmos along the shore. Alkidamas laughed, "Ah yes, we take the ferry straight over to windy Naupaktos. No Gastêr this time, just an honest ferryman and his barge. We stay the night over there on the high eastern road by the water. Then up a day through the olive groves of Amphissa to Delphi and we will pass along by the snake oracle of Trophonios into Boiotia, coming up on Helikon on her backside. Once across the water we are safe. Done with the deed—at least for this season."

Mêlon and Ainias were mostly quiet on the broad-bottomed ferry-boat over to Naupaktos. The late-spring sea of the fickle month Theilouthios was choppy. But the aged tiller was no fat one-armed running mouth, but an expert young sailor from Zakynthos with his father's boat, who crisscrossed to the opposite side despite the white tops on the waves. Even with a strong northern headwind in their faces, they reached the northern shore by the noon, and then made the sixty stadia to Naupaktos in less than a day.

There Alkidamas rented a large common room, an *andron* with six wooden couches and reed mats. He had ordered food brought in to sup together a final time—olives, garlic, some dried fish, and an octopus or two, with four *kratêres* of black wine and greens and spring *horta* from the well-watered slopes above Naupaktos. He had on either side of him flute girls. Two porters brought in torches and a long low table. "Well," Alkidamas began as he leaned on his elbow, chewing a tip of raw wild asparagus, "well, well, we have a sort of symposion with girls and couches. Let the wine and eating and boasting begin. I am the *symposiarchos*, and preside over our talk session. Look. I have bought laurel wood for a roaring fire." A short Akarnanian girl in a see-through cloak of light linen kept their cups full. Another with a large backside from Ithaka walked around the table with an *aulos*. On the prompt of Ainias, she took up a soft song of Erinna of Athens. Ainias had no smile on his face as he leaned forward. Rather than drop a raisin in his mouth he threw several across at the beard of Alkidamas.

"So we ended the Spartans," he growled. "Don't lie to me that we left something better. You saw the mess at Messenê. Lichas was right. We miss him—and can't bring him back to right things." Alkidamas wiped a dribble of wine from his chin, clicked his fingers, and the Akarnanian girl—Skylaki, they called her—brought in a new calyx of red, the third of the night, and a towel for his face. "I am hog at the symposion and won't let any of you speak, no, not just yet," Ainias announced. "There is an army still left with Agesilaos. Even after Leuktra he is enough alive. He sits safe on his acropolis. I think we will all be back in the vale of Lakonia—and more than once."

The other four were fidgeting. Ainias looked away from them. They were unsure how much the wine rather than Ainias was talking and looked over to see that his spear was on the floor. They signaled for the music to begin again, in soft fashion, as they heard him out, hoping the five-foot tune would calm him and that they themselves would not be persuaded by his anger. Ainias was a slave himself to Dionysos and would not calm. He kicked up his feet and jumped back up in the lamplight, spilled an entire *kratêr* of the white, and almost turned over the table itself. "Will your ox Aias pull the yoke any better, Mêlon, because there are no more helots? Will that big press work better without a Chiôn? I think not. Who challenges all this? All vanity. It was all about the vanity of Pythagoras, this notion you could play god, and make some serfs free so to make yourselves feel more something—what I don't quite know."

The drunken Ainias knocked over his couch and walked around the table, along the backside of the couches. Not one of the four was reclining. Mêlon might have agreed with some of this nonsense of Ainias. Now he kept quiet, for he had a half-thought to cross swords with Ainias, and more than a half that he would take down the Stymphalian. The piper Skylaki started on her flute and began to dance and lead Ainias back to his couch. It was the writer of *historia* among them, the yellow-haired *malthakos* Ephoros, who challenged the mercenary. How odd that the twig-armed Ephoros cared little about a spear-thrust from the drunken hoplite. He was even redder from the winter sunburn he had acquired on the trip down, but his voice came out through his nose in his affected Attic. There is courage in writers on occasion, especially if there is a story to come of it. Ephoros had learned to endure slights and an occasional slap as he questioned the helots for his great saga of their liberation to come. For all his perfumed locks, he was no coward. Ephoros had said little in fear that the veterans would scorn his white skin and soft hands—and his support for a war that he had not fought in.

He had come late with Alkidamas. So he missed all the battles north or south. His only battle scars? The vomiting from the long boat to the Peloponnesos and some scratches from fighting off a big helot rower on Gastêr's boat. Now he had no intention of letting the friendship of all be turned sour by a good man gone bad in his drink—not now, right before they set out on the last road to holy Delphi at sunrise. So better to prompt the battle of words with Ainias here in friendly Naupaktos. That way their bile would rise and pass. Then they could march east in easy quiet to Delphi. All could enjoy the hike up to Apollo's shrine. As sober friends once more, the five would descend from the high meadows to Trophonios and the borders of home.

Ephoros poured himself a calyx of warm unmixed wine and began. "Sit down, dear Ainias, just as our dear Akarnanian Skylaki orders. Please, let us all sit down and recline, and show some respect to one another and the idea of a proper symposion, as we do in Ionia. Where is our *symposiarchos* to impose order? Girls. You two bring in more wine, and play something soft on the lyre as we speak, an elegy perhaps, and do some of your twists and leg raises for the men over there." To the general surprise, the Arkadian Ainias did just as he was told.

"Is that what Lophis and Kalliphon, the son of our Alkidamas, fell for at Leuktra? Chiôn, and Proxenos and all the other best men of Boiotia whose names I have written on my scrolls? Did they all die to just kill Lichas, the better man? Was it only to kill Kleombrotos and his henchmen at Leuktra?" He picked up some cucumber relish and spread it on his bread and then again looked up. "The helots are free and yet they squander their liberty in license? My, my—they loot. They steal, Ainias. By Zeus, they even plunder their own temples, or so you shriek." Ephoros leaned on his elbow and somehow raised his squeaky voice even another notch higher. "We laid out their walls. They sleep on them rather than build them higher. We died for Messenians. And, oh my, they have no government, no laws, no rules on stone. Spartans at least kept order with their *kryptes* and their chasm of death." He may have been fragile, this papyrus leaf, but Ephoros nonetheless looked over at the drunken killer Ainias and faced him down.

"This is your writ—that you prefer order to freedom, the rules of the pit of the Kaiadas to the chaos of the unruly assembly? Hah. So you think if we were smart, we would bring back a Spartan harmost, and have Antikrates and Lichas and his braids back again?" Ephoros looked around to his right. He wanted to see if any in their sorrow and drink agreed with the bitter Ainias and might prick his backside with a spear tip. So he went on to provoke Mêlon right across the table, although he was unsure of his reaction. "Was that the goad for you too Mêlon, son of Malgis, only to keep Agesilaos on his acropolis and out of the vineyards and wheat fields of others around Helikon? You had no thought of the helots or the cities of the Peloponnesos?"

Now the pale Ephoros broke his own rules of the symposion. He leaped up, but much more violently than even Ainias had. He stalked, yes, stalked to the wall and back. He had feather arms and even smaller legs. Yet he paced to the back of the Arkadian's couch and took on Ainias, and showed the greater courage for standing right over the reclining killer.

"Ainias, you will return to your old fire soon enough and lead Arkadia onto the path of its old renown—once you hear the voice of your Proxenos and the whispers of your Pythagoras. We are in the north again, across the gulf now, Ainias Taktikos. So obey your oath to the dead. Fill your wine flask with spring water. Cut off your filthy mane and bathe in the nearby Mornos tomorrow, and if you are man enough to go to Plataia, as you boast, go and raise the children of Proxenos. Otherwise keep still and join the other drunkards on the corners and the alley beggars with their coin cups, or go back down to Taygetos and take up where Chiôn finished."

Mêlon finally looked up. "All of us sit down, lounge back, and have some relish and more wine." Mêlon spoke rapidly and with confidence. "Nêto is not a mere cripple. She is not ugly or feral. No. She is free. She has whispered that it will be this angry Ainias, who alone will become the tyrant slayer of the Peloponnesos, who will deal with Lykomedes yet—who may prove the great traitor of us all as he colludes with old Agesilaos. Yes, in your pride and zeal, you will go south there again—I fear for you— and settle up with our backstabber Lykomedes in Mantineia. You are the biggest liberator of us all." He went on. "Erinna is not dead. Her song lives on. Epaminondas hums and sings it as we speak. So, yes, all that has been a good thing to die for, Ephoros, for the freedom of the Hellenes. I am at last proud to be a Hellene. I won't stay on my mountain." Mêlon wanted to finish and get it all out, and show that he was one with Epaminondas at last, no difference between the two of them. "Let the others talk of your Pythagoras as the evil *daimôn* that addled the wits of the democrats of Boiotia. Or say that he sent them south on this mad dream of a dead philosopher. What is it for me who has no love for that sect and likes to eat meat as much as beans? It was the freedom of the Messenians that I now know was worth the blood of the Malgidai. We ended the Spartans who marched into the land of others. I have no regrets. Not one. Not ever. Not since I came down Helikon to fight at Leuktra for Epaminondas. For I too was freed from a different sort of slavery, one worse in some ways: a slavery of the mind—and of the soul that once believed in nothing other than itself. Nothing is worse than the cynic who is disappointed by the world about him for not appreciating in his own genius, for being less than perfect. I know that now from years of wilderness."

Pale Ephoros from across the table, behind his large *kratêr* of warm wine, looked over at Mêlon. "It will be sung a thousand seasons and more from now that the stones that grew out of the Peloponnesos this season prove who was the better man after all—and who the worse. What will they say of Sparta? What will they say when one day when we are ashes, and the Hellenes to come conclude, 'Why look. There is nothing here, no stones on the acropolis of Agesilaos. The Sparta of song was nothing. But the walls of its subjects, why over at Messenê are they looming over the Peloponnesos?' "

Melissos twitched. He for some reason was not tired of these talkers. He liked them and what they said. What was this Hellas, this notion of no city-state, but one people—one language, the same gods, from Thessaly to Crete? "Please, don't speak of our ruin. Think of the ruined at Sparta. They feel their own misery far more. Isn't that enough? The world is split between those who apologize for killing their enemies and those who take pride in it. What we did was good, right as you say. Surely you taught me that much." Gone was his half-Makedonian slang. He had wanted to fight with Mêlon at Taygetos, die even if need be. So he had earned their attention. Now he spoke as clearly as any Boiotian three times his age.

"Antikrates is not feasting with Agesilaos. More likely the two are serving their own table. They drown their tears in bad wine of their own bad making—with a dead king Kleombrotos, and a dead Lichas, and a dead Kleonymos, and all those others dead at Leuktra. Their helots are gone. And bald Kuniskos is ash in the high *aithêr*." This new boy Melissos was making good sense, as he turned and signaled the girl from Ithaka to sit by his feet and rub his upper leg. He turned to the Akarnanian who continued with her lyre and grabbed her cloak. He scarcely had a beard but he had known such women since his second teeth had grown in. The year of apprenticeship of this Melissos was coming to an end. Alkidamas had told the young man, on the word of Pelopidas, that there was a ship waiting for him at Kirrha over the hill, below Delphi. They would fight the wind out of the gulf and then battle more of it northward along the coast, and row him home up the west side of Makedonia.

The treaty had held through the late spring as summer approached. None of the northern Makedonian folk of Melissos had attacked them from the rear when the Boiotians went south. So the northern kings had kept their word—at least for now—and the year of his guaranty and truce was honored. Melissos, along with the other Makedonians held at Thebes, was once again a free man. He was already feeling once more his privilege and birth rank, and yet he was learning from these Hellenes who bled and died so well for nothing other than helots, than helots no less. Alkidamas jumped up from his couch, then clapped his hands and dismissed the servants. He ordered all to get ready their beds and end this symposion, since it had gone just as he had planned. The once surly and tired banqueters had let their *daimones* out, and would return with one story as friends, with four empty *kratêres* as proof of their amity. Ainias, he knew, would shortly bathe and cut off his matted hair of mourning. Mêlon had come down at last from Helikon and would never really go back up again. Ainias nodded at Alkidamas and put away his wine, the goblet half full. He felt relieved that his own bitterness had at least not spread to others. He pointed at Ephoros and then picked up his own spear and broke it over his knee as if it were a tooth-picker.

"For a while longer," Ainias promised, "I will be your captain. Sleep and wake sober. We have a long march to the port of Delphi. Then there is a steep climb up to the temple. There we can gaze down at the pass into Boiotia. On our last day we pass through the hill of the Sphinx and near that dreadful snake goddess at Lebadeia. Like it or not, the age of Epaminondas, and of men like Lichas, and of Chiôn—and us here tonight—is over with."

The returning veterans left the lodging the next morning and set out into the hard winds of the mouth of the gulf, pressing to get on the road to the east and home. The travelers fell in soon with yet another band of Messenians along the coast road. These were the children of free men. Forty years earlier they had settled in Naupaktos to the north, when they fled Pylos during the Athenian war. The helots walked briskly as if for the first

time in their lives it was a thing of pride to be known as Messenians and
not mere helots of Sparta. All seven of these wayfarers were stonecutters
and likewise were climbing to Delphi. Or so said their leader Artemido-
ros. He boasted to the Boiotians that the new assembly of the Messenians,
under the direction of the rebel Nikôn, *polemarchos* of Messenê, right after the liberation had sent them on a ship with black marble of the type
the Athenians quarried at Eleusis. The transport was at the dock in Kirrha. These Messenians were to guide the rough stones with the teamsters
up the mountain to the Sacred Way of the sanctuary. There they would
set up the great altar of the liberated Messenians. This work was, as Ainias
knew, the last design of Proxenos, the final scroll found in his pack after
his end on the Eurotas, so confident had he been that there would be a
need for a victory monument of a free Messenê at Delphi. None of these
helot folk now at his side even knew the name of the benefactor who had
perished to plan their new city; much less had they any idea of the hide-
clad Nikôn who once had poached his way to freedom on the slopes of
Ithômê.

At the notion of a Messenian polis with a sanctuary at Delphi, Mêlon
now thought as they hiked that it was the Boiotian farmer, the horny-
handed plowman who had hated war and had drunk his cool red and
napped beneath his arbors, who had nonetheless gone willingly southward for the freedom of these helots. These lowly men from the marshes
of Boiotia had chased the Spartans, the very taskmasters of war, across the
Eurotas. With Epitêles they had marched amid the high ice into Messenia
and built a city out of stone. Now they were ready to go home and blend
back into the black soil of Boiotia, in hopes the great shaking-up in the
south would mean that the northerners would never again worry about
Spartans, who would instead always worry about the Messenians. These
were the true Hellenes, the *geôrgoi*, these rocky stones like Philliadas, and
Antitheos and Staphis, who, immovable on the banks that anchored the
poleis, kept it alive a bit longer, while the city folk joined the deluge that
was carrying all the lesser pebbles headlong over the falls. For a while
longer they would trudge into town and warn their betters that their
right spear arms, not walls, kept the enemy distant, that the Makedonian and the Persian would always come from the north unless stopped,
and that the more *gymnasia* and *palestrai* the city built, the softer the

citizens became. Yes, the burning of Lakonia to the south was the win of the farmers, the *mesoi* who had proved stronger than the lords of Sparta, who had shown they could hold their shields as high as those at Marathon.

Mêlon himself remembered little of the next day's trek along the coast to Kirrha—other than that for most of this last leg of the march he worried as he stared at the familiar massif of Parnassos. His farm: Had it been overrun or abandoned in these few days following the death of Chiôn? Was it even his farm anymore, with Malgis long gone, and Lophis dead, and himself absent? Who would the Boiotians charge with treason for fighting well past the new year: the five Boiotarchs who followed Epaminondas and Pelopidas? Or perhaps Alkidamas and Ainias, who, the jurymen would allege, had planned the campaign? Surely he too as well would be stoned or cut down for joining? A democracy—or so Mêlon well knew Backwash would allege—could not survive should its leaders trample the laws as they pleased. And they were all lawbreakers of their own as much as liberators of others.

Once the band reached the Delphians' harbor at Kirrha and could look up the Gorge of the Pleistos and far to the right at the shadows of the peaks of Arkadia across the water, the four finally took leave of their hostage Melissos. As arranged, the youth would go back on board the Messenian ship—*Eleutheria*—to sail out of the gulf. It would row up the coast on the west side of Hellas to Epiros. The crew, after dropping their marble at Kirrha, had planned to continue north past Akarnania to fetch more Messenians who were eager to reach their liberated homeland. None of these Messenian seamen seemed to mind taking the boy along for ballast, especially as Mêlon flipped them four silver owls for their trouble.

At the docks, Alkidamas first saw a fat man grab the silver from his steward—and with his one hand, no less—even as he called back from across the boarding plank. "Old man. I thought you'd be dead now, you, my partner, and your Spartan-killers." It was Gastêr. Gastêr who never aged, and never worried, and cared not a whit whether you were Athenian or spoke Doric, won or sat out the great war, if only you had four-piece silver owls from Athens in your palm. Yes, Gastêr was here, the anti-Epaminondas. "I'm afraid I sold our *Theôris* to the Messenians, Alkidamas. Or at least sort of. Why, that cutthroat Nikôn and his council, they gave me this merchant boat instead. I got marble and ferrying business with it to boot. Not a bad trade. Some shiny coins came with the ship swap. Those helots of yours learned to row and stayed with me on this boat too, better sailors than they proved wise men. So we meet again. I took the risk. You don't want a cut out of my *Eleutheria*, though the *rhêtôrs* might argue it came from your money to begin with. I have proof of sale. Here, take it."

Alkidamas took the rumpled tiny papyrus and gave it to Mêlon without thinking to throw it away. "Fine, fat man. No need of proof. You beat those Korinthians out to the gulf, and we all got to Messenê as bargained for. As for your trade for the *Theôris*—well, there's money to be made even in Messenia, it seems. Take it as the spoils of war."

"I already have," announced Gastêr as he waved for their passenger to board his deck. Alkidamas then escorted the Makedonian to the quay and laughed. "You remind me of clever Kuniskos, Melissos, if you don't mind me saying. Now that you're both gone, as it were. Like him, you were not like you seemed—with your rickety thin bones and bad eyes. Or maybe you're a Gastêr, as smart as you are ugly, who can tiptoe on a rolling deck with one arm and a pot belly. Yet I think you see better than the rest of us who don't squint so. Tell the kings of Makedon that Alkidamas took good care of you, as you did him."

The four gave their ward a final good-bye. Melissos walked on board, just as Ainias called out across the gangway. He had thought he disliked this half-Hellene and had not believed in his eye blurs or even his stutter, but instead had studied his airs and darting eyes. Now he was not so sure, and he wanted others to see the boy's true insides here at the end, since they were more good than bad. Indeed, Ainias would not slit the Makedonian's gullet, even if the voices in his head warned him that thousands of Hellenes not born would live if only this buzzing bee from the north were swatted right here before he ever began.

Ainias grabbed his sword. "Not so fast up on your hind legs, our little Makedonian upstart. One last order. It won't require you to carry our shields any longer. Just tell me a final thing, down-beard northerner. What exactly did you learn from your year with our Alkidamas, and with us as well?" A wind came up, so Ainias yelled out even louder to the departing ship. "So hostage boy, give me something that I can tell our general on his return. You claim to be half-blind, but like no-eyes Oidipous you see more than the seeing can."

Melissos sensed that Ainias meant him more good than bad. On the final walk along the gulf he had been going over just such questions and how to answer them when his father King Amyntas at home pressed him for wisdom—and for the walls and passes and armies of the Hellenes they would soon conquer in the south. He was safe, and even Ainias would not kill him now. The boy thought that he wanted to say that they were all second-thoughters like Mêlon, who would hesitate to strike the first, or maybe even the second, blow—dreamers who thought we had souls and so died for something other than loot and fame; makers of grand walls and bronze armor, but without the sense to put them to proper use. But that was not at all what came out from the departing Melissos, not at all.

Melissos turned to Ainias and spoke no longer in the role of hostage servant of Alkidamas and Mêlon, but as the future king of a warrior tribe who was coming of age. Melissos stared at the Arkadian. "I figured out many things, Taktikos, as you will soon fancy yourself as you write down your exploits for the rest of us. Of your democracy, it is not so silly as I thought—even if the dirtiest and loudest like Backwash shout down their betters. There are, I learned, lords like poor Nikôn and Nêto and cowards like well-born Antikrates. How would we know that if birth trumped merit? Any of those who whined in the hall of the Thebans we would have strung up, and yet they fight for something far better than my father's wage, though he would have kicked them into the barns for their braying."

They laughed at that boy's high talk. Then even Ainias stopped, for he saw that this new Melissos was no fool, and was no longer what he had been before the great march. He went on with the airs of the Makedonian prince that he was again: "Was there some gold or a secret shipment of slaves in the bargain for you? I think not, though I was once convinced that there must be cartloads. Instead, I think here of Proxenos and your Chiôn and lame-footed Nêto and all the wild men like Nikôn and the rest who rot, who taught me, their slave, that I was as good as they with no idea that I was supposed to have been born far better than them all. I too in Lakonia and in the hut on Taygetos would have died for the dream of all them, and for crippled Nêto and my crippled master Mêlon, who taught me that I was the real cripple, after all."

The four were struck dumb as Melissos went on. "I will also tell my father that we too will fight deep in the phalanx like you smarter Thebans. Very soon we will carry spears longer even than yours, *sarissas* we know them as. We will kill from five ranks in, not your three. We are tough, foul folk as you know, who worry only about killing in the north—not dying. Yes, I fear my Makedonians will be far better killers than you in your phalanxes. All that is written as the sun will set tonight in the west."

Now Melissos was shouting as the wind came up. Then, as the *Eleutheria* left the pier and floated out from its mooring, Melissos ended. "A last warning, my friends: I fear you have no more Chiôns that I can see. No more giants of the soil to come, men like Mêlon and Ainias. When I come back down here as king, as I must, I will honor you all even as I must end you all."

Then even as his voice was carried off by the wind, the youth yelled to the clouds a last time. "Oh, and you will know me next time I come back, but not I fear by your dear Melissos the Honeybee. For you see, I was and am Philippos, the lover of horses of the royal House of Pella. Yes, I am the son of Amyntas and the royal Eurydikê, the future King Philippos of all of Makedon and all of Hellas to come and Persia perhaps as well—I who carried your baggage and would do it if I could ten times and more again."

# CHAPTER 36

# The Restoration

With that the teary-eyed boy was gone, although none on the pier could quite fathom the last boasts of Melissos that were lost on the gusts—something about a Philippos and kings and Persia but just a few words without sense. Mêlon would remember only that the last time they saw Melissos he was waving, the one arm of Gastêr still around his shoulder. Gastêr, no doubt, had not liked the end of his speech, but at least he was buoyed by the boy's spirit and saw money ahead for both. As for this Melissos-Philippos, he really was seen again in the south and in about thirty seasons thence, when the grandsons of Mêlon and the men of Thespiai would fall before his phalanx of *sarissas* and Philippos's eighteen-year-old son to be born, Alexandros, *ho Megas Alexandros*. The dream of Epaminondas would end in the narrow valley of Chaironeia, not more than a day's walk from where they all stood, where a balding Philippos would build a great lion monument to the Thebans he had killed. There would lie the better men of the polis, the sort that decades earlier in Boiotia the hostage prince wished to become—and might have become, had he only stayed longer as Melissos at the side of Mêlon and Epaminondas.

Ainias and Ephoros were happy enough to see the odd northern boy leave, and on the ship of Gastêr, no less—though he had been handy on the road and had carried far more than they had thought he would from the look of his small arms. Mêlon told them, "He proved at the end as good as any of us, a mirror as he hinted that we too went from bad to good once we set foot at holy Leuktra and then crossed the Isthmos. The next big war, mark my words, will come from his Makedonians and by land from the north. I miss him already—though I should not, since we may have trained a cub that will return a lion. Still, with Nêto gone, and Lophis and Chiôn dead, there is not much left. And without the Spartans I wonder whether our children can stop anyone as the old ones once routed Xerxes and his Medes."

Alkidamas turned to them and looked over at Mêlon. "Are we ready for our climb up to the sanctuary? Don't worry about our Melissos or whatever his name was or shall be. I too believe that he may not quite be a killer, although he proved to be a killer enough still. We did our best to tame him so he wouldn't learn just our warcraft but also the rule of law, our *nomoi*, as well and the voice of Pythagoras, which I think I heard in him beneath his strange speech. What he does with that knowledge rests on his soul, not ours. The One God sorts it all out in the end. Enough; each man fights the battles of his own day. Ours are mostly over, and his will begin soon." The four laughed at that and spent their second day out from Naupaktos ascending through the valley of the orchards to Parnassos. They walked in shade up the hills amid the olive groves of the men of Amphissa, who waved at them from the tall pruning ladders as word had gone ahead that the slayers of the Spartans this day were climbing to Delphi.

At last they rested beneath the shiny Phaidriades cliffs, not far from the ravine at the spring of Kastalia, happy to spend their last night together in the nearby tavern beneath the upper sanctuary of Apollo. In the morning the four headed down the Boiotian road with an escort of Phokians who were eager to hear of the victories in the south as the wage of their escort—and who pressed them for news of booty and more to be had. Rumors had already reached them that the army of Epaminondas would come up from the Isthmos in a new moon with wagons of Spartan plunder and gold from the Messenians. Ephoros and Alkidamas were to go on to Athens. Ainias would accompany the two as far as the shadows of Kithairon and take the fork off to Plataia and the farm of Proxenos. So Mêlon would be the first to part in the evening at Helikon, whose looming silhouette brooded on their right. Finally at dusk the four came to the crossroad that led on to Askra and Thespiai. The wheat of the upper fields was about milk ripe, not quite in full ear—just as Epaminondas had promised the previous winter when he assured the men they would be home from Ithômê for high harvest in Boiotia. The other three said little at their parting, for Ainias wished to see Aretê of the yellow hair, the widow of Proxenos, by nightfall. He had at last bathed as promised in the icy Mornos above Naupaktos, and then shaved at the inn below Parnassos. Each in Boiotia and beyond would now talk up the virtues of Epaminondas and ready the countryside for his return.

Ainias knew that he always would be a mere day's walk from the farm of Malgis and that he and Mêlon were yoked as the twin oxen team who, for all their grunts, would still once more, side-by-side, willingly pull the hard plow of Epaminondas. Ephoros and Alkidamas were anxious as well to get to Thebes by dark. Ephoros had to meet two Athenian scribes and was ready to dictate from his dirty scrolls all that he could remember and all that Alkidamas could relate of the great march to the south. He was soiled with mud on his chiton and his cloak was thick with burrs. The writer wanted a long bath to wash and pleat his hair and get the road stink off before he took a carriage over Kithairon to his salon at Athens, the lone brave voice to take on Platôn and his friends on behalf of Epaminondas. The great adventure that had begun so long ago with a marching into the spears of Kleombrotos at Leuktra ended quietly in the spring sunshine a few stadia away. Alkidamas told the Thespian, "I wish you would come to Athens to hear my speech on the liberation of the Messenians. I could use a strong arm since I have no friends at Athens and I hear a number of enemies would like this head off its shoulders. Their democracy is much more of a free-for-all than anything at our Thebes."

"No, not Athens," Mêlon laughed, "I would rather go back to Sparta than that. So good-bye to you three and farewell. I will see you at our trial. Don't listen to the signs of your doom this year, Alkidama. I wager you will die in your sleep in your eighth decade." Mêlon slowly made his way up the winding road to the flanks of Helikon. He was alone, just as he had begun on that cold day five months earlier when he had made the long detour to the monument of Epaminondas on his way to the great debate at Thebes. And Nêto? He had left her somewhere at Ithômê, lost in the forests above the schoolhouse of Erinna. He should have stayed, even if he had sensed that she could see him through the glens and glades and would not come out and not come home.

He recoiled at the thought of the disorder of the farm. Would it be worse than the mess that he left when he had loitered in town with Phrynê? Of course, it must. After his half-year of neglect, there would be chaos—the weeds choking the fields, mud clogging the great drain. Perhaps the stones of Chiôn's walls fallen to the ground. The worst of it? There would not be even a one-armed Chiôn to make right what would take other lesser men years to finish. The three boys of his dead Lophis had only the half-wit Myron to guide them. Damô was twice-widowed now with a young son. She would be locked in the tower as before, now with two husbands to mourn—and, with her young Chiônikos, now four children to raise. The tower's roof probably leaked and its whiteness had probably long since peeled off. In her frenzy, Damô would blurt out the cold voice of reason: Why die for helots far to the south? Still, Mêlon remembered that there was at least no more Dirkê. No more Thrattos or Medios, or Hippias or maybe others like Hipponichos, who had coveted the farm of the Malgidai or even plotted it harm. The final rage from the outlaw Chiôn had settled those accounts. He had played Zeus on Olympos—as Mêlon had feared both Chiôn and Gorgos might have if they had been freed—meting out final justice to any of those he thought had lived far too long.

Mêlon felt how hard the great ideas of Epaminondas, noble as they were, had fallen on the household of Malgis. He wondered what he would do as he aged, with the bad leg and without the arms of Chiôn, or even the bitter obedience of Gorgos—and with the pipe-playing of his Nêto a distant memory. A wretched farmer without son or a wife finally grows decrepit by the tiny fire and alone ends in hunger on the floor, without the energy to fetch even a light twig for the last flame. Mêlon half-expected to meet around the next turn of the road the Spartan Antikrates in his armor and tall crest to take a life for the life of Lichas. Or maybe Dirkê's satyrs and centaurs had come down from the high slopes of Helikon and overrun his vineyard, as it went back to the wild savagery of the strawberry trees in his absence, as in the days before Malgis had cut it out from Helikon. Or would the ghost of the hag herself float up with tears and rents on her chest and arms, howling at the night for the knife work of Chiôn? Nothing is worse for a wayfaring farmer than that last day before home when the mind conjures up thoughts of ruin and mayhem of the long absence.

But none of this proved so. One hundred fifty days and more had it been since the army had left Sparta to march into Ithômê. On each, it was Myron, freed at Leuktra, who had stomped about with manure between his toes, and earned the scars and cuts from the slapping canes as he tied the pruned vines back onto the trellises and lifted the stones back onto the walls after the hard rains. In the evenings as soon as the winter freezes ceased, Myron had begun whitewashing the tower, perched on a long ladder, but bending his neck often backward, always toward the south and east to catch at least a glimpse of the homeward trek of the Boiotians. So in the last months the farm, it turned out, had improved with the absence of Mêlon. That so often happens when those of the land, the petty tyrants of our ground, think they are irreplaceable and learn on return that the truth is even far worse than that for them. Things often prove better with their departure, as liberated dependents learn to fend for themselves without the overbearing hand of the worried overseer. Or perhaps it was the work of Pythagoras all along that made the farm thrive as it did—as its symmetry entranced all who worked in it, and for their toil gave them calm in return. Myron at last found that farm work suited him, and that he was not as dull as his long arms and stooped back made him appear.

The wheat was already drooping with the weight of the ripening grains. The olive pressing that Mêlon had left before the new year was long finished, the oil safe in the vats with another even heavier new crop on the trees. The sons of Lophis would meet their grandfather in the courtyard— since they wagered Mêlon at least for now had survived the Peloponnesos and come home safely. They would be eager to boast that Myron had laid out the new pressing room on the slope near the first threshing floor as Chiôn had once envisioned.

After his first night back on Helikon, Mêlon said little in the morning to the boys, who were accustomed to rise with the sun if they were to eat one more day. Myron, it seemed, was more himself on a level with the boys. He worked alongside them rather than, like Chiôn, leading the sons of Lophis to the fields. He knew far better the lore of the neighbors and was liable to go off the farm to listen and stop the rumors that had grown up with the death of Lophis and the flight of Chiôn.

Mêlon only now grasped that folk like Chiôn and he are the worn hobnails that finally ruin the boot and hurt the wearer from the inside. In the end they must be either pulled out or hammered down, however much they have once softened the cruel wear of the hard road for others. These two were the goads of war that are useful only to stop men like Kleonymos or Lichas when such brutes threaten to run amok and hurt the weaker sort. But in peace? They must be watched or better yet kept at a distance, until bloody Ares crashes in and the more civilized and frightened call them back to bar the gate. So Mêlon noticed the worried glances of his own kin at his scars and grim look that had not yet left him. On the second night back in his bed in the shed behind Damô's tower, Mêlon finally pulled off his old cloak, and then saw the tiny scroll that fell to the dirt—the proof of sale of the *Theôris* that Gastêr had quickly handed to Alkidamas on the quay below holy Delphi.

Mêlon got ready to put it in the flame of the lamp, but for some reason unrolled it to see how much that scoundrel Nikôn had made off the exchange of Alkidamas's ship, if there were even a bill of sale rather than a blank scroll. Yet there was writing, but it was no receipt at all.

Nikôn salutes the men of Boiotia.

The secretary Hêlos, grammateus of the Boulê writes this. You are home safe if that one-armed Gastêr gives you this papyrus. Rejoice. We are free now. In a free Messenê, under a free Ithômê—with gratitude only to grandfather Alkidamas, and our father Epaminondas, and you, our apple, Mêlon, and dark-eyed Ainias and the souls of Chiôn and Proxenos, and wandering lame Nêto, and all you others from the north. Don't be cross with us. The polis Messenê is better. This month looting stopped. The helots will soon be Messenians. We were worthy of your blood sacrifice. Free men elected me first citizen of the Messenians, archon Basileus, friend of the Boiotians, friendlier still to the men of Helikon. Know that we Messenians, as long as I am archon, are the first and last friends of the Boiotians.

Nikôn, son of Nikostratos, archon of the Messenians.
And Hêlos wrote this too.

Mêlon rolled back the tiny paper, tied it carefully, and put it in his small wooden box on the three-legged table next to the bed, where he could find it in his evenings by his lamp and so reread the letter from the archon of the greatest city of Hellas—who could neither read nor write. In half a month's time as the summer solstice came on, Mêlon wondered whether he had ever been south at all, so well the farm looked as the grain harvest was continuing in the lower fields and the goats were ready to eat the stubs bare. No one came to disturb him from town. None asked who was free and who not. Mêlon's fame from Leuktra had passed on in his absence. That Chiôn was dead was lamented, and then almost immediately forgotten. The memory of Chiôn rested only in the hearts of a few kindred great-hearted souls, the *megalopsychoi* who must remain the strong links in the otherwise weak chain of civilization. All Mêlon could do was frown when the agora lounger and wall-borers harangued at the smithy and butcher shop: "Old Chiôn had some run-in, a falling out with that runaway Gorgos, his helot slave, and went down there to fetch him, I gather. Got more than he asked for, he did. Both ended up butchered, as the slaves usually are when they have no business being freed."

To the crowd at the agora of Thespiai, Lichas and Antikrates might as well have been cold stone hoplites, nameless on the temples at Thebes. None knew that a stone lion known as Chiôn now guarded the Arkadian Gate at holy Messenê. The farmers of the bottomland around Kopais up until the plain of Chaironeia, had they even known of tall Messenê, would have only yawned at the business of folk far to the south and of no import for the Boiotians. Yet they would never again fight men from the south on the slopes of their Ptôon or Messapian. That there would never be Spartans in their fields—never Spartans in anyone's fields in all of Hellas—they just by rote and habit assumed, as if it were their birthright and not a gift paid for with the lives of Lophis, Staphis, Proxenos, and Chiôn.

Mêlon was through with the world of petty repute, the town's whispers of the larger coin chest in the well, and the rolling gossip of the agora; and yet in these first ten days of his return he was restless too on his mountain. Damô and Myron asked him little about the fighting to the south, as he returned to the chores of the farm. He heard even Phrynê was to flee to Attika, in disgust at Epaminondas who had emptied the countryside of her customers and ruined her colony of *erôs,* and whose army might torch her salon of gossip and treason should they catch her still in Boiotia. At that thought Mêlon at last hiked down to pay her a final visit. She had received word of his visit, and so his Sphêx was sitting under the plane tree by the lion-head fountain in a bright white chiton, with her breasts tucked high, and her hem hiked to the upper thigh.

She had come out to watch her carts go with her load of love gear, both her girls and the rich baggage of the *porneiai* that headed back under the guidance of Eurybiades to Athens. In the past at Athens, when Phrynê was in trouble in the courts, she simply bared her breasts and won her freedom. Now? If she had stripped naked, it would have done no good in winning a pass to stay at her palace in Thespiai, as both her breasts and her audience were not as they once had been. "You could have stayed the hero of Leuktra, my Mêlon," she sighed. "I would have had all thoughts of that know-nothing virgin girl Nêto out of your breast the moment my cloak dropped. Instead you were helot-crazy. Too eager to kill your fellow Hellenes. All for man-footed slaves like that Nêto of yours, whom I hear didn't come out so well after all. I could have used her, it seems, but not now, I hear at any rate, unless it is for some depraved sport among the bad ones. So you took away my clients on the long march south and soon the city here will turn against me. Yes, the army will return with no goodness in their heart for those of us who opposed bitterly your Epaminondas. They say I gave silver to Backwash to stop this madness. They claimed I offered free *erôs* at Athens to Kallias and Iphikrates for their words and weapons to save Hellas from your bloodlust. They say I sent runners to Lichas to ready the Spartans for Epaminondas, and they say your Gorgos was in my pay."

Mêlon turned away, happy that he had never mounted this woman. Do that, he thought, and he would have been thinking of his terraces and vines, and the need to get home before he was even done. Only now he knew why men called her "Toad." Still, as he turned away, he spoke to her. "They say? No, no, so I say. I say that the Boiotians who come back will not have patience with any of you. None of you traitors they like. As for helot-crazy, I suppose I was. Yes, I found out that I was, both for the freedom of the Messenians and for the company of Nêto." He then got up and ended, "Not you, not me—not any of us have ever been helots. Have we, Phrynê? Cutting down the wheat stalks, only to give flour to masters on the other side of Taygetos—as thanks each year that they might kill only a few hundred not thousands of our kin?" Now Mêlon turned wild and raised his hand to slap her hard if she even squeaked back a slur. "No, you go from here. Go. Leave from out Thespiai. Your lust, your sway is nothing. It leaves your customers hating you as much after their pleasure as they flatter you for it before. So, no, I have no apologies. Maybe only one: We should have battled the ice of the Eurotas and killed Agesilaos when we could have. Or stayed on Taygetos and hunted down that Antikrates. Or stayed in the high country until I carried my Nêto back kicking on my shoulder."

"My, my, even face-to-face with my beauty, you still miss your helot girl, Mêlon, I can see that well enough." And with that, the Toad left Thespiai—at least until the town's zeal for the Pythagoreans and democracy for helots might pass.

# CHAPTER 37

# Epaminondas Returns

Then before the summer came on, all gossip stopped. At last the grand army of the tired Boiotians trudged in from the south—a thousand stadia and more of tramping from Ithômê to the hike down Kithairon, a month and more after Mêlon himself had reached Thespiai. Tired and dirty, the Boiotians had pushed their way through the Athenians at the Isthmos and marched proudly over the Megarid on the heels of Iphikrates as he scampered in fright back with his army to Attika.

Epaminondas had smashed Iphikrates at the Isthmos, like a farmer's boot flattens the dung beetle. So the army came into Boiotia dirty and ragged, but with another triumph still and in perfect order. The long snake wound through the pass just as it had left nearly half a year earlier, but with Pelopidas and Epaminondas singing Erinna's songs at the head and worrying little about what their war had been for. The Boiotians came down over the crest of Kithairon at precisely the time the *rhêtôres* in Thebes were swearing their sons had been lost in the land of Pelops and the harvests would rot in the fields for want of men. Menekleidas of Aulis, in the middle of his peroration to confiscate the property of Epaminondas and Pelopidas, ran from the *bêma*. All the Athenian silver and gold of Kallistratos did him no good. Backwash was unsure whether the rumors were true that the veterans were about to storm the *ekklêsia* and hang the seers of doom like himself from the plane trees in the central courtyard. So he fled over to Euboia, always in fear the island was too close to Epaminondas.

In the plain below the Kadmeia, smoke arose off to the east above

Plataia as the army broke up and spilled over the plain. The Thebans in the agora cheered as they saw the morning campfires of the horde that was already nearing and filling the roads of Boiotia in the thousands. A long line of creaking wagons came down the pass, full of pots and tools, and Peloponnesian herds behind to enrich the villages of the flatlands. Immediately upon his formal report of the army's return to the Boiotarchs, Epaminondas was ordered by the council of the Boiotians to be tried within thirty days. First, the stay-at-home Boiotarchs had in their fear immediately ordered his army to disband, to scatter to their harvests and homes. Perhaps they could try him in the night, and stone him at the Kadmos Gate, before the thousands who followed him even knew he was in the jail on the order of the *rhêtôres*.

On these first days of the army's return, Mêlon figured that Epaminondas had no retainers to bar his arrest. Bluster and boast had not yet filtered through the countryside about the size and beauty of the not finished new cities of Mantineia, Megalopolis, and Messenê. No one knew of the terrified Agesilaos trapped on his acropolis, with Lichas and the others of Sparta's worst all dead, with twenty-five myriads of helots free and full of hatred for Lakonia. Yet, Mêlon guessed, once the truth of free Messenia was out, and the extent of the plunder from Lakonia seen, tempers would soften. The truth would spread that thousands of Boiotian hoplites were wealthy, with good pay from the Peloponnesians and plenty of plunder in their sacks and gifts from the Messenians. Yet in these initial days after the arrival of the army, few had any love for the generals who had marched their men south to help others when their own fields needed tending.

So it is with all wars, that both supporters and critics weave and warp until the final story is known—and alike then go back with their plumb strings to line up their past principles with the final verdict of the last battlefield. This Epaminondas knew and shrugged off as the price of leading rather than watching events go by. While he feared he had not yet ruined Sparta as he wanted, he also accepted that his men thought he had, and so would always follow a leader who gave them victory, and whose own sense of achieving less than he hoped was more than they had dared imagine. At last, the day of the trial of Epaminondas came. He was standing in the dock alone; if he were found guilty, the other generals would follow. If he were freed, the others would never need to come before the popular courts. Six hundred jurymen chosen by lot and eager for the drachma daily wage poured into the jury hall. Mêlon was determined to ride the lame Xiphos over from Helikon to Thebes to speak out at this twisting of justice. On the Kadmeia, he was to meet Alkidamas and Ainias, who swore that they would not have the Boiotians do to Pelopidas and Epaminondas what the Spartans had not been able to do.

Then all Boiotia was on fire with word that thousands of hoplites would march into the *dikastêrion*. The armed would file in who had known the Spartan on the Eurotas and had lifted stone for the Messenians. Few of them had been lost despite the ordeal. Most were rich from their victories in the south, but, like all good soldiers, were already bored with the luxury of peace in their hamlets. Had Epaminondas nodded, these hoplites in their torn cloaks and battered shields would have gladly crossed the pass into Attika for him and taken down the Athenian temples of Perikles if only for sport and to fulfill his boast. So for now, fickle war had proven sweet to all the Boiotians, even for those who had stayed home—as they counted all the plunder and noted that their fathers and sons came back with eyes that blinked and arms that had all five fingers. Even marching in dead winter at Boukatios had proved wise, since all came home just in time to cut their barley and scythe the wheat.

The courtroom of Thebes was an armed camp pitted against the slackers and men left behind. On this day of the trial Mêlon had gotten off his tired and lame Xiphos about halfway to Thebes. The once sleek warhorse's hooves were cracked, and Mêlon was leading him the rest of the way, worried that he would miss the opening indictment. Then, just as he passed the fork to Leuktra, a hooded horseman, with a cloak of green frayed wool that the old men of Thebes wore, galloped his way. "Mêlon, son of Malgis, one of the renegades, aren't you?" the covered traveler yelled out. "You are late—and you soon to be a defendant as well."

Mêlon halted and led the pony to the orchard on the side of the road. "Why, I guess I am. Say your thing. Be careful what your tongue may earn, stranger. I know my way around iron."

Then the horseman, as if Mêlon were no stranger, started right in, "So I hear you do. Your master has been freed. No trial, man—for him or you. Hear the story." The hooded rider had his pony's nose at Mêlon's chest. "Epaminondas walks up to the jurymen, all six hundred, Epaminondas does. A thousand hoplites roar to his rear. He pleads guilty. Yes, guilty to the charge of holding his command beyond the new year. He says to the jurymen of Boiotia to punish him as they please. As his dog, little Eurotas, barked a second for him, they voted to pardon this Epaminondas and all the stalwarts who went with him to the south. You too. How? All the accused did was to recite a poem of sorts. The funny song was in the poet's six-foot and said to be the work of the fallen Amazon Erinna, whose ashes they scattered amid the winds below Ithômê.

> By my plans Sparta was shorn of her glory.
> And holy Messenê at last received back her children.
> By the arms of Thebes Megalopolis was girded with walls—
> and all Hellas was independent and free.

Then the rider laughed and finished, "Our Epaminondas offered the jurymen a final warning: 'Put that song on my statue at Leuktra should you kill me this day.' Then he was carried out on the shoulders of the army, guilty of nothing other than freeing the helots, burning Lakonia, and building three great fetters of Sparta in the south."

With that story, Mêlon smiled at the rider's bold familiar voice. "I like that line—'and all Hellas was independent and free.' I thought I would be arriving too late at Thebes to do much, wasting my days away at the long trial before watching the stoning of the man who freed the Hellenes of the Peloponnesos—and waiting all the time for the tug on my own sleeve for my own moment to face the stones." Mêlon laughed louder now. "I can turn around and lead tired Xiphos home by dark. Still, you false man, throw off your hood. I have heard this voice and words of yours before. They are not of an old man, a *gerôn* who needs wool in the heat. After all, there is no reason for your cover. We are now in the hot season."

"Always the clever man." The horseman laughed, stuck out his hand, gave Mêlon a firm grasp, and then reined in his horse to gallop on by. Mêlon smiled, since Pelopidas was a poor actor and a worse jokester. But Mêlon was pleased that this good general had left the court and headed his way to break the good news first to the Malgidai. The rider galloped out and yelled, "Until the late summer, in the late summer . . ." as he quickly left Mêlon far behind.

As Mêlon had set out to Thebes at dawn, he already had gone a good forty stadia toward the city when Pelopidas had stopped him. He turned Xiphos around on the road to head home to the farm, trying to make sense of the acquittal of Epaminondas. The vote meant not just that the liberators were not hanged or stoned, but perhaps that the people even wanted them to do again what they had just finished. Yet as Mêlon left the Theban behind, he turned back for a moment one last time, and far off he spied yet another man galloping his way—as it was now an apparent rule that when one of the Malgidai set out to Thebes he was to be accosted on the road by strangers. This time the horseman came more quickly and with maybe ten or so riders at his side. He thought he should not press his luck with strange riders twice. Were these not robbers or worse? The army was back and thousands were thick in the countryside and had, as Pelopidas warned, become used to the easier life of plunder and assault. Or so Mêlon thought as he got off his hobble-footed horse.

Mêlon walked Xiphos off the road. He sat hidden under an oak with green, early summer leaf to let the band pass by. He had come without a spear, much less his heavy breastplate. For all his bluster to the hooded Pelopidas, he carried only a knife. Mêlon had no wish to try the lame Xiphos against this new horde of horsemen. The riders halted right where Mêlon had left the road. This time there were no hoods and Mêlon saw bare-headed Epaminondas with the throng, sitting proud back on his Boiotian red pony. Mêlon called out to them from his seat beneath the shade tree. "You are not even back for long, and your riders dash up to Helikon to tear folks from their farms and fill their heads with talk of three-day-rations and campfires. I hear that jurymen of Boiotia have decided not to cut your throat or crush your head with rocks, Theban. No, you will end your days by the fire with your dog Eurotas as you sing to the Thebans of freedom and the helots."

"Hardly. You know how all this ends as well as I do, Mêlon of the afterthought. I leave to Thessaly in the north. Those folk up there would invade us the moment we go to the south in late summer." He may have been on his horse and in a hurry, but the general kept smiling not at his reprieve, but at the cure of the once-lost Mêlon. Now he wanted to talk more than to leave. "They jabber up north of our sinister plots of Pythagoras, and of their sadness at the end of Sparta. They threaten us with Nemesis. They cry that their own serfs, the *penestai,* have been stirred up by the evil Epaminondas. They say up in Thessaly that I favor the sheep and dogs and other unfree folk to walk with heads higher than the freemen of Hellas."

What was all this "they say"? Mêlon wondered why Epaminondas cared, Epaminondas who had raised whole new cities out of the very mud. The general went on. "They say that we have left a democracy with children and we opened the chest of Pandora and then went home as all the foul things belched forth. So no. I will not sit by the fire in Thebes and spin the tall tales about our past glory. Why would I, when I have unfinished affairs at summer's end back down in the Peloponnesos? Or have you forgotten that Agesilaos and the son of Lichas, that Antikrates, have lived too long and that oily ingrate Lykomedes bears us a grudge for too many good turns? He will soon join his new Mantineia with Sparta. Remember as well that they say that there are still some serfs in Lakonia on the Eurotas."

Mêlon laughed, "Who are 'they?'—your 'they' that are always saying something? Folks like you always have a half-meal uneaten somewhere. You won't let yourself—or anyone else—relax and enjoy the leisure of peace. So after the serfs are freed, north and south, no doubt it will be all the slaves, and then, as they charge, our goats and sheep as well to be liberated."

At that Epaminondas laughed, reined around his horse, and turned it to ride on past Helikon and out through the narrows at Chaironeia. He paused as he passed by. "So we will see you Mêlon, after all, next time? On our late summer's march back, our second one this year to the south to finish things up in the vale of Lakonia? I halted that cold day on the Eurotas and won't make that same mistake twice. I need good men, just a few is all it takes, but there are not too many of them left."

Even more to his own surprise, Mêlon did not pause, but even louder answered back, as the cured patient to his doctor: "When the red is on the grapes, then I come down to meet you. Or maybe even earlier to the marching yard of Thebes. We will have a far better descent than the first, my general, though in the heat rather than the dead of winter when cruel Boukatios is upon us. So yes, I follow you. Maybe to Hades and back if need be. It seems you're my Orpheus."

Mêlon laughed at his own words. He would march that summer, and for years more, the once most reluctant now the most zealous of the liberators. His general Epaminondas was not surprised at all by that final outburst from the quiet Thespian, but still finished, "That we will, Mêlon, first citizen of Hellas, that we will."

Epaminondas bent over a little from his horse. The two men clasped arms and then the riders were gone.

# CHAPTER 38

# *The Anabasis*

On this strangest of mornings, Mêlon once more led Xiphos toward the mountain on the road that Lophis had once ridden down to Leuktra. There would be no third group of riders. Still, he wished an Alkidamas and Melissos would roust him on the road, as they had at the monument to Leuktra, since these days he had only himself for company. Instead it was a mere breeze that snapped him out of his trance, as he noticed that he was almost home and had been walking in thought at a fast clip. Finally, off on the horizon he could see the roof-tiles of the tower of Malgis, and the shiny whitewash work of Myron. The tower from bottom to top glistened as the sun picked up its glaze. The lame veteran headed for that beacon, this lighthouse that drew him home. He limped hard to close the final distance to the farm, once again walking with the hobbled horse at his side. Mêlon thought he saw Damô. The boys—weren't they waving in his direction out the window? Why, when he had more than two stadia to go to the first high vineyard of Malgis?

His eyes were getting as bad as those of Melissos. And everything he touched—horse or woman—seemed to end up as hobbled as he was. He was eager to tell them all of Pelopidas and the trial of Epaminondas and his meeting with the Thebans and that all was over for now and that he was free from punishment. That he was now a Panhellene, no mere farmer of Thespiai but a *hoplitês* of Thebes pledged to come down his mountain and follow his Epaminondas back into the labyrinth to the south.

In response to his sudden zeal came a good wind, stronger than the late spring breezes, but so unlike the cold northern blast that had once blown at the backs of the army as it started out over Kithairon. It nudged him up the long bend of the trail. Mêlon warmed with that late spring heat and blowing and the odd voices from the birds above, and the squirrels of the new season, and even the oaks and ferns below. They all had music and speech in them, as loud in their song as they had always been mute before. Now as a Pythagorean, he heard sounds, a symphony of a nature alive as he had never sensed before. In the very air itself Mêlon could pick up, amid the ferns, and elms, and squirrels of the road, the war cry of his dead Chiôn as he once dashed out from the hut of Gorgos after Antikrates. The shouts of his good son Lophis followed too as he had ridden Xiphos, head-to-head against Lichas at Leuktra.

Even the specter of rich Proxenos who overturned an aristocracy came upon him, laughing in the great theater at Mantineia about the massive gates hung awry. There was the soft chanting of what he thought must be Erinna, hiking up to the slope of Ithômê and her schoolhouse, singing of her hero Epaminondas, son of Polymnis—whom she had never met. Where did such women come from to give up their all to hike up into the cold of Ithômê to free the Messenians? Why would a branded slave on Helikon think he could kill, as if he were all-seeing Zeus who dispenses divine justice, all who needed killing? All these voices of the dead were just as he had been promised back in Messenê when the cult of the green-eaters warned him that he had already seen the one way of Pythagoras and heard the promise of the souls as they prepare to return among us whether as majestic oaks or tiny worms.

As Mêlon, son of Malgis, neared the farm of Malgis, he felt the power of the symmetry of the grain fields, of the vines and of the orchards especially, the grid of files and rows of Pythagoras's perfect numbers, and knew he was back where it had all begun as planned. Now he could sense also the indomitable strength of the triangle's golden ratios, as strong in their order even as the streets and blocks were of the grids of Mantineia, Megalopolis, and Messenê. He looked this way and then up; not a vine, not a tree was out of line. He saw squares and triangles and more still in the layout of the farm.

The whispers grew stronger in his head. They reminded him of the one way that had made the farm grow and sent them all south and would keep Mêlon safe until the end without fear. The voices with assurance told him that there were no shades in Elysion. There was no mythical Sisyphos, or Tantalos of children's song in the rungs of Hades. No silly Hades even. No marble Zeus throned on snowy Olympos. Nothing like that at all. Instead those fables and bogeymen could do no harm to the good man on this earth or his soul on the next. His own choices and his faith in the One God, they alone determined the one life to come. Now one voice, everywhere at once, prophesied to him that there would be no peace for five or even ten years in Messenê as the ripples of three hundred and fifty years of servitude battered the helots still, and those of Lakonia who had done such evil would not quit with a trip or two. So confess it, you Mêlon. Epaminondas and his Thebans would have to go back to the south this very summer, and then twice more before the helot democracy was safe from others—and from itself. It seemed as stupid a thing to have marched south to liberate such wild childish folk as ten years hence it would seem wise to have done so. Men really are not, as Lichas boasted, born as slaves. The helotage of Sparta had to cease, if by the most unlikely tool of the farmers of Boiotia and their one-cloak childless general Epaminondas.

As Mêlon made the last bend to the big house, he let lame Xiphos go with a slap to his flanks. The murmuring of his own friends and lost son in the air and in his head and in the trees and bushes about and the parables of Epaminondas in the wind at last ceased. Silence and quiet everywhere—but for a moment only.

Now in their place, as if on some eerie cue, he heard sweeter music or something faint like the distant chords of a single *aulos* that always came to strengthen him when things to come seemed most forbidding. Mêlon shuddered at the familiar strains from Thisbê that so often went into his ear as healing sounds. He took a second glance back, half-thinking it was Epaminondas who had dismounted and followed him up with his reed—as before when the general had played the same tune of the Thisbeans in his wild talks about cutting the head off the Spartan snake. Or perhaps the melody was the sound of the ghost initiates, who, in the upper *aithêr*, were celebrating that Epaminondas had brought such fame to the way of Pythagoras and had saved the soul of Mêlon, son of Malgis, of the line of Antander on Helikon. Or was it the dirge of the dead?

But the sound marked nothing at all like that. Epaminondas was even now far away. The general was racing out the narrows of Chaironeia, hoping to raise the countryside to free the serfs of Thessaly ahead—and so to offer the poor *penestai* of the north what he had bequeathed to the *heilôtai* of the south. Instead, the sound came from a faint figure below on the edge of the plain, though off in a different direction to his right. Mêlon turned to make out this solitary shape behind him, who was ascending with an unsteady gait the same southwest road up to his Helikon.

Perhaps if the sound were real, the phantom—was it the shade of an avenging Dirkê?—would prove only some slow-moving woman playing a pipe to calm her goats. The shadow moved more slowly than he did, with a walking stick. Or was it more likely that after the voices, and the disguise of Pelopidas and the riders of Epaminondas, he was completely in the grip of a god, *enthusiastikos*—and so now he saw and heard divine things from Pythagoras that others did not?

He wanted to awake from all this. Yet he already was awake in the sun and climbing and almost home. As he neared the courtyard gate of the lower fields and headed for the gravestones of Malgis and Lophis and the marker stone of the farm with the new high cenotaph of Chiôn, Mêlon could see into the big window of the tower with the shutters thrown wide open. No dream this. Damô and the children above were looking east beyond him, staring off with hands on their brows in the direction of the bright sun and the music, waving to that something well below him—not far to the south where Epaminondas and Pelopidas had raised the dust below as they had joined and galloped off together in the distance to hard battle with the horse-lords of Thessaly.

Then all was lucid. Once again the Thisbean melody and the breeze kicked up. All those cobwebs of the past, the dusts of bitter memory of loss and regrets of choices not followed were blown away with the late spring wind on Helikon. With that, lame Mêlon, without needing to turn around, raised his right arm high and kept it there, opening all five fingers to catch the warm wind, slowing at last and entering the courtyard.

As if on cue, a familiar keen-scented dog yelped in answer off in the distance, below and down the hill path. With that greeting, not far behind, Nêto of Messenia—now more beautiful even than before, as she would say too of the lame and bald Mêlon now made whole—took her fingers from the pipe, smiled, and then she too hobbled ahead as her Thisbean strain ceased. And with stiff Kerberos back as old Porpax at her heels, Nêto in her hood and shawl made it up to that final well-known turn, and onto the farm of the Malgidai.

## A Historical Postscript

The historian Xenophon's *Hellenica*, our primary historical source for events of earlier-fourth-century-B.C. Greece—in his apparent anger at the rise of a democratic and powerful Thebes—makes no mention of the presence of Epaminondas at Leuktra. He is silent also about his role in the first invasion of Sparta, or the Theban effort to free the helots of Messenia and to found the citadel of Messenê. Xenophon does, however, in his *Anabasis* ("The March Up-Country"), talk of a Boiotian Proxenos who had advised Xenophon to join the Ten Thousand, though he says nothing of our son of the same name. The loss of Plutarch's "Life of Epaminondas," together with Xenophon's bias, explains in large part why today we do not fully appreciate the reasons why the classical Greeks and Romans considered Epaminondas the greatest man of the age.

In contrast, the Roman-era Diodorus—based on the lost histories of an Ephoros, Xenophon's contemporary—much more frequently mentions and praises Epaminondas and his invasions to the south. Thanks to Ephoros—I have no idea whether he had long yellow hair and lisped and was fond of the Boiotians—and the lost historians Theopompos and Kallisthenes, something about the achievement of Epaminondas survives in bits and pieces in the Roman-era traveler Pausanias and Plutarch's *Life of Pelopidas*.

Much of what we know about siege warfare of the age is found in "On the Defense of Fortified Positions," written by one Ainias of Stymphalos, a shadowy general of the Arkadian federation. His larger corpus,

"On Military Preparations," is unfortunately lost and we otherwise know very little of the general and writer Ainias Taktikos, who may have played a considerable role in the politics of the Peloponnesos in the mid fourth century B.C.

We don't know exactly all the reasons why Plato (Platôn) so distrusted democracy and favored the Spartans, but it was more than just the democracy's execution of Sokrates and his own exile.

"The Oration on the Messenians" (*Logos Messêniakos*) by Alkidamas does not survive either, but a fragment of the great speech on the liberation of the helots, "No man is a slave by nature," seems to be the only explicit condemnation of slavery that survives from classical Greek literature. Perhaps Aristotle had Alkidamas in mind when he later attacked those who taught that there was no such thing as a man suited to slavery at birth.

We hear from Plutarch and others that an adolescent Philip of Makedon spent a year as a hostage with the Thebans. Though it is not recorded that he was known at Thebes as Melissos, the adult Philip bore no antipathy for the Messenians and when, more than thirty years later, he invaded Boiotia, he spared the helot city to the south after his victory at Chaironeia. He did, however, finish the job of subjugating Greece by ending the Sacred Band at Chaironeia—but supposedly lamented the sight of their corpses that littered the battlefield. Scholars are still unsure why Philip erected a proud lion on the battlefield to honor the dead of the Sacred Band, but the monument sits there today guarding the old road to Thebes as it skirts the foothills of Mt. Parnassos.

Pausanias says in his own days of the first century B.C. that there was an iron monument of Epaminondas at Messenia. Both Pausanias, and Plutarch in his life of Agesilaos, record that the offspring of Antikrates were forever known as the "swordsmen" for the thrust of their ancestor that killed the hated Epaminondas. They add that the great liberator was brought alive out of battle to die in 362 B.C. on the hilltop of Skopê, overlooking the battlefield of Mantineia, after Epaminondas's fourth and last invasion of the Peloponnesos, more than nine years after the victory at Leuktra. They mention none who died with him, not even Mêlon, son of Malgis, farmer of Helikon.

Black limestone steles of the heroes of Boiotia can be seen in the modern museum of Thebes, carved, we believe, by the sculptor Aristides.

Archaeologists argue about the architecture of the great cities of Mantineia, Megalopolis, and Messenê, but by general consent the stones seem to reveal the work of now anonymous Boiotian architects whose work resembles the contemporary rebuilt walls of Plataia and Thespiai. Much of the massive Arkadian Gate at Messenê survives, though no one has yet found among the best-preserved city in Greece any fragments of the two stone lions with the likenesses of Chiôn and Proxenos—nor the iron statue of Epaminondas himself.

Of the final end of Phrynê, little is known. Athenaeus in the thirteenth book of *The Deipnosophists* relates a tradition that she returned to Thespiai and offered her own great riches to rebuild the city walls after Alexander the Great had torn them down—if only they would inscribe her own name on the fortifications.

I have hiked over much of Hesiod's Mt. Helikon, but so far I have not discovered the highland farm of Mêlon, son of Malgis, father of the good Lophis—the master of godlike Chiôn and Nêto, hero of Leuktra, slayer of Kleombrotos, who in the following decade went south three more times after the founding of Messenê to fight the Spartans and, more than nine years after Leuktra, to die on Skopê above Mantineia at the side of his friend—and of his savior—Epaminondas, son of Polymnis, general of Thebes, first man of Greece.

## The Peoples and Places of Fourth-Century B.C. Greece*

**Attika:** the territory surrounding the city of Athens, and, with the polis proper, comprising the city-state of the Athenians on the southern border of the Boiotians.

**Boiotia:** a geographical region in central Greece whose capital city was Thebes. Its rich farmlands, cities, and hamlets were federated into a political union in the late sixth century B.C. and were made democratic in the fourth.

**Doric:** the dialect of Greek that the Spartans and most in the southern and eastern Peloponnesos spoke—supposedly derived from the mythical Dorians who swept from the north into the Peloponnesos.

**Epaminondas:** the Theban hero and victor at the battle of Leuktra (371 B.C.) who subsequently led Boiotian armies on four invasions of the Peloponnesos before dying at the second battle of Mantineia (362 B.C.).

---

\* Ease of recognition and pronunciation, rather than absolute consistency, has guided the spellings of Greek names. Some less well known Greek names and places are transliterated rather than Latinized—for example, Korinthos for Corinth, Leuktra for Leuctra, and Thespiai for Thespiae—while more common names like Epaminondas and Thebes seemed preferable to Epameinôndas and Thêbai. I use Hellas for Greece, which derives from Roman nomenclature for Hellas.

**Ephoros**: a fourth-century-B.C. student of Isokrates who wrote a universal history of the Greeks, from mythical times to the advent of Philip of Makedon. Now lost, many books of Ephoros's history survive in part through the extant work of the Roman-era compiler Diodorus Siculus.

**Helikon**: the prominent mountain of Boiotia, almost 6,000 feet in elevation, birthplace of the poet Hesiod and said to be the home of the Muses.

**Hellas**: what the Greeks (or Hellenes) called their own country.

**helots**: (*heilôtai*, "those taken") indentured Greek serfs who were obligated to raise food for the Spartan state. Although there were thousands of helots in Lakonia surrounding Sparta, the great worry was instead the far more numerous thousands of Messenian helots who lived on the other side of Mt. Taygetos, and who for centuries revolted both frequently and unsuccessfully.

**hoplites**: the class of Greek small farmers who, as middling citizens of the polis, fought as heavily armed infantry soldiers in the phalanx, with spear, body armor, and round shield.

**Lakonia**: a geographical region in the southern Peloponnesos surrounding Sparta, and thus along with the city comprising the Spartan state, which in turn was also known as Lakedaimon.

**Lokrians**: inhabitants of two regions in central Greece, to the west on the Korinthian Gulf north of Boiotia and to the east south of Thermopylai. They usually joined the Boiotian horse in battle.

**Messenia**: large territory in the southwestern Peloponnesos, home to thousands of helots and controlled by Sparta—not to be confused with Messenê, the capital city of a free Messenia.

**Pelopidas**: Theban general and political leader, partner with Epaminondas in spreading democratic fervor beyond the borders of Boiotia. He died in 364 B.C., two years before Epaminondas, while fighting in Thessaly.

**Peloponnesos**: the southern and largely mountainous peninsula of Greece connected to the northern mainland by the Isthmos at Korinthos.

**Philip II**: famous fourth-century B.C. king of Makedon who united its warring tribes and then moved south to end the freedom of the Greek city-states. His dream of leading a panhellenic army into Asia was to be completed by his son Alexander the Great.

**Phokians**: inhabitants of Phokis in central Greece, near and to the north of Boiotia. They were often distrusted as robbers of the temples at Delphi and fickle neighbors.

**Phrynê**: "Toad," the nickname given to the famous courtesan Mnesaretê and model of the sculptor Praxiteles.

**Plataia**: a Boiotian city at the southern frontier, nestled on the slopes of Mt. Kithairon, usually an ally of Athens and so often at war with the Thebans.

**Polis**: the Greek city-state, of which at the time of Epaminondas there were some 1,000 to 1,500 on the Greek mainland and the islands in the Aegean and west to Sikily. The concept of a polis included both the urban center (*astu*) and the surrounding countryside (*chôra*).

**Pythagoras**: the famous philosopher, mathematician, and mystic of the sixth century B.C. whose followers believed in one divinity, the reincarnation of souls, and a reality explicable by mathematics and music. Cult members were chastised for embracing vegetarianism, the nobility of the left hand, the equality of the sexes, voluntary poverty, and communalism.

**Sparta**: both the city on the Eurotas River and the state that encompassed most of Lakonia, and, through alliance and conquest, controlled much of the southern Peloponnesos. Lakedaimon is probably the closest synonym.

**Taygetos**: the large mountain wall between Lakonia and Messenia, ranging some 60 to 70 miles in extent and rising nearly 8,000 feet at its peak.

**Thebes**: the largest city and capital of the federated region of Boiotia in central Greece. Not to be confused with Egyptian Thebes. On occasion Thebes and Boiotia were used, if inexactly, interchangeably.

**Thespiai**: a city-state in Boiotia, in the foothills of Mt. Helikon, and nearly always at odds with the larger capital Thebes a few miles away. Thespians were residents of Thespiai but bore no relation to Thespis, the legendary sixth-century-B.C. founder of tragic drama, from whom derives the modern notion of "thespians" as actors.

**Xenophon**: famous Greek historian of fourth-century-B.C. Greece and veteran of the retreat of the Ten Thousand from Asia, as well as author of treatises on topics as diverse as horsemanship and the economics of household management. He was exiled from Athens, lived in Triphylia as a friend of the Spartans, and was banished after the invasion of Epaminondas.

# Principal Characters

**Ainias:** ("praiseworthy") the Arkadian mercenary and tactician who came north to join Epaminondas

**Alkidamas:** ("strength of the people") the aged rhetorician and champion of the Messenians

**Chiôn:** ("snowy" or the "Chian") the huge slave from the island of Chios bought in infancy by Malgis from the Spartans, and raised on the farm on Mt. Helikon

**Damô:** wife of Lophis and custodian of the farm

**Dirkê:** aged neighbor of Mêlon on Mt. Helikon

**Epaminondas:** Boiotarch and general of the Boiotian army and leader of the allied army

**Ephoros:** historian and resident of Athens, at work on a general history of the Greeks

**Gastêr:** ("belly") captain of the *Theôris* and veteran sailor of the Korinthian Gulf

**Gorgos:** ("dragon") captured helot slave of Mêlon, veteran of the Spartan wars against Athens

**Lichas:** ephor and warrior of Sparta

**Lophis:** only son of Mêlon

**Malgidai:** the descendants of Malgis who continued to work his farm on Mt. Helikon

**Malgis:** the one-eyed Thespian veteran, father of Mêlon, who first carved out the farm on Mt. Helikon

**Melissos**: ("bee") the young boy hostage from Makedon, who spent a year with the Thebans as a guarantor of the northern peace

**Mêlon**: ("apple") the son of Malgis, the lame farmer on Mt. Helikon and the "apple" of various prophecies promising the end of Sparta

**Myron**: ("perfume") farm slave on Mt. Helikon, recruited by Nêto on the eve of Leuktra

**Nêto**: the Messenian slave of Mêlon, bought as a small girl from the Spartans

**Nikôn**: ("victor") leader of the helot insurgents

**Pelopidas**: head of the Sacred Band, and co-general of the allied army

**Phrynê**: ("toad") courtesan and owner of a rest-stop at Thespiai

**Porpax**: ("shield-strap") the older of the two great hounds of the Malgidai

**Proxenos**: ("consul") the wall builder from Plataia and chief architect to Epaminondas

**Sturax**: ("butt-spike") the younger and friskier of the two dogs of the Malgidai

# Timeline

(ALL DATES B.C.)

454  Birth of Malgis, founder of the farm on Mt. Helikon

431  War between Athens and Sparta breaks out. Thebes joins the Spartans.

424  Battle of Delion. Malgis becomes famous for his bravery in the battle.

423  Thebes levels the walls of Thespiai.

423  Malgis scouts out Mt. Helikon and begins to carve out a farm with his father Antander.

422  Battle of Amphipolis. Sixteen-year-old Gorgos fights for the Spartans under Brasidas.

420  First visits of Alkidamas to the farm on Mt. Helikon

419  Birth of Mêlon, son of Malgis

415–13  Malgis campaigns in Sikily with the Spartans, leaves his father Antander in charge of the new farm.

413  First visit of young Lichas to the farm in search of Mêlon

412  Death of Antander; Malgis plants the high vineyards in Sikilian fashion.

404  Malgis and young Mêlon raid the Attic borderlands; the Peloponnesian War ends.

401–400  Malgis fights with the Ten Thousand in Asia Minor.

399  Malgis on his way home at Chios buys Chiôn from a Spartan trader.

395 Boiotians defeat the Spartans at Haliartos. Malgis strips the armor of the dead Lysander.

394 Thebans battle the Spartans at the Nemea River and Koroneia. Gorgos is captured at Nemea. Death of Malgis at Koroneia.

389 Mêlon buys the child Nêto from a Spartan trader.

380 Kleombrotos becomes the Agiad king at Sparta.

379 Pelopidas and other Thebans expel the Spartans and establish a democracy for the Boiotians.

378 The Spartan king Agesilaos invades Boiotia.

377 Boiotia is invaded again by Agesilaos.

375 Thebes beats Sparta in a small battle at Boiotian Tegyra.

## 371 The Great Year

**SUMMER**

Spartans invade Boiotia. Battle of Leuktra and defeat of the Spartans

**AUTUMN**

Monument at Leuktra is begun. Proxenos and Ainias work on walls of Thespiai and continue visits to the rising walls at Mantineia.

**WINTER**

Phrynê moves back to Thespiai. Foundations are established of Megalopolis.

## 370

**SPRING**

Uprising at Messenia is begun by Nikôn and Doreios.

**SUMMER**

Nêto and Erinna leave for the Peloponnesos; Chiôn marries Damô.

**AUTUMN**

Nêto and Erinna arrive in Messenia.

**WINTER**

Muster of the Boiotians, arrival in the Peloponnesos. Fight at the Eurotas. Voyage of the *Theôris* to Messenia

## 369

**WINTER/SPRING**

Epaminondas, with the Argive and Theban armies, heads over Mt. Taygetos to Messenia; Chiôn disappears on Mt. Taygetos. The walls of Messenê rise on Mt. Ithômê. The Thebans head home.

**369–68**

Second invasion of the Peloponnesos by Epaminondas.

**366**

Epaminondas invades the Peloponnesos a third time.

**364**

Pelopidas dies in battle at Cynoscephalai in Thessaly.

**362**

Final Boiotian invasion of the Peloponnesos; Mêlon and Epaminondas die on Skopê after the Theban victory at Mantineia.

# A Note on the Author

**Victor Davis Hanson** is the Martin and Illie Anderson Senior Fellow in Residence in Classics and Military History at the Hoover Institution, Stanford University, and the codirector of the Group in Military History and Contemporary Conflict; a professor of classics emeritus at California State University, Fresno; and a nationally syndicated columnist for Tribune Media Services. He is also the Wayne & Marcia Buske Distinguished Fellow in History, Hillsdale College, where each fall semester he teaches courses in military history and classical culture. He received his Ph.D. from Stanford University in classics, was a member of the American School of Classical Studies, Athens, and received his B.A. with highest honors in classics from the University of California, Santa Cruz. He lives on his farm in Selma, California, where he was born in 1953.